Robin Hobb is one of the world's f...
She was born in California in 1952...
she learned how to raise a wolf cub, to skin a moose and to survive in the wilderness. When she married a fisherman who fished herring and the Kodiak salmon-run for half the year, these skills would stand her in good stead. She raised her family, ran a small-holding, delivered post to her remote community, all at the same time as writing stories and novels. She succeeded on all fronts, raising four children and becoming an internationally best-selling writer. She lives in Tacoma, Washington State.

Contact Robin:
www.robinhobb.com
Facebook: www.facebook.com/robin.hobb
Twitter: @robinhobb

'Hobb is one of the great modern fantasy writers . . . As addictive as morphine'
The Times

'A little slice of heaven'
The Guardian

'The feelings of anguish, ambiguity, fear and failure [in her novels] are as familiar as those in a novel by Jonathan Franzen'
Independent on Sunday

'Hobb is always readable. But the elegant translucence of her prose is deceptive . . . That is the ambition of high art. The novelists in any genre are rare who achieve it with Hobb's combination of accessibility and moral authority'
Sunday Telegraph

'A series that recalls HBO's *Game of Thrones*, and *The Lord of the Rings*'
The Telegraph

'In today's crowded fantasy market Robin Hobb's books are like diamon... ...R. Martin

'Hobb i... ...plots from pure im... ...n Iggulden

BY ROBIN HOBB

THE FARSEER TRILOGY
Assassin's Apprentice
Royal Assassin
Assassin's Quest

THE LIVESHIP TRADERS
Ship of Magic
The Mad Ship
Ship of Destiny

THE TAWNY MAN
Fool's Errand
The Golden Fool
Fool's Fate

THE SOLDIER SON
Shaman's Crossing
Forest Mage
Renegade's Magic

THE RAIN WILD CHRONICLES
Dragon Keeper
Dragon Haven
City of Dragons
Blood of Dragons

FITZ AND THE FOOL
Fool's Assassin
Fool's Quest

The Inheritance
The Wilful Princess and the Piebald Prince

WRITING AS MEGAN LINDHOLM
The Reindeer People
Wolf's Brother

Harpy's Flight
The Windsingers
The Limbreth Gate
Luck of the Wheels

Wizard of the Pigeons
Cloven Hooves
Alien Earth

Fool's Quest

ROBIN HOBB

Book Two of Fitz and the Fool

HARPER
Voyager

HarperVoyager
An imprint of HarperCollinsPublishers
1 London Bridge Street
London SE1 9GF

www.harpervoyagerbooks.co.uk

This paperback edition 2016
1

First published in Great Britain by
HarperCollinsPublishers 2015

A catalogue record for this book
is available from the British Library

ISBN: 978-0-00-744424-3

This novel is entirely a work of fiction.
The names, characters and incidents portrayed in it are
the work of the author's imagination. Any resemblance to
actual persons, living or dead, events or localities is
entirely coincidental.

Set in Goudy Oldstyle Std by Palimpsest Book Production Ltd,
Falkirk, Stirlingshire

Printed and bound in Great Britain by
Clays Ltd, St Ives plc

MIX
Paper from
responsible sources
FSC™ C007454

FSC™ is a non-profit international organisation established to promote
the responsible management of the world's forests. Products carrying the
FSC label are independently certified to assure consumers that they come
from forests that are managed to meet the social, economic and
ecological needs of present and future generations,
and other controlled sources.

Find out more about HarperCollins and the environment at
www.harpercollins.co.uk/green

To Rudyard. Still my Best Beloved
after all these years

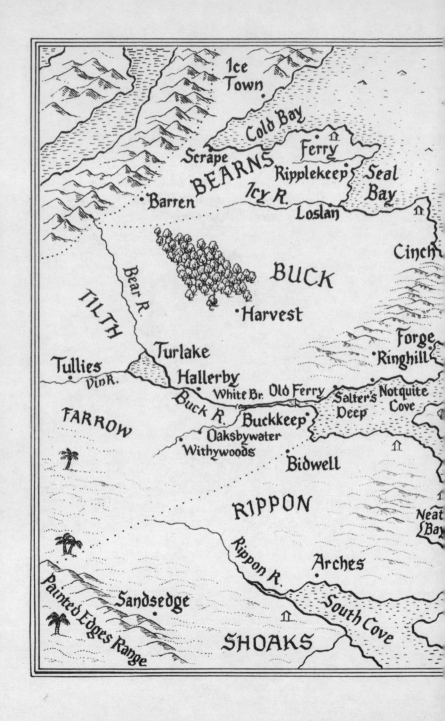

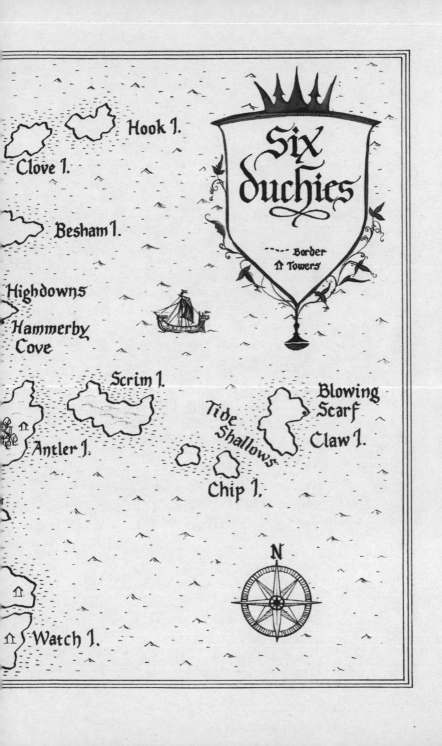

ONE

Winterfest Eve at Buckkeep

I am warm and safe in the den, with my two siblings. They are both heartier and stronger than I am. Born last, I am smallest of all. My eyes were slow to open, and I have been the least adventurous of the cubs. Both my brother and my sister have dared, more than once, to follow my mother to the mouth of the den dug deep in the undercut bank of the river. Each time, she has snarled and snapped at them, driving them back. She leaves us alone when she goes out to hunt. There should be a wolf to watch over us, a younger member of the pack who remains with us. But she is all that is left of the pack, and so she must go out to hunt alone and we must stay where she leaves us.

There is a day when she shakes free of us, long before we have had enough of her milk. She leaves us, going to the hunt, leaving the den as evening starts to creep across the land. We hear from her a single yelp. That is all.

My brother, the largest of us, is filled with both fear and curiosity. He whines loudly, trying to call her back to us, but there is no response. He starts to go to the entrance of the den and my sister follows him, but in a moment they come scrabbling back to hunker down in fear beside me. There are strange smells right outside the den, bad smells, blood and creatures unknown to us. As we hide and whimper, the blood-smell grows stronger. We do the only thing we know to do. We hunch and huddle against the far back wall of the den.

We hear sounds. Something that is not paws digs at the mouth of our den. It sounds like a large tooth biting into the earth, biting and tearing, biting and tearing. We hunch even deeper and my brother's *hackles rise. We hear sounds and we know there is more than one creature outside the den. The blood-smell thickens and is mingled with the smell of our mother. The digging noises go on.*

Then there is another smell. In years to come I will know what it is, but in the dream it is not smoke. It is a smell that none of us understands, and it comes in driven wafts into the den. We cry, for it stings our eyes and sucks the breath from our lungs. The den becomes hot and airless and finally my brother crawls toward the den opening. We hear his wild yelping, and how it continues, and then there is the stink of fear-piss. My sister huddles behind me, getting smaller and stiller. And then she is not breathing or hiding any more. She is dead.

I sink down, my paws over my nose, my eyes blinded by the smoke. The digging noises go on and then something seizes me. I yelp and struggle, but it holds tight to my front leg and drags me from the den.

My mother is a hide and a bloody red carcass thrown to one side. My brother huddles in terror in the bottom of a cage in the back of a two-wheeled cart. They fling me in beside him and then drag out my sister's body. They are angry she is dead, and they kick her about as if somehow their anger can make her feel pain now. Then, complaining of the cold and oncoming dark, they skin her and add her small hide to my mother's. The two men climb onto the cart and whip up their mule, already speculating at the prices that wolf cubs will bring from the dog-fighting markets. My mother's and sister's bloody hides fill my nose with the stench of death.

It is only the beginning of a torment that lasts for a lifetime. Some days we are fed and sometimes not. We are given no shelter from the rain. The only warmth is that of our own bodies as we huddle together. My brother, thin with worms, dies in a pit, thrown in to whet the ferocity of the fighting dogs. And then I am alone. They feed me on offal and scraps or nothing at all. My feet become sore from pawing at the cage, my claws split and my muscles ache from confinement. They beat me and poke me to provoke me to hurl myself against bars I cannot break. They speak outside my cage of their plans to sell me for the fighting-pits. I hear the words but I do not understand them.

I did understand the words. I spasmed awake, and for a moment everything was wrong, everything was foreign. I was huddled in a ball, shuddering, and my fur had been stripped away to bare skin and my legs were bent at the wrong angles and confined by something. My senses were as deadened as if I were wadded in a sack. All around me were the smells of those hated creatures. I bared my teeth and, snarling, fought my way out of my bonds.

Even after I landed on the floor, the blanket trailing after me and my body asserting that I was, indeed, one of those hated humans, I stared in confusion around the dark room. It felt as if it should be morning, but the floor beneath me was not the smooth oaken plank of my bedchamber, nor did the room smell as if it belonged to me. I came slowly to my feet, my eyes striving to adjust. My straining vision caught the blinking of tiny red eyes, and then translated them to the dying embers of a fire. In a fireplace.

As I felt my way across the chamber, the world fell into place around me. Chade's old rooms at Buckkeep Castle emerged from the blackness when I poked at the embers and added a few sticks of wood. Numbly, I found fresh candles and kindled them, awakening the room to its perpetual twilight. I looked around, letting my life catch up with me. I judged that the night had passed and that outside the thick and windowless walls, day had dawned. The dire events of the previous day – how I had nearly killed the Fool, left my child in the charge of folk I did not fully trust, and then dangerously drained Riddle of Skill-strength to bring the Fool to Buckkeep – rushed over me in a sweeping tide. They met the engulfing memories of all the evenings and nights I'd spent in this windowless chamber, learning the skills and secrets of being the king's assassin. When finally the sticks caught flame, enriching the thin candlelight in the room, I felt as if I had made a long journey to return to myself. The wolf's dream of his horrific captivity was fading. I wondered briefly why it had come back in such intensity, and then let it go. Nighteyes, my wolf, my brother, was long gone from this world. The echoes of him lived on in my mind, my heart and my memories, but in what I faced now, he was no longer at my back. I stood alone.

Except for the Fool. My friend had returned to me. Battered, beaten, and possibly not in his right mind, but he was at my side again. I held a candle high and ventured back to the bed we had shared.

The Fool was still deeply asleep. He looked terrible. The marks of torture were written on his scarred face, hardship and starvation had chapped and chafed his skin and thinned his hair to broken straw. Even so, he looked better than when first I had seen him. He was clean, and fed, and warm. And his even breathing was that of a man given a fresh infusion of strength. I wished I could say I had given it to him. All unwitting, I had stolen strength from Riddle and passed it to my friend during our Skill-passage through the standing stones. I regretted how I had abused Riddle in my ignorance but I could not deny the relief I felt to hear the Fool's steady breathing. Last night he had had the strength to talk with me, and he had walked a bit, bathed himself and eaten a meal. That was far more than I would have expected of the battered beggar I had first seen.

But borrowed strength is not true strength. The hasty Skill-healing I'd practised on him had robbed him of his scanty physical reserves, and the vitality I had stolen from Riddle and given to him could not long sustain him. I hoped the food and rest he had taken yesterday had begun to rebuild his body. I watched him sleeping so deeply and dared to hope he would live. Moving softly, I picked up the bedding I had dragged to the floor in my fall and arranged it warmly around him.

He was so changed. He had been a man who loved beauty in all its forms. His tailored garments, the ornaments in his chambers, the hangings for his bed and windows, even the tie that had held back his immaculately groomed hair had all been chosen with harmony and fashion in mind. But that man was gone. He had come back to me as a ragbag scarecrow of a man. The flesh of his face had fallen to skin-coated bones. Battered, blinded, wearing the scars of torture, the Fool had been so transformed by hardship that I hadn't recognized him. Gone was the lithe and limber jester with the mocking smile. Gone, too, elegant Lord Golden with his fine clothes and aristocratic ways. I was left with this cadaverous wretch.

His blind eyes were closed. His mouth was a finger's width ajar. His breath hissed in and out. 'Fool?' I said and jogged his shoulder cautiously. His only response was a slight hitch in his breathing.

4

Then he sighed out, as if giving up on pain and fear, before resuming the even respiration of deep sleep.

He had fled torture and travelled through hardship and privation to meet me. His health was broken and he feared deadly pursuit. I could not grasp how he had managed it, broken and blind. But he'd done it, and for one purpose. Last night, before he had surrendered to unconsciousness, he had asked me to kill for him. He wanted us to return to Clerres, to his old school and to the people who had tormented him. And as a special favour, he had asked that I use my old assassin's skills to kill them all.

He knew that I'd left that part of my life behind me. I was a different man, a respectable man, a steward of my daughter's home, the father of a little girl. Assassin no more. I'd left killing behind. It had been years since I'd been lean, the muscles of my arms as hard as the heart of a killer. I was a country gentleman now. We had both changed so much.

I could still recall the mocking smile and flashing glance that had once been his, charming and enraging at once. He had changed, but I was confident I still knew him in the important ways, the one that went beyond trivial facts such as where he had been born or who his parents had been. I'd known him since we were young. A sour smile twisted my mouth. Not since we were children. In some ways I doubted that either of us had ever truly been children. But the long years of deep friendship were a foundation I could not doubt. I knew his character. I knew his loyalty and dedication. I knew more of his secrets than anyone, and I had guarded those secrets as carefully as if they were my own. I'd seen him in despair, and incapacitated with terror. I'd seen him broken with pain and I'd seen him drunk to maudlin. And beyond that, I'd seen him dead, and been him dead, and walked his body back to life and called his spirit back to inhabit that body.

So I knew him. From the bones out.

Or so I had thought.

I took a deep breath and sighed it out, but there was no relief from the tension I felt. I was like a child, terrified of looking out into the darkness for fear of what I might see. I was denying what I knew was true. I did know the Fool, from his bones out. And

I knew that the Fool would do whatever he thought he must do in order to set the world in its best track. He had let me tread the razor's edge between death and life, had expected me to endure pain, hardship and loss. He had surrendered himself to a tortured death he had believed was inevitable. All for the sake of his vision of the future.

So if he believed that someone must be killed, and he could not kill that person himself, he would ask it of me. And he would freight the request with those terrible words. 'For me.'

I turned away from him. Yes. He would ask that of me. The very last thing I ever wanted to do again. And I would say yes. Because I could not look at him, broken and in anguish, and not feel a sea-surge of anger and hatred. No one, no one could be allowed to hurt him as badly as they'd hurt him and continue to live. Anyone so lacking in empathy that they could systematically torment and physically degrade another should not be suffered to live. Monsters had done this to him. Regardless of how human they might appear, this evidence of their work spoke the truth. They needed to be killed. And I should do it.

I wanted to do it. The longer I looked at him, the more I wanted to go and kill, not quickly and quietly, but messily and noisily. I wanted the people who had done this to him to know they were dying and to know why. I wanted them to have time to regret what they'd done.

But I couldn't. And that tore at me.

I would have to say no. Because as much as I loved the Fool, as deep as our friendship went, as furiously hot as my hatred burned, Bee had first rights to my protection. And dedication. Already I had violated that, leaving her to the care of others while I rescued my friend. My little girl was all I had left now of my wife Molly. Bee was my last chance to be a good father, and I hadn't been doing very well at it lately. Years ago, I'd failed my older daughter Nettle. I'd left her to think another man was her father, given her over to someone else to raise. Nettle already doubted my ability to care for Bee. Already she had spoken of taking Bee out of my care and bringing her here, to Buckkeep, where she could oversee her upbringing.

I could not allow that. Bee was too small and too strange to survive among palace politics. I had to keep her safe, with me, at Withywoods, in a quiet and secure rural manor, where she might grow as slowly and be as odd as she wished. And as wonderful. So although I had left her to save the Fool, it was only this once and only for a short time. I'd go back to her. Perhaps, I consoled myself, if the Fool recovered enough, I could take him with me. Take him to the quiet and comfort of Withywoods, let him find healing and peace there. He was in no condition to make a journey back to Clerres, let alone aid me in killing whoever had done this to him. Vengeance, I knew, could be delayed, but the life of a growing child could not. I had one chance to be Bee's father and that time was now. At any time, I could be an assassin for the Fool. So for now, the best I could offer him was peace and healing. Yes. Those things would have to come first.

For a time, I quietly wandered the assassin's lair where I had spent many happy childhood hours. The clutter of an old man had given way to the tidy organizing skills of Lady Rosemary. She presided over these chambers now. They were cleaner and more pleasant, but somehow I missed Chade's random projects and jumbles of scrolls and medicines. The shelves that had once held everything from a snake's skeleton to a piece of bone turned to stone now displayed a tidy array of stoppered bottles and pots.

They were neatly labelled in a lady's elegant hand. Here was carryme and elfbark, valerian and wolfsbane, mint and beargrease, sumac and foxglove, cindin and Tilth smoke. One pot was labelled OutIslander elfbark, probably to distinguish it from the far milder Six Duchies herb. A glass vial held a dark red mixture that swirled uneasily at the slightest touch. There were threads of silver in it that did not mingle with the red, yet did not float like oil on water. I'd never seen such a mixture. It had no label and I put it back carefully in the wooden rack that kept it upright. Some things were best left alone. I had no idea what karuge root was, nor bloodrun, but both had tiny red skulls inked next to their names.

On the shelf below were mortars and pestles, knives for chopping, sieves for straining and several small heavy pots for rendering. There were stained metal spoons, neatly racked. Below them was a row of small clay pots that puzzled me at first. They were no bigger than my fist, glazed a shiny brown, as were their tight-fitting lids. They were sealed shut with tar, except for a hole in the middle of each lid. A tail of twisted waxed linen emerged from each hole. I hefted one cautiously and then understood. Chade had told me that his experiment with his exploding powder had been progressing. These represented his most recent advance in how to kill people. I set the pot back carefully. The tools of the killing trade that I had forsaken stood in rows like faithful troops. I sighed, but not out of regret, and turned away from them. The Fool slept on.

I tidied the dishes from our late night repast onto a tray and otherwise brought the chamber to rights. The tub of bathwater, now cold and grey, remained, as did the repulsively soiled undergarment the Fool had worn. I did not even dare to burn it on the hearth for fear of the stench it would emit. I did not feel disgust, only pity. My own clothing from the day before was still covered in blood, both from a dog and the Fool. I told myself it was not all that noticeable on the dark fabric. Then, thinking again, I went to investigate the old carved wardrobe that had always stood beside the bed. At one time, it had held only Chade's work robes, all of them of serviceable grey wool and most of them stained or scorched from his endless experiments. Only two work robes hung there now, both dyed blue and too small for me. There was also, to my surprise, a woman's night robe and two simple shifts. A pair of black leggings that would have been laughably short on me. Ah. These were Lady Rosemary's things. Nothing here for me.

It disturbed me to slip quietly from the rooms and leave the Fool sleeping, but I had errands to carry out. I suspected that someone would be sent in to do the cleaning and to supply the room afresh, and I did not like to leave him there unconscious and vulnerable. But at that point, I knew I owed Chade my trust. He had provided all for us the previous evening, despite his pressing duties.

The Six Duchies and the Mountain Kingdom sought to negotiate alliances, and to that end powerful representatives had been invited to come to Buckkeep Castle for the week of Winterfest.

8

Yet even in the middle of an evening of feasting, music and dancing, not only Chade but King Dutiful and his mother, Lady Kettricken, had found time to slip away and greet me and the Fool, and Chade had still found a way to have this chamber well supplied with all we needed. He would not be careless of my friend. Whoever he sent to this chamber would be discreet.

Chade. I took a breath and reached for him with the Skill-magic. Our minds brushed. *Chade? The Fool is asleep and I've some errands that I'd like—*

Yes, yes, fine. Not now, Fitz. We're discussing the Kelsingra situation. If they are not willing to control their dragons, we may have to form an alliance to deal with the creatures. I've made provisions for you and your guest. There is coin in a purse on the blue shelf if you need it. But now I must put my full attention to this. Bingtown claims that Kelsingra may actually be seeking an alliance with the Duchess of Chalced!

Oh. I withdrew. Abruptly, I felt like a child who had interrupted the adults discussing important things. Dragons. An alliance against dragons. Alliance with whom? Bingtown? And what could anyone hope to do against dragons save bribe them with enough meat to stupefy them? Would not befriending the arrogant carnivores be better than challenging them? I felt unreasonably snubbed that my opinion had not been consulted.

And in the next instance, I chided myself. Let Chade and Dutiful and Elliania and Kettricken manage the dragons. Walk away, Fitz.

I lifted a tapestry and slipped away into the labyrinth of secret corridors that wormed its way behind the walls of Buckkeep Castle. Once I had known the spy-ways as well as I knew the path to the stables. Despite the passing years, the narrow corridor that crept through interior walls or snaked along the outer walls of the castle had not changed.

But I had. I was no longer a skinny boy or even a youth. I was a man of sixty, and though I flattered myself that I was fit enough still to do a hard day's work, I was no longer limber and lithe. The narrow corners that I had once ferreted past without a thought now required a bit of negotiating. I reached the old pantry entrance and hunched by the concealed door, ear pressed to the wall, waiting for a quiet moment before I emerged behind a meat rack full of dangling sausages.

I was saved only by the benign chaos of Winterfest. When I stepped out of the pantry into the corridor, a large woman in a flour-dusted apron demanded to know what was taking me so long. 'Did you find the goose-grease for me, or not?'

'I, I didn't see it there,' I replied and she responded tartly, 'That's because you went into the wrong pantry! Go along two more doors, down a flight of steps and take the second door to the cold room and look for it there, in a big brown crock on a shelf. Hurry up!'

She spun around and left me standing. As she walked away, she muttered loudly about hiring new help right before a feast-day. I blew out a nervous breath and turned to find a fellow of about my height and build labouring up the corridor with a heavy brown crock in his arms. I followed him and as he went into the kitchens, I stepped past the kitchen door and its exhaled aroma of fresh bread, steaming soups and roasting meats and hurried outside.

In the teeming courtyard of Buckkeep Castle on a wintry day, I was just one more man hurrying on an urgent errand. I looked up at the sky in surprise. Past noon. I had slept far longer than I'd intended. A brief break in the storms had bared the noon sun, but more snow was surely coming our way. Now I regretted how impulsively I had discarded my cloak the day before. I'd be lucky to regain the keep before the snow came down.

I went first to the infirmary, hoping to apologize to Riddle privately. But it was busier than usual, for apparently some of our guardsmen had got into a bit of a brawl last night. No great damage to any of them, save for one fellow who had been bitten on the cheek. The ugliness of that was enough to make anyone wince. Again, the noise and disorder were my allies as I swiftly discovered that Riddle was no longer there. I left, hoping that he was well recovered by now but surmising that he was actually recuperating someplace that was more conducive to rest. I stood outside the infirmary deciding what I should do next.

I hefted the purse Chade had left me. The coins I had hoped to spend to delight my little daughter still weighted it heavily – now supplemented by what Chade had left me. I had loaded my purse well at Withywoods in the belief that I would indulge her in every possible way on that market-day in Oaksbywater. Had it been only yesterday? Bleakness washed over me. What I had intended as a day of pleasure and indulgence had ended in violence and bloodshed. To save the Fool's life, I had sent her home without me, in the dubious guardianship of Scribe FitzVigilant and Lady Shun. Little Bee, only nine and looking more like a six-year-old. I wondered what sort of day she was having. Nettle had promised to send a bird to let her know I had arrived safely at Buckkeep, and I knew that my elder daughter would never fail me at such a task. So, later today, I would write letters, to FitzVigilant and Revel, but most especially to Bee. A top-notch messenger on a good horse could have them there in three days. Four if more snow fell . . . For now, the bird message would have to suffice. And while I had this time, I would take myself to Buckkeep Town, not just to buy myself a fresh set of garb with what coin I had from Chade but also to buy gifts for Bee. Winterfest gifts, I decided, to show her I had thought of her even if I could not be with her. I'd brought Chade's purse with me. I'd indulge myself by indulging her! Even if my gifts would reach her days late.

I chose to hike down to the town rather than Skilling to Dutiful or Nettle to arrange a horse from the stables. Horses did not do well on the steeply cobbled streets, and Dutiful was doubtless still fully engaged with entertaining his trade delegations. Nettle was probably still very angry with me, as I well deserved. No harm in letting time cool her temper a bit.

I found the road wider than I recalled it, with trees cut back from the margin on both sides, and far fewer potholes and muddy swathes than I recalled. And the town was closer than it had been, for its sprawl of houses and shops had begun to crawl up the road to the castle. An area that once had been forest was now the outskirts of the town, with merchants of all sorts, a cheap tavern called the Buck Guard and what I suspected was a whore-house behind it. The door of the Bawdy Trout was off its hinges and a scowling innkeeper was repairing it. Past it, old Buckkeep Town was decked out for the feast-day to come, with garlands and evergreen boughs and brightly-coloured pennants. The streets were busy, not just with deliveries to taverns and inns, but with all the travellers and tradesfolk that prospered during a holiday.

It took some time for me to find the items I needed. In one shop that was obviously accustomed to catering to sailors and guardsmen, I found two cheap ready-made shirts that almost fitted, a long vest of brown wool, a heavy cloak and some trousers that would do for a time. I had to smile as I realized I had become accustomed to a much better quality of clothing. After giving that a thought, I went to a tailor's shop where I was swiftly measured and clothing was promised before two days had passed. I feared I would be in Buckkeep at least that long, but mentioned that if the clothing was ready faster, I would pay a bonus. I fumbled my way through estimating the Fool's height and greatly diminished girth, and they told me that if I returned by late afternoon, they would have smallclothes and two serviceable house-robes for him. I told them he was ill and that soft fabrics would be appreciated. The coins I left with them promised swift work.

With that necessary shopping out of the way, I took myself down to where music and merry chaos dominated the streets. Here was the Winterfest of my youth: puppetry and juggling, song and dance, vendors offering sweets and savoury treats, hedge witches selling potions and charms, girls in holly wreaths and every noisy joy the heart could hope for. I missed Molly, and longed ardently to have Bee at my side, experiencing this with me.

I bought things for her. Ribbons with bells on them, sticks of candy, a silver necklace with three amber birds on it, a packet of spiced nuts, a green scarf with yellow stars woven into it, a small belt-knife with a good horn handle, and then a canvas bag to carry it all in. It came to me that a messenger could just as easily take this bag to her as a simple letter from me, and so I filled it. A necklace made from speckled seashells from some faraway beach, a pomander for her winter woollens chest, and on, until the bag would barely close. For the moment, it was a blue-sky day, with a fresh wind that tasted of the ocean. A gem of a day, and I enjoyed imagining her delight in all the trinkets she would discover in this bag. As I loitered amid the merriment, I thought of the words I would write on the letter to go with it, letters written plain and clear that she might read my thoughts herself and know how much I regretted leaving her. But soon the wind brought a fresh bank of dark grey snowclouds scudding in. Time to return to the castle.

I stopped by the tailor's shop on my way back and was rewarded with garments for the Fool. As I left, lowering clouds that had been on the horizon stole in. Snow began to fall and the wind bared its teeth as I hurried up the steep road back to the castle. I was passed in at the gate as easily as I had left: the trade delegation and the merrymaking of Winterfest meant that the guards had been ordered to be generous in whom they admitted.

But it reminded me there was still a problem I'd soon have to solve. I needed an identity. Since I had shaved my beard to please my daughter, not only the staff of Withywoods but even Riddle had been astonished at my youthful appearance. After all the years I'd been absent from Buckkeep Castle, I feared to introduce myself as Tom Badgerlock, and not just because the streak of white in my hair that had prompted that name was long gone. The folk who recalled Tom Badgerlock would expect a man of sixty years, not someone who looked to be in his middle thirties.

Instead of using the kitchen entrance, I went about to a side hall and entered through a door mostly reserved for couriers and higher status servants. My bulging bag gained me entry, and to the one under-steward who asked me my business, I replied that I had a parcel for Lady Nettle and I was allowed to pass.

The wall-hangings and furniture of the castle had changed over the years, but the basic hierarchy of chambers remained as it had been since my boyhood. I went up a servant's stair, gained the floor reserved for lesser nobility, spent a small amount of time apparently waiting for someone to let me into an apartment there and, as soon as the corridor was cleared, successfully gained access to the next floor and the door to Lady Thyme's old chambers. The key turned smoothly and I entered the room. The concealed entrance to Chade's old chamber was through a wardrobe of musty old women's clothing.

My crawl through the wardrobe was as ungainly as it had been the night before, and I found myself wondering if all Chade's secrecy was truly needed. I knew the Fool had asked for these rooms because he still feared pursuit, but I trusted that our passage through the stones would thwart anyone who had been following him. Then I recalled how the White girl had died, with parasites eating her eyes, and decided that caution was ever the better path. Keeping the Fool well hidden could do no harm.

One of Chade's secretive minions had visited those chambers while I was gone. I needed to meet him. Or her. The Fool's filthy garments had been taken and the tub had been emptied and pushed into the corner. Last night's dishes and glasses had been tidied away. A heavy stoneware pot was lidded deep in the hearth, but the smell of braised beef had still escaped to flavour the room. A cloth had been spread on the table, and a loaf wrapped in a clean yellow napkin reposed next to a small dish of pale winter butter. There was a dusty bottle of red wine and a couple of cups, alongside plates and cutlery.

Kettricken was probably responsible for the two sensible linen nightgowns draped over the chair. Two pairs of loose trousers in the same weave were with them. Lambs' wool bed stockings were neatly rolled into balls. I smiled, considering it quite possible that the former queen had raided her own wardrobe for these soft things. I gathered the clothing and set it on the foot of the Fool's bed.

The garments left on the second chair were more puzzling. A sky-blue dress, with dagged sleeves and dozens more buttons than any garment required to close it was on the chair back. On the seat of the chair, almost-sensible trousers of black wool terminated in cuffs of blue-and-white stripes. The slippers beside them resembled a pair of small boats, with pointed and upturned toes and a thick heel. I thought they were too large for the Fool even if he had been well enough to walk around Buckkeep.

I had been aware of his deep and steady breathing since I entered the chamber. It was good that he still slept and I suppressed my boyish impulse to wake him and ask him how he felt. Instead, I found paper and sat down at Chade's old worktable to compose my note to Bee. I was full of words, managed a greeting, and then stared at the paper for a time. There was so much I needed to say, from reassurances that I would quickly return to advice for dealing with FitzVigilant and

Shun. Could I be certain that hers would be the only eyes to read what I wrote? I hoped so and yet my old training came to the fore and I decided not to commit to paper any words that could create ill feeling toward her. So I wrote only that I hoped she would enjoy these small things. As I had long promised, there was a knife for her belt, which I trusted she would use wisely. I reminded her that I would return home as soon as I could, and that I hoped she would use her time well while I was gone. I did not command her to study hard with her new tutor. In truth, I rather hoped that between my absence and the winter holiday, they would set lessons aside for a time. But I did not commit that thought to paper either. Instead I closed my message with hoping that she had enjoyed Winterfest and that I missed her terribly. Then I sat for a time promising myself that Revel at least would be sure that there was some festivity for the holiday. I had intended to find some minstrels that fateful day in Oakshywater. Cook Nutmeg had proposed a menu that Revel had embellished. It was somewhere on my desk at home.

I had to do better by my daughter. I had to, and so I would. But there was little I could do about it until I returned home. The gifts would have to suffice until I could be there for Bee.

I spindled my note and tied it with some of Chade's twine. I found his sealing wax and melted a bit onto the knot, and imprinted the blob with my signet ring. No charging buck for FitzChivalry Farseer, only the badger's footprint that belonged to Holder Tom Badgerlock. I stood and stretched. I'd need to find a courier.

My Wit prickled. My nostrils flared, trying to find a scent. I did not move, but I let my gaze rove about the room. There. Behind a heavy tapestry of hounds pursuing a deer that concealed one of the secret entryways to the chamber, someone breathed. I centred myself in my body. My own breathing was silent. I did not reach for a weapon but I shifted my weight to my feet so that I could stand, move, leap or drop to the floor in an instant. I waited.

'Don't attack me, sir, please.' A boy's voice. The words had a country lad's drawn-out vowels.

'Come in.' I made no promises.

He hesitated. Then, very slowly, he pushed the tapestry to one side and stepped out into the dim light of the chamber. He showed me his hands, the right one empty, the left holding a scroll. 'A message for you, sir. That's all.'

I assessed him carefully. Young, perhaps twelve. His body had not yet turned the corner to manhood. Bony, with narrow shoulders. He'd never be a large man. He wore the Buckkeep blue of a page. His hair was brown and as curly as a water dog's, and his eyes were brown as well. And he was cautious. He'd shown himself but not stepped far into the room. That he had sensed danger and announced himself to me raised him in my estimation.

'A message from whom?' I asked.

The tip of his tongue wet his lips. 'A man who knew to send it to you here. A man who taught me the way to come here.'

'How do you know I'm the one it's for?'

'He said you'd be here.'

'But anyone might be here.'

He shook his head but didn't argue with me. 'Nose broken a long time ago and old blood on your shirt.'

'Bring it to me, then.'

He came like a fox thinking of stealing a dead rabbit from a snare. He walked lightly and did not take his eyes from me. When he reached the table's edge, he set the scroll down and stepped back.

'Is that all?' I asked him.

He glanced around the room, at the firewood and the food. 'And whatever else you might wish me to fetch for you, sir.'

'And your name is . . .?'

Again he hesitated. 'Ash, sir.' He waited, watching me.

'There's nothing else I need, Ash. You may go.'

'Sir,' he replied. He stepped back, not turning nor taking his eyes from me. One slow step after another he retreated until his hands touched the tapestry. Then he whisked himself behind it. I waited, but did not hear the scuff of his steps on the stairs.

After a moment, I rose silently and ghosted toward the tapestry. But when I snatched it back, empty air met my gaze. He was gone as if he'd never been there. I permitted myself a nod. On his third try, Chade seemed to have found himself a worthy apprentice. I wondered how much of the training he did, or if Lady Rosemary taught the boy, and where they had found him . . . and then I set it firmly out of my thoughts. None of my business. And if I were wise, I'd ask few questions and become as little involved in the current state of assassinations and politics at Buckkeep as I could. My life was complicated enough already.

I was hungry, but thought I'd wait a bit longer to see if the Fool would awaken and eat with me. I went back to the worktable and drew Chade's scroll toward me. Within the first two lines, I felt the webs of Buckkeep intrigue tightening around me again. 'As you are here, with little to do other than wait for his health to improve, perhaps you are willing to make yourself useful? Clothing has been provided, and the expectation has been planted that the court will be visited by Lord Feldspar of Spiretop, a small but well-established holding in the far northwest corner of Buck. Lord Feldspar is as stony as his name, fond of drink, and there is a rumour that a copper mine on his holding has recently begun to produce very fine grade ore. Thus he has come to Buckkeep to be a party to the current trade negotiations.'

There was more. I was never once addressed by name, the handwriting was not recognizably Chade's, but oh, the game clearly was. I finished reading the scroll and went to consider the outlandish dress that had been left for me. I sighed. I had some time yet before I would be expected to join them for an evening meal and conversation in the great hall. I knew my role. Talk little, listen a great deal, and report back to Chade all details as to who sought me out to make an offer and how rich the offer was. I could not imagine what the greater game was. I knew that Chade would have decided what I needed to know and given me exactly that much. Weaving his webs as he ever did.

And yet despite my annoyance, I felt a stirring of the old excitement as well. It was Winterfest eve. The castle kitchen would have outdone itself, there would be music and dancing and folk from all over the Six Duchies. With my new identity and in dress that would both draw attention to me and mark me as a stranger, I would once more spy for Chade as I had when I was a youth.

I held the dress up against me. No. Not a dress, a fussy and foppish long jacket, to go with the impractical shoes. The buttons were dyed bone, carved into little blue posies, and they were not just on the front but on the long cuffs as well. Lots of buttons. Buttons that did no buttoning, but were mere ornamentation. The fabric was soft, a kind I had not seen before, and when I held the garment by the shoulders, it proved far heavier than I had expected it to be. I frowned, then quickly realized that the secret pockets had already been loaded for me.

I found a very nice set of small burglary picks and a tiny fine-toothed saw blade. In another pocket, there was an extremely sharp blade of the sort favoured by cutpurses. I doubted I was deft enough to ply that trade. The few times I'd done it for Chade it had not been for the coins but to see what love-notes were in Regal's purse, or which servant seemed to possess far more wages than an honest serving-man would carry. Years ago. So many years ago.

I heard a low moan from the Fool's bed. I slung the jacket over my arm and hastened to his side. 'Fool. Are you awake?'

His brow was lined, his eyes tightly closed, but at my voice something almost like a smile bent his mouth. 'Fitz. It's a dream, isn't it?'

'No, my friend. You're here at Buckkeep. And safe.'

'Oh, Fitz. I am never safe.' He coughed a bit. 'I thought I was dead. I became aware, but then there wasn't any pain, and I wasn't cold. So I thought I was dead, finally. Then I moved, and all the pains woke up.'

'I'm sorry, Fool.' I was to blame for his most recent injuries. I hadn't recognized him when I saw him clutching Bee. And so I had rushed to save my child from a diseased and possibly mad beggar, only to discover that the man I had stabbed half a dozen times was my oldest friend in the world. The swift Skill-healing I'd imposed on him had closed the knife wounds and kept him from bleeding to death. But it had weakened him as well, and in the course of that healing, I'd become aware of the multitude of old injuries and the infections that still raged inside him. Those would kill him, slowly, if I could not help him gain strength enough for a more thorough healing. 'Are you hungry? There's beef cooked to tenderness by the hearth. And red wine, and bread. And butter.'

He was silent for a time. His blind eyes were a dull grey in the dim light of the room. They moved in his face as if he still strove to see out of them. 'Truly?' he asked in a shaky voice. 'Truly all that food? Oh, Fitz. I almost don't dare to move, lest I wake up and find the warmth and the blankets all a dream.'

'Shall I bring your food there, then?'

'No, no, don't do that. I spill so badly. It's not just that I can't see, it's my hands. They shake. And twitch.'

He moved his fingers and I felt ill. On one hand, all the soft pads of his fingers had been sliced away to leave thickly-scarred tips. The knuckles of both hands were overly large on his bony fingers. Once he had had such elegant hands, such clever hands for juggling and puppetry and woodcarving. I looked away from them. 'Come, then. Let's take you back to the chair by the fireside.'

'Let me lead, then, and you only warn me of a disaster. I'd like to learn the room. I've become quite clever at learning rooms since they blinded me.'

I could think of nothing to say to that. He leaned heavily on my arm but I let him make his own groping way. 'More to the left,' I cautioned him once. He limped, as if every step on his swollen feet pained him. I wondered how he had managed to come so far, alone and blinded, following roads he could not see. Later, I told myself. There would be time for that tale later.

His reaching hand touched the chair back and then felt down it to the arm. It took him some time to manoeuvre himself into the chair and settle there. The sigh he gave was not one of contentment but of a difficult task accomplished. His fingers danced lightly on the tabletop. Then he stilled them in his lap. 'The pain is bad, but even with the pain, I think I can manage the journey back. I will rest here, for a time, and heal a bit. Then, together, we will go back to burn out that nest of vermin. But I will need my vision, Fitz. I must be a help to you, not a hindrance, as we make our way back to Clerres. Together, we will bring them the justice they deserve.'

Justice. The word soaked into me. Chade had always called our assassin's tasks 'quiet work' or 'the king's justice'. If I took on this quest of his, what would it be? The Fool's justice? 'Food in just a moment,' I said, letting his worry go unanswered for now.

I did not trust him to be wise enough to exercise restraint with how much food he took. I dished the food up for him, a small portion of meat cut into little bites and bread buttered and cut into strips. I poured wine for him. I took his hand, thinking to guide it to the dish, but I had not warned him, and he jerked back as if I had burned him with a poker, nearly oversetting his dishes. 'Sorry,' we exclaimed in unison. I grinned at that, but he did not.

'I was trying to show you where your food was,' I explained gently.

His head was bent as if he were looking down in shame. 'I know,' he said quietly. Then, like timid mice, his crippled hands crept to the edge of the table, and then ventured cautiously forward until he found the edge of his plate. His hands moved lightly over the dish, touching what was there. He picked up a piece of the meat and put into his mouth. I started to tell him there was a fork at the side of his plate. I stopped myself. He knew that. I would not correct a tormented man as if he were a forgetful child. His hands crabbed over to the napkin and found it.

For a time, we ate together in silence. When he had finished what was on the plate, he asked softly if I would cut more meat and bread for him. As I did that, he asked suddenly, 'So. How was your life while I was gone?'

For a moment, I froze. Then I transferred the cut meat to his plate. 'It was a life,' I said, and was amazed at how steady my voice was. I groped for words; how does one summarize twenty-four years? How does one recount a courtship, a marriage, a child, and a widowing? I began.

'Well. That last time I left you? I became lost in the Skill-pillar on the way home. A passage that had taken but moments on my previous journeys took me months. When the pillar finally spat me out, I was near senseless. And when I came to my wits, some days later, I found you had been and gone. Chade gave me your gift, the carving. I finally met Nettle. That did not go well, at first. I, uh, I courted Molly. We married.' My words ground to a halt. Even telling the tale in such bald terms, my heart broke over all I had had, and all I had lost. I wanted to say we had been happy. But I could not bear to put that in the past tense.

'I'm sorry for your loss,' he spoke the formal words. From him, they were sincere. It took me aback for a few moments.

'How did you . . .?'

'How did I know?' He made a small incredulous sound. 'Oh, Fitz. Why do you think I left? To leave you to find a life as close as possible to the one that I had always foreseen would follow my death. In so many futures, after my death, I saw you court Molly tirelessly, win her back, and finally take for yourself some of the happiness and peace that had always eluded you when I was near. In so many futures, I foresaw that she would die and you would be left alone. But that does not undo what you had, and that was the best I could wish for you. Years with your Molly. She loved you so.'

He resumed eating. I sat very still. My throat was clenched so tight that the pain nearly choked me. It was difficult even to breathe past that lump. Blind as he was, I think he still knew of my distress. For a long time he ate very slowly, as if to stretch out both the meal and the silence I needed. Slowly he wiped the last of the meat juices from his plate with his final bite of bread. He ate it, wiped his fingers on the napkin, and then walked his hand over to his wine. He lifted it and sipped, his face almost beatific. He set the cup down and then said quietly, 'My memories of yesterday are very confusing to me.'

I held my silence.

'I had walked through most of the previous night, I think. I remember the snow, and knowing that I must not stop until I found some sort of shelter. I had a good stick, and that helps more than I can say when a man has no eyes. And bad feet. It's hard for me to walk without a stick, now. But I did. I knew I was on the road to Oaksbywater. Now I remember. A cart passed me, with the driver cursing and shouting at me to get out of the way. So I did. But I found his cart-tracks in the snow and knew that if I followed them, they had to lead me to some sort of shelter. So I walked. My feet got numb, and that meant less pain, but I fell more often. I think it was very late when I reached Oaksbywater. A dog barked at me, and someone shouted at it. The cart-tracks led to a stable. I could not get inside, but there was a pile of straw and manure outside.' He folded his lips for a moment and then said wryly, 'I've learned that dirty straw and manure are often warm.'

I nodded, then realized he could not see me. 'They are,' I conceded.

'I slept a bit, and then woke when the town started to stir around me. I heard a girl singing and recognized one of the old Winterfest songs from when I lived at Buckkeep. And so I knew it might be a good day to beg. Holidays bring out the kindness in some people. So I thought I would beg and try to get some food in me and then, if I encountered someone who seemed kind, I would ask them to put me on the path to Withywoods.'

'So you were coming to find me.'

He nodded slowly. His hand crept back to his wine cup. He found it, drank sparingly and set it down. 'Of course I was coming to find you. So. I was begging, but the shopkeeper kept ranting at me to move on. I knew I should. But I was so tired, and the place where I had settled was out of the wind. Wind is a cruel thing, Fitz. A day that is cold but bearable when the air is still becomes a constant torment when a wind rises.' His voice fell away and he hunched his shoulders as if even the memory of wind could freeze him now.

'Then, hmm. A boy came by. He gave me an apple. Then the shopkeeper cursed me and shouted at her husband to come and drive me off. And the boy helped me to move away from the door. And . . .' The Fool's words trailed away. His head moved, wagging from side to side. I did not think he was aware of it. It reminded me of a hound casting about for a lost scent. Then plaintive words burst from him. 'It was so vivid, Fitz! He was the son I was seeking. The boy touched me and I could see with his vision. I could feel the strength he might have, some day, if he were trained, if he were not corrupted by the Servants. I'd found him and I could not contain my joy.' Yellowish tears spilled slowly from his eyes and began to track down his scarred face. All too well, I recalled the request that he had sent his messengers to give me: that I search for the 'Unexpected Son'. His son? A child he had fathered, despite all I knew of him? In the time since his messenger had reached me and then died, I'd mulled over a dozen possibilities as to who the mother of such a son might be.

'I found him,' the Fool continued. 'And I lost him. When you stabbed me.'

Shame and guilt washed over me in a wave. 'Fool. I am so sorry. If only I had recognized you, I never would have hurt you.'

He shook his head. One clawlike hand found his napkin. He mopped his face with it. His words came out as hoarse as a crow's caw. 'What happened, Fitz? What . . . provoked you to try to kill me?'

'I mistook you for someone dangerous. Someone who would hurt a child. I came out of the tavern, looking for my little girl.'

'Your little girl?' His words broke through my explanation in an incredulous shout.

'Yes. My Bee.' Despite all else, I smiled. 'Molly and I had a child together, Fool, a tiny girl.'

'No.' His denial was absolute. 'No. Not in any future I saw did you have another child.' His brow was furrowed. Scarred as his face was, it was not easy to read his emotions, but he looked almost furious. 'I KNOW I would have seen that. I am the true White Prophet. I would have seen that.' He slapped his hand on the table, jerked with the pain and cradled it to his chest. 'I would have seen that,' he insisted more quietly.

'But we did,' I said softly. 'I know it's hard to believe. We thought we couldn't. Molly told me her time for bearing was past. But then she had Bee. Our little girl.'

'No.' He said the word stubbornly. He pinched his lips flat together, and then abruptly his chin trembled like a child's. 'It can't be. Fitz, it can't be so. How can that be true? If I did not see such an immense event in your life, what else did I miss? How wrong can I have been about so many other things? Was I wrong about myself?' He fell silent for a time. His blind eyes shifted back and forth, trying to find me. 'Fitz. Do not be angry that I ask this, for I must.' He hesitated and then asked in a whisper, 'Are you sure? Can you be positive? Are you certain the child was yours, and not just Molly's?'

'She is mine,' I said flatly. I was astonished at how much insult I took at his words. 'Definitely mine,' I added defiantly. 'She has a Mountain look to her, like my mother.'

'The mother you scarcely remember.'

'I remember her enough to say that my child looks like her. And I remember Molly well enough to know that Bee is my daughter. Without question. Fool, this is not worthy of you.'

He lowered his eyes and bowed his head. 'So few things are, any more,' he decided. He rose with a lurch that shook the table. 'I'm going back to the bed. I don't feel well.' He shuffled away from me, one knotted hand feeling the air before him while the other curled protectively near his chin.

'I know you're not well,' I replied, suddenly repentant for how harshly I'd rebuked him. 'You are not yourself, Fool. But you will be again. You will be.'

'Do you think so?' he asked. He did not turn toward me but spoke to the empty air in front of him. 'I am not certain of that myself. I've spent over a decade with people who insisted that I was never who I thought I was. Never the White Prophet, only a boy with vivid dreams. And what you have just told me makes me wonder if they did not have the right of it.'

I hated seeing him so defeated. 'Fool. Remember what you told me so long ago. We move now in a time that you never foresaw. One where we are both alive.'

He made no response to my words. He reached the bed, groped along the edge, then turned and sat down on it. Then he more crumpled than lay down, pulled the covers up over his head and was completely still.

'I tell you the truth, old friend. I have a daughter, a small girl who depends on me. And I cannot leave her. I must be the one to raise her, to teach her and protect her. It's a duty I can't forsake. And one I do not want to abandon.' I tidied as I spoke, wiping away the food he had spilled, corking the remainder of the wine. I waited and my heart continued to sink as he made no response. Finally I said, 'What you asked me to do last night. I'd do it for you. You know that. If I could, I would. But now I ask you, as you asked me last night; for my sake, understand that I must say no to you. For now.'

The silence unspooled like a dropped ball of yarn. I'd said the words I must, and the sense of them would soak into him. He was not a selfish man, nor a cruel one. He'd recognize the truth of what I had told him. I couldn't go anywhere with him, no matter how badly someone needed to be killed. I had a child to raise and protect. Bee had to come first. I went to the bedside and smoothed the bedclothes on my side of the bed. Perhaps he'd fallen asleep. I spoke softly.

'I can't be here this evening,' I told him. 'Chade has a task for me. It may be very late before I come back. Will you be all right alone here?'

Still no response. I wondered if he truly had fallen asleep that quickly, or if he were sulking. *Leave it alone, Fitz,* I counselled myself. He was a sick man. Rest would do more for him than anything else.

TWO

Lord Feldspar

What is a secret? It is much more than knowledge shared with only a few, or perhaps only one other. It is power. It is a bond. It may be a sign of deep trust, or the darkest threat possible.

There is power in the keeping of a secret, and power in the revelation of a secret. Sometimes it takes a very wise man to discern which is the path to greater power.

All men desirous of power should become collectors of secrets. There is no secret too small to be valuable. All men value their own secrets far above those of others. A scullery maid may be willing to betray a prince before allowing the name of her secret lover to be told.

Be very chary of telling your hoarded secrets. Many lose all power once they have been divulged. Be even more careful of sharing your own secrets lest you find yourself a puppet dancing on someone else's strings.

Confidence Mayhen – *The Assassin's Other Tool*

I'd not eaten much, but my appetite was gone. I tidied our table. The Fool was either asleep or feigning it perfectly. I resigned myself to silence from him. With some trepidation, I dressed myself in the clothing that Chade had provided for Lord Feldspar. It fitted me well enough, though it was looser around the chest and belly than I had expected it to be. I was surprised at how comfortable it was. I transferred a few of the items from one concealed pocket to another. I sat down to put on the shoes.

They had more of a heel than I was accustomed to, and extended far past my foot before terminating in upcurled toes decorated with little tassels. I tried a few steps in them, and then walked the length of the chamber five times until I was certain that I could move with confidence and not trip myself.

Chade had a large looking-glass of excellent quality, as much for his own vanity as for the training of his apprentices. I recalled one long night when he had me stand in front of it for most of a watch, trying to smile first sincerely, then disarmingly, then sarcastically, then humbly . . . his list had gone on and on, until my face ached. Now I lifted a branch of candles and looked at Lord Feldspar of Spiretop. There was also a hat, rather like a soft bag, edged with gilt embroidery and a row of decorative buttons and incorporating a fine wig of brown ringlets. I set it on my head and wondered if it was supposed to wilt over to one side as much as it did.

Chade kept a tinker's tray of odd jewellery in the cupboard. I chose two showy rings for myself and hoped they would not turn my fingers green. I warmed water and shaved and inspected myself again. I had just resigned myself to creeping out of the room under the smelly garments in Lady Thyme's old room when I felt a slight draught. I stood still, listening, and at just the right moment, I asked, 'Don't you think it's time you entrusted me with the trick of triggering that door?'

'I suppose I will have to, now that you are Lord Feldspar and inhabiting the room below.' Chade stepped around the corner, halted, and then nodded his approval at my attire. 'The trigger is not where you'd think it would be. It's not even on this wall. Look here.' He walked to the hearth, swung a brick aside, mortar and all, and showed me a black iron lever. 'It's a bit stiff. I'll have the boy grease it later.' And so saying, he pulled the lever and the draught was abruptly closed off.

'How do you open the door from my old room?' I'd lost count of how many hours I'd spent searching for that trigger when I was a boy.

He sighed and then smiled. 'One after another, my secrets have fallen to you. I'll confess, I've always been amused by your inability to find that one. I thought that surely you would stumble on it by accident if nothing else. It's in the drapery pull. Close the curtains completely, and then give a final tug. You won't see or hear a thing, but then you can push the door open. And now you know.'

'And now I know,' I agreed. 'After half a century of wondering.'

'Surely not half a century.'

'I'm sixty,' I reminded him. 'And you started me in the trade when I was less than ten. So, yes, half a century and more.'

'Don't remind me of my years,' he told me, and then sat down with a sigh. 'It's unfair of you to prate of passing time when it seems to touch you not at all. Tip your hat a bit more to the back. That's it. Before you go, we'll redden your nose a little and give you higher colour in your cheeks so it will appear you've begun your drinking early. And we'll thicken your brows.' He tilted his head to consider me critically. 'And that should be enough to keep anyone from recognizing you. What's this?' he demanded, pulling Bee's parcel toward him.

'Something that I'd like to dispatch immediately to Withywoods. Things for Bee. I had to leave her quite abruptly, in a very peculiar way. It's the first Winterfest since her mother died. I'd hoped to be there with her.'

'It will be on its way within the day,' he promised me gravely. 'I sent a small troop of guards there this morning. If I'd known you had a message, I would have sent it with them. They'll travel swiftly.'

'It has little gifts for her from the market. For a late Winterfest surprise. Wait, you sent a troop of guards? Why?'

'Fitz, where are your wits? You've left Shun and FitzVigilant there, unprotected. You haven't even doorguards. Luckily I've one or two fellows about the place who know their business. Not much muscle among them, but keen eyes. They'll warn Lant if they see anything threatening. And weather permitting, my troop will be there in three days or so. They're a rough band, but I've seen that their commander is bringing them around. Captain Stout keeps them on a taut lead, until he lets them loose. And then nothing stops them.' He sounded very satisfied with his choice. He drummed his fingers on the table edge. 'Though the daily bird hasn't arrived, but sometimes that happens when the weather is foul.'

'Daily bird?'

'Fitz, I am a thorough man. I watch over my own. That includes you, for all your years there. And now when a messageless bird arrives, I know that all is well for Lant and Shun as well. It's only sensible.'

I'd known he had at least one watcher in place at Withywoods. I hadn't realized that a daily report had been sent to him. Well, not a report. A bird with no message meant all was well. 'Chade, I'm ashamed that I gave no thought to Shun and FitzVigilant when I brought the Fool here. You entrusted them to me. It was a dire situation: I'm afraid it drove all other thoughts out of my head.'

He was nodding as I spoke, his face grave and his mouth without expression. I'd disappointed him. He cleared his throat and very deliberately shifted the topic. 'So. Do you think you can masquerade as Lord Feldspar for an evening or three? It would be very handy for me if I had a man mingling with the crowd who knew how to listen and how to steer a conversation.'

'I think I can still do that.' I felt abashed at failing him. This was the least I could do. 'What were you hoping to discover?'

'Oh, the usual. Anything interesting. Who is trying to make deals out of sight of the crown? Who has been offering bribes to get better trading terms; who has been taking bribes? What is the general feeling about placating the dragons? Of course, the most valuable information you can discover would be any little facts that we aren't expecting.'

'Do I have any specific targets?'

'Five. No, six, perhaps.' He scratched his ear. 'I trust you to find a trail and follow it. I'll make some suggestions, but keep your ears open for any interesting propositions.'

And for the next few hours he educated me in the various seesaws of power currently in play in the Six Duchies. He described each of the four men and two women that he wished me to spy upon, right down to their preferences for drink, which ones used smoke and the two that were rumoured to be meeting behind their spouses' backs. Chade gave me a swift tutoring on copper mining so that I could at least appear knowledgeable, and advised me to maintain a crafty silence should anyone ask me detailed questions about my operations or the new vein of ore we had reportedly discovered.

And for a time, I put my life and time back in the old man's hands. It would not be fair to say that I forgot my grief at losing Molly or stopped worrying about Bee or resigned myself to the Fool's declining health. What I did was to step outside of my real life and step back into one in which all I had to do was obey Chade's directives and report back to him what I had learned. There was deep comfort in that. It was almost healing to discover that despite all I had been through, all my losses and all my daily fears and worries, I was still Fitz and this was something I was still very good at.

When he had finished informing me for my task, he tilted his head toward the Fool's bed. 'How is he?'

'Not himself. In pain and emotionally frail. I upset him and he went back to his bed. And immediately fell asleep.'

'Not surprising. You're wise to let him sleep.' He picked up Bee's parcel, weighed it in his hand and smiled indulgently. 'I doubt that any child in Buckkeep Castle will get a heftier sack of holiday loot than this. I've an excellent courier. He'll ride out tonight with this.'

'Thank you,' I said humbly.

He wagged a dismissive finger at me and then left, taking the package with him. I descended the hidden staircase to the room that had been mine when I was young and closed the door behind me. I halted there briefly to admire the staging of the room. There was a travelling case, of good quality, but dusty and battered as if it had come a long way. It was open and partially unpacked, with items of clothing draped carelessly over the chair. Several of the new-appearing items featured a plenitude of buttons. I made a cursory examination of the trunk's contents. In addition to a selection of clothes that would fit me and were not obviously new, there was all that a man would be likely to pack for an extended stay. Anyone who sought to slip the lock on my room and inspect my things would most likely be convinced that I was indeed Lord Feldspar, right down to my monogrammed kerchiefs. I tucked one of those into my pocket and descended to the merrymaking of Winterfest Eve in Buckkeep.

And, oh, how I loved it. There was music and excellent food and drink of all manner flowed freely. Some people were enjoying smoke in tiny braziers at their tables. Young ladies in their best dresses flirted outrageously with young men in bright and impractical garb. More buttons. And I was not the only one in heeled slippers with twirled toes. Indeed my footwear was among the more modest in that regard. It made the lively dances of Winterfest a true contest of agility, and more than one youngster was brought low by an untimely slip.

I had only one bad moment, and that was when I glimpsed Web across the room. I became aware of Buckkeep's Witmaster in a way that I can't describe. I think as he quested toward me with his Wit, wondering why I seemed familiar, I somehow became aware of the magic's touch on me. I turned away and made an excuse to leave that area of the room. I did not see him again that evening.

I located those Chade had bid me find, and insinuated myself into conversations. I appeared to drink a great deal more than I really did, and thoroughly enjoyed playing the role of a mildly inebriated lordling who bragged indiscreetly about the newfound wealth of his holdings. I moved among the merchants and tradesfolk rather than near the dais where the nobility and royalty congregated to socialize with trade delegates from Bingtown, Jamaillia and Kelsingra. I caught only passing glimpses of Lady Kettricken, dressed in a simple gown of pale yellow with trim of Buckkeep blue.

King Dutiful and Queen Elliania passed through the chamber, pacing sedately, accepting and bestowing greetings from the lesser nobles and well-placed merchants. King Dutiful was appropriately solemn and kingly. He had recently begun to cultivate a well-groomed beard which added to his gravitas. The queen smiled, and her hand rode on the back of Dutiful's forearm. Her crown rode on a short crop of black curls not much longer than mine; I'd heard she had not allowed her hair to grow since she had lost a girl infant. This marked sign of her continued mourning troubled me even as I too well understood it, but I was glad to see her at the gathering.

The wild girl I had once watched leaping her pony over obstacles was a child no longer. She was small and dark and one might have expected tall, blonde Kettricken, the former Queen of the Six Duchies, to dominate the festivities. But she did not. The two had come into an accord years ago, and balanced one another well. Whereas Kettricken urged the kingdom to embrace new ways, new trading partners and new ways of doing things, Elliania was a traditionalist. Her matriarchal upbringing in the OutIslands had imbued her with confidence in her right to rule. Her two sons walked behind her, impeccably attired in Buckkeep blue, yet every silver button on their garments featured their mother's leaping narwhal. I'd known them as babies and as small boys. Those days were long gone now. They were young men now, and Prince Prosper wore the simple crown of the King-in-Waiting. Prince Integrity favoured his OutIslander mother but had developed the Farseer brow. I smiled as the royal family passed, tears of pride stinging my eyes. Our doing, the Fool's and mine. Peace between the Six Duchies and the OutIslands at last. I feigned a cough to dab at my watering eyes. I turned aside hastily and pushed my way deeper into the crowd. That sort of behaviour would never suit Lord Feldspar. *Control yourself, Fitz.*

Lord Feldspar, Chade and I had decided, bore a greedy merchant's heart beneath his noble title. He would have no tender feelings toward his rulers, only a stony resolve to retain as much of his tax-money as he could. I played my role well. To every minor noble that deigned introduce himself to me, I muttered disconsolately over how much of my taxes had gone to fund these festivities and snarled at the thought of my money used to subsidize meat herds for dragons. Dragons! Those with the bad fortune to live near the dragons' hunting territories should feed them. Or move. It was not up to me to pay for their poor choices! I insinuated myself into conversations near my targets, and made sure my complaints were audible.

I had expected that one of our noble guests would be the one to propose bypassing the tax collectors of the Six Duchies, but when I was finally targeted it was by a young man from Farrow. He was not a lord or a merchant, but the son of a man who operated freight barges on the river. He smiled and spoke me fair and made a dedicated effort to ply me with stronger drink. He was not one of Chade's targets, but his sly hints that there was money to be made by a man who knew how to bypass the taxing agents at the river- and sea-ports made me think that he was a thread that would bear following. I used the Skill to reach out mentally to Chade and became aware that my old mentor was using Thick's strength to help him be fully aware not only of King Dutiful but of several of the coterie members. I kept my sending to him private and small as I drew his attention to my drinking partner.

Ah. Well done. That was all he Skilled back to me, but I shared his sense of satisfaction and knew I had given him the bit of information that made sense of some puzzle he had been working to solve.

I separated myself from the young man and mingled and wandered for several hours more. Winterfest was a significant holiday and the dukes and duchesses of all the Six Duchies were in attendance. I saw and was not seen as I recognized many an old friend or acquaintance from my earlier years. Duchess Celerity of Bearns had aged gracefully. Several lifetimes ago she had taken a fancy to FitzChivalry. I hoped she had had a good life. The little lad trotting at her heels was probably a grandson. Perhaps even a great-grandson. There were others, not just nobles but serving folk and tradesmen. Not as many as I would have recognized a score of years ago. Time's nets had dragged many of them from this life.

The night grew deep, and the room was warm with the press of bodies and the sweat of the dancers. I was not surprised when the young river trader sought me out to introduce me to a very friendly sea captain from Bingtown. He introduced himself as a New Trader, and immediately shared with me that he had little patience for the Bingtown system of tithes and levies on foreign goods. 'The Old Traders are wedged in their ways. If they will not shake off the past and realize they must open their doors to less restricted trade, well, there are those who will find a window.' I nodded to him and asked if I might call on him the day after Winterfest. He gave me a small shingle of wood with the name of his ship and his own name lettered onto its smooth surface. He was staying at the Bloody Hounds near the warehouse docks and would look forward to my visit. Another fish for Chade's net.

For a time, I indulged myself and took a seat at one of the lesser hearths to hear a minstrel recite one of the traditional Winterfest tales. When I went seeking some chilled cider, a young woman who had had too much to drink caught me by the arm and demanded that I dance the next measure with her. She could not have been more than twenty, and to me she suddenly seemed a foolish child in a dangerous place. I wondered where her parents were and how they could leave her drunken and alone in the midst of the festival.

But I danced with her, one of the old partner-dances, and despite my fancy toes and lifted heels managed to keep to the steps and mark the time correctly. It was a merry dance and she was a pretty girl with dark curls and brown eyes and layers upon layers of skirts, all in shades of blue. Yet by the end of the dance I was filled to brimming with loneliness and a deep sadness for all the years that were now behind me. I thanked her and escorted her to a seat near the hearth and then slipped away. My Winterfest Eve, I thought, was over and I suddenly missed a little hand in mine and big blue eyes looking up at me. For the first time in my life, I wished my little girl had the Skill so that I could reach out to her across the snowy distance and assure her that I loved her and missed her.

As I sought my room, I knew that Chade would be as good as his word. Doubtless a messenger was already in the saddle on his way to Withywoods, my parcel and note in his pack. Yet it would be days before she received it and knew that I had thought of her in the midst of the festivities. Why had I never accepted Chade's offer to give me a Skilled apprentice at Withywoods, one who could, in my absence, relay news and messages from there? It would have still been a poor substitute for holding my child in my arms and whirling her in a dance at midnight, but it would have been something.

Bee, I love you I Skilled out, as if somehow that errant thought could reach her. I felt the soft brush of both Nettle's and Chade's shared thought: I'd had as much drink as was good for me. And perhaps I had, for I Skilled to them, *I miss her so.*

Neither one had a reply to that, so I bade them goodnight.

THREE

The Taking of Bee

Sometimes, it is true, a great leader arises who, by virtue of charisma, persuades others to follow him into a path that leads to greater good. Some would have you believe that to create great and powerful change, one must be that leader.

The truth is that dozens, hundreds, thousands of people have conspired to bring the leader to that moment. The midwife who delivered his grandmother is as essential to that change as is the man who shod his horse so that he might ride forth to rally his followers. The absence of any one of those people can tumble the leader from power as swiftly as an arrow through his chest.

Thus, to effect change does not demand military might nor the ruthlessness of murder. Nor must one be prescient. Gifted with the records of hundreds of prescient Whites, anyone can become a Catalyst. Anyone can precipitate the tiny change that tumbles one man from power and boosts another into his place. This is the change that hundreds of Servants before you have made possible. We are no longer dependent on a single White Prophet to find a better path for the world. It is now within the power of the Servants to smooth the path we all seek to follow.

Servant Imakiahen – *Instructions*

Snow was falling, white stars cascading down from the black sky. I was on my back, staring up at the night. The cold white flakes melting on my face had wakened me. Not from sleep, I thought.

Not from rest, but from a peculiar stillness. I sat up slowly, feeling giddy and sick.

I had been hearing the sounds and smelling the smells for some time. In my dazed state, the roasting meat of Winterfest had been enticing, and the crackling was the sound of the huge logs in the grand hearth in the Great Hall. A minstrel was tuning some sea-pipes, the deepest voiced of traditional wind instruments.

But now I was awake and I stared in horror. This was no celebration of Winterfest Eve. This was the opposite of a gathering to drive darkness from our homes. This was a wallowing in destruction. The stables were burning. The charring meat was dead horses and men. The long low tones that had seemed to be the slow awakening of musical instruments were the confused moaning of the folk of Withywoods.

My folk.

I rubbed my eyes, wondering what had happened. My hands were heavy and floppy with no strength in them. They were stuffed into immense fur mittens. Or were they huge white furry paws? Not mine?

A jolt. Was I me? Was I someone else, thinking my thoughts? I shivered all over. 'I'm Bee,' I whispered to myself. 'I'm Bee Farseer. Who has attacked my home? And how came I to be here?'

I was bundled warmly against the cold, enthroned like a queen in the bed of an open sleigh I did not recognize. It was a marvellous sleigh. Two white horses in red-and-silver harness waited stoically to pull it. To either side of the driver's seat, cleverly wrought iron hangers held lanterns with glass sides and worked iron scrolls as decorations. They illuminated the cushioned seat for the driver and a passenger, and the gracefully curved edges of the sleigh's bed. I reached out, thinking to run my hand over the finely polished wood. I could not. I was rolled and wrapped and weighed with blankets and furs that bound my sleepy body as effectively as knotted ropes. The sleigh was drawn up at the edge of the carriageway that served the once grand doors of Withywoods. Those doors were caved in now, broken and useless.

I shook my head, trying to clear my mind of cobwebs. I should be doing something! I needed to do something, but my body felt heavy and soft, like bags of wet laundry. I could not remember how I had been returned to Withywoods, let alone dressed in a heavy fur robe and bundled into a sleigh. As if I were backtracking my day, trying to find a lost glove, I set what I could remember in order. I'd been in the schoolroom with the other children. Steward Revel, dying as he warned us to run. I'd hidden the other children in the secret passage in the walls of Withywoods, only to have the door closed to me. Fleeing with Perseverance. He'd been shot. I'd been captured. And I had been so happy to be captured. I recalled no more than that. But somehow I'd been brought back to Withywoods, buttoned into a heavy fur coat and swaddled into a dozen blankets. And now I was here, in a sleigh, watching my stables burn.

I turned my eyes away from the leaping orange flames of the burning stable and looked toward the manor. People, all the people I had known all my life, were gathered in front of the tall doors of Withywoods. They weren't dressed for the snow. They wore the clothes they had donned that morning for the day's work inside the manor. They huddled together, hugging themselves or clinging to one another for warmth. I saw several shorter figures and finally my blurry vision made out that they were the children I had earlier concealed. Against my stern admonition, they had come out and betrayed themselves. My slow thoughts put together the burning stable and the hidden children. Perhaps they had been wise to come out. Perhaps the raiders would next burn the house.

The raiders. I squeezed my eyes shut and opened them again, fighting for clarity of vision and thought.

This attack made no sense to me. We had no enemies that I knew of. We were far inland in the duchy of Buck, and the Six Duchies were not at war with anyone. Yet these foreigners had come and attacked us. They had battered their way into our halls.

Why?

Because they wanted me.

The thought made no sense, and yet it seemed to be true. These attackers had come to steal me. Armed men on horseback had run me down. Run us down. *Oh, Perseverance.* His own blood leaking between his fingers. Was he dead or hiding? How had I ended here, back at Withywoods? One of the men had seized me and dragged me back. The woman who seemed to be in charge of this raid had rejoiced at finding me, and told me that she was taking me home, to where I belonged. I frowned. I'd felt so happy at those words. So cherished. What had been wrong with me? The fog-man had greeted me and welcomed me as his brother.

Even though I was a girl. I had not told them that. I had been so suffused with happiness to see them that I could scarcely speak. I had opened my arms to the fog-man, and to the plump, motherly woman who had rescued me from the raider who had been choking me. But after that . . . I remembered a warm whiteness. That was all. The memory made no sense but it still filled me with shame. I'd embraced the woman who had brought these killers to my home.

I turned my head slowly. I felt as if I could not do anything quickly. I could not move quickly or think quickly. I took a bad fall, I remembered slowly. From a running horse. Had I struck my head? Was that what was wrong with me?

My unseeing eyes had been focused on the burning stables. Two men approached it now, carrying something. Withywoods men, dressed in our yellow and green, in their best clothes. For a Winterfest Eve that had become a winter slaughter. I recognized one as Lin, our shepherd. They were carrying something between them. Something that sagged. A body. Around the burning stables, the snow had melted to slush. They trudged on. Closer and closer. Would they walk right into the flames? But as they drew closer, they halted. 'One, two, three!' Lin's voice cracked on the count as they swung the body and then, on three, they let go. It flew into the red mouth of the burning building. They turned. Like puppets traipsing across a stage, they walked away from the flames.

Was that why the stable was burning? To get rid of the bodies? A good hot bonfire was a very effective way to get rid of a body. I'd learned that from my father. 'Papa?' I whispered. Where was he? Would he come to save me? Could he save all our people? No. He'd gone to Buckkeep. He'd left me and gone off to Buckkeep Castle, to try to save the blind old beggar. He wasn't going to save me, or our people. No one was.

'I am cleverer than this.' I whispered the words aloud. I had not known I was going to say them. It seemed as if some part of me strove to awaken the dull, deadened creature I had become. I looked around fearfully to see if anyone had heard me speak. They must not hear me speak. Because . . . if they did . . . If they did, they would know. Know what?

'Know they aren't controlling me any more.'

My whisper was even softer this time. The parts of me were coming back together. I sat very still in my warm nest, gathering my mind and my strength. I mustn't betray myself until I could do something. The sleigh had been heaped with furs and woollen blankets from the manor. I was wrapped in a heavy robe of white fur, thick and soft, too big for me. It was not from Withywoods. It was no type of fur that I knew and it smelled foreign. A hat of the same fur covered my head. I moved my mittened hands, shifting my arms free of the heavy blankets. I was loaded up like a stolen treasure. I was what they were taking. Me and very little else. If they had come to plunder, I reasoned, the teams and wagons of Withywoods would be standing full of loot and the riches of my home. I saw none of that, not even our riding horses bunched to steal. I was the only thing they were carrying off. They had killed Revel to steal me.

So what would happen to everyone else?

I lifted my eyes. The huddled folk of Withywoods were limned against smaller fires. They stood like penned cattle in the snowy centre. Some were held up by their fellows. Faces were transformed by pain and horror into people I dared not recognize. The fires, built of the fine furniture of Withywoods, were not there to warm them but to light the night so they could not elude their captors. Most of the raiders were mounted on horses. Not our horses, nor our saddles. I'd never seen saddles like those, so high in the back. My numbed mind counted them. Not many, perhaps as few as ten. But they were men of blood and iron. Most of them were fair, with yellow hair and stained pale beards. They were tall and hard and some walked with bared blades in their hands. Those men were the killers, the soldiers that had come to do this task. Those men, with fair hair like mine. I saw the man who had chased me down, the one who had dragged me, half-strangled, back to the house. He stood face to face with the woman who had shouted at him, the plump woman who had made him drop me. And next to them, there, make my eyes see him, yes, there. He was there. The fog-man.

Today was not the first time I had seen him.

He had been in Oaksbywater, at the market. He had been there, fogging the whole town. No one who had seen him had turned to look at him. He'd been in the alley, the one that no one was choosing to walk down. And what had been behind him? The raiders? The soft, kind woman with the voice and words that made me love her as soon as she spoke? I was not sure. I had not seen through his fog, had barely seen the fog-man himself. I could scarcely see him now. He stood by the woman.

He was doing something. Something hard. It was so hard for him that he had had to stop fogging me to do it. Knowing that helped me to peel my mind clear of his. With every passing moment, my thoughts were more my own. My body was more my own. I felt now the bruises of the day, and how my head ached. I ran my tongue around inside my mouth and found the place where I had bitten my cheek ragged. I pushed my tongue against it, tasting blood and waking the pain and suddenly my thoughts were my own and only my own.

Do something. Don't sit still and warm and let them burn the bodies of your friends while Withywoods folk stand shivering in the snow. They were helpless, I perceived, their minds almost as fogged as mine had been. Perhaps I was only able to find myself because of my years of experience at withstanding the pressure of my father's mind on mine. There they stood, in distress, as indecisive as sheep in a blizzard and as helpless. They knew something was wrong, and yet there they stood. They moaned, they lowed like penned cattle awaiting slaughter. Save for Lin and his partner. Here they came again, out of the darkness, a body slung between them. They trudged, wooden-faced, men carrying out an assigned task. One they had been told not to think about.

I looked at the fog-man. More of a fog-boy, I decided. His round face had the unfinished, chinless look of a boy. His body was soft, unused. Not so his mind, I suspected. His brow was wrinkled in concentration. The soldiers, I realized suddenly. He was ignoring the Withywoods folk, trusting that the haze he had left them in would not disperse quickly. He held the soldiers still, keeping them listening to the woman with the trustworthy words. His fog wrapped the old man who sat on a black horse.

The old man held his sword in his hand, and the tip that pointed at the ground dripped blackness. The fog was almost a haze I could see. Then I realized that actually I could not quite see through it. It reflected light, so the old man had an aura of red firelight around him. His was a terrifying face, old and fallen, as if he had melted. The bones were hard and his eyes were pale. He radiated bitterness and hatred of everyone who was not as miserable as he was. I groped within my mind and made a tiny hole in my wall so that I could feel what the fog-man told the old soldier. The fog-man was wrapping him in triumph and success, was feeding him satisfaction and satiation. The task was done. He would be well rewarded, rewarded far beyond his expectations. People would know what he had done. They would hear of it and remember who he had been. They'd regret how they had treated him. They'd grovel before him and beg for him to be merciful.

But now? Now it was time to turn away from the pillaging and raping, time for him and his men to take what they had come for and begin the journey home. If they delayed here, it could only cause complications. There would be more conflict, more killing . . . no. The fog shifted suddenly. *Don't feed him that prospect.* Instead the fog became full of the cold and the darkness and how weary he was. The sword was heavy in his hand, his armour bowed his shoulders. They had what they had come for. The sooner they turned back toward Chalced, the sooner he would be in warmer lands with his well-earned prize. The sooner he would look down from his horse on the folk who would regret how they had scorned him.

'We should burn it all. Kill all of them and burn it all,' one of his men offered. He was mounted on a brown horse. He smiled, showing good teeth. His pale hair was bound back from his face to fall in two long braids. His brow was square and his chin firm. Such a handsome man. He rode the horse into the huddled people and they parted like butter melting before a hot spoon. In the midst of them, he wheeled his mount and looked at his commander.

'Commander Ellik! Why should we leave one timber standing here?'

The plump woman spoke clearly into the night. 'No. No, Hogen, that would be foolishness. Do not be hasty here. Listen to your commander. Ellik knows what is wise. Burn the stable and the bodies. Allow Vindeliar to take care of all the rest. Let us journey home knowing that no one will remember us or pursue us. We have what we came for. Let us go now. With no pursuit to worry about, we can move swiftly back to the warm lands.'

I struggled out of the wallow of blankets and rugs. My boots, they had pulled my boots off my feet and left only my socks. Find my boots or lose my chance to escape? The long robe of heavy white fur reached past my knees. I hiked it up, crawled to the far side of the wagon and dropped over the side. My legs crumpled under me and my face plunged briefly into the snow. I struggled to get up by pulling on the edge of the sleigh. I hurt all over, but it wasn't just that. I felt as if I'd been disconnected from my muscles. I wasted precious moments working my legs until I felt I could walk without falling.

And then I stood up. I could walk. But what good would that do? At that moment, I hated being small more than I had ever hated my stature in my life. Yet even if I had been a tall and mighty warrior on a powerful horse, what could I do against so many armed men?

I felt sick and helpless as I realized the larger truth. Not even an army could undo what had been done. Nothing and no one could bring back Steward Revel or unspill FitzVigilant's blood from the snow or unburn the stables. It was all broken. I might still be alive but I was just a salvaged piece of a life that had been shattered. Not one of us was whole. There was no going back, not for any of us.

I could not decide what to do. I was already getting cold. I could get back into the wagon, burrow under the blankets and let happen to me whatever might happen. I could run away into the darkness and try to find Perseverance under the snow and the cloak. I could flee to the captured people, and be once more dragged to the wagon. I wondered if I could steel myself and run into the burning stable deep enough to die there. How badly would it hurt?

Cornered wolves fight. Even the cubs.

That thought seeped into my brain, then was frozen and shattered by a long, shrill scream. It seemed so odd that I could recognize who the scream belonged to. It was Shun. I peeked around the side of the wagon. The man who had defied the plump woman gripped Shun by her hair. 'We'll go,' he agreed affably. 'But first I enjoy a prize of my own.' He tugged Shun up on her toes. She squealed, sounding like a piglet. At any other time, it would have been a funny sound. Both her hands were on top of her head as she gripped her own hair, trying to take the pressure off her scalp. Her torn blouse gaped wide. It was as red as blood, that dress, with an overlay of white lace in a snowflake pattern. He shook her, not gently. 'This one. This little cat tried to stick a knife in me. She's still got some fight in her. I haven't had her yet. And in some things, I am not a hasty man.'

Still gripping Shun by the hair, he dismounted. She tried to pull free of him but he just shifted his grip to the back of her head. He was taller than she was and when he held her at arm's length her swinging fists could not touch him. The men of Withywoods just stood and watched. Their eyes were dull, their mouths slack. No one moved to help her. FitzVigilant would have tried to protect her. But I'd seen him earlier, sprawled in his blood in the snow. Shun struggled against her captor, as helpless against him as I would be. He laughed, and shouted over her shrieks, 'I'll take special care of this one, and then I'll catch up with you. Before morning.'

The other mounted soldiers were stirring, suddenly interested, fighting the fog-man's calm. Their eyes fixed on the struggling woman like housedogs watching a man tear the last meat from a bone.

The plump woman shot the fog-man, Vindeliar, a desperate look. He pursed his mouth until his lips thrust out like a duck's beak. Even where I stood, ignored by them, I felt the suffocating drag of what he did. My thoughts softened at the edges like candles too near a flame. I had been about to do something, but it could wait. It would have been too much bother. Too much effort. The day had been long, and I was tired. It was dark here, and cold. It was time to find a quiet, safe place and rest. Rest.

I turned back to the sleigh and reached for the edge of it to climb back over the side. My hands in the immense fur mittens slipped and my forehead jolted hard against the wood.

Wake up! Fight. Or run. But do not fall asleep. Wolf Father shook my awareness as if he shook the life from a hare. I came back to myself with a shudder. *Push it back. Push it away. But softly, softly. Don't make him aware that you fight him.*

It was not easy advice to act on. The fog was like cobwebs. It clung and muffled and dimmed my sight. I lifted my head and stared over the sleigh. Vindeliar had the others under his control. It was not that he was forcing them to do anything. It was that he had put their thoughts into a place where rest and sleep sounded more enticing than anything else. It was affecting even the captives. Some were sinking down where they stood, to fall on their sides in the snow.

Shun had ceased her struggles but the fog did not seem to be touching her. She looked up at her captor, her teeth bared. Hogen stared at her, shook her, and then slapped her. She regarded him with hatred, but she refused to fight. She had realized it only amused him. He laughed, a cruel and brittle sound. Then he seized her by the throat and threw her violently backwards. She lay where she landed. The skirts of her dress floated wide, like rose petals on the snow. The fog-man's efforts rolled past her attacker. The handsome man stepped on Shun's skirts to pin her down as his hands went to his belt-buckle.

His mounted commander looked at him with no interest. He lifted his voice and spoke to his men. It was an old man's thin shout but that did not matter. He knew he would be obeyed. 'Finish here. Put the bodies into the fire when you are done. Then follow. We are leaving now.' He spared a glance for the handsome man. 'Do not be long, Hogen.' Then he turned his horse's head and lifted his hand. His mounted men followed him without a backward glance. Others came from the shadows, some on horses, some on foot. More than I had counted. The plump woman and Vindeliar looked around. That was when I realized they were not alone. The others had been unnoticeable to me, as the fog-man had intended.

They were dressed in white. Or so I thought. But as they passed the firelight and ranged themselves around the plump woman and Vindeliar, I realized their garments were shades of yellow and ivory. They were all dressed alike, as if their close-tailored coats and quilted trousers were a strange livery. They wore knit hats that covered their ears with flaps at the backs of their necks that could be wrapped around their throats. I had never seen such hats. Their faces were as alike as if they were siblings, all pale of skin and hair, round-chinned and rosy-lipped. I could not tell if they were men or women. They moved as if silenced by exhaustion, their mouths downturned. They walked right past the handsome man struggling with his cold, stiff belt as he stood over Shun. They looked at Shun as they passed, pitying her but with no mercy.

The plump woman spoke as they gathered around her. 'I am sorry, luriks. I wish as much as you that this had been avoided. But that once begun cannot be undone, as we all know. It was seen that this might happen, but there was no clear vision of the path that would lead both to this not happening and us finding the boy. And so today we chose a path that we knew must be bloody but would end in the necessary place. We have found him. And now we must take him home.'

Their youthful faces were stiff with horror. One spoke. 'What of these ones? The ones that didn't die?'

'Have no fear for them.' The plump woman comforted her followers. 'The worst is over for them, and Vindeliar will ease their minds. They will remember little of this night. They will invent reasons for their bruises and forget what befell them. Gather yourselves while he works. Kindrel, go for the horses. Take Soula and Reppin with you. Alaria, you will drive the sleigh. I am weary beyond saying and still must tend to Vindeliar when all is finished here.'

I saw Shepherd Lin and his fellow leave the circle of huddled folk. They carried another body slung between them. Their faces were unconcerned, as if they carried a sack of grain. I saw the handsome man drop to his knees in the snow. He'd opened the front of his trousers and now he pushed Shun's beautiful red skirts up to bare her legs.

Had she been waiting for that? She launched a tremendous kick at him, aiming for his face. It struck his chest. She gave a deep-throated, wordless cry of refusal and tried to roll to her side and flee, but he seized her by one leg and jerked her back. He laughed out loud, pleased that she would fight because he knew that she would lose. She grabbed one of his dangling braids and jerked it hard. He slapped her, and for an instant she was still, stunned by the force of that blow.

I did not like Shun. But she was mine. Mine as Revel had been, and never would be again. As FitzVigilant had been. They had died for me, trying to stop these strangers from taking me. Even if they hadn't known it. And I knew, quite clearly, what the handsome man would do after he had hurt and humiliated Shun. He would kill her, and Shepherd Lin and his helper would throw her into the stable-fire.

Just as my father and I had burned the body of the messenger. I moved. I ran, but I ran as a small person in wet and freezing socks, wearing a long, heavy fur robe. That is, I surged and trudged against a low wall of heavy wet snow. It was like trying to run in a sack. 'Stop!' I shouted. 'Stop!' And the roaring of the flames and the mutters and groans of the gathered folk of Withywoods and Shun's desperate wordless cries swallowed my words.

But she heard me, the plump woman. She turned to me, but the fog-man was still looking at the huddled people and doing whatever magic he was doing to them. I was closer to the handsome man than I was to the plump woman and her followers. I ran at him, screaming wordlessly in a strange harmony with Shun's cries. He was dragging at her clothes. He had ripped her embroidered Winterfest blouse to loose her bared breasts to the cold and falling snow and now he was tugging and tearing at her scarlet skirts, but he was trying to do it with one hand. His other hand was fending off the desperate blows and clawing efforts she was making at his face. I was not moving fast but I did not slow down as I thrust at him with the full force of my braced arms.

He grunted slightly, turned a snarling face toward me and clouted me with an outflung arm. I do not think he even used his full strength, for most of it was devoted to holding Shun on her back. He did not need his full strength. I flew backwards and landed in the deep snow. He had struck the air out of my lungs, but even so, I was more humiliated than hurt. Gasping and choking, I rolled and wallowed in the snow, finally managing to get to my hands and knees. I drew painful breath and shouted words that scarcely made sense to me, the most frightening words I could think of. 'I will make myself dead if you hurt her!'

The rapist paid no attention to me, but I heard the outraged cries of the plump woman's followers. She was shouting something in a language I didn't know, and the pale-faced people suddenly swept in as a mob. Three seized me and set me on my feet, sweeping snow off me so anxiously that I felt like a carpet that was being beaten. I pushed them away from me and tottered toward Shun. I could not see what was happening to her, save that there was fighting there. I fought free of my rescuers, shouting, 'Shun! Help Shun, not me! Shun!'

The knot of struggling people seemed to trample Shun and then the fight moved away. The pale folk were not faring well, except that there were so many of them and only one rapist. Time after time, I heard the solid smack of fist on flesh, and someone would cry out in pain. Then one of the plump woman's minions would fall back, holding a bleeding nose or bending over and clutching a stomach. By sheer numbers they overcame him, flinging their bodies over him and holding him down in the snow. One cried out suddenly, 'He bites! Beware!' prompting a sudden reshuffling of the bodies on top of him.

All this took place as I wallowed forward, fell, rose and finally burst free of the deep snow onto the trampled ground. I flung myself to my knees beside Shun, sobbing, 'Be alive! Please, be alive!'

She wasn't. I felt nothing from her. Then, as I touched her cheek, her staring eyes blinked. She looked up at me without recognition and began to utter short, sharp shrieks as if she were a hen on a threatened nest. 'Shun! Don't be scared! You are safe now! I'll protect you.' Even as I made those promises, I heard how ridiculous they were. I tugged at her opened top and the torn lace, getting snow from my mittened hands onto her bare chest. She gasped and suddenly gripped the ripped edges of the fabric. She sat up, holding her collar closed. She looked down at the fabric in her hands and then said brokenly, 'It was the finest quality. It was.' She bowed her head. Sobs rose from her, terrible shaking sobs without tears.

'It still is,' I assured her. 'You still are.' I started to pat her comfortingly, then realized the mittens were still laden with snow. I tried to drag my hands free of them, but they were fastened to the sleeves of my fur robe.

Behind us, the plump woman was talking to the man on the ground. 'You cannot have her. You heard the words of the shaysim. He values her life beyond his own. She must not be harmed lest he do harm to himself.'

I turned my head to look at them. The plump woman was nudging her charges and they were slowly getting off the man. The rapist responded with curses. I did not need to know the language to understand the depth of his anger. The pale folk were tumbling away from him, falling back and stumbling through the deeper snow as he came to his feet. Two were bleeding from their noses. He spat snow, cursed again, and then strode off into the darkness. I heard him address something angrily, the heavy stamping of a startled horse and then the sounds of a horse pushed abruptly into a gallop.

I had given up on the mittens. I crouched beside Shun. I wanted to talk to her but had no idea what to say. I would not lie again, and tell her that she was safe. None of us were safe. She huddled as deep into herself as she could, pulling her knees up to her chest and bowing her head over them.

'Shaysim.' The plump woman crouched in front of me. I would not look at her. 'Shaysim,' she said again and touched me. 'She is important to you, this one? Have you seen her? Doing important things? Is she essential?' She put her hand on Shun's bent neck as if she were a dog, and Shun cowered away from the touch. 'Is she one you must keep beside you?'

The words sank into me like FitzVigilant's blood had sunken into the trampled snow. They made holes in me. The question was significant. It had to be answered and it had to be answered correctly. What did she want me to say? What could I say that would make her keep Shun alive?

I still did not look at her. 'Shun is essential,' I said. 'She does important things.' I flung an arm wide and shouted angrily, 'They are all essential. They all do important things!'

'That's true.' She spoke gently, as if I were a little child. It came to me that perhaps she thought I was much younger than I was. Could I use that? My mind tumbled strategies frantically as she continued to speak. 'Everyone is significant. Everyone does important things. But some people are more significant than others. Some people do things that make changes. Big changes. Or they make tiny changes that can lead to big changes. If someone knows how to use them.' She hunched even lower and then thrust her face below mine and looked up at me. 'You know what I'm talking about, don't you, Shaysim? You've seen the paths and the people who are the crossroads. Haven't you?'

I turned my face away. She reached out and took me by the chin to turn my face back to hers, but I put my gaze on her mouth. She could not force me to meet her eyes. 'Shaysim.' She made the name a gentle rebuke. 'Look at me, now. Is this woman significant? Is she essential?'

I knew what she meant. I'd glimpsed it, when the beggar had touched me in the marketplace. There were people who precipitated changes. All people made changes, but some were a rock in the current, diverting the waters of time into a different channel.

I did not know if I lied or told the truth when I said, 'She is essential. She is significant to me.' Or if it was inspiration or deception that prompted me to add, 'Without her, I die before I am ten.'

The plump woman gave a small gasp of dismay. 'Take her up!' she cried to her followers. 'Treat her gently. She must be healed of every hurt, comforted of every wrong she has felt today. Be cautious, luriks. This one must live, at all costs. We must keep her out of Hogen's hands, for thwarted as he is now, he will want her more than ever. He will be most determined. So we must be even more determined, and we must search the scrolls to know what we must do to hold him at bay. Kardef and Reppin, it will be your task tonight to confer with the memorizers and see if they can tease out any wisdom for us. For I fear nothing comes to mind.'

'May I speak, Dwalia?' A youngster in grey bowed deeply and held that posture.

'Speak, Kardef.'

Kardef straightened. 'The shaysim has called her "Shun". In his language, it is a word that means to avoid or beware of a danger. There are many dream-scrolls that caution us, over and over, to avoid casting significant things into the flames. If translated into his language, could not the dreams have been telling us, not shun the flames, but Shun not into the flames?'

'Kardef, you are reaching. That way lies corruption of the prophecies. Beware and beware again of twisting the ancient words, especially when you do it so blatantly to make yourself look more learned than your partner Reppin.'

'Lingstra Dwalia, I . . .'

'Do I look as if I have time to stand in the snow and argue with you? We should have been away from here before the night fell. With every moment that we linger the greater the chance that someone may see the flames from a distance and come to see what has happened here. And then must Vindeliar spread his talents even wider, and his control grows more tenuous with each passing moment. Obey me now. Convey the shaysim and the woman to the sleigh. Mount your horses, and two of you assist Vindeliar to the sleigh as well. He is nearly spent. We must away right now.'

Her orders issued, she turned and looked down at me where I crouched by Shun. 'Well, little shaysim, I think you have what you wished now. Let's get you onto the sleigh and be on our way.'

'I don't want to go.'

'And yet you will. We all know you will, just as clearly as you do. For, from this point in time, only two possible outcomes have been documented. You go with us. Or you die here.' She spoke with calm assurance, as if pointing out that rain could not fall on a cloudless day. I heard her absolute belief in her own words.

Once, my foster-brother Hap had amused me for almost an hour by showing me how, long after he had plucked a string, the wood of his harp still vibrated to its song. I felt it then, how the woman's words woke a harmony inside me. She was right. I knew it was true, and that was why I had threatened them with my death. Tonight, I would either leave my home with them or I would die here. All the circumstances that might lead to another outcome from this moment were too remote, too fantastic to hope for. And I knew that. Perhaps I had known it since I woke up this morning. I blinked and a shiver ran down my back. Was this happening now, or was it the remembrance of a dream?

Strong arms were plucking me out of the snow, and voices exclaimed in dismay at the frost coating my wet socks. The one who carried me spoke comforting words I did not understand. I lifted my head and saw that four of them were carrying Shun. It was not that she was heavy but she struggled in a disconnected way as if her legs and arms were all different creatures.

The woman they called Dwalia had proceeded to the sleigh. She was already in the back, making a fresh nest in the furs and blankets. I was handed up to her, and she set me between her legs and facing away from her with my back warmed by her front and her arms around me. I did not like being so close to her, but I was wedged there. Shun they loaded like freight, and then heaped blankets over her. Once they let go of her she ceased struggling and lay like dead meat under the mounded wraps. Part of her skirt had snagged on the edge of the sleigh. The flap of red was like a mocking tongue.

Someone spoke to the horses and they moved off. I was facing backwards. I listened to the sounds of their hooves dulled by the falling snow, the squeaking of the wide wooden runners and the fading crackle of the flames that ate the stable. The folk of Withywoods, my folk, were slowly re-entering the house. They did not look at us. We left the light of the burning stables behind and entered the long carriageway that led away from Withywoods. The lanterns swung and a bubble of light danced around us as we flowed down the avenue of arched, snow-laden birches.

I did not even realize the fog-man was in the sleigh until he spoke to Dwalia. 'It's done,' he said and heaved a big sigh of satisfaction. Definitely a boy, I realized. He spoke with a boy's voice as he added, 'And now we can go home, away from the cold. And the killing. Lingstra Dwalia, I did not realize there would be so much killing.'

I felt her turn her head to look at him where he sat, up front with the driver. She spoke softly, as if I were asleep. I wasn't. I didn't dare try to hide in sleep. 'We did not intend for there to be any killing. But we knew that the chances of avoiding all killing were nearly impossible. We had to use the tools we had, and Ellik is a man full of bitterness and hate. The wealth and comfort he expected in his elder years escaped him. He lost his position, his fortune and all his comforts. He blames the whole world for that. He seeks to rebuild in a few years what it took him a lifetime to acquire. And so he will always be more violent, more greedy, more ruthless than he need be. He is dangerous, Vindeliar. Never forget that. He is especially dangerous to you.'

'I don't fear him, Lingstra Dwalia.'

'You should.' Her words were both a warning and a rebuke. Her hands moved, pulling more blankets over both of us. I hated the touch of her body against mine but could not find the will to shift. The sleigh lurched forward. I stared at the passing forests of Withywoods. I did not even have the heart to bid it a tearful farewell. I had no hope. My father would not know where I had gone. My own people had given me up, simply standing up and going back into Withywoods Manor. None had shouted that they would not let me go. No one had tried to take me back from my captors. I faced what my strangeness had done to me: I had never really belonged to them. Losing me was a small price to pay for the invaders to leave with no more bloodshed. They were right. I was glad they had not fought to keep me. I wished there had been a way to save Shun without having her carted off with me.

The corner of my eye caught a movement. The swaying lanterns made the trees at the edge of the drive cast iron bars of blackness on the snow. But this was not a movement born of that light. This motion was standing snow, gripped by a hand black with blood and above all, a pale face with staring eyes. I did not turn my head, or cry out, or catch my breath. I let nothing in me betray to anyone that Perseverance stood in my Elderling cloak and watched us pass him by.

FOUR

The Fool's Tale

When winter's clutch is cold and dark
And game is scarce and forest stark
This songster to the hearth retreats
To warm his cheeks and icy feet.

But on the hill and in the glen
Are hunters hardier than men.
With lolling tongues and eyes that gleam
They surge through snow with breath like steam.

For in the hunt there is no morrow,
Time does not wait. There is no sorrow
As blood spills black and snarls are rife.
For life is meat, and death brings life.

A song for Nighteyes and
his friend – Hap Gladheart

The stairs seemed steeper than I remembered. When I reached my old bedchamber, I entered it as cautiously as befit an erstwhile assassin. I closed and locked my door, put wood on the fire and for a short time considered simply getting into the bed and going to sleep. Then I drew the curtains shut and inspected the area where they were fastened to the rod. Yes. I saw it now, as I had not in all those years. Another tug on the drapery-pull triggered the door panel, but no sound nor crack betrayed that. It was only when I pushed on it that it swung silently open and the narrow black staircase appeared before me.

I climbed the risers, stumbling once when my curly toe hooked on the step. Up in Chade's old workroom, Ash had come and gone. Our dirty dishes had been tidied away, and a different pot simmered at the edge of the hearth. The Fool had not moved since I left him, and I crossed the room anxiously to lean over him. 'Fool?' I said softly, and with a cry he flung his arms wide and sat up to cower behind his raised hands. One flying hand glanced off my cheek. As I stepped back from his bed, he cried, 'I'm sorry! Don't hurt me!'

'It's only me. Only Fitz.' I spoke calmly, trying to keep the anguish from my voice. *Eda and El, Fool, will you ever recover from what you endured?*

'I'm sorry,' he repeated breathlessly. 'So sorry, Fitz.' He was breathing hard. 'When they had me . . . they never woke me gently. Or allowed me to sleep until I woke. I so feared sleep I would bite myself to stay awake. But always, eventually, one sleeps. And then they would wake me, sometimes just a few moments later. With a little barbed blade. Or a hot poker.' His grimace had barely the semblance of a smile. 'I hate the smell of fire now.' He dropped his head back on the pillow. Hatred surged in me and then passed, leaving me empty. I could never undo what they had done to him. After a time, he rolled his head toward me and asked, 'Is it day now?'

My mouth had gone dry and wordless. I cleared my throat. 'It's either very late at night or very early in the morning, depending on how you think of such things. We spoke last in early afternoon. Have you been sleeping all this time?'

'I don't exactly know. Sometimes it's hard for me to tell. Give me a few moments, please.'

'Very well.'

I retreated to the far end of the room and studiously ignored him as he tottered from the bed. He found his way to the garderobe, was there for some time and when he emerged, he called to ask if there was washwater.

'In a pitcher next to the bowl on the stand by your bed. But I can warm some for you if you wish, too.'

'Oh, warm water,' he said, as if I had offered him gold and jewels.

'Shortly,' I replied. I set about my task. He groped his way to the chair by the fireside and sat down. I marvelled at how quickly he had learned the room. When I brought the warmed water and a washing cloth, he reached for it immediately and I realized that his silence had been so he could track my activity by what he could hear. I felt as if I spied on him as he washed his scarred face and then repeatedly scrubbed his eyes to clear the gummy mucous from his lashes. When he had finished, his eyes were clean but reddened at the rims.

I spoke without apology or preamble. 'What did they do to your eyes?'

He set the cloth back in the bowl and clutched his damaged hands together, gently rubbing the swollen knuckles. He was silent as I cleared the table. Very well, then. Not yet. 'Are you hungry?' I asked him.

'Is it time for a meal?'

'If you're hungry, it's time for your meal. I've eaten too much already. And possibly drunk more than I should have as well.'

His response shocked me. 'Do you truly have another daughter beside Nettle?'

'I do.' I sat down in my chair and pulled one of the shoes off. 'Her name is Bee. And she is nine years old now.'

'Truly?'

'Fool, what purpose could I have for lying to you?' He made no answer to that. I reached down and unfastened the second shoe. I pulled it free and put my foot flat on the floor. My left calf cramped abruptly and I exclaimed in pain and bent to rub it.

'What's wrong?' he asked in some alarm.

'Ridiculous shoes, courtesy of Chade. Tall heels and pointed tips curling up at the toes. You'd laugh if you could see them. Oh, and the jacket has a skirt that goes nearly to my knees. And buttons shaped like little blue flowers. And the hat is like a floppy sack. Not to mention the curly wig.'

A small smile quirked his mouth. Then he said gravely, 'You've no idea how much I'd love to see it all.'

'Fool. It's not idle curiosity that makes me ask about your eyes. If I knew what was done to you, it might help me undo it.'

Silence. I removed my hat and set it on the table. Standing, I began to unbutton the jacket. It was just slightly too tight in the shoulders and suddenly I could not endure how it bound me. I gave a sigh of relief, draped it on the chair back and sat down. The Fool had picked up the hat. His hands explored it. Then he set it, wig and all, upon his head. With apparent ease, he twitched the hair into place and then effortlessly arranged the hat into an artful slouch.

'It looks far better on you than it did on me.'

'Fashion travels. I had a hat almost like this. Years ago.'

I waited.

He sighed heavily. 'What have I told you and what haven't I? Fitz, in my darkness, my mind slips around until I scarcely trust myself at all any more.'

'You've told me very little.'

'Have I? Perhaps you know very little, but I assure you that night after night, in my cell, I spoke with you at length and in detail.' A wry twist of his mouth. He lifted the hat and set it on the table where it crouched on its wig like a small animal. 'Each time you ask me a question, it surprises me. For I feel that you were so often with me.' He shook his head, then leaned back suddenly in his chair and for a time appeared to stare at the ceiling. He spoke into that darkness. 'Prilkop and I left Aslevjal. You know that. We journeyed to Buckkeep. What you may never have guessed is that we used the Skill-pillars to do so. Prilkop spoke of having learned it from his Catalyst, and I, I had my silvered fingertips from when I had touched Verity. And so we came to Buckkeep and I could not resist the temptation to see you one last time, to have yet another final farewell.' He snorted at his own foolishness. 'Fate cheated us both of that. We lingered for a time but Prilkop was anxious to be on his way. Ten days he allowed me, for as you recall I was still very weak, and he judged it dangerous to use the pillars too frequently. But after ten days he began to chafe to be on our way again. Nightly he urged me to leave, pointing out what I knew: that together you and I had already worked the change that was my mission. Our time together was over, and long past over. Lingering near you would only provoke other changes in the world, changes that might be far less desirable. And so he persuaded me. But not completely. I knew it was dangerous, I knew it was self-indulgent even as I carved it. The three of us together, as we once had been. You, Nighteyes and I. I shaped it from the Skill-stone and I pressed my farewell into it. Then I left my gift for you, knowing well that when you touched it, I would be aware of you.'

I was startled. 'You were?'

'I told you. I have never been wise.'

'But I felt nothing of you. Well, there was the message of course.' I felt cheated by him. He had known that I was alive and well, but had kept his own situation concealed from me.

'I'm sorry.' He sounded sincere. After a moment, he continued. 'We used the pillars again when we left Buckkeep. It was like a child's game. We jumped from one standing stone to the next. Always he made us wait between our journeys. It was . . . disorienting. It still makes me queasy to think of it. He knew the danger of what we did. On one of our leaps . . . we travelled to an abandoned city.' He halted and spoke quietly. 'I hadn't been there before. But there was a tall tower in the middle of it, and when I climbed those stairs, I found the map. And the broken window and the fingerprints in the soot from the fire.' He paused. 'I am sure it was the map-tower you visited once.'

'Kelsingra. So the Dragon Traders name it now,' I said, not wanting to divert him from his revelations.

'At Prilkop's insistence, we stayed there five days. I remember it . . . strangely. Even knowing what the stone can be and do, having it speak to one continually is wearing. I felt I could not escape the whispers no matter where I went. Prilkop said it was because of the silver Skill on my fingertips. The city drew me. It whispered stories to me when I slept, and when I was awake it tried to draw me into itself. I gave in once, Fitz. I took off my glove and I touched a wall in what had been a market, I think. When next I knew myself as myself, I was lying on the ground by a fire and Prilkop had all our things packed. He wore Elderling garb and had found some for me as well. Including the cloaks that help one hide, one for each of us. He demanded that we leave immediately, declaring that travel through the pillars was less dangerous to me than spending another day in the city. He said it had taken him a day and a half to find me, and that even after he had dragged me away I had slept for another full day. I felt I have lived a year in Kelsingra.

'So we left.' He paused.

'Are you hungry?' I asked him.

He considered the question carefully. 'My body has not been accustomed to regular meals for quite some time. It is almost strange to know that I can ask you for food and you give it to me.' He coughed, turning aside as he did so and hugging his belly against the strain. The coughing went on for some time. I fetched him water and he sipped from the cup, only to go off into an even worse spate of coughing and wheezing. When he could draw a full breath and speak, tears had tracked down his cheeks from the effort. 'Wine, if we have it. Or brandy. Or more water. And something to eat. But not a lot, Fitz. I must go slowly.'

'That's wise,' I told him, and found that the pot held a creamy chowder of whitefish and onions and root vegetables. I served him up a shallow bowl of it and was relieved when his groping fingers found the spoon I'd placed within his reach. I set a cup of water next to it. I regretted that his eating would put an end to his tale-telling, for it was rare beyond rare for the Fool to be so forthcoming. I watched him spoon up soup carefully and convey it to his mouth. Another spoonful . . .

He stopped. 'You're watching me so closely that I can feel it,' he observed unhappily.

'I am. I apologize.'

I rose and poured a small amount of brandy into a cup. Then I arranged myself in the chair with my feet outstretched toward the fire and took a measured sip of the brandy. When the Fool spoke, it surprised me. I continued to watch the fire, and listened without comment as he spaced his tale out with slow mouthfuls of the chowder.

'I remember how you warned the prince . . . well, he's King Dutiful now, isn't he? How you warned him about using the

Skill-pillars to go to an unfamiliar destination. You are right to worry about that. Prilkop assumed the pillars would be just as they were the last time he used them. We stepped into the pillar in the map-city and suddenly found ourselves face down on the ground with barely room to struggle out from under the stone.' He paused to eat more chowder.

'The pillar had been toppled. Deliberately, I suspect, and we were fortunate that whoever had done it had not been more thorough. It had fallen so that the top of it rested on the rim of a fountain's bowl. Long dry and deserted: that city was not like Kelsingra. It showed the signs of ancient war and more recent pillaging. Deliberate damage. The old city was on the highest hills on an island. As to where exactly that island is, I could not tell you. It was unfamiliar to me. Decades ago, when I first travelled here, I did not pass through that old city. Nor did I on my return journey here.' He shook his head. 'When we journey back, I do not think we can rely on that path. What would happen to us if there were no room to emerge from a stone? I've no idea. And no wish to discover it.'

More soup, and a bit spilled. I said nothing, and watched only out of the corner of my eye as he groped for the napkin, found it, and wiped at his chin and nightshirt. I sipped more brandy and took care that my cup made a small sound as I set it back on the table.

'When we had bellied out from under the pillar, it took us half a day to hike through the ruins. The carvings, what little remained of them, reminded me of what I'd seen in Kelsingra and on Aslevjal. Most of the statues had been shattered and many of the buildings had been raided for stone. The city was broken. I'd hear a shout of laughter, and half a sentence whispered by my ear, and then a distant bit of music. The discord rang terribly against me. I tell you, if I had had to remain there any longer than we did, I would have gone mad. Prilkop was heartsick. Once, he said, it had been a place of beauty and peace. He hurried me through it despite how weary I was as if he could not bear to witness what it had become.

'Are you drinking brandy without me?' he asked suddenly.

'Yes. But it's not very good brandy.'

'That's the worst excuse I've ever heard for not sharing with a friend.'

'It is. Will you have some?'

'Please.'

I fetched another cup and poured him a small measure. While I was up, I added a log to the fire. I suddenly felt very comfortable and weary in a good way. We were warm and dry on a winter night, I'd served my king well this evening, and my old friend was at my side and slowly recuperating. I felt a twinge of conscience as I thought of Bee, so far away and left to her own devices but comforted myself that my gifts and letter would soon be in her hands. She had Revel and I liked her maid. She would know I was thinking of her. And surely after I had spoken to both Shun and Lant so severely, they would not dare to be cruel to her. And she had her riding lessons with the stable lad. It was good to know she had a friend, one she had made on her own. I dared to hope she had other household allies that I knew nothing about. I told myself I was foolish to worry about her. She was actually a very capable child.

The Fool cleared his throat. 'That night, we camped in the forest at the edge of the broken city, and the next morning we hiked to where we could look down on a port town. Prilkop said it had grown greatly since last he had seen it. Its fishing fleet was in the harbour, and he said there would be other ships coming from the south to buy the salted fish and fish oil and a coveted leather made from very heavy fish-skin.'

'Fish-leather?' The question leapt from me.

'Indeed, that was my reaction. I'd never heard of such a thing. But there is a trade in it, for the rougher pieces are cherished for polishing wood or even stone, and the finer pieces are used on the grips of knives and swords; even soaked in blood, they don't become slippery.' He coughed again, wiped his mouth and took more brandy. When he drew breath to go on, it wheezed in his throat. 'So. Down we went, in our winter clothes to that sunny town. Prilkop seemed sure of a welcome there, so he was surprised when the folk stared at us and then turned away. The city on the hilltop was regarded as being haunted by demons. In that town, we saw abandoned buildings that had been built from the stone salvaged from the city but were now considered haunted by dark spirits. No one welcomed us, even when Prilkop showed them silver coins. A few children followed us, shouting and throwing pebbles until their elders called them back. We went down to the docks, and there Prilkop was able to buy us passage on an ill-kept vessel.

'The ship was there to buy fish and oil and stank of it. The crew was as mixed a lot as I've ever seen; the youngsters aboard looked miserable and the older hands were either tremendously unlucky or had suffered repeated rough treatment. A missing eye here, a peg for a foot on another man, and one with only eight fingers left to his hands. I tried to persuade Prilkop that we should not board, but he was convinced that if we did not depart that town we'd lose our lives that night. I judged the ship just as poor a choice, but he was insistent. And so we went.'

He paused. He ate some more soup, wiped his mouth, sipped his brandy, and carefully wiped his mouth and fingers again. He picked up the spoon, and set it down again. Sipped again from his brandy cup. Then he pointed his blind eyes my way, and for the first time since we had met again, a look of pure mischief passed over his face. 'Are you listening?'

I laughed aloud, to know he still had that spirit in him. 'You know I am.'

'I do. Fitz, I feel you.' He held up his hand, showing me the fingertips that had once been silvered with Skill and were now sliced away to a smooth scar. 'I took back my link to you long ago. And they cut the silver from my fingertips, for they guessed how powerful it was. So, in the years of my confinement, I thought I imagined my bond with you.' He tipped his head. 'But I think it's real.'

'I don't know,' I admitted. 'I've felt nothing in all the years we were separated. Sometimes I thought you must be dead and sometimes I believed you had forgotten our friendship entirely.' I halted. 'Except for the night your messenger was killed in my home. There were bloody fingerprints on the carving you had left for me, the one of you, Nighteyes and me. I went to brush them away, and I swear that something happened.'

'Oh.' He caught his breath. For a time, he stared sightlessly.

Then he sighed. 'So. Now I understand. I did not know what it was, then. I did not know one of my messengers had reached you. They were . . . I was in great pain, and suddenly you were there, touching my face. I screamed for you to help me, to save me or to kill me. Then you were gone.' He blinked his blinded eyes. 'That was the night—' He gasped for air suddenly and leaned on the table. 'I broke,' he admitted. 'I broke that night. They hadn't broken me, not with the pain or the lies or the starvation. But that moment, when you were there and then you were not . . . that was when I broke, Fitz.'

I was silent. How had he broken? He had told me that when the Servants tormented him, they wanted him to tell them where his son was. A son he had no knowledge of. That, to me, had been the most horrific part of his tale. A tortured man who is concealing knowledge retains some small portion of control over his life. A tortured man who has no knowledge to barter has nothing. The Fool had had nothing. No tool, no weapon, no knowledge to trade to make his torment cease or lessen. The Fool had been powerless. How could he have told them something he didn't know? He spoke on.

'After a time, a long time, I realized there was no sound from them. No questions. But I was answering them. Telling them what they needed to know. I was screaming your name, over and over. And so they knew.'

'Knew what, Fool?'

'They knew your name. I betrayed you.'

His mind was not clear, that was obvious. 'Fool, you gave them nothing they did not know. Their hunters were already there, in my home. They'd followed your messenger. That was how the blood got onto the carving. How you felt me there with you. They'd already found me.' As I said those words, my mind went back to that long-ago night. The Servants' hunters had tracked his messenger to my home and killed her there before she could deliver the Fool's words to me. That had been years ago. But only weeks ago another of his messengers had reached Withywoods and conveyed his warning and his plea to me: Find his son. Hide him from the hunters. That dying messenger had insisted she was being pursued, that the hunters were hot on her trail. But I'd seen no sign of them. Or had I not recognized the sign they had left? There had been hoofprints in a pasture, the fence rails taken down. At the time, I'd dismissed it as coincidence, for surely if they'd been tracking the messenger, they would have made some attempt to determine her fate.

'Their hunters had not found *you*,' the Fool insisted. 'They'd trailed their prey there, I think. But they were not looking for you. The Servants who tormented me had no way of knowing where their hunters were at that moment. Not until I screamed your name, over and over, did they know how important you were. They had thought you were only my Catalyst. Only someone I had used. And abandoned . . . For that would be what they expected. A Catalyst to them is a tool, not a true companion. Not a friend. Not someone who shares the prophet's heart.' We both held a silence for a time.

'Fool, there is something I do not understand. You say you have no knowledge of your son. Yet you seem to believe he must exist, on the word of those at Clerres who tormented you. Why would you believe they knew of such a child when you did not?'

'Because they have a hundred, or a thousand, or ten thousand predictions that if I succeeded as a White Prophet, then such an heir would follow me. Someone who would wreak even greater changes in this world.'

I spoke carefully. I didn't want to upset him. 'But there were thousands of prophecies that said that you would die. And you did not. So can we be sure that these foretellings of a son are real?'

He sat quietly for a time. 'I cannot allow myself to doubt them. If my heir exists, we must find him and protect him. If I dismiss the possibility of his existence, and he does exist and they find the child, then his life will be a misery and his death will be a tragedy for the world. So I must believe in him, even if I cannot tell clearly how such a child came to be.' He stared into darkness. 'Fitz. There in the market. I seem to recall he was there. That I touched him and in that moment, I knew him. My son.' He drew a ragged breath and spoke in a shaky voice. 'All was light and clarity around us. I could not only see, I could see all the possibilities threading away from that moment. All that we might change together.' His voice grew weaker.

'There was no light, Fool. The winter day was edging toward evening, and the only person near you was . . . Fool. What's wrong?'

He had swayed in his chair and then caught his face in his hands. Then he said in a woeful voice. 'I don't feel well. And . . . my back feels wet.'

My heart sank. I moved to stand behind him. 'Lean forward,' I suggested quietly. For a wonder, he obeyed me. The back of his nightshirt was wet with something that was not blood. 'Lift up your shirt,' I bade him, and he tried. With my help, we bared his back, and again he did not protest. I lifted a candle high. 'Oh, Fool,' I said before I could think to control my voice. A large and angry swelling next to his spine had split open and was leaking a thin, foul fluid down his scarred and bony back. 'Sit still,' I told him and stepped away to the water warming by the fire. I soaked my napkin in it, wrung it out and then warned him, 'Brace yourself,' before applying it to the sore. He hissed loudly, and then lowered his forehead onto his crossed arms on the table.

'It's like a boil. It's opened and draining now. I think that might be good.'

He gave a small shudder but said nothing. It took me a moment to realize he was unconscious. 'Fool?' I said, and touched his shoulder. No response. I reached out with the Skill and found Chade. *It's the Fool. He's taken a turn for the worse. Is there a healer you can send up to your old rooms?*

None that would know the way, even if any were awake at this hour. Shall I come?

No. I'll tend to him.

Are you certain?

I'm sure.

Probably better not to involve anyone else. Probably better it was only he and I, as it had been so often before now. While he was unaware of pain, I lit more candles to give me light, and brought a basin. I cleansed the wound as well as I could. He was limp and still as I trickled water into it and sponged away the liquid that flowed out. It did not bleed. 'No different from a horse,' I heard myself say once through my gritted teeth. Cleaned, the split boil gaped on his back as if some vile mouth had opened in his skin. It went deep. I forced myself to look at his abused body. There were other suppurations. They bulged, some shiny and almost white, others red and angry and surrounded by a network of dark streaks.

I was looking at a dying man. There was too much wrong with him. To think that somehow food and rest could bring him closer to healing was folly. It would prolong his dying. The infections that were destroying him were too widespread and too advanced. He might even now be dead.

I set my hand to the side of his neck, placing two of my fingers on the pulse point there. His heart was still beating: I felt it there in the feeble leaping of his blood. I closed my eyes and held my fingers there, taking a peculiar comfort in that reassuring beat. A wave of dizziness passed through me. I had been awake too long, and drunk too much at the feast long before I'd added brandy with the Fool to the mix. I was suddenly old, and tired beyond telling. My body ached with the years I'd heaped on it and the tasks I'd demanded of it. The ancient, familiar ache of the arrow scar in my back, so close to my spine, twitched to wakefulness and grew to an unavoidable deep ache, as if someone's finger were insistently prodding the old injury.

Except that I no longer had that scar. Or the pain from it. That realization whispered into my awareness, light as the first clinging snowflakes on a window. I did not look at it, but accepted what was happening. I let my breathing slow and remained very still inside my own skin. Inside *our* skin.

I slipped my awareness from my own body into the Fool's and heard him make a soft sound, a wounded man disturbed in deepest sleep. *Do not worry. I am not after your secrets.*

But even the mention of secrets roused him. He struggled, a little, but I remained still and I do not think he could find me. When he subsided, I let my awareness tendril throughout his body. *Gently. Go softly*, I told myself. I let myself feel the pain of his back injury. The boil that had drained was not as dangerous as the ones that had not. It had emptied itself but the poisons from some of the others were working deeper into his body and he had no strength to fight them.

I turned them back. I pushed them out.

It did not take that much effort. I worked carefully, asking as little of his flesh as I could. In some other place, I set my fingers to the sores and called up the poison. Hot skin strained to the breaking point opened under my touch and the poisons trickled out. I used my Skill-strength in a way that I had not known it could be used, yet it seemed so obvious to me there and in that moment. Of course it worked this way. Of course it could do this.

'Fitz.'

'Fitz!'

'FITZ!'

Someone seized me and jerked me back. I lost my balance and fell. Someone tried to catch me, failed and I struck the floor hard. It knocked the wind out of me. I gasped and wheezed and then opened my eyes. It took a moment for me to make sense of what I saw. The dying firelight illuminated Chade standing over me. His face was seized with horror as he stared down at me. I struggled to speak and could not. I was so weary, so very tired. Sweat was drying on my body, and my clothing clung to me where it was soaked. I lifted my head and became aware that the Fool was slumped forward on the table. The red light of the fire showed me pus oozing from a dozen injuries on his back. I rolled my head and my gaze met Chade's horrified stare.

'Fitz, what were you doing?' he demanded, as if he had caught me in some foul and disgusting act.

I tried to draw breath to respond. He looked away from me and I became aware that someone else had entered the room. Nettle. I knew her as she brushed against my Skill-sense. 'What happened here?' she demanded, and then as she stepped close enough to see the Fool's bared back, she gasped in dismay. 'Did Fitz do this?' she demanded of Chade.

'I don't know. Build up the fire and bring more candles!' he ordered in a trembling voice as he sank into the chair I had left empty. He set his shaking hands on his knees and leaned down toward me. 'Boy! What were you doing?'

I'd remembered how to pull air into my lungs. 'Trying to

stop . . .' I pulled in another breath, 'the poisons.' It was so hard to roll over. I ached in every fibre of my body. When I set my hands to the floor to try to lever myself up, they were wet. Slippery. I lifted them and brought them up to my eyes. They were dripping with watery blood and fluid. Chade shoved a table napkin into my hands.

Nettle had thrown wood on the fire and it was catching. Now she kindled fresh candles and replaced the ones that had burned to stubs. 'It stinks,' she said, looking at the Fool. 'They're all open and running.'

'Heat clean water,' Chade told her.

'Shouldn't we summon the healers?'

'Too much to explain, and if he dies it were better that it did not have to be explained at all. Fitz. Get up. Talk to us.'

Nettle was like her mother, stronger than one expected a small woman to be. I had managed to sit up and she seized me under my arms and helped me to my feet. I caught my weight on the chair and nearly overset it. 'I feel terrible,' I said. 'So weak. So tired.'

'So now perhaps you know how Riddle felt after you burned his strength so carelessly,' she responded tartly.

Chade took command of the conversation. 'Fitz. Why did you cut the Fool like this? Did you quarrel?'

'He didn't cut the Fool.' Nettle had found the water I'd left warming by the fire. She wet the same cloth I'd used earlier, wrung it out, and wiped it gingerly down the Fool's back. Her nose wrinkled and her mouth was pinched tight in disgust at the foul liquids she smeared away. She repeated the action and said, 'He was trying to heal him. All of this has been pushed from the inside out.' She spared me a disdainful glance. 'Sit on the hearth before you fall over. Did you give a thought to simply putting a pulling poultice on this instead of recklessly attempting a Skill-healing on your own?'

I took her suggestion and attempted to collapse back to the hearth in a controlled fashion. As neither of them was looking at me, it was a wasted effort. 'I didn't,' I said, beginning an attempt to explain that I had not, at first, intended to heal him. Then I stopped. I wouldn't waste my time.

Chade had suddenly sat forward with an enlightened expression on his face. 'Ah! Now I understand. The Fool must have been strapped to a chair with spikes protruding from the back, and the strap slowly tightened to force him gradually onto the spikes. If he struggled, the wounds became larger. As the strap was tightened, the spikes went deeper. These old injuries appear to me as if he held out for quite a long time. But I would suspect there was something on the spikes, excrement or some other foul matter, intended to deliberately trigger a long-term infection.'

'Chade. Please,' I said weakly. The image he painted made me queasy. I hoped the Fool had remained unconscious. I did not really want to know how the Servants had caused his wounds. Nor did I want him to remember.

'And the interesting part of that,' Chade went on heedless of my plea, 'is that the torturer was employing a philosophy of torment that I've never encountered before. I was taught that for torture to be effective at all, the victim must be allowed an element of hope; hope that the pain would stop, hope that the body could still heal, and so on. If you take that away, what has the subject to gain by surrendering his information? In this case, if he was aware that his wounds were deliberately being poisoned, once the spikes had pierced his flesh, then—'

'Lord Chade! Please!' Nettle looked revolted.

The old man stopped. 'Your pardon, Skillmistress. Sometimes I forget . . .' He let his words trail away. Nettle and I both knew what he meant. The type of dissertation he had been delivering was fit only for his apprentice or fellow assassin, not for anyone with normal sensibilities.

Nettle straightened and dropped the wet cloth in the bowl of water. 'I've cleaned his wounds as well as water can. I can send down to the infirmary for a dressing.'

'No need to involve them. We have herbs and unguents here.'

'I'm sure you do,' she responded. She looked down on me. 'You look terrible. I suggest we ask a page to fetch you breakfast in your room below. He'll be told that you over-indulged last night.'

'I've just the lad for the job,' Chade declared abruptly. 'His name is Ash.'

He flicked a glance at me and I did not betray to Nettle that

I'd already met the lad. 'I'm sure he'll do fine,' I agreed quietly, even as I wondered what plan Chade was unfolding.

'Well, then I'll leave you two. Lord Feldspar, I've been informed by Lady Kettricken that you begged for a brief audience with her tomorrow afternoon. Don't be late. You should join those waiting outside her private audience chamber.'

I gave her a puzzled glance. 'I'll explain,' Chade assured me. More of his plans unfurling. I held in a sigh and smiled weakly at Nettle as she left. When Chade rose to seek out his healing herbs and unguents, I unfolded myself gingerly. My back was stiff and sore and the elegant shirt was pasted to me with sweat. I used what water was left in the pot to cleanse my hands. Then I tottered over to claim a seat at the table.

'I'm surprised Nettle knew the way here.'

'Dutiful's choice. Not mine,' Chade replied brusquely. He spoke from across the room. 'He's never liked my secrets. Never fully understood how necessary they are.'

He came back from a cupboard with a blue pot with a wooden stopper in it, and several rags. When he opened it, the pungency of the unguent stung my nose and somewhat cleared my head. I rose and before he could touch the Fool, I took the rags and medicine from him. 'I'll do it,' I told him.

'As you wish.'

It troubled me that the Fool was still unaware of us. I set my hand to his shoulder and quested slightly toward him.

'Ah-ah!' Chade warned me. 'None of that. Let him rest.'

'You've grown very sensitive to Skill-use,' I commented as I scooped some of the unguent onto the rag and pushed it into one of the smaller wounds on the Fool's back.

'Or you've grown more careless in how you use it. Think on that, boy. And report to me while you repair what you've done.'

'There's little to tell that I didn't Skill to you from the festivities. I think you have a quiet but effective pirate trade on the river that is avoiding all tariffs and taxes. And a sea captain ambitious enough to try to extend it to trade with Bingtown.'

'And you know full well that is not what I need reported! Don't quibble with me, Fitz. After you asked me about a healer, I tried to reach you again. And I could not, but I could sense how intensely involved you were elsewhere. I thought I was not strong enough to reach you, so I asked Nettle to try. And when neither of us could break in on you, we both came here. What were you doing?'

'Just,' I cleared my tight throat, 'trying to help him heal. One of the boils on his back had opened by itself. And when I tried to clean it for him, I became aware that . . . that he's dying, Chade. Slowly dying. There is too much wrong with him. I do not think he can gain strength fast enough for us to heal him. Good food and rest and medicine will, I believe, only delay what is inevitable. He's too far gone for me to save him.'

'Well.' Chade seemed taken aback by my bluntness. He sank down into my chair and drew a great breath. 'I thought we had all seen that, down at the infirmary, Fitz. It was one reason why I thought you'd want a quieter place for him. A place of quiet and privacy.' His voice trailed away.

His words made what I faced more real. 'Thank you for that,' I said hoarsely.

'It's little enough, and sad to say, I doubt that there is more that I could do for either of you. I hope you know that if I could do more, I would.' He sat up straight, and the rising flames of the fire caught his features in profile. I suddenly saw the effort the old man was putting into even that small gesture. He would sit upright, and he would come up all those steps in the creaking hours before dawn for my sake, and he would try to make it all look effortless. But it wasn't. And it was getting harder and harder for him to maintain that façade. Cold spread through me as I faced the truth of that. He was not as near death as the Fool was, but he was drifting slowly away from me on the relentless ebb of aging.

He spoke hesitantly, looking at the fire rather than at me. 'You pulled him back from the other side of death once. You've been stingy with the details on that, and I've found nothing in any Skill-scroll that references such a feat. I thought perhaps . . .'

'No.' I pushed another dab of unguent into a wound. Only two more to go. My back ached abominably from bending over at my task, and my head pounded as it had not in years. I pushed aside thoughts of carryme powder and elfbark tea. Deadening the body to pain always took a toll on the mind, and I could not afford that just now. 'I haven't been stingy with information, Chade. It was more a thing that happened rather than something I did. The circumstances are not something I can duplicate.' I suppressed a shudder at the thought.

I finished my task. I became aware that Chade had risen and was standing beside me. He offered me a soft grey cloth. I spread it carefully over the Fool's treated back and then pulled his nightshirt down over it. I leaned forward and spoke by his ear. 'Fool?'

'Don't wake him,' Chade suggested firmly. 'There are good reasons why a man falls into unconsciousness. Let him be. When both his body and his mind are ready for him to waken again, he will.'

'I know you're right.'

Lifting him and carrying him back to the bed was a harder task than it should have been. I deposited him there on his belly and covered him warmly.

'I've lost track of time,' I admitted to Chade. 'How did you stand it in here, all those years, with scarcely a glimpse of the sky?'

'I went mad,' he said genially. 'In a useful sort of way, I might add. None of the ranting and clawing the walls one might expect. I simply became intensely interested in my trade and all aspects of it. Nor was I confined here as much as you might suspect. I had other identities, and sometimes I ventured forth into castle or town.'

'Lady Thyme,' I said, smiling.

'She was one. There were others.'

If he had wanted me to know, he would have told me. 'How long until breakfast?'

He made a small sound in his throat. 'If you were a guardsman, you'd likely be getting up from it by now. But for you, a minor noble from a holding that no one's ever heard of, on your first visit to Buckkeep Castle, well, you'll be forgiven for sleeping in a bit after last night's festivities. I'll pass the word to Ash and he'll bring you food after you've had a bit of a nap.'

'Where did you find him?'

'He's an orphan. His mother was a whore of the particular sort patronized mostly by wealthy young nobles who have . . . aberrant tastes. She worked in an establishment about a day's ride from here in the countryside. A useful distance from Buckkeep Town for the sorts of activities a young noble might wish to keep secret. She died messily in an assignation gone horribly wrong, for both her and Ash. An informant thought I might find it useful to know which noble's eldest son had such proclivities. Ash was a witness, not to her death but to the man who killed her. I had him brought to me and when I questioned him about what he had seen, I found he had an excellent eye for detail and a sharp mind for recalling it. He described the noble right down to the design of the lace on his cuffs. He'd grown up making himself useful to his mother and others in her trade, and thus he has a well-honed instinct for discretion. And stealth.'

'And the collecting of secrets.'

'There is that, too. His mother was not a street whore, Fitz. A young noble could take her to the gaming tables or the finer entertainments in Buckkeep Town, and not be shamed by her company. She knew poetry and could sing it to a small lute she played. He's a lad who has walked in two worlds. He may not have court manners, yet, and one can hear he's not court-born when he speaks, but he's not an ignorant alley rat. He'll be useful.'

I nodded slowly. 'And you want him to page for me while I'm here so . . .?'

'So you can tell me what you think of him.'

I smiled. 'Not so he can watch me for you?'

Chade opened his hands deprecatingly. 'And if he does, what would he see that I don't already know? Consider it part of his training. Set him some challenges for me. Help me hone him.'

And again, what was I to say? He was doing all for the Fool and me that could be done. Could I do less for him? I had recognized the unguent I'd pushed into the Fool's wounds. The oil for it came from the livers of a fish seldom seen in our northern waters. It was expensive, but he had not flinched from giving it to me. I would not be chary of giving him whatever I could in return. I nodded. 'I'm going down to my old room to sleep for a bit.'

Chade returned my nod. 'You have overtaxed yourself, Fitz. Later, when you've rested, I'd like a written report on that healing. When I reached for you . . . well, I could find you, but it was as if you were not yourself. As if you were so immersed in healing the Fool that you were becoming him. Or that the two of you were merging.'

'I'll write it down,' I promised him, wondering how I could describe for him something I didn't understand myself. 'But in return, I'll ask you to select for me new scrolls on Skill-healing and lending strength. I've already read the ones you left for me.'

He nodded, well pleased that I'd asked for such things, and left me, slipping out of sight behind the tapestry. I checked on the Fool and found him deeply asleep still. I hovered my hand over his face, loath to touch him lest I wake him but worried that my efforts might have wakened a higher fever in him. Instead, he seemed cooler and his breathing deeper. I straightened, yawned tremendously and then made the error of stretching.

I muffled my yelp of pain. I stood still for a long moment, then carefully rolled my shoulders. I hadn't imagined it. I reached behind myself and gingerly tugged my shirt free of where it had adhered to my back. I peeled it free and found Chade's mirror. What I saw confounded me.

The oozing wounds on my back were far smaller than those on the Fool's, nor were they puffed and reddened with infection. Instead they gaped, seven small injuries as if someone had repeatedly stabbed me with a dagger. They had not bled much; I judged them shallow. And given my propensity to heal quickly, they might very well be gone by the end of tomorrow.

The conclusion I had to reach was obvious. In Skill-healing the Fool's wounds, I had taken on these small twins. A sudden memory stirred, and I examined my belly. There, just where I had closed the wounds my knife had made on the Fool's body was a series of reddened dents. I prodded one and winced. Not painful but tender. My whirling thoughts offered me a dozen explanations. In sharing strength with the Fool, had I actually shared flesh with him? Were his wounds closing because mine were opened? I draped my shirt around me, added wood to the fire, gathered my buttony jacket and scuffed down the dusty steps to my old bedchamber.

I hoped I would find some answers in the scrolls that Chade had promised me. Until I did, I would keep this small mishap to myself. I had no desire to participate in the experiments that Chade would doubtless envision if he knew of this.

I shut the door and it became undetectable. A glance out of my shuttered window told me that a winter dawn was not far away. Well, I would take what sleep I could still get and be grateful. I added a log to the dying fire on my hearth, draped my ruined finery on a chair, found Lord Feldspar's sensible woollen nightshirt and sought my boyhood bed. My drowsy eyes travelled the familiar walls. There was the wandering crack in the wall that had always reminded me of a bear's snout. I had made that gouge in the ceiling, practising a fancy move with a hand axe that had flown out of my grip. The tapestry of King Wisdom treating with the Elderlings had been replaced with one of two bucks in battle. I preferred it. I drew a deep breath and settled into the bed. Home. Despite all the years, this was home, and I sank into sleep surrounded by the stout walls of Buckkeep Castle.

FIVE

An Exchange of Substance

I am curled warm and snug in the den. Safe. I am tired and if I shift too much, I feel the marks of teeth on my neck and back. But if I am still, then all is well.

In the distance, a wolf is hunting. He hunts alone. It is a terrible sound he makes, desperate and breathless. It is not the full-throated howling of a wolf that calls to his pack. It is the desperate yipping and short breathless howls of a predator who knows his prey is escaping. He would be better to hunt silently, to save his failing strength for running instead of giving tongue.

He is so far away. I curl tighter in the warmth of my den. It is safe here and I am well fed. I feel a fading sympathy for a wolf with no pack. I hear the broken yipping again and I know how the cold air rushes down his dry throat, how he leaps through deep snow, extending his full body, literally flinging himself through the night. I remember it too well, and for an aching moment, I am him.

'Brother, brother, come, run, hunt,' he beseeches me. He is too distant for me to know more of his thought than this.

But I am warm, and weary, and well fed. I sink deeper into sleep.

I awoke from that dream a lifetime away from the last time I had hunted with the wolf. I lay still, troubled and feeling the fading threat of it. What had wakened me? What needed to be hunted? And then I became aware of the smell of hot food, bacon and meal-cakes and the reviving fragrance of tea. I twitched fully awake and sat up. The sound that had awakened me had been the closing of my door. Ash had entered, set down a tray, stirred up my fire and fed it, taken my soiled shirt and done it all so silently that I had slept through it. A shudder of dread ran over me. When had I become so complacent and senseless as to sleep through intruders in the room? That was an edge I could ill afford to lose.

I sat up, winced, and then reached behind me to touch my own back. The wounds were closing and had stuck to the mildly itchy wool. I braced myself and plucked the nightshirt free of them, all while berating myself for sleeping too soundly. Ah. Too much to eat, too much to drink, and the exhaustion of a Skill-healing. I decided I could excuse my lack of wariness on those grounds. It did not totally banish the chagrin I felt. I wondered if Ash would report my lapse to Chade, and if he would praise the lad and if perhaps they would laugh about it.

I stood up, stretched cautiously, and told myself to stop being such a child. So Ash had fetched my breakfast and I'd slept through it. It was ridiculous to let it bother me.

I had not expected to be hungry after all I'd eaten the night before, but once I sat down to the food, I found I was. I made short work of it and then decided I would check on the Fool before taking a bit more sleep. The Skill-work I had done last night had taxed me far more than any other endeavour I'd taken on recently. He had been the receiver of that work: had it exhausted him as it had me?

I latched the main door to my room, triggered the secret door and went softly up the stairs, back into a world of candles and hearth-fire twilight. I stood at the top of the steps and listened to the fire burning, something muttering and tapping in a pot on the hearth-hook, and the Fool's steady breathing. All trace of last night's activities had been cleared away, but at one end of Chade's scarred worktable, clean bandaging, various unguents and a few concoctions for the relief of pain had been left out. Four scrolls rested beside the supplies. Chade seemed always to think of everything.

I stood looking down at the Fool for some time. He lay on his belly, his mouth slightly ajar. Lord Golden had been a handsome man. I recalled with the regret of loss the clean planes of his face, his light-gold hair and amber eyes. Scars striated his cheeks and thickened the flesh around his eyes. Most of his hair had succumbed to ill health and filth; what he had left was as short and crisp as straw. Lord Golden was gone, but my friend remained. 'Fool?' I said softly.

He made a startled sound somewhere between a moan and a cry, his blind eyes flew open and he lifted a warding hand toward me.

'It's just me. How are you feeling?'

He took a breath to answer and coughed instead. When he had finished, he said hoarsely, 'Better. I think. That is, some hurts have lessened, but the ones that remain are still sharp enough that I don't know if I'm better or just becoming more adept at ignoring pain.'

'Are you hungry?'

'A bit. Fitz. I don't remember the end of last night. We were talking at the table, and now I'm waking up in the bed.' His hand groped toward his lower back and cautiously touched the dressings there. 'What's this?'

'An abscess on your back opened. You fainted, and while you could not feel the pain, I cleaned it out and bandaged it. And a few others.'

'They hurt less. The pressure is gone,' he admitted. It was painful to watch his progress as he manoeuvred his body to the edge of the bed. He worked to get out of the bed with as few motions as possible. 'If you would put the food out?' he asked quietly, and I heard his unvoiced request that I leave him to care for himself.

Under the hopping kettle lid I found a layer of pale dumplings over a thick gravy containing chunks of venison and root vegetables. I recognized one of Kettricken's favourite dishes and wondered if she were personally selecting the Fool's menus. It would be like her.

By the time I had set out the Fool's food, he was making his way to the hearth and his chair. He moved with more certainty, still sliding his feet lest there be an obstacle, still leading with an outstretched hand, tottering and wavering, but not needing nor asking my help. He found the chair and lowered himself into it. He did not allow his back to rest against the chair. As his fingers butterflied over the cutlery, I said quietly, 'After you've eaten, I'd like to change the dressings on your back.'

'You won't really "like" to do it, and I won't enjoy it, but I can no longer have the luxury of refusing such things.'

'That's true,' I said after his words had fallen down a well of silence. 'Your life still hangs in the balance, Fool.'

He smiled. It did not look pretty: it stretched the scars on his face. 'If it were only my life, old friend, I would have lain down beside the road and let go of it long ago.'

I waited. He began to eat. 'Vengeance?' I asked quietly. 'It's a poor motive for doing anything. If you take vengeance it doesn't undo what they did. Doesn't restore whatever they destroyed.' My mind went back through the years. I spoke slowly, not sure if I wanted to share this even with him. 'One drunken night of ranting, of shouting at people that were not there,' I swallowed the lump in my throat, 'and I realized that no one could go back in time and undo what they'd done to me. No one could unhurt me. And I forgave them.'

'But the difference, Fitz, is that Burrich and Molly never meant to hurt you. What they did, they did for themselves, believing you dead and gone. And for them, life had to go on.'

He took another bite of dumpling and chewed it slowly. He drank a bit of yellow wine and cleared his throat. 'Once we were a good distance offshore, the crew did what I had known they would. They took whatever we had that they thought was of value. All the little cubes of memory-stone that Prilkop had painstakingly selected and carried so far were lost to him then. The crew had no idea what they were. Most could not hear the poetry and music and history that were stored in them. Those who could were alarmed. The captain ordered all the cubes thrown overboard. Then they worked us like the slaves they intended us to become once they found a place to sell us.'

I sat silent and transfixed. The words came from the usually reticent Fool in a smooth flow. I wondered if he had rehearsed his tale during his hours alone. Did his blindness accentuate his loneliness and propel him toward this openness?

'I was in despair. Prilkop seemed to harden every day, muscled by the work, but I was too recently healed. I grew sicker and weaker. At night, huddled on the open deck, in the wind and rain, he would look up at the stars and remind me that we were travelling in the correct direction. 'We no longer look like White Prophets, we two, but when we make shore, it will be in a place where people value us. Endure, and we will get there.'

He drank a bit more wine. I sat quietly and waited while he ate some food. 'We got there,' he said at last. 'And Prilkop was almost correct. When we reached port, he was sold at the slave auction and I . . .' His voice trickled away. 'Oh, Fitz. This telling wearies me. I do not wish to remember it all. It was not a good time for me. But Prilkop found someone who would believe him, and before many days had passed, he came back for me. They bought me, quite cheaply, and his patron helped us complete our journey back to Clerres and our school.'

He sipped his wine. I wondered at the gap in his story. What was too terrible for him to remember?

He spoke to my thought. 'I must finish this tale quickly. I have no heart for the details. We arrived at Clerres, and when the tide went out, we crossed to the White Island. There our patron delivered us to the gates of the school. The Servants who opened the doors to us were astonished for they immediately recognized what we were. They thanked our patron and rewarded him and quickly took us in. Collator Pierec was the Servant who was in charge, now. They took us to the Room of the Records, and there they leafed through scrolls and scripts and bound pages until they found Prilkop.' The Fool shook his head slowly, marvelling. 'They tried to reckon how old he was, and failed. He was old, Fitz, very old indeed, a White Prophet who had lived far past the end of his time of making changes. They were astonished.

'And more astonished when they discovered who I was.'

His spoon chased food around his bowl. He found and ate a piece of dumpling, and then a piece of venison. I thought he was making me wait for the tale, and taking pleasure in my suspense. I didn't begrudge him this.

'I was the White Prophet they had discarded. The boy who had been told he was mistaken, that there was already a White

Prophet for this time, and that she had already gone north to bring about the changes that must be.' He clattered his spoon down suddenly. 'Fitz, I was far more stupid than the Fool you have always named me. I was an idiot, a fatuous mindless . . .' He strangled on his sudden anger, knotting his scarred hands and pounding them on the table. 'How could I have expected them to greet me with anything except horror? For all the years they had kept me at the school, confined me, drugged me that I might dream more clearly for them . . . For the hours they spent needling her insidious images into my skin to make me unWhite! For all the days they tried to confuse and confound me, showing me dozens, hundreds of prophecies and dreams that they thought would convince me I was not what I knew myself to be! How could I have gone back there, thinking they would be glad to see me, and quick to acknowledge how wrong they had been? How could I think they would want to know they had made such an immense error?'

He began to weep as he spoke, his blinded eyes streaming tears that were diverted by the scars on his face. Some detached part of me noted that his tears seemed clearer than they had been and wondered if this meant some infection had been conquered. Another, saner part of me was saying softly, 'Fool. Fool. It's all right. You are here with me now, and they cannot hurt you any more. You are safe here. Oh, Fool. You are safe. Beloved.'

When I gave him his old name, he gasped. He had half-risen to stand over the table. Now he sank back down into Chade's old chair, and heedless of his bowl and the sticky table, put his head down on his folded arms and wept like a child. For a moment, his rage flared again and he shouted, 'I was so stupid!' Then the sobbing stole his voice again. For a time, I let him weep. There is nothing useful anyone can say to a man when such despair is on him. Shudders ran over him like convulsions of sorrow. His sobs came slower and softer and finally ceased, but he did not lift his head. He spoke to the table in a thick, dead voice.

'I had always believed they were mistaken. That they truly had not known.' He gave a final sniff, a sigh and lifted his head. He groped for his napkin and wiped his eyes with it. 'Fitz, they knew. They had always known I was the one. They knew I was the true

White Prophet. The Pale Woman was the one they had made. They made her, Fitz, as if they were trying to breed a pigeon with a light head and tail. Or as if you and Burrich were breeding for a colt with the stamina of the stud and the temperament of the dam. They'd created her, there in the school, and they'd taught her and filled her with the prophecies and dreams that suited their purposes. They'd made her believe and twisted her dreams to make them foretell what they wanted to happen. And they'd sent her out. And held me back.' His head sank down. He pillowed his brow on his forearms and fell silent.

One of Chade's exercises when he was training me was to put the pieces of something back together. It began with simple things: he'd drop a plate, and I would have to reassemble it to the best of my ability. The challenges advanced. The plate would fall, and I had to look at the pieces and mentally assemble it. Then I would be presented with a bag of pieces of something, broken crockery or cut harness or something of that ilk, and I had to put it back into a whole. After a time, the bag would hold not just the destroyed item but other random bits of things that looked as if they belonged with it. It was a physical exercise to teach my mind to assemble bits of facts and random gossip into a comprehensible whole.

So now my mind was at work, assembling bits so that I could almost hear the snicking of pieces of a teapot being put back together. The messenger's tale of bearing children who were taken from her meshed with the Fool's tale of the Servants creating their own White Prophets. The race of Whites with their gift of prescience had vanished from our world long ago; the Fool had told me that when we were still boys. He claimed the Whites had begun to intermarry with humans, diluting their bloodlines until those who carried that heritage showed no sign of it and often were unaware of it. And he had added that only rarely was a child born who, by chance, reflected that ancient heritage. He had been one such, and was fortunate enough that when he was born his parents knew what he was. And they knew there was a school at Clerres where children who showed the physical traits of Whites were taken and taught to record their dreams and their flashes or visions of the future. Vast libraries of recorded visions were held there and studied by the Servants so that they might learn the events that the future of the world would turn upon. And so, while he was very young, his parents had given him to the Servants to be taught to use his talents for the good of all mankind.

But the Servants had not believed he was the one true White Prophet. I had known a little of that. He had confided that they had held him there long past the time when he felt he needed to be out, changing the world's events to set us all on a better path. I had known that he had escaped them and set out on his own, to become what he had believed he must be.

And now I knew the darker side of that place. I had helped Burrich to select breeding lines for dogs and horses. I knew how it was done. A white mare and a white stallion might not always yield a white foal, but if they did, chances were that if we bred that white offspring to another white horse, or bred it back to a sibling, we would get a white foal. And so, if King Shrewd desired it, he could have generations of white horses for his guard. Burrich had been too wise a horse-breeder to inbreed our stock too deeply. He would have been shamed to have a crippled or malformed foal born due to his negligence.

I wondered if the Servants shared his morality in that regard. Somehow I doubted it. So if the Servants desired it, they could likewise breed children with the pale skin and colourless eyes of White Prophets. And in some, prescience would manifest. Through those children, the Servants could gain the ability to glimpse the future and the various paths it might take, depending on events large and small. By the Fool's account, they had been doing it for generations, possibly since before he was born. So now the Servants had a vast reservoir of possible futures to study. The future could be manipulated, not for the benefit of the world at large, but for the comfort and good fortune of the Servants alone. It was brilliant, and it was obscene.

My mind made the next leap. 'How can you fight people who know your next move before you do?'

'Ah.' He sounded almost pleased. 'You grasp it quickly. I knew you would. Even before I give you the final bits, you see it. And yet, Fitz, they don't. They didn't see me returning at all. Why?

Why would they resort to something as crude as physical torture to find out what I knew? Because you made me, my Catalyst. You created me, a creature outside of any future ever seen. I left you because I knew how potent we were together. I knew that we could change the future of the world, and I feared that if we remained together, with me blind to the future, we might set terrible things in motion. Unintentionally, of course, but all the more powerful for that. So I left you, knowing it tore your heart as deeply as it tore mine. And blind, even then, to the fact that we had already done exactly that.'

He lifted his head and turned his face toward me. 'We blinded them, Fitz. I came seeking you, a lost Farseer. In almost every future I could foresee you either never existed or you died. I knew, I *knew* that if I could see you through and keep you alive, you would be the Catalyst to set the world into a new and better path. And you did. The Six Duchies remained intact. Stone dragons rose into the air, the evil magic of Forging was ended, and true dragons were restored to the world. Because of you. Every time I snatched you back from the brink of death, we changed the world. Yet all those things the Servants had also glimpsed, even if they believed they were unlikely to come to pass. And when they sent out their Pale Woman to be the false White Prophet, and kept me confined to Clerres, they thought they had guaranteed the outcome they wished. You would not exist

'But we thwarted them. And then you did the unthinkable. Fitz, I died. I knew I would die. In all the prophecies I'd ever read in the Clerres library, in all the dream-visions I'd ever had, I died there. And so I did. But in no future foreseen by anyone, ever, in all their trove of prophecies, was I pulled back alive from the other side.

'That changed everything. You flung us into a future unseen. They grope now, wondering what will become of all their plans. For the Servants do not plan for decades, but for generations. Knowing the times and means of their own deaths, they have extended their lives. But we have taken much of that power from them. The White children born since my "death" are the only ones who can look into the future from that time. They grope through the futures where once they galloped. And so they must seek that which they most fear now: the true White Prophet for this generation. They know he is out there, somewhere, beyond their knowledge and control. They know they must seize him soon, or all they have built may come tumbling down.'

His words rang with his conviction. And yet I could not keep a smile from my face. 'So you changed their world. You are the Catalyst now. Not I.'

All expression fled his face. He stared past me, his filmed eyes fixed and distant. 'Could such a thing be?' he asked in wonder. 'Is that what I glimpsed, once, in the dreams where I was not a White Prophet?'

'I have no answer for that. I may no longer be your Catalyst, but I am certain I am not a prophet either. Come, Fool. The dressings on your back have to be changed.'

For a time he was very silent and still. Then, 'Very well,' he acceded.

I led him across the room to Chade's table. He sat down on the bench there and his hands fluttered, settled and then explored the tabletop, finding the supplies Chade had set out for me. 'I remember this,' he said quietly.

'Little has changed here over the years.' I moved to the back of his seat and studied his nightshirt. 'The wounds have oozed. I put a cloth on your back, but they've soaked through that as well. Your nightshirt is stuck to your back. I'm going to fetch warm water, soak it loose, and clean them again. I'll fetch you a clean nightshirt now and set the water to warm.'

By the time I returned with the basin of water and the clean shirt, the Fool had arranged my supplies for me. 'Lavender oil, by the scent of it,' he said, touching the first pot. 'Bear grease with garlic in here.'

'Good choices,' I said. 'Here comes the water.'

He hissed as I sponged it onto his back. I gave the half-formed scabs time to soften and then gave him the choice. 'Fast or slow?'

'Slow,' he said, and so I began with the lowest one on his back, a puncture far too close to his spine. By the time I had painstakingly freed the fabric from the oozing wound, sweat had plastered his hair to his skull. 'Fitz,' he said through clenched teeth. 'Just do it.'

His knotty hands found the table's edge and gripped it. I did not rip the shirt free, but I peeled it away from him, ignoring the sounds he made. At one point he hammered on the stone table with his fist, then yelped at that pain and dropped his fist to his lap and his brow to the table. 'It's done,' I told him as I rolled the lifted shirt across his shoulders and let it drape there.

'How bad are they?'

I pulled a branch of candles closer and studied his back. So thin. The bones of his spine were a row of hummocks down his back. The wounds gaped bloodlessly at me. 'They're clean, but open. We want to keep them open so that they heal from the inside out. Brace yourself again.' He kept silent as I wiped each injury with the lavender oil. When I added the bear grease with garlic, the scents did not blend well. I held my breath. When each had been tended, I put a clean cloth over his back, trusting the grease to hold it in place. 'There's a clean shirt here,' I said. 'Try not to displace the dressing as you put it on.'

I walked to the other end of the room. His injuries had spotted his bedding with blood and fluid. I would leave a note asking Ash to bring fresh linens. Then I wondered if the boy could read, and decided it was likely so. Even if his mother had not demanded it of him for her business, Chade would have immediately set him to learning. For now, I turned his pillows and tugged the bedding straight.

'Fitz?' he called from the worktable.

'I'm here. Just straightening your bedding.'

'You'd have made a fine valet.'

I was silent for a moment, wondering if he mocked me.

'Thank you,' he added. And then, 'Now what?'

'Well, you've eaten and we've changed the dressings. Perhaps you'd like to rest some more.'

'In truth, I am tired of resting. So weary of it, in fact, that I can do nothing except seek my bed again.'

'It must be very boring.' I stood still and watched him haltingly totter toward me. I knew he did not want me to offer help.

'Ah, boredom. Fitz, you have no idea how sweet boredom can be. When I think of endless days spent wondering when next they would return to take me, and what new torment they might devise and if they might see fit to give me food or water before or afterwards . . . well, boredom becomes more desirable than the most extravagant festival. And on my journey here, oh, how I longed for my days to be predictable. To know if the person who spoke to me was truly kind or cruel, to know if there might be food that day, or if I would find a dry place to sleep. Ah.' He had almost reached me. He halted where he was, and the emotions that passed over his face tore me. Memories he would not share with me.

'The bedstead is right there, to your left. There. Your hand is on it.'

He nodded to me, and patted and felt his way back to the side of the bed. I had opened the blankets to the linens for him. He turned and sat down on the bed. A smile crossed his face. 'So soft. You've no idea, Fitz, how much this pleases me.'

He moved his body so carefully. It reminded me of Patience toward the end of her years. It took him time to manoeuvre so that he could lift his legs up onto the bed. The loose trousers bared his meagre calves and the distorted knobs of his ankles. I winced as I looked at his left foot. To call it a foot was a charity. How he had walked on that I did not know.

'I had a stick to help me.'

'I didn't speak that aloud!'

'I heard that little sound you made. You make it when you see anything hurt. Nosy with a scratch on his face. Or the time I had a sack put over my head and took a beating.' He lay on his side and his hand scrabbled at the bedcovers. I pulled them up over him with no comment. He was silent for a minute and then said, 'My back hurts less. Did you do something?'

'I cleaned out the injuries and put dressings on them.'

'And?'

And why should I lie? 'When I touched you to clean the first boil that had broken, I . . . went into you. And encouraged your body to heal itself.'

'That's . . .' He groped for a word, 'interesting.'

I had expected outrage. Not his hesitant fascination. I spoke honestly. 'It's a bit frightening, too. Fool, my previous experiences with Skill-healings were that it took a real effort, often the effort of an entire coterie, to find a way into a man's body and provoke his body to work harder at healing itself. So, to slip into awareness of your body so easily is unsettling. Something is strange there. Strange in the same way that it was too easy to bring you through the Skill-pillars. You took back our Skill-bond, many years ago.' It was a struggle to keep rebuke from my voice. 'I look back on the night when we came here and I marvel at my foolhardiness in deciding to make the attempt.'

'Foolhardiness,' he said softly, and laughed low. He coughed then and added, 'I believe my life was in the balance that night.'

'It was. I thought I had burned Riddle's strength to bring you through. But the degree of healing you already showed when we arrived here makes me wonder if it weren't something else.'

'It was something else,' he said decisively. 'I can't claim to know this and yet I feel certain I am right. Fitz, all those years ago when you brought me back from the dead, you found me and put me into your own flesh while you entered my dead body and forced it back into life as if you were lashing a team to pull a wagon from a swamp. You were ruthless in what you did. Much as you were when you risked all, not just you and me, but Riddle, to bring me here.'

I lowered my head. It was not praise.

'We passed one another as we each resumed life in our own bodies. Do you remember that?'

'Somewhat,' I hedged.

'Somewhat? As we passed, we merged and blended.'

'No.' Now he was the one who was lying. It was time to speak the truth. 'That is not what I recall. It was not a temporary merging. What I recall is that we were one. We were not wholes blending as we passed. We were parts, finally forming a whole. You, and I, and Nighteyes. One being.'

He could not see me and yet he still averted his face from me, as if I had said a thing that was too intimate for us to witness. He bowed his head, a small affirmation. 'It happens,' he said softly. 'A mingling of beings. You've seen the results, though you may not have recognized it. I certainly didn't. That tapestry of the Elderlings that once hung in your room.'

I shook my head. I'd been a child the first time I'd seen it.

It was enough to give anyone nightmares. There was King Wisdom of the Six Duchies, treating with the Elderlings, who were tall, thin beings with unnaturally coloured skin and hair and eyes. 'I don't think that has anything to do with what I'm talking about now.'

'Oh, it does. Elderlings are what humans may become through a long association with dragons. Or more commonly, what their surviving offspring may become.'

I saw no connection. 'I do recall, long ago, when you tried to convince me that I was part dragon.'

A smile twisted his weary mouth. 'Your words. Not mine. But not so far from what I was theorizing, even if you've phrased it very poorly. There are many aspects of the Skill that put me in mind of what dragons can do. And if some distant ancestor of yours was dragon-touched, so to speak, could it be why that particular magic manifests in you?'

I sighed and surrendered. 'I've no idea. I don't even know quite what you mean by dragon-touched. So, perhaps. But I don't see what that has to do with you and me.'

He shifted in the bed. 'How can I be so tired, and not one bit sleepy?'

'How can you start so many conversations and then refuse to finish any of them?'

He went off into a coughing fit. I tried to tell myself he was feigning it but went to fetch him water anyway. I helped him sit up and waited while he drank. I took the cup while he lay back down and waited. I said nothing, simply stood by the bed with the cup. After a time I sighed.

'What?' he demanded.

'Do you know things you aren't telling me?'

'Absolutely. And that will always be true.'

He sounded so much like his old self and took such obvious pleasure in the words that I felt almost no annoyance. Almost.

'I mean about this. About what bonds us in such a way that I can take you with me through a Skill-pillar, and almost without effort enter your body to heal it?'

'Almost?'

'I was exhausted afterward, but that was from the healing, I think. Not from the joining.' I would say nothing of what it had done to my back.

I thought he would detect I was holding something back. Instead he spoke slowly. 'Because perhaps the joining already exists and always does.'

'Our Skill-bond?'

'No. You haven't been listening.' He sighed. 'Think again about the Elderlings. A human lives long in the company of dragons, and eventually he begins to take on some of the traits of the dragon. You and I, Fitz, lived in close company for years. And in that healing that was actually a snatching back from death, we shared. We mingled. And perhaps we became, as you claim, one being. And perhaps we did not completely sort ourselves back into our own separate selves as thoroughly as you think. Perhaps there was an exchange of our very substances.'

I thought about this carefully. 'Substances. Such as flesh? Blood?'

'I don't know! Perhaps. Perhaps something more essential even than blood.'

I paused to sort the sense from his words. 'Can you tell me why it happened? Is it dangerous to us? Something we must try to undo? Fool, I need to know.'

He turned his face toward me, took a breath as if he were going to speak, then paused and let it out. I saw him thinking. Then he spoke simply, as if I were a child. 'The human that lives too long near the dragon takes on aspects of the dragon. The white rose that is planted for years beside the red rose begins to have white blossoms threaded with red. And perhaps the human Catalyst who is companion to a White Prophet takes on some of his traits. Perhaps, as you threatened, your traits as a Catalyst have infected me as well.'

I studied his face for signs of a jest. Then I waited for him to mock me for my gullibility. Finally I begged him, 'Can you just explain?'

He blew out a breath. 'I'm tired, Fitz. And I've told you as clearly as I can what I think may be happening. You seem to think we are becoming or were "one thing" as you so gracefully put it. I think that our essences may be seeping across to the other, creating a bridge between us. Or perhaps it's a vestige of the Skill-bond we once shared.' He leaned his poor head back on the pillows. 'I can't sleep. I'm weary and tired, but not sleepy. What I am is bored. Horribly bored with pain and darkness and waiting.'

'I thought you just said that being bored—'

'Is lovely. Horribly lovely.'

Well, at least he was showing signs of his old self. 'I wish I could help you. Sadly, there isn't much I can do about your boredom.'

'You already did something for me. The sores on my back are much better. Thank you.'

'You're welcome. And now I fear I must leave you for a time. I'm supposed to meet with Lady Kettricken, as Lord Feldspar of Spiretop. I will need to dress for that role.'

'And you must go right now?'

'I should, if I'm to be properly dressed and in line for a private audience with her. I'll come back afterwards. Try to rest.'

With regret, I turned away. I knew how the time must drag for him. He had always been a lively fellow, a juggler, a tumbler, adept at sleight-of-hand, with a mind as quick and clever as his fingers. He had cavorted through King Shrewd's court, quick with a witty retort, always a part of the gay whirl that Buckkeep society had been when I was very young. Now sight and clever fingers and agile body had all been taken from him. Darkness and pain were his companions.

'After Prilkop's benefactor bought me from my "owner", at an insultingly low price I might add, we were fairly well treated. His new patron was not a noble but a fairly wealthy landowner. It was only by the greatest of good fortune that the man was well-versed in the lore of the White Prophets.'

He paused. He knew I had halted, intrigued by his words. I tried to calculate how much time had passed. It was difficult to tell in the perpetual twilight of the room. 'I have to leave soon,' I reminded him.

'Do you truly?' he asked, a mocking lilt in his voice.

'I do.'

'Very well.'

I turned.

'For ten days, we rested and were well fed in his home. He arranged new garments for us, packed provisions, and then he himself drove the horse and cart to Clerres. It was a journey of nearly a month to get there. Sometimes we camped, and at other times we were able to stay at inns. Both Prilkop and I worried greatly at what the man was sacrificing of pocket and time to get us there, but he would always say he was honoured to do it. Our road led us through a mountain pass, nearly as frozen and cold as a Buckkeep winter, and then down, down we went. I began to recognize the scents of the trees and I knew the names of the wayside flowers from my boyhood. Clerres itself had grown a great deal since last I had seen it, and Prilkop was astounded that the place he remembered as the simple village of Clerres had grown to an edifice of walls and towers and gardens and gates.

'Yet so it was. The school had prospered, and in turn the city had prospered, for there was a trade now in the searching of prophecies to give advice to merchants and would-be brides and builders of sailing ships. From far and near they came, to pay a fee in the hope of getting an audience with the Head Servant, and then to tell their tale to him. And if he judged them worthy, they could buy a licence for a day or three or twenty, and cross the causeway to the White Island. There, one of the acolyte Servants would be put to researching the prophecies to see if any pertained to that particular venture or wedding or voyage.

'But I am getting ahead of myself.'

I clenched my teeth and then let him win. 'Actually, you've gone backward in your telling, as you well know. Fool, I desperately want to hear this story, but I must not be late to my audience.'

'As you wish.'

I had taken four steps when he added, 'I only hope I am not too weary later to tell you the rest.'

'Fool! Why are you being like this?'

'Do you really want to know?' The old lilt of mockery was back in his voice.

'Yes.'

He spoke more softly and soberly than he had before. 'Because I know it makes you feel better when I mock you.'

I turned to look back at him, denial on my lips. But some trick of the firelight showed him to me as he was. Not at all like my friend of old. He looked like a badly-carved puppet of himself, something as battered and ragged as a beloved old toy. The light touched the scars on his face, the grey-painted eyes and straw-thatch of hair on his skull. I couldn't utter a word.

'Fitz, we both know I teeter on a knife's edge. It's not if I will fall, but when. You are keeping me balanced there and alive. But when it happens, as I fear it must, it will not be your fault. Nor mine. Neither of us could have steered this fate.'

'I'll stay if you want me to.' I threw aside all thoughts of courtesy to Kettricken and duty to Chade. Kettricken would understand, and Chade would have to live with it.

'No. No, thank you. Suddenly I am feeling ready to sleep.'

'I'll be back as soon as I can,' I promised him.

His eyes had closed, and perhaps he already slept. I left quietly.

SIX

The Witted

When Regal the Pretender retreated to the inland duchies, the coastal duchies were left rudderless. Strong as the dukes of Bearns, Shoaks and Rippon were, they were each too engrossed in defending their own coasts to mount any meaningful unified response to the Red Ships. The titular Duke of Buck, a cousin to the Pretender Regal, was little more than a place-holding puppet, who could do nothing to rally the nobles.

It was at this time that Lady Patience, queen of the former King-in-Waiting Chivalry, rose to prominence. What began with the selling of her jewels to keep the warships of Buck manned and active soon consumed almost all of her personal fortune as she worked to keep up the spirits of her farmers and miners as well as rallying the lesser nobility to organize their own forces to repel the invaders.

This was the situation to which Queen Kettricken returned. Pregnant with the Farseer heir, she and her minstrel, Starling Birdsong, were transported from the Elderling lands to the battlements of Buckkeep Castle, flown there by an immense dragon. King Verity escorted her to the safety of the castle before rejoining his dragon mount. With the other Elderling warriors astride their dragon steeds, he took to the air to resume the great battle he had begun against the Red Ships. Few were present to witness the king's return to Buckkeep, and had his queen not been there to assert to the truth of his presence with the minstrel Starling Birdsong to swear truth to it, her sudden appearance would have seemed almost magical. The sparkling dragons that filled the sky had been a terrifying sight to the defenders of Buck until the queen revealed that they were no danger to the folk of Buck, but instead were at the command of their rightful king, and had come to defend them.

On that day, before nightfall, all the Red Ships were driven from the shores of Buck. The legions of dragons swiftly spread out, securing the entire coastline of the Six Duchies before the moon had waxed twice full again. Many a shoreline defender and doughty sailor can attest to how the dragons would appear as distant sparkling lights in the sky, that grew larger and larger until their power and majesty sent the raiders fleeing.

Against this backdrop, the Mountain princess turned Six Duchies queen returned to accept her crown. Lady Patience remained at her side for the remaining months of the war, advising her and putting the reins of power securely into her hands. With the birth of the heir, the succession was secured.

A Brief History of the Monarchs of the Six Duchies

I descended, shut the door, peeked out through my shuttered window and was horrified. Truly the morning had fled while I was with the Fool. I was still in my nightshirt, unwashed, unshaven, and possibly already late for my audience with Kettricken. To add to my annoyance, Ash had visited my rooms again. The fire was freshly stirred and a new outfit for Lord Feldspar had been draped on the chair. His rescued brown wig had been transferred to a fresh hat and carefully brushed. Well, growing up the son of a courtesan had at least taught Ash some useful valet skills. I knew I had latched my door. I wondered if Chade had given him a key or if he had slipped the lock. It wasn't an easy lock to jigger. I tried not to let that question distract me as I quickly washed, shaved, staunched the bleeding from my hasty blade, and dressed in the fresh garments.

One of the scabbed wounds on my back had broken open as I took off my nightshirt. I put on Lord Feldspar's long-sleeved tunic and a gaudy vest over it and hoped the stripes of bright colour were in honour of Winterfest. I dreaded the idea that the imaginary lord dressed this way every day. The leggings were moderately comfortable, and the vest admirably concealed no less than six tiny pockets of various nasty things. Settling the wig and the ridiculously tiny hat pinned to it consumed more minutes than I liked, and yet I knew it was the one piece that must be done perfectly. I pinched and scratched at my nose until it was the appropriate shade of red. Soot from the fire with a few drops of water made my brows heavier. The heeled shoes with the silly toes slipped onto my stockinged feet and the moment I stood up one of my feet cramped abominably. I kicked the shoes off and stamped around the room until it passed. Then, muttering curses on Chade, I put them back on and left my room, locking the door behind me.

My foot cramped again twice before I reached the bottom of the stairs, and it was all I could do to keep my steps steady and betray no sign of how badly I wanted to hop and stamp. Kettricken's audience chamber had once served Queen Desire as a private parlour for herself and her ladies. This I knew only because I had been told of it; that woman had never tolerated me within her sight, let alone within her private chambers. I dismissed the last clinging shreds of childhood dread as I approached the tall oak doors. They were closed. Outside on several benches perched those hopeful of currying influence with the king by bestowing their attentions and gifts upon his mother. I took my place at the end of a lavishly cushioned bench and waited. Eventually, the door opened, a young noblewoman was ushered out and a rather bored page in white-and-purple livery approached the next aspirant and ushered him in. When the page returned, I made myself known to her and resumed my wait on the bench.

I had rather expected that I would not have to wait in line, but Kettricken was true to her Mountain roots. Each petitioner was invited in turn and allotted time with Lady Kettricken, and then was ushered out. I sat and waited, with my foot spasming inside the evil shoe and a pleasant and hopeful expression on my face. When finally the page beckoned to me, I rose and managed to follow her into the room without limping. As the tall doors closed behind me, I allowed myself a smile. There was a cosy hearth, several comfortable chairs, and a low table with cushions around it. A collection of curious or beautiful objects from every one of the Six Duchies was displayed on various tables about the room. Some might have seen it as a blatant display of wealth, but I divined the truth of it. Kettricken had never had any great use for possessions. These gifts, these tokens of esteem from the lords and ladies of the Six Duchies and from foreign lands and emissaries must not be discarded. And so she kept them here, in a casual and cluttered display that ran counter to her austere Mountain upbringing. I let my eyes wander over them briefly before making my obeisance to Kettricken.

'Courage, you may go. Let the kitchen know my guests and I are ready for our refreshment. Please let Witmaster Web also know that I am ready to see him at his earliest convenience.'

I remained standing until the little page had left the room, and was grateful when Kettricken wearily gestured me to a seat. She pursed her lips as she regarded me and then asked, 'Is this mummery yours, Fitz, or another puppet show from Chade?'

'Lord Chade facilitated it, but I agreed that it was the prudent thing to do. As Lord Feldspar I am able to move about Buckkeep Castle as your guest for Winterfest without exciting comment.'

'After all these years, I should be resigned to the need for such deceptions. But they only make me long for simple truth. One day, FitzChivalry Farseer, I would like you to stand before the court and be acknowledged as yourself and given credit for your many years of service to the crown. One day you should take your rightful place at Dutiful's side, and be openly recognized as his mentor and protector.'

'Oh, please don't threaten me with that,' I begged her, and she smiled tolerantly and drew her chair a bit closer to mine.

'Very well, then. But what of your daughter. What of clever little Bee?'

'Clever little Bee.' I repeated her words. They numbed my mouth.

'So I have heard, in the missives Lant has sent Nettle. She received one just two days ago. She was quite relieved to hear her sister was doing so well at her lessons. Indeed, that in some areas, such as her reading and writing, she scarcely needs his instructions.'

'I think she is a bright child,' I conceded. Then, disloyally, I added, 'But I am sure that all fathers think their daughters are clever.'

'Well. Some fathers do. I hope you are one of them. Nettle was startled that her sister was developing very differently from how she had feared. When the news reached me, I was very pleased. And intrigued. I had feared the child would not survive, let alone prosper. But my intent is that we will send for her, and then I can see for myself.' She folded her hands and rested her chin on her fingers. She waited.

'Perhaps the next time I come to Buckkeep, I will bring her with me,' I offered. I hoped my desperation did not sound in my voice. Bee was too little, too different to be brought to court. How much did I dare tell Kettricken?

'Then you do not intend to stay long with us?'

'Only until the Fool is hearty enough to endure a Skill-healing.'

'And you think that will be so soon that your little daughter will not miss you?'

Oh, Kettricken. I did not meet her eyes. 'Probably later rather than sooner,' I admitted reluctantly.

'Then we should send for her now.'

'Travelling conditions are so harsh now . . .'

'There is that. But in a comfortable carriage, accompanied by my personal guard, she might do well. Even through the storms. I am sure they will manage to find respectable inns every night.'

'You've given this a lot of thought.'

The look she gave me implied her plan was immutable. 'I have,' she said, and with that settled, she changed the topic. 'How fares Lord Golden?'

I started to shake my head and then shrugged instead. She had made her plans for Bee, but I would let her distract me while I planned my own campaign. 'Better than he was, in some ways. Warm, clean, fed, and some of his lesser injuries have begun to heal. But he is still closer to death's door than to the gates of health.'

For a moment, her years showed on her face. 'I could scarcely believe it was him. If you had not been there to vouch for it, I would never have suspected it. Fitz, what happened to him? Who did this?'

I wondered if the Fool would want his tale shared. 'I am still drawing the full tale out of him.'

'When last I saw him, years ago, he said he would return to the place where he was taught.'

'And he did.'

'And they turned on him.'

Kettricken could still take me by surprise with her leaps of intuition. 'So I believe. Lady Kettricken, I am sure you recall how private a man the Fool was.'

'And is. I know what you will next suggest, that I visit him myself. And I shall. In truth, I have already called on him twice, and each time found him sleeping. But my visits would be much easier for me if you and Lord Chade had not squirreled him away into your old den. I'm a bit old to be stooping and scuttling through narrow hideaways. Surely he would be better off in a chamber that offered him light and air.'

'He is fearful of pursuit, even within the stout walls of Buckkeep. I think he will sleep best where he is right now. And as for light, well, it means little to him now.'

She shuddered as if my words were arrows that had struck her. She turned her face away, as if to hide from me the tears that filled her eyes. 'That grieves me beyond words,' she choked out.

'And I.'

'Is there any hope that with the Skill . . .?'

The very question I still pondered. 'I do not know. He is very weak still. I do not wish to restore his sight if it takes the last of his strength and he dies of it. We will have to be very cautious. We have made some small progress already, and as he eats and rests and gains strength, we will do more.'

She nodded violently to that. 'Please. But, oh, Fitz, why? Why would anyone treat him so?'

'They thought he knew something, and was keeping it from them.'

'What?'

I hesitated.

She turned back to face me. Weeping seldom makes a lady lovelier. Her nose had reddened and the rims of her eyes had gone pink. She no longer tried to disguise the tears running down her face. Her voice was harsh. 'I deserve to know, Fitz. Do not play Chade with me. What secret could possibly be worth resisting what they did to him?'

I looked at my feet, ashamed. She did deserve to know. 'He knew no secret. He had no knowledge to give them. They demanded to know where his son was. To me he has said that he has no knowledge of any such son.'

'A son.' A strange look came over her face, as if she could not decide whether to laugh or weep. 'So. Are you finally giving a definite answer to the question Starling put to him so many years ago? He is, then, a man?'

I took breath, paused, and then replied, 'Kettricken, he is what he is. A very private person.'

She cocked her head at me. 'Well, if the Fool had given birth to a son, I think he would remember that. So that leaves him only the male role.'

I started to say that not every child was fathered in the same way. The thought of how King Verity had borrowed my body to lie with her, leaving me for a night in his old man's skin, swept through my mind like a storm. I folded my lips on my words and looked aside from her.

'I will visit him,' she said quietly.

I nodded, relieved. There was a tap at her door. 'I should go now, so you may meet your next supplicant.'

'No, you should stay. The next visitor concerns you.'

I was not entirely surprised when a page ushered Web into the room. He halted inside the door while two serving girls entered with trays of refreshments. They arranged everything on a low table while we all looked at one another. Web scowled briefly at my disguise, and I saw him reorder his impression of the man he had glimpsed last night. It was not the first time he had witnessed me assume a different character. As he evaluated me in my new guise, I studied him as well.

Web had changed since last we had spoken. For a number of years following the death of his Wit-bird Risk, he had not re-partnered. That loss had wrought a change in him. When I had lost my wolf, I felt as if half my soul had gone missing, as if there was too much empty space in both my mind and my body. For a time,

I had seen that same emptiness in Web when he and Nettle's brother Swift would visit Molly and me at Withywoods. His eyes had lost their bird-brightness, and he had walked as if he were anchored to the earth. He had seemed to age decades in a matter of months.

Today he walked with his shoulders squared, and his gaze darted quickly around the room, taking in every detail. The difference was a good one, as if he had rediscovered youth. I found myself smiling at him. 'Who is she?' I greeted him.

Web's eyes met mine. 'He. Not she. A young kestrel named Soar.'

'A kestrel. A bird of prey. That must be different for you.'

Web smiled and shook his head, his expression as fond as if he spoke of a child when he said, 'We both have so much to learn of one another. We have been together less than four months. It is a new life for me, Fitz. His eyesight! Oh, and his appetite and his fierce joy in the hunt.' He laughed aloud and seemed almost breathless. There was more grey in his hair and deeper lines in his face, but his laugh was a boy's.

I felt a moment of envy. I recalled the headiness of the first days with a new partner. As a child, I had joined myself to Nosy without the least hesitation, and experienced a summer with the full senses of a young hound amplifying my own. He had been taken from me. Then there had been Smithy, the dog I had bonded to in complete defiance of Burrich and common sense. Lost to me when he gave his life defending my friend. They had been companions to my heart. But it had been Nighteyes the wolf who had wrapped his soul around mine. Together we had hunted and together we had killed, both game and men. The Wit bonded us to all life. From him, I had learned to master both the exhilaration of the hunt and the shared pain of the kill. Recalling that bond, my envy faded. No one could replace him. Could another woman ever be to me what Molly had been? Would I ever have a friend who knew me as the Fool did? No. Such bonds in a man's life are unique. I found my tongue, 'I'm happy for you, Web. You look a new man.'

'I am. And I am as sad for you as you are glad for me. I wish you had a Wit-companion to sustain you in your loss.'

What to say to that? There were no words. 'Thank you,' I said quietly. 'It has been hard.'

Kettricken had kept silent during our exchange but she watched me keenly. The Witmaster found a cushion and lowered himself to sit beside the table. He offered Kettricken a wide smile and then regarded the food with interest.

Kettricken smiled in return. 'Please, let us not wait for formalities. Be at ease, my friends. It has given me great pleasure to watch Web recover his spirits. You should meet Soar, Fitz. I do not say that he might make you reconsider your decision to remain alone, but he has certainly given me reason to doubt my own un-partnered status.' She gave a small shake of the head. 'When I saw the pain you felt at Nighteyes' passing, I thought I wanted none of that, ever. And again, when Web lost Risk, I told myself that I had been wise to refrain from sharing my heart with an animal, knowing eventually I must feel the tearing pain of departure.' She lifted her eyes from watching Web pour tea for all of us and met my incredulous gaze. 'But witnessing Web's joy in Soar, I wonder. I have been alone so long. I grow no younger. Must this be a regret I take to my grave, that I did not understand fully the magic I possessed?'

She let her words trail away. When she turned to meet my gaze, there were echoes of hurt and anger in her eyes. 'Yes. I am Witted. And you knew, Fitz. Didn't you? Long before I suspected, you knew. And you knew the Wit that so endangered Dutiful when he was a boy came from me.'

I chose my words carefully. 'My lady, I think it as likely that it came from his father as from you. And ultimately, it mattered little where it came from. Even now, to possess the Wit can bring—'

'It mattered to me,' she said in a low voice. 'And it matters still. What I felt between Nighteyes and me was not imaginary. If I had known that during our sojourn in the Mountains, I would have let him know what that support meant to me.'

'He knew,' I said, recklessly interrupting her. 'He knew, never fear.'

I saw her take a breath, her breast rising and falling with the emotion she contained. Her Mountain training was all that kept her from berating me. Instead, she said quietly, 'Sometimes thanking someone is more important to the person giving the thanks than the one who receives it.'

'I'm sorry.' Words I was heartily sick of saying. 'But there was so much else we were struggling with. I had only the barest understanding of the Wit then and even my grasp of what the Skill could be was tenuous. If I had told you that I suspected you were Witted, then what? I certainly could not have taught you how to manage a magic that I did not myself control well.'

'I understand that,' she said. 'But nonetheless I think my life has been less fulfilling than it might have been.' In a lower voice she added, 'And much lonelier.'

I had no response. It was true. I had known of the loneliness that devoured her once King Verity was transformed into a stone dragon and taken from her forever. Could an animal companion have helped her to bear that? Probably. Yet it had never occurred to me to tell her that I had sensed a feeble pulsing of the Wit in her. I had always believed it so slight that it did not matter. Unlike myself, where the Wit had demanded from my earliest childhood that I find a soul to share my life. I moved slowly across the room and sat down at the low table. Kettricken came to take her place. She spoke to me in a calmer voice as she picked up her cup. 'Web tells me that it is not too late. But also not a thing for me to rush into.'

I nodded and sipped from my own cup. Was this discussion why she had summoned me? I could not imagine where it was leading.

Web looked up at Kettricken. 'The bond must be mutually beneficial,' he said. He darted a glance at me as he continued, 'Kettricken's duties often confine her to the castle. Were she to bond with a large animal, or a wild creature, it would limit their time together. So I have suggested to her that she consider beasts that would be comfortable sharing her lifestyle. Cats. Dogs.'

'Ferrets. Parrots,' I pointed out, relieved to move the conversation to a different arena.

'And that is why I've a favour to ask of you, Fitz,' Web said abruptly.

Startled, I met his gaze.

'I know you will say "no", but I am pressed to ask you anyway. There is no one else who can help her.'

I looked at Kettricken in dismay, wondering what she needed.

'No. Not Lady Kettricken,' Web assured me.

My heart sank. 'Then who is she and what does she need?'

'She's a crow. If you two come to an understanding, she'll share her name with you.'

'Web, I—'

He spoke over my objection. 'She has been alone for about six months. She was sent to me, seeking my help. She was hatched with a defect. When she fledged out, several of her pinions in each wing were white. At an early age, she was driven out of her murder. Assaulted and badly injured by her own family, she was found by an elderly shepherd. He took her in and helped her heal. For eight years they were companions. Recently, he died. But before he died, he contacted me and then sent her on to me.'

He paused, waiting for the question he knew I would ask.

'She left her Wit-partner?' I was incredulous at such faithlessness.

Web shook his head. 'No. The shepherd was not Witted. He was simply a man with a kind heart. And due in no small part to the efforts of the Farseer crown, he was able to reach out to the Old Blood community to find her a new home. No, don't speak, let me finish my tale. Crows are social creatures. If she is forced to live a solitary life, she will go mad. Furthermore, with her striped wings, she cannot join other crows. They will turn on her for her differences. And finally, she does not seek a Wit-bond, only a human companion. For company and for her protection.'

Kettricken dropped words into my silence. 'It seems the perfect fit to both of us.'

I drew breath to respond and then sighed it out silently. I knew why Web could not take her on. Nor could Lady Kettricken be seen with a crow upon her shoulder: battlefield scavenger and bird of ill omen, a crow companion would not do for her. I already knew I would not do it. I would find someone else, but for now, instead of outright refusing, I said, 'I will think about it.'

'You should,' Web approved. 'Even simple companionship with an animal is not a thing to take lightly. A crow can live a score of years, and it is not unheard of for one to reach thirty. Having met her, I judge you two would be well matched in temperament.'

Knowing what Web thought of my temperament, I was more convinced than ever that I wanted nothing to do with that bird. I would find her an appropriate companion. Perhaps Tallerman would not mind a crow in the stables at Withywoods. So I nodded without speaking.

They both took it as surrender. Kettricken poured more tea for us and the next hour passed with us speaking of old times. Web told, perhaps, too many stories of Soar, but Kettricken and I both understood. And from those stories, it was natural that the talk turned to Old Blood, and Kettricken's feeble command of the Wit-magic and what it might mean to her. What it had meant to her she shared more fully now; she had reached out to my wolf and he had accepted that faint connection. His friendship had sustained her more than I had realized.

Then, as if it were the most natural thing in the world, Kettricken asked if Bee had either the Wit or the Skill. I cannot say why it was so unsettling for her to ask that question. Certainly I had few secrets left from either of them. Yet in some odd way, Bee felt like a secret, something private and precious that I did not want to share. I had to fight not to lie. I told them that, as far as I could determine, my little daughter possessed neither of those magics in any strength. At most, she could sense the Skill in Nettle and me, but I received no sense of it from her. Then I added that, as young as she was, it was hard to tell such a thing.

Web quirked an eyebrow. 'Usually the Wit manifests young in children. She has shown no predilection for bonding with an animal? No intrinsic understanding of their ways?'

I shook my head. 'But, to be honest, I've kept her away from such dangers. I know what it is to bond too young and without guidance.'

Web frowned. 'So there are no animals in her life?'

I hesitated, trying to decide what answer he would like to hear. I pushed myself toward the truth. 'She has been learning to ride her horse. At an early age, when we first tried to teach her, she seemed uncomfortable with such an idea. Frightened, even. But of late, she has made good progress. She does not dislike animals. She likes kittens. The shepherd's dog likes her.'

Web was nodding slowly. He looked at Kettricken when he said, 'When she arrives, I would like to speak with her. If she has inherited Old Blood from her father, then the sooner we all know, the better for her to master her magic.'

And Kettricken inclined her head gravely, as if the permission were hers to give. I felt a wave of misgiving but decided that, for now, I would say nothing. I made a note to myself that Web had known that Kettricken desired to bring Bee to Buckkeep before I did. With whom else had she discussed this? I needed to find what was behind her resolution. But discreetly. Boldly, I turned the conversation. 'What of the princes? Has either Prosper or Integrity shown signs of the Wit or the Skill?'

Kettricken's smooth brow furrowed. She took a breath and considered well her words before she replied, 'We believe both princes have the Skill, their heritage magic as Farseers. But it does not seem that either one has a strong talent for it.' She did something with her eyes as she met my gaze. It was not a wink or an eye roll toward Web, but only the slightest flicker of movement that let me know this was not a topic she wished to discuss before the Witmaster. So, my erstwhile queen had learned discretion and secrecy. Perhaps Buckkeep had changed her as much as she had changed it.

She turned the talk to other topics and I let her. Web was garrulous as ever, and astute at getting other people to talk. I tried to stay to safe topics; sheep and orchards and the repairs I'd been making to Withywoods but I am sure I told him far more about myself and my situation than I intended. The food was long gone and the last of the tea standing cold in our cups when Kettricken smiled at both of us and reminded us that others awaited her attention outside the audience chamber.

'Please tell Lord Golden that I will come to call on him this evening. Late, I fear, for there will be yet more celebration of the dark's turning and I must attend. But when I may, I will come to him, and hope that he does not mind too much if I wake him.

If he prefers not, leave a note for me, to say he does not desire company.'

'Boredom besieges him in his infirmity. I daresay he will welcome the company.' I decided it for him. It would be good for him.

Web spoke. 'And Fitz, when can I expect a visit from you? I'd like to introduce you to the crow. I will not say that her company is a burden to me, but Soar does not regard her with welcome . . .'

'I understand. I will come tomorrow morning, if Lord Chade does not give me any other errands. I may have to spend my day in Buckkeep Town.' I rebuked myself for being reluctant to help him. I would go. I was confident that the crow would find me an unsuitable partner.

Web smiled at me. 'Excellent. I've told her a great deal about you and shared Wit-knowledge of you. Within a day or so, I must be on my way. So she may find you before then. She's eager to meet you.'

'And I as eager to meet her,' I replied politely. And with that I made my bows and left Lady Kettricken's audience chamber wondering if Riddle had ever considered having a pet bird.

SEVEN

Secrets and a Crow

With the Red Ships at our doors and our noble King Shrewd
    failing in both body and mind
The young bastard saw his opportunity. He felled him. With
    magic and might of muscle,
He took from the duchies the king they needed. And from
    Prince Regal he stole
His father, his mentor, his rock of wisdom.
    The kindness bestowed on a bastard felled him.

And the Bastard laughed. In his murderous triumph, sword
    bared and bloody, he soiled with murder
The keep that had sheltered his worthless life. Cared he
    nothing for the great hearts
That had fostered him, fed him, clothed and protected him.
    He loved only bloodshed.
No loyalty did the Bastard cede to king or country.

Wounded in heart, sorrowing as a son, burdened with the
    concerns of a country at war,
The prince, now king, stepped forward to his tasks. His
    brothers dead or fled, to him fell
The heavy crown. To him fell the mourning, and to him, the
    protecting. The last son,
The loyal son, the brave prince became the king of the
    wracked and troubled land.

Robin Hobb

'Vengeance first!' weary King Regal cried. To his shelter flocked
  his dukes and nobles.
'To the dungeons with the Bastard!' they pleaded with one
  voice. And so King Regal
Did his duty. To cell and chains went the conniving Bastard,
  the Witted One, the Regicide.
To dark and cold he was sent, as befitted such a dark and
  cold heart.

'Discover his magic,' the king bade his loyal men. And so they
  tried. With questions and fists,
Clubs and iron, with cold and dark, they broke the traitor.
  They found no nobility, no cleverness,
Only wolf-greed and dog-selfishness. And so he died, the
  Traitor, the Witted One, the Bastard.
Of no use to anyone but himself had his life been. His death
  freed us from his shame.

King Regal's Burden – a song
                                    by Celsu Cleverhands,
                                    a Farrow minstrel

I tottered back to my room, silently cursing my painful shoes. I
needed to sleep. Then I would check on the Fool, and after that,
I thought with a sigh, I would once more assume my role as Lord
Feldspar. There would be feasting, dancing, and music again
tonight. My mind wandered to Bee, and I felt that sudden gulf
of guilt. Revel, I told myself sternly. He would see that Winterfest
was well kept at Withywoods. And surely Shun would not allow
the holiday to go by without appropriate foods and festivity. I
hoped only they would include my child. I wondered again how
long I would be away from her. Was Kettricken wiser than I?
Would it be best to send for her?

I was chewing my lip at that thought as I reached the top of
the stairs. When I looked down the corridor and saw Riddle
standing outside my door, my heart lifted as it does when one
sees an old friend. Then as I drew closer it sank again, for his

face was solemn and his eyes opaque as when a man hides his feelings. 'Lord Feldspar,' he greeted me gravely. He bowed, and I took care that the bow I gave him was little more than a nod. Further down the hallway, two servants were replenishing the corridor lamps.

'What brings you to my door, good man?' I took care that my words held the right amount of disdain for a messenger.

'I bring you an invitation, Lord Feldspar. May I step within your chambers and recite it for you?'

'Of course. A moment.' I patted about in my garments, found my key and, opening the door, I preceded him into the room.

Riddle shut the door firmly behind us. I removed the wig and hat gratefully, and turned to him, expecting to see my friend. But he still stood at the door as if he were no more than a messenger, his face both grave and still.

I said the words I hated most. 'I'm so sorry, Riddle. I had no idea what I was doing to you. I thought I was giving the Fool my strength. I never intended to steal from you. Have you recovered? How do you feel?'

'I'm not here about that.' He spoke flatly. My heart sank.

'Then what? Sit, please. Shall I summon someone to bring us food or drink?' I asked. I tried to keep my words warm, but his manner warned me that his heart was sealed against me right now. I could not blame him.

He worked his mouth, took in a deep breath and then let it out. 'First,' he declared, in a voice almost hard despite its shaking, 'this is not about you. You can be offended. You can offer to kill me, you're welcome to try to kill me. But it's not about you or your pride or your place at court, or who Nettle is or my common parentage.' His words grew more rushed and impassioned as he spoke, and the colour rose higher in his face. Anger and pain sparked in his eyes.

'Riddle, I—'

'Just be quiet! Just listen.' He took another breath. 'Nettle is pregnant. I will not let her be shamed. I will not let our child be shamed. Say what you will, do what you will, she is my wife and I will not let our joy be dirtied with politics and secrets.'

I was the one who sat down. Luckily, the bed was behind me

when I did so. If he had driven the air out of me with a blow to my belly, the impact could not have been stronger. Words rattled in my head. *Pregnant. Shamed. Wife. Dirtied. Secrets.*

A baby.

I found my voice. 'I'm going to—'

Riddle crossed his arms on his chest. His nostrils flared and he exclaimed defiantly, 'I don't care what you do. Understand that. Do whatever you wish, but it won't change anything.'

'—be a grandfather.' I choked on the word. Incredulity melted his face and he stared. It gave me the moment I needed to organize my thoughts. Words tumbled from my lips. 'I have money saved. You can have it all. You must leave soon, before travel is too difficult for her. And I think you must flee the Six Duchies entirely. She is the Skillmistress; she is too well known for you to . . .'

'We are not leaving!' Anger tightened his slack face. 'We refuse. We were lawfully wed—'

Impossible. 'The king forbade it.'

'The king can forbid whatever he likes, but if a man and a woman make their vows before the Witness Stones, with at least two witnesses—'

'Only if one is a minstrel!' I interrupted him. 'And the witness must know both parties.'

'I wager the Queen of the Six Duchies knows us both,' he said quietly.

'Kettricken? I thought Kettricken was a party to forbidding the marriage.'

'Kettricken is *not* the queen of the Six Duchies. Elliania is. And she comes from a place where a woman can marry whoever she wishes.'

It all fitted together as tightly as the blocks that make up an arch. Almost. 'But your other witness had to be a minstrel . . .' My words trickled away. I knew who their minstrel had been.

'Hap Gladheart.' Riddle confirmed it quietly. A smile almost twisted his face. 'Perhaps you've heard of him?'

My fostered son. He'd been delighted to call Nettle 'sister'. I found I had clamped both hands over my mouth. I tried to think. So. Married. In public and yet in secret. Yes, Elliania would do it, and possibly not realize that in flaunting her husband's authority she was doing far more than simply asserting her belief that a woman should have complete control over who she wed. Or didn't wed, and merely slept with.

I let my hands fall away from my mouth. Riddle still stood as if he expected me to leap to my feet and pummel him. I tried to recall if I'd even felt that impulse. I hadn't. No anger: that was drowned in dread.

'The king will never accept this. Nor Kettricken, nor Chade. Oh, Riddle. What were the two of you thinking?' Joy warred with tragedy in my voice. A child, a child that I knew Nettle wanted. A child that would change their lives completely. My grandchild. And Molly's.

'Babies happen. For years, we have been cautious. And lucky, I suppose. And then we were neither. And when Nettle realized she was pregnant, she told me she intended to be happy about it. No matter what she must do.' His voice changed and suddenly my friend spoke to me. 'Fitz. We are neither of us youngsters. This may be our only chance for a child.'

No matter what she must do. I could almost hear Nettle's voice saying those words. I took a deep breath and tried to re-order my thoughts. So. This was something done. They were wed, they were going to have a baby. Useless to advise them against having a baby, useless to remonstrate with them over defying the king. Begin now, where they are.

In danger. Foolishly defiant.

'What does she plan to do? Go to the king, tell him she is both married and pregnant?'

Riddle's dark eyes met mine and I saw something like pity there. 'She shared her news with Queen Elliania only. Only we four know that Nettle is with child. And only five people know that we are truly wed. Not even to her brothers has she confided the news. But she told Elliania. And the queen is ecstatic. And full of plans for the child. She did some sort of needle-dangling magic over Nettle's palm, and she is certain our child will be a girl. Finally, a daughter born to the Farseer's mothershouse. And hence a future narcheska.'

'I'm confused,' I said after a silence.

'As well you should be. As I was when they first told me. First, you must understand how close Nettle and Queen Elliania have become over the years. They are nearly of an age. Both felt like outsiders when first they came to Buckkeep Castle court: Elliania an OutIslander, and Nettle a simple country girl made a lady. When Elliania realized that Nettle was her husband's cousin, she claimed her as kin.'

'Her husband's second cousin?'

Riddle shook his head. 'A member of her new mothershouse.' At my puzzled expression, he added, 'You have to think of it from Elliania's perspective. In the OutIslander culture, the mother's lineage is what matters. It was terribly hard for Elliania to leave her mothershouse and come here to be the Farseer queen. If she had stayed in her own land, she would have become the narcheska of her mothershouse. Equivalent to a queen. She bartered that away to save her mother and her little sister Kossi. And to finally ensure peace between the Six Duchies and the OutIslands. That she and Dutiful came to love one another was simply the kindness of fate.

'You know how Elliania has grieved that she has borne only two sons. Her grief at her failure to provide a daughter to send back to the OutIslands and reign after her mother as narcheska consumes her.'

'What of Kossi? Surely her younger sister would be next in line for that title?'

Riddle shook his head. 'No. We saved Kossi's life, but her health never recovered. She was nearly two years in the Pale Woman's captivity. Two years of starvation, cold and mistreatment. She is a brittle woman, frail as dried twigs. And she has shown a marked dislike for the company of men. She will bear no children.'

'I recall she had a girl cousin . . .'

'Disliked by both Elliania and her mother. One of the reasons for her desperate desire to present a girl to her mothershouse.'

'But Nettle's child is no kin to Elliania at all!'

'She is if Elliania says she is. There is a saying there. "Every mother knows her own child." Thus, when Elliania draws up genealogies, you are Patience's son.'

I was hopelessly befuddled. 'What does that have to do with it?'

He smiled. 'You Farseers are an inbred lot. And yet pitiable by OutIslander standards. Generations without a female child. It left Elliania wondering if there were any true descendants of the original Farseer Mothershouse. In her desperate quest for a female of true lineage, she had the most doddering of the minstrels singing themselves hoarse with genealogies. Do you know who Queen Adamant is?'

'No.'

'The first Farseer to stake a claim on the cliffs of Buck was Taker. He himself was an OutIslander, and is seen as something of a rogue there, for he forsook his own mothershouse to establish a new one here. He took a wife from among the people he conquered. Her name was Adamant. We now call her Queen Adamant. The first of the Farseer's mothershouse.'

'Very well.' I didn't see where any of this was going.

'Patience and Chivalry were very distant cousins, according to Elliania. Both descended by wandering lineage from Adamant. She of the "copper-gleaming hair and violet eyes", according to one very old ballad. Hence you are doubly descended from that mothershouse. That makes Nettle the rightful "narcheska" of the Farseer line. The mothershouse that Elliania joined. Her kin. And hence a possible source of an heir for Elliania.

'The thought that there have been generations with no female offspring to refresh the line troubles her. And at the same time, it has comforted her. She now feels the fault is with the Farseer males, who cannot seem to seed girls in their wives' wombs. For years, she tormented herself that it was her own failing that she had borne only two males. She has known for years about Nettle's true parentage and sees her opportunity to raise Nettle's child as a narcheska as righting a great wrong done to Nettle. After a dearth of females, Nettle was born, finally, a true daughter of the Farseer Mothershouse. But instead of being celebrated, she was hidden in the shadows. Concealed from the royal court. Her parentage denied. And only brought to Buckkeep when she became useful to the Farseers.'

I was silent. I could not deny the truth of his words. It stung badly to hear them uttered by her husband and my friend. I had believed I was protecting her. As I was protecting Bee by keeping her away from Buckkeep? There was an uncomfortable thought. I tried to justify myself.

'Nettle is the bastard daughter of a bastard son of an abdicated prince, Riddle.'

A flash of anger. 'Here, perhaps. But in the OutIslands our child might well be seen as a princess of their line.'

'You and Nettle would do that? Leave Buckkeep and the court and go to the OutIslands?'

'To save my daughter being seen as a shame and a bastard? Yes. I would.'

I found I was nodding in agreement. 'And if the child is a boy?'

He heaved a sigh. 'That will be a different battle, on a different day. Fitz. We were friends before I fell in love with your daughter. I've felt guilty that I did not come to you before this. That I did not reveal our marriage to you.'

I didn't hesitate. I'd had too much time in the last few days to remember all sorts of decisions that had been taken out of my hands. 'I'm not angry, Riddle.' I stood and held out my hand. We clasped wrists and then he embraced me. I spoke by his ear. 'I thought you had come here in fury over what I did to you as we passed through the Skill-pillars.'

He stepped back from me. 'Oh, I'll leave that to Nettle. If she hasn't blasted the skin from your flesh with her words yet, then you've that to look forward to. I don't know what will come of this, Fitz, but I wanted you to know that I've done my best to be honourable.'

'I can see that. As you always have. Riddle. No matter what comes of this, I will take your side and Nettle's.'

He gave a tight nod, then heaved a heavy sigh and went over to sit on the chair I had offered him earlier. He clasped his hands and looked down on them.

'There's more, and it's bad news,' I guessed.

'Bee.' He said her name, took a deep breath and then sat, wordless.

I sank back down onto the bed. 'I remember what you said at the tavern, Riddle.'

He looked up at me suddenly. The muscles in his face were

tight. 'And the situation hasn't changed, Fitz. Nor the outcome. Nettle said she would talk to you, that this wasn't my burden. But it is. Even if I were not married to your daughter, as your friend it would still be my duty. Fitz, you have to give her up. You have to bring her here, to Buckkeep, where she can be properly supervised and educated. You know that. You do.'

Did I? I clenched my teeth to hold back my angry response. I thought back over the last month. How many times had I resolved to do better with Bee? And failed. How many times had I set her aside to deal with disasters and mayhem? I'd involved my nine-year-old daughter in disposing of a body and concealing a murder – even if she didn't know I'd killed the messenger. For the first time I thought of the potential danger to my child, if, indeed, there were pursuers still searching for the messenger. Or assassins seeking Shun and FitzVigilant. Chade had put those two with me for safekeeping, secure in his belief that I would protect them. I'd given no thought to that at all when I'd left everyone to bring the Fool to Buckkeep. No consideration that Bee might be in danger from assassins seeking their targets in my home. That last attempt on Shun's life had been a poisoning. The assassin had killed a kitchen boy instead of Shun. A sloppy job. And what if his next attempt was just as sloppy? Winterfest would open the doors of Withywoods to all sorts of folk. What if the assassin poisoned more than a single dish in his next try for Shun?

Why hadn't I seen this before?

'I've lost my edge,' I said quietly. 'I'm not protecting her.'

Riddle looked puzzled. 'I'm talking about your being a father, Fitz, not her guardsman. I think you're more than capable of protecting her life. But someone has to make sure she has that life, for you to protect. Give your daughter an education and the opportunities appropriate to her station. The manners, the dress, the social experiences. She is the daughter of Lady Molly, as well as the child of Holder Badgerlock. It would be very appropriate for her to come to court and spend time with her sister.'

He was right. But, 'I can't give her up.'

Riddle stood, squared his shoulders and spoke firmly. 'Then don't. Come with her, Fitz. Find a new name and come back to

Buckkeep. This is where Bee belongs. And where you belong. And you know that.'

I stared at the floor. He waited some time for me to speak, and when I did not, he said more softly, 'I'm sorry, Fitz. But you do know that we're right.'

He left quietly and as he shut the door behind him I wondered how difficult that had been for him. We'd known each other a long time. He had begun as a sort of spy for Chade and a bodyguard for when I needed someone to watch my back. He'd become a comrade and someone I'd trusted as we'd experienced terrible things. And then, somehow, he'd become the man who courted my daughter. Riddle would be the father of my grandchild. Strange. I'd trusted him with my life, more than once. I had no choice now in that he must be trusted with not just my daughter's heart but the fate of the child they would have. I swallowed. And with Bee? Because I was failing her.

If I gave Bee to Riddle and Nettle, I could undertake the Fool's vengeance.

That traitorous thought made me want to vomit.

I got up suddenly. I could not think about it at the moment. I tried so hard, but there was just not enough time or enough of me. And trying was not doing. 'Oh, Molly,' I said aloud and then clenched my jaws together. There had to be an answer, but I couldn't see it. Not now.

Time to go check on the Fool. I went to the window and looked out. I felt as if it should be late afternoon bordering on evening. Too much had happened already today. Kettricken was Witted. She was interested in Bee. Web wanted me to adopt a crow. I was to be a grandfather, possibly the grandfather of a narcheska. And Riddle believed I was a failure as a father and wished to take my child from me. As I turned to head toward the stairs, Nettle tugged on my thoughts.

Riddle told me. No point in pretending I did not know. She would feel the current of concern in my thoughts.

I knew he would, though I wish he had left it to me. Something about manly honour. Did you shout at him? Tell him he had shamed me and therefore you?

Of course not! Her prickly sarcasm stung me. *Need I remind you that I am a bastard and know what it is to be seen as my father's shame?*

Which is why you have always denied me entirely.

I . . . what? I never denied you. Had I? Uncertainty flavoured my thoughts. Memories flooded in. I had. Oh, yes, I had. *Only to protect you,* I amended. *Times were harsher then. To be, not just the Bastard's daughter, but the child of the Witted Bastard, possibly possessing that dirty magic . . . some folk would have seen fit to kill you.*

So you let Burrich claim me.

He kept you safe.

He did. Her words were relentless. *And it kept you safe, when you chose to pretend you were dead. It kept the Farseer reputation safe, too. No inconvenient bastards to muddle the line of succession. Safe. As if 'safe' were more important than anything else.*

I hemmed my thoughts tightly from her. I was not sure what she was trying to tell me, but I was certain of one thing. I didn't want to hear it.

Well, my child will know who her parents are! And she will know who her grandparents were! I will see to that, I will give her that, and no one will ever be able to take it away from her!

Nettle, I— But she was gone. I didn't reach after her. There was another daughter I had failed. I'd let her grow up believing she was the daughter of another man. I'd let her mother and Burrich believe I was dead. I'd told myself, all those years, that I was keeping her safe. But she had felt denied. And abandoned.

I thought of my own father as I seldom did. I'd never even looked in his eyes. What had I felt, that he had abandoned me in Buckkeep to the care of his stablemaster? I stared at nothing. Why had I done the same to my elder daughter?

Bee. It wasn't too late for me to be a good father to her. I knew where I should be right now, and if I used the Skill-pillar, I could be there before nightfall. It was a little dangerous, but hadn't I risked more than that bringing the Fool through? It would be days before I dared risk any more healing on him. I should go home, gather Bee, and bring her back to Buckkeep with me. Not to give her up to Nettle, not for us to stay here, but to have her by me while I had to be here to tend the Fool. It made sense. It was what I should do.

The upper chamber was dark save for the reddish light from the fire. The Fool sat in the chair in front of it. I bit my tongue before I could ask him why he was sitting in the dark. He turned his face toward me as I approached. 'There's a message for you. On the table.'

'Thank you.'

'A young man brought it. I'm afraid that when he walked in, I was half-asleep. I screamed. I don't know which of us was more terrified.' His voice reached for a note of mockery, and failed.

'I'm sorry,' I said, trying to rein in my wayward thoughts. There was no sense in sharing my anguish with him. There was nothing he could do to help me, except feel ashamed that he had pulled me away from my child.

I made myself focus on his string of anxious words.

'And now I'm afraid to go back to sleep. I didn't think of other people coming and going from here. I don't know how it could have escaped me. I know they must. But I can't stop thinking about them. What if they talk to others? People will know I'm hiding here. It won't be safe.'

'I'm going to light some candles,' I told him. I did not say that I needed to see his face because I could not tell how serious he was. As I kindled the first one, I asked him, 'How are you feeling? Better than yesterday?'

'I can't tell, Fitz. I can't tell yesterday from early this morning. I can't tell early this morning from midnight. It's all the same for me, here in the dark. You come and you go. I have food, I shit, I sleep. And I'm frightened. I suppose that means that I'm better. I remember when all I could think about was how badly every part of my body hurt. And now the pain has subsided to where I can think about how scared I am.'

I lit a second candle from the first one and set them in the holders on the table.

'You don't know what to say,' he observed.

'I don't,' I admitted. I tried to set my own fears aside to deal with his. 'I know you are safe here. But I also know that no matter how often I say that, it won't change how you feel. Fool, what can I do? What would make you feel better?'

He turned his face away from me. After a long moment, he said, 'You should read your message. The boy blurted out it was important before he ran away.'

I picked up the small scroll on the table. Chade's spy-seal was on it. I broke the wax free and unrolled it.

'Fitz. Do I look that frightful? When I sat up in my chair and screamed, the boy screamed, too. As if he'd seen a corpse rise from the grave and shriek at him.'

I set the scroll aside. 'You look like a very ill man who was deliberately starved and tortured. And your colour is . . . odd. Not tawny, as you were in the days of Lord Golden, nor white as you were when you were King Shrewd's jester. You are grey. It's not a colour one would expect a living man to be.'

He was silent for so long that I turned my eyes back to the scroll. There was to be another festive gathering tonight, the final one of the Winterfest before our nobility once more dispersed to their own duchies. Queen Elliania urged everyone to attend and asked everyone to wear their best to celebrate turning toward the growing light. Chade suggested that perhaps Lord Feldspar should make a trip to town and purchase some finery for the occasion. He suggested a tailor's shop, and by that I knew that the garments would have been ordered and rushed to be prepared for me.

'You're an honest man, Fitz.' The Fool's voice was dull.

I sighed. Had I been too honest? 'What good would it serve for me to lie to you? Fool, you look terrible. It breaks my heart to see you this way. The only thing I can offer myself or you is that as you eat and rest and grow stronger, your health will improve. When you are stronger, I hope to use the Skill to urge your body to repair itself. That is the only comfort that either of us have. But it will take time. And demand our patience. Haste will not serve either of us.'

'I don't have time, Fitz. Rather, I do. I have time to get better or time to die. But somewhere, I am sure, there is a son who needs to be rescued before the Servants of the Whites find him. With every day, with every hour, I fear they have already secured him. And with every day and every hour, I am mindful of the continued captivity of a hundred souls in a faraway place. It may seem it has little to do with us and Buckkeep and the Six Duchies, but it does. The Servants use them with no more thought than we give to penning up a chicken, or wringing a rabbit's neck. They breed them for their insights into the future, and they use those insights to make themselves omniscient. It bothers them not at all when a baby is born who will never walk or can barely see. As long as they are pale and have prescient dreams, that is all they care about. The power of the Servants reaches even to here, twisting and turning events, bending time and the world to their will. They have to be stopped, Fitz. We have to go back to Clerres and kill them. It must be done.'

I said what I knew was true. 'One thing at a time, my friend. We can only attempt one thing at a time.'

He stared sightlessly at me as if I had said the cruellest thing in the world to him. Then his lower jaw trembled, he dropped his face into his broken hands and began to sob.

I felt sharp annoyance and then deep guilt that I'd felt it. He was in agony. I knew it. How could I feel annoyed at him when I knew exactly what he was experiencing? Hadn't I felt that way myself? Had I forgotten the times when my experiences in Regal's dungeons had washed over me like a wave, obliterating whatever was good and safe in my life and carrying me right back into that chaos and pain?

No. I tried to forget that, and in the last decade of years, for the most part I had. And my annoyance with the Fool was not annoyance but extreme uneasiness. 'Please. Don't make me remember that.'

I realized I'd said the betraying words out loud. His only response was to cry louder, in the hopeless way of a child who has no hope of comforting himself. This was misery that could not yield, for he sorrowed for a time he could not return to, and a self he would never again be.

'Tears can't undo it,' I said and wondered why I uttered the useless words. I both wanted to hold him and feared to. Feared that it would alarm him to be touched and feared even more that it would draw me tighter into his misery and wake my own. But at last I took the three steps that carried me around the table. 'Fool. You are safe here. I know you can't believe it just yet, but it's over. And you are safe.' I stroked the broken hair on his head, rough as the coat of a sick dog, and then pulled him closer to cradle his head against my sternum. His clawlike hands came up and clutched my wrist and held himself tighter against me. I let him have his tears. They were the only things I could give him then. I thought of what I had wanted to tell him, that I had to leave him for a few days to get Bee.

I couldn't. Not right now.

He was slow to quiet and even when his sobs ceased, the breath shuddered in and out of him. After a time, he patted my wrist tentatively and said, 'I think I'm all right now.'

'You aren't. But you will be.'

'Oh, Fitz,' he said. He pulled away from me and sat up as straight as he could. He coughed, and cleared his throat. 'What of your message? The lad said it was important.'

'Oh, it is and it isn't. The queen wishes us to be dressed in our finest for the last night of Winterfest revelry, and that means I must make a trip down to Buckkeep Town to secure some clothing.' I scowled to myself as I reflected I would have to go as Lord Feldspar in his awful garb. But not in those shoes. Oh, no. I wasn't walking on icy cobbles in those shoes.

'Well. You'd best be on your way, then.'

'I should,' I agreed reluctantly. I didn't want to leave him alone in his darkness. Yet I didn't want to stay where his despondency could infect me. I had come up the stairs thinking that I could safely confide Nettle's news to him. For a moment, I had seen him as my friend and counsellor of our youth. Now the news was ash on my tongue. Here was another Farseer he had not foreseen. His talk of deformed babies had chilled me; how could I tell him my first grandchild was expected? It might plunge him into yet another dark spiral. Worse would be to tell him I had to be gone for six to eight days. I could not leave him to fetch Bee. But I could agree to having her brought here. I would talk to Kettricken about it tomorrow. Together we would arrange it.

You do your duty to your friends. How often had Nighteyes sat beside me when I had sought to lose myself in futile Skilling attempts? How often had Hap staggered me back to the cabin and deliberately given me less than the amount of stunning drugs I commanded him to fetch for me? I did not even want to think of the weeks, and then months, Burrich had spent trying to help me make the transition back from wolf to human. My friends had not abandoned me, and I would not abandon the Fool.

But he could still abandon me. And he did. He levered himself up from the table. 'You should go and do your errand, Fitz,' he said. He turned and almost as if he were sighted walked back to the bed.

As he clambered into it and drew up the blankets I asked him, 'Are you certain you want to be alone now?'

He did not reply. And after a time I realized he wasn't going to. I felt unreasonably hurt at this. A dozen scathing comments went unsaid by me. He had no idea of what I had given up for him. Then the moment of anger passed and I was grateful I had not spoken. I never wanted him to know what I had sacrificed for him.

And there was nothing left for me to do but my duty. I went back down the stairs, freshened my appearance as Feldspar and defiantly put my own boots back on.

Winterfest might celebrate the lengthening of the days but it did not mean that we were on the road to spring. Yesterday's clouds had snowed themselves to nothing. The sky overhead was as deep and pure a blue as a Buck lady's skirts but more clouds clustered on the horizon. Frost coated the festive garlands that festooned the shopfronts. The packed snow on the street squeaked under my boots. The cold had subdued the holiday spirit, but scattered vendors of winter sweets and toys still shouted their wares to hasty passers-by. I passed a miserable donkey with icy whiskers, and a hot-chestnut vendor who could barely keep his brazier lit. He warmed his hands over his wares, and I bought a dozen just to carry them in my chilled fingers. Overhead, the gulls wheeled and screamed as they always did. Crows were noisily mobbing a tardy owl they had found. By the time I reached the street of the tailors, my drunkard's nose was as red from the cold as Chade could ever have wished it. My cheeks were stiff and my lashes clung together briefly each time I blinked. I gathered my cloak more closely around myself and hoped that the new clothing that awaited me was not as foolish as what I was wearing.

I had just located the correct shop when I heard a voice call, 'Tom! Tom! Tom!'

I remembered in time that I was Lord Feldspar. So I did not turn, but a boy on the street shouted to his friends, 'Look, it's a talking crow! He said "Tom".'

That gave me the excuse to turn and look where the lad was pointing. Perched on a signboard across the street was a bedraggled crow. It looked at me and screamed shrilly, 'Tom, Tom!'

Before I could react, another crow dived on it, pecking and flapping and cawing. In response to that attack, a dozen other birds appeared as if from nowhere to join in the mobbing. As the beleaguered bird took flight, I caught a glimpse of white pinions among her black ones. To my horror, one of the other crows struck her in mid-air. She tumbled in her flight and then in her desperation took refuge under the eaves of a nearby shop. Two of her attackers made passes, but could not reach her. The others settled down on nearby rooftops to wait. With the instincts of all bullies, they knew that eventually she would have to emerge.

Then, in the way of their kind, they would peck her to death for being different.

Oh, Web, what have you got me into? I could not, *could* not, take in another orphan. She would have to fend for herself. That was all. I would have to hope that she would make her way back to him. I wished he had not sent her in search of me. I hardened my heart and went into the tailor's shop.

My new accoutrements were a very short blue cape with a trim of snowflake lace in layers on it. I wondered if the tailor had jumbled Chade's order with one for a lady, but the tailor and her husband gathered around me to try it on and make some adjustments to the ties. They then brought out the matching cuffs for my wrists and ankles. The tailor made a mouth at the sight of my distinctly unfashionable boots but agreed that they were probably more suitable for the snow. I promised her that the lace cuffs would be worn with my most fashionable bell-toed shoes, and she appeared mollified. The lad that had delivered the order had paid them in advance, so all I had to do was accept the package and be on my way.

As I came out of the shop, the light of the short winter afternoon was starting to leak away. Cold was settling on the town, and the traffic in the streets had thinned. I did not look toward the crow hunched under the eaves nor at her gathered tormentors. I turned my steps toward Buckkeep. 'Tom! Tom!' she cried after me, but I kept walking.

Then, 'Fitz! Fitz!' she cawed shrilly. Despite myself, my steps faltered. I kept my eyes on the path before me as I saw others turning to stare at the crow. I heard the frantic beating of wings and then heard her shriek, 'Fitz—Chivalry! Fitz—Chivalry!'

Beside me, a thin woman clasped her knotted hands to her breast. 'He's come back!' she cried. 'As a crow!' To that, I had to turn, lest others mark how I ignored this sensation.

'Ar, it's just some fellow's tamed crow,' a man declared disdainfully. We all turned our eyes skyward. The hapless bird was flying up as high as she could, with the mob in pursuit.

'I heard you split a crow's tongue, you can teach it to talk,' the chestnut vendor volunteered.

'Fitz—Chivalry!' she shrieked again as a larger crow struck her. She lost her momentum and tumbled in the air, caught herself, and flapped bravely, but she had fallen to a level below the murder of crows and now they all mobbed her. In twos and threes they dived on her, striking her, tearing out feathers that floated in the still air. She fought the air to try to stay aloft, helpless to protect herself from the birds that were mobbing her.

'It's an omen!' someone shouted.

'It's FitzChivalry in beast form!' a woman cried out. 'The Witted Bastard has returned!'

And in that instant, terror swept through me. Had I thought I recalled earlier what the Fool was enduring? No. I had forgotten the icy flood of certainty that every hand was against me, that the good people of Buck dressed in their holiday finery would tear me apart with their bare hands, just as the flock of crows was tearing that lone bird apart. I felt sick with fear, in my legs and in my belly. I began to walk away and at every step I thought they must see how my legs quivered, how white my face had gone. I gripped my package with both hands and tried to walk on as if I were the only one uninterested in the aerial battle overhead.

'He's falling!' someone shouted, and I had to halt and look up.

But she wasn't falling. She'd tucked her wings as if she were a hawk and was diving. Diving straight at me.

An instant to see that, and then she had hit me. 'I'll help you, sir!' the chestnut vendor shouted and started toward me, his tongs raised to strike the flapping bird tangled in my cloak. I hunched my shoulders and turned to take the blow for her as I wrapped her in the fabric.

Be still. You're dead! It was the Wit I used to speak to her, with no idea if she would hear my thoughts. She had become still as soon as I covered her and I thought it likely she actually was dead. What would Web say to me? Then I saw my foolish hat and flopping wig lying in the street before me. I snatched it up and under the guise of catching my parcel to my chest I held the crow firm as well. I whirled on the well-meaning chestnut vendor. 'What do you mean by assaulting me?' I shouted at him as I jammed hat and wig back onto my head. 'How dare you humiliate me like this!'

'Sir, I meant no ill!' the vendor cried, falling back from me. 'That crow—!'

'Really? Then why did you charge at me and nearly knock me to the ground, if not to expose me to ridicule?' I tugged vainly at my lopsided wig, settling it oddly on my head. I heard a boy laugh, and a mother rebuke him with barely-contained merriment. I glared in their direction and then one-handedly made my wig and hat worse. There were several guffaws from behind me. I whirled, letting my hat and wig nearly leave my head again. 'Imbeciles! Ruffians! I shall see the Buckkeep town guards know about the dangers on this street! Assaulting visitors! Mocking a guest of the KING! I want you to know, I am cousin to the Duke of Farrow, and he will be hearing about this from me!' I puffed out my cheeks and let my lower lip tremble in feigned rage. My shaking voice I did not have to manufacture. I felt half-sick with fear that someone would recognize me. The echo of my name seemed to hang in the air. I turned on my heel and did my best to flounce with indignation as I strode hastily away. I heard a little girl's voice ask, 'But where did that bird go?'

I did not loiter to see if anyone would answer her. My apparent discomfiture at losing my hat and wig seemed to have provided them with some amusement, as I had hoped. Several times before I was out of sight I made seemingly vain attempts to adjust both. When I judged I was far enough away, I stepped into an alley and drew up the hood of my cloak over my hat and wig. The crow was so still within the fold of my cloak that I feared she was truly dead. She had struck me quite hard, hard enough to break a bird's neck I surmised. But my Wit told me that while she might be stunned and stilled, life still beat in her. I traversed the alley and walked down the winding way of Tinker Street until I found another, narrower alley. There I finally unfolded the wrap of cloak that cradled her still black body.

Her eyes were closed. Her wings were clapped neatly to her body. I have always been impressed with how birds could fold two limbs so smoothly that, had you never seen a bird before, you would believe it only had legs. I touched her gleaming black beak.

She opened a shining eye. I put a hand on her back, trapping her wings to her side. *Not yet. Stay still until we are somewhere safe.*

I felt no return of the Wit from her, but her obedience made me believe she had understood me. I arranged crow and parcel under my cloak and hurried on toward Buckkeep Castle. The road was better maintained and more travelled than it had once been, but it was still steep and icy in some places. The light was fading and the wind rising. The wind picked up snow crystals as scathing as sand and blasted them at me. Carts and wagons bearing provisions for this final evening of merry-making passed me. I was going to be late.

Inside my cloak, the crow had become restive. She shifted and clung to my shirtfront with beak and claws. I reached in to touch her and offer her support. She fluttered violently and the hand I drew back had fingertips of blood. I reached her with the Wit. *Are you hurt?*

My thought bounced back to me as if I had thrown a pebble at a wall. Despite that, her pain washed against me and prickled up my spine. I spoke aloud in a quiet voice. 'Stay under my cloak. Climb up to my shoulder. I'll keep still while you do that.'

For a time, she did not move. Then she gripped my shirt with her beak and climbed up me, reaching to claim a fresh beak-hold with every few steps. She became a lump on my shoulder under my cloak and then moved around to make me a hunchback. When she seemed settled, I straightened up slowly.

'I think we'll be fine,' I told my passenger.

The winds had shepherded the clouds in and now they released a fresh fall of snow. It came down in thick clumps of flakes that whirled and danced in the wind. I bent my head and trudged up the steep hill toward the keep.

I was admitted back into the castle grounds without question. I could hear the music and the murmur of voices from the Great Hall. Already so late! The crow-mobbing had delayed me more than I had realized. I hastened past servants bearing trays, and well-dressed folk who were less late than I was and up the stairs. I kept my hood up, my gaze down and greeted no one. The moment I was inside my room, I lifted my snowy cloak away. The crow gripped the back of my collar and my wig was tangled in her feet. As soon as she was uncovered, she lifted from the nape of my neck and attempted to fly. With my wig and hat weighing her down, she plummeted to the floor.

'Keep still. I'll free you,' I told her.

After several minutes of struggling, she lay on her side, one wing half-open and the hair of the wig snarled around her feet. The white pinions interspersed with the black ones were clearly visible now, the feathers that meant every other crow in the world would attempt to kill her. I sighed. 'Now keep still and I'll free you,' I repeated. Her beak was open and she was gasping. One bright black eye stared up at me. I moved slowly. It seemed impossible that she had tangled her feet so thoroughly in such a short time. Drops of her blood were scattered on the floor. I spoke to her as I tried to untangle her. 'Are you hurt badly? Did they stab you?' With my Wit I tried to radiate calm and reassurance to her. *Are you hurt?* I offered the question, trying not to press against her boundaries. Her pain washed against me. She fluttered wildly, undoing much of my untangling effort, and then fell still again. 'Are you hurt badly?' I asked her again.

She closed her beak, looked at me and then croaked, 'Plucked! Plucked my feathers!'

'I see.' Wonder at how many human words she knew mingled with relief that she could give me information. But a bird was not a wolf. Trying to interpret what I felt from her was difficult. There was pain and fear and a great deal of anger. If she had been my wolf, I would have known exactly where she was injured and how badly. This was like trying to communicate with someone who spoke a different language. 'Let me try to get you free. I need to take you to a table and better light. May I pick you up?'

She blinked. 'Water. Water. Water.'

'And I will get you water, too.' I tried not to think of how time was fleeting. As if in response to my worry, I felt a questioning twinge from Chade. Where was I? The queen had asked Dutiful to be sure I was present, a most unusual request from her.

I'll be there soon, I promised, fervently hoping I would be. I triggered the secret door and then scooped the crow from the floor, holding her safely but loosely in my hands as I carried her up the dark stairway.

'Fitz?' the Fool asked anxiously before I had reached the last step. I could just make out his silhouette in the chair before the fire. The candles had burned out hours ago. My heart sank at the worry in his voice.

'Yes, it's me. I've an injured crow with me, and she's tangled in my wig. I'll explain in a moment, but for now I just need to set her down and get some light and give her water.'

'You have a crow tangled in your wig?' he asked, and for a wonder, there was a trace of both amusement and mockery in his voice. 'Ah, Fitz. I can always trust you to have some sort of bizarre problem that breaks my ennui.'

'Web sent her to me.' In the darkness, I set her down on the table. She tried to stand, but the strands of hair wrapped her too well. She collapsed onto her side. 'Be still, bird. I need to get some candles for light. Then I hope I'll be able to untangle you.'

She remained quiescent, but day birds often go still in the

dark. I groped through the dimly-lit chamber to find additional candles. By the time I had lit them, put them in holders and returned to the worktable, the Fool was already there. To my surprise, his knotted fingers were at work on the locks of hair that were wrapped so securely about the bird's toes and legs. I set my candles down at the far end of the table and watched. The bird was still, her eyes occasionally blinking. The Fool's fingers, once long, elegant and clever, were now like knotted dead twigs. He was speaking to her softly as he worked. The hand with the deadened fingertips gently bade her feet be still as the fingers of his other hand lifted and pulled at strands of hair. He spoke in a murmur like water over stones. 'And this one must go under first. And now we can lift that toe from the loop. There. That's one foot almost clear. Oh, that's tight. Let me push this thread of hair under . . . there. There's one foot cleared.'

The crow kicked the free leg abruptly, and then subsided as the Fool set his hand to her back. 'You will be free in a moment. Be still, or the ropes will just get tighter. Struggling against ropes never works.'

Ropes. I held my silence. It took longer than a moment for him to untangle her second foot. I nearly offered him scissors, but he was so intent on his task, so removed from his own misery that I banished my concerns about the passing time and let them be. 'There you are. There,' he said at last. He set the hat and battered wig to one side. For a breath, she lay still. Then, with a twitch and a flap, she was on her feet. He didn't try to touch her.

'He will want water, Fitz. Fear makes one so thirsty.'

'She,' I corrected him. I went to the water bucket and filled a cup and brought it back to the table. I set it down, dipped my fingers in it and held them up so the bird could see water drip back into the cup and stepped away. The Fool had taken up the hat and the wig that was fastened to it still. Wind, rain, and the crow-struggle had taken a toll on the wig. Parts were tangled into a frizz while other locks hung lank and wet.

'I don't think this can be easily mended,' he said. He set it back on the table. I took it up and ran my fingers through the hair, trying to bring it back to some semblance of order. 'Tell me about the bird,' he requested.

'Web asked me if I could take her in. She had, well, not an owner. A friend. Not a Wit-bond, but a human who helped her. She was hatched with some white feathers in her wings—'

'White! White! White!' the bird suddenly croaked. She hopped over to the water, a typical crow's two-footed hop and stuck her beak deep into the cup. As she drank thirstily, the Fool exclaimed, 'She can talk!'

'Only as birds do. She repeats words she has been taught. I think.'

'But she talks to you, through your Wit?'

'Not really. I can sense her feelings, distress, pain. But we are not bonded, Fool. I do not share her thoughts nor she mine.' I gave the hat and wig a shake, trying to mend them. The crow squawked in surprise and hopped sideways, nearly oversetting the water. 'Sorry. Didn't mean to startle you,' I said. I looked woefully at the wig and hat. There was no mending them. 'A moment, Fool. I must speak to Chade.' I reached out to Chade through the Skill. *My wig has been damaged. I do not think I can appear as Lord Feldspar tonight.*

Then come however you may, but make it soon. Something is brewing, Fitz. Queen Elliania bubbles with something. At first I thought she was angry, for when she greeted me, her eyes were cold and bright. But she seems oddly warm, almost jubilant, leading the dancing with an enthusiasm I've never seen before.

Did you ask Dutiful if he had any idea what is brewing?

Dutiful does not know. I felt him throw his Skilling wide, including Dutiful in our mental conversation.

Perhaps Dutiful does not think there is anything wrong with his queen so obviously enjoying herself this evening. The king suggested sarcastically.

There is something in the wind. I feel it! Chade replied.

Perhaps I might know my wife's moods better than you do? Dutiful retorted.

I wanted no more of their fractiousness. *I will be down as soon as I can, but not as Lord Feldspar. The wig is ruined, I fear.*

At the least, dress fashionably, Chade ordered me irritably. *If you come down in a tunic and trousers, you will turn every head. Nor can you wear what was ordered for Lord Feldspar. There must be*

*items in Lord Feldspar's wardrobe that he has not yet worn. Choose
from among them, and quickly.*

I shall.

'You have to go.' The Fool spoke into the silence after my
Skilling.

'I do. How did you know?'

'I learned to read your exasperated little sighs long ago, Fitz.'

'The wig is ruined. And with it, my identity as Lord Feldspar.
I must go to my room, sort through clothing, dress and go down
as someone entirely different. I can do it. But I do not delight in
it as Chade does.'

'And as I once did.' It was his turn to sigh. 'How I would love
to have your task tonight! To choose clothing and go down well-
dressed, with rings and earrings and scent, and mingle with a
hundred different folk, and eat well-prepared food. Drink and
dance and make jests.' He sighed again. 'I wish I could be alive
again before I have to die.'

'Ah, Fool.' I began to reach for his hand, and then stopped.
He would startle back in terror if I touched him, and when he
did that, it woke hurt in both of us.

'You should go right now. I'll keep the bird company.'

'Thank you,' I said, and meant it. I hoped she would not panic
suddenly and dash herself against the chamber walls. As long as
it was mostly darkened, I thought she would be fine. I had nearly
reached the top of the stairs when his query reached me.

'What does she look like?'

'She's a crow, Fool. A grown crow. Black beak, black feet, black
eyes. The only thing that sets her apart from a thousand other
crows is that she was hatched with some white upon her feathers.'

'Where is she white?'

'Some of her pinions are white. When she opens her wings,
they are almost striped. And there were a few tufts of white on
her back or head, I think. The others ripped out some of her
feathers.'

'Ripped,' the Fool said.

'White! White! White!' the bird cried out in the darkness.
Then, in a soft little mutter, so that I was barely sure I heard it,
she muttered, 'Ah, Fool.'

'She knows my name!' he exclaimed in delight.

'And mine. More's the pity. It was how she forced me to stop for her. She was shouting, "FitzChivalry! FitzChivalry!" in the middle of the Tailors Street.'

'Clever girl,' the Fool murmured approvingly.

I snorted my disagreement and hurried down the stairs.

EIGHT

Farseers

And back to back those brothers stood
And bade farewell their lives
For round them pressed the Red Ship wolves
A wall of swords and knives.

They heard a roar and striding came
The bastard Buckkeep son.
Like rubies flung, the drops of blood
That from his axe-head spun.

A path he clove, like hewing trees
As bloody axe he wielded.
Blood to his chest, the bastard came,
And to his blade they yielded.

'Twas Chivalry's son,
His eyes like flame,
Who shared his blood
If not his name.
A Farseer son,
But ne'er an heir
Whose bloodied locks
No crown would bear.

Antler Island Anthem
– Starling Birdsong

I was pulling off my clothes before I was halfway down the stairs. I emerged into my room, shut the door, and hopped from one foot to the other as I pulled off my boots. None of what I wore today could I wear down to the gathering in the Great Hall. All it would take would be one style-obsessed idiot to recognize that I wore a garment he had earlier seen on Lord Feldspar.

I began to drag garments from his wardrobe, then forced myself to stop. I closed my eyes and visualized last night's gathering. What had they had in common, all those peacocks parading their finery? The long-skirted jackets. A plenitude of buttons, most of them decorative rather than functional. Fussy lace at throat and wrist and shoulder. And the clash of bright colours. I opened my eyes.

Scarlet trousers, with rows of blue buttons down the outsides of the legs. A white shirt with a collar so high it near choked me. This long blue vest with tufts of red lace at the shoulders and red buttons like a row of sow's nipples down the chest. A massy silver ring for my thumb. No. None of that. My own trousers from Withywoods, laundered and returned, thanks to Ash. The plainest of the fussy shirts in a foresty green. A brown vest, long, with buttons, but ones of horn. And that was all I had time for. I looked in the glass and ran my hands through my rain-damp hair. It lay down, for now. I chose the plainest of the small hats: to go bareheaded would attract more stares than any hat. It would have to do. I hoped to look poor enough that no one would seek to be introduced to me. I chose the least uncomfortable of the shoes and pulled them on. Then, with the reawakened expertise of my youth, I rapidly loaded my concealed pockets, transferring my small weapons and envelopes of poison and lock-picks from the jacket I had worn earlier today, trying not to wonder as I did so if I would use them if Chade ordered me to. If it came to that, I'd decide then, I promised myself, and turned away from that stomach-churning question.

On my way! My Skilling to Chade was tight and private.

Who are you? His question reminded me of our old game. Create an identity in the space of a heartbeat.

I'm Raven Kelder. Third son of a minor lord in rural Tilth. I've never been to court before, I've only arrived at Buckkeep tonight, and I'm dazzled by all I see. I'm dressed plainly and rather unfashionably. I'll be full of foolish questions. My father died late, my brother only recently inherited, and he's pushed me off the holding and told me to seek my own way in life. And I'm more than happy to be having an adventure and spend my share of my small inheritance.

Good enough! Come, then.

And so Raven Kelder hurried down the wide stairs and immersed himself in the crowd thronging the Great Hall. Tonight was Last Night for Winterfest. We'd celebrated the turning from dark to light, and tonight was our final feast before we settled down to outlast the storms and cold of winter. One more night of fellowship, song, feasting and dancing, and tomorrow the nobility of the Six Duchies would begin to drain out of Buckkeep Castle and trickle back to their own holdings. Usually it was the most subdued of the Winterfest nights, for it was a time of bidding farewell to friends for the winter as harsh weather cut down on travel. When I was a lad, the nights that followed Last Night were for indoor pursuits: the fashioning of arrows, weaving, carving and sewing. The younger scribes would bring their copy work to the Great Hearth and listen to the minstrels as they worked.

I had expected slow ballads from the minstrels, mulled drinks and quiet conversations. Instead I walked into a hall where folk were once more dressed in their best garments and jewellery, and minstrels played lively tunes that set toes to tapping and brought dancers out onto the floor. And as I entered, the middle of the dance floor was dominated by the King and Queen of the Six Duchies. The plague of buttons that had attacked my wardrobe had not spared the royal couple. Hundreds of buttons, in silver and ivory and mother of pearl, decorated the queen's dress. They ticked and rattled against one another as she trod the lively steps. Dutiful's garments were burdened with multiple buttons of horn, ivory, bone, and silver in a more sedate but no less rattling display. I stood several layers of folk back in the crowd and watched them. Dutiful's eyes had not left Elliania's face: he seemed as entranced with her as he had when they were courting. The queen's cheeks were flushed and her lips parted as she breathlessly kept the pace of the lively dance. As the music skirled to a close, he lifted her and whirled her around as she braced her hands on his shoulders.

The applause of the crowd was unrestrained and unfeigned. His grin was white in his dark beard and Elliania's cheeks were red. Both of them were flushed and laughing as they left the dance floor and retreated to their elevated thrones at the end of the room.

I drifted in the crowd like a bit of seaweed caught on a tide change. Chade, I decided, was correct. There was an undercurrent of excitement tonight, a spice of curiosity in the air. The queen's request that all attend in their best finery had been heeded. Clearly something special was to occur, perhaps a bestowal of honours, and the room simmered with expectations.

I had time to visit a wine cask and secure a glass for myself before the musicians began to fuss with their instruments prior to choosing the next tune. I manoeuvred myself into a position where I had a clear view of the high dais and yet remained at the edges of the crowd. Dutiful said something to the queen; she smiled and shook her head. Then she stood, and with a gesture, silenced the minstrels. The quiet rippled out until the entire gathering had stilled and all attention had focused on her. Dutiful, still seated on his throne, looked askance at her. She smiled at him and patted his shoulder reassuringly. She took a breath and turned to address her nobility.

'Lords and ladies of the Six Duchies, I have excellent news to share with you. And I fondly believe you will celebrate it with me as jubilantly as I shall!' After her years in the Six Duchies, her OutIslander accent had faded to a charming lilt. Dutiful was watching her with one raised eyebrow. At a nearby table, Lord Chade was looking somewhat concerned, while Kettricken's face was full of speculation. The Skillmistress sat at Lord Chade's left hand. Nettle's face was grave and thoughtful. I wondered if she even heard Elliania's speech or if her mind was full of her own dilemma. The queen took a few moments to survey her listeners. No one spoke; the servants stood still. She let the silence build. Then the queen cleared her throat.

'I have long agonized that there have been no females born to the Farseer line during my reign as queen. Heirs I have given my king. I am proud and glad of our sons, and believe they will reign here well after their father. But for my own land a princess is required. And such I have been unable to bear.' Her voice faltered and broke on the last words. King Dutiful was looking at her with concern now. I saw the Duchess of Farrow lift a hand to her mouth. Tears started down her cheeks. Evidently our queen was not the only one who struggled to bear a living child. Was that what she would announce tonight? That she was with child again? Surely Dutiful would have been told, and the announcement delayed until the pregnancy was assured.

Queen Elliania lifted her head. She glanced at Dutiful as if to reassure him and then said, 'But of course, there *is* a Farseer princess. She has long dwelt among us, tacitly known to many and yet unacknowledged by her dukes and duchesses. Two days ago, she gave me portentous news. She will soon bear a child. I myself swung a needle on a thread over her palm, and my heart leapt with joy when its swinging foretold a girl child in her womb. Ladies and gentlemen of Buckkeep Castle, my dukes and duchesses of the Six Duchies, you will soon be blessed with a new Farseer princess!'

What had begun as gasps of astonishment was now a rising mutter of voices. I felt faint. White-faced, Nettle stared straight ahead. Chade had a stiff smile of feigned puzzlement on his face. Dutiful, mouth ajar, stared in horror at his queen and then betrayed Nettle by swinging his gaze to her.

Elliania seemed completely immune to the catastrophe she was wreaking. She looked out over her audience with a wide smile and then laughed aloud. 'And so, my friends, my people, let us acknowledge what many of us have long known. Skillmistress Nettle, Nettle Farseer, daughter of FitzChivalry Farseer, cousin to my own dear husband, and a princess of the Farseer line, stand forth, please.'

I had folded my arms across my chest. At the mention of my daughter's rightful name, and my own, I had to fight to keep breathing. Whispering in the hall rose to the level of chirring summer insects. I scanned the faces. Two young ladies exchanged delighted glances. One grey-haired lord looked scandalized while his lady held her hands before her mouth in horror at the disgrace. Most of Elliania's audience was simply dumbstruck, waiting for whatever might happen next. Nettle's eyes were wide, her mouth ajar. Chade's face was ashen. Kettricken's slender fingers covered her mouth but could not conceal the joy in her eyes. My gaze flickered to King Dutiful. For a long moment, he was frozen. Then he rose, to stand beside his queen. He extended a hand to Nettle. His voice shook but his smile was genuine as he said, 'Cousin, please.'

Fitz. Fitz, please. What . . . The desperate Skilling that reached me from Chade was nearly incoherent.

Be calm. Let them handle it. What other choice did we really have? If it had been someone else's life, someone else's secret, I might have found the tableau charming. The queen, her cheeks flushed and eyes bright with delight at honouring Nettle, Dutiful, his hand outstretched to welcome his cousin to the most dangerous moment of her life, and Nettle, her teeth showing in something not quite a smile, her gaze fixed, unmoving at the table.

I saw Riddle, too. He had always had a talent for moving unobserved in crowded situations. Now he carved through the melee like a shark through water. I saw the determined look on his face. If they turned on Nettle, he would die fighting to protect her. By the set of one shoulder, I knew he already had his hand on the haft of his knife. Chade, too, marked his passage. I saw him make a small motion. *Wait,* his hand said, but Riddle moved closer.

Lady Kettricken moved gracefully to stand behind Nettle's chair, bent down and whispered something to her. I saw Nettle take a breath. She rose, her chair scraping back on the floor. The erstwhile queen paced at her side as she escorted Nettle to the throne dais. There, as was proper, they both curtseyed deeply. Kettricken remained at the bottom of the steps while Nettle managed to ascend all three. Dutiful took her hands in his. For a moment, their bowed heads were close together. I am sure he whispered something to her. Then they straightened, and Queen Elliania embraced her.

Nettle had locked her thoughts down so firmly that I could not even reach out to her with reassurance. Whatever she felt on the inside, she betrayed only pleasure as she thanked the king and queen for congratulating her on her child. She said nothing of the revelation of her parentage. Truly, Elliania had the right of it when she said it was a secret already known to many. The stamp of the Farseer line was on Nettle's face and many of the older folk had known of the scandalous gossip about FitzChivalry and Lady Patience's maid. Patience's transfer of Withywoods to Lady Molly, supposedly in honour of Burrich's selfless sacrifice to the Farseer family, would have only confirmed that Molly's daughter was mine. A larger omission was mention of Nettle's marriage or the father of her child. Those ripe bits of gossip would be well chewed tomorrow. I watched my daughter as she began to turn and return to her seat, but Kettricken stopped her and held her there, her hands on her shoulders. I saw Riddle look up at her, white-faced, a mere man among many as the woman he loved was proclaimed a princess. My heart went out to him.

Kettricken spoke now, her voice cutting through the rising murmur. 'For years many have persisted in believing that FitzChivalry Farseer was a traitor. Despite what I have recounted of that fateful night when I fled Buckkeep, the taint on his name has lingered. So I would ask if any minstrel here knows of a song, sung but once in this hall? Tagson, son of Tag, son of Reaver, sang it. It was the true tale of the doings of FitzChivalry Farseer, when he came to the aid of his king in the Mountains. Do any minstrels here know it?'

My mouth went dry. I'd never heard the song, but I'd been told of it. In my lifetime, I'd been the subject of two songs. One, 'Antler Island Tower' was a rousing ballad that recounted how I had fought against the Red-Ship Raiders when by treachery they had managed to gain a foothold on Antler Island. It had been composed during the Red-Ship Wars by an ambitious young minstrel named Starling Birdsong. The melody was pleasing and the refrain was memorable. When first it had been sung, the folk of Buckkeep Castle had been willing to believe that enough Farseer blood ran through my bastard veins that I might be a hero, of sorts. But that had been before my fall from grace, before Prince Regal had convinced all of my treachery. It had been before I'd been thrown into his dungeon on the accusation of killing King Shrewd. Before I had supposedly died there, and vanished from Buckkeep history and public knowledge forever.

Yet there had been a second song, one that celebrated not

only my Farseer blood and Witted magic, but asserted that I had risen from my grave to follow King Verity on his wild quest to wake the Elderlings and bring their aid to the Six Duchies. Like the Antler Island song, strands of truth had been braided with poetry and exaggeration. To my knowledge, only one minstrel had ever sung it in Buckkeep, and he had done so to assert that those with the Old Blood Wit-magic could be as loyal and noble as anyone else. Many of the listeners of that day had not welcomed such an opinion.

Kettricken's eyes roved over the gallery where the minstrels were gathered. I watched with relief as they exchanged puzzled glances and shrugs. One fellow folded his arms on his chest and shook his head in disgust, evidently displeased that anyone would wish to sing the praises of the Witted Bastard. One harper leaned over the railing to consult a greybeard below. The fellow nodded and even though I could not hear him, I suspected he admitted to having heard the song once, but the eloquent lift of his shoulders denied any real knowledge of the words, tune or authorship. Just as my heart began to slow and the look of disappointment to settle on Lady Kettricken's face, a matronly woman dressed in an extravagant gown of blue and green stepped from the crowd. As she made her way forward into the open space before the royal dais, I heard a scattering of applause and then someone cried out, 'Starling Birdsong! Of course!'

I wondered if I would have recognized my old lover without that call. Her body had changed with the years, her waist thickening and her curves growing. In the be-buttoned layers of lush fabrics that made up her gown, I did not recognize the tough and pragmatic wandering minstrel who had also followed Verity into the Mountain Kingdom to wake the Elderlings. She had let her hair grow long, and the streaks in it were silver, not grey. She wore jewels on her ears and wrists and fingers, but as she advanced, she was stripping the rings from her fingers.

The look of disappointment on Kettricken's face had been replaced with one of delight. 'Well, here is a minstrel of yore who has let many years pass since we last heard her lift her voice. Our own Starling Birdsong, now Lord Fisher's lady wife! Do you remember the song of which I spoke?'

Despite her years, Starling flourished a curtsey and then rose gracefully. Age had lowered the timbre of her voice but the music had not left it. 'Lady Kettricken, King Dutiful and Queen Elliania, if it please you, I have heard the song sung but once. And do not think me a jealous minstrel when I say, while the threads of truth ran strong through it, the words rattled against one another as painfully as gravel in a boot, and the tune was one stolen from an ancient ballad.' She shook her head, lips folded, and then said, 'Even if I recalled every word and note, I would not think it a kindness to you if I sang it.'

She paused, head lowered respectfully. Despite all my misgivings, I almost smiled. Starling. So well she knew how to whet the appetite of an audience! She waited until precisely the moment when Kettricken drew breath to speak; then she raised her head and offered, 'But I can sing you a better song, if you would, my lady and once my queen. If you with a nod allow me; if my king and my queen grant permission, my tongue can be freed from its long-imposed silence, and sing to you I shall, of all I know of the Witted Bastard. Of FitzChivalry Farseer, son to Chivalry, loyal to King Verity and, to the last breath of his days, a true-hearted Farseer, despite his ignoble birth!'

The music rose and fell in her words: she was tuning and preparing her voice. I saw her husband now, Lord Fisher, standing at the edge of the crowd, a proud smile on his face. His shoulders were as broad as ever; he wore his greying hair in a warrior's tail. Ever he had gloried in the popularity of his wild minstrel wife. The look of enjoyment on his face was not feigned; he basked in her reflected glory. She had not come to the festival tonight as Starling the minstrel but as Lady Fisher. And yet this was the moment she had dreamed of, for all those years. She would not let it pass her by and he would rejoice in it with her. She looked around at her audience as if to ask them, 'Shall I sing?'

She could and she must. The lords and ladies of the Six Duchies already hung on her every word. How could King Dutiful forbid it, when his own queen had revealed the bastard daughter of the bastard Farseer, sheltered and then exalted as Skillmistress at Buckkeep Castle? Lady Kettricken exchanged a look with her son and his wife. And then she nodded, and the king spread his hands in permission.

'Does my harp come?' Starling turned to her husband, and he in turn gestured wide. The doors to the Great Hall opened and two healthy lads appeared, a grand harp supported between them. I had to smile. For it to appear so quickly, she must have ordered it the moment Kettricken asked if any recalled that song. And such a harp! This was no wandering minstrel's harp! Sweat stood out on the boys' faces and I wondered how far and fast they had lugged the beast. She had timed her delaying perfectly for its arrival. They brought it forward and set it down: it stood as high as Starling's shoulder. She glanced toward the minstrel gallery, but someone had already stepped forward, bearing his own stool. He placed it before the harp, and then I saw the only awkward moment in her performance. Her gown had never been cut for her to be seated behind a harp with the instrument leaned back on her shoulder. With a fine disregard for modesty, she lifted her skirts and bundled them out of the way, displaying legs still shapely and stockinged in bright green, and dainty blue slippers with silver buttons. She woke the harp, running her fingers lightly up and down the strings, letting them barely speak, as if they whispered to her that they were in tune and waiting for her.

Then she plucked three strings, one after another, as if she were dropping gold coins on a path and bidding us follow. The notes became a chord, and her other hand began to pluck a lilting melody. Then she lifted her voice.

This, I knew, was the song she had waited a lifetime to sing. Always, always, she had wanted to leave a song that would linger in Six Duchies' memory and be sung over and over. When first I had met her, she had spoken with hungry ambition of how she would follow me and record my deeds and fate so that she might be witness to a turning point in Six Duchies' history. And witness she had, but her lips had been stilled and her song unsung, by royal decree that what had happened in the Mountains must ever after be kept secret. I was dead and must remain so until the Farseer throne was returned to stability.

Now I stood and I listened to my own tale. How long had

she honed those words, how many times had she practised the music that flowed effortlessly and faultlessly from her fingers? This was her highest achievement. I knew that before she was two verses into the song. I had heard her sing other minstrels' work, and I had heard her sing songs and play music of her own composing. Starling was good. No one could ever deny that.

But this was better than good. Even the minstrel who had earlier scowled seemed bespelled by her words and notes. This was the music she had saved, and these were the words she had turned and shaped as if she were a woodcarver. I knew the story of my own life, and most of the court would know at least some of it. But she sang me from an abandoned bastard child to a hero, to a shameful death in a dungeon and a crawl out of a forgotten grave, until I stood before a stone dragon, one that had drunk the life from King Verity, and looked up at her as she and Queen Kettricken departed.

For a time she plucked strings and wove chords, letting that part of the tale sink in. It was not how it had been sung before, and many a face was puzzled. Then, with a sudden sweep of her fingers, she struck up a martial air and finished the tale. I myself had told her what happened after they had departed astride a single dragon with the heart of a king bearing them back to Buckkeep. Verity-as-Dragon had set out to pit himself against the whole of the OutIslander fleet, to save his queen, his unborn child and his entire beloved kingdom from the ravages of the Red Ships. Tears rolled down Kettricken's cheeks as she listened, and King Dutiful was rapt, his mouth slightly ajar.

And so it was I, and my Wit-companion – my wolf Nighteyes – who had wakened the other sleeping dragons. We had battled Regal's corrupt Skill-coterie and their hapless apprentices, and in shedding blood we had wakened the stone dragons to a semblance of life and sent them winging after Verity, a veritable army at his back. She gave three verses to how the dragons had followed the king, describing half a dozen of their varied shapes, and then recounted how swiftly the Red Ships had been driven from our shores. Verity-as-Dragon had led and the other dragons had followed, taking the battle to their islands. Queen Elliania, of

OutIslander blood, listened with her face grave and nodded as if to confirm all that Starling told of those bloody days.

Again, an interlude of only music. Gradually, the tempo slowed and the chords deepened. She sang then of how the Bastard and his wolf, knowing they were dead to all, knowing that the name of FitzChivalry Farseer would ever be tarnished with shame and accusations of treachery and cowardice, walked away into the depths of the Mountain forests. Never again, she sang, would they hunt the green hills of Buck. Never could they come home. Never would their deeds be known. Never. Never. The tale and the song slowed, and became a trickle of wistful notes. They dwindled. Silence.

I do not know how long the song lasted. I came back to the Great Hall and the gathered nobles of the Six Duchies as if I had been on a long journey. Starling sat before her tall harp, her head bent forward and her brow resting on its dark wood. Her face glowed with perspiration. She breathed as if she had run over nine hills. I stared at her. She had been a stranger, a lover, a nemesis, and a betrayer to me. And now she was my historian.

When the applause came, it began as a whisper and rose to a roar. Starling lifted her head slowly and I followed her gaze as she looked around at her audience. Tears tracked down the faces of many, and anger sat on some. I saw a stony-faced woman who sneered at the emotion of the lady next to her. Another noble shook his head and leaned close to whisper to his companion. Two young women were embracing one another, overcome with the romance of the story. The Duchess of Bearns hugged herself tight, her clasped hands under her chin, her head bent over her hands. The Duke of Rippon appeared to be telling the people around him that, 'I knew it. I always knew it,' as his big hands beat against one another.

And I? How to describe that vindication? I stood among them, unknown and unseen, but feeling as if we had finally come home, my wolf and I. I felt a sharp pang that the Fool had not been here to hear this, and realized I was trembling, as if I had come in from somewhere very cold and was shaking as the warmth finally came back into my body. I was not weeping, and yet the water ran from my eyes until I could scarcely see.

Dutiful's gaze scanned the crowd, and I knew he was looking for me, but he was searching for me in the guise of Lord Feldspar. Lord Chade stood and moved slowly from his place at the high table. I thought he was going to Kettricken, but then his steps wavered and he began to wend his way through the crowd. I watched him, puzzled, and then with horror realized that he had seen me and was coming straight toward me.

NO, I Skilled to him, but he was sealed tight – not to keep me out but to keep whatever he was feeling in. When he reached me, he took a firm hold of my arm. 'Chade, please, no,' I begged him. Had the old man's mind turned?

He looked at me. His cheeks were wet with tears. 'It's time, Fitz. Time and past time. Come. Come with me.'

The people standing closest to me were watching and listening. I saw one man's eyes widen and his face went from puzzlement to shock. We were in the midst of the crowd. If they turned on me now, they could tear me apart. There was no retreat here. And so, as Chade tugged at my arm, I let myself be led. My knees felt loose: I felt as if I walked like a puppet, jouncing with every step.

No one had expected this. Queen Elliania smiled joyously, but all colour had drained from Nettle's face. Kettricken's chin trembled and then her face crumpled and she wept as if I were King Verity himself walking toward her. As we passed Starling, she lifted her head. When she saw me her hands flew to her mouth. Her eyes went wide and greedy, and some part of me thought, already she plans what song she will make of this.

The empty space between the crowd and the king and queen's dais was an endless desert we crossed. King Dutiful's face was white and stark. *What are you doing? What are you doing?* He demanded of us, but Chade did not hear him and I had no answer to give. A tumultuous roar of confusion, whispers, speculations and then shouts rose behind us. Nettle's eyes were black in a face carved of ice. Her fear soaked me. When we stood before my king, I went to my knees more out of sudden weakness than from any sense of propriety. My ears were ringing.

Dutiful saved us all.

He shook his head slowly as I stared up at him. 'Never is over,' he proclaimed to the crowd. He looked down at my upturned face. I stared up at him. I saw King Shrewd, and King Verity there. My kings, looking down at me with earnest sympathy. 'FitzChivalry Farseer, too long have you sojourned among the Elderlings, your memory spurned by the very people you saved. Too long have you been in a place where the months pass as if days. Too long have you walked among us in false guise, deprived of your name and your honour. Rise. Turn and face the folk of the Six Duchies, your folk, and be welcomed home at last.' He bent and took my arm.

'You're shaking like a leaf,' he whispered by my ear. 'Can you stand up?'

'I think so,' I muttered. But it was his strength that pulled me to my feet. I stood. I turned. I faced them all.

The roar of acclaim broke over me like a wave.

NINE

The Crown

As I have risked my life for this knowledge, I expect that for my next piece of information, I will be paid more handsomely! When you first approached me for these 'small tasks' as you called them, there at Buckkeep Castle, I had no idea what sorts of missions you would be assigning me. As I have said in the past, I will continue to convey interesting information to you, but nothing that I feel undermines or exploits my friendships.

Kelsingra is indeed a city of wonders past imagining. Information is stored in almost every stone there. I have heard that there is even more to be found in the Elderling archives recently discovered in the city, but I am not invited to enter there, and I won't risk my friends' trust by attempting to go there. A great deal of information about Elderlings is available in the walls of the old market space and one can't help but be aware of it, even just strolling by on an evening. If you wish to advance me some coin and ask specific questions, I will answer the ones that I can. Had I not lost a hand to a windlass, I would not be in need of your funds. Nonetheless, I will remind you that I have my pride. A simple sailor you may think me, but I have my own code of honour.

But to your most pressing question. I have seen no 'silvery river or stream'. And as I travelled there on the Rain Wild River and then up one of its tributaries, I assure you that I saw a great many rivers and streams feeding into that vast waterway. They were grey with silt. I suppose they might appear silvery in some lights.

However, I think I have had tidings of what it is that you seek. It is not a river, but a well. Silvery stuff rises within it, and the dragons seem to find it almost intoxicating. The location of this well and its very existence is supposed to be a great secret, but for one who can hear dragons, their clamour when the stuff rises close enough to the surface for them to drink betrays it. At other times, I imagine it must be drawn up in a bucket for them. I was obliged to keep my questions on this topic oblique. Two of the young keepers have very little tolerance for brandy, and we had a lovely wandering conversation until their commander arrived and berated them and threatened me. This Rapskal seems a very unsettled sort of person, capable of carrying out his various threats against me if he found me encouraging his men to drunkenness. He demanded that I leave Kelsingra, and the next morning I was escorted from my accommodations to the next departing ship. He did not ban me from the city as I have heard other travellers and entrepreneurs have been banned, but I think I shall let some time pass before I attempt another visit.

I will anticipate your next letter of credit and your queries. I am still quartered at the Splintered Fid, and messages sent to that inn will reach me.

Jek

It was dawn when I fell face down on my bed. I was exhausted. I had climbed the stairs, eager as a boy to tell the Fool all that had transpired, only to find him soundly asleep. For a time, I had sat by his bed, wishing he could have been there with me. When I dozed off in the chair, I'd surrendered and tottered down the stairs to my bed. I closed my eyes and slept. I sank into sweet oblivion, and then jerked awake as if someone had stuck a pin in me. I could not free myself from the sensation that something was wrong: terribly, terribly wrong.

I could not sleep. Danger, danger, danger thrummed through my nerves. I seldom felt such unease without a reason. Years ago, my wolf had always been at my back, using his keener sense to warn me of lurking intruders or unseen watchers. He was long gone these many years, but in this he remained. When something prickled against my senses, I had learned to pay attention.

I remained perfectly still on my bed. I heard only what I

expected to hear, the winter wind outside my window, the soft sounds of the fire, my own breathing. I smelled nothing beyond my own smells. I opened my eyes to slits, feigning sleep still, and studied what I could of the room. Nothing. There was nothing to be alarmed about. Wit and Skill, I sensed all around me. There was nothing to alarm me. And yet I could not shake my anxiety. I closed my eyes. Sleep. Sleep.

I slept, but I did not rest. My heart was a wolf, hunting over snow hills, not for prey but for his lost pack. Hunting and hunting and hunting. Howling out my pain to the night, I ran and ran and ran. I awoke sweaty and still in my clothes. I had a moment of stillness and then heard the tiny scratch at my door. My senses were still wolf-sharpened from my dream. I crossed the room and opened the door while Ash was still poking at my lock.

Without a trace of embarrassment, he removed the pick from the lock, stooped, picked up the breakfast tray and carried it into my room. Moving efficiently, he set out my breakfast for me. Then he moved a small table that had been by my bed. He unslung a pouch from his shoulder, removed papers from it and set them out in orderly rows.

'What are those? Are they from Chade?'

He pointed to each category. 'Letters of congratulation. Invitations. Petitions for you to use your influence. I did not read them all, only the ones that looked useful. I expect you will have a host of them every day now.'

My unwanted correspondence arranged, he looked around my chamber for his next task. I was still grasping that reading my private correspondence was part of what he considered his duty. I saw only a shadow of disapproval in his eyes as he took in my rumpled clothes before he offered, 'Have you any washing, my lord? I should be happy to take it to the laundry folk.'

'Yes, I suppose I do. But I don't think guests use the washerfolk that way. And I am not your "lord".'

'Sir, I do believe that all of that changed last night. Prince FitzChivalry, I should be greatly honoured to convey your dirty smallclothes to the washerfolk.' A grin twitched and then disappeared.

'Are you being cheeky with me?' I was incredulous.

He lowered his eyes and observed quietly, 'Not cheeky, sir. But one bastard may rejoice at another lowborn's good fortune, and dream of better days for himself.' He cocked his head at me. 'Chade has had me hard at learning the history of the Six Duchies. Did you know that one queen-in-waiting actually gave birth to a bastard, and that he rose to be King of the Six Duchies?'

'Not quite. You are thinking of the Piebald Prince. And that did not end well for him at all.' His cousin had killed him for being Witted and had taken the throne.

'Perhaps not.' He glanced at my breakfast tray and tugged the napkin straight. 'But he had a moment, didn't he? Some day, I'd like a moment. Does it seem fair to you that how we are born determines how we are seen for the rest of our lives? Must I always be the son of a whore, a bawdyhouse errand boy? A few promises and a ring, and you might have been the king. Did you never think of that?'

'No,' I lied. 'It was one of the first lessons I had from Chade. Think of what is and don't let what might have been distract you.'

He nodded to that. 'Well, being Lady Rosemary's apprentice is definitely a step up in my life. And if the opportunity presents itself, I will imagine a better status for myself. I respect Lord Chade, but if one only remains what one is today, well . . .' He tipped his head at me with a speculative look.

That stung, a bit. 'Well. No offence taken, Ash, and if you continue with your lessons and your present master then, yes, I think you can rightly dream of better days.'

'Thank you, sir. Your clothes, then?'

'A moment.' As I began to strip off my sweaty shirt and crumpled trousers, Ash went to Lord Feldspar's travelling trunk and began to pull out garments. 'This won't do,' I heard him mutter. 'Nor this. Not now. What's this? Perhaps.'

But when I turned back to him to accept the clothing he was offering me, his eyes were very wide. 'What's wrong?'

'Sir, what happened to your back? Were you attacked? Should I request a private guard for you? One on your door?'

I reached around to touch the sore spots on my back. I was startled that they were not completely healed. One was still oozing and two others were sore to the touch. And I could not think of a ready lie to explain what must look like a number of small puncture wounds on my back. 'A bizarre accident, not an attack. My shirt, please.' I tried to sound as if I were accustomed to having some young man as my valet. Wordlessly, he shook it out and held it open for me. I turned, and met his eyes. He glanced away. He knew I was lying about my back. But was I? It had been, after all, a bizarre accident. I said nothing as I accepted clean smallclothes, trousers and stockings. I was pleased that he had chosen clothes that were far more sensible than those Lord Feldspar had been flaunting. There were still a multitude of buttons, but fewer that poked me. My boots, newly cleaned, were ready for me. I felt a measure of relief as I sat down to put them on. 'Thank you. You're good at this.'

'I served my mother and the other women of the house for years.'

I felt a little sinking of my heart. Did I want to know more about this apprentice of Chade's? But that sort of an invitation could not be heartlessly ignored. 'So I heard.'

'Lord Chade was never my mother's patron, so you need not fear he is my father. But he was always kinder to me than most. I began running errands for him when I was about ten. So, when my mother was . . . killed, and I was forced to flee, he sent someone to find me. And he saved me.'

Tumbling facts falling into place. Chade was a patron of the house where his mother worked, just not his mother's patron. Some kindness, and probably the boy had begun spying for him without even knowing he was doing it. Some coins to run an errand, and a few casual questions, and Chade would learn things about the other patrons. Enough to put the boy's life in danger when his mother died? A story there. Too many stories. Which noble son had taken his deviation too far? I didn't want to know. The more I knew, the more involved I would become. Last night, I'd been netted as neatly as a fish. I already knew that the more I thrashed, the tighter the web would become. 'I'm tired,' I said, and then amended it to a weary smile and, 'I'm already tired and the day has only just begun. I'd best check on my friend. Ash, count me among the friends you could run to, did you ever need that again.'

He nodded gravely. Another noose of spiderweb wrapped around me. 'I'll take these to the washerfolk for you, and bring them back this afternoon. Do you require anything else of me?'

'Thank you. That will be all for now.'

I heard a distant echo of Verity in my voice. Verity dismissing his man who always attended him. Charim. That had been his name. So long ago. I half-expected Ash to be offended at my dismissal, but he bobbed a bow and went out of the door with my laundry over his arm. I sat down to the tray of food that he had brought and made a start on it. Was the food better today? Was FitzChivalry Farseer supplied a better breakfast than Lord Feldspar? And if he was, what did that say for the expectations folk would have, both low and high? Would nobles try to curry favour with me? Underlings seek employment with me? I sampled some of the missives Ash had left. Favour begged, fawning invitations and overly kind congratulations on my return. I closed my eyes tight and opened them again. The stack of correspondence was still there. Eventually, I'd have to deal with it. Or perhaps that was one of Ash's duties. He'd said he'd read most of it, without apology.

Where would I fit into Dutiful's court now? And how could I leave it? What of my Bee? I still had not had a chance to tell Kettricken to send for her, but it seemed that I must, for it came to me suddenly that those who connected me with Tom Badgerlock would know there was a second, secret, Farseer daughter. Did I control any aspect of my life any longer? The life I had led for the past forty years was suddenly shattered to fragments. Lies and deceptions had been swept aside. Well, some lies and deceptions. I needed to talk to Chade: a tale must be concocted about what I had been doing all those years. Would we admit my part in the freeing of IceFyre, the black dragon? Reveal that I had snatched Dutiful back from a misadventure with the Witted and preserved him for the throne? How did Tom Badgerlock intersect with FitzChivalry Farseer? It suddenly seemed to me that truth-telling was just as hazardous as lying. One little bit of truth might lead to requiring another revelation. Where would it end?

I concentrated on the eating, not letting myself dwell on all the questions crowding into my brain. I had no intention of leaving my room today until someone Skilled to me or sent me a message.

So when I heard the light tap at my door, I set down my cup and stood immediately. The tap came again. And not from the chamber door, but from the concealed door that led to Chade's old lair. 'Fool?' I queried softly, but no one replied. I triggered the door.

But it was not the Fool who waited there, but the crow. She looked up at me, turning her head to regard me with one bright eye. Then, as if she were the queen herself, she hopped gravely down the remaining steps and into the centre of the room.

It is common for folk who are not Witted to think that those of us with Old Blood can talk to any animal. We can't. The Wit is a mutual exchange, a sharing of thoughts. Some creatures are more open than others; some cats will not only talk to anyone, but will natter on or nag or pester with absolutely no restraint. Even the person with only the tiniest shred of the Wit will find themselves standing to open the door before the cat has scratched at it, or calling the cat from across the room to share the best morsel of fish. Having been bonded to a wolf for so many years set my thoughts in a pattern that, I believed, made all creatures of that family more open to me. Dogs, wolves and even foxes have communicated with me from time to time. One hawk I have spoken with, at the bidding of her mistress. One small ferret, ever a hero in my heart. But no Witted one can simply arrow thoughts at a creature and expect to be understood. I considered trying, but the Wit swiftly becomes an intimate sharing. And I had little desire to develop such a bond with this bird. So I did not use the Wit, but only words as I said to her, 'Well, you look much better than the last time I saw you. Would you like me to open the window for you?'

'Dark,' she said, and I was astonished at the clarity of the word, and how appropriate it was. I had heard birds trained to speak, but usually the human words they uttered were simple repetitions bereft of sense or context. The crow walked rather than hopped across the room and studied the window before fluttering to the top of my clothing chest. I did not stare at her. Few wild creatures are comfortable with that. Instead, I stepped carefully past her and opened the window.

Wind and chill came in: the storms of the past few days had paused but clouds promised more snow tonight. For a moment I stood and stared out over the castle walls. It had been years since I had studied this view. The forest had retreated. I could see farm cottages where once there had been only the sheep pastures, and pastures where there had been forest, and stumplands beyond that. My heart sank; once we had hunted there, my wolf and I, where now sheep pastured. The world had to change and for some reason the prosperity of men always results in them taking ever more from wild creatures and places. Foolish, perhaps, to feel that pang of regret for what was gone, and perhaps it was only felt by those who straddled the worlds of humans and beasts.

The crow fluttered to the windowsill. I stepped back carefully to give her room. 'Fare well,' I wished her and waited for her to go.

She cocked her head and looked at me. In that quick way birds have, she twisted her head again and looked out over the world. Then she opened her wings and with a flutter crossed the room and landed with a rattle of crockery on my breakfast tray. Wings spread wide, as if to remind me, she said, 'White! White!' Then without hesitation she snatched up and swallowed a shred of bacon. She stabbed at a bit of leftover bread and with a shake scattered it over the floor. She eyed it for a moment, and then disregarded it as she clattered her bill in a dish that had held apple compote.

While she dismembered my breakfast, I went to Lord Feldspar's trunk. Yes, Chade had supplied him well. I found the bottle of ink. And a quill pen. I thought for a bit, then cleared the correspondence from the table. I reversed the quill and dipped the feathered end into the ink bottle and studied it. It would do. 'Crow. Come here. I'll paint you black.'

She dropped the piece of bacon she'd been trying to shred. 'White! White!'

'No white,' I told her. I focused my Wit. *No white.*

She cocked her head and pointed one bright eye at me. I waited. With a clatter that sent my spoon to the floor, she lifted from my tray and hopped to the table.

'Open your wings.' She stared. I slowly lifted my arms wide. '*Open. Show me the white.*'

To understand what someone wants is not the same as trusting. She tried. She opened her wings. I tried to dab black on, but she fluttered her wings and spattered ink all over us. I tried again. I talked to her as I worked. 'I've no idea if this will stand up to rain. Or wind. Or if your feathers will stick together. *Open them. No, leave them open. So the ink dries. That's it!*'

By the time I began work on the second wing, she was more cooperative. My arms and my correspondence were freckled with ink. I finished her second wing and went over the first one again. Then I had to make her understand that I had to paint the undersides of her wings as well. 'Now dry!' I warned her, and she stood, wings outstretched. She rattled her pinions to put them in order and I was glad to see little spatter of ink. And when she folded them, she looked to me like an ordinary black crow.

'No white!' I told her. She turned her head and preened her feathers to smoothness. She seemed satisfied with my work, for she hopped abruptly back into the middle of my plate.

'I'll leave the window open for you,' I told her, and left her there, making a mess of my unfinished breakfast.

I pulled the door shut behind me, for what Chade had told me once was true. That open window and this opened door together created a terrific draught in the apartments about.

I climbed the steep steps wondering how I could convey to the Fool all that had happened in one night. A foolish grin took command of my face. For the first time, I allowed myself to admit that part of me rejoiced. So long, so long, I had stood at the edge of the forest, looking at the lit windows in the distance. Buckkeep Castle was my home, had always been my home. Despite all my misgivings and fears, I allowed myself to imagine, for one delicious moment, that I could stand to my king's left side during his judgments or be seated at the high table during a banquet. I imagined my small daughter dancing with me in the Great Hall. I would tell the Fool and he would understand my torn feelings. Then, with a rush of regret, I wished again that the Fool had been there last night, to see and hear Starling singing of my courage and brave and selfless deeds.

But he would have seen nothing of it. And like a hunted stag run off a cliff over a frozen lake, my mood plummeted into dark and cold. My exultation vanished and I almost dreaded telling him. Yesterday I had not mentioned Nettle's pregnancy. Today I feared to tell him of King Dutiful's public recognition of me.

My steps had slowed and by the time I reached the top of the stairs, I was plodding. So I was not prepared to see the Fool seated at Chade's table, six candles burning bright in a tight circle before him. I was even less prepared for the lopsided smile with which he greeted me. 'Fitz!' he exclaimed, almost merrily, the scars on his face contorting his smile to a puppet's grin. 'I've news to share!'

'And I,' I rejoined, my spirits daring to lift a bit.

'It's good news,' he told me, as if I could not have guessed that. I wondered if he was going to tell me my own tidings, and immediately resolved that if he wished to do so and take pleasure in it, then I would let him.

'So I see,' I told him, taking a seat at the table opposite him.

'No, you don't!' he rejoined, his laughter bubbling up at a jest I didn't share yet. 'But I do!'

I sat for a long moment in silence, waiting for him to add words to that. Then, as often had happened in our youths, I suddenly grasped the meaning he intended. 'Fool! You can see?'

'I just told you that,' he responded, and burst into hearty laughter.

'Look at me!' I commanded him, and he lifted his eyes but they did not meet my gaze. To my deep disappointment, they were still clouded and grey.

The smile on his face faded a little. 'I can see light,' he admitted. 'I can tell light from darkness. Well, that's not it exactly. Being blind isn't darkness as you know darkness. Oh, it doesn't matter, so I won't try to explain it except to say, I know there are candles burning on the table before me. And when I turn my face away, I know there are not candles over there. Fitz, I think my eyesight is coming back. When you used the Skill on me that night . . .

I knew that the sores on my back began to heal. But this is so much more than that.'

'I did nothing to your eyes that night. It may simply be that a natural healing process has begun.' I bit back the warning that nearly burst from me. *Don't hope too much.* I knew how tenuous his health was. And yet, he could now perceive light. That had to mean he was starting to rally. 'I'm glad for you. And we must keep you on the path. Have you eaten today?'

'Oh, yes. I've eaten. Chade's boy brought food, and seemed less fearful of me. Or perhaps more fascinated by the bird. And then Chade himself came by, with a parcel of things for you. Fitz! He told me all. And I am . . . befuddled. And happy for you. And frightened. How can such a time be, such a world where things happen that I never foresaw! And he told me that Starling played your story and sang it beautifully! Is it truly so? Did I dream it?'

A lurch of disappointment. I had not known how much I wished to tell him myself until I found he already knew. But his smile at my good fortune was everything I could have wished for.

'No. It was all true. It was wonderful.' And with him, I shared the moments that few others would have understood. I told him how Celerity, the Duchess of Bearns, heir to her sister Lady Hope, had set her hands on my shoulders. I had stared into her clear eyes. There were lines at the corners of her eyes and framing her mouth, but still a determined girl met my gaze. 'I never doubted you. You should not have doubted me,' she had said, and kissed my mouth softly before turning and walking quickly away, her husband shooting me a puzzled glare before he hastened after her. I recounted how Queen Elliania had cut a silver narwhal button from her cuff and given it to me, bidding me wear it always. He smiled to that, and then his face grew thoughtful when I told him that people that I scarcely recalled had taken my hand and pressed it, or slapped my shoulder. Some had smiled incredulously, a few had wept. Very disconcerting were those who tipped me a wink or leaned in to whisper, 'Remember well that I kept your secret,' and messages of that ilk. Worst of all was a young guardsman who strode boldly past the waiting nobility. Sparks of anger had danced in his eyes as he said, 'My grandfather died thinking he had sent you to your death. To the end of his days, Blade believed he had betrayed you. He, I think, you might have trusted.' Then he had turned on his heel and was engulfed by the crowd before I could speak a word to him.

I found myself speaking softly as if I were telling an old tale to a young child. And giving it a happy ending, when all know that tales never end, and the happy ending is but a moment to catch one's breath before the next disaster. But I didn't want to think about that. I didn't want to wonder what would happen next.

'Did Chade say why he had done it?' he asked me.

I gave a shrug he could not see. 'He said it was time. That both Shrewd and Verity would have wanted it to happen. Having emerged from the shadows himself, he said he could not leave me there.' I rummaged on one of Chade's shelves and then another before I found what I sought. Spirits of wine. I lit my own candle at the fire and found a rag. I damped the rag and began to remove my ink freckles. They were hard to get off. Good for the crow, annoying for me. I moved to Chade's mirror, scrubbing at the spots on my face.

'What is that smell? What are you doing?'

'Getting ink off my face. I was painting the crow's white feathers black so she could go out without being pecked and chased.'

'Painting a crow. Prince FitzChivalry amuses himself painting crows the day after his acknowledgment by the throne.' He laughed. A very good sound.

'Chade left a package for me?'

'At the end of the table,' he said. He had fixed his gaze once more on the candles, revelling in whatever trace of their brilliance he could perceive. And so I did not take any of them, but moved the parcel to their vicinity and began to unfasten it. It smelled of earth. It was wrapped in leather, and tied with leather straps. The knots were green with disuse and the white-edged stains on the leather were from damp. The ties had not been undone in a very long time, and I suspected that at some point it had been stored outside, perhaps for a winter. Possibly buried somewhere. As I worked on the knots, the Fool observed, 'He left you a note as well. What does it say?'

'I haven't read it yet.'

'Shouldn't you read it before you open the parcel?'

'Did he say I should?'

'He seemed to take a very long time to think about it, and then he wrote only a few words. I heard the scratching of his pen, and many sighs.'

I stopped working on the straps. I tried to decide which made me more curious, the letter or the parcel. I lifted one candle and saw the single sheet of paper on the table. I'd missed it in the dimness. I reached, trapped it and slid it toward me. Like most of Chade's missives there was no date, no greeting and no signature. Only a few lines of writing.

'What does it say?' the Fool demanded.

'*"I did as he bade me. The conditions were never met. I trust you to understand. I think you should have it now."*'

'Oh. Better and better,' the Fool exclaimed. And added, 'I think you should just cut the straps. You'll never get those old knots out.'

'You already tried, didn't you?'

He shrugged and tipped a grin at me. 'It would have saved you the trouble of struggling with them.'

I tormented both of us by working at the stubborn knots for some little time. Leather that has been knotted, wet, and then left to dry can seem as hard as iron. In the end, I drew my belt-knife and sawed through the straps. I tugged them off the parcel and then struggled to unfold the leather that surrounded whatever it was. It was not soft leather, but heavy, the sort one would use for a saddle. It creaked as I pried it open and brought out something wrapped in a still-greasy cloth. I set it with a thunk on the table.

'What is it?' the Fool demanded, and reached to send his fingers dancing over the concealed item.

'Let's find out.' The greasy cloth proved to be a heavy canvas sack. I found the opening, reached in and pulled out . . .

'It's a crown,' the Fool exclaimed, his fingers touching it almost as soon as my eyes saw it.

'Not exactly.' Crowns are not usually made of steel. And Hod had not been a maker of crowns but a maker of swords. She had been an excellent weaponsmaster. I turned the plain circlet of steel in my hands, knowing this was her work though I could not have explained to anyone how I recognized it. And there, there was her maker's mark, unobtrusive but proud inside the circlet.

'There's something else here.' The Fool's hands had gone questing like ferrets into the opened leather parcel and now he held out a wooden tube to me. I took it silently. We both knew it would contain a scroll. The ends of the tube were plugged with red wax. I studied it in the candlelight.

'Verity's seal,' I told him softly. I hated to mar the imprint, but nonetheless I dug the wax out with my belt-knife, and then tipped the tube and shook it. The scroll was stubborn. It had been in there a long time. When it finally emerged I just looked at it. Water had not touched it.

'Read it,' the Fool's whisper urged me.

I unrolled the vellum carefully. This was Verity's hand, the careful lettering of a man who loved to draw, to make maps and chart terrain, to sketch fortifications and draw battle-plans. He had written large, dark and plain. My king's hand. My throat tightened. It was a moment before I could speak. My voice was higher as I spoke past tightness.

'Be it known by my seal on this document and by the testimony of the trusted bearer, Chade Fallstar, that this scroll is the true desire of King-in-Waiting Verity Farseer. In plain words let me say, I leave today on a quest from which I may not return. I leave my queen, Kettricken of the Mountains, with child. If in my absence my father, King Shrewd, should die, I commend my lady to the protection of my nephew, FitzChivalry Farseer. If word of my death be returned, then I desire that he be recognized formally as protector of my heir. If my queen perish and my heir survive, then I stipulate that FitzChivalry Farseer is to reign as regent until such time as my heir is able to assume the throne. And if none survive me, neither father, nor queen nor heir, then it is my will that FitzChivalry Farseer be recognized as my heir. It is not my wish that my younger brother Regal Farseer inherit my crown. I do most ardently urge that my dukes recognize and affirm my will in this matter.' I paused to catch my breath. 'And his signature is below it.'

'And this would have been your crown.' The Fool's scarred fingertips traced the rim of the simple circlet. 'Not a jewel to be touched. And sword-steel, by the feel of it. Wait, wait! Not so plain, perhaps. Here. What is this?'

I took the crown from him and tilted it to the candlelight. It was engraved into the plain circlet. 'A charging buck.'

'He gave you that emblem.'

'Verity did,' I said quietly. My voice tightened up a notch as I observed, 'It's just the charging buck. There is no slash across it to mark me a bastard.'

There was a very long silence. The candles burned and at the other end of the room a log slumped on the hearth. 'Do you wish it had come to pass?' the Fool asked me.

'No! Of course not!' That would have been like wishing death on Shrewd and Kettricken and her unborn child. 'But . . . I do wish I had known. There were times when it would have meant a great deal to me.' A tear tracked down my cheek. I let it fall.

'And not now?'

'Oh, and still now. To know he thought me worthy, to guard his queen and his child. And to step up and claim the throne after him.'

'Then you never wished to be king?'

'No.' Liar. But the lie was so old and so oft repeated that most of the time I believed it.

He gave a small sigh. When I realized it was of relief, not sadness for the smallness of my ambitions, I wondered why. He answered before I asked.

'When Chade told me you had been formally acknowledged, and that most of the folk there were inclined to lionize you and welcome you home, I worried. And when my fingers touched your crown, I feared.'

'Feared what?'

'That you would want to stay here at Buckkeep Castle. That you would enjoy being seen as what you have always been, not the King-in-Waiting but the King-in-the-Shadows.'

Such a title to give me. 'And that made you fear . . . what?'

'That you would be reluctant to leave the acclaim you had finally earned. That you would go without heart to my errand.'

His errand. A return to my old role as assassin. To deflect him from any thoughts of the murders he'd assigned me, I hastily mentioned his other errand. 'Fool. I will do all I can to find the son you suspect you have left somewhere. Doubtless it would make my task much easier if you could recall for me the women you have lain with who might have borne such a child, and when it might have happened.'

He gave a snort of displeasure. 'Fitz! Have you listened not at all to what I told you? There is no such woman, nor a child conceived in that way. I told you that.'

My mind reeled. 'No. No, you didn't. I am sure that if you had told me such a thing, I would have remembered it. And that I would have immediately asked, as I do now, then how have you made a son?'

'You don't listen,' he said sadly. 'I explain things, quite clearly, but if it's not what you expect to hear, you set it aside. Fitz. This crown. Would it fit?'

'It's not a crown, not really.' He had changed the subject again. I knew that he would not explain until he decided to do it. I tried to conceal my relief that he'd let me get away with my deflection as I turned the cold steel in my hands. The last time I'd worn a crown, it had been wooden and decorated with roosters. *No. Don't summon that memory now.* I lifted the circlet and set it on my head. 'It fits, I suppose. I'm not sure how it's supposed to fit.'

'Let me touch it.' He rose and groped his way around the end of the table to where I sat. His hands felt for me, found a shoulder, the side of my face and then fluttered up to my head and the crown there. He lifted it slightly, and then, with no self-consciousness at all, measured the length of my hair. He walked his fingers down my face, touching the break in my nose, the old scar, the scruff of beard on my chin. If anyone else had done it, it would have felt invasive. Insulting. But I knew he was comparing what I looked like now to what he recalled.

He cleared his throat then lifted the circlet in his hands. He spoke more gravely than I had ever heard him as he uttered the words, 'FitzChivalry Farseer. I crown you King-in-the-Shadows of the Six Duchies.' He set the circlet on my head, settling it carefully. The steel was cold and heavy. It settled there as if it would never move again. He cleared his throat once more and after a pause he added, 'You're a handsome man still, Fitz. Not as pretty as before Regal broke your face. But you've aged well, I judge.'

'That old Skill-healing,' I shrugged. 'My body just keeps repairing itself, whether I wish it or not.'

I took off the steel crown and set it on top of the oily canvas that had sheltered it. Light ran along the edge of it like blood on a swordblade.

'I wish that were my situation,' the Fool returned. His gaze went back to the candles. For a long time, we were both silent. Then he said softly, 'Fitz. My eyes. Being blind . . . they used that. To make me fearful and cowering. I need to see. I dread the thought of setting out on our quest still blinded. I will if I must. But . . . Could you . . .'

So much for my deflection. He was still planning murders. I had told him I could not go on his quest, but he persisted in ignoring what I'd said. Let it go. 'Tell me what they did to your eyes,' I said as quietly.

He held up a helpless hand. 'I don't know. Perhaps they did not even intend to do it, but once it was done, they made full use of it. They . . . oh, Fitz. There was a beating. And another one. My eyes were swollen shut. And another beating. And—'

I stopped him. 'And when the swelling went down, you could no longer see.'

He drew in a deep breath. I saw how he fought to tell me a tale of things he wanted only to forget. 'At first, I kept thinking it was night. Or that I was in a dark cell. They did that some times. If you are in the dark always, you can't tell how much time has passed. I think, I think that sometimes they brought me water and food at very long intervals, and sometimes they brought me food quickly. To confuse me about time passing. It was a long time before I realized I couldn't see. And a longer time before I knew it wasn't going away.'

'That's enough. I just needed to know a bit, to help me.'

Another silence. Then he whispered, 'Will you try now?'

I was silent. To do so would risk my own vision. Could I tell him that now, while such hope burned in his face? He looked more like my old Fool than he had since Aslevjal. His vision was so important to him. Restoring it was key to his locating his son, and his ridiculous quest to assassinate all the Servants was the only purpose that he had left to him. Last night I'd had the triumph of a dream I'd never allowed myself to dream. Could I destroy his hopes today?

I'd be careful. So careful. Surely I'd be able to tell if I were endangering myself?

Was I more like Chade than I wished to be? Did I always want to find out how far I could push the magic, what I could do if no one restrained me? I pushed aside the itching question.

'Now? Why not?' I said. I pushed my chair back and walked around the table to him. 'Face me,' I told him quietly. Obediently, he turned away from the candles. I pulled one of them closer and studied his face in its flickering light. He had scarring on the tops of his cheeks, right below the deep hollows under his eyes. It was the sort of puckering seen on the faces of men who have been in many fist-fights. The skin splits easily where flesh is a thin layer over bone. I moved my chair, placing it so that I faced him. I sat down. 'I'm going to touch you,' I warned him and took his chin in my hand. I turned his face slowly from side to side, studying the scars that meticulous torture and crude battering had left there. I remembered suddenly how Burrich had studied my face after Galen had beaten me. I set two fingers to his face and pressed gently as I traced a circle around his left eye. He winced more than once. Then the right. It was the same. I guessed at bone that had fractured and healed unevenly. In one place, there was a definite dent in his facial bones near his temple. Touching that made me feel queasy. But could that have been what blinded him? I didn't know. I took a deep breath. I would be careful this time. I vowed I would not risk either of us. I set my hands to both sides of his face. I closed my eyes. 'Fool,' I said softly. And just that easily, I found him.

And the Fool was there. The last time, he had been deeply unconscious, unaware of how I moved through him with his blood. Now I felt his hands come to rest on mine. That would help. I knew how his face had looked but he would recall how his face had felt. I started with my fingertips under his eyes. I called to mind the drawings in Chade's old scrolls from the Flayer, and the human skull that probably still reposed in the cabinet in the corner. I whispered as our hands moved together. 'When adjacent bone breaks, sometimes it fuses incorrectly. Here. Feel that? We need to undo that.'

And so we worked, not quickly. We moved bone, bit by tiny bit. Where his face had broken, it had healed with ridges and seams. Some reminded me of the cracks one makes when one taps a hard-boiled egg before shelling it. It was not something to be hurried, the painstaking exploration of the bones of his face. As we worked, touch and Skill combined, and we followed one fine crack down from the lower rim of his left eye to his upper jaw. The tops of his cheekbones were a maze of tiny cracks. At the outer corner of his right eye, a hard blow had crushed bone, leaving an indentation that pressed on the tissue beneath it. We worked for some time, moving tiny bits of bone to both ease pressure and fill the hollow.

To describe it makes it seem a simple thing. It wasn't. The tiny movements of minuscule motes of bone were still a breaking away and a reforming. I clenched my jaws against the Fool's pain until my own head pounded with it. We did no more than the lower expanses below both his eyes. My strength was flagging and my determination failing me when the Fool lifted his hands from the backs of mine.

'Stop. Stop, Fitz. I am so tired now. It hurts. And the pain wakens all the memories.'

'Very well,' I agreed hoarsely, but it took some time for me to separate my awareness from his body. I felt as if I returned to my own flesh from a long and vivid nightmare. The last step of that withdrawal was my lifting of my hands from his face. When I opened my eyes to regard him, the room swam before me. I felt a moment of terror. I'd gone too far and damaged my sight! But it was only weariness. As I stared, the dim room yielded to my vision. I shuddered with relief. The candles had burned down to half their length. I did not know how much time had passed, but my shirt was sweated to my back and my mouth as dry as if I had run to Buckkeep Town and back. As soon as I released the Fool from my touch, he dropped his face into his hands and cradled it, his elbows on the table.

'Fool. Sit up. Open your eyes. Tell me if we accomplished anything.'

He obeyed me but he shook his head as he did so. 'I did not close my eyes. I kept them open. Hoping. But nothing changed.'

'I'm sorry.' And I was. I was sorry he was blind and fiercely glad I had not lost my own sight trying to heal his. I had to ask myself how hard I had truly tried. Had I been holding back? I didn't want to think I had, but I could not find an honest answer. I thought of telling the Fool my fear. What would he ask of me? That I help him regain sight in one eye by giving up one of mine? Would he demand that much of me? Would I agree or deny him? I measured myself and found I was less courageous than I'd believed. And more selfish. I leaned back in my own chair and closed my eyes for a time.

I jolted awake when the Fool touched my arm.

'So you were asleep. You suddenly became very quiet. Fitz. Will you be all right?' There was apology in his voice.

'I will. I'm just very tired. Last night's . . . revelation exhausted me. And I didn't sleep well.' I reached up to rub my eyes, and flinched at my own touch. My face was swollen and warm to the touch, as if I'd been in a fight.

Oh.

I gingerly prodded the tops of my cheekbones and the outer sockets of my eyes. Even if I had not given him his vision back, I would pay a toll for what I had done for him.

Why?

None of the other Skill-healings I'd assisted with had affected me this way. Thick had done a prodigious amount of healing on Aslevjal Island and shown no ill-effects at all. The only difference that came to my mind was my connection to the Fool. It was far more than a Skill-connection: when I had called him back from the other side of death we had had a moment of profound joining. Perhaps we had never truly parted.

I blinked and measured my vision again. I noticed no difference, no hazing. I was almost certain that while we had repaired bone we hadn't done anything that would benefit his eyesight. I wondered if I would have the courage to attempt any further healing of him. I thought of all I had glimpsed that was broken inside him, all the lingering infections and badly healed damage. How much of that must I take on if I continued my attempts to heal him? Could anyone fault me for refusing to make such a sacrifice? I cleared my throat.

'Are you certain there is no difference in your vision?'

'I can't really tell. Perhaps I perceive more light. My face is sore, but in a different way. The soreness of healing, perhaps. Did you find anything when you were . . . inside my body? Could you tell what stole my sight?'

'It's not like that, Fool. I could tell that there were breaks in your facial bones that hadn't healed properly. And I put them on the path to healing, and tried to undo some of the places where the bones were not aligned as they should be.'

He lifted questioning hands to his face. 'Bones? I thought the skull was one bone, mostly.'

'It's not. If you wish, later I can show you a human skull.'

'No. Thank you. I'll take your word for it. Fitz, I can tell by your voice that you found something else. Is more wrong with me than you wish to tell me?'

I chose my words carefully. No lies this time. 'Fool, we may have to go more slowly with your healing. The process is demanding for me. We must employ good food and rest as much as we can, and save magical efforts for the more difficult injuries.' I knew those words were true. I tried not to follow that thought to its logical conclusion.

'But—' he began and then halted. I watched the brief struggle in his expression. He so desperately needed to be well and on his quest and yet, as a true friend, he would not ask me to exert myself past my strengths. He'd seen me exhausted from Skill-efforts, and knew what the physical demands could be. I did not need to tell him that the healings might do actual injuries to me. He did not need to bear the guilt for what I'd already done to myself. That was my own doing. He turned his clouded gaze back to the candles. 'Where did Motley go?'

'Motley?'

'The crow.' He seemed embarrassed to reply. 'Before she went down to you, we were talking, well, not really, though she knows quite a few words and almost seems to make sense some times. I was asking her, "What's your name?" Because, well, because it was so quiet up here. At first she said random things in reply. "Stop that!" and "It's dark" and "Where's my food?" And finally she said back to me, "What's your name?" It rattled me for a moment, until I realized she was just mimicking me.' A tentative smile dawned on his face.

'So you named her Motley?'

'I just started calling her Motley. And shared my food with her. You said she came down to you and you painted her. Where is she now?'

I hated to tell him. 'She came down the stairs and tapped at the secret door. I let her into my room, where she ate half my breakfast. I left the window open for her; I suspect she's gone by now.'

'Oh.' The depth of disappointment in his tone surprised me.

'I'm sorry.' He said nothing. 'She's a wild creature, Fool. It's for the best.'

He sighed. 'I am not certain you are correct about that. Eventually the ink will fade and then what? Her own kind attacks her, Fitz. And crows are flock birds, unaccustomed to being solitary. What will become of her?'

I knew he was right. 'I don't know,' I said quietly. 'But I also don't know what else I can do for her.'

'Keep her,' he suggested. 'Give her a place to be and food. Shelter from storms and her enemies.' He cleared his throat. 'The same things that King Shrewd offered to a misfit creature.'

'Fool, I scarcely think that's a valid comparison. She's a crow, not a youngster alone in the world.'

'A youngster. In appearance. Young in terms of my kind, yes. Naïve and unlearned in the wider world in which I found myself. But almost as different from King Shrewd as a crow is from a man. Fitz, you know me. You've been me. You know that you and I are as much unlike as we are alike. As like and unlike as you and Nighteyes were. Motley, I think, is as like me as Nighteyes was like you.'

I pinched my lips shut for a moment and then relented. 'I'll go and see if I can find her for you. And if I can find her, and if she will come, I'll bring her up here to you. And set out water and food for her.'

'Would you?' His scarred smile was beatific.

'I will.' And I rose in that moment, and went down the steps and opened the door to my room. Where I found Motley waiting.

'Dark,' she informed me gravely. She hopped up a step, then the next one, and on the third one she turned to look back at me. 'What's your name?' she demanded of me.

'Tom,' I said reflexively.

'Fitz—Chivalry!' she squawked derisively, and continued her hopping ascent.

'FitzChivalry,' I agreed, and found myself smiling. I followed her to make her comfortable.

TEN

Tidings

Report for my master
Befriending the scarred man has not been as difficult as we thought it might be. I have realized that part of my reluctance for this assignment was that I feared his appearance. My greatest hurdle, I now perceive, was that I needed to overcome my fear of him before I could lull his fear of me.

It has not been easy to observe him while remaining unobserved as you requested. His blindness seems to have enhanced his other senses. Sometimes, if I arrive before he awakens, I can spend some little time before he is aware of me, but thrice now he has turned his face unerringly toward me and asked 'Who is there?' And his fearfulness is such a sad thing to behold that I have not had the will to pretend I am absent. Once, when I crept into the chamber, I found him fallen by the bed and unable to rise. In his distress and pain, he was unaware of me and struggled for some time. I judged that, although he still possesses some strength, he is in such pain that he is unable to raise his body from certain positions. I tried to be an observer only, but when I could stand it no longer, I scuffed my feet as if I had just entered and immediately called out to him that I would be happy to help. It was still difficult for me to put my hands on him and harder still for me to allow him to grip onto me to help him rise. But I overcame my dislike of his touch, and I think it gained me a great deal of regard and trust from him that I did so.

He has not been as reticent to speak to me as you said he might, but instead has shared many tales of his boyhood as King Shrewd's jester, and stories of himself and Prince FitzChivalry when they were boys. He has also told me tales of his journey to the Mountain Kingdom with Queen Kettricken and his days there when all believed that King Verity was dead and the true Farseer lineage come to an end. And I have heard of the days he spent in the Mountains helping to seek the king, and of his times with Prince FitzChivalry there. Truly, they are tales of heroism and courage beyond any I could have imagined. And I have undertaken to write them down in a separate document, for I think there may be events there that even you have not heard about previously.

For now, I judge I have completed this assignment. I have gained his trust and his confidence. I know that was the sole aim of this exercise, but I will tell you also that I feel I have gained a friend. And for that, my good master, I thank you as much as I thank you for my other instruction.

As you bade me, I have kept my secret and neither seems to have perceived it. The test will be, of course, when they meet me in my true guise. Will either recognize me? I will wager the blind will perceive more than the sighted one.

The Apprentice

After I'd left the Fool with Motley, I had returned to my room, intending to think. But instead, exhausted by the Skill-healing, I had slept. And when at last I awoke, I had no idea what time of day it was.

I rubbed the sleep from my face, wincing at the tenderness around my eyes, then went to the looking-glass and discovered that indeed I looked as bad as I felt. I had feared to find darkness and bruising. Instead my face was puffy and swollen, with a few spatters of ink still. Well, I supposed that was better than looking as if I'd had both eyes blacked in a tavern brawl. I went to the window, opened the shutters and looked out on the setting sun. I felt rested, hungry and reclusive. The idea of leaving my room and venturing out into Buckkeep Castle to find food daunted me.

What was my role to be, now that I was FitzChivalry once more? Even now that I was rested, my efforts to put what had happened into political, social and familial context had failed. In truth, I'd been expecting that someone would summon me. I'd expected a missive from Kettricken, or a Skill-nudge from Chade or Nettle or Dutiful, but there had been nothing. Slowly it came to me that perhaps my relatives were waiting to hear from me.

I damped a towel in my ewer and put the cool bandage over my swollen face. Then I sat down on the edge of my bed, composed myself, stiffened my resolve and reached out to Nettle.

How are you? A question that might have been banal at any other time was now freighted with significance.

How are you? she echoed me. *You've been so quiet!*

I'm stunned, still.

Are you happy it happened?

I had to think about that for a long moment. *I think I am. But I'm probably as frightened as I am happy. And you?*

It changes so many things in such profound ways. We shared a time of quiet awareness of each other. Her thoughts touched me hesitantly. *Yesterday. I am so sorry for the things I said. Today, when I think of how I struck at you, I'm appalled. Mother, when she was carrying, would have bursts like that. Lightning strikes of wild emotions. Burrich would send me out with the older boys and he would stay and face her and weather her storm. It always ended with her weeping in his arms. I felt so annoyed with her, for being so emotional and weak.* Wryly she added, *Why does understanding come so late to us?*

Poor Burrich.

I felt her amusement. *And poor Riddle, I suppose?*

He can withstand it. As Burrich did. And so can I, Nettle. Your mother and I had a few moments like that when she was carrying Bee. It almost comforts me to imagine that they weren't entirely my fault!

Actually, I'm certain they were. She was gently mocking me, I realized with surprise. And enjoyment.

You're probably right, I admitted. I pulled my thoughts away from Molly before my sorrow could rise. Then I thought again of Bee. Now was not the time to insist to Nettle that I could be a good father and that I was determined to keep Bee at my side, because all of that would be balanced on the issue of what happened next to the resurrected FitzChivalry Farseer. Back to the matter at hand. *At some point, we must gather to speak of what has happened.* The quiet had begun to seem ominous to me.

We did. We wondered why you did not join us, and Lord Chade said that it was probably a very large shock for you. He urged us to give you time to reach your own decisions.

No one summoned me.

A moment of startled silence. *No one summoned me, either. Not Chade, nor Dutiful. We simply gathered in Verity's Tower early this morning and tried to make sense of what must come next.*

Oh. I pondered that for a moment. Not including myself was not the same as being excluded. Of course they would meet there and at that hour. I pulled my thoughts back on course. *Who was there?*

Who you might expect. The king and queen, Lord Chade, Lady Kettricken, myself. Lady Rosemary. Riddle of course.

Of course? That last name had not seemed obvious to me at all. *And what was decided?*

About you? Nothing. We had much else to discuss. Your situation is worth an entire meeting on its own.

So, what was discussed?

I wish you had been there. Summarizing is not going to convey all the currents and tides that moved there. Lord Chade came thinking he might rebuke the queen for her headlong action and thinking that perhaps I had influenced her. Queen Elliania rapidly cleared those thoughts from his mind and I am pleased to say that both her husband and Lady Kettricken sided with her. Lady Kettricken then spoke of Riddle's long service to Chade, to you, to the crown in general, and said that as it was completely within her power to do so, he is now Lord Riddle of Spruce Keep.

I've never heard of Spruce Keep.

Evidently it exists on the older maps of the Mountain Kingdom, with a different name in the Mountain tongue. It's deserted now, and probably has been for several generations. The fortification there may not be standing at all, any more. But as the Mountain Queen pointed out, it matters little what is there. He now has title to it. Evidently it was one of her brother's holdings and has sat empty since before his death. And she says that 'lord' is not an appropriate translation of the Mountain concept of what that title would be, but that also matters little. Riddle has the appropriate attitude of being willing to sacrifice himself for the sake of others.

I sat and silently pondered that. Bitter mixed with the sweet. Kettricken was right. In the Mountains, the rulers were not named king or queen, but Sacrifice. And they were expected to be willing to do anything, even to accepting death, in the service of those they ruled. Had not Riddle done that, and more than once? And yet he had been judged too common to marry a Farseer daughter, even one that was a bastard. Denied for years. And in a night, solved. Why had it taken so long? Anger rumbled through me like thunder in the distance. Useless anger. Let it go.

Will you wed officially now?

It will be recognized that we are wed.

She was safe. My daughter and her unborn child were safe. The level of relief that washed through me must have reached Nettle.

You were that concerned for me?

It has long bothered me that you were not allowed to wed as you wished. And when Riddle told me there would be a child, well. I have been a bastard Farseer in Buckkeep Castle, Nettle. I would not wish it on anyone.

Have you eaten today?

Some breakfast. A crow took the rest.

What?

A long tale. One that involves Web.

Are you hungry? Come eat with us.

Where?

The high table. In the Great Hall. Suppressed amusement.

I may. I pulled my thoughts back into my own mind and stared at the wall. How could I do this? Just leave my room, walk down the stairs, enter the Great Hall and seat myself at the high table. Would a place be waiting for me? Would people stare at me and whisper behind their hands?

Impulsively, I Skilled to Chade. *Was it hard to come out of the labyrinth and into the light?*

Whatever are you talking about? Fitz, are you well?

Nettle invited me to join you for dinner. At the high table.

My heart beat twelve times before he responded. *It is what will be expected, yes. Your absence today has been rather dramatic and suspenseful for some. A few nobles who had planned to depart early today, now that Winterfest is over, have delayed their departures. I think they hope for a second glimpse of the mysteriously young and alive FitzChivalry Farseer. Given all that happened last night, it will cause far more speculation if you do not appear at dinner. And your question makes sense to me now. For me, the only difficulty was to ease back into society rather than exploding into it. I was a rat lurking behind the walls for many years. Longing for society, for light and moving air. My transition was less abrupt and strange than yours will be. But as I told you last night, Fitz, it is time and past time. I will expect to see you at dinner.*

I veiled my thoughts from him. Anxiety twisted my guts.

Dress appropriately, he suggested.

What? I felt a rush of dismay.

I could almost hear his sigh. *Fitz. Straighten your thoughts. Tonight you will be FitzChivalry Farseer, the Witted Bastard, abruptly revealed as the hidden hero of the Red-Ship War. It's your new role here at Buckkeep Castle, just as Lord Chade is mine. And Dutiful is the king. We all parade our roles, Fitz. Sometimes, in the comforts of our own chambers, we are who we are with old friends. Or at least who our old friends expect us to be. So, think well on it, and live up to the expectations of the folk of Buckkeep Castle, both noble and humble. It is not a time for you to be unremarkable. Prepare.*

I found your note. And the crown.

Do not wear that!

I laughed out loud. *It had not even crossed my thoughts to do so! I just wanted to thank you. And to let you know I understand.*

He sent me no words, only a shared emotion that I had no name for. Snapping my teeth after meat I could not kill, Nighteyes might have named it. The poignant regret of nearly claiming something. I wondered what Chade had dreamed of claiming.

He departed from my mind. I sat, blinking. Slowly it came to me that Chade was completely right. So, my role was the mysterious returning Witted Bastard, wronged all those years ago. What part of that was untrue? So why was I so acutely uncomfortable at being that? I put my elbows on my knees and lowered my face into my hands, and then jerked upright when my fingers touched my swollen eyes. I got up and fetched my looking-glass and studied my reflection again. Could I have chosen a worse time to look peculiar?

I looked down at the clothing that Ash had chosen for me that morning. Then I scooped an armful of extra clothing from the travelling trunk, triggered the door and went back up to the lair. I did not have much time. I took the stairs two at a time and was speaking before I entered the room. 'Fool, I need your help!'

Then I felt foolish. For both Ash and the Fool turned toward me. They had been seated at the table, feeding things to the crow. She had made a remarkable mess of bread bits and scattered grain and was now holding down a chicken bone as she stripped meat from it.

'Sir?' Ash responded as the Fool turned to me and said, 'Fitz?'

I did not have time for subtleties. 'I'm not sure my clothing is right. I'm to join the king and queen at the high table, with Lord Chade and Lady Nettle. There will be others there, looking on. And I must present myself as FitzChivalry Farseer, the Witted Bastard, returned from his sojourn among the Elderlings. Last night was one thing. They were taken by surprise. But tonight, Chade has said I must give them—'

'The hero,' the Fool said quietly. 'Not the prince. The hero.' He turned to Ash and spoke as if I were incompetent to answer. 'What is he wearing?'

Ash bristled, just a trifle. 'The clothing I chose for him earlier in the day.'

'I'm blind,' the Fool reminded him tartly.

'Oh. I beg pardon, sir. He has on a brown vest decorated with buttons of horn, over a white shirt, the sleeves cut full, with a dozen or so buttons on long cuffs. The collar is open at the throat. He is wearing no jewellery. His trousers are a darker brown, with a line of buttons, also horn, down the outer seams. He's wearing heeled shoes with a plain but lifted toe.' He cleared his throat. 'And his face is splotched with mud.'

'It's ink!' I objected.

'As if that matters,' the boy muttered.

The Fool interrupted. 'The buttons. How recent a fashion are they here?'

'A few folk were wearing them last summer, but now everyone—'

'Fitz, come here. Stand before me.'

I did as he told me, amazed to see that he almost looked animated. I wondered when anyone had last demanded his help. When he felt me standing before him, he lifted his hands and ran them over my garments as if I were a horse he was considering buying. He felt the fabrics, touched the rows of buttons, tugged at my collar and then touched my chin.

'Don't shave,' he instructed me abruptly, as if I had been poised with razor in hand. 'Ash. Can you cut the buttons from the trousers and leave no trace they were ever there?'

'I think so.' The boy sounded a bit sullen.

'Come, Ash,' the Fool cajoled him. 'You grew up in a bawdy-house, where daily women presented themselves to be what men fancied. This is the same thing. We must give them what they want to see. Not a fashionable gentlemen dressed to impress, but a hero returned from the outskirts of society. He has been hidden amongst us since he returned from the Elderlings, living as a humble rural landholder. Slice the buttons off the trousers! We must make him look as if he has not mingled in court society for close to two score years. Yet we must also make it appear that he has tried to dress to the style. I know that Chade knows well how to play this sort of a game. We will need powder and paint, to emphasize the old break in his nose and the scar on his face. Some jewellery, but nothing too fine. Silver suits him better than gold.'

'My fox pin,' I said quietly.

'Perfect,' the Fool agreed. 'Ash?'

'A hat. Almost no one goes bareheaded any more. But simpler. Without feathers, perhaps.'

'Excellent. Go fetch. I think you've the head for this game. Indulge yourself.'

As easily as that, he had stroked the boy's pride smooth. The lad flashed a smile at me as he rose and then vanished, headed toward the crawlway that would exit into Lady Thyme's chamber.

'The fox pin,' the Fool demanded of me.

'And there is now a silver narwhal button that the queen gave me last night,' I remembered.

I took the button from my pocket and the fox pin from inside my shirt, where habit had placed it when I dressed. His crippled hands worked awkwardly at the collar of my shirt, folding the fabric and then securing it with the pin so that it suddenly looked and felt like a different garment to me. By the time he had finished and I had scrubbed the last of the ink spots from my face, Ash was back with a full armload of belts, vests, paint, powder and a very sharp knife. The lad sheared the buttons from my trousers and then plucked the loose threads away. He was good with face paint; I almost asked if he had applied it for his mother, and then bit back the question. He traded my belt for a heavier one, and my belt-knife for a more substantial blade, one that verged on being a short sword. The hat that he produced for me had undoubtedly been one for a lady, sixty or seventy years ago. Ruthlessly, he stripped the feathers from it before handing it over to the Fool, who felt it carefully, and then commanded the boy to restore two small feathers and add a leather strap with a showy buckle to the crown. The silver button they threaded with heavy twine and fastened to my wrist. 'We should order a fine silver chain for that,' the Fool suggested and the boy grinned, dug in a small box and produced one.

'Excellent choice!' the Fool praised him as he fingered the fishscale links, and in a trice they had redone the narwhal.

By the time they finished, they were both chortling and congratulating one another. Ash seemed to have lost all uneasiness around the Fool; indeed, they seemed to have established a swift camaraderie. 'The final touch for the Witted Bastard,' the Fool exclaimed. 'Motley. Will you ride on his shoulder and be his Wit-beast for the evening?'

'No,' I said, appalled, even as the bird cocked her head at me and responded, 'Fitz-Chivalry!'

'She can't, Fool. She's not my companion. It will offend Web if I pretend she is. And I have no way to reassure her that she is safe in such a crowded and noisy space.'

'Ah, well.' The Fool understood immediately, even if he could not conceal his disappointment.

Ash had tilted his head and was looking at me speculatively.

'What?' I asked, thinking that he'd found something awry in my garments.

He glanced away from the Fool but tipped a nod toward him. 'He says he was there. With you, in the Mountains, when you woke the dragons and sent them to aid King Verity.'

I was startled both by the lad being brave enough to ask such a question and the idea that the Fool would have spoken so freely to him of our time together. 'It's true,' I managed to say.

'But the minstrel didn't mention him at all last night.'

The Fool gave an abrupt caw of laughter, and the crow immediately mimicked him.

'And that is true also,' I agreed.

'But Lady Starling said she sang true.'

'Everything she sang was true. I will leave it to you as to whether the truth can exist with details omitted, or if those lacks make a lie of it.'

'He told me that he rode a dragon behind a girl who had been carved from the same stone as the dragon and that they flew up into the sky and saw some of the battles.' The lad was getting bolder. The Fool gave me a sightless glance.

'I myself saw him fly away on the back of a dragon. Girl-on-a-Dragon we called her. And if he has favoured you with an account of battles he saw, well, then you know more of it now than I've ever heard.'

A slow smile spread over the boy's face. 'Then he's a hero, too.'

I nodded. 'Without him, Queen Kettricken would never have reached the Mountains alive. And I would have died of an arrow wound before ever we went on our quest to seek King Verity. So yes, he is a hero, too.' I glanced over at the Fool. His face was very still, his fingers perched on the table's edge.

'She left out a lot.'

'She did.'

'Why?'

Before I could respond, the Fool intervened. 'Perhaps some day you should ask her that.' I did not miss the lilt of amusement in his voice as he imagined such an encounter.

'I have to go.' A thought came to me and I dared it. 'Fool,

you should dress and come with me. I think you are strong enough to manage it, at least for an hour or so.'

'No.' His response was swift and strong.

I regretted my words instantly. The old light that had shone so briefly in his face, his pleasure in helping me and telling Ash stories, had vanished as if it had never been. The fear was back and he cringed back in his chair. I looked at him and wondered how he had ever managed to muster his courage to travel so far to find me, alone, hurt and blind. Had he expended the last of his spirit to do so, and would he never recover to be once more the Fool I had known?

'You don't have to,' I said quietly.

He spoke swiftly, his words tumbling out. 'I'm still in danger, Fitz. I know you think I'm foolish. I know you can't possibly believe that here, in Buckkeep Castle, they could not only come after me but take me back. But they could. I know this as clearly as I know . . . as I know that you are my friend. There are very few things I know any more, Fitz. Few things I am certain about, but you are one of them. And the other is that the danger to me is real.' His voice had become softer and softer as he spoke. On his last words, he folded his hands and looked down at them as if he could see them. Folded, they no longer resembled hands. There were knots of white and lumps of red and speckles of scars. I looked away from them.

'I'll stay with him, sir,' Ash said quietly. I hadn't asked him to, and wouldn't have thought of it, but the moment he volunteered, I was grateful.

'I know you have to go,' the Fool said. Quiet desperation was in his voice.

'I do.' I'd felt several nudges from Chade, and Nettle was now pressing against my thoughts. It was important that I appear. Dutiful and Elliania were delaying their entrance until I could walk in with them. Much longer and it would appear that we slighted our nobles.

I'm coming now, I Skilled back to them and then closed my thoughts to them. 'I'll be back as soon as I can,' I assured the Fool, and 'Soon!' the crow echoed me. She hopped closer to the Fool and tilted her head as if she were trying to look into his face.

'Motley's worried about you,' Ash said as gently as if he were coaxing a child. 'She's trying to look into your face.'

I did not think it would work. I was not sure of what I felt as the Fool's clenched hands slowly opened. He beckoned to the bird and she hopped closer. 'Here's a bit of bread for her,' Ash whispered, and dropped a torn crust into the Fool's hand. He closed his fingers on it, forcing the bird to stand near and take it in chunks as he held it.

'Soon,' I promised the Fool, and rose and left the table. I was halfway down the steps when Ash caught up with me.

'Sir, sir,' he called in a carrying whisper. 'Let me adjust your collar.' But when he was closer to me, he spoke other words by my ear, for me alone to hear. 'He is not as strong as he tries to show himself to you. Earlier today, I found him on the floor near the hearth, trying to rise. It was hard for him to make himself take my hand. Harder for him to endure the pain as I helped him back to his feet. You see him walk, and he can rise from a bedside or a chair. But once on the floor, he could not lift himself.' And again in his whisper, he added, 'There, that's much better.'

'Thank you,' I told him, letting my voice carry as he did. I caught his hand and gripped it briefly; I knew he understood my unvoiced gratitude. Hard news for me to hear, and harder to know that my friend concealed his infirmity from me. I went the rest of the way down the stairs to my old room with a heavy heart.

No sooner had I closed the hidden door behind me than I heard a forceful rap at the chamber door. 'A moment,' I called, and Riddle spoke through the door, saying, 'That's a moment more than I'm to give you.' As I opened the door, he told me, 'I've been sent to fetch you and bring you down to dinner regardless of objections or appearance. But actually, I'll think you've done very well with yourself.'

'And you,' I returned his barbed compliment, for truly Riddle looked little like his normal self. His white shirt was cuffed and collared in purple. Kettricken's Mountain colours. His trousers were black. He was allowed to wear simple boots. I felt envy.

He lifted his chin and showed me his profile. 'You don't think I look more noble-blooded already? It's Kesir Riddle now, which Kettricken explains would translate more as "servant" than "lord" given the Mountain Kingdom philosophy on the duties of rulers. But tonight they will call me Kesir Riddle and I will sit at the high table.'

'Were you sent to escort me there, lest I fail to arrive on time? Or am I to be seen with you to impart my paternal approval of your marriage to my daughter?'

'Both, perhaps. Though I will admit it seems a bit odd that you should be in that role when you actually appear to be younger than I am.'

I had just shut the door behind me and locked it, or I think I would have insisted he stand beside me before the looking-glass. I turned my gaze on him and studied him in silence. Riddle was Riddle, and so I had seen him through the years. While he was scarcely a greybeard, when I surveyed him I noted the lines that now framed his mouth and that his hair was retreating from his brow. He grinned suddenly.

'You've missed your moment to charitably disagree with me, Tom. Oh. It's time to abandon that, too, isn't it? Come, Prince FitzChivalry Farseer. It's time to descend and face the hordes of well-wishers.' He linked his arm through mine and marched me off with him as if he were escorting me to the gallows. As we walked the corridor and descended the stair, I pulled my awareness in. Prince FitzChivalry Farseer. Hero. Humble hero, coming out of a long exile in Withywoods after spending decades amongst the mythical Elderlings. I was the son of Chivalry Farseer, nephew to Verity. Cousin to King Dutiful. Defender of the crown. What would the folk, common and noble, want to see in this hand-crafted hero?

By the time we were striding past folk in the halls, I knew that I was taciturn, but not too grave. I would be as interested in people as Web was, and whenever possible I would turn the conversation to who they were and what they had done. I would talk little and listen well. Modesty about my exploits would serve me until Chade and I could take counsel and decide exactly which ones were for public discussion.

Ah, that evening. I had made us all tardy, and I realized belatedly that I had significantly heightened Nettle's anxiety by doing so. I walked at her left side and Riddle on her right, and as we processed through the corridors to the Great Hall, she whispered to me that I must come to the dawn meetings in Verity's tower if I was to understand what was happening in Buckkeep Castle. For tonight, follow Chade's lead and if in doubt, Skill to her for direction. I successfully concealed my amusement at her dictatorial tone by watching Riddle endeavouring to master his nervousness.

The Great Hall had been rearranged for the occasion. There was the high table, on its dais so all might watch the king and queen dine. A second, lower, dais had been erected before it for chosen favourites and the dukes and duchesses in attendance. I found it reassuring as it might act as a sort of barricade for any lesser assassin who might try to eliminate me. In the centre of the hall, there was a third dais, bedecked with evergreen and holly thick with berries, as if we were just now commencing to celebrate Winterfest. Starling was seated there, before her harp, in the most extravagant minstrel's garb that I had ever seen. As we entered, she struck a series of chords connected by stair steps of notes. She continued to play as we were seated, softening her volume as a page announced each of us as we took our places on the dais. I was introduced after Nettle and before Riddle, so the ripple of talk at my name muffled any astonishment there might have been to hear him named not only as a landed noble but wed to Lady Nettle.

The food was brought to us swiftly. I am sure it was excellent, though I barely noticed. I ate little and drank less and looked around with wide eyes as if I had never seen the Great Hall before. And in truth, I had not ever seen it from that vantage point. As the dishes were being cleared and wine and brandy brought, Starling struck up her harp more aggressively, and soon launched into a second rendition of last night's song. I noted that she had modified it somewhat, and wondered if that had been Chade or Kettricken's work. This night, there was mention of King Shrewd's jester and how he had aided Kettricken's escape and accompanied her on her flight to her father's house. The Fool was given credit for rescuing me when I was injured and restoring me to Kettricken's side. He was even mentioned as aiding me to wake the stone dragons that had risen to Verity's aid. It pleased

me to hear him given his due before such an august company
and I wished he had been there to hear it.

I was even more astonished at the end, when after her final
notes had nearly finished vanishing to a whisper, she suddenly
struck up a reverential air. From the far end of the hall came
Lady Rosemary, bearing what appeared to be a jewel-studded
casket. As she approached, Starling sang of Verity's regard for me,
and how he had left me a final token of that respect, to be claimed
by me if ever I returned to Buckkeep Castle. I divined what was
in the box even before Lady Rosemary presented it to the king
and queen. Dutiful opened the chest and lifted from it the steel
circlet. It had been polished and it shone. With trembling hands
he took out his father's scroll. I knew with heartfelt certainty that
he had never seen or read it before, for his voice shook as he
read Verity's words. He carried the crown with his lady beside
him until he stood in the centre of the room near Starling's harp.
As she played, he called me forth, to kneel before him while he
set it on my brow. 'Prince FitzChivalry Farseer, son of King-in-
Waiting Chivalry Farseer,' he publicly named me.

And so I was crowned twice that day.

Then he bade me rise and embraced me. A roar of acclaim
rose and for a time faces and sounds seemed to recede around
me. Then, 'Don't faint!' my king exhorted me quietly, and I drew
a deep breath lest that happen. I followed them back to the high
dais, the circlet cold and heavy on my brow.

A long evening followed. The tables were cleared and carried
away. Kettricken's guard was formed up around me, to honour
me, as every duchy was named and their nobility summoned to
greet me. Duchess Celerity was hardest for me to face, but she
had said her words the evening before, and so she but took my
hands and wished me well as her husband offered me a stiff bow.

The Duke and Duchess of Tilth presented another difficulty,
as they escorted their daughter, a sturdy girl of perhaps seventeen
years, and introduced her as Lady Meticulous, 'unspoken for' as
yet. They told me that she enjoyed riding and hawking and
extended an immediate invitation that I might join them on the
morrow for a winter hunt. The girl looked at me with such frank
and undismayed appraisal that I barely managed to respond that

I had a previous engagement and regrettably could not join them. The duchess immediately suggested that perhaps I would be free the next day. I was horribly grateful when Nettle leaned over to say that as she had not seen me for some time, she hoped to occupy most of my days for the next month.

'Ah, then we shall have to invite you to Tilth in the spring,' the girl's father observed brightly as his wife folded her lips in disappointment, and I managed to nod acquiescence to that.

I do not know how many hours we were there. People came, presented themselves, commented on past connections, many of them extremely tenuous, and then moved on. The noise of conversation in the hall was a constant. I looked up to see that Starling had her own circle of admirers asking questions about her adventures. Both she and her husband appeared to be basking in the crowd's adoration. As I was not. I envied them their ability to relax and be flattered. I watched the crowd with an assassin's eyes, noting faces and names, alert for signs of hidden hostility, storing information and connections until I thought my brain would burst. The stares and glares that I noted were not many, but I suspected that for every minor noble who openly disdained the Witted Bastard there would be six who would smile to my face while imagining putting a knife in my back.

The smile on my face felt stiff and aching long before King Dutiful declared that we were all sated with too much good food, good wine and good fortune and that we would now retire. We left as we had arrived, a formal exit from the Great Hall accompanied by the Buckkeep Blue Guard all the way to his private chamber.

It was a large and comfortable room with many cushioned chairs, a wide hearth with a hearty fire in it, and a table laden with yet more refreshments and a selection of brandy and wines. Even when King Dutiful had assured the serving staff that we were fine and dismissed them, I still felt somewhat constrained by the company. They were my closest friends and my family, and it took me a few silent moments to identify my problem. I had been a different person to every single one of them. What role was I expected to play this night? And if I decided to simply be myself, which self was that? The killer Chade had trained, Dutiful's protector and mentor, Riddle's brother-in-arms, Nettle's negligent father? All me and all not me.

Kettricken looked directly at me and heaved a great sigh. 'Oh, my friend, I'm so glad it's all over,' she said, and went to a chair and sat down.

'It's never over,' Dutiful observed wearily.

'But the worst of it is,' his mother asserted. 'For years it has been like a barbed thorn in my heart that Fitz did so much, sacrificed so much, and only a few knew of it. Now they know at least some of what he did. Now he can come home to us, can eat meals with us and walk in the gardens and ride in the hunt, and answer to his rightful name. And his little girl will soon arrive here and come to know the rest of her family!'

'Then will we reveal that Badgerlock is also Fitz? It may bring the rest of his deeds to light if we do, for there are many who know that Badgerlock and Riddle were among those who accompanied Prince Dutiful to Aslevjal. Will people be offended that Lady Molly of Withywoods was married to the Witted Bastard and they lived right under their noses all those years?' Nettle posed her query to all of us.

'But,' Kettricken said, and then fell unhappily silent.

'Let people make up their own explanations,' Riddle chuckled. 'I imagine there will be many who will claim to have known all along, and they will be the ones least likely to ask questions.'

I shot him a gaze of pure admiration. I looked to Chade to see him share that approval, but the old man looked distracted and displeased.

'It will all be sorted out,' Dutiful said comfortingly, 'but it will take time. And simply because Fitz can now move openly within Buckkeep Castle does not mean that he will joyfully give up his quiet life and private ways.' Regretfully, he added, 'Or that all will be glad to see the Witted Bastard return to Buckkeep and polite society.'

Chade abruptly interrupted. 'Nettle, I must ask you to apply your Skill for me. It's Sildwell. I sent him with messages and gifts to Withywoods. He was to Skill to me when he arrived safely. All this evening, I've felt him pecking at my thoughts like a woodpecker on a tree, but his Skill ebbs and flows as if blown by the wind.'

'Sildwell? The apprentice who left the Silver Coterie?' She looked startled and my heart sank a bit. What had Chade been up to?

'Yes. As he seemed unable to get along with his fellows in the coterie and you gave him leave to depart, I thought to train him as a messenger, one that could occasionally employ his Skill-talents as well. He's a tough young man and an excellent horseman.'

'His Skill was erratic,' Nettle observed somewhat acerbically. 'And his manners appalling.'

'Practice may improve both of those things,' Chade replied. 'In any case, I sent him off to Withywoods with messages and small gifts for FitzVigilant and Bee and so on. And he seems to be trying to tell me he has reached Withywoods but he cannot find Bee. And FitzVigilant has been injured. Or burned. I cannot make out what he is trying to convey to me. If you would reach to him?'

'He can't find Bee?' I interrupted.

Nettle shook her head at me, her mouth pinched with disapproval. 'Take no alarm. Sildwell is disorganized and ill mannered. And possibly drunk. There were a number of reasons I chose to discontinue his Skill-training. Let's not panic.'

I took a breath. Chade was scowling. He'd been caught going behind Nettle's back to co-opt a former apprentice as his personal Skilled messenger. I wondered if he'd intended more than that. I noticed he'd mentioned Lant but said nothing of Shun. Was she a bigger secret than I'd realized?

Nettle took a seat on the divan. 'Let's resolve this swiftly and put everyone's mind at ease. Dutiful, will you join us? Fitz?'

Although a joining of Skill-strength did not require physical proximity, each of us moved to be seated beside her. Chade came to stand behind her. As I took my place and opened my Skill to theirs, it felt rather like wading into a river. No. Being a stream merging with a river. Together, we rushed out toward the messenger.

I knew nothing of Sildwell, so I let the others guide us. We reached, I felt the connection, and then it failed and faded. I had never felt such a thing in the Skill. I tried not to let my puzzlement be a distraction. Nettle gathered us as if she were plaiting a rope and again she reached.

Skillmistress! Sildwell seemed as startled as he was relieved. *I cannot . . .* And he was gone, like a voice swept away by wind or the glimpse of someone in a heavy snowfall. *Fog . . . stables fire . . . no one knows of . . . strange folk.*

Fire in my stables? Fear leapt in me and I shoved it down relentlessly. I glanced at Chade. His eyes were wide with fear. I reached behind Nettle, took his hand and squeezed it. Small and tight, I sent a thought to him. *Don't distract the others. First we discover the truth.* I felt his assent but his fear did not abate. I tried to wall in mine. Nettle was taking control of Sildwell. I felt her reach and try to shape him into himself.

Apprentice Sildwell. Gather yourself. Focus. Choose one thought to convey. Be calm. Form the thought in your mind. Hold it. Polish it. Now. Slowly. Extend the thought to me.

So calm and structured. As she instructed Sildwell, I felt Nettle reinforce his awareness of himself as a solid and separate entity from the Skill-current that we all navigated. She abruptly spoke aloud to me. 'Da. Calm yourself. I need your strength right now. Lord Chade. Now is not the time for this panic.' Then, I felt her dismiss us and put her focus back on the youngster. I tried to help her as she attempted to wrap him in confidence. And, *Now,* she invited him.

There is no Lady Bee here. Some folk died in a fire. They all are strange. Then, as if something else flowed and washed against us, his thoughts were swept away. All was fog, as if we were on a grey sea in a grey fog in a constant wash of grey rain. *Frightening . . .* That thought broke through stronger than the others, and then there was nothing. No sense of anyone, anywhere in the Skill-current.

Chade's grip on my hand had tightened. In that physical touch, our rising fears became one thing. I could hear his shuddering breath.

Later. Rest now. Nettle arrowed the thought at Sildwell with a fierce strength, but it was an arrow sent toward a target that no one could see.

We were abruptly seated on a divan in the comfortable chamber in Buckkeep. I shot to my feet. 'I'm going now.'

'Yes,' Chade confirmed. He gripped the back of the divan with both hands.

'What was that?' Dutiful demanded of all of us. I scarcely heard him. Dread was rising in me like cold water in a flood. Something was terribly wrong at Withywoods. A fire in the stables? Lant injured? Bee was there, as good as alone if Lant were injured. So far away from me. 'I'm leaving,' I repeated. My voice had no strength. Chade nodded and reached for me.

'Perhaps a dragon,' Nettle said softly. 'We know that the Stone Dragons often distorted memory and perception when they over flew a battle.'

'The confoundment,' Elliania confirmed. 'Many of our warriors spoke of it. The battle would be lost and over, and few had more than fragmentary memories of what had happened.'

'And the living dragon Tintaglia was able to bend our thoughts and change our Skilling,' Nettle recalled slowly. 'Dragons have visited Bearns. It may be that one had descended on Withywoods. We should wake Thick and see if he can reach through the fog and get some sense out of Sildwell.'

Chade gripped my arm, leaned heavily on me for a moment. 'To my room. I have everything you need there.' He suddenly pulled himself up straight. 'There is no time to lose.'

As we moved toward the door, his strength seemed to come back to him. 'Da?' Nettle asked in consternation.

'I go to Withywoods tonight, via the stones. Riddle, arrange a horse for me, please.'

'Don't you think that—'

I didn't want to waste words or time. I spoke over my shoulder. 'No Lady Bee there? A fire? Regardless of his Skill-ability, all is not well there. I should never have left her there alone.' I reached the door, Chade beside me.

'FitzVigilant is with her,' Nettle reminded me. 'He's young but he has a good heart, Fitz. He would not let harm come to her. I think something or someone has befuddled Sildwell. His talent was always uneven.' She tried to speak calmly but her voice was a notch too high.

'He said Lant was injured. Or burned? If he's injured he can't protect anyone. I'm going now. By the pillars.' The unease I had felt was building to a panic in my chest. I tried to push it down. Be calm. No wild imaginings. Just get there and find out what was real. But the messenger's words stabbed me with a thousand fears. A fire. Bee missing. Had the fire spread to the manor? Had she hidden in the walls and died there, unseen? I dragged in a deep breath and tried to sound reasonable. And calm. 'Once I am there, I will let you know what has happened.'

Nettle opened her mouth to object but Riddle spoke quickly. 'Fitz is right. Let him go. Fitz. Do you want me with you?'

I did. He had Skill-strength to lend and was good with a sword and I had no idea what I was going into. But I would not again leave a daughter unguarded. 'No. But thank you, my friend. Guard what we love here and my mind will be easier for that.'

I had one glimpse of Nettle's grateful face and then the door closed behind us.

'Let's get you on your way,' Chade insisted. From somewhere he had summoned the strength of a much younger man. He hastened down the corridor and up the grand stairs. He took them two at a time and I kept pace with him.

'Chade?' I began and 'Not yet,' he replied breathlessly. His stride lengthened. He ran and I followed. He slammed into his room, startling his valet and a servant stoking the hearth-fire. He dismissed them both abruptly, and they went with much bowing to me, a performance that made me uncomfortable until Chade shut the door on them. Once we were alone, he threw open his wardrobe. 'Your feet are smaller than mine. Can you manage in my boots still?'

'I imagine so,' I said, and he pulled out a heavy pair of riding boots. A thick cloak and a woollen shirt followed, billowing as he threw them toward me.

'Change while I talk,' he instructed me, and his voice was fraught with emotion. I was already dragging on the boots.

'I had bits of Skilling from Sildwell before I asked Nettle to help me. All of it was disturbing. He could find no sign of Lady Bee or Lady Shun. "They are unknown here" he said at one point. Or seemed to say, through a fog and a roaring. He described a "great fire" and I think he told me that your folk there seemed unconcerned by it. You experienced what it was like, trying to receive his thoughts.'

'When?' I demanded. How dare he hide that from me! 'How long ago?'

He stared at me, his anger rising to meet mine. 'Moments before I asked Nettle for help. Did you think I would wait?' He handed me a very plain sword in a leather sheath. There was dust on it, and the belt that held it was stiff. I buckled it around me without comment. I drew it out, looked at it, and sheathed it again. Plain but very well made.

'Give me that,' Chade suggested, and I realized I was still wearing the sword crown. I pulled it free and handed it to him. He tossed it on his bed. I dragged the woollen shirt over my head and shoved my arms out of the sleeves. As I swept the cloak over my shoulders, I told him, 'Tell the Fool why I've gone. He'll understand.'

'Skill to me as soon as you arrive there. Please.'

'I shall.'

I did not care who turned as I passed or who stared after me as I pounded down the great stair and through the halls of Buckkeep Castle and out into the courtyard where a boy held the reins of a fine roan mare. Her eyes were bright with intelligence, her long legs straight and strong. 'Thank you,' I called as I seized her reins and mounted. As I wheeled her toward the gate, the lad shouted something about Lord Derrick's horse, and I saw that a long-legged black was being led toward the steps. I'd taken the wrong horse. But too late. Nothing would turn me back now.

'Go!' I told her, voice and heels, and leaned forward.

ELEVEN

Withywoods

To Prince FitzChivalry
Sir. For many years I have held your secret as closely as you have
held mine. My king entrusted it to me that I might better understand
all that you did in that difficult time. My pride had been gravely injured
by the ruses that you and your friend Lord Golden had played upon
me. I would let you know that for years now I have better understood
your role in those events. I do not forget all you have done for me. I
recall well that but for you I would not be alive today. I write to you
to remind you that I remain ever in your debt, and that if there is ever
any way in which I can serve you, I beg that you will ask it of me.
*   Please know I make this offer with all sincerity.*
*   Lord Civil Bresinga*

The roan mare lifted herself into a gallop and we were through the
gate before anyone had a chance to either challenge us or wave
us through. She was a spirited creature and seemed to relish
the idea of a night gallop. Her Wit shimmered between us, seeking
a confirmation from me that we would become the best of friends.
But my heart was frozen with fear and I held myself small and
still. Her hooves threw up chunks of packed snow from the
carriageway, and the wind of our passage squeezed my face in an
icy grip. A cart trail turned off toward the Witness Stones. The
snowy road was less packed and her pace slowed despite my
efforts to hurry her. I blessed the brief break in the storms that

let the moon and starlight reflect from the snowy fields. I pressed her and as the trail became just a rumpling in the deep snow, she lunged and surged through it. Long before we reached the stones, I had made my decision. Regal's apprentices and journeymen had taken horses through Skill-pillars before. True, some had lost their wits doing it, but I was far more seasoned at the Skill than they had been. And my need was far greater.

At the summit of the hill, I pulled her in, let her breathe, and then reined her close to the stones. *Roan. With me.* I pressed my Wit against all her senses, and it shocked me when she welcomed me. She tossed her head and showed me one white-rimmed eye as I slapped the stone with a bared hand and simultaneously wheeled her in. For a long moment she leapt through a starlit sky, and then we plunged out and she landed, stiff-legged and heaving under me, on the top of Gallows Hill. A three-day journey done in an instant. Wind and falling snow had erased almost every trace of my previous passage. The roan tossed her head, eyes and nostrils wide. Her strange exhilaration swept through me. I fought through a wave of vertigo before I found both common sense and my Wit, then wrapped her in reassurance and comfort, praised her and promised her warmth and oats and fresh water. I walked her down the snowy hill. A small bit of patience now would pay off in the stamina to finish the ride.

Once our path met with a packed trail, I nudged her to a trot, and then as we came to a road, I pushed her up to a gallop. When I felt her begin to labour beneath me, I pulled her in, and again we walked. I had never had a deep faith in either Eda or El, but that night I prayed to Eda that I would find my child hidden but safe. I tormented myself with a thousand theories as to what might have happened. She had been trapped in the walls without food or water. She had been in the stables when they burned. Smoke had overcome her. Shun had done something dreadful to her and then fled after setting the house afire.

But none of my wild theories would explain why my household staff would claim to know nothing of Lady Bee or Lady Shun. I chewed my information a dozen different ways but made a meal from none of it. The night was cold and weariness welled in me. The closer I came to Withywoods, the less inclination I felt to be there. I should have stopped at Oaksbywater for the night. The thought surprised me and I shook my head to clear it from my mind. I pushed the mare back to a gallop, but I felt more heavy-hearted than ever when I saw the lights of Withywoods through the trees.

Steam was rising from the roan's withers when I pulled her in before the manor house. Even in the cold night, I could smell the stench of the burned stables and the animals that had been in it. The loss of the building and the horses were a separate stabbing blow that made real the possibility that I had lost my little daughter as well. But as I swung down from the saddle, shouting for servants and stableboys, my heart lifted that I could see no damage to the house. The fire had not spread. I suddenly felt incredibly weary and woolly-witted. *Bee*, I said to myself, and pushed the haze of sleepiness away.

Chade. I'm here. Stables burned.

My Skill-message went nowhere. It was a terrible sensation, as if for one moment I was smothered and fighting for breath. *Chade! Nettle! Dutiful! Thick!* With each effort, the sense of suffocation increased. The Skill-current was there, I could almost touch it, but something shredded my sending into scattered threads. Exhaustion rose like a tide, stifling my terror. My fear became despair and I abandoned the effort. I shouted again and was relieved to hear my own voice.

A houseman pulled the door open for me and I heard it drag across the threshold. In the light from the lamp he lifted, I saw the damage that had been done to it. Someone had beaten the doors of my home in. That stung me to full alertness again. 'What's happened here?' I demanded breathlessly. 'Where's Revel? Where's FitzVigilant? And Bee and Shun?'

The man goggled at me. 'Who?' he demanded. And then, 'The scribe is long abed, sir. Since his accident, he has been poorly. The whole household is abed, except for me. I can fetch Steward Dixon, but Holder Badgerlock, you look exhausted. Mayn't I build up the fire in your chamber and see you there? And in the morning—'

'How did the stable burn down? Where is my daughter? Where is Lord Chade's messenger Sildwell?'

'Lady Nettle?' the man queried me earnestly, and I gave him up for an idiot. Don't ask questions of idiots: find the likeliest person to have an answer. 'Wake the steward and have him meet me in my private study immediately. Not the estate study, my private study! Have him bring FitzVigilant!'

I strode past the man, snatching the lamp from his hands and shouting over my shoulder, 'And find someone to see to that horse!' before I broke into a run. Bee would be there. I knew she would be there. It was the one place she always felt safe, the secret that only she and I shared. I tried to ignore other damage to the house as I raced through corridors and up stairs. I passed a door that had been forced and still hung off its hinges. A tapestry had sustained a slash and hung crookedly, one corner puddled on the floor. My mind could not encompass it. My stables had been burned, someone had attacked Withywoods and marauded through its corridors, my daughter was missing and the door servant seemed completely at ease with whatever had happened. 'Bee!' I shouted as I ran, and I continued to shout her name until I reached the door of the study. Throughout the house, I heard doors opening and querying voices raised. I didn't care who I roused. Why should anyone be sleeping when the daughter of the house was missing?

The doors of my study had been forced, the fine wood splintered. Two of my scroll-racks leaned drunkenly against one another, their contents spilled to the floor. My desk had been ransacked, my chair overturned. I cared nothing for that destruction nor for any stolen secrets. Where was my little girl? I was panting as I strove to align the doors so that I could close them and work the catch to the hidden labyrinth. 'Bee,' I told her, my voice cracking with hope. 'Papa's home, I'm coming. Oh, Bee, please be there.'

I worked the catch hidden in the door hinge and then hunched over to enter the secret spy-ways that wended their ways behind the panelled corridors of Withywoods. I found her tiny hidey-hole. It was empty and looked untouched, her cushions and pens just as she had left them. The fragrance of one of her mother's candles still hung in the air. 'Bee!' I called, still hoping I might hear an answer from her. Hunched over, I followed her chalk marks toward the entry in the pantry. I was horrified to see other markings on the walls, her clear letters indicating passageways that I'd never explored.

I saw a litter of objects on the floor of the passage ahead and smelled urine. When I reached a spill of unused candles and the mouse-gnawed remains of a loaf of bread, I was completely puzzled. I travelled on toward the pantry exit. There were burned candle stubs discarded on the floor, a wet shawl that was not Bee's mouldering in a pile and then I found the pantry entry door ajar. I shouldered it wider and squeezed out, then shut it firmly behind me. Not even I could see where it had been.

This time of year, there should have been a store of hams and smoked fish and strings of sausages swinging from the storage hooks. There was nothing. Taken as plunder? Sausages? It made no sense. I knew of no one who would attack Withywoods. Adding that the culprits had stolen sausages only made the riddle ridiculous.

I stepped from the pantry into the kitchen. A scullery maid was there, her winter shawl flung around her shoulders over her nightdress. Lark. That was her name, a second cousin to Cook Nutmeg and a recent hire. 'Oh! Holder Badgerlock! Where did you come from? We didn't expect you home so soon, sir!'

'Obviously not! Where is my daughter? And where is Lady Shun?'

'Sir, I'm sure I don't know. I thought you had gone to Buckkeep Castle to see Lady Nettle. And I don't know Lady Shun. Still new here, sir.'

'What happened here while I was gone?' I met her question with one of my own.

She pulled her shawl more warmly around her shoulders. 'Well, sir, you went to town. Scribe FitzVigilant returned and told us you had decided to travel on to Buckkeep Castle. And then we had the Winterfest. And the fire in the stables. And that fight, though no one saw that. Someone was drunk probably, or several someones. Scribe Lant couldn't even say who stabbed him or why. Some of the other men were knocked about, a black eye here, a tooth gone there. You know how menfolk are. And then we had that messenger, who I think is less than a half-wit, with his parcels for folk no one's heard of. And now, tonight, you popping out of the pantry. And that's all I know, sir. Oh, and the steward, shouting us out of bed and telling us to bring you a tray with hot tea and some food to your study. Is that why you're here in the kitchen, sir? Was there something else you wanted?'

I turned away from her prattling and ran once more through the halls of my home. My heart pounded in my ears and I was thirsty but there was no time to stop to drink. I was trapped in a hideous, twisted nightmare, a dragon-tainted dream in which nothing made sense and I could not awaken. Bee's room was empty, the hearth-fire burned out to ashes and the stones long cold, her wardrobe dragged open and her little tunics flung about. I looked under her bed, crying her name hopelessly. I felt I could not drag enough air into my lungs. I could not order my thoughts. I suddenly, desperately wanted to just curl up on her bed and sleep. Not think about any of this.

No. Onward.

I opened Lady Shun's door to the same sort of chaos it always was. I could not tell if her room had been ransacked. Her bed was cold and unslept-in, the bedding dragged half onto the floor. One of the hangings had been torn loose. On I went. My chamber had been rummaged through as well. I didn't care. Where was my child? I left the corridors of bedrooms and ignored the few sleepy and frightened servants I passed in the hall as I ran again to the schoolroom and the scribe's quarters adjacent to it. I flung open the door to FitzVigilant's room and felt an unmanning wave of relief when he sat up in his bed. 'What is it?' he demanded, face pale and eyes wide. 'Oh. Badgerlock! Back so soon?'

'Thank Eda! Lant, where are they, where are Shun and Bee? What happened to the stables?'

The growing consternation on his face made me want to strike him. 'The stables burned down on Winterfest eve. I suppose someone was careless with a lamp. Shunanbee? What is that?'

I was gasping for air now. 'Lady Shun. My daughter, Lady Bee, my little girl. Where are they? Did they perish in the fire?'

'Holder Badgerlock, calm yourself. I do not know the ladies you speak of. Surely your step-daughter is Lady Nettle, the Skillmistress at Buckkeep Castle?'

He sat up slowly and painfully, his blankets falling back to reveal heavy bandaging around his chest. It startled me. 'What happened to you?' I demanded.

His eyes flew wide and for a moment his pupils became so large I felt I looked into blackness inside his head. Then he rubbed his face with both hands and when he looked at me again, a sickened and awkward smile spread over his face. 'So embarrassing to admit this. I drank too much on Winterfest eve. I was found after the fire. Somehow I took a stab wound. Possibly from a hayfork or a tool of some kind during the fire? It seems to have missed anything vital, but given the injuries I was already recovering from, it has made me an invalid again. I must apologize to Lady Nettle that I have been quite unable to function as an instructor for the children since then.'

I staggered to a chair and sat down. The room whirled around me. Lant regarded me with deep concern. I could not stand his stupefied sympathy. I wanted to pound his face to a bloody ruin with my fists. I closed my eyes and reached out to the king's Skill-coterie.

I have been in howling storms in which a shout is reduced to a whisper, moved across the sea's featureless face in a grey fog that does not yield to human eyes. That was what I found. My Skill was quenched, damped like wet firewood that will not catch regardless of the flame put to it. I focused, I strained my Skill to a needle-point, then flung it wide to the sky. Nothing. I was trapped in my body. I could not reach for help. I wondered suddenly how I could be sure I was not in a dream of a dragon's making. Could I be sure I was not trapped inside the Skill-pillar and this all some insane illusion of my own making? What test could I give myself?

'Where is Revel?' I demanded of FitzVigilant. Again he stared at me blankly. 'I told Dixon to bring you and Revel, and meet me in my private study. Oh.' Perhaps it was unreasonable to expect him to find me here in Lant's room. I rose. 'Get up, Lant. I need you with me.'

Something flickered in his eyes. I thought he would whine and protest that he was hurt and it was the middle of the night. Instead I think I glimpsed, finally, the man that Nettle and Riddle had claimed him to be. 'Give me a moment,' he said quietly. 'And I will be with you. In your private study?'

'The estate study,' I amended.

I left him there, rising slowly and stiffly from his bed. My boots rang in the halls as I strode back to the study. Time after time, I saw the marks that suggested there had been armed invaders in my home. A long score down the panelling as if an edged weapon had been parried aside and dragged there. A broken wall sconce.

The double doors to the estate study had been battered open. Inside the room, a tray with a steaming pot of tea and sliced meat, bread and cheese awaited me. There were slashes in the hangings that covered the doors to the garden and something dark had stained the carpet. The wolf in me woke. I took a deep snuff of the room. Old blood. That was blood, on the floor of my study. The wolf within me crouched low and every sense I possessed suddenly flared. There was danger here still. *Be still, be silent, and watchful.*

Dixon, Revel's assistant arrived, bearing a tray with brandy on it. 'It's so pleasant to have you home again, sir, even on such short notice. I went to your private study, but when you were not there, I brought your food here.' His words said one thing, his tone quite another. He was a short stout man, dressed impeccably, even at this late hour. He smiled at me.

Contained. Time to be contained. Everything I felt was compressed into a cold stone box. I needed answers. 'Thank you. Put it on the table and sit down, Dixon.'

I waited until he had tentatively settled on a chair. He looked around and gave a tiny sigh of disapproval. The put-upon servant summoned late by the unworthy master. I watched him with every fibre of my being as I asked him, 'Where is Steward Revel tonight?'

I got what I had feared. That wash of confusion across his face, his dilated pupils and then a shamed laugh as he said, 'Sir, I don't know of whom you speak. I am steward for Withywoods. Or have I displeased you so that this is how you tell me I am replaced?'

'Not at all. Revel was steward before you, of course. Do you recall him now?'

The confusion again and a flickering of fear on his features.

Then his face smoothed. 'I'm sorry, sir, I do not. I think . . . perhaps he had left before I was hired?'

'Lady Shun spoke highly of you.'

Confusion crawled toward panic. 'Sir, I don't know—'

'And little Lady Bee.' I pressed blindly on, not knowing what I was seeking, but willing to crack the man like a nutshell to get at the knowledge I needed.

'Bee . . .'

'Who set fire to the stables?'

He made a sound without words.

'Who attacked the manor? Did they take Lady Bee and Lady Shun? Kill them? What happened?'

The man's head bobbed and his chest heaved. His lips puffed in and out with his audible breathing. He rocked back and forth in his chair, his mouth working wordlessly. Froth began to gather at the corner of his mouth.

'Holder Badgerlock! Sir! Please!' A shrill young voice full of anxiety. Out in the corridor, another outraged voice shouted, 'You, boy, come back here! Don't you dare go in there!'

I turned my head away just as Dixon collapsed to the floor. He twitched and shuddered. A fit. I'd had many in my lifetime. My conscience squirmed but I kicked it aside and left him jerking as I turned to see who had interrupted me.

It was Tallerman's son. The stableboy with the unlikely name. His face was white and strained, and he carried one arm curled protectively against his chest. He darted toward me as the study door was snatched wide open by an outraged Bulen. Lant's manservant had obviously dressed hurriedly, for his shirt was half-buttoned. 'Your pardon, Holder Badgerlock. This boy is ill and half-mad, and this is how he repays our care of him! Young sir, come with me immediately, or risk being turned out in the morning.'

'Holder Badgerlock! Say you know me! Please, say you know me!' The boy's voice had gone shrill and broken as Bulen advanced on him. He leaned away from Bulen's grasping hand as he made his plea.

'Of course I know you. You're Tallerman's son, from the stables.' I turned to Bulen and spoke severely. 'And it is not your place to turn out any of my people, Bulen!'

Bulen halted where he stood. He had not been long employed at Withywoods. I had assigned him to be Lant's manservant. He was still learning his duties. And his place. He looked at me uncertainly as he protested, 'Sir, the boy is a beggar, found injured and taken in. He insisted on speaking with Scribe FitzVigilant when we found him, and the scribe summoned a healer and has allowed him to stay in the classroom during his recovery. But he speaks wild and fearsome and . . .'

'Leave, Bulen. Take Dixon with you and put him in his bed. I'll deal with the boy. Perseverance. That's it, that's your name, isn't it?'

'Oh, thank the gods, you know me, I'm not mad! I'm not a beggar! Sir, sir, they came and they killed and burned, and I tried to get away with her, I got her on a horse and we rode, but they shot me and I fell. And I didn't know any more until they were leaving and they went past me in a sleigh drawn by white horses and I saw Bee, all wrapped in white furs, in the sleigh. They took her, sir, and they left the stables afire, and no one here but me even tried to put out the flames. Some of the horses got out and some were stolen I think and some burned in their stalls. With my pa and grandpa's bodies, sir! I saw them dead there! And my own ma does not know me and says she never had such a son as me! Oh, sir, they took Bee, they took her and no one knows me. No one!'

'I know you,' I said in a trembling voice. 'I know you, boy. Oh my Bee! Was she hurt? Who were they? Where did they go?'

But the lad had begun to shake as if he had an ague, and when I put my arms around him to steady him, he fell toward me, crying like a much younger child. I gathered him to my chest and held him, my thoughts racing. He spoke against my chest. 'They shot me. I felt the arrow go right through me. Through my shoulder,' he sobbed. 'I woke up under a cloak. Her cloak. She hid me with it, I think. I kept it. So fine and light. I was trying to save Bee and she saved me.'

My mind leapt. 'A butterfly cloak.'

'Yes sir.'

'Come over by the fire. Sit down.' I looked around. Bulen still stood in the doorway, eyes wide. Dixon lay on the floor, no longer jerking, but lying half-curled on his side, staring at nothing. 'Bulen!' I snapped and the young man jumped. 'See to Dixon. Take him to his bed. Then ask Scribe FitzVigilant to give me bandages and some of the salves Lord Chade gave him, if he has any left. Go quickly.'

'I can fetch the salves for you, if you wish.' That was Lant, holding onto the doorframe with one hand. He looked pale and as his gaze took in Dixon on the floor, he demanded, 'What is going on here? Is this boy bothering you with his wild tales?'

'Lant. Just the salves and bandages, please. Let Bulen deal with Dixon. He's had some sort of fit.' Then I ignored all of them as I steered the stable-lad toward the fire. I hooked a chair with one foot and dragged it close to the hearth. 'Sit here, Perseverance. And let me see your injury.'

The boy sat down as soddenly as an armful of wet laundry. He hunched there, staring at the fire. I left him and went to the brandy. I poured a jot, tossed it down, and then poured another and took it to the boy. 'Drink this,' I told him. He didn't respond. I leaned down to look in his face. He shifted his eyes to meet mine. I put the glass in his hand.

'They said I was a beggar. And crazy. My own Ma wouldn't let me in the door. I was all blood and she sent me up to the manor and wouldn't take me in.' His voice rose higher and higher on each word until it ended in a strangled squeak.

I said the only words I had to comfort him. 'I know you,' I said. 'You are Perseverance, son of Tallerman, grandson of Tallman, and you worked in my stables. You cared for my daughter's horse and you've been teaching her to ride. Drink that.'

He lifted the glass and smelled it. He took a sip, shuddered, but at a look from me, drank the rest in a gulp. He gasped and took three breaths before he could speak. 'What happened to them? What's wrong with them? All of them? I told them Steward Revel was dead and they said, "Who's Revel?" I said, "They took Bee. We have to go after her!" and they said they didn't know her. And when I tried to go after her by myself, they accused me of trying to steal her horse.'

I refilled his glass. 'You went after them?' Did he know where they'd taken her?

'I tried, sir. But the snow and the wind erased everything. I had to turn back. I was still bleeding. I'm so sorry, sir. I'm sorry I didn't bring her back.'

'Perseverance. I don't know what happened here, but we will puzzle it out. First you have to think back to the very beginning. I saw you watching us as we left for Oaksbywater. You were about to exercise a horse. Tell me everything from there. Every single thing. As it happened. Each and every thing you remember from that moment on. Go on. Drink the brandy. One gulp and it's down. There. Oh, it wasn't that bad, was it? Now. Talk to me. Just talk.'

I thudded a chair down facing him and sat, our knees almost touching. I focused myself on him, Wit and Skill. I felt almost nothing from him with my Skill-sense. Some folk were like that. But all of us live inside animals and even though I did not know him well, we had both loved Bee. So I did as Burrich had done so often to me, breathing calmness and safety at him, willing that he would smell and sense that I was here to protect him and he was safe. I forced my own body to relax as well and I slowed my breathing. In a few moments, I saw his shoulders ease. Brandy and the Wit. 'Just talk to me,' I suggested again. He nodded slowly.

He was well into describing a day of ordinary stablework when Lant brought the bandages and salves. I motioned the scribe to be silent and sit down. He was grateful to do so. As Perseverance spoke of his routine day and the tears for things lost rolled down his cheeks, I opened his shirt and looked at his shoulder. I doubted the bandage had been changed today. He winced as I peeled it off him. The wound was ugly. The arrow had gone through his shoulder, but not as cleanly as I'd hoped. His injury had been given all the careful attention that I'd expect most healers to devote to a beggar-child.

I set out salves and bandaging and washed the wound front and back with wine. He gritted his teeth when I picked at a scrap of his shirt fabric working out of the wound. I got a grip on it and tugged it out. Blood followed. He looked down at it and went paler. 'Keep talking,' I told him and he recounted how a man had come with a donkey and cart and some abused bull-pups. I nodded, and washed his shoulder again with the wine.

I was pushing salve into the wounds when he told me what I didn't know, which was how Lant and Lady Shun and Bee had returned late that night. Lant had escorted Shun into the house and left my Bee in the cold and snowy wagon. Lant's brow wrinkled at the tale, and when the boy told of the house steward coming to carry her inside, Lant stood up and said stiffly, 'I don't know why you are listening to the boy. He's either mad or malicious beyond explaining. I know nothing of a Lady Shun, nor a child named Bee. Call the house steward and see what Dixon has to say of this wild tale.'

'Sit down,' I said to Lant through gritted teeth. Something had been done to his mind, and I could forgive him not recalling Bee or Shun, but I could not forgive how he had left my child to the care of a stableboy and a house steward after I had placed her in his care. 'Be absolutely silent. And no, you are not dismissed to your room. Stay until I tell you that you may go.'

'Do you speak this way to me because I am a bastard? For my blood is just as good as yours and—'

'I doubt that. I am Prince FitzChivalry, as you well know, son of King-in-Waiting Chivalry Farseer, and now recognized as such by the king. So sit and be silent.'

Such a dark moment to flaunt my grand new status. He looked at me, uncertain how to react. Then he closed his lips. I took out my belt-knife and began to cut bandaging to the proper size. 'You are truly him? The Witted Bastard?' Those words came from Perseverance. The boy's eyes were wide.

'I am.'

I did not expect what he next said. A tremulous smile broke on his tear-stained face. 'He was right. He did know. My grandfather said as much, for he knew your father and said no one could be mistaken who had seen him. My father used to agree with him, but I think it was only so he would stop insisting on it. Sir, I am proud to serve you, as my family has served your family for generations. And here and now, I vow my loyalty to you. And to your daughter, Princess Bee. Forever and ever.'

'Thank you.' What else does one say when a boy promises his life and loyalty? I closed my heart to the storm of emotions his words woke in me and spoke soothingly. 'Continue telling me what happened, Perseverance.'

'I mean it, sir.' A boy's tender feelings that such an offer might be disdained as childishness rode in his words.

'I know you do.' I spoke severely. 'And right now, I am holding you to it. I need what you are doing now. I need to know every bit of what you know. Keep talking.'

And so I heard of how he had gone to his lessons the next day, and my daughter had been there. He spoke of his conversation with Bee and how she had told him what I'd done. She'd been proud of me. Proud. I glanced at Lant as the lad spoke. His face was a mixture of emotions. Did he remember snatches of that day, scrubbed clean of Shun's presence? But as Perseverance began to tell of the sounds they had heard and how Lant had gone to see what they were, the scribe began shaking his head again. I gave him a look and he stopped.

So I learned that Revel had spent the last moments of his life trying to save the Withywoods children. Truly, I'd never given the man the credit he deserved. And as the tale wound on, I heard of my Bee hiding the children where she had believed they would be safe, only to be deprived of that safety herself. Perseverance told me of the slaughter he'd seen in the stables, slain men sprawled with their throats cut as they did their daily chores, his own father and grandfather among them, and of stepping over bodies to saddle Priss, and the wild ride he and Bee had made in the hope of getting help.

His detailed account of the attack ended with the arrow. He had come to consciousness only in time to see them leaving with Bee. He had returned to the manor, to the stables still on fire and the folk he had known all his life denying that he had ever existed. I stopped him there. He had begun to shake as he spoke of it. 'That's enough. Let it go for now, Perseverance. I know the truth of your words. Now. I want you to think, but not speak, of the people you saw. Think about each one of them, and when you are ready, tell me about them, one at a time.' This, I had been taught by Chade, was the best way to gain information from one who had not been trained to report as I had. A question such as 'was he tall?' or 'was he bearded?' could

carry the untrained mind to imagining something that had not
been there.

He was silent as I bandaged his shoulder. It was infected, but
no worse than such wounds always were. When I had finished, I
helped him with his shirt and then brought him food and another
jot of brandy. 'Drink that first. Down in a gulp. Then you can
eat while you talk to me.'

He took the brandy down, gasped and choked even more than
he had on the first two, and quickly took a piece of bread to clear
the taste from his mouth. I waited. He was as close to drunk as
I wanted him, his thoughts wide and unguarded. And he told me
what I would expect a stableboy to notice. White horses, with
peculiar flat saddles and big horses suited for men who might wear
chainmail. Saddles on the big horses that sounded almost
Chalcedean in design.

They spoke a foreign tongue. I asked no question, but he told
me of a man on a horse who shouted, '*krintzen, krintzen!*' over
and over.

Kar inte jhen. Chalcedean for 'sit down'.

Chalcedeans in Buck. A raiding force? One that had crossed
Shoaks Duchy and Farrow to raid an isolated manor in Buck?
Why? To steal my daughter? It made no sense. Not until he told
me that a pleasant-faced woman was with them, seeking a pale
boy or young man. Then I knew what they had come seeking.
The Unexpected Son, the child that the Fool's messenger had
urged me to find and protect. I still had no idea who or where
that lad might be, but the puzzle began to make sense. Hostages
to exchange. Who better to take than the daughter of the house
and a noble lady?

When he spoke of how markedly pale some of the younger
invaders were, the ones who wielded no weapons but aided those
who did, when he spoke of their light hair and pale eyes and
their pale garments, my blood ran cold. Were these the messenger's pursuers? Of course they were. She had said she was being
hunted. The Fool's wild warnings were suddenly solid and real.
These pale folk must be Servants from Clerres. As the Fool had
warned me, the Servants had been tracking the messenger. And
following him as well? Would they want to recover the Fool as

well as find this Unexpected Son? Did they think I had found and concealed him at Withywoods and so sought him there? But what were they doing with Chalcedeans? Were they mercenaries in their hire? How had they come so far and deep into Buck Duchy without being reported to anyone? There was a regular patrol that rode the king's highways, mostly to discourage highwaymen, but also to take reports of unusual events. A troop of horses of that size, ridden by obvious foreigners would certainly have been reported to them. If people remembered seeing them.

'That's all I remember, sir.' The boy looked drained. And suddenly appeared as tired as I felt. I doubted that he had been sleeping well.

I sorted the information I had and tried to find sense in it. They would have taken Bee and Shun as hostages. They would want the Unexpected Son in trade for them. I did not have him, but I did have the Fool. Could I use him as bait to lure them in? Did he have the strength to agree to such a gambit?

And then my logic fell into discordant pieces. If Bee was a hostage, their power was in dangling her before me, not vanishing without a trace and clouding the memories of those they left behind. Unless they had a stronghold close by, a secure place from which to negotiate. What would I do in their place? Take the hostages to the Chalcedean border or the seacoast? Negotiate from there, demand that we bring the Unexpected Son there? Perhaps. 'Eat some food. I'll be back in a moment.' I turned and pointed a finger at Lant. 'Stay there. I want to talk to you.'

He didn't say a word.

As I walked down the corridor to the chamber that had been Bee's nursery, the enormity of the disaster suddenly swept through me. I staggered to one side and caught myself on the wall. I stood for a moment, my vision black at the edges. Then with a surge I slashed at my weakness, damning it for daring to overcome me just when I most needed to be calm and rational. All emotion must be contained until I had all the information I needed with which to plan a course of action. Now was not the time to hate myself or give in to useless wishes for what I should have, might have, could have done. There was only the now, and I must be keen and remorseless if I was to find and follow their trail. I entered the nursery. Here, at least, no one had bothered to toss furniture and search for plunder. Perhaps no one had hidden here, perhaps the room had been missed. Why couldn't Bee have hidden here and been safe? Useless question.

I found cushions and a blanket and went back to my study. I threw them down on the hearth, refusing to feel anything about Molly's pretty things so roughly used. I pointed at them. 'Perseverance. After you've eaten, rest there. Try to sleep. If you recall anything more, no matter how trivial it might seem, I want to hear it.'

'Sir,' he said. He put his attention back on the food, hunching over it like a half-starved hound. He'd probably been unable to eat much the last few days. Now he would eat and then he'd be able to sleep. I looked at him for a moment. Fatherless, unknown to his mother, and I was the only one in his world who remembered his name. Mine, now, sworn to me. First vassal for the bastard prince. So fitting, somehow.

I seized my chair, dragged it across the room and sat down facing Lant. I'd moved so close that he had to sit up straight to avoid his sprawled legs tangling with mine as I sat down. 'It's your turn. Tell me everything you remember from the time I cut the dog's throat.'

He stared at me and then licked his lips. 'We had gone to town. And a man was cruel to his dog, so you knocked him down and gave the dog a quick death.'

'Why had we gone to town, Lant?'

I watched his face, saw his mind skip and jump, finding what he was allowed to recall. 'To get some more tablets for my students.'

I nodded. 'Then we went to the inn to eat. And both Riddle and I left in a hurry. Why?'

He swallowed. 'You didn't say.'

I nodded again. I moved toward him, not with my body, but first with my Wit, sensing him as another living creature, and then with my Skill. I did not know if I could push into his mind, but I suspected someone had. I recalled a brief conversation I'd had with Chade. He'd asked me if I thought the Skill could be used to make a man forget something. I'd told him I didn't want to consider ever using the magic that way. Both times I'd seen it done had been disastrous for me. When my father Chivalry had made the Skillmaster Galen forget how much he hated him, the man had turned his hatred for my father onto his son. The irony was that Galen had used the magic in a similar way on me. He'd invaded my mind and left me 'misted' as Verity had put it. Galen had used his Skill to convince me that I had little talent for the magic. Even after my king had done his best to clear the clouds from my mind, I'd never had full confidence in my abilities again. I'd always wondered if that forced forgetting had been what made my Skill-magic so erratic.

I didn't want to invade the man's mind. My repeated questioning of Dixon had not given me any information and had pushed him into a seizure. I couldn't risk that with Lant. From what Perseverance had told me, Lant had taken that stab wound when he'd been held captive with the others in the carriageway. Did that mean he'd tried to fight them? Perhaps that was where I should begin.

'Let me see your injury,' I requested.

He startled and leaned back from me. 'The healer has treated it. It's healing as well as could be expected.'

'And what did he say it looked like?'

'It's a puncture. From a tine.'

'Or a blade. He said it looked like a sword thrust, didn't he?'

His eyes went very wide. He began to shake his head, a small denial at first and then a more frantic one.

'Sir? Prince FitzChivalry Farseer?'

I turned my attention from him to the man who stood in the doorway, startled at how he had named me. He was young, scarcely past his teens and dressed in the livery of a royal messenger. His nose and the tops of his cheeks were bright red with cold and he looked exhausted. 'Sildwell,' I greeted him.

He looked mildly surprised that I knew his name. 'Yes. They told me to come back here and talk to you.'

I heaved a sigh. 'Come in, get warm by the fire, and please start this conversation as if you have at least a little training as a messenger.'

'It's the fog,' he said. He walked to the fire and stood beside Perseverance. 'It makes it hard to care. All I want to do is sleep and not think about anything.' I became aware the boy had curled up and was deeply asleep on the floor. The messenger looked down at him, glanced at the glowering FitzVigilant, and then stood straighter. Reaching into the satchel at his side, he took out the baton that proclaimed him a true messenger. He held it as he spoke. 'Sir, I bring you tidings from Lord Chade of Buckkeep Castle. I was to deliver these tidings and gifts to Lady Bee, Lady Shun and Scribe FitzVigilant of Withywoods. But on arriving here, I was told that two of those recipients were unknown here. I endeavoured to Skill this information to Lord Chade to request his further instructions. Although I am not highly Skilled, I have never encountered difficulties with the simple relaying of information. This time, however, I was not able to make myself understood. I next undertook to send a messenger bird. I asked for one to be brought to me and was told the manor had no such birds. I knew that was untrue. I found all the birds dead on the floor of the pigeon-house. Throttled, their necks broken. No one had even cleared the bodies away. When I endeavoured to bring this to the attention of the steward, he said that the manor had no pigeon-house. He said this as he stood looking at it with me.

'I believe you were with the others when Lady Nettle attempted to Skill to me. You already know how little success we had. After a long and frustrating day of disbelief and lies, I decided to go down to Withy and have a glass of ale. My insistence that I had a message for two non-existent ladies had not made me the most welcome fellow here. But as I rode, the fog and heaviness that seemed to fill the air began to dissipate. By the time I reached Withy, I was able to communicate clearly with Lord Chade and the King's Own Coterie. They directed me to return here as swiftly as possible and say that Thick and Lord Chade hope to arrive here by morning. He directed me to arrange to have mounts waiting for them at the Judgment Stone on Gallows Hill as soon as there is daylight. So I did.' He looked uneasy for a moment. 'I feared no one here would obey me, so I hired horses in Withy, to be taken to the Gallows Hill in the morning. I said you would pay very well.'

'Thank you,' I said. 'Will Lady Nettle not accompany Lord Chade and Thick?'

He raised his brows. 'Sir, I was told she is with child. Hence she cannot use the pillars.'

'And why not?'

'It was in a recent translation that Lord Chade brought to our attention. Perhaps you have not heard of it. A pregnant Skill-user who moves through the stones often emerges, er, unpregnant.'

'She miscarries her child?'

'No, sir. It's darker than that. Her pregnancy vanishes. There are two accounts of it happening. And a third account of a fine mare that was led through a Skill-portal to be serviced by a stallion. Close to her time to bear, she was taken home again, but emerged from the Skill-pillar empty-wombed.'

Cold rose in me. I had never heard of such a thing. It came to me again that we knew nothing of how the portals worked. An unborn child vanished. To where? How? It didn't matter in some ways. Gone was gone. I spoke faintly. 'Thank Eda Chade found that scroll!'

'Yes sir. So Lady Nettle will stay behind. Lord Chade and Thick will come here to experience this fog I've described. And perhaps to see if Thick can prevail against it.'

I tried not to feel hope. I dreaded seeing Chade and telling him that I had no idea what had become of Shun. Time to dig a bit more. I rang for a servant and waited. When some small time had passed, I stepped out into the hall and shouted for Bulen. As I re-entered the room, FitzVigilant asked, 'Are you finished with me? Can I go back to my bed now? I am not well, as you can see.'

I tried to speak kindly. 'I can see that, Lant. And I see something that you cannot see. Your mind has been hazed. Things have happened here in the last few days that you can no longer recall. You know what the Skill-magic is; you've heard of it. Someone has used the Skill or something very like it to confuse you. You walk past carpet stained with blood, and doors that have been battered open and you see nothing odd. Servants have been slaughtered and you do not miss them. Two of our household are missing. Lady Bee, my young daughter, has been taken, and Lady Shun has vanished. I don't know if she was killed and her body burned in the stable fire, or if she is also kidnapped.' My voice had begun to shake. I paused and took several long breaths. 'Tonight I will try to find out if anyone in our household recalls any detail of that night. For that sleeping lad is truly a stableboy born and bred here, the third generation of his family to serve mine. And he spoke the truth, a truth you cannot recall.'

FitzVigilant's face had grown more and more still as I spoke. Halfway through my speech, he had begun to shake his head. When I had finished, he sat back in his chair and folded his arms on his chest. 'Holder Badgerlock, you sound as mad as he does.'

'I'm sure I do. But I assure you, I am not. Where is Bulen?'

'Gone back to bed, I imagine. As I wish I could.'

I wanted to strike him. Then, as swiftly as the hot anger had come, it drained out of me. He could not help how clouded his mind was. I looked at Sildwell. 'It's hopeless,' he said. 'Perhaps Lord Chade and Thick will be able to get through to him. But I have never felt anything like this myself. As if I think and move through a thick soup of weariness and discouragement.'

I was silent for a moment. 'I thought it was only me,' I said.

He shook his head. 'No. The further I got from this place, the more my spirits lifted and my mind cleared. Making myself come back was difficult. I simply did not want to travel up the road. It's like someone placed a magical spell over all of Withywoods to discourage visitors.'

'Maybe they did,' I wondered grudgingly. I looked at FitzVigilant and tried to make my voice kind. 'Go to bed, Lant. I'm sorry for all that has befallen you, for what you know and what you don't know. Go to bed and sleep while you can. Tomorrow will be a long and weary day for all of us.'

Lant needed no more urging. He rose and glared at me with narrowed eyes. 'Wakened in the middle of the night to be insulted and ordered about. This is not why I came here.'

He was angry. As I would have been angry, I imagined. I tried to keep my voice level. 'If you could remember that Nettle and Chade actually sent you here as a tutor for young Lady Bee . . .' Then I gave it up as hopeless.

He turned from me and went out of the door without a word. I turned to Sildwell. 'Did they give you a chamber?'

'They did.'

'Then I suggest you get what rest you can as well.'

'Thank you, sir.' He tipped his head toward the brandy. 'Would you mind if I took that with me for company?'

He was certainly not a shy fellow. Appalling manners indeed. I liked him. 'Go ahead. And thank you for all you have done today.'

'You're welcome, sir. But I shall be very happy to leave your home as soon as I possibly can.' He sketched me a bow and hooked the bottle of brandy on his way to the door.

I sat down in the chair that Lant had vacated and stared at the fire. I could not feel anything. I tried to find my heartache over Bee, my anger at what had happened, but not even my guilt came to torment me. Discouragement as thick as soup. I felt useless, helpless and weary. Sildwell was right. A cloud of dullness and discouragement hung over Withywoods. Sadness was all I could provoke in myself. I should be furious. I should thirst for vengeance. Instead I thought of killing myself. No. Not yet. I rose and covered the stableboy more warmly. My vassal.

I took a candle and wandered the halls. I went first to my own room, but could not settle there. I went again to Lady Shun's room, but if there were clues in that disorder, they escaped me. I did not like the woman, but had no desire to see her kidnapped or dead and burned. I went to Bee's room. Amongst the scattered possessions I glimpsed the seashells we had bought for her strewn across the floor. And the warm red shawl sprawled across a chair. The kerchiefs she had intended for Revel rested undisturbed on a table by her bed. She'd never had the pleasure of gifting them to him.

I left her room and drifted through the halls until I came to my ruined study. I entered and almost thought of building a fire there and ordering my thoughts by writing them down. Instead, I triggered the secret door and returned to Bee's tiny hidden chamber. As I turned the corner to enter it, my Wit told me that someone awaited me there. I felt a sudden leap of hope only to confront a small black cat blinking resentfully at my candlelight. He was curled on the cushions in perfect ease and regarded me as an annoying but unimportant intruder. We looked at one another.

She's not here.

She is Bee?

The girl who promised me fish and sausage if I would catch rats and mice for her.

I contained my impatience. *Someone stole her. Can you tell me about the people who took her?*

They took all the fish. And the sausages, too.

I noticed that. What else?

Some of them stank. Some did not.

I waited for a time. Cats themselves may be very chatty, but they seem to resent it in anyone else. Cats like listeners. But when he had sat regarding me for some time, I dared to ask, *Anything else?*

They came for her. The ones that did not stink.

What?

A silence fell between us. My question went unanswered. Finally I said aloud, 'I wonder if they found all the fish and sausages? I think I shall go down to the pantry to find out.'

I took my shortened candle and left him, eeling my way through the wandering passages. I stepped over the gnawed bread, and took up one of the fallen candles and kindled it from my failing one. It had been nibbled by mice, but not badly. I listened at the door before pushing it open and emerging into the storage room. The sacks of beans and peas and grains had been left. The raiders had taken meat and fish, the two supplies that any traveller depletes first. Could I deduce anything from that?

Gone. Confirmed the cat.

'Do you care for cheese at all? Or butter?'

The cat looked at me speculatively. I pushed the door to the labyrinth closed and went into the cold room. It was down a short stairway into a room lined with stone. Here on shelves were crocks of summer butter and wheels of cheese. Either the raiders had not fancied these or they had not discovered the cold room. I took out my belt-knife and carved a wedge of cheese. As I did so, I became aware that I was hungry. I felt shamed by that. My child and Lady Shun had vanished from Withywoods. Carried off by brutes into the cold and dark. How could I feel such ordinary things as hunger? Or sleepiness?

Yet I did.

I pared off another generous wedge and went back to the kitchen. The cat followed me and when I sat down at the table, he leapt up and sat down on it. He was a handsome fellow, very tidy in black and white, the picture of health save for the kink in his tail. I broke off a chunk of the cheese and set it down before him. By the time I returned to the table with a piece of bread and a mug of ale, he had finished it and hooked a second slab toward himself. I ignored that. We ate together and I tried to be patient. What could a cat know, I wondered, that would do me any good?

He finished before I did and sat cleaning his whiskers and dabbing at his face. When I set my mug down on the table, he stopped and looked at me. *The ones that didn't stink had no scent of their own at all.*

A shiver ran up my spine. The Scentless One, my wolf had called the Fool. Because he had no scent. And he was invisible to my Wit. Would that be true of all folk with White in their bloodlines?

Once they had her, they stopped killing. They took only her. And one other.

I did not appear too interested. I rose and went back to the cold room. I emerged with more cheese. I sat down at the table, broke off a respectable piece and placed it before the cat. He looked down at it, and then up at me. *They took a woman.*

Lady Shun.

I do not bother with the names of humans. But that might have been her name. He bent his head to eat his cheese.

'The girl who promised you fish and sausages. Did they . . . hurt her?'

He finished part of the cheese, sat up, and then suddenly decided to groom his front claws. I waited. After a time, he looked up at me. *I scratched her once. Hard. She took it.* He hunched over the remainder of the cheese. *Pain is not the thing she fears.* I teetered between feeling comforted and horrified. I left him eating and went back to the estate study. The boy did not stir as I put the last of the wood into the fire. With a sigh, I took up Chade's wet cloak and the lantern I'd earlier taken from the door servant. I lit it again and carried it down the hall.

My errand had been firewood, but when I stepped outside into the clear night, my mind cleared. The bite of the cold seized me and the terrible lassitude that was misting my mind receded a bit in the physical discomfort. I walked instead to the burned ruin of my stables. As I did so, I crossed the drive in front of Withywoods. Snow had fallen recently. There were no tracks to read. I moved in wide circles around the stable and then between the house and stables, looking for sleigh tracks. But the fresh snow had gentled all tracks to dimples. The tracks the runners had left were indistinguishable from the marks of the carts and wagons we used on the estate. I walked through the darkness down the long drive that led up to Withy. Somewhere, Per had bled and somewhere Bee had been captured. But I found no traces of either event. I found my horse's tracks, and the hoofprints of Sildwell's horse. No others. No one else had come this way for days. Falling snow and wind had softened all traces of the raiders' passage as smoothly as whatever magic had misted my people's memories of them.

I stood for a time staring off into the darkness as the wind chilled and stiffened my body. Where had they taken my child and why? What good was it to be a prince if he was as helpless as a penniless bastard?

I turned and walked slowly up the carriageway to the manor, feeling as if I breasted an icy winter storm. I did not want to go to this place. With every step, I felt more downhearted. I went slowly to one of the firewood stacks and filled a sling of my cloak with enough wood for what remained of the night. My steps dragged as I carried it up the steps of my home.

TWELVE

The Shaysim

Corioa, the first Servant, wrote thus of his White Prophet: 'He is not the first to come, nor will he be the last. For to every generation is given one who walks amongst us and by virtue of his ability to see all the possibilities, guides us to the best future there may be. I have chosen to call myself his Servant, and to record the dreams of my pale master, and to keep count of the ways in which he makes the crooked path straight and safe.'

So Corioa was the first to name himself Servant. Some think he was also Terubat's Catalyst. As to that, the records from that day are so fragmented that this Servant thinks it an unsafe assumption.

And contrary to many Servants who have gone before me, and been the primary recorders of the deeds of the White Prophet of their days, I will state clearly what some may rebuke me for. Must there be only one? And if this is so, who determines who that single White Prophet is from among those who show us a pale face and colourless eyes? And exactly when, pray tell, does a 'generation' begin and end?

I ask these questions not to spread discord or doubt, but only to plead that we Servants open our eyes as wide as those of the White Prophets we serve. Let us admit there are many, many futures. At countless crossroads, the future becomes the past and an infinite number of possibilities die as an infinite number are born.

So let us no longer call the pale child Shaysa, Who Is The One, as we used to name him in our most ancient tongue. Let us call him Shaysim, Who May Be The One.

Let us no longer be blind to our own vision. Let us recognize that

217

when the Servants select, as we must, the Shaysa, then we have determined the fate of the world.

Servant Cetchua, of the 41st Line

We travelled.

They were a bigger group than I had thought. There were the soldiers, about twenty of them, and Dwalia's followers, also about twenty. I rode in the big sleigh, and we followed two other smaller ones full of supplies. The soldiers and Dwalia's followers rode horseback. We travelled by night for the most part. We did not move quickly for we avoided the king's highway, instead crossing pastures and following wandering farm roads. We seemed to skirt forest and cross unsettled land, avoiding the farmsteads I sometimes glimpsed. Darkness and cold and the steady thudding beat of the trotting team filled my senses. At other times, the team dragged us through unbroken snow, surging forward with the sleigh sawing and tipping behind them.

I felt cold all the time, even when I was well bundled in furs and robes. When they put up the tents during the day and told me to sleep, I was so cold I could not relax my muscles. Yet the cold I felt had nothing to do with my body. I think it was the same cold that had stilled Shun. She was still as ice on a lake. Even when she moved, she walked like a stiffened corpse. She didn't speak and scarcely tended to herself. One of Dwalia's girls took it upon herself to drape Shun in a heavy white fur coat. The same girl, Odessa, would put food into her hands, or push a mug of hot soup into her grip. Then sometimes Shun would eat and sometimes she would sit and hold the mug until the hot soup went scummy and cold. Odessa would take the mug and dump the soup back into the shared pot. And Shun, cold and empty, would crawl across the blankets and skins back to the far corner of the tent.

Odessa had long dark hair that was thin and patchy, and pale white skin and eyes the colour of sour milk. One of her eyes wandered in its socket. Her bottom lip sagged open. It was hard for me to look at her. She looked diseased, and yet she moved as if she were healthy and strong. She sang softly as she rode her white horse by our sleigh, and sometimes laughed aloud with her companions at night. Yet there was a wrongness about her, as if she had been born half-finished. I tried not to stare at her. It seemed that whenever I did turn my head to look at her, her wandering eye was already gazing at me.

By day, we camped in the forest, usually well away from the road. Even in the darkest night, when snow fell and the wind blew, the teams and the riders pushed on. One of the pale folk was always at the front, and they followed her without question. A dim part of my mind speculated that they were retracing their steps, returning as they had come. I tried to wonder where they had come from, and why, but my thoughts were as thick as cold porridge.

White. There was so much white. We travelled through a world cloaked in white. Snow fell almost daily, softening and smoothing the land. When the wind blew, it sculpted the snow into flows and mounds as pale as the faces of Dwalia's followers. Their tents were white, and many of the robes and blankets were white, and the fogs that seemed to billow and bloom around us as we travelled were white. Their horses were white and fog-grey. My eyes were always weary. I had to peer to make the shapes of the people separate from the general whiteness of the icy world.

They spoke to one another, but their conversations flowed past me and made no more sense than the sound of the sleigh's runners sliding over the snow. The language they spoke rippled and flowed, the words running into one another as their voices trilled up and down, as if they sang their words to one another. I learned a few of their names, but only by repetition. The name they gave to me was Shaysim, a whispery, shivery sort of a sound. Either few of them spoke my language or they did not think it worth trying to speak to me. They talked above me and around me as they chivvied me from the sled and into the tent and back again. They put bowls of food into my hands and then took them away. They gave me almost no privacy, though they had the decency to allow Shun and me to move away from them when the pressure of bladder or bowel had to be answered.

Since I had spoken out for Shun, they had not questioned that I wanted her to be beside me at all times. I chose to sleep beside her, and during the day she rode near me in the big sleigh. Sometimes Dwalia and Odessa and the fog-man, Vindeliar, rode with us. Sometimes they rode horses, or one of them would sit up front beside the driver. I did not like them to be near me, yet I felt safer when they rode in the sleigh. They spoke to one another in low voices, making a harmony with the sound of the creaking harness, hooves and shushing runners. When they were not there, the dark pressed closer. Several times I came out of my daze to realize that soldiers were riding alongside our sleigh. Some of them stared at Shun as if they were dogs circling an abandoned table, trying to decide if they dared snatch a bone left on a plate. She did not seem to see them, but they made my blood run cold. There was one with hair the colour of ripe acorns; he was the one I noticed most often because once or twice he moved up to ride alone by the sleigh. The others always came in pairs or as a trio, to stare at Shun and talk and laugh in short, harsh bursts. They would stare at her for a time, or me. I would try to stare back at them, but it was hard when my thoughts were so woolly and soft. Soon their faces would soften, their mouths sometimes hanging slightly ajar, and then they would drop back to join the soldiers that rode behind us. The fog-boy did that to them, I think.

We travelled through the long winter nights, in the darkest hours when most folk were asleep. Twice, as we emerged from forest toward a country road, I saw other folk riding past us. I saw them, but I did not think they saw us. Into my mind drifted the old tales, of worlds that brushed against ours but only touched for a moment. It was like that, as if a pane of misty glass separated us. It never occurred to me that I should cry out for help. This was my life now, sitting in Dwalia's sleigh and being carried off through a snowy world. My life had been placed in a narrow track and I moved on it as surely as a hound following a scent.

Shun and I shared a corner of the big tent at night. I would have welcomed her back against mine, for even on the mounded furs and beneath the heavy robes, I felt cold. I think Shun felt at least as cold as I did, but when I once rolled against her in my sleep, she gave a short, sharp shriek that woke me, Dwalia and Odessa. Shun did not say anything, but she moved as far away from me as she could, taking most of the furs with her. I didn't complain. It was not a thing to question, any more than I questioned the thin, dark soup that accompanied every meal, or the way that Odessa groomed my scruff of hair and rubbed lotions into my hands and feet at dawn before we went to bed. Her hands were cold and so was the lotion, but I could not find the will to resist her. 'So your skin will not crack, Shaysim,' she would say, her words soft and wet from her mouth that never quite closed. Her touch chilled me as if Death herself caressed my hands.

So quickly the harsh days became routine. Captivity dazed me. I did not ask questions or speak to my captors. I rode in silence, too full of confusion to object to being stolen. We would halt, and I would be left in the sleigh while Dwalia's helpers scurried around us like ants. Fires were built and tents erected. Ellik's raiders had their own tents and their own camp a short distance from ours. Dwalia's people cooked and took food to them in a three-legged pot, but the soldiers and the pale folk never ate together. I wondered vaguely if Captain Ellik kept them separate from us or if Dwalia insisted on it. When the food was ready, I was summoned from the sleigh. They fed me, we all slept during the short winter day, and as each evening deepened, we rose, ate again, and journeyed on.

On a snow dawn several days into our journey, I finished eating the food in my bowl. I did not want the thin brown brew they gave me to drink but it was warm and I was thirsty. I drank it, and almost as soon as I swallowed the last of it, I felt my stomach protest. I rose and followed Shun, who evidently had the same mission. She led me some small distance from the camp to an area of bushes cloaked in snow. I squatted behind them to relieve myself when she suddenly spoke to me from close by. 'You have to be more careful. They think you are a boy.'

'What?' I was as startled that she finally spoke as at her words.

'Sshh! Speak softly. When you come with me to piss. You should stand for a time and fumble at your trousers as if you are pissing, then walk a short way and squat to do the real thing. They all believe you are a boy, someone's lost son. That's the only thing that saved you, I think.'

'Saved me?'

'From what happened to me.' She bit off each word savagely. 'From the raping and beating. If they find out you are not a boy, not the lost son, they'll do it to you, too. Before they kill us both.'

My heart pounded high up in my chest and throat. I felt as if I could not get a breath.

'I know what you are thinking, but you're wrong. You are not too young for it to happen to you. I saw one of them chasing one of the kitchen girls after they came out of whatever place they had hidden in. I heard her scream.'

'Who?' I pushed the word out on the small puff of air left in me.

'I don't know their names,' she spat at me, as if I'd insulted her by insinuating she might know the names of servants. 'And what does it matter now? It happened to her. It happened to me. They came into my room. One seized my jewellery box. Two others came after me. I threw things at them and screamed and hit them. My maid fought, but only for a moment. Then she stood like a cow and watched when they attacked me. She didn't make a sound when they pushed her down on the floor and took her. It took two of them to hold me down. I fought them.' A tiny bit of pride in those words, and then it became ash as she choked. 'But they laughed while they did it to me. Mocked me because they were stronger. Afterwards, they dragged me out to be with the others. The only reason it didn't happen to you was because they think you're a boy and special somehow.' She looked away from me. How angry she was at me, that they had not hurt me as they had hurt her! She stood slowly, letting her skirts fall around her. 'You probably think I should thank you for saving me. Well, I'm not sure you did. Maybe that last man would have left me alive, and at least I'd still be at home. Now, when they find out you're female, I think we'll both face a lot worse.'

'Can we get away?'

'How? Look. That woman stands and watches where we've gone. If we don't come back soon, she'll send someone after us. And when else can we slip away?'

My belly did not like their food, but there was nothing to wipe myself with. I braced myself, took a handful of snow, and cleaned my bottom with that before pulling my leggings back up. Shun watched me dispassionately with no regard for my privacy. 'It's that brown soup,' she said.

'What?'

'Can you say something besides "what" or "who"? The brown soup they give us. It goes right through you. I started pretending to drink it yesterday. Then I didn't fall asleep right away. It has something in it to make you sleep so they can rest during the day and not have to watch us.'

'How do you know all this?'

'Training,' she said tersely. 'Before I came to live with you, I had some training. Lord Chade saw to that. He sent this awful old woman named Quiver to teach me all sorts of things. How to throw a knife. Where to hit someone who grabs you. Chade said she was preparing me to be an assassin. I don't think she did very well at it, but I do know how to protect myself.' She stopped speaking and her face sagged. 'A little,' she amended.

I didn't point out that she hadn't done very well at that back at the manor. No sense stinging her pride. I wanted to know more, but I heard Dwalia call to one of her helpers and point toward us.

'Pretend to be sleepy. Droop your eyes and walk slowly behind me. And don't try to talk to me, unless I talk to you first. They can't know.'

I nodded, folding my lips tight. I wanted to tell her that I could be just as alert and wary as she was, just as clever at knowing when it was safe for us to talk. But Shun had already let her face droop into that unresponsive mask she had been wearing since she was hauled to the sleigh. I wondered if she had been pretending all that time. A wave of panic rose up in me. I wasn't as perceptive as she was. I'd heard them saying I was a boy, but hadn't had the will to care that they were wrong. Nor the experience to be afraid that they would find out I wasn't who or what they thought I was. I hadn't feared what would happen when they found out. Now I did. My heart was leaping and thudding. The brown soup tried to make me sleepy and my fear tried to make me be awake. How could I look sleepy when I could scarcely catch my breath?

Shun stumbled, or pretended to stumble against me. As she

caught herself on my shoulder, she pinched me hard. 'Sleepy,' she warned me on a breath. Her mouth barely moved.

'Shaysim, are you well? Did your bowels move in a satisfactory way?' Odessa spoke as if chatting about my bowels were as courteous a topic as the weather.

I shook my head at her and put my hands low on my belly. I felt sick with fear. Perhaps I could disguise fear as discomfort. 'I just want to sleep,' I told her.

'Yes, that's a good idea. Yes. I will tell Dwalia of your bowel problem. She will give you an oil for that.'

I didn't want her to give me anything. I bowed my head and walked slightly bent over so no one could look into my face. The tents were awaiting us. Their roofs were rounded on their half-hoops, the canvas bleached white, and I supposed that from a distance they could have been mistaken for mounds of snow. Yet we had not bothered to move that far from the road, and the horses were hobbled and pawing up the snow, searching for frozen grass. Any passing traveller would surely note them, and the brightly-painted sleighs. And the tents of the soldiers were brown and pointed, and their horses a mix of colours. So why bother disguising our tents? Something niggled at me about it, and then as I drew closer, a wave of sleepiness spread over me. I yawned hugely. It would be good to rest. To get into my warm blankets and sleep.

Shun was plodding along beside us. As we drew closer to our tent, I became aware of several soldiers watching us. Hogen, the handsome rapist, still sat his horse. His long golden hair was smoothly braided, his moustache and beard carefully combed. He smiled. He had silver hoops in his ears and a silver clasp to his cloak. Was he keeping watch? He looked down at us, a predator watching prey and said something in a low voice. Standing near Hogen's horse was a warrior with half a beard; his cheek and chin on the other side were sliced like a pared potato, and not a whisker grew out of the smooth scar. He smiled at Hogen's jest but the young soldier with the hair as brown as ripe acorns just followed Shun with dog's eyes. I hated them all.

A growl bubbled up in my throat. Odessa turned her face sharply toward me and I forced a belch up. 'Pardon,' I said, trying to sound sleepy, embarrassed and uncomfortable.

'Dwalia can help you, Shaysim,' she comforted me.

Shun moved past us and into the tent, trying to move as if she was still dead to all things, but I had seen the tightening in her shoulders when the gawking soldiers had spoken. She was a small cat walking bravely past snuffing hounds. By the time I stood in the entrance, shedding my snowy boots, Shun had burrowed under the blankets and was out of sight.

I was very certain I did not want Dwalia to help me with anything. The woman frightened me. She had an ageless face, round and yet lined. She could have been thirty or even older than my father. I couldn't tell. She was as plump as a fattened hen; even her hands were soft. If I had met her as a guest in my home, I would have guessed she was someone's genteel mother or grandmother, a woman who had seldom done physical work. Every word she had spoken to me had been in a kindly voice, and even when she had rebuked her followers in my hearing, she had sounded grieved at their failure rather than angered by it.

Yet I feared her. Everything about her set Wolf Father to snarling. Not noisy growling but the silent lifting of the lip that made the hair on the back of my neck prickle. Since the night they had taken me, even in my foggiest moments, I was aware that Wolf Father was with me. He could do nothing to help me, but he was with me. He was the one who counselled silence, who bade me conserve strength and watch and wait. I would have to help myself, but he was there. When the only comfort one has is a thin comfort, one still clings to it.

Strange to say, despite Shun's whispered words, I still felt that I was the one more competent to deal with our situation. What she had said had awakened me to a danger I had not considered, but they had not given me the sense that she was going to be the one who would save us. If anyone could save us. No. Instead her words had sounded to me as if she bragged, not to impress me but to bolster her own hopes. Assassin's training. I'd seen small sign of that in her during our weeks together at Withywoods. Instead I had seen her as vain and shallow, focused on obtaining as many pretty things and delightful distractions as coin could buy. I'd seen her wailing and weeping in terror at the supposed moaning of a ghost that was actually a trapped cat. And I'd seen her flirting with FitzVigilant, and attempting to do the same to Riddle and even, I felt, my father. All in the name of getting what she wanted. Flaunting her beauty to attract attention.

And then men had come who had turned her own weapons against her. The beauty and charm and pretty clothes she had deployed to her own ends could not save her from them. Indeed, they had made her a target. I wondered now if beautiful women were not more vulnerable, more likely to be chosen as victims by such men. I turned it over in my mind. Rape, I knew, was injury and pain and insult. I did not know the full mechanics of it, but one does not have to know swordplay to understand a stab wound. Shun had been hurt, and badly. So badly that she was willing to accept me as some sort of ally. I had thought I was helping her when I had claimed her that night. Now I wondered if, indeed, I had dragged her out of the frying pan and down into the flames with me.

I tried to think of skills I had that might save us. I could fight with a knife. A little bit. If I could get one. And if there was only one person to fight. I knew something they didn't know. They spoke to me as if I were a much younger child. I had not said anything to correct them. I had not said much to any of them, at all. That might be useful. I could not think how, but it was a secret I knew that they did not. And secrets could be weapons. I had read that, or heard that. Somewhere.

The sleepiness rolled over me again, putting blurred edges on the world. Something in the soup, or the fog-man or both. *Don't struggle*, Wolf Father warned me. *Don't let them know that you know.*

I took a deep breath and feigned a yawn that suddenly became real. Odessa was crawling into the tent behind me. I spoke in a sleepy voice. 'They look at Shun in a bad way. Those men. They give me dark dreams. Cannot Dwalia make them stay away?'

'Dark dreams,' Odessa said in soft dismay.

I held very still inside myself. Had I gone too far? She said nothing more and I dropped to my knees, crawled across the spread bedding and burrowed under it adjacent to Shun. Beneath the blankets, I wriggled out of the bulky fur coat, crawling out of the bottom instead of unbuttoning it and bundled it into a pillow. I closed my eyes almost all the way and let my breathing slow. I watched her through my eyelashes. Odessa stood still for a long time, watching me. I felt she was deciding something.

She went away, letting the tent flap drop behind her. That was unusual. Usually when Shun and I settled to sleep, Odessa lay down beside us. We were seldom out of her sight, save when Dwalia was watching over us. Now we were alone. I wondered if that meant it was our chance to escape. It might be. It might be our only chance. But my body was warming, and I felt heavy. My thoughts moved more and more slowly. I raised my hand beneath the covers and reached for Shun. I would wake her, and we would crawl out under the tent side. Into the cold and the snow. I didn't like cold. I liked warmth and I needed sleep. I was so weary, so sleepy. My hand fell, short of reaching Shun, and I did not have the will to lift it again. I slept.

I awoke as if I were a swimmer surfacing from water. No. More like a bit of wood that bobbed to the surface because it had to. My body shed sleep and I sat up, clear-minded. Dwalia was sitting cross-legged at the foot of my bed. Odessa knelt slightly behind her and to one side. I looked over at Shun. She slept on, apparently oblivious to what was going on. What was going on? I blinked my eyes and caught a flash of something at the corner of my eye. I turned to look, but there was nothing there. Dwalia was smiling at me, a kind and reassuring smile. 'Everything is fine,' she said comfortingly. By which I knew that it was not.

'I just thought that we should talk, so that you understand that you do not have to fear the men who guard us. They will not hurt you.'

I blinked my eyes and in the moment before they focused on Dwalia, I saw him. The fog-man was sitting in the corner of the tent. I slowly, slowly shifted my gaze in that direction, moving only my eyes. Yes. He was beaming a fatuous smile at me, and when his eyes met mine, he clapped his hands happily. 'Brother!' he exclaimed. He laughed heartily, as if we had just shared a wondrous joke. The way he smiled at me let me know that he wanted me to love him as much as he already loved me. No one had loved me that openly since my mother had died. I did not want his love. I stared at him, but he continued to smile at me.

Dwalia scowled, just for an instant, her buttery face melting into sharp disapproval. When I looked at her directly, her smile was in place. 'Well,' she said, as if glad of it, 'I see that our little game is finished now. You see him, don't you, Shaysim? Even though our Vindeliar is doing his best, his very best, to be hidden?'

Praise, question, or a rebuke was all twisted together in that question. The boy's moon-face only grew jollier. He wriggled from side to side, a happy dumpling of a boy. 'Silly. Silly. My brother looks with a different kind of eyes. He sees me. He's seen me, oh, since we were in the town. With the music and the sweet food and the people dancing.' He scratched his cheek thoughtfully, and I heard the sound of shorn whiskers against his nails. So he was older than I thought, but so boyish. 'I wished we had that festival to keep, with dancing and singing and eating sweet things. Why are we not a festival folk, Lingstra?'

'We are not, my lurik. That is the answer. That we are not, just as we are neither cows nor thistles. We are the Servants. We stay to the path. We are the path. The path we walk is for the good of the world.'

'When we serve the world, we serve ourselves.' Dwalia and Odessa spoke these words in harmony. 'The good of the world is the good of the Servants. What is good for the Servants is good for the world. We walk the path.'

Their voices ceased, but they stared at Vindeliar almost accusingly. He lowered his eyes and some of the brightness went out of his face. He spoke in a measured cadence, words I was certain he had learned from his cradle days. 'He who leaves the path is not a Servant but an obstacle to the good of the world. An obstacle in the path must be evaded. If it cannot be evaded, it must be removed. If it cannot be removed, it must be destroyed. We must stay to the path, for the good of the world. We must stay to the path for the good of the Servants.' He took a huge breath at the end. His round cheeks puffed as he sighed it out. His lower lip remained pushed out in a baby's pout and he looked at the mounded blankets, not at Dwalia.

She was relentless. 'Vindeliar. Has anyone seen a festival for you on this part of the path?'

'No.' A soft, low denial.

'Has anyone ever seen, in any dream, Vindeliar merrymaking at a festival?'

He drew a short breath and his shoulders slumped as he said, 'No.'

Dwalia leaned toward him. Her kind look was back on her face. 'Then, my lurik, there is no festival on Vindeliar's path. For Vindeliar to go to a festival would be for Vindeliar to leave the path, or bend it awry. And then what would Vindeliar be? A Servant?'

He shook his blunt head slowly.

'What then?' She was remorseless.

'An obstacle.' He lifted his head and before she could press him, added, 'To be evaded. Or avoided. Removed. Or destroyed.' He dropped his voice and his eyes on that last word. I stared at him. I had never seen a man who believed so completely that someone who apparently loved him would kill him for breaking a rule. With a cold rush up my spine, I discovered that I believed it, too. She would kill him if he veered from the path.

What path?

Did they think I had a path? Was I in danger of veering from it? I shifted my stare to Dwalia. I believed she would kill Vindeliar if he veered from the path. Would she kill me, too?

Dwalia's gaze snapped to mine and I could not look away from it. She spoke softly, kindly. 'It's why we came, Shaysim. To rescue you and keep you safe. Because if we did not, you would become an obstacle to the path. We will take you home, to a safe place where you cannot leave the path by accident, nor change it. By keeping you safe, we will keep the path safe, and keep the world safe. As long as the world is safe, you are safe. You don't have to be afraid.'

Her words terrified me. 'What is the path?' I demanded. 'How can I tell if I am staying to the path?'

Her smile stretched. She nodded slowly. 'Shaysim, I am pleased. This is the first question we always hope to hear from a Servant.'

A lurch and my belly went cold. A servant? I had seen the lives of servants. I'd never imagined being one, and suddenly knew I never wanted to be one. Did I dare say that? Was that leaving the path?

'So, to hear it from a shaysim of your years is remarkable. Shaysims are often blinded to the idea that there may be a path. They see possibilities, and ways that lead to so many divergent paths. Shaysims born out here in the wide world often have difficulty accepting that there is only one true path, a path that has been seen and charted. A path that we all must strive to bring into the world, so that the world may be a better place for all of us.'

The understanding of what she meant rose in me like a tide. Was it a thing I had always known? I recalled with clarity how the beggar in the marketplace had touched me, and suddenly I had seen an infinity of possible futures, all depending on the decision of a young couple I had glimpsed in passing. I had even thought to nudge the future into a direction that seemed wise to me. It would have involved the young man being murdered by highwaymen, and the woman suffering rape and death, but I had seen her brothers riding to avenge her, and encouraging others to join them, and how they had made the highways safe for travellers for decades after their sister had died. Two lives gone in pain and torment, but so many saved.

I came back to the present. The blankets I had clutched had fallen away from me and the winter cold gripped me.

'I see you understand me,' Dwalia said in a honeyed voice. 'You are a shaysim, my dear. In some places, they would call you a White Prophet, even if you are not nearly as pale as one of them should be. Still, I trust Vindeliar when he tells me that you are the lost son that we seek. You are a rare creature, Shaysim. Perhaps you have not realized that. Few are the folk who are given the gift of seeing what may be. Even rarer are the ones who can look and see the tipping points, the tiny places where a word or a smile or a swift knife set the world on a different course. Rarest of all are the ones like you. Born, it would seem, almost by chance, to folk who do not know what you are. They cannot protect you from making dangerous mistakes. They cannot save you from leaving the path. And so we came to find you. To keep you, and the path, safe. For you can see the moment when all things change, before it happens. And you see who it is, in any cycle, who will be the Catalyst for that time.'

'Catalyst.' I tried the word on my tongue. It sounded like a spice or a healing herb. Both of those were things that changed other things. A spice that flavoured a food or an herb that saved a life. Catalyst. Once it had meant my father, in some of his scrolls that I had read.

Dwalia used the word to pry at me. 'The one you might use to set the world on a different path. Your tool. Your weapon in your battle to shape the world. Have you seen him yet? Or her?'

I shook my head. I felt sick. Knowledge was welling up in me like vomit rising in my throat. It burned me with cold. The dreams I'd had. The things I'd known to do. Had I provoked the manor children to attack me? When Taffy had struck me, the web of flesh that had kept my tongue tied to the bottom of my mouth had been torn free. I'd gained speech. I'd gone out that day, knowing it must happen if I was going to be able to speak. I rocked in my wrap, my teeth chattering. 'I'm so cold,' I said. 'So cold.'

I had been ready to trigger that change. Taffy had been my tool to do that to myself. Because I could see the tumbling consequences of being where the other children would see me. I had placed myself where they could catch me. Because I had known that I had to do that. I had to do that to put myself on my path. The path I'd seen in glimpses since before I was born. Anyone could change the future. Every one of us changed the future constantly. But Dwalia was right. Few could do what I could do. I could see, with absolute certainty, the most likely consequences of a particular action. And then I could release the bowstring and send that consequence arrowing into the future. Or cause someone else to do so.

The knowledge of what I could do dizzied me. I didn't want it. I felt ill with it, as if it were a sickness inside me. Then, I was ill. The world spun around me. If I closed my eyes, it went faster. I clutched at the blankets, willing myself to stillness. The cold gripped me so hard I thought I had already died from it.

'Interesting,' Dwalia said. She made no move to aid me, and when Odessa shifted behind her she flung her hand out and down in a sharp motion. The lurik froze where she was, hunching her head between her shoulders like a scolded dog. Dwalia looked at

Vindeliar. He cowered into himself. 'Watch him. Both of you. But no more than that. This was not predicted. I will summon the others and we will pool our memories of the predictions. Until we know what has been seen of this, if anything has been seen, it is safest to do nothing.'

'Please,' I said, not knowing what I begged of them. 'I'm sick. And I'm so cold.'

'Yes.' Dwalia nodded. 'Yes, you are.' She moved an admonishing finger at both her luriks, and then she left the tent.

I sat very still. If I moved the spinning became unbearable. But I was cold, so cold. I wanted to reach for the blankets and furs, to pull them up around me. But any motion awakened the vertigo. I braved it, and then, for my bravery, I retched. I vomited on myself and it soaked my shirtfront and made me colder. Neither the fog-man nor Odessa moved. She watched me with sour milk eyes and Vindeliar watched me with tears brimming his eyes. They watched until I was retching a thin yellow fluid that I could not spit clear of my mouth. It clung to my lips and chin, and still the tent spun and I was so cold. I wanted to be away from the wet and the stink of my vomit.

Do it. Move away. The dizziness would be bad no matter if I moved slow or fast. So just move.

I scooted back and dropped over on my side. The vertigo that struck me was so severe I could not tell up from down. I moaned, I think.

Someone lifted a blanket and tucked it around me. It was Shun. I could not bear to look at her for the spinning, but I knew her scent. She put another something over me. A fur, a heavy one. I felt a tiny bit warmer. I drew my body up into a ball. I wondered if I could speak without vomiting. 'Thank you,' I said. Then, 'Please. Don't touch me. Don't move me. It makes the dizziness worse.'

I focused my eyes on a corner of the blanket. I willed it to be still, and for a miracle, it was. I breathed slowly, carefully. I needed to be warm but even more, I needed the spinning to stop. A hand touched me, an icy hand on my neck. I cried out wordlessly.

'Why don't you help him? He's sick. He burns with fever.' Her voice sounded sleepy but I knew she was not. Not really. Her anger was too strong for her to be sleepy. Could the others hear that, too?

Odessa spoke. 'We are to do nothing until Lingstra Dwalia returns to instruct us. Even now, you may have disrupted the path.'

Another blanket settled over me. 'Do nothing then. Don't stop me.'

Shun lay down beside me. I wished she wouldn't. I feared that if she nudged me or moved me, the vertigo would come roaring back.

'We obeyed.' The fear in Vindeliar's voice was like a bad taste in the air. 'Lingstra cannot be angry with us. We obeyed and did nothing.' He lifted his hands to cover his eyes. 'I did nothing to help my brother,' he moaned. 'I did nothing. She can't be angry.'

'Oh, she can be angry,' Odessa said bitterly. 'She can always be angry.'

Very carefully, I let my eyes close. The spinning slowed. It stopped. I slept.

THIRTEEN

Chade's Secret

This is the dream of the flame horses. It is a winter evening. It's not night but it's dark. An early moon is rising over the birch trees. I hear a sad song with no words, and it is like a wind in the trees. It keens and moans. Then the stables burst into flames. Horses scream. And then two horses race out. They are on fire. One is black and one is white, and the flames are orange and red, whipped by the wind of the horses' own passage. They race out into the night. The black one falls suddenly. The white one races on. Then suddenly, the moon opens its mouth and swallows the white horse.

This dream makes no sense to me and no matter how I try, I cannot draw a picture for it. So this dream is recorded only in words.

Bee Farseer's Dream Journal

I woke on the floor of the study, not far from where the stableboy slept on. I had not wanted to sleep, and I certainly could not have borne sleeping in my own room. But I had taken blankets from my bed, and Bee's book from her hiding-place, and returned to the estate study. I'd fed the fire to sustain it through what was left of the night and then spread my blankets. I'd settled down and held her book in my hands. I thought about reading it. Was that breaching her trust in me? I'd leafed through it, not settling on any section but marvelling at her tidy lettering, precise illustrations and how many pages she had filled.

In a bizarre hope that she might have had time to leave some account of the attack, I went to the last page of her journal. But it stopped well short of our trip to Oaksbywater. There was a sketch of a barn cat. The black one with the kinked tail. I'd closed the book, pillowed my head on it, and fallen asleep. The sound of footsteps in the corridor had awakened me. I sat up, aching and discouraged and the weight of my worries fell on me again. Bleak discouragement soaked me. I'd already failed and there was nothing I could do to change that. Bee was dead. Shun was dead. Perhaps they were worse than dead. It was my fault and I could find neither anger nor ambition to do anything about it.

I went to the window and pushed back the drape. The skies were finally clear and blue. It was an effort to gather my thoughts. Chade would be coming today, with Thick. I tried to make plans, to decide to ride to meet him or make preparations for his arrival. I couldn't find the mental order to do either. On the hearth, Perseverance slept on. I made myself cross the room and add wood to the fire. I welcomed the blue sky but knew it meant the days would be colder.

I left my study and went to my room. I found clean clothing. I went to the kitchen. I dreaded who I might not find there, but Cook Nutmeg was there, and Tavia and the two little kitchen maids Elm and Lea. Tavia had a black eye and a swollen lower lip, but seemed unaware of both. Elm had a peculiar hobble to her gait. I felt sick with dread and refrained from asking any questions. 'So good to have you home again, Holder Badgerlock,' Cook Nutmeg greeted me, and promised to serve me breakfast very quickly.

'We should expect company here soon,' I warned them. 'Lord Chade and his man Thick will be arriving in the next few hours. Please prepare something for all of us to eat when they get here. I will ask you to let the other servants know that I expect Thick to be treated with the same respect as Lord Chade. His appearance and mannerisms may give you the impression he is a half-wit. But he is an indispensable and loyal servant to the Farseer throne. Treat him as such. For now, if you'd send a tray of food and some hot tea to my study, that would be very welcome. Oh, and please send up enough food for the stableboy Perseverance, too. He will breakfast with me this morning.'

Cook Nutmeg knit her brow but Tavia nodded at me. 'It's kind you are, sir, to take on that poor benighted lad as a stableboy. Having work to do may settle his mind.'

'Let us hope so,' was all I could find the will to say to her. I left them there, fetched a cloak and walked out to where the Withywoods stables had once stood. Cold crisp air, blue sky, white snow, blackened wood. I walked around what remained. I could see at least one horse corpse, half-baked and crow-scavenged, sprawled in the wreckage. The fire appeared to have burned unchecked. A survey of the grounds around the stable showed me nothing more than what I'd seen in the night. The only tracks were of folk on foot, most likely Withywoods folk going about their tasks.

I found the remaining horses and the mount I'd stolen the night before housed in one of the sheep shelters. They had feed and water. A dazed-looking girl was taking care of them, and one of the bull-pups had survived. The girl sat on a heap of straw in the corner, the pup in her lap, and stared at nothing. She was probably struggling to make sense of a world in which her masters were gone and she was suddenly in charge of the remaining horses. Could she remember that she'd had masters? Seeing her alone there made me wonder how many of the stablehands had perished alongside their charges. Tallman and Tallerman were gone, I knew. How many others?

'How's the pup?' I asked her.

'Well enough, sir.' She started to struggle to her feet. A motion of my hand excused her from that. The puppy reached up to lick her chin. His raggedly cut ears were healing.

'You've done a good job with his injuries. Thank you.'

'You're welcome, sir.' She looked up at me. 'He misses his mother, sir. He misses her so badly I can almost feel it myself.' Her eyes were very wide. She swayed slightly.

I nodded. I was too great a coward to ask after her mother. I doubted she would remember if she'd had one. 'Take good care of him. Comfort him all you can.'

'I will, sir.'

I found the pigeon-cote as the messenger had warned me I would. Rats or some other scavenger had been at the small, feathered bodies. A single live pigeon with a message tied to its leg was perched on one of the higher ledges. I caught it and opened the message to discover it was from Nettle to FitzVigilant, wishing him a happy Winterfest and asking for news of her sister. I swept the bird bodies out of the coop area. I found corn for the pigeon, checked that it had water and left it there.

By the time I re-entered the manor, I was chilled to the bone and heartsick. Everything I had seen convinced me of the accuracy of Perseverance's tale. The men who had seized Bee were ruthless killers. I desperately hoped she was a hostage, one they would value and care for. I made my way back to the study and found the stableboy awake. Someone had brought him washwater, and he'd attempted to tidy himself. The tray of food rested on my desk, untouched. 'Aren't you hungry?' I asked him.

'Starving, sir,' he admitted. 'But I didn't think it right to eat it without your leave.'

'Lad, if you're to serve me, the first thing I require of you is that you behave in a practical way. Didn't the kitchen lass tell you it was for you? Didn't you see two cups there, and two plates? You're hungry, the food is there, and you had no idea when I was coming back. You should have eaten.'

'It didn't seem polite, sir. My family always ate at table together.' He closed his mouth suddenly, his lips tight. For an instant, I hoped Thick would be able to clear his mother's mind. Then I wondered if the woman deserved to face all that she had lost. I opened my mouth twice before I spoke.

'I see your point. Let's sit together and eat, then. We have to be ready to face this day. I'll need your help to put what remains of our horses back into comfortable situations. Lord Chade and Thick will be arriving later, to help us consider what has happened here.'

'The king's own adviser?'

I was startled that the boy knew of Chade. 'Yes. And Thick will be with him. He's a sort of adviser, too. Don't be put off by his appearance and ways. His mind may not work exactly as ours do, but he's an old friend of mine and has helped me more than once.'

'Of course, sir. Any guest in your house must be treated with respect.'

'Excellent. Now let's stop talking for a bit and get some food down both of us.'

The boy excelled at that. The haunted look had receded a bit from his eyes, but his cheeks were still flushed with fever from his wound. I excused myself from the table, left him eating and came back with a generous dose of ground willowbark that I added to the rest of his tea. After he had eaten, I told him to go to the steams. I thought of sending someone to his mother's house to get clean garments for him, but decided it would only cause more distress for everyone.

A tap at the study door was FitzVigilant. He looked little better than he had the night before. 'Did you sleep?' I asked him.

'Nightmares,' he replied brusquely.

I didn't ask questions. 'How's your shoulder?'

'Somewhat better.' He looked at the floor, and then back up at me. His words came slowly. 'I can't make my days fit together. Not just Winterfest Eve. That whole day at Oaksbywater is fragmented. And not just that day but many that came before it. Look at this. I remember buying it. But I don't recall why.' He held up a bracelet of delicate silver links. 'I would never choose anything like this for myself. And I feel ashamed and I don't know why. I did something terrible, didn't I?'

Yes. You didn't protect my daughter. You should have died before you let them take her. 'I don't know, Lant. But when Lord Chade is here with Thick, perhaps we can—'

'Sir!' It was Bulen, bursting into the room. For one crooked moment, I wanted to rebuke Revel for not training him better. But Revel was gone.

'What is it?'

'A troop of soldiers, sir, coming up the carriageway! Twenty or more!'

I was on my feet in the instant. My eyes went to the sword over the mantel. Gone. Looted. No time to care about that. I reached under my desk and jerked free the nasty short sword that I'd long ago fastened to the underside of it. I looked at Lant. 'Arm yourself and join me. Now.' I went out of the door without looking back to see if he or Bulen was following. I had a target and at that moment I was fully convinced that I could slay twenty men with my anger alone.

But the mounted men advancing up the drive were in the livery of the Buckkeep Rousters. They wore black with only a touch of blue, and had a reputation as dark for recklessness and violence. The leader wore a helm that left only his eyes and a great expanse of beard and moustache exposed. I stood in the open door, panting, my bared sword in my hand and returned their incredulous looks as they pulled their horses to a halt. Belatedly, it came to me. The troop of guards that Chade had dispatched had finally arrived. The messenger, travelling alone, had braved the snow and storms to reach Withywoods before they had. Their captain's eyes met mine, evaluating me coldly. His eyes flickered to the burned stable and then back to me. He knew he was too late and was already assembling reasons for why it was not his fault. This was the guard company Chade had chosen to send to Withywoods? The Rousters? What had he expected them to face? Had the men who had taken Bee actually been targeting Shun? Too many new ideas rattled through my head. Slowly I lowered my sword until it pointed at the ground.

'Captain, I am Holder Badgerlock, master of Withywoods. Welcome. I am aware that Lord Chade sent you to supplement my folk here. I am afraid we were all too late to prevent a disaster.' Such bland and formal words for what had happened here. I'd reverted to my former identity, giving a name they might expect to hear.

'Captain Stout is my name. My lieutenant is Crafty.' He gestured at the younger man beside him. His beard and moustache were patchy but ambitious. 'Given the weather, we travelled as swiftly as was possible to be here. It is unfortunate that we were not placed here before you left your home unguarded.'

Not his fault, and he was making sure I knew it. He was right, but it was salt in a fresh wound, and his disrespect was unhidden.

A thin, almost-familiar music crept into my thoughts. I lifted my eyes. Thick? From the ranks of the men, he and Chade emerged. Chade pushed his horse forward to demand, 'What tidings? Is she here? What happened?'

'It's hard to say. There was a raid here, on Winterfest Eve. Bee was taken. My stables were torched, and some of my folk killed, but something has clouded the minds of everyone who was here. They recall nothing of it. Except for one stableboy.'

'And Lady Shun?' His question was desperate.

'I'm sorry, Chade. I don't know. She isn't here. I don't know if she was taken or is among the dead.'

His face changed. He aged. I swear the flesh sagged on his skull and his eyes dimmed. 'And Lant?' His voice was faint with despair.

'I'm fine, Lord Chade. A bit the worse for a new hole in my shoulder, but I'll live.'

'Thank Eda for that.' The old man dismounted as Lant handed his sword to Bulen and went forward to meet him. Chade embraced him wordlessly, closing his eyes. I think I saw Lant flinch as Chade's arms enfolded him but he made no sound.

'Fitz. Hey!' Thick, looking uncomfortable on a very tall horse. He dismounted awkwardly, sliding on his belly down the horse's shoulder. His round cheeks were red with cold. His music, the harbinger of his incredible Skill-strength, was a muted anthem today. Nonetheless, as it reached my senses more strongly, I felt a slight lift of my heart. He came to me and stared up at me. He reached up and patted my chest as if to make certain I saw him. 'Fitz! Look! We met the soldiers and we rode with them. Like an army coming to your door! I'm cold! I'm hungry! Can we go inside?'

'Of course, all of you, please.' I looked up at the mounted men. 'You must be cold and hungry. Um, Bulen, can you find some help to take care of the horses?' I had no idea where we would stable the beasts. And I had given cook no notice that we might have twenty hungry guardsmen dropping in. Thick reached out and took my hand.

And Bee was stolen!

The knowledge hit me like a blow to the head. What was I doing here? Why hadn't I already set off in pursuit?

'There you are! Why were you hiding in the fog? Now we can feel each other,' Thick told me companionably. He squeezed my hand and smiled up at me.

The cold shock of reality seizing me was like being flung directly from a fever back to health. Everything that had seemed distant and vaguely sad now assaulted me full force. My child stolen by folk cruel enough to burn horses alive in my stables. My people dulled down to the sensibilities of sheep. A killing rage rose in me and Thick took a step back from me. 'Stop,' he begged me. 'Don't feel that much!'

As soon as he released my hand, the choking miasma of despair sought to fill me. I looked at the ground. Putting up my Skill-walls at that moment was like attempting to lift the real walls of Withywoods. I felt too much to contain it: too much anger, frustration, guilt and fear. My emotions circled each other like savage dogs, tearing at my soul in passing. Block by block, I built my Skill-walls. When I looked up, Thick was nodding at me, his tongue resting on top of his lower lip. Lant was speaking softly and quickly to Chade, who held him by the shoulders and stared into his face as he spoke. And the Rousters were looking very unhappy at being here at all. I looked at their captain and used my Skill to push my words as well as my voice.

'You didn't want to come here. You were fine travelling down the road until you got to the carriage lane that leads here. Then you wanted to go anywhere else. Now that you are here, you feel miserable and unsettled. You see the signs, as I do, that this holding was attacked by armed men. They came and they went, and left the signs of their passage but no memory of it with my folk. There is a spell . . . an evil magic has been put over Withywoods, specifically to keep away those who could help us.' I took a steadying breath and straightened my back. 'Please, if two of your fellows would find stabling for the horses in the sheep pens and give them whatever fodder you can find, I would be grateful. Then come inside, get warm, have food. Then we will discuss how best to follow people who have left no tracks.'

The captain of the guard regarded me with reservation. His lieutenant rolled his eyes and did not bother to conceal his disdain. Chade lifted his voice. 'After you have eaten, go out in pairs and ask of the folk round and about. Look for tracks of a party of mounted soldiers. There will be a reward, in gold, for any who bring me back solid information.'

That motivated them and they were obeying orders before

their captain had finished issuing them. Then Chade was beside me hissing, 'Inside. Somewhere private. I need to talk to you.' He turned to FitzVigilant. 'Take Thick, please, and see he is warmed and fed. Then come and find us.'

Bulen hovered until I pointed at him. 'Find Dixon. Tell him to take care of everything, now. Feed those men, see that their horses are treated properly. Tell him I said he should have been at the door. Let him know I am not happy.' In all my days at Withywoods, I'd never spoken that sharply to a servant. Bulen stared at me and then set off at a run.

I led Chade past my splintered doors. His face grew grimmer as we passed a sword-scored wall and a slashed tapestry. We entered my study and I shut the door. For a moment, Chade just looked at me. Then he asked, 'How could you have let this happen? I told you I needed her protected. I told you that. I've suggested, over and over, that you have a few house-soldiers or at least a Skilled apprentice here who could have summoned help. You've always been so stubborn, so insistent that you must have everything your way. Now look what you've done. Look what you've done.' His voice trailed and broke on the last words. He staggered to my desk and sat down in my chair. He bowed his face into his hands. I was so stunned by his rebuke that it took me a short time to realize he was weeping.

I had no words to offer in my own defence. It was true. Both he and Riddle had urged me to have some sort of guard, but I'd always refused, believing that I'd left violence behind me at Buckkeep Castle. Believing I could always protect my own. Until I'd left them all without a thought to save the Fool.

He lifted his face from his hands. He looked so old. 'Say something!' he ordered me harshly. Tears were wet in the lines of his cheeks.

I bit back the first words that came to my mind. I would not utter another useless apology. 'The minds of everyone who was here have been fogged. I don't know how it was done, nor how a Skill-suggestion lingers here to turn folk away and make them discouraged. I don't know if it is even the Skill or a different magic used against us. But no one here recalls an attack, even though the evidence is plain throughout the house. The only one who seems to have clear memory of Winterfest Eve is a stableboy named Perseverance.'

'I need to talk to him,' Chade interrupted me.

'I sent him to the steams. He took an arrow through the shoulder. And he has been rattled badly by days of folk who no longer recall him and treat him as if he were mad.'

'I care nothing for that!' he shouted. 'I want to know what has become of my daughter!'

'Daughter?' I stared at him. Anger burned in his eyes. I thought of Shun, her Farseer features, even her green eyes. So obvious. How could I not have seen it before?

'Of course my daughter! Why else would I go to such lengths? Why else would I have sent her here, to you, to the one person who I thought I could trust to keep her safe? Only to have you abandon her. I know who did this! Her damned mother and her brothers, but worst of all her stepfather! They've the family feeling of snakes! For years I paid Shun's family and paid them well to care for her. But it was never enough for them. Never. They always wanted more – more money, honours at court, grants of land, more than I could possibly give them. Her mother never had any feelings for the child! And once the grandparents were gone, her mother began to threaten her. Her pig of a husband, trying to put his hands on Shun when she was little more than a girl! Then when I removed Shun, and cut off the money, they tried to kill her!' He sputtered to a halt. There was a tap on the door. He brushed his cuff over his eyes and composed his face.

'Enter,' I called, and Tavia came in to announce that there was hot food and drink waiting for us. Even in her deadened state, she seemed to sense the tension in the room, for she withdrew swiftly after her announcement. Chade stared at her bruised face and after she left, his gaze remained fixed on the door, his thoughts miles away. I spoke into the quiet that followed. 'And you never saw fit to share any of that with me?'

He flung his attention back to me. 'There was never a good time to talk with you! I no longer trust our Skilling to be private, and that first evening at the inn, when I needed to talk to you, you were in such a damnable hurry to leave—'

'To get home to *my* daughter, I might point out!' My guilt was giving way to my own anger. 'Chade. Listen to me. This was not an attack by Shun's family. Not unless they are capable of hiring Chalcedeans to do their dirty work. And have a stable full of white horses, and a troop of pale folk to ride them. I believe that whoever came here was actually in pursuit of the Fool. Or the messenger who preceded him.'

'A messenger preceded him?'

'There is much that I have not had a good time to share with you. So, listen to me. We both need to drop our anger and contain our fear. We'll share every scrap of information we have, and then we'll act. Together.'

'If there is anything for me to act upon. You've already told me that my Shine may be dead.'

Shine. Not Shun. Shine Fallstar. It was not a smile but I showed my teeth to him. 'We will discover the truth. And face it. And whatever it is, we will go after them. And we will kill them all, like the bastards we are.'

He caught a ragged breath at that, and sat up a bit straighter. I wanted to tell him that I thought perhaps Shun had been taken with Bee. But I did not want to tell him I believed that because a cat had said it might be so. The word of a cat was not to be relied upon. Another tap at the door, and FitzVigilant entered. 'I don't mean to intrude, but I'd like to be included.'

I stared at him. How blind I'd been. And how stupid. Of course that was what was special about him. I looked at Chade and spoke recklessly. 'And he's yours, too, isn't he?'

Chade stiffened. 'And fortunately for you and your careless speech, he knows he is my son.'

'Well, it would have explained a lot to me if I had known!'

'I thought it was obvious.'

'Well, it wasn't. Not for either of them.'

'Would it have made a difference? I gave them into your care. Would you have taken better care of them if you had known?'

'Them?' FitzVigilant broke into our sparring. He looked at his father, and in profile, I saw Chade was right. Obvious. If one were looking for it. 'Them? Do you have another son? I have a brother?'

'No,' Chade replied shortly, but I was in no mood to harbour his secrets any longer.

'No, you don't have a brother. You have a sister. And for all I know, perhaps there are other brothers and sisters that I haven't been informed about.'

'And why would I be required to inform you?' Chade raged at me. 'Why is this so surprising to you, that I had lovers, that children were born? For years, I lived in near-isolation, a rat behind the walls of Buckkeep Castle. When finally I could come out, when finally I could eat an elegant meal, dance to music and yes, enjoy the company of lovely women, why would I not? Tell me this, Fitz. Is it not purely luck on your part that you don't have a child or two from your past? Or did you remain chaste all those years?'

After a moment, I closed my mouth.

'I thought not,' Chade said acerbically.

'If I have a sister, where is she?' Lant demanded.

'You do have a sister. Shine Fallstar, once known to you as Shun. As to where she is, that is what we are here to discover. She was here, supposedly safe in Fitz's care. And now she has vanished.' His bitter words stung me.

'As has my own daughter, a much younger and less capable child,' I pointed out angrily. Then wondered if Bee were truly less capable than Shun. Or Shine. I glowered at him.

At that moment, there was yet another knock on the door. Chade and I both composed our faces. It was a reflex. 'Enter,' Chade and I chorused, and Perseverance opened the door and stood there, confused. He looked somewhat better, despite still wearing a bloodstained shirt. 'This is the stableboy I told you about,' I said to Chade. And to Perseverance, 'Come in. I know you've told me your story, but Lord Chade will want to hear it all again, and with every detail you can summon to mind.'

'As you wish, sir,' he replied in a subdued voice and came into the room. He glanced at FitzVigilant and then at me.

'Are you uncomfortable speaking about him while he is here?' I asked. The boy gave a short nod and dropped his head forward. He stared at the floor.

'What did I do?' FitzVigilant demanded in a voice both agonized and affronted. He crossed over to Perseverance so swiftly that the boy shrank back from him while I took two steps forward. 'Please!' he cried in a strained voice. 'Just tell me. I need to know.'

'Boy, sit down. I need to talk with you.'

I wondered how Chade felt when Perseverance looked at me to see if he was to obey. In response, I nodded at a chair. He sat and then looked up at Chade with very wide eyes. FitzVigilant hovered, his eyes full of trepidation. Chade looked down at Perseverance. 'You needn't be afraid, as long as you tell me the exact truth. Do you understand that?'

The lad gave a nod and then dredged up a, 'Yes, sir.'

'Very good.' He looked at FitzVigilant. 'This is too important for me to delay. Would you go and arrange to have food brought here to us? And ask Thick to join us if he has finished eating?'

Lant met his father's eyes. 'I'd like to stay and hear what he has to say.'

'I know you would. But just your being in the room would colour the boy's tale. As soon as I've finished speaking to him, Fitz and Thick and I will be sitting down with you to see if we can clear the cobwebs from your mind. Oh, and I've one more errand for you. Lad,' and here he turned back to my stableboy, 'tell me what sort of tracks we should be looking for.'

His eyes flickered to me again. I nodded. 'They rode horses, sir. Big ones, to carry heavy loads, the soldiers did, the ones who spoke a foreign tongue. Big hooves, shod well. And there were smaller mounts, white horses, very graceful but sturdy, too. The white horses that pulled the sleighs were taller than the ones the pale folk were riding. Matched pairs. The soldier troops led first, and then the sleighs went with the riders on white horses following and then only four soldiers at the very end. But it was snowing that night and the wind was blowing. Almost before they were out of sight, the snow was filling in their tracks and the wind was blowing it smooth.'

'Did you follow them? Did you see which direction they took?'

He shook his head and looked down. 'I'm sorry, sir. I was bleeding still, and dizzy. And very cold. I went back to the manor house to try to get help. But no one recognized me. I knew Revel was dead, and my dad and granddad. I went to find my mum.' He cleared his throat. 'She didn't know me. She told me to go back up to the manor house and get help there. Finally, when they opened the door, I lied. I said I had a message for Scribe FitzVigilant. So they let me in and took me to him, but he was as bad off as I was. Bulen cleaned up my shoulder and let me sleep by the fire. I tried to talk to them, to get them to go after Bee. But they said they didn't know her, and that I was a crazy beggar-boy. The next morning, when I could walk a bit, I saw her horse had come back, so I took Priss and tried to go after her. But they called me a horse thief! If Bulen hadn't told them I was crazy, I don't know what would have happened to me!'

Chade's voice was calming. 'You've had a hard time of it, I can tell. I know you told Fitz that you saw Bee in the sleigh. We know they took her. But what of Lady Shun? Did you see aught of her that day?'

'When they were leaving? No, sir. I saw Bee because she looked right at me. I think she saw me looking at her. But she didn't give me away . . .' A moment later, he continued, 'There were other people in the sleigh. A pale man was driving it, and a round-faced woman was sitting in the back holding Bee on her lap like she was a baby. And there was a man, I think, but with a boy's face . . .' His words ran down. Both Chade and I were silent, waiting. Expressions slowly moved across his face. We waited.

'They were all dressed in pale colours. Even Bee was wrapped in something white. But I saw the edge of something. Something red. Like the dress the lady was wearing earlier.'

Chade dragged in a ragged breath, a sound of dread, or hope. 'You saw her earlier?' he pressed the boy.

He gave a single nod. 'Bee and I were hiding behind the hedge. The raiders had herded all our folk out of the manor and into the courtyard in front of the house. Bee hid the children in the wall, but when she went to follow them after we hid the tracks, they'd shut the door. So she went with me. And we hid behind the hedge and went to see what was happening. The soldiers were shouting at everyone, telling them to sit down, even though they were in house-clothes and the wind was blowing and the snow was falling on them. When we saw them like that, I thought Scribe Lant was dead. He was face down in the snow, and it was red all around him. And Lady Shun was there, with the others, in a torn red dress, with two of the housemaids. With Caution and Scurry.'

I saw those words hit Chade. A torn dress. Deny what it might mean but the knowledge would still burrow into him like a worm. Her dress torn, and then she was carted away like plunder. At the very least, there had been violence. Rape was likely. Damage done. He swallowed audibly. 'Are you certain?'

Perseverance paused before he answered. 'I saw something red on the sleigh. That's all I can be certain about.'

Thick entered without knocking, with FitzVigilant behind him. 'I don't like this place,' he announced to us. 'They all sing the same song, *no, no, no, don't think about it, don't think about it.*'

'Who does?' I asked him, startled.

He stared at me as if I were the half-wit. 'Everyone!' He flung his arms wide. Then he looked around the room and pointed at Perseverance. 'Everyone except him. He makes no song. Chade says, don't make your music loud. Keep your music inside a box. But they are not keeping their song in a box and it makes me sad.'

My gaze met Chade's. We shared the same suspicion. 'Let me listen for a moment,' I said to Thick.

'For a moment?' Thick exclaimed, outraged. 'You listened and listened. When I got here, you were listening to it so much you couldn't hear me and I couldn't feel you. And you are doing it again, right now.'

I touched my fingers to my lips. He scowled at me, but was still. I listened, not with my ears but with my Skill. I heard Thick's music, the constant Skill-sending that was so much a part of him that I now blocked it without even thinking about it. I closed my eyes and sank deeper into the Skill-current. And there I found it, the roaring whisper of a hundred minds reminding each other not to think about it, not to remember who had died, not to remember the screams or the flames or the blood on the snow. I pressed on the whispers and behind them I could glimpse what they hid from themselves. I retreated. I opened my eyes and found Chade watching me.

'He's correct,' Chade confirmed quietly.

I nodded.

The Skill is popularly believed to be the magic of the royal Farseer line. And perhaps it is true that in our bloodlines it runs stronger and more potent. But when a summoning goes out that will reach only those who already possess the Skill to a useful degree, it is answered as often by a shoemaker or a fisherman as it is by a duke's son. I had long suspected that all people possessed at least a rudimentary level of this magic. Molly was unSkilled, yet how often had I seen her rise and go to Bee's crib moments before the child awoke. The man who 'had a bad feeling' at the moment that his soldier son was wounded or the woman who opened the door before her suitor could knock all seemed to be utilizing the Skill even if they were unaware of it. Now the unspoken agreement that no one would remember the terrible events that had happened at Withywoods hummed like a hive of angry bees once I let myself be aware of it. All the folk of Withywoods, shepherds, arbour- and orchard-folk and house-servants breathed the same forgetfulness. The fury simmered with their ardent desire that no one come to Withywoods, that no one awaken them to what had befallen them. It flooded me with their lost hopes and dreams.

'They have to be made to remember,' Chade said softly. 'It is our only hope for recovering our daughters.'

'They don't want to,' I protested.

'Ya,' Thick agreed morosely. 'Someone told them not to, and then made it seem like a good idea. They don't want to remember. They all keep telling each other, *don't remember, don't remember.*'

Once aware of it, I could not clear it from my senses. It was a ringing in my ears.

'How do we stop it? If we stop it, will they remember? If they remember, can they live with it?'

'I'm living with it,' Perseverance said softly. 'I'm living with it alone.' He crossed his arms on his chest. 'My mum is strong. I'm her third son and the only one that lived. She wouldn't want to have turned me away from her door. She wouldn't want to forget my da and my granddad.' Hope and tears stood in his eyes.

What would deaden the Skill and still that forgetful song for them? I knew. I knew from years of indulging in the herb. 'I have elfbark. Or had it. With some other herbs in my private study. I doubt it was taken.'

'What are you doing with elfbark?' Chade was aghast.

I stared at him. 'Me? What are you doing with elfbark? And not just Six Duchies elfbark, but that OutIslander strain they used on me on Aslevjal? Delvenbark. I saw it on your shelf.'

He stared at me. 'Tools of the trade,' he said quietly. 'Elliania's father obtained it for me. Some things I have and hope never to use.'

'Exactly.' I turned back to Perseverance. 'Find Bulen. Tell him to go to your mother's cottage and ask her to come here to the house. To this study. I'll fetch the herb. After Bulen is on his way, go to the kitchen and tell them I need a teapot, cups and a kettle of boiling water.'

'Sir,' he said. He halted by the door and turned back to me. 'Sir, it won't hurt her, will it?'

'Elfbark is an herb that has been used for a long time. In Chalced, they feed it to their slaves. It gives them a jolt of strength and endurance, but with it comes a bleak spirit. The Chalcedeans claim they can get more work out of their slaves and few have the will to attempt to escape or rise against their masters. It can deaden a severe headache. And Lord Chade and I together discovered that it can dampen a person's ability to use the Skill. The variety from the OutIslands can completely close a person's mind to Skill-communication. I do not have that kind. But it may be that what I have will be strong enough to free your mother from the Skill-suggestion that she forget about you and your father. I cannot promise you that, but it may.'

FitzVigilant stepped forward suddenly. 'Try it on me first. See what it does.'

'Perseverance, go on your errands,' I said firmly. The boy left. Chade and I were left alone with Lant and Thick.

I studied Lant. His resemblance to Chade and his other Farseer forebears was not nearly as clear as Shun's, but now that I knew of it, it was impossible for me not to see it. He also looked terrible. His eyes were sunken but bright with a wound fever, his lips chapped. He moved like a decrepit old man. It had not been that long ago that he had been given a severe beating in Buckkeep

Town. For his own safety, Chade had sent him to me, ostensibly to be my scribe and tutor my daughter. Haven with me had won him a sword thrust in the shoulder and considerable blood loss. And a memory wiped as bland as blowing snow.

'What do you think?' I asked Chade.

'It may lessen his pain, if nothing else. And I do not think his spirit could sink lower than it is. If he is willing, we should let him try it.'

Thick had been drifting about my study, picking up the few curios I had on display, then lifting the curtain to peer out at the snowy grounds. He found a chair and perched on it and suddenly said, 'Nettle can send you the Aslevjal bark. She says she has a journeyman who could bring it through the stones.'

'You can Skill to Nettle?' I was astounded. The keening of the multitude kept me from hearing Chade's Skill at all, and we were in the same room.

'Ya. She wanted me to tell her if Bee was okay, and Lant. I told her Bee is stolen and Lant is crazy. She is sad and scared and angry. She wants to help.'

Not how I would have chosen to convey those tidings, but Nettle and Thick had their own relationship. They spoke plainly to one another.

'Tell her, yes, please. Tell her to ask Lady Rosemary to pack some of each blend of elfbark, and to send them through with her messenger. Tell her we will send a guide and a mount for her courier to the stone on Gallows Hill.' Chade turned to Lant. 'Go to the Rousters' captain, and ask that he dispatch a man with a mount to Gallows Hill outside Oaksbywater.'

Lant looked directly at him. 'Are you sending me out of the room so you can discuss me with Fitz?'

'I am,' Chade replied pleasantly. 'Now go.'

When the door had closed behind him, I said evenly, 'He has his mother's forthright way.'

'Huntswoman Laurel. Yes. He has. It was one of the things I loved about her.' He watched me as he said it, challenging me to be surprised.

I was, a little, but I covered it. 'If he is yours, why is he not FitzFallstar? Or simply a Fallstar?'

'He should have been Lantern Fallstar. When we discovered Laurel was with child, I was willing to wed. She was not.'

I glanced at Thick. He appeared uninterested in what we were saying. I lowered my voice. 'Why?'

There was pain in the lines at the corners of Chade's mouth and in his eyes. 'The obvious reason. She had come to know me too well, and knowing me could not love me. She chose to leave court and go to where she could give birth quietly and out of sight of all.' He made a small sound. 'That hurt the worst of all, Fitz. That she did not want anyone to know the child was mine.' He shook his head. 'I could not stop her. I made sure she had funds. She had an excellent midwife. But she did not survive his birth for long. The midwife called it a childbed fever. I had left Buckkeep as soon as the messenger bird reached me that the boy was born. I still hoped to persuade her to try having a life with me. But by the time I reached her, she was dead.'

He fell silent. I wondered why he was telling me, and why he was telling me now, but did not ask either question. I got up and put more wood on the fire. 'Are there ginger cakes in your kitchen?' Thick asked me.

'I don't know but there is bound to be something sweet there. Why don't you go and ask for something nice. Bring some back for Lord Chade and me, too.'

'Ya,' he promised, and left with alacrity.

Chade spoke as soon as the door had closed around him. 'Lant was a healthy, wailing boy. The midwife had found a wet nurse for him as soon as Laurel began to fail. I gave a great deal of thought to his future, and then I approached Lord Vigilant. He was a man in a great deal of trouble. Debts and stupidity will do that to a man. In exchange for his claiming the boy and raising him as a nobleman, I paid off his debts and found him a clever steward to keep him out of trouble. He had an excellent holding; all it required to prosper was good management. I visited my son as often as I could, and saw that he was taught to ride, to read, swordplay and archery. All a young aristocrat should master.

'I thought it an ideal arrangement for all of us. Lord Vigilant lived well on a now-prosperous estate, my son was safe and well taught. But I did not allow for that man's stupidity. I'd made him too attractive. A stupid man with a well-run estate and money to spare. That bitch plucked him like low-hanging fruit. She never even pretended to like the boy, and as soon as her son was born, she proceeded to drive Lant out of the nest. By then, he was old enough for me to have him at Buckkeep Castle, as a page. And an apprentice. I did hope he would follow in my footsteps.' He shook his head. 'As you saw, he had not the temperament for it. Still, he would have been safe if that woman had not seen him as a threat to her sons' inheritance. She saw him well liked at court and could not stand it. And she made her move.'

He fell silent. There was more to that tale and I knew it. I could have asked after her health, or the well-being of her sons. I chose not to as I did not want to know. I could accept what Chade would do for his family; doubtless to avenge his son, he had done the sort of thing that had guaranteed that Laurel could never love him.

'And Shine was bad judgment.' It shocked me to hear him admit that. Perhaps he'd longed to tell someone. I kept silent and let no sign of judgment show on my face.

'A festival. A flirtatious, pretty woman. Wine and song and carris seed cakes. My daughter has been told one version of the incident of her conception. The truth is quite another. Her mother was neither that young nor that innocent. We danced together, we drank together, we spent time at the gaming tables. We took my winnings and went down to Buckkeep Town and spent them on trinkets and trifles for her. We drank some more. For one evening, Fitz, I was the young man I might have been, and we finished the evening in a cheap inn room under the rafters with the noise of revelry coming up through the floor planks and the sounds of another couple coming through the walls. For me, it was wine and impulse. For her, I am not so sure that she did not have more in mind.

'A month and a half later she came to me to tell me she would bear my child. Fitz, I tried to be honourable. But she was a stupid, vain woman, pretty as a picture and vapid as a moth. I could not hold a conversation with her. Ignorance I could have forgiven. We both know it's a temporary state. But her level of greed and self-indulgence appalled me. My excess on the night of Shine's conception was festival, wine and carris seed. But for Shine's mother, it was how she always was! I knew if I wed her and brought her to court, she would quickly bring scandal down on me and her child. It would only be a matter of time until Shine was used against me. Her parents swiftly saw that. They did not want us to wed, but they did want the child, to hold her over my head and extort money for her. I had to pay to see her, Fitz. They did not make it easy. I could not oversee her upbringing as I had with Lant. I sent tutors, and her mother sent them away as "unsuitable". I sent money for tutors; I've no idea what they spent it on. Her education has been sadly neglected. And when the grandparents finally died, her mother snatched her up, thinking to wring yet more money from me. They held Shine as their hostage. When I heard that the brutish lout her mother had married had begun to mistreat Shine, I stole her. And saw that her stepfather got what he deserved for looking at my daughter in that way.' He paused. I didn't ask. His face sagged with sadness and weariness. He spoke more slowly.

'I put her somewhere safe and tried to repair some of her lacks. I found a capable bodyguard for her, a woman who could teach her the ways a woman can protect herself. And a few other skills as well.

'But I misjudged her stepfather. Her mother would have swiftly forgotten her: she is as maternal as a snake. But I underestimated the thwarted greed of her husband, and his cleverness. I was certain I had concealed Shine. I still do not know how he found her, but fear I have a rat within my spy ranks. I did not fully grasp the lengths her stepfather would go to repair the blow to his pride, though her mother is not innocent either. They tried to poison Shine and killed a kitchen-boy instead. Did they mean to kill her, or simply make her ill? I don't know. But the dose was enough to kill a small boy. So again, I had to move her, and again I had to show them that I am not someone to trifle with.' He folded his lips tightly. 'I have had him watched. He simmers with hate and dreams of vengeance. I intercepted a letter that bragged he would be avenged upon both Shine and me. So you see why I am convinced this is his hand at work again.'

'And I am almost certain it is linked to those who pursue the

Fool. But soon we shall know.' I hesitated, then asked, 'Chade. Why do you tell me these things only now?'

He gave me a cold stare. 'So you will understand the lengths that I will now go to in order to protect my son and regain my daughter.'

I met his gaze angrily. 'Do you think I will do less to bring Bee back?'

He looked at me for what seemed a long time. 'Perhaps you will. I know you wonder if it is a kindness to force your folk to remember. I tell you this plainly. Kind or unkind, I will open each of their minds and find what they know, down to the youngest child or oldest gaffer. We have to know every detail of what happened that day. And then we must act on it, without delay. We cannot undo whatever has befallen them. But we can make the culprits pay in pain. And we can bring our daughters home.'

I nodded. I had not let my mind go to those dark places. Bee was young and very small. No one could think her a woman. But for some men, that did not matter. I thought of Elm's tottering gait and was sickened. Must we indeed force the little kitchen-girl to remember what had been done to her?

'Go fetch the elfbark,' Chade reminded me. 'It will take time to brew.'

FOURTEEN

Elfbark

. . . *and worst of all, hemlock is likely to grow next to the useful and pleasant watercress. Mind that the lads and lasses sent to gather watercress are mindful of this.*

Carris seed is an evil herb; there is little excuse ever to use it. The practice of sprinkling a bit of it on tops of cakes at festivals is an abomination. The user will experience exhilaration and a sense of physical well-being. While using it, a man or woman may feel the heart beat faster, feel warmth in the cheeks of the face and in the organs of the groin. The urge to dance, to run, to sing loudly or to rut without regard for the consequences becomes strong. The effects of the seed wear off suddenly, and then the user may drop in exhaustion and sleep a full day through. In the next handful of days, the user will be weary, disgruntled and sometimes feel pain in the spine.

Of evil herbs, the next culprit is elfbark. It is, as the name implies, bark scraped from the elf tree. The more potent bark will be on the tips of the newest growth. The elf trees that grow in pleasant valleys produce the mildest bark, while those that grow in more rigorous circumstances, such as on sea cliffs or windswept mountainsides, produce a bark that is more dangerous to the user.

The most common use for elfbark is to make a strong tea of it. This gives the user a burst of stamina and can enable the weary traveller or fieldworker to persevere through the most difficult conditions. But stamina is not spirit. While elfbark may mask the pain of an injury or the aching of weary muscles, it brings with it a heavy heart and a discouraged spirit. Those who use it to extend the hours of their work

must have a strong will to continue to pursue their tasks, or an over-
seer who is merciless.

Twelve Unfortunate Herbs – unsigned scroll

I walked through the halls of Withywoods. The Skill-whispering
to *forget, forget, it didn't happen, they are not dead or gone, they
never were,* was like an icy wind in my face. Away from conversation with others, it sapped my will to do anything save the most
rudimentary tasks. I desperately longed to take a nap by a warm
fire with a soft blanket, and perhaps a glass of mulled cider to
ease me into sleep. Shaking off that impulse was like pulling my
sleeve free of plucking ghost-fingers.

The doors of my private study sagged slightly, the elegant wood
around the latches splintered. I scowled. It hadn't been locked,
simply latched. There had been no need for that destruction, save
for the glee of brutes in the grip of battle.

Inside, I looked around as I had not earlier. Dim winter sunlight
reached in a single pointing finger where the draperies were not
quite closed across the window. It fell in a sword-slash of light
across my splintered desk. I walked past the drunken scroll racks
that leaned against one another. Verity's blade that had hung so
long above the mantel was gone. Of course. Even the most rudimentary man-at-arms would have recognized the quality of that
weapon. I fell into a gulch of pain, but quickly I sealed my heart
against that loss. Verity's sword was not my child. It was only a
thing. I retained the memory of the man and the day he had
given it to me. The triptych of Nighteyes, the Fool and me
remained in place on the centre of the mantel, apparently
untouched. The Fool's gift to me before he left for Clerres, the
one that had led to him 'betraying' me. I could not bear the Fool's
knowing half-smile.

I did not look to see what else was broken or stolen. I went
to my desk, pulled the drawer all the way out, and then reached
in to take out the box that fitted snugly behind it. I opened it.
The second compartment held the corked pot of elfbark. I took
it out and started to restore the box to its hiding-place in the
broken desk. Instead, I tucked it under my arm and dropped the

drawer to the floor. I found myself not thinking about anything as I walked back to the estate study. *Forget, forget, forget* thrummed the song. I summoned the will to set a Skill-block against it. The moment I had it in place, I felt a wave of panic hit me. Bee had been taken, and I had not a clue as to where to seek her. The drive to do something, do anything, lashed me like a whip. But this drug in my hand was the most I could do right now, and that shamed me. Almost I fled back to the whispering of *forget, forget*. Like seizing a sharpened blade, I gripped my anger and fear and clutched it hard. *Feel the pain and feed the fury.* What could my fear be to whatever she was enduring?

In the study, a kettle had been hung over the hearth: I heard the seething of boiling water. Perseverance sat dejectedly beside the fire. The tops of his cheeks were red, but his mouth was pinched white with pain. A teapot and cups were set out on a tray. Someone in the kitchen had sent along little cakes with it. A pleasant touch, I thought savagely. Remember a night of terror, and then, oh, do have a sweet cake to go with it. Chade took the box of herbs from my hands, opened it, and scowled at the contents. I offered no apologies for sometimes indulging myself. He opened the pot of elfbark and shook some into his hand. 'It looks old.' He glanced up at me, the displeased teacher.

'It's not exactly fresh,' I admitted. 'But it will have to do.'

'It will.' He put a generous measure into the pot and handed it to me. I pulled the kettle back from the flames and tipped boiling water into the teapot. The once-familiar scent of elfbark tea rose to greet me, and with it a hundred memories of how often I had drunk it. There had been a time when the effort to Skill had cost me pounding and nauseating headaches, the sort where spots and lines of light would dance before my eyes and every sound was a new jolt of agony. Only when the coterie had accidentally loosed that spectacular healing upon me had I become able to Skill with little to no pain. I'd never known whether to blame my earlier agonies on the beating that Skillmaster Galen had given me, or on the magical block he had put in my mind, one that fogged me and made me believe I had no talent for the Skill and little personal worth to the world. But until that healing, elfbark tea had been my consolation after serious Skill-sessions.

'Let it brew,' Chade advised me and my mind leapt back to the present. I set the pot down on the tray. At almost the same moment, FitzVigilant returned. 'I've sent a man on his way, and told him to take an extra mount. I could not give the best directions to the Gallows Hill, but I am sure anyone in Oaksbywater can point him on his way.'

'Excellent,' Chade told him and I nodded. I was putting a measure of ground willowbark into one of the cups. I added some valerian. Chade watched me curiously. I flicked a glance at the boy. He nodded, and then reached past me to add an additional pinch of valerian. 'Your valerian looks stale, too,' he chided me. 'You should renew your stock more often.'

I said nothing to that, but nodded as I added hot water to the cup. I knew the old man would not apologize for his earlier remarks; this was his way of trying to put us back to our old foundation. I'd take it. I set the cup on the floor by Perseverance. 'Let that brew for a time, and then drink it all. It won't taste good, but it's not about taste.'

'Is that elfbark?' he asked anxiously.

'No. It's willowbark for your fever, and valerian to take some of the pain away. How's your shoulder?'

'It throbs,' he admitted. 'All the way to my back and up my neck.'

'The tea will help.'

He looked up at me. 'Will that other tea hurt my mother? When she remembers?'

'I expect it will be hard for her. But the choice is to leave her alone for the rest of her life. She wouldn't remember your father dying, but she'd never recall she'd had a son.'

'She'd have my aunt, and my cousins. They live down in Withy.'

'Boy?' It was FitzVigilant, cutting into our conversation. 'I'll be drinking it first. We'll see what it does to me. Then you can decide about giving it to your mother.'

Perseverance stared up at him. 'Thank you, sir,' he said doubtfully.

Lant spoke to his father. 'Is it brewed enough?'

'We'll see,' Chade said quietly. He poured some into a cup,

looked at it, smelled it, and then filled the cup the rest of the way. He handed the cup to Lant. 'Go slowly with it. Let us know if you sense a difference, or start to remember that night.'

Lant sat down. He looked at the tea in the cup. We were all watching him as he raised it and took a sip. He made a face. 'It's a bit too hot. And it tastes bitter.' But almost immediately he took another sip. He lifted his eyes. 'Could you not stare?' he said to me. I shifted my eyes. A moment later, he said, 'It's so quiet.'

Chade and I exchanged a glance. I stole a look at Lant. He was staring at the liquid in his cup. He took a breath, as if daring himself, and then drained it down. He made a pained face and then sat still, holding the cup. He closed his eyes. His brow wrinkled and then he hunched in on himself. 'Oh, sweet Eda,' he groaned. 'Oh, no. Oh, no, no, no!'

Chade went to him. He set his hands on Lant's shoulder and with a tenderness I'd seldom seen in him, leaned down to say softly by his ear, 'Let yourself remember. It's the only way you can help her now. Remember it all.'

Lant bowed his face into his hands, and I suddenly saw how young he was. Not even twenty. Raised far more gently than I had been. The beating from his stepmother's thugs might well have been the first real violence he'd experienced in his life. He'd never pulled an oar on a war galley, let alone swung an axe through a man's midsection. Chade had already told me that Lant hadn't been able to kill. And I'd entrusted him with Bee's life. And Shun's.

'Tell me what happened,' Chade said quietly. I leaned back to sit on the edge of my desk and kept perfectly still.

Lant's voice was tight. 'Well. We came back here after Badgerlock and the beggar went into the Skill-pillar. I, and Shun—' His voice broken on her name. 'And Bee. We didn't understand any of what had happened in Oaksbywater, not why he killed a dog and then bought its puppies, nor why he stabbed the beggar and then took him by magic to Buckkeep. We, that is, Shun and I, were both rather angry about all of it. First he had said I was not competent to teach Bee and then he had gone off and left her completely in my care. And he had insulted Lady Shun as well!' Lant was suddenly just a youngster, pouring out his wrongs to Chade. The old man shot me a questioning look. I met his stare with a flat gaze of my own.

'Get to the next day,' I suggested.

At my tone, Lant straightened his back. 'Yes. Well. As you might imagine, the servants including Steward Revel were very confused when the master of the house did not return. Shun and I assured them that we were very capable of looking after Withywoods for a few days. Despite how tired we were, Shun and I sat up that night, and she undertook to plan the festivities for Winterfest. We were up very late. And so we did not rise early the next morning. I regret to say that I was late joining my students in the schoolroom. Bee was there, looking tired but otherwise fine. And when we parted that morning, Shun had said that she would be speaking with the staff about decorating the house and talking to the musicians who had come and seeing if she could not send for more entertainers.' He looked suddenly at Chade. 'You said my sister was taken, earlier.' For two breaths, I watched the knowledge spread through him. 'Shun is my sister? Truly? By blood?'

'You are both my offspring, both Fallstars,' Chade assured him.

Could Chade ignore the deep dismay that washed over Lant's features? I wondered what had passed between him and Shun on the evening they had stayed up so late. I decided I never wanted to know.

'Continue,' Chade reminded Lant. The scribe had lifted his hand to cover his mouth. When he took it away, his mouth trembled for a moment before he mastered himself. He tried to sit up straighter, then winced at his wound. Chade looked at me. 'Valerian and willowbark,' he requested. I took Lant's cup and made the requested tea while I listened.

'Well, I had just settled my students when we heard noises. I was not alarmed, but puzzled. I thought it might be some sort of altercation among the servants, with pot throwing. I told my students to stay and study and went into the hallway. I soon realized the sounds were coming from the front entrance, not the kitchens. I heard Revel's voice raised, and I ran toward the commotion. When I got to the hall, I saw Revel there and two of the serving-boys. They were trying to hold the doors closed, but someone was pounding on them and shouting. I thought perhaps we had drunken tinkers at the door. Then someone shoved a sword through the crack of the door and caught one of the serving-boys in the hand. I shouted at Revel to hold the door while I got help. I went to find a sword, calling to the servants to warn Shun and to arm themselves. I took the old sword that used to be there, over the mantel. And I ran back.' He wet his lips. His gaze went distant and his breathing deepened.

'Fitz,' Chade said quietly. 'Perhaps some more elfbark in that mix.'

Before I could move, Perseverance was on his feet. He brought the teapot to Lant, took the cup from his hand and added the elfbark brew. Lant was sitting very still. Chade still stood behind him. He leaned down and said quietly, 'Son, take the cup. And drink it.'

A peculiar pang passed through me. It could not have been jealousy.

Lant did as his father told him. This time, his expression scarcely changed as he set the cup back down. 'I've never been a fighter. You know that. You both know that!' His admission sounded more like an accusation. Then his voice dropped. 'I'm just not. A friendly bout, with practice blades, on a summer day with a friend and comparing bruises later is one thing. But when I went running back, the door had already given way. I saw Revel stagger past me, holding his gut. And one of the lads was on the floor in a pool of blood. The other youngster was trying to hold them off with his belt-knife. The first man through the door laughed, and cut his head off. And then it was only me in the hall, facing first one, then three, and then at least six of them. I tried to fight. I did. I was shouting for help and I tried to fight, but this wasn't fencing, man against man. There were no rules! I engaged with one man, and a second stepped forward. I managed to hold my own but the entry hall is wide. The invaders just went around us, and I heard them running down the halls behind me. And I heard screams, and things breaking. And the man in front of me suddenly laughed.'

He looked down suddenly.

I hazarded a guess. 'A man behind you attacked you? He knocked you unconscious?'

'No. No one touched me. I dropped my sword to the ground. And the two men I'd been fighting just stood and laughed at me. One gave me a hard push as I walked by him, and I didn't care. And I walked outside and stood in the snow in front of the manor. And I still don't know why.'

Skill-suggestion? Chade's thought brushed lightly against mine.

I nodded, unwilling to make the effort to do more. To Skill to him, I'd have to drop my walls and let in that fog of *forget, forget, forget.* I would not forget. 'Don't worry about what you don't know,' I suggested gently. 'It's obvious magic was at work. You had no way to resist it. Just tell us what you do know.'

'Yes,' he said unwillingly. But he was shaking his head 'no'.

'Do you want more of the elfbark?' Chade asked.

'No. I remember what happened that day, and on the days since. I don't understand it, but I recall it. I'm just ashamed to speak it aloud.'

'Lant, Fitz and I have both known our share of defeats. We've been burned, poisoned, beaten. And yes, we've been buffeted by Skill and made fools of and done things we're ashamed to admit. No matter what you did or didn't do, we won't think less of you. Your hands were bound, even if there was no rope you could see. If we are to rescue your sister and little Bee you have to set your pride aside and just tell us what you know.'

Chade's voice was comforting. A father's voice. Something cynical inside me wondered if he would have been that forgiving of me but I quenched it.

It took Lant a little time. He rocked in his chair once or twice, cleared his throat, and then said nothing. When he spoke again, his voice was higher and tighter. 'I stood with the others out in the snow. People walked out of the manor and came and stood near me. There were a few men on horseback but I didn't feel that they were keeping me there. I was afraid of them but mostly I was afraid to do anything except stay there with the others. No. Not afraid, not even reluctant. It just seemed that what I was doing was the only possible thing I could do. Everyone was there, milling about. Lots of people were weeping and agitated, but no one was talking to anyone else. No one resisted. Even the injured just stood and bled.' He paused again, his mind going back.

Bulen tapped on the door. 'Sir? I am so sorry to disappoint you. I have been down to the cottages where the stableworkers live. No one there has any recollection of a lad named Perseverance or admits to being his family.'

I felt like a ninny. I looked at the boy. His eyes were dark with sorrow. He spoke softly. 'It's the third cottage. There is a hedge witch charm over the door for good luck. And my grandfather made a doorknocker out of a carthorse's shoe. My mother's name is Diligent.'

Bulen was nodding. I amended his orders. 'Do not make mention of her son at all. Tell her we wish to speak to her to see if she will take on some extra tasks in the kitchen.'

'Oh, she'd like that,' Perseverance said quietly. 'She's always after Da to build her an oven behind the cottage so she could bake whenever she wanted.'

'Very well, sir. And Steward Dixon sends to tell you that the guardsmen are eating everything within sight. As our larders were not well stocked this fall . . .'

Our larders had been overflowing before the raid. 'Tell him to send a man and wagon to Withy and stock whatever he thinks we need for now. Next market day, he can make a trip to Oaksbywater. I will settle with the merchants later. They know we are good for it.'

'Very good, sir.' Bulen cast a worried look at FitzVigilant. He had only served him for a short time, but there was already a bond between the young men. 'Is there anything I can bring for Scribe Lant?'

Lant did not even shift his eyes toward Bulen. Chade shook his head silently and the man withdrew. 'Lant?' he said softly.

FitzVigilant drew a deep breath and took up his tale as if it were a heavy burden. 'We were all there. And they brought out Shun and her maid. I remember I noticed that Shun was fighting them, because no one else was. She was kicking and screaming at the man who dragged her. Then from somewhere, she had a knife and she stabbed his hand. She almost broke free. He grabbed her by the shoulder and slapped her so hard that she fell. He still had to throttle the knife out of her hand. He pushed her toward us and walked away. Then she looked all around and when she saw me, she came running to me. She was screaming, "Do something! Why isn't anyone doing anything?" She threw her arms around me, but I just stood there. Then she asked me, "What's wrong with you?" And I couldn't think of anything wrong at all. I said we should just stand with the others. It was what I wanted to do. And she asked, "If it's what they want to do, why are they moaning?"' He stopped and swallowed. 'I listened, then. And they were. Moaning and weeping but in a disconnected way. And I realized I'd been doing it, too.'

Only Shun had fought back. Why? Had the training Chade had provided for her made her bolder than the others? I'd hired no servants for their skill with arms, but I was sure my stable-folk had seen a brawl or three. But no one had fought back. Except Shun. I looked at Chade. He didn't meet my eyes and I was forced to set the question aside for later.

'The guards on horseback started shouting at us to "sit down, sit down". Some yelled in Chalcedean, some in our tongue. I didn't sit, because I was already too cold and there was snow on the ground. And I felt that as long as I stayed with the others in the carriage turn-around, I was doing what I should be doing. One of the men started making threats. He was looking for someone, a pale boy, and said he would kill us all if we did not turn him over to them. I knew of no such lad, and apparently no one else did. There was Oak, who you had hired as a serving-man. He was blond, but scarcely a boy. But someone said to one of the men that he was the only tow-head working at Withywoods. He was standing not far from me. And the man who was asking rode his horse over to Oak, looked down on him, and then pointed at him. "Him?" he shouted at this other man. He was dressed all in white, and though he looked like a prosperous merchant, his face was a boy's. He shook his head and the man on the horse was suddenly very angry. "Not him!" he shouted and then he leaned down and slashed Oak's throat with his sword. And he fell into the snow, with the blood leaping from the wound. He lifted his hand to his throat, as if he could hold it back. But he couldn't. He looked right at me until he died. Blood steams when the day is that cold. I never knew that. And I just watched.

'But Shun didn't. She screamed, and cursed the man on the

horse, saying she would kill him. She started to run at him. And I didn't know why, but I caught hold of her arm and tried to hold her back. I struggled with her. And a man on a horse rode over and kicked me hard in the head, so I let go of her. Then he leaned down and thrust his sword through me. And he laughed as I fell right onto Oak's body. His blood was still warm. I remember that.'

Oak. A young man hired to help serve the dinners. A smiling young man, unlearned at serving in a house, but always smiling, and so proud of his new livery. Oak, a lifeless body, seeping red into white snow. He had come to us from Withy. Did his parents wonder yet why he had not come home to visit?

There was a noise at the door. It was Thick, coming back with a platter of little raisin cakes. He was smiling as he offered them to us. He looked puzzled when Chade and I and Lant shook our heads. Perseverance took one, but held it in his hand. Thick smiled and sat down on the hearth with the plate on his lap. He made a great show of choosing one. His simple enjoyment of a little cake rang sharply against my heart. Why could not it be my little girl, my Bee, sitting there with a whole plate of cakes to herself and no worries?

Lant had paused, his brow furrowed. He looked up at Chade, as if to find what the old man thought of his words. Chade's face was expressionless. 'Go on,' he said in a voice both quiet and wooden.

'I don't remember anything after that. Not until I woke very late at night. I was alone in the carriageway. Oak's body was gone, and it was fully dark night, except for the light from the stables. They were burning. But no one was paying any attention to the fire. I didn't think about any of that, then. I didn't notice Oak's body was gone or that the stables were burning. I got up. I felt very dizzy and the pain in my arm and shoulder was terrible, and I was so cold I was shaking all over. I staggered inside and went to my room. Bulen was there, and he said he was glad to see me. And I told him I'd been hurt. And he bandaged me and helped me to bed, and said Old Rosie the shepherd's granny was in the manor doing some healing. And she came and saw to my shoulder.'

'Bulen didn't ride to Withy to get a real healer? Or to Oaksbywater?' Chade was obviously appalled that someone's granny had tended to his son's sword wound.

Lant knit his brows. 'No one wanted to leave the house and grounds. And no one wanted any strangers to come in. We all agreed on that. Just as we agreed that someone must have been drunk and careless to burn the stables. But none of us really cared. I could not recall how I had been injured. Some said there had been a drunken brawl, others that there were injuries from the stable fire. But no one was clear about what had happened. And we didn't care, really. It wasn't something to dwell on.' He looked up at Chade suddenly, a piercing, pleading look. 'What did they do to me? How did they do that?'

'We think they imposed a strong Skill-suggestion on you and the others. And then suggested that you keep reinforcing it with one another. You were all to refuse to remember, to not think about it, to be unwelcoming to outsiders and to have no desire to leave the estate. It was the perfect way to cover up what had happened here.'

'Was it my fault? Was I weak, that they could do that to me?' There was agony in that question.

'No.' Chade was very certain. 'It was not your fault. A person with great Skill-talent can impose his will on another and make him believe almost anything. It was one of King Verity's best weapons against the Red Ships during the war.' More softly he added, 'I never thought to see it used like this, within Buck's boundaries. It took tremendous strength and Skill to do this. Who has that sort of knowledge of the magic? And that sort of talent for it?'

'I could do that,' Thick announced. 'I know how to do it, now. Make a music to forget, forget, and make them all sing the same song, over and over. Probably not hard. I just never thought of doing that before. I could do that if you want?'

I don't think I have ever heard more chilling words. Thick and I were friends now, but in the past, we had had our differences. For the most part, the simple man had a generous heart. But crossed, he had proved he was capable of making me so clumsy that I constantly barked my shins or bumped my head in doorways. His magical strength was far beyond my own. Should he ever decide that I should forget something, would I even know he had done it? I lifted my eyes and met Chade's gaze. I saw the same thought in his eyes.

'Didn't say I would do it,' Thick reminded us. 'Just said I could do it.'

'I think taking someone's memories is wrong and bad,' I said. 'Like taking someone's coins or their sweets.'

Thick's tongue had curled over his upper lip. It was his thinking expression. 'Ya,' he replied gravely. 'Probably bad.'

Chade had picked up my teapot and was weighing it thoughtfully in his hand. 'Thick. Could you make a song that let people remember? Not one that forced people to remember, but one that told them they could remember if they wanted to.'

'Don't do it yet!' I intervened. 'Think about it, and tell us if you think it can be done. But maybe we shouldn't do that, either.'

'Do you think we have enough elfbark to make tea for all of Withywoods? Even if a courier brings my supply also? Fitz, with every minute, every hour, Bee and Shine may be in greater danger. At the very least, they are moving away from us. At worst, well I refuse to consider the worst. But we need to know what happened after Lant was knocked unconscious. We both know that their tracks are totally obscured by now, with all the snow and wind we've had. And if the raiders can make Withywoods folk forget what happened here, can they make folk forget they've seen them passing? As we've had no news of strangers in this part of Buck, I consider that likely. So our only hope is to find out who they were and what their plans were. They came a long way and apparently made very elaborate plans to get something. What?'

'Who,' Lant corrected him. 'They wanted a pale boy.'

'The Unexpected Son,' I said quietly. 'From the White prophecies. Chade, the Fool told me that was why he was tortured. The Servants are looking for the next White Prophet, and they thought the Fool would know where to find him.'

A tap at the door turned my gaze that way. Bulen poked his head in. 'Sir, I've brought her.'

'Please bring her in,' I invited him. As Bulen opened the door and the woman entered, Perseverance came to his feet. He stared at her with dog's eyes. I saw his lip quiver and then he clenched his jaws.

I had possibly met his mother when I first came to Withywoods, but I doubted our paths had crossed much since then. She was a typical Buck woman, with curly black hair bundled into a lace net at the back of her head, and soft brown eyes. She was slender for a woman of her years, and her clothing was well cared for. She bobbed a curtsey to us and politely but eagerly asked about the position in the kitchen. I let Chade reply.

'This lad who has worked in the stables says you have a reputation as an excellent baker.'

Diligent turned a polite smile on Perseverance but showed no sign of recognition. Chade continued, 'I understand that you live in the cottages used by the stablehands. We are looking into the stable fire that happened on Winterfest Eve. Lives were lost in that fire, and we are trying to get an accurate accounting of how it may have started. Did you know any of the stablehands?'

Such a direct question. It was as if someone had flapped a black rag behind her eyes. There was a moment when she did not seem to see us or be in the room with us. Then she was back. She shook her head. 'No, sir, I don't believe I do.'

'I see. And I've forgotten my manners, asking you here on such a cold day and offering you no comfort. Please. Do sit down. We've some cakes here. And may I pour a cup of tea for you? It's a special brew from Buckkeep Castle itself.'

'Why thank you, sir. That would be kind.' Bulen brought her a chair and she sat carefully, arranging her skirts so they fell smoothly. As Chade poured tea and brought it to her, she offered, 'You know, you might ask Hawthorn at the end of the lane. Her boy works in the stables; they might know.'

Chade brought her the cup himself. 'It can be a bit strong. Let us know if you'd care for some honey,' he said as he gave it to her.

She smiled as she accepted the pretty china cup. 'Thank you,' she said, and took a sip. She puckered her mouth in surprise at the bitterness, but she smiled. 'It is a bit strong,' she said politely.

'It's something of a tonic,' Chade told her. 'I enjoy the vigour it seems to give me, especially on chill winter days.' He gave her his most charming smile.

'Indeed, does it?' she asked. 'At my age, I could use a bit of that!' She smiled back at him and took a second, polite, sip. As she lowered the cup to the saucer, her face changed. The cup chattered on the saucer as her hand began to tremble. Chade rescued it from her failing grip. Her hands rose to cover first her mouth, and then to picket her whole face. She bowed forward from the waist. She began to shake badly and the first sound that came out of her was not a woman weeping but an animal's low cry of agony.

Perseverance flew across the room. He knelt before her and put his good arm around her. He did not tell her that it would be all right. He said nothing, but put his cheek beside hers. No one in the room spoke as she continued to grieve. After a time, she lifted her head, put her arms around her son and said, 'I sent you away. How can you ever forgive me? You were all I had left, and I sent you away.'

'I'm here now. Oh, Ma, I thank Eda you know me.' He lifted his head and looked at me. 'Thank you, sir. I've got my ma back. Thank you.'

'What happened to me?' The query was a shaking moan.

'A bad magic,' the stableboy comforted her. 'The same bad magic that happened to everyone else here. It made everyone forget what happened on Winterfest Eve. Everyone but me.' He knit his brows. 'Why not me?'

Chade and I conferred with a look. Neither of us had an answer. Thick spoke in a soft voice. 'Cause they didn't have you with the others. When they told them to sing the forgetting song. So they couldn't make you forget. And you don't hear the song at all. Not any songs.' He looked sad for the boy.

Bulen startled us all when he strode forward. I'd almost forgotten he was in the room. Without a word, he lifted the cup from the saucer Chade still held. He drained off the cup of tea, stood like a statue, and then unbidden, sank into a nearby chair. For a time, he simply sat. When he looked up, his face was pale. 'I was there,' he said. He rolled a glance at Lant. 'I saw them kick you in the head, after they stabbed you, and I stood there.

I saw that same horseman knock Lady Shun to the ground. He called her filthy names and said if she dared to get up, he would—' He paused, obviously sickened. 'He threatened her. Then they herded us into a tighter group, as if we were sheep being bunched. And other people came to join us there, the folk from the cottages. A lot of the children had been hiding somewhere, but they came out in a group. And the soldiers began to shout at us about a pale boy.

'Then a woman came out of the manor. I'd never seen her before. She was dressed all in white, very warmly. At first she scolded the old man in charge. He was cruel and seemed to care little about what she said. She was angry that people had been killed. The bodies would have to be dealt with, and it would make everything harder to conceal. She said he had done it badly, that it was not the path she had wanted. And he told her to leave him to the business of war, that she had no idea how territory was captured. And that when they had finished, they could set fire to the stables and get rid of the bodies that way. I could tell she was not happy with him.

'But when she turned to us, she was calm and smiling. She didn't yell. She spoke so kindly that all I wanted to do was find whatever would please her. She was seeking for a boy or a young man who had come recently to stay with us. She promised they were not there to hurt him, only to take him back to where he belonged. Someone, Tavia I think, shouted that they'd killed the only young man who had recently joined us. But the woman began to walk among us, looking each of us in the face. I think someone was with her . . .' Bulen's voice and expression went bland. I sensed he pushed against a barrier he could not pass. There was yet another layer to all this.

'You!' Bulen said suddenly. He pointed a finger at Perseverance. 'It was you on the brown horse, and Lady Bee on the grey, wasn't it? Everything changed in the instant. The woman was urging and urging us to think of a boy who had come recently, and then one of the soldiers shouted and pointed, and we all looked. And you were running the horses dead out, and then three of the soldiers wheeled their horses about and went after you. Including that cruel old man. And one was drawing his bow and shooting as he rode. I remember seeing him do that, guiding the horse with his knees.'

'He got me, too,' Perseverance said quietly. He lifted his good hand to his bandaged shoulder. His mother gave a gasp and pulled him closer.

'For a short time, while they were chasing you, there were just a few soldiers guarding us. And I remember that we started talking, asking each other what was going on, how had this happened? It was like waking from sleepwalking . . .' His gaze was unfocused. 'But then we all calmed down. And there were other people there, younger and, well, softer people in the pale clothing. They were walking among us, telling us to be calm, be calm. They looked worried, but were trying to reassure us. But for a time, I think I knew how wrong everything was. I knelt down by Lant because Shun was there, crying over him. And I told her he wasn't dead. Then the round-faced woman came back and she had Bee with her. But Bee looked as if she were asleep with her eyes open. She was calling to everyone that they had found him, they'd found an unexpected son. I remember now, I thought they meant the stableboy. But she had Bee with her and . . . someone else. Someone . . .'

Again he floundered, reaching after something buried beyond his ability to recall it. I heard his words with a rising chill in my heart. They'd captured Bee. And spoken of the Unexpected Son, the child from the White Prophecies. The boy upon whom the fate of the world turned. Once, the Fool had believed that was me. And now he thought it was a son he'd left behind, a child he had fathered without knowing he'd done it. However he meant those peculiar words, I could not imagine why anyone might think it was my daughter. The drive to do something, to do anything, was rising in me, an irrational storm that insisted I could not simply wait and gather information.

Bulen was speaking again. 'They wrapped her in white robes and put her on their sleigh, as if she were a princess. By then the soldiers were back, circling us. And I couldn't think of anything else to do but wait and see what would happen. It just seemed the only proper thing to do, was to be in that huddle of people.'

I asked the question. 'You think they thought Bee was the boy they were looking for? The Unexpected Son?'

Bulen hesitated. 'So they behaved, sir. After they had her, they stopped seeking for him.'

'I remember all that,' Diligent said as I was still trying to picture Bee as a boy. 'I was in the cottage, putting a mend in Tallerman's good jacket, and thinking about the fun we'd have at Midwinterfest. He was such a dancer!' Her voice caught on a sob, but she went on, 'I was fretting that Perseverance had outgrown his good shirt and wondering if I could let it out any more for one more wearing. Then, suddenly, for no reason I can think of now, I decided I wanted to go up to the manor. I didn't wait, I left the cottage just as I was and walked up to the manor. Everyone from the cottages was going, just as if it were time for Winterfest, but no one was laughing or talking. We just all wanted to go to the manor. On the way, I walked right past the stables. They were on fire but I didn't think that was terrible. I didn't stop or call out to anyone . . .' Her voice faltered and I saw her wonder if her husband and father-in-law had still been alive, if she could have had one last word with them.

'Everyone was already dead, Ma.' Perseverance spoke the words aloud and the woman gave a sudden sob. She clutched her son as if he were the last bit of floating wreckage in a stormy sea. Her grief strangled her into silence.

Bulen spoke into that gulf. 'Yes. The cottage folk came, and the children. The children were coming willingly, but some of the soldiers were mocking them. I saw one of the men seize a little kitchen girl . . .'

The colour left his face and his mouth fell ajar. For a time, none of us spoke. 'They were brutes,' Diligent said at last. 'And we were like sheep. I watched the stables burn, and we heard the screams of the horses left inside. Some of the beasts must have broken loose, for a few fled. I just watched the flames and I didn't even wonder where my husband was, or my son. It was just a thing that was happening.'

'Did they take Lady Shun?' Chade's voice was heavy with fear. It was unlike him to interrupt anyone giving such a complete telling of events, but I knew he could not stand the suspense. He had to know. I didn't blame him.

'Yes. They did.' Bulen spoke with certainty. 'It happened later. It was evening. They had placed Bee on the sleigh. I seem to remember the woman urging the soldiers to leave as soon as possible. But the soldiers were looting and feasting on food from the kitchens and . . . taking the young women. The women were . . . empty. As if they did not care or notice, and one man complained it was not . . . satisfactory. The kind woman finally talked them into leaving, but the angry soldier dragged Shun away from the others. She was resisting, when no one else was. He threw her down in the snow. And he, he began to, he intended to rape her.'

Lant made a sound in the back of his throat. I glanced at him. His face was in his hands. Chade was as pale as chalk but silent.

'She was fighting back, but not with any hope of winning. And I, I was just watching it happen. As you watch snow fall or wind move in the trees. I am so ashamed to say that. Not a man of Withywoods objected or raised a hand to stop him. But suddenly Bee came running and threw herself on the man. He flung her aside, but Bee was shouting that she would die if they hurt Shun. And a whole swarm of the pale people attacked the soldier then and dragged him off Lady Shun.'

'Then she was not violated?' Chade barely had breath to push the words out.

Bulen looked at him. He flushed a deep scarlet and lowered his eyes in shame. 'Then? No. But before then, or after they took her, I cannot say.' He lifted his gaze and met Chade's eyes with honest pain. 'I consider it likely.'

Lant groaned aloud.

Chade rose abruptly. 'A moment,' he said in a voice I did not recognize, and hurried out of the room.

'Lad.' Bulen spoke quietly. 'Please forgive me for doubting you.'

Before Perseverance could speak, his mother let out a loud wail. 'All I had left, and I turned you from my door! What would your father have said to me? Oh, son, son, whatever shall we do now? How shall we earn our bread?' She clutched at Perseverance and sobbed against him. The boy had gone pale. He gave me a look and then spoke to her bowed head.

'I've sworn myself to Badgerlock, mother. I'll earn our keep. Only he's not Badgerlock. Grandfather was right. He is truly FitzChivalry Farseer and he's accepted me into his service. I will take care of you.'

'Truly?' It was Bulen who spoke. 'He is truly FitzChivalry, the Witted . . . Farseer?' He near fell over his tongue dodging the word 'bastard'.

'He is,' Perseverance said proudly before I could think of a sufficient lie.

'He is,' Lant echoed. 'But I thought it was to be kept always a secret.' He stared at me in consternation.

'It was an interesting Winterfest at Buckkeep Castle,' I said, and his eyes grew rounder.

'Then everyone knows?'

'Not in full.' But now they would. The woven lies of decades were suddenly unravelling. How much of the truth could I bear?

Before anyone could speak again, Chade walked back into the room. He looked cadaverous. His voice was hoarse and thick. 'They seem to have struck first at the stables and then destroyed the messenger birds. We must now speak with anyone who may have survived that first part of the attack.' He cleared his throat. 'Eventually we will speak with everyone who endured this. But first we must start at the beginning.'

FIFTEEN

Surprises

Let there be made a great record of every dream that has been recorded. Even more important, as the shaysims share dreams with us, let each dream be recorded, not once, but for each element of the dream. Let there be a record of dreams of horses, of trees, of acorns or apples, and so on. So that when there is a mustering of cavalry, or a fire sweeps through the forests, we can look and see if this event was foretold. And soon, as the Servants study well the dreams, I foretell that we shall see the patterns for ourselves, and then make ourselves the judgments as to what must be enabled and what must be hindered.

Servant Cetchua of the 41st Line

Chade was true to his word. Long after I thought we had every bit of information that we could use, he continued to summon my folk to the study and offer them elfbark tea. In a soft conversation, we had decided against Thick's 'remembering song'. The tea was working and we needed results more than we needed to experiment with the Skill. We took the safe road. Nettle's courier from Buckkeep arrived with the supply of OutIslander elfbark known as delvenbark from Chade's hoard. When my older and less potent stock gave out, Chade began to brew tea with the more virulent form of the herb. Even the smell of it made me giddy and Thick left the study and would not return. Dixon returned with supplies from Withy and demanded to know how many folk the kitchen should expect for dinner. I was less patient with him than I might have been. Pragmatically, Chade and I decided that neither Dixon nor any of the kitchen staff were to be restored until after the evening meal was prepared and served.

The captain of the Rousters returned to report to us that no one they had encountered on any of the main roads or even the lesser trails had any recollection of a troop of soldiers and several large sleighs. He was obviously disappointed that no one would claim Chade's reward but by that time, neither Chade nor I were surprised at his news. With every piece of evidence of how well they had planned their attack and escape, my heart sank. I was virtually certain the raiders were the Servants that the Fool had described. He had said they would stop for nothing in their quest for the Unexpected Son.

'So why take our daughters?' Chade demanded in an almost-quiet moment between victims of our tea.

I spoke aloud my only theory. 'As hostages. They think we know where this other child is, and so they take our daughters to hold hostage. If I am correct, they will soon send some sort of a message, offering to exchange our children for the boy they seek.'

Chade shook his head. 'They should have sent the message already, then. Or left it here for us to find. Why cover their tracks so well if they only wanted to frighten us? And why brutalize Shine, if they hope to sell her back to me? Why treat Bee like a princess and drag Shine off as if she were plunder?'

I had one possible theory. 'Bulen said they seemed to think Bee was the boy they sought. The Unexpected Son.'

He frowned at me in consternation. 'You think that is possible? Does your daughter look like a boy?'

'Not to me,' I said tersely. Then I had to add, 'But she is not fond of ruffles or lace. Nor is she the most feminine of little girls.' I thought of her in her tunic and leggings, with dirt on her knees. Her hair chopped short for mourning. 'I'm going back to Buckkeep,' I announced, surprising even myself.

'Why?' Chade demanded.

'Because I need to talk to the Fool. I need to tell him what has happened here, and describe the people involved and see if he has any insights into what they might want and where they might take our daughters. I doubt you will wring much more from my folk.' I did not admit that I dreaded hearing what my kitchen servants would recall, especially little Elm. Several of the stable-folk had been reduced to incoherency when given the tea and allowed to recall what they had experienced. Families had been decimated by the silent slaughter in the stables. With each retainer reawakened to that horror, the susurrus of *forget, forget, forget* lessened. Even those who had not yet been dosed appeared uneasy now, and as each person who entered my study emerged later weeping or silent or drained, the atmosphere of dread in the manor increased. When I left my study, I noticed servants now staring at the damaged doors or slashed tapestries as each came to terms with what they had experienced, forgotten and now recalled.

Chade cleared his throat, drawing my wandering attention back. 'We will both return to Buckkeep. I suggest that after the evening meal we summon all the remaining servants and offer them the tea together. We can ask then for specific information about the appearance of the invaders and the fate of Shine and Bee. I doubt that we shall discover much that is new, but we would be foolish to ignore the chance that any one of them might hold one more hint of what we are up against.'

I resented that he was right. I longed to do something more than sit and listen to my people recount how they had been brutalized. I excused myself from the remainder of his tea parties, knowing that if he discovered anything of great significance, he would summon me. I checked on Thick to be sure he was occupied and comfortable, and found him with FitzVigilant. No. Lant, I reminded myself. A bastard, but never Vigilant's. They were well known to each other from their time together at Buckkeep and I was pleased that Lant seemed genuinely fond of Thick. A somewhat subdued Lant was allowing him to draw on the wax tablets we had acquired for his students, and Thick was fascinated that he could scribe onto the surface and then watch it smoothed away.

I left them and moved slowly through Withywoods. Nowhere could I hide from the disaster that had befallen me. The faces of the servants I encountered were pale and troubled. The raiders had wantonly destroyed items too large to carry off with them. Blinded by forgetfulness, my people had not cleaned or repaired any of the damage. An arc of blood droplets on one wall spoke of someone's death; I did not even know whose.

My people and my home, I would have said at one time. I'd been proud of how I'd taken care of the folk here, paid them well and treated them well. Now that illusion was as broken as a smashed egg. I'd failed to protect them. The pretty rainbow of rooms that we had restored for Bee and Shun seemed a useless vanity now. The heart of my home had been stolen; I could not even bring myself to visit the mounded snow on Molly's grave. As a holder and as a father, I had failed miserably. I'd grown slovenly and careless, let my guard down so far that it had protected nothing at all. I could not distinguish the shame I felt from the fear that coiled and writhed in my guts. Was Bee alive and abused and terrified? Or dead and discarded in the snow at the edge of some seldom-used road? If they believed her the son and discovered she was a girl, how would they react? None of my answers to that question pleased me. Would they torment her before they killed her? Did they torture her even now, as they had tortured the Fool? I could not stand to consider those questions and I could not afford to focus on them.

I put people to work. It was the only exercise I knew that might occupy their minds as they absorbed what had been done to them. I visited the temporary quarters for what horses remained to us and found my stableworkers already mustering there. I spoke briefly of our losses, and listened longer to what they had to tell me. None of them faulted me, and somehow that woke the coals of my shame and guilt to a hotter fire. I told Cinch to step up to being stablemaster for Withywoods. He'd served under Tallerman and I valued Perseverance's tight nod to my decision. I gave him the authority to send for carpenters and lumber, and to order the clean-up of the burned building.

'We'll set a fire and burn what remains, then,' he informed me. 'There are bodies of men in there, alongside the burned remains of creatures they cared for. We'll let them go to smoke and ash together, and this time as they burn, we'll remember well who they were.'

I thanked him. My hair had not grown much in the months since I'd sheared it for Molly's death; I could not even band it into a warrior's tail. But with my knife I cut as long a lock as I could from my scalp and gave it to Cinch, asking that he be sure it was burned when they torched the stable again. He took my emblem of mourning from me gravely and promised me it would burn alongside his own.

I asked for a keeper for the messenger birds, and a woman of perhaps fourteen years presented herself, saying it had been her parents' task and now it would be her own. A shy young man from the stables said he'd be certain to help her tidy the dovecote and she accepted his offer gratefully.

And so it went. Dixon was blithely forgetful still, but many of my household staff had begun to get back to work. By the time I returned to the manor, I found that several damaged tapestries had been removed, and the front entry doors temporarily repaired so that they could fully close.

The evening meal was a gloomy affair. The captain of the Rousters joined us at table with his lieutenant. Captain Stout was a match for me in years and had belatedly connected that Tom Badgerlock and FitzChivalry Farseer were one and the same. He surprised me by recalling my duties against the Forged during the Red-Ship Wars. 'That was dirty, bloody work. Dangerous, too. I admired you then. Not always true in the years that followed, but I always knew you had grit.' Plainspoken he was and direct. He'd been commander of the Rousters for two years now and was well on the way to making something of them other than a band of brigands and horse thieves.

His lieutenant, Crafty, however, was a different sort of fellow. He seemed quite satisfied with himself and smiled and winked at every serving-maid who ventured into the hall. For their part, they were either horrified or terrified at his flagrant flirtation, a reaction that at first seemed to puzzle and then insulted him. The food set out was plain and simple, products of a greatly reduced larder and the captain looked pained when Crafty observed that they were accustomed to better fare at Buckkeep Castle. I refrained from replying that we were accustomed to better manners at Withywoods. The serving staff moved awkwardly through their duties, scarcely able to keep their minds on their tasks, and I was quietly incensed to see Crafty's barely-masked disdain for our rural hospitality.

But what followed was worse. We summoned everyone who served in Withywoods, tall or small, to gather in the Great Hall. There we brewed the elfbark tea in a great cauldron in the hearth. Those who had already imbibed stood grim-faced and silent, ready to offer comfort to those who would soon share what they knew. Tattered remnants of the Winterfest decorations, hung for a celebration that never had been, still dangled on the walls. I ordered spirits and ale and wine, not judging any who might wish to find courage in those. Chade, Thick, and I took seats at the high table. Lant and Bulen were placed in charge of ladling tiny servings of the potent tea into cups. Together they gravely bore the hard task of watching folk, one by one, transform from confused to grieved or shattered. Of each they asked two questions: Do you recall anything that might identify the raiders, and Did you see aught of Lady Shun or small Lady Bee?

Most of what we sieved from them was useless, or information we already had. One avaricious rapist was described to us in detail four times. So handsome, and so cruel. Golden hair worn in two long braids, blue eyes and a finely-trimmed moustache and beard. But it was an older man with dirty hands who stank that my kitchen maid remembered vividly. Little Elm became hysterical and the healer carried her off to a warmed bed and valerian tea laced with brandy, her mother tottering along beside her.

The Rousters and their officers withdrew to one end of the hall, with a keg of ale. Chade requested that the captain keep order among their men. Captain Stout seemed to grasp the situation, and sternly ordered his men not to mingle with the Withywoods folk. They obeyed, but even from a distance, I was aware of their coarse humour and callous attitude toward my shattered people. War and hardship had hardened them; I understood that, but it did not mean that I wished to see my own folk mocked or disdained that they were not likewise hardened.

Was it only a day ago that I had stood in Buckkeep Castle and been hailed as Prince FitzChivalry, crowned with steel and welcomed home? And now, here in my own home, I listened to wailing and shrieks, or saw men struck dumb by the memory of what they had witnessed and done. Shepherd Lin stood before me and begged my forgiveness for how, at the bidding of the pleasant woman, he had helped to gather bodies and throw them into the flames. It shamed me to see the man so broken by what he had done under a magical influence. Chade confirmed with him that Shun had not been among those he had burned.

And so that long evening went. As the undercurrent of tiny Skill-voices muttering *forget, forget* faded, I was able to reach for Nettle. She locked her mind to mine, and looked through my eyes and heard with my ears the full tale of the woes of Withywoods. It was not long before I felt Riddle lending her strength, and soon Dutiful joined us, with Steady supporting the coterie. There was a thin comfort in opening my mind to theirs and letting them know all I had gleaned. I felt Nettle's agony at the uncertainty of Bee's fate, and Dutiful's fury that such a thing could happen within Buck, and no one the wiser. I felt a deep and agonized sorrow for the death of Revel and was surprised to sense it was Riddle's. I offered them no excuses for my failure. I had none. Like a travesty of Winterfest, the gathering was a dance of sorrow and horror, a feast of bitter tea and tears.

But all fires, of wood or grief, burn down to ashes eventually. The Great Hall emptied slowly. Folk returned to cottages or bedchambers, some emptier than they should have been. Some went drunk, some coldly sober. Even the Rousters eventually trundled drunkenly from my hall to their beds in the servants' wing. Lant sent Bulen to get what rest he could, and I firmly insisted that Perseverance return to his mother's cottage. 'But I'm sworn to you now,' he insisted, and I had to tell him, 'And I tell you where your duty is this night. Go.' At last only Chade and I and Lant remained. Thick had been long abed. The little man tired easily these days, and I had seen no reason to expose him to such pain. Chade and I sat together on a cushioned bench before the last of the fire. Lant sat morosely alone, staring into the dying flames.

So. What is the plan? This from King Dutiful.

Tomorrow, early, I return to Buckkeep. I intend to share all this with the Fool and see if he can make sense of it.

Is it wise, to use the stones again so soon? This from Nettle.

Need demands it, I responded.

And I, also, Chade surprised me.

I started to object and then silenced myself. His daughter was at as great a risk as my own. Who was I to warn him to avoid using the stones again?

Lord Golden, Dutiful began, and then halted the thought.

What of him? I demanded, my heart sinking.

He was extremely upset that you were gone. Dutiful's dismay was plain. *There was no reasoning with him. He shouted and ranted like a spoiled child.*

Like a terrified child, I thought to myself.

He said that he must go with you, that you must not leave him. We did our best to calm him, but to no avail. At last he became exhausted and went back to his bed. We thought he would sleep long, and we left him alone. But he must have arisen shortly after we left him. And somehow, he tottered from Chade's old lair out into the main corridors of Buckkeep and almost to the stables. He was found in the morning, face down in the snow there. Fitz, he is worse, much worse, than when you left here. I'm sorry. Dutiful's apology betrayed what he expected. The Fool was dying.

I'd lost everything. Not just my friend, but any clues to what the kidnappers would do with my daughter. A terrible weariness engulfed me, followed by numbness. I could think of no response.

Inform Ash that he is to keep a constant watch on the Fool, and do all he can for his comfort and well-being. We will come in the morning, Chade replied decisively.

I felt their confusion and despair, but could make no reply. *Enough for tonight,* Chade added, and I felt our connections ebb and fail.

I drew breath but Chade spoke before I could. He took my forearm in a grip that still retained a great deal of iron. 'I know what you are thinking. No. Tonight we will sleep, tomorrow we will eat, and then we will set forth for the stone on Gallows Hill. We both know we dare a danger. We will do it, but together and not in a stupid fashion. You can do nothing for the Fool that is not already being done. Our daughters depend on us. We go as competent assassins, not as panicked fathers.'

I hated his words because they made sense. Delaying was the last thing I wanted to do, but he had not released my arm. 'Doing something stupid and reckless is not a better proof of your love than doing something measured and powerful. You are no longer the boy who chased Regal's coterie through the halls of Buckkeep Castle with a bared blade. You are Prince FitzChivalry Farseer. And we will make them pay with every drop of their blood.'

Isn't it strange how wise counsel can cool the hottest head? He made sense but my heart screamed protest. I nodded slowly.

'I'm off to bed,' Chade said. He tilted his head and looked at his son. 'Lant? You mustn't blame yourself.'

Lant nodded but did not look away from the flames. I left them there and went to my bedchamber.

But that does not mean that I slept well in my bed that night. The damage in my room snagged my eyes and I imagined the men who had ransacked my home. I rose in the hours before dawn and went to Bee's room. Someone had been in there. Her new wardrobe had been righted, and the vandalized room tidied as much as was possible. I sat down on her bed and then sprawled there, hugging the pillow that had cradled her head. No scent of her remained to comfort me. I did not sleep again. Before dawn, I returned to my room and packed a handful of items. A change of clothing, the tools of my trade, Bee's journal. I went to her room and selected a change of clothing for her and her new cloak. When I found her, perhaps these things would be a comfort to her, a promise of normality again.

Chade and I were joined at our early breakfast by Captain Stout and Lieutenant Crafty. They would accompany us to Gallows Hill while Sergeant Goodhand would be left in charge of the Rousters. They would return our mounts to Withywoods. We had decided to leave Thick behind. Chade wished to have easy contact with Lant, and we did not wish to risk Thick in another trip through the stones so soon. It was agreed that when we judged enough time had passed, Thick would return through the stones with Nettle's journeyman Skill-user and Sildwell. Chade had arranged it all, including mounts to meet us when we emerged at the Witness Stones near Buckkeep.

I gave Dixon instructions to summon back the carpenters

and joiners and have them begin repairs immediately. Lant begged to go with us, but we both judged him too weakened and commended him to Bulen's care. Privately, I knew that we wanted to go alone, men on a mission. As we waited for our horses to be brought round, I looked at the old man, so bravely trussed into his girdle that he might stand straight, and knew that there was no one else I would rather have at my side. We would not judge one another in what we intended to do to those who had taken our daughters. I did not know if his health would stand up to our task, and also knew there was no way to persuade him to stay behind. I clung firmly to the belief that the Fool would have some clue that would put us on the trail of the kidnappers. And when we found them, we would kill them.

Perseverance brought the horses. Chade looked at Lord Derrick's roan mare and an almost-smile twitched his mouth. 'A fine mount,' he observed.

'I only steal the best,' I admitted.

To my surprise, Perseverance was mounted and leading Bee's grey. His arm was bound across his chest, but he sat his horse firmly. 'We don't need Bee's horse,' I told him.

'I should bring her, sir. Bee will want to ride her home.'

I gave the boy a look. 'You aren't coming with me, lad. You're hurt and your mother needs you.'

'I told her I was sworn to you. She understood.' He sat a little straighter. 'And Lady Bee will expect it of me.'

That choked me. I spoke past the tightness in my throat. 'We are not going by a road where anyone can follow. We are not even going to take the horses we are riding. You can't go with us Perseverance, though I admire your courage. When it is time for Bee to ride again, I promise you will be with her.'

Just the slightest tremble of his lower lip betrayed him. 'Sir,' he said, not agreeing but obeying. I nodded to him, then Chade and I mounted and joined the waiting officers. Once I had loved the carriageway in winter, the white-barked birches burdened with snow arching over it. But today, in the dim morning light, I felt we travelled through a tunnel of gloom. The two Rousters were happy to precede us. They rode side by side, conversing sporadically. Chade and I rode stirrup to stirrup, not speaking as the cold stiffened our faces.

By the time we entered the main road, the sun had summoned a bit more strength. The day warmed, but not appreciably. At any other time, the roan mare would have been a pleasure to ride. I wondered idly how many people knew that Prince FitzChivalry had stolen a horse, or if Dutiful had somehow smoothed it over. I tried to feel shame, but could not. I had needed her and I took her. I would do it again. I sensed agreement from my mount but chose to ignore it.

I glanced over at Chade. Once my teacher had been a faded old man, the burn-pocks obvious on his pale face. When he had finally emerged into Buckkeep society after years in the spy-warren he had seemed to drop more than a score of years. He had laughed, eaten elaborate meals, ridden to the hunt and danced as lively as a youth. For a short time, he had recaptured a few of the years denied to him. Now he was truly old, aged by years rather than circumstance. But he sat his horse well and held his head high. He would display no weakness to the world. No stranger would have suspected he was a man agonizing over a missing daughter. He had dressed precisely, in fine Buck-blue garments and gleaming black boots. He had a classic profile, his beard trimmed neatly, his leather-gloved hands holding his reins easily.

'What?' he demanded in a soft voice.

I'd been staring at him as I mused. 'I'm glad of you. That's all. In this hard time, I'm glad of you. That we'll ride together.'

He gave me an unreadable glance. Even more softly, he said, 'Thank you, my boy.'

'A question?'

'Why bother asking me that when you know you'll ask it anyway?'

'The boy Ash. Your apprentice. Is he yours, too?'

'My son, you mean? No. I've only the two, Lant and Shine.' In a lowered voice, he added, 'I hope I still have two.'

'He's a fine apprentice.'

'I know. He'll stay with me, that one. He's got the edge.' He glanced at me. 'Your boy. That Perseverance. He's a good one. Keep him. When you were out of the room, I asked him,

"If all the others were summoned to come to the front of the manor and assembled, why weren't you?" And he said, "I felt that I wanted to go there and be with the others, but I knew my duty was to guard Bee. So I didn't go." He resisted what I suspect was a strong Skill-suggestion to do his best to protect your daughter.'

I nodded, and wondered if a stableboy had known his duty better than I had known mine.

A silence fell between us. *Oh, Bee, where are you? Do you know I'm coming after you?* How could she? Why would she think I'd bother coming after her when I'd abandoned her before? I fenced the question with stone. Focus on finding her and bringing her home. Don't let your agony cloud your thoughts.

We heard hoofbeats behind us and I turned in my saddle. Four of the Rousters were catching up with us. 'A message from Withywoods?' I hazarded.

But they came on at a gallop, and then pulled their horses in hard when they were alongside their captain. One of them, a youngster with orange hair and freckles greeted his captain with a grin. 'Sir, it's boring as old maids at tea back there. Mind if we ride along?'

Lieutenant Crafty laughed aloud and leaned over to clasp wrists with his man as he shot a glance at his captain. 'I told you we had a lively one when we found him, sir! And you've brought a few like-minded friends, I see. Excellent.'

Their captain was not as merry about it. 'Well. If you must ride along, form up and try to look like you've a bit of discipline.'

'Sir!' the redhead agreed with a shout, and in a moment Chade and I were in the centre of an honour guard. I sat straighter on the roan, suddenly uncomfortable with such a status. I felt a tendril of Wit-quest from the mare. Were we safe? We were fine, I assured her, and scowled to myself. She was becoming too attuned to me. Chade glanced over at me and misinterpreted my expression.

Become accustomed to it, Prince FitzChivalry. The tone of his Skilling was wry.

They know me only as Badgerlock, I objected.

I doubt that. Gossip flies swiftly. But even if they name you

*Badgerlock now, that will change when they return to Buckkeep Castle.
So conduct yourself as a prince now.*

It was good advice and hard to follow. I was not accustomed
to being at the centre of anything. Assassins lurk at the edges,
looking like no one in particular.

*And you will learn now to do that while being at the centre of
scrutiny,* Chade suggested.

We rode on, not speaking aloud now. Out of the forest and
on the open road, the day was blue and white. Farmsteads set in
their fields plumed smoke from their chimneys. The road was
little travelled on this fine cold day, and when we reached the
turn for Gallows Hill, the only tracks were the soft dimples from
Chade and Thick's and Nettle's journeyman when they had arrived
the day before. We followed them.

'What's up this trail?' the redhead asked curiously. He looked
to me for an answer.

'Not much of anything. The old gallows for Withy and
Oaksbywater. And a standing stone.'

'Then no one comes up here much?'

'True,' I affirmed. 'And I am glad of it.'

We rode a bit further in silence.

'As good a place as any, then,' the lad said.

Amateur. The betrayal was in his arrogant tone, his confidence
allowing him to bait us. The bit of braggadocio cost them their
surprise. Chade was pulling his sword even as the boy tried to
wheel his horse into Chade's. I felt the flash of Chade's Skill as
he arrowed a message to Dutiful. *We are attacked!* I sensed a
startled response from the king but had no time to pay attention
to it. In front of us, the lieutenant thrust his sword deep into
his captain's side below his ribs, and then pulled his foot from his
stirrup to kick the dying man off his horse. I saw it as I urged the
roan so that she surged forward and carried me out of the jaws
of danger as my two 'guards' tried to trap me between them.
One shouted, 'Witted Bastard!' The roan chested the lieutenant's
horse hard. His foot had not returned to the stirrup and she
caught him off-balance. I shoved him hard, he fell sideways,
and his startled horse dragged him a short way before his foot
came free and he fell. Down but not dead.

Chade.

I wheeled the roan tightly and was in time to see Chade and the redhead exchange sword thrusts. The tip of Red's sword skittered across Chade's belly before slicing into his side. Chade's thrust was surer. He gave a low cry and bared his teeth as his blade sank into the youngster's belly. I echoed it with a horrified shout of my own. As Red fell away from Chade, another guard closed with him from the other side.

I had no time to see more. The banked rage I had felt at Bee's kidnapping and the rape of Withywoods roared to life in me, and I let it. I had two adversaries of my own. I wore the nondescript sword Chade had armed me with before I left Buckkeep. I've never been an excellent swordsman, but as there was no axe handy and since the situation did not seem suited to poison or garrottes, I began to draw the blade. Then I leaned far back in my saddle to allow one sword to pass through the air that occupied the place where my midsection had been a moment before. Snapping myself upright again was far harder than it should have been but it enabled me to slam the pommel of my sword into one opponent's mouth. There was a satisfying crunch of teeth.

Kicking. The roan's warning was instantaneous with her action. I had no time to prepare for her sudden motion, but I did manage to stay in the saddle. Resourceful man, that Lord Derrick, and I suddenly knew he was very unlikely to forgive me the theft of such a horse. I'd seen warhorses trained for battle, but the roan was a palfrey that looked built more for running than fighting. She wheeled under me and kicked out powerfully with her hind legs. I held on and felt the blow impact solidly with the other horse. I gave less than a heartbeat's thought to the realization that I had not signalled her to do this: she had undertaken it herself. As her hind legs came down under her again, she gave a great leap forward. She'd carried me out of range of the swords. I scarcely needed to guide her as she swung tightly to face our attackers. I had a moment to see that Red was down and unmoving, and Chade's other opponent was draped forward on his mount with his blood running freely down his horse's neck as his mount paced in a confused circle. Chade was off his horse, locked tight with Lieutenant Crafty. I was dimly aware of the captain sitting up in the snow, cursing at them.

The roan crashed chest to chest with one of the Rouster's mounts. I leaned in time and his sword sliced only the good wool of my cloak and glanced off the point of my shoulder. I was more accurate. This time I used the pointed end of my weapon, pushing it deep into the chest of the very young and very surprised guardsman. So satisfying to finally shed blood, to let the anger rage! My Wit shared his agony with me. I blocked it even as I took satisfaction in it. The attack had brought me close to him. As I seized his throat to push him off my blade, I smelled on his breath the breakfast he'd eaten at my table. His two front teeth overlapped slightly. Probably younger than Lant. And much deader as he fell from his horse.

'You bastard!' his partner shouted.

'Yes!' I responded. I turned in the saddle, ducked, and the tip of his blade etched fire across my brow instead of beheading me. The pain was shockingly sharp. We were knee to knee. Blood from my earlier blow ran over his chin, but I knew that in a moment the flowing blood from my brow would blind me and my sword would be useless. I nudged the roan. She responded. I kicked free of my stirrups as she wheeled into the other horse. I needed to get my hands on him while I could see. I dropped my sword and shook my hands out of my gloves, then launched myself at him.

It was possibly the last thing he'd expected me to do. I was inside the range of his sword. He kept hold of his weapon and hit me with the hilt, with little impact. He had stayed in his saddle but my sudden extra weight sent his horse staggering sideways. The Rouster fought to keep his balance. He had a fine beard and moustache and I seized two great handfuls of it and let myself fall. He came after me, shouting curses and delivering several solid punches to my chest. He lost his sword as we went down. As we fell together from his horse into the deep snow, I twisted, hoping to land on top of him. I didn't. I heard a muffled shout and knew Chade's voice. 'Wait!' I shouted stupidly, as if Chade and his enemy would delay their fight for me, and the man on top of me hit me in the jaw. Even as we fell, I had not released his beard and now I did my best to pull out as big a handful as I could. He roared with the pain, a very satisfactory sound. I let go of his beard and boxed both his ears as hard as I could with the heels of my hands.

Then I fastened my hands to his throat. Strangling a man with a heavy beard and a high collar is difficult. I worked my fingers through the beard, slid them under his collar. The warm column of his throat was mine, and I sank my fingers into it. Doing this while the man was on top of me, pummelling me while blood ran into my eyes, meant that it took much longer for me to kill the man than I care to recall. When he stopped hitting me and seized my wrists, I darted my head in and bit his hand as hard as I could. He roared and then screamed with pain and outrage. Assassins take no pride in fighting fairly. We take pride in winning. As I spat out a piece of finger, I told myself Nighteyes would have been proud. I'd kept my grip and I felt the flesh of his throat standing in ridges between my fingers. 'BEE!' I gasped and squeezed harder. Throttling someone while being struck requires focus. I knew that as long as I had his throat and kept squeezing, there was a limit to how long he could do whatever painful things he could think of as I inexorably cut off his breath. I jerked him close enough to me that he couldn't make a large swing, while keeping his broken teeth away from my face. He tried to find my throat, but I locked my chin to my chest and hung on. It had been a long time since I'd had to fight this way, but some things a man does not forget. His blows began to lose force. He gripped my wrists. *Hold tight*, I reminded myself. All I had to do was keep squeezing. When he collapsed on me the first time, I knew he was feigning death. He did not fake it for long. He stirred enough to lift his hands and pry at mine. It was a feeble effort. The second time he collapsed I knew he was truly unconscious. I squeezed. When I knew he was dead, I let go and pushed him off me.

I rolled away, my ribs aching, my jaw burning where I'd clenched it against his blows. I staggered to my knees and dragged my cuff across my bloodied vision. When I could see, I got to my feet and looked for Chade. The horses had scattered. The captain was curled on his side, calling faintly for help. The four guardsmen were down, three dead and one dying. Chade was still on his feet. Blood from his side had darkened his coat and dripped red on the snow. The tough old bastard was behind the lieutenant, his arm locked around the man's throat. The lieutenant was wasting time clawing at Chade's arm. I brought out my knife to make a quick end to him.

'No!' Chade forbade me breathlessly. 'My kill.' Never before had my old mentor sounded so much like my wolf. I took a respectful two steps back and without remorse dispatched the fourth guardsman and then went to the captain's aid.

He was dying and he knew it. I didn't try to move him. I went down on my knees and leaned on my hand to look in his face. He could barely focus on me. He tried to lick his lips, then said, 'Not traitor. Not me. Not the rest of my boys. My Rousters.'

I thought he was finished. 'I'll tell Lord Chade,' I assured him.

'That son of a mangy bitch,' he said, anger lending him strength. 'Leave their bodies . . . on the gibbet. That dung-eating bastard Crafty. Led them astray. My boys. Mine.'

'The others won't be punished,' I promised him, but knew I lied. The reputation of the Rousters, never sterling, would be dirtied. No one would want to join that guard company, and the other guardsmen would avoid them at table. But it was what I could say, and he closed his eyes and let go of life.

I went back to Chade. He knelt by Crafty. The man was not dead. He was unconscious from being choked, and Chade was finishing hamstringing him. He'd pushed the man face down, pulled up the legs of his trousers and cut the big tendons behind his knees. As I watched, he trussed the man's wrists behind his back with a length of cord he materialized from his sleeve. Then with a grunt, he rolled Crafty onto his back. With those tendons cut, Crafty wasn't going to stand, run or fight. Chade was pale and breathing hard as he settled back on his haunches. I didn't tell him to finish the man or ask him his intent. Assassins have a code of their own. Bee was at stake as well as Shun, and if this man's attempt on us had to do with her abduction, then whatever we had to do to extract his information was acceptable.

Crafty was drawing deeper breaths, a scratchy sound. His eyelids fluttered, then opened. He gasped loudly and then looked up at us, me standing, and Chade kneeling beside him with a bloody knife. Chade didn't wait for him to speak. He set his knife to the hollow of the man's throat.

'Who paid you? How much? What was your mission?' Chade spoke the words as if he were counting aloud.

Crafty didn't answer immediately. I observed the standing stone. My roan stood at a distance, watching me closely. The other horses had bunched together, confused and taking comfort in her company. I suspect Chade did something with his knife because Crafty gasped high. I muffled my Wit not to share what he felt. I heard him struggle and then demand, 'What did you do to my legs, you bastard?'

Chade spoke again. 'Who paid you? How much? What was your mission?'

'Don't know his name! He wouldn't say!' The man was breathless with pain. 'What did you do to my legs?' He tried to sit up, but Chade pushed him roughly back. I eyed the old man critically. He was still bleeding, the red melting the snow beside him. Soon, I'd have to intervene, if only to bandage him.

'What did he tell you to do? How much did he offer you to do it?'

'Kill you. Five gold for me, and two for any man who helped. He came to us in a tavern in Buckkeep. Actually, he came to the captain, but he cursed him and said no. Is he dead? Captain Stout?'

I couldn't tell if it was fear or regret in his voice.

'Only me?' Chade asked him.

'Kill you. Kill you slow if we could but kill you and bring back your hand. To prove it.'

'When?' I interrupted Chade's questioning. 'When did you get this job?'

He rolled his eyes to look at me. 'In Buckkeep. Before we left. Right after we got word that we were leaving, that we would miss Winterfest to come out here. No one was happy about that.'

I spoke. 'It's not connected, Chade. Whoever bribed them had no way of knowing you'd be here: he'd have been hoping they could somehow kill you at Buckkeep. Bee and Shun were taken the same day they were bribed. And why send these traitors if they already had a force on its way here? It's two different things. Kill him and let me see to your side.'

Chade shot me a look that silenced me. 'What did he look like, the man who offered the money?'

'My legs hurt so bad, I can't think. I want a healer before I talk any more. Sweet Eda!' He lifted his head a short way and then let it fall back in the snow. 'You killed everyone? All four of them?'

'What did he look like?' Chade was relentless. The man was bleeding to death. Chade and I knew it, but Crafty seemed unaware of it.

'A tall man, but not thin. Tall but with a stomach like a barrel. Just a Buckman, like any other. I don't know. It was an easy deal. Bring the hand with your ring on it, the innkeeper at the Bawdy Trout gives us the money. When you showed up, it was like the gods handed you to us. So damn easy. If the captain had said yes, you'd be a dead man, and him, too.'

'Tell me about his teeth.'

'I'm not saying nothing more until you take me to a healer. I'm getting cold, so cold. What did you do to my legs?'

Chade set the tip of his knife to the man's nostril. 'Talk to me, or I cut your nose,' he said coldly. He inserted the blade up the man's nostril until he felt the edge of it.

Crafty's eyes went very wide. 'His teeth, one of the front ones, was grey. Is that what you meant?

Chade nodded to himself. 'Did he mention a girl?'

'The girl you stole. Ya. Said if we found her with you, we could have her. Or if we could make you tell us where she was. Said she'd make a good whore. Aaaaah!'

The nose is sensitive. Very sensitive. Chade had always maintained it was as good or better a target for torment than a man's genitals. Not only is there pain, but disfiguring a man's face will affect him for the rest of his life. Crafty was writhing in the snow, one of his nostrils sliced open and bleeding profusely. He began to weep. Abruptly, I wanted this to be over.

'He said it.' The blood and the pain of his sliced nose thickened his voice. 'Not me. And no one even saw the girl, so no one did her. Eda, help me!' He called on the goddess, as I doubted he'd ever done before, and snorted wildly, spraying blood.

I was fairly certain this was all about Shun, and Chade's vendetta with her stepfather, but I would be certain. 'Did he mention a little girl?' I demanded of him. 'A child?'

He halted his thrashing and stared up at me. 'A little girl? No. Gods, we're not monsters!'

'Liar,' Chade said. Crafty had wallowed away from him. Chade hitched himself closer, and very slowly, almost gently, drew his blade across the man's throat. Crafty's eyes flew wide open in the sudden knowledge that he was dead. His mouth worked but the sounds were not words. Cutting a man's throat isn't an instant death for him, but it's a certain one. Chade knew that. So did Crafty. He was still moving when Chade said to me, 'Give me a hand up.'

I held my hand out to him. 'All of that to confirm what you already knew?'

'I got a bit extra. The name of the inn.' He took my hand. His was slippery with blood. I stooped and slid my arm around him and pulled him upright. He grunted with pain as he came to his feet. 'It wasn't about information, Fitz. It was payback. For Captain Stout. Treachery deserves great pain.' He made a bad sound. I stood very still until he could catch his breath. 'And daring to think he could try to kill me.'

My bared hand felt the warmth of the blood on his clothing. 'I'll sit you down and catch a horse. There's a healer in—'

'The stone,' Chade said decisively. 'Better healers in Buckkeep.'

Nettle once compared having the Skill to having a sense of smell. One does not mean to intrude on people any more than one wants to sniff someone, but in proximity, you sense the smell of someone. Or Skill tells you of his pain. In this case, it was the Wit that told me Chade was a creature in desperate need of healing. And he was right. The best healers would be in Buckkeep. I reached out to Nettle. *We were attacked. Chade is injured. Coming through the stones in a few moments. Please have a healer ready to tend him. He's taken a sword wound to his side.*

We knew of the attack. And then you both blocked us out! What is going on? Were they Bee's kidnappers? Have you found her, is she safe? Anger and frantic questions that I had no time for.

No Bee. We are coming through the stones. Our attackers are dead. I'll explain when I get there.

This time the block I threw up against the Skill was deliberate. King Verity had always complained that whenever I became fully

engaged in battle or any dangerous activity, I blocked my Skill.
Evidently Chade did the same. Interesting. But not as compelling
as the blood that had now soaked my hand and sleeve, nor my
own blood that was still dripping down my brow and gumming
up my eyes.

Master?

*Go back to where you had oats today. Get the others to follow you
if you can. But go back and be safe there.*

Go with you.

No.

I closed my Wit to her. The roan was a beautiful horse, shim-
mering with spirit and intelligence. She was reaching for me
strongly, seeking a bond I could not allow. I had no time to be
that important to any creature, not until I had regained my little
girl. And perhaps not then. I sensed the horse's confusion and
disappointment. I could not let it touch my heart. Nothing could
touch my heart until Bee was safe again.

'The stone,' I told Chade. He nodded, saving his breath. The
snow was deep and the path to the stone only partially broken.
I waded side-on in the deep snow, letting Chade benefit from the
path I made. He moved his legs, but I was taking most of his
weight. My shoulder reminded me of the slice on the tip of it.
We reached the stone with Chade leaning heavily on me. 'Catch
your breath for a minute,' I suggested. He managed to shake his
head.

'No.' He barely breathed the word. 'Going to faint. Get through
while I'm conscious.'

'Too dangerous,' I objected, but he lifted the bloody hand that
had been clutching his side. I couldn't stop him, and I barely had
time to focus my Skill before he slapped the stone and we were
snatched inside.

It was wrong. For an instant, I was clutching Chade as we
entered the stone. But as he dragged me in behind him, my Skill-
sense of him winked out. I gripped naught but dead weight. I
could not sense him and I fell through the sea of stars, plummeting
in a place that had no bottom.

SIXTEEN

The Journey

When a shaysa appears, the Servants must be ready to welcome the child. Often the parents will be filled with sadness at having to give up the child they have nourished and sheltered for years. When parents bring a shaysim to the gates, let them be welcomed and offered rest and refreshment. Gifts, too, should be offered but it must never appear that the gifts are given in exchange for the child. No shaysim should be purchased nor taken by force. If the parents are reluctant to surrender the child, allow them as much time as they need. If the child is an infant, gently remind them that such a child can require years of intense care. If the child be older, speak of the needs of the child to be raised where he can be accepted, taught and cherished.

If they cannot bear to immediately surrender the child, be patient. Offer them lodgings for the night, let them walk in the gardens and see the libraries. Allow them to see that no matter how long the child's infancy or childhood, she will be cherished here, educated, and yes, loved by those Servants who tend her. Do not forget that every White child is a gift given by the family to the world. Be grateful.

Above all, be patient. Remember that it is the child's destiny to come to us, and that destiny is never denied. It may happen in a way none of us has foreseen, but happen it will. To interfere too much may set the child's life on a path unforeseen and unfortunate. Once the child is with us, it is important to let the shaysa's life unfold as it will. The future cannot be rushed. Allow time to work its will upon us all.

Buffeni, Servant of the 3rd line

I do not know how long I was ill. It was like a terrible vertigo from which no one could rescue me. I was sick upon myself, and soiled myself, more than once. Shun tended me fiercely, without gentleness and certainly not because she wished to do so. She battled relentlessly for privacy in which she washed me with cold, snowmelt water. She gave my dirtied garments over to the pale people for them to wash and attempt to dry. She was uncompromising in insisting that only she could tend me. It was not devotion to me, although she claimed that to them. It was fear, plain and simple. She thought that if they discovered I was a girl, they would have no further use for me. Or her.

And so she took care of me, as best she could. They gave her no help. There was no willowbark tea brewed for my fever, no rest from our relentless travelling. They simply allowed me to be ill while they continued their journey. Every evening, Shun carried me from the tent to the sleigh. We travelled all night. As dawn approached, they made camp and she moved me from the sleigh to the tent. They prepared no special food for me, no broth or gruel. Shun increased my misery by insisting that I eat and drink, sometimes forcing the spoon into my mouth. My lips were chapped and sore from the fever. Her ministrations made them bleed.

But I didn't die, and one night I felt slightly better. I kept my eyes open and watched the stars as they appeared and then vanished again behind the wind-driven clouds. Dwalia no longer held me on her lap. None of the luriks seemed to want to touch me. So Shun held me, and I heard her little gasp when we crested a hill and saw the lights of a small town below us. We followed the road down the hill, directly toward the town. The fog-boy sat beside the driver and I could feel how hard he strove to keep anyone from seeing us. Commander Ellik and the handsome rapist led the way. The other soldiers rode close beside the sleighs and the luriks on their white horses were bunched close behind us. A dog barked and barked at us, hackles raised, until his owner came out and shouted at him to be quiet.

I felt Shun tighten her grip on me. 'Could you run?' she breathed by my ear, and I knew what she was thinking.

So did Dwalia. She did not whisper but spoke in a normal voice. 'If you leapt from the sleigh and ran to any of those houses, the soldiers with us would kill everyone you spoke to. The rest we would bind to forgetfulness. Then we would burn the house down around the bodies, and on you would go with us. Much simpler for all if you simply stay where you are and enjoy this picturesque little town.' She gave a sideways glance, and Reppin and Soula both shifted to sit between us and the edge of the sleigh.

Shun did not loosen her grip on me, but I felt the spirit go out of her. We drove right past a team and waiting wagon outside an inn. The horses whickered a greeting to us, but on we went. We passed through the town as if we were the wind, and we continued past the outlying farmsteads and up another hill and back into woodlands again. We left the road and followed a dimpled cart-trail into the forest. And on until dawn.

That morning, I could eat a little food on my own, and follow Shun when she went aside from the others to piss. I remembered what she had told me, and mimed standing to piss as if I were a boy, before crouching to relieve myself. When we went back in the tent, the luriks whispered to one another behind their hands. 'I told you he would live, if he was meant to live. And we knew he was. That was why we did not interfere.' Dwalia spoke those words to her underlings, and once more she held a kindly smile on her face whenever she looked at me. She was pleased that I hadn't died, but even more pleased, I thought, that she hadn't helped me to stay alive.

We camped well off the road that dawn. The fog-boy stumbled when he clambered down from the sleigh. Then he held on to the side of the sleigh and stood there with his head bent. Dwalia frowned but as soon as she realized I'd seen her expression, she changed it to a look of motherly concern. 'Come, Vindeliar. It was not that hard, was it? And we have spared you that work as much as we can. But travelling cross-country is taking far too much time. You must be strong and determined. We need to return to the ship as swiftly as we can, lest the work you did there begin to weaken and fade. Come. I will see if we cannot get a bit of meat for you tonight.'

He nodded, his head a heavy stone on a reed neck. She held out her arm with a sigh and he took it. She escorted him to a place where others were building the fire and commanded that a fur be folded for him to sit upon. That dawn he did no chores but only sat by the fire and went early to his bed.

Shun and I slept more closely together than ever we had that day. I was too weak still to stay awake for long, but I could tell that she had not eaten enough of the brown soup to make her sleep. She feigned sleep with one arm flung over me, as if she feared they might take me from her.

I woke toward nightfall, itching everywhere. I scratched myself but it brought only slight relief. When the others stirred and we went out by the fires, Shun flinched back at the sight of me. 'What is wrong with you?' she demanded. I had been scratching my cheek. I lowered my hand, startled, and saw tendrils and flaps of dry white skin clinging to my fingers.

'I don't know!' I exclaimed, and still weak from being ill so long, I began to weep. Shun sighed over my uselessness. But Dwalia came quickly to my side.

'Silly,' said Dwalia. 'You shed your old skin. That is all. You've taken a step forward in your path. Let me look at you!' She seized me by the sleeve and pulled me closer to the fire. She pushed back the cuff of the fur coat, and then my shirt. Her nails were rounded and clean. She matter-of-factly scratched at my arm, and then shook the threads of dangling skin from her fingertips. She leaned in to look closer at my new skin.

'That is not right!' she exclaimed, and then clapped a hand over her own mouth.

'What isn't right?' I asked anxiously.

'I didn't hear you, dear? Does something worry you?' Her voice was warm with concern for me.

'You said something wasn't right. What's wrong?'

Her brows drew together and her voice radiated warmth. 'Why, dear, I said nothing. Do you think something's wrong?'

I looked at the patch of skin her nails had cleared. 'I'm turning white. Like a dead person.' I had nearly said 'like the messenger'. I shut my lips tightly and tried not to sob. I'd said too many words. I wasn't good at this pretending to be younger and stupider than I was.

'Did he dream in his change time?' a thin-faced lurik lad asked, and Dwalia shot him a look far sharper than a slap. He hung his head and I saw him take a quick, anxious breath. Alaria had been sitting next to him. She hitched herself away from him.

They were all watching me to see if I would answer. Even Dwalia. 'No dreams,' I said quietly, and I saw a puzzled look wash through her eyes. 'None that made sense,' I amended. 'Silly dreams.' I hoped I sounded childish. I gave a small sigh and seated myself on the fallen log that was serving us as a bench. Odessa immediately came to sit close beside me.

For a short time I listened to the crackling of the fire. No one else spoke, but I could almost feel them wishing for me to go on. I didn't. Dwalia made a little sound in her throat and left the fireside. I was suddenly tired. I leaned my head forward, my elbows on my knees and my face in my hands and looked into the darkness there. I wanted Revel to come and pick me up and carry me in to where it was warm.

But Revel was dead.

I thought about my father. Did he care that I'd been stolen? Would he come after me?

I'm right here, Wolf Father said. *I've never left you.*

My other father.

We are one.

'Shaysim?'

I felt queasy. I lifted my head slowly. Dwalia crouched before me. I said nothing.

'Look what I have for you, Shaysim.' She held out to me something rectangular and covered in bright fabric. I looked at it without comprehension. She opened it, and inside were pages of thick, creamy paper. It was a book, not a simple ledger such as my father had given me, but a book bound in rich cloth. I itched to touch it.

Danger! Wolf Father's warning brushed against my mind. I kept perfectly still.

'And this.' It was like a quill, but made of silver. 'The ink I have for this is as blue as a summer sky.' She waited. 'Don't you want to try them?' she asked me.

I tried to restore childishness to my voice. 'Try them how? What do they do?'

Dismay crept over her face. 'You write with the pen on the paper. You write down your dreams. Your important dreams.'

'I don't know how to write.' I held my breath, hoping my lie would protect me.

'You don't . . .' She let her words trail away. Then she smiled her warmest smile. 'That doesn't matter, Shaysim. When we get to Clerres, you will be taught. Until then, you can tell me about your dreams, and I will write—'

Temptation surged in me. Tell her I had dreamed of a wolf tearing white rabbits into bloody shreds. Tell her of a man with a battleaxe chopping the heads of squirming white snakes.

NO. Wolf Father was adamant. In a breath of awareness, he added, *Do not provoke another predator until your pack is ready to tear it apart. Be small and still, cub.*

'I don't remember any dreams now.' I scratched my face, looked at the bits of dangling skin, wiped them on my shirt and then pretended to pick my nose until she made a small sound of dismay. She moved away from me taking book and quill with her. I looked carefully at my finger and then put it in my mouth. Odessa moved away from me. I did not let myself smile.

SEVENTEEN

Blood

There are seventy-seven known medicinal uses for dragon parts, and fifty-two unsubstantiated ones. The seventy-seven are listed in the scrolls called Trifton Dragon-killer's Remedies. Of great antiquity, this scroll has been translated many times, to the extent that seventeen of the remedies make no sense. For instance, we are told that 'ground dragon scales applied to the upple with brighten coal a maiden's eyes'. Yet, mistranslated as these remedies may be, for each one the original scribe provided the name and apparently the attestation from someone who had used the remedy to good effect.

The fifty-two unsubstantiated remedies are those with no attestations, and ones that seem unlikely to be real. As they are at the end of the translation I have, I suspect they are a later addition by someone seeking to present the medical properties of dragon parts as having more wondrous uses. There are potions made from various bits of dragons that are said to render a man invisible, to give a woman the gift of flight, ones guaranteed to bring twins to term, healthy and strong, in three months and one startling remedy that assures the user of being able to see anyone whose name he speaks aloud, regardless of the distance or if that person is still alive.

With the reappearance of dragons in our corner of the world, perhaps these remedies may again become available, but I hypothesize that they will remain exceedingly rare and expensive. Thus the opportunity to test the beneficial effects of Trifton's remedies may evade us still.

Chade Fallstar, unfinished manuscript

When one misses a stair in the dark and begins to fall, one feels that terrible lurch of wrongness combined with fear of the impact that will surely follow. I fell with the same horrid sensation of moving in the wrong direction but my fear was that there would never be any impact. Only endless falling. The points of light were like dust. Bodiless, I flailed at them. Never before had I retained such a sense of self, such a sense of mortality inside a Skill-pillar.

And when I recognized that I had a self, I suddenly sensed I was not alone. He was beside me, streaking endlessly down like a comet as his being unravelled in brightness behind him. That was wrong. That was very wrong.

Between knowing it was wrong and wanting to do something about it, an indeterminate amount of time passed. Then I struggled to know what to do. Limit him. Define him. How? Name him. One of the oldest magics known to men. Chade. Chade. But I was tongueless, voiceless. I wrapped him in my self, containing him with all I knew of him. Chade. Chade Fallstar.

I held him. Not his body, but his awareness. We fell together. I held my awareness of my separate self and hoped without reason that there was an end, somewhere, some time, to this endless falling. Despite my efforts, Chade was leaking away from me. Like a basket of meal in a high wind, he seemed to waft away, carried off by the Skill. Worse, I had no sense of him resisting it. I held him, gathered back what I could of him, but I also felt myself shredding in the constant blast of that place that was neither a place nor a time. The very timelessness of it was terrifying. The journey through the star-studded vastness of the stone passage seemed to slow. 'Please,' I breathed, terrified that we might never emerge, that no one would ever know what became of us, that Bee would live or die believing that her father had never attempted to rescue her. But that agony was fleeting.

Merge, whispered something that was Chade but both more and less than he was. *Let go. It doesn't matter.* And he surrendered to that glittering attraction of the spaces between, to the darkness that was neither a distance nor a location. Like a seedhead that, at the whisper of the wind, launches itself into a thousand pieces, so was Chade. And I, I was not a sack to hold him, but a net.

With the least part of the will that remained to me, I strove to hold him together within myself, even as the lure of the sparkling darkness sought to disperse us into bits of light.

Chade. Chade Fallstar.

His name was not enough to bind him. He had hidden himself from it for too long.

Chade Fallstar. Brother to Shrewd Farseer. Father to Lant Fallstar. Father to Shine Fallstar. Chade! Shaper of FitzChivalry Farseer. I settled loop after loop of identity around him as if I were wrapping line to tie up a storm-tugged ship. But I could not enclose him without opening myself to the pull of the current.

I have them!

I did not wish anyone to have me, but then I was clutching at Dutiful and felt myself drawn from the stone that sucked at me like thick mud. Chade came with me whether he would or not, and suddenly we were both shaking with cold on the snowy hillside above Buckkeep as dawn was breaking.

Dawn.

King Dutiful grasped me by the wrist, and Kettricken, swathed from head to foot in a purple wool cloak edged in white fox fur, gazed at me. Six of her guards in purple and white stood by. Near them was a wagon, made comfortable with blankets and cushions. Steady was slouched on the seat, holding his face in his hands. Nettle sat in the wagon, swaddled in blankets like an old tinker. Riddle was beside her, haggard, his face red with cold. Lending her his strength with no thought of the cost. They both looked worn, as if aged by years.

Years?

I turned my head and looked at Dutiful. His beard was grey and his shoulders bowed.

How long? I asked, and then remembered that speech came from my mouth. 'How long?' I asked again, croaking the words from my dry throat.

Every Skilled person there startled. Dutiful spoke. 'Easy, Fitz. Gently. Half a day and all the night.' He lifted a hand and rubbed his cheek. Frost. His dark beard was hoared grey with frost. Days. Not years. But still, days.

He put his hand on my shoulder, awakening me to him. 'Fitz.

What happened?' He added, 'You need not Skill so powerfully. We are right here to hear your words.'

'But you are all still here?' I was astounded.

'Where else would we be?' Nettle demanded angrily. 'You Skilled to us that you were attacked and then we heard nothing. You both blocked us. Then you suddenly Skilled that you'd be coming through the stone. But you didn't! What happened?'

There was too much to explain. I moved my mouth but could not find words intricate enough to explain anything. I had told him we were attacked. How could that encompass the betrayal, the swords, the cuts, pain, gasping for breath, the many motions our bodies had made? My thoughts slid and slipped like cartwheels in mud. As Dutiful put an arm around Chade to lift him, two guardsmen joined him, carrying him drooping between them to the wagon. Kettricken took my arm. I felt her so strongly. Such a brave woman, so true and intelligent. Nighteyes had loved her so much.

'Oh, Fitz,' she said softly and her cold-reddened cheeks flushed hot. I leaned on her unabashedly. She would help me. She'd always helped me, never failed me. They all had. I simply opened my mind to Nettle and Dutiful and let my tale flow from my thoughts to theirs. I was too weary and it was all too complex to hold anything back. I gave it all to them, everything that had happened since I had left Buckkeep. Skilling was so much easier than talking. I finished with the most awful truth I knew. *'You were right, you and Riddle. I'm a terrible father. I should have given her to you. This would never have happened if I'd listened to you and given you Bee.'*

I saw Nettle recoil from me. She lifted her hands to cover her ears and then it was suddenly harder to reach her. I groped for her, but she tried to wall me out. She could not. I seeped through. I turned my slow glance to Dutiful. Another wall. Why?

'You're still bleeding.' Kettricken shook out her handkerchief and pressed the silky thing to my brow.

'It only happened a few moments ago,' I told her, knowing she had not been a party to our shared thoughts.

'A day, at least,' she reminded me. I stared at her. Wit or Skill? What was the difference, I abruptly wondered. Were not we all animals in some sense of that foolish word?

'*I am not sure that time is the same for us,*' I said aloud, and then was glad of Riddle's strong hand gripping my wrist and pulling me up into the wagon. He leaned close to me. 'Let go of Kettricken. Walls up, Fitz,' he said quietly. 'I've not the Skill, but even I can sense you spilling.' Then he left me to help Dutiful arrange Chade. The old man lay on his side, clutching at his wound and groaning. The driver spoke, the horses started the wagon with a lurch, and I passed out.

I came back to awareness somewhat on the stairs inside Buckkeep Castle. A serving-man was helping me walk up the stairs. I didn't know him. I felt alarm, and then a wash of Skill from Dutiful assured me that all was well. I should just keep climbing the stairs. *Do not try to Skill back to me, please. Or to anyone. Please put up your walls and try not to spill.* I could feel Dutiful's weariness. I seemed to recall that he had asked me to look to my walls several times. He was not with me. I wondered why.

In my room, a different serving-man, one I had never seen before, offended me by insisting on helping me remove my bloody clothes and putting on a clean nightshirt. I did not wish to be further bothered, but a healer came into my room and asserted that he must clean both the wound on my shoulder and the slash on my brow and then suture my brow closed with many a, 'Beg your indulgence, Prince FitzChivalry,' and 'If my prince would be pleased to turn his face toward the light,' and 'It grieves me to ask you to endure this pain, Prince FitzChivalry,' until I could scarcely stand the man's unctuousness. When all was done, he offered me tea. At the first sip, I knew it was too strong with valerian, but I had little will to resist his insistence that I drink it. And then I must have slept again.

I awoke to the fire burned low and the room full of darkness. I yawned, stretched against the ache of my muscles and gazed dully at the short flames that licked lazily across the surface of the last log in my hearth. Slowly, slowly, I found myself in place and time. And then my heart jumped in my chest and began to hammer. Chade, injured. Bee, stolen. The Fool, possibly dying. The disasters vied to dominate my fear as being the most terrifying. I groped out with the Skill and touched Nettle and Dutiful simultaneously. *Chade?*

Softly, Fitz. Softly. Hold yourself in. It isn't good, Dutiful responded glumly. *The stays of his girdle deflected the sword but it still penetrated his side. He lost a great deal of blood and seems disoriented from his experience within the Skill-pillar. The only sense we have had from him is that he is angry with you for divulging that he, too, has a daughter who has been stolen. I am still trying to settle that bit of news in my mind!*

I pushed my weary thoughts back. Had I divulged Chade's secret? Probably when I had spilled myself, it had cascaded out. I was appalled that I had been so careless, but could not dwell on that. It had been when I had given Nettle and Dutiful access to my mind to explain the situation. Even now, I felt too weary for detailed conversation. *Is Nettle all right? She looked so worn.*

I am better, now that you and Chade are here. I am coming to your room. Now. Try to be very still until I get there.

I had forgotten that our minds were touching. *Am I that addled still?* I asked myself, and felt my question echo off into the Skill-current.

I am coming also. And yes, you are that addled, so please, if you can, put up your walls. Be still. You are alarming the other coteries. You seem to have gained strength and lost control of your thoughts during your passage. You are battering our apprentices. And you seem to not be entirely within yourself, if you can conceive what I mean. As if you are still caught in the Skill-current.

Barricading my thoughts back into my own mind was like building a drystone wall. Fit each piece into place. Hold back the cascading thoughts, stop the chaining thoughts of worry, fear, desperation and guilt. Stop them, hold them, guard them.

When I thought I was safe once more behind my walls, I became aware of my body's complaints.

Several of my stitches were too tight. The slightest change in my facial expression made them pull. The rest of my body ached, and I was suddenly, horribly hungry in a way I could not control.

There was a tap on my door but before I could rise from my bed, Nettle entered. 'You're still spilling,' she whispered. 'Half of Buckkeep Castle will be having nightmares tonight. And eating like ravenous dogs. Oh, Da.' Sudden tears stood in her eyes. 'Out there, by the stones. I could not even speak to you afterwards . . .

our poor folk at Withywoods. That fight! And how much agony you feel about Bee. How hurt you were that I asked for her, and how guilty . . . How you love her! And how you torment yourself. Here. Let me help you.'

She sat down on the edge of my bed and took my hand. As if I were a child being taught to wield a spoon, or an old man leaning on a youngster's shoulder, her Skill flowed into me, mingled with mine, and she set my walls. It was good to be contained again, as if someone had buttoned a warm coat securely around me. But even after I found that the clamour of the lesser Skill-stream of strangers had been sealed out of me and my own thoughts fenced in, Nettle kept hold of my hand. I turned my head slowly to look at her.

For a time, she just looked at me silently. Then she said, 'I've never really known you, have I? All these years. The things you kept hidden from me, lest I think less of Burrich or my mother. The reserve you held because you felt you did not deserve to intrude into my life . . . Has anyone ever really known you? Known what you felt and thought?'

'Your mother did, I think,' I said, and then I had to wonder. *The Fool*, I nearly said, and then *Nighteyes*. That last answer, I knew would have been the truest truth. But I did not say it.

She sighed a small sigh. 'A wolf,' she said. 'A wolf best knew your heart.' I was certain I had not shared that thought with her. I wondered if, having been so vulnerable to her, she now could tell when I held things back. I was trying to summon words to say to her when there was a second tap on the door and Riddle entered, bearing a tray. King Dutiful, looking less than regal, was behind him.

'I brought food,' Riddle announced even as the scent of it dizzied me with longing.

'Just let him eat first,' Dutiful advised as if I were an ill-mannered dog or perhaps a very small child. 'He's sharing his hunger with the whole castle.' And again, I could think of no words. Thoughts were too fast for words and too complex. There was too much to say, more than anyone could ever say in a lifetime about even the simplest things. But before I could despair about that, Riddle put the food in front of me. I recognized it as having come from the guards' mess, the simple hearty food one could find there at any hour of the day or night. A thick brown soup, lumpy with vegetables and chunks of meat, good brown bread with a chewy crust. Riddle had not skimped when he had buttered two chunks of that, nor on the wedges of orange cheese beside them. The flagon of ale on the tray had spilled over a bit, wetting the edge of the bread. I didn't care.

'He's going to choke,' someone said, but I didn't.

'Fitz?' said Dutiful.

I turned to look at him. It was strange to remember that there were people in the room. Devouring the meal had been such a consuming experience that it was startling to discover that the world could hold more sensory information than that. My eyes wandered over his face, finding my features in his, and then Kettricken's.

'Are you feeling a bit more yourself?' he asked. I wondered how much time had passed. I found I was breathing hard. Eating that fast was hard work. No one else had spoken since he had last spoken. Was that how time was truly measured? In how many people spoke, in how much information was shared? Perhaps it was measured in how much food one ate. I tried to pare my thoughts down to something that might fit in words.

'I think I feel better,' I said. No. That wasn't true. I thought nothing of the kind. Better than what? My thoughts raced away from me again. Someone was touching me. Nettle. She had moved behind me and set her hands on my shoulders. She was making my walls stronger. Making me one thing, one separate person instead of the taste of the bread and the sound of the fire crackling. Separating me out from everything else.

'I'm going to talk,' Dutiful said. 'And I'm going to hope you are listening, and that you can find the sense of my words better than Chade can. Fitz. Fitz, look at me. You were almost a day in the stones. You told us you were coming, and we waited for you, and you didn't emerge. Nettle was the one who reached out to try and find you, and with Steady's strength and Riddle helping her she found you and held you together until I could reach into the stone and draw you out. Eda and El, that was strange! I felt I found your hand and pulled you out of the earth itself!

'Chade was still bleeding, and so were you, but not as badly. If you are concerned for the bodies you left behind, well, that has been tended to. Chade's emissary was still at Withy, and we gave him the mission of conveying to the rest of the Rousters that unknown persons had attacked you, and that their fellows had given their lives to win you safe passage to the stones. For now, they need hear nothing of treachery, though I'll wager that some of them will know or suspect there were traitors in their band. I required them all to take an oath of silence on the topic of what happened at Withywoods, witnessed by FitzVigilant in my stead. There is no sense panicking folk over the idea that invisible raiders may attack anywhere. And after brief thought, I have directed Lady Rosemary to undertake whatever quiet work she feels is needed to bring justice to Shun's stepfather. Shun! Such a name!

'And I have put out a notice to all our patrols to be looking for sleighs bearing a small girl and a young woman, and folk on white horses, and also to ask at every ferry crossing and ice bridge if anyone like that has been seen. They cannot simply vanish, and I think it unlikely they can have passed our borders yet. We will find and recover both Bee and Lady Shun.'

The words he spoke made pictures in my mind. I looked at all of them carefully. They were things we wished to be so, and perhaps might never be. Nonetheless, they were pictures that pleased me greatly. 'Thank you,' I said at last. The words were thin, insubstantial as wind. They didn't convey what I felt. I took a breath. '*Thank you.*'

Riddle slapped his hand over his heart and gawked at me. Nettle lowered her face and breathed deeply for several breaths. Dutiful sank down slowly to sit on the floor.

'Is that what it feels like? The Skill?' Riddle spoke.

Nettle shook her head. 'No. I don't know what to call that. Well, yes, it is the Skill, but it is the Skill as a hammer's blow rather than as a fingertap. Dutiful, what can we do? He's more dangerous than Thick. If he goes on like this, he may damage some of the newer Skill-apprentices who cannot wall him out.'

Even with my walls raised, I sensed their agitation. 'It's coming clearer,' I offered them. 'I'm coming back to myself. I will be better by morning, I think.' I used only the words, sliced thin as paper. They all looked relieved.

I attempted a question. 'How is Chade?'

Nettle shook her head. 'He is caught in fascination. With everything. The weave of the blanket. The shape of his spoon. His wound is bad. We would like to do a Skill-healing on him once he has rested a bit, but Thick is still at Withywoods, and we are reluctant to let anyone use the stones to travel now. We were hoping you would feel well enough to help, but . . .'

'Tomorrow,' I said, and hoped it would be true. I was remembering how to do this. Package a tiny bit of thought in a word and let it out of my mouth. Strange. I had never known that when I spoke I Skilled a tiny bit with the words, to make the meaning more clear. But only the tiniest bit. I'd opened my heart and let them feel the rush of gratitude I felt that they would try to help me. I should not do that. I could not recall when I had learned that. Had I ever learned it, or had it just always been so? They were all staring at me. Words. Use words.

'I hope to have recovered more by tomorrow. And perhaps be able to tell you what I experienced inside the stones. And help to heal Chade.'

An urgent thought bubbled up in me. How could I have forgotten him? 'The Fool. Does he live still?'

A glance between Dutiful and Nettle. A secret fear. 'What's happened? He's dead, isn't he?' It was a terrible thing for me to even imagine. A tremor of sorrow rose bubbling in me. I tried to catch it, to hold it in.

Dutiful paled. 'No, Fitz. He's not dead. Please, don't feel that! Such sorrow. No, he's not dead. But he's . . . changed.'

'He's weak? Dying?' I thought of the secret Skill-healings I'd practised on him. Had they gone wrong, come undone somehow?

Dutiful spoke quickly, as if to stem my emotions by giving me information. 'Ash was tending to him. Lord Chade had told him to do whatever the Fool needed, to give the Fool whatever might do him good. Or so the lad took his command. You know that in his zeal to follow you, Lord Golden escaped his room and somehow managed to get as far as the stables. How, I cannot imagine. When he was found the next morning, he was nearly dead of the cold and his injuries.'

'I knew that,' I affirmed.

Dutiful looked relieved at my swift response. 'You are coming back to us, aren't you? You sound clearer in your words. More alert. Thank Eda you are better. I feared that neither one of you would completely return to us.'

'Yes. Better.' It was a lie. I wasn't better. I was becoming duller. Slower. The complexities of the world that had danced and blossomed all around me but a few moments before were fading to dim simplicity. The chair was just a chair, all echoes of the tree and the forest that had produced it muted to insignificance. Nettle sat on the chair, and she was only Nettle, not a tributary of the rivers that Molly and I had been, or the quiet water where her unborn child turned and formed. I was not better. I was simpler, slower, duller. Human again. As to what I had been in the previous hours, I had no name for it.

I lifted my eyes to Dutiful. He was watching me expectantly. 'The Fool,' I prompted him.

'He was near dead. When first he was found, he was mistaken for a beggar or wandering madman. He was taken to the infirmary and given a clean bed to die in. But a young apprentice there recognized him from the night you brought him in. She raised quite a fuss before her master would listen to her, but finally a runner was sent to me.

'By then, Ash had raised the alarm that Lord Golden was missing. We had servants searching the guest wings, but no one had expected him to have got as far as the stables. My mother and her personal healer reached the infirmary before I did. She collected him and had him brought to her private parlour. There, her healer attempted to tend to him. At the woman's touch, he awoke shrieking and found enough strength to object strenuously to her efforts. My mother acceded to his wishes and dismissed her healer. Before he lapsed into unconsciousness, he asked to be brought back to Chade's old den. This was done. And my mother settled herself beside him to keep his death-watch. She left him only when she heard that you and Chade had been attacked, and then lost. She is back with him now.'

'I wish to go to him.' I didn't need to hear any more. I tried to keep the despair from my voice. I was losing my friend, and possibly my last link to my Bee. If anyone had any clue as to why the Servants of the White Prophets would come to Withywoods and take my daughter and what their intentions for her were, it was the Fool.

'Not yet,' Nettle asserted. 'You need to know what happened before you see him.'

I had not thought my fear could deepen, but it did. 'What happened?' I imagined treachery.

'I went to see him, of course,' Dutiful took up his tale. 'Whatever strength and life he'd had left in him he'd expended battling my mother's healer. He was unresponsive to me. I tried to reach him with the Skill, and could not. And to my Wit, he remains invisible. My mother was at his side, tending him. And Chade's lad, Ash. And a crow?'

There was the slightest inflection of a question on his last words. I ignored it. Later, perhaps, there would be time to explain the crow. For now she did not matter.

'The lad was grieved beyond telling. Nearly prostrate with remorse, I thought. I tried to comfort him, telling him that no one blamed him and that I would intercede with Lord Chade to be sure he was not held responsible. But I was mistaken. It was not fear that he had failed in his duty but genuine mourning. My mother told him that we had done all that could be done, and that the Fool himself had decided to let go of this life. The lad kept saying that the Fool was a hero and should not die in such an ignoble way. He wept. We agreed with him but I could tell he was heartsick and our agreement brought him no comfort.

'I knew they would keep a good watch on him, and that I would be summoned if needed. My mother told me that all we could do was comfort his body, and this she was doing, with cool damp cloths to ease the burning of his fever. There was nothing I could do for him. And so I left them there.'

The Fool with a fever. Serious indeed for a man who was usually chill to the touch. Dutiful's words were an apology. I could not imagine why. He paused in his telling and exchanged a look with Nettle.

'What?' I demanded.

Riddle lifted his head and spoke. 'To make it short, Lady Kettricken left to come to the Skill-pillar. And while we were gone, Ash took it upon himself to give Lord Golden something. He won't say what; evidently it was an elixir or potion or some rare healing draught. He won't reveal what it was, but only repeats that Lord Chade told him to give the man whatever he might need, and so he did. Whatever he gave him . . . it changed him.'

Now they were all staring at me as if they expected me to understand something they did not. 'It revived him? It killed him?' I was sick of useless words, such thin slices of meaning. 'I'm going to him.'

Dutiful opened his mouth, but Riddle was bold enough to shake his head at his king. 'Let him go. Words won't explain it. What a man doesn't understand, he cannot tell. Let him see.'

I stood, staggered sideways a few steps and was glad to catch myself before Dutiful could seize my arm. When a man's pride is all he has left, he holds it closely. I did not care that they watched as I went to the drapes and triggered the hidden door. I was sick of secrets. Let them all spill out into the daylight. But it wasn't daylight now. It was night. Let the secrets spill into the night? I shook my head. I had been doing something. Going to the Fool. I clutched my thoughts tightly.

I ascended the stairs. I knew they followed. The room above was yellow with candlelight and hearth-fire. I smelled the resinous fragrance of the Mountain forests and suspected that Kettricken burned incense from her home. It cleared my mind and as I entered the chamber, it struck me that I had never seen it so warm and welcoming. My eyes swept over the changes. The crow perched on one of the chairbacks, dozing in the warmth from the fire. 'Fitz—Chivalry!' she greeted me. Ash sat on the floor by the hearth at Kettricken's feet. He gave me a doleful look and then turned his gaze back to the fire. My former queen was ensconced in Chade's old chair. She had draped a colourful Mountain coverlet over it. On the table beside her, a fat blue teapot painted with leaping hares steamed. Her braided hair was pinned high on her head, and the cuffs of her simple blue gown were folded back as if she were ready to do the day's scrubbing. She turned to me, a mug of aromatic tea in her hands. Her eyes were concerned but her mouth smiled. 'Fitz! I am so relieved you have returned to us, and so worried for little Bee! And for Chade's daughter!'

I made no answer to her greeting. My gaze was snagged on the man who sat beside her. He was slender and upright, but his posture was still uncertain. An invalid still, he was robed in soft grey wool and a loose hood covered his head. I could not tell if he could see me or not. The eyes he turned on me were no longer clouded and grey; they gleamed a faint gold as if the firelight reflected in them. He extended a hand toward me. The knuckles were still swollen and his hands were bone-gaunt, but his fingers moved with a shadow of their old grace. He turned his hand palm up and reached toward me. 'Fitz?' he asked, and I knew then he could not see me. Yet I had the uncanny feeling he could sense me.

I crossed the room and seized his hand in both of mine. It was slightly cool, as the Fool's flesh had ever been cool. 'You are better!' I exclaimed, full of relief at the sight of him upright and moving. I had expected to see him grey and failing in the bed. I turned his hand over in mine; the flesh of the back of it was strangely puckered. It reminded me of an unfledged squab.

'I am alive,' he rejoined. 'And more vital. Better? I do not know. I feel so different that I cannot say if I am better or not.'

I stared at him. Chade had an apothecary supply that would rival any shop in Buck, and possibly even Bingtown. I knew most of what he had, and I'd had the use of some of it. Carryme. Elfbark. Nightshade. Cardomean. Valerian. Willowbark. Carris seed. Poppy. On more than one occasion, I'd had recourse to those supplies. In the course of my training, Chade had occasionally deliberately exposed me to the effects of some of the lesser poisons, soporifics and a wide array of stimulants. Yet I knew of nothing in his arcane array that could call a man back from death's gate and put a golden glint in his blinded eyes.

Ash's gaze had been flickering between the two of us. His eyes were dog-dark, his shoulders hunched as if expecting the snap of a switch. I regarded him severely. 'Ash. What did you give him?'

'The lad believed he was following Chade's orders. And it seems to have worked,' Kettricken said mildly.

I did not speak aloud what I feared. Many treatments were temporary. Carris seed might lift a man's vigour to unusual heights for a day or even two. but it would be followed by a devastating drop to total exhaustion as the body demanded the debt be repaid. Elfbark gave energy, quickly followed by deep despair. I had to know if Ash had saved the Fool's life or merely given him a false lease on it.

Chade's apprentice had not answered my question. I put a growl of command into my voice. 'What did you give him, Ash? Answer me.'

'Sir.' The boy rose awkwardly to his feet and bowed to me gravely. His gaze roved uneasily past Kettricken, glided over Nettle and Riddle, and then faltered before King Dutiful's severe expression. He looked back at me. 'May I speak to you alone?'

Dutiful's voice was deceptively mild as he asked him, 'And what is it that you can tell to Lord FitzChivalry but not to your rightful king?'

The boy looked down, abashed but determined. 'Sire, Lord Chade has made me his apprentice. When he asked if I wished to learn his skills, he warned me that in our trade, there might be times when my king would have to deny me. And times when my silence must protect the honour of the Farseer reign. He said that there are secrets that those who practise our trade do not inflict on the nobility.'

I well recalled the same lecture. It had not come early in my training. Evidently the boy was deeper in Chade's confidence than I had thought.

Dutiful pinned him with a stare. 'Yet Lord FitzChivalry can be a party to your secret?'

Ash stood his ground though the blood flushed his cheeks. 'If it please my king, I have been told that he was one of my kind for many years before he was elevated to being one of yours.' He gave me an apologetic look. 'I had to act on my own judgment. Lady Rosemary was called away. So I had to do as I thought Lord Chade would have wanted done.'

I did not hold the power here. I waited for Dutiful to free the boy from his dilemma. After a long pause, Dutiful sighed. I saw Lady Kettricken give a small nod of approval, while the crow made several courting bows and announced, 'Spark! Spark!' That made no sense to me, but I had no time to pursue a bird's thought. Dutiful spoke. 'I permit this. This once. My honour should not be preserved by those who serve me doing dishonourable things.'

Ash started to speak. I put a hand on his shoulder to silence him. There would always be dishonourable things done to preserve the honour of any power. Silence now, as Dutiful never needed his nose rubbed in that dirt. Something like a shadow of a smile bent the Fool's lips. Riddle and Nettle remained silent, acceding to Dutiful. The relief on the boy's face was evident. It took courage for him to make a low bow to Dutiful and add, 'It is respect for the Farseer line that bids me take this course, my king.'

'Be it so.' Dutiful was resigned.

I gestured to Ash and he followed me. We moved away from the light and warmth of the fire, to the dark and shadowy end of the room. Back to the shadows where assassins belonged, I thought to myself. Back to where the old worktable still bore the scorches and scars of my own apprenticeship.

As I moved, I thought about the task Lady Rosemary had been dispatched to carry out. The man who had hired killers to assassinate the royal assassins would soon experience the king's quiet justice. Would it be subtle: a fall down the stairs, or poisoning from a bit of bad meat? Or would she choose to be sure he knew who was killing him and take her time about it? Would his body be left in such a way as to warn others, or would no corpse ever be found? And I suspected the Bawdy Trout might catch fire. Or possibly experience a very destructive brawl. Cod oil in their wine casks? I reined my thoughts away. It was her task and her assignment came from the king himself. Professional courtesy demanded that I not interfere or judge her decisions. As Ash would learn, some secrets we held back, even from those who shared our trade.

The boy was standing silent near the darkest end of the table. 'Well?' I demanded.

'I was waiting for you to be seated, sir.'

I felt a moment's exasperation. Then I sat, looked at him, and chose Chade's tone as I ordered him quietly, 'Report.'

He licked his lips. 'Lord Chade told me that I should do all in my power to keep your friend comfortable. Anything he might need, I was to furnish him. And I was told that he had Skilled that directive to me from Withywoods, as well. Any desire he expressed, I was to fulfil as well as I might. But sir, it was not just my master's order that made me do as I did. I did it for that man – I scarcely know what name to call him by! But he spoke me kind, even when I first frightened him. Even when I continued to fear and almost loathe his appearance, if I am honest!

'And when he became accustomed to me, he talked to me. As if he were full of words and they must pour out! And the stories he told! At first I thought he was making up such things. Then I went to the scrolls you had written from those times and there I found the tales told again, almost exactly as he had said.'

He paused expectantly, but his words had snatched the speech from my lips. He'd been reading the accounts I'd written and entrusted to Chade, my reports on the hidden history of the Red-Ship Wars, and how Dutiful had been won back from the Old Blood faction and the dragon IceFyre released from the glacier on Aslevjal. The fall of the Pale Woman. It astonished me, even as I felt a bit foolish. Of course he was reading them. Why did I imagine that Chade had asked me to record them, if not to use in the education of his new apprentices? Had I not read scroll after scroll in Verity's hand, and King Shrewd's, and even those from my father's pen?

'But, if you don't mind my saying, his tellings were more exciting than your writing. Hero tales, told by one of the heroes himself. Not that he didn't tell your part in all he did, but . . .'

I nodded, wondering if the Fool had indulged in a bit of embroidery or if the true tales of our exploits had been enough to fire the boy's imagination.

'I took the best care of him that I knew how, preparing his food, keeping his linens clean, changing the dressings on his injuries, the few times he would allow it. I thought he was getting better. But when he received the news that you had gone off to Withywoods, he became a different creature. He ranted and wept.

He said that he should have gone with you, that only you and he could protect one another. I could not calm him. He got up from his bed and stumbled about, demanding that I find garments and boots for him, that he must follow you however he could. And so I obeyed him, but very slowly, for I knew this was not what was best for him. And I am ashamed to say I brought him a tea, one of those that taste of sweet spices and milk but hide a sleeping draught. He drank it down and calmed somewhat. He asked for toasted cheese and bread and perhaps some pickles and a glass of white wine.

'I was so relieved to see him calm and so sure of my tea that I promised to fetch it right away. I left him sitting on the edge of the bed. I took my time in preparing the food and putting it on a tray, and when I returned, my hopes were rewarded. I saw him well bundled in the bed and sleeping soundly. So I did not disturb him.'

'But he wasn't there at all.'

The boy looked only mildly surprised that I had guessed the Fool's ruse. 'No. He wasn't. But it was quite a time before I discovered that. When he did not wake when I thought he should, I thought to see if his fever had come back. But he was only bunched bedding and a pillow stuffed into the hooded cloak I had brought him.'

'I know the rest. What did you give him to revive him?'

'An unproven elixir. I knew that it was all my fault, that my sleeping tea had overcome him as he neared the stables. If he died from the cold and exposure, it would be my fault. Lord Chade had obtained the potion some time ago, at great expense. He did not say directly, but I believe it was stolen from a courier who was bearing it to the Duke of Chalced.'

'That would have been years ago!' I objected.

'Yes, sir. I took that into account. The potion was old and often things like that lose their potency. So I doubled the dosage in the scroll. I gave him two full spoons of it.'

'Two spoons full of what?'

He left me then and went to Chade's cupboard. When he came back, he bore the small glass vial I had seen there earlier. Half its contents were gone, but what remained of the dark red potion had silvery threads that crawled and squirmed through it in a way that made me queasy.

'What is it?'

Ash looked astonished that I did not know at a glance. 'Dragon's blood, sir. It's dragon's blood.'

EIGHTEEN

The Changer

Given that dragons have speech, as men have, and trade their thoughts with us, how can we even consider commerce in their body-parts? Would you ask us to sell you babies' fingers or the livers of slaves? The tongues of women or perhaps men's flesh? It is the considered decision of the Bingtown Traders' Council that to traffic in the parts of dragons is an immoral trade, and one that we as Traders cannot countenance.

It seems unnecessary to add that it is a dangerous trade as well, one that only the foolish would seek to engage in. To slay a dragon for its body-parts would be to invite the full wrath of all dragons falling upon any Trader so reckless as to do it. And doubtless that wrath would include any who indulged in secondhand commerce of such parts. In the course of defending Bingtown from the Chalcedean invaders, our fair city took extreme damage from a single dragon defender. This body refuses to consider what the concerted wrath of the Kelsingra dragons might do to our city.

Hence it is decided and declared that no Bingtown Trader may legally engage in any aspect of trade or commerce that involves the harvesting or marketing of goods sourced from dragons.

Resolution 7431, Bingtown Traders' Council

'He gave you dragon's blood.'

I had persuaded the others there that, while I had concerns over the medicine that Ash had administered to the Fool, there was little to be done save wait and see. I had not told them precisely what that potion was. There was nothing to be gained by involving the king in the knowledge of Chade's illegal trade. I was already appalled on his behalf. When Ash had first spoken of it, I had felt astonished. And then almost immediately, I had known that yes, if Chade were curious about the properties of dragon's blood, he would obtain it, however he could. I only wished that Chade were not incapacitated right now. I had no idea if the suggested dosage Ash had located in Chade's scroll was correct, let alone what side-effects we should beware. And unfortunately for me, my best course was to keep all those worries to myself.

Fortunately for me, Dutiful had a kingdom to rule. Nettle needed rest, and seeing that she got it would occupy Riddle. And Kettricken had excused herself from the Fool's bedside to go to Chade's. I promised her that I would join her there soon, sent Ash off to fetch food for the Fool and me, and seated myself in the chair Kettricken had vacated. Then I had told him.

'What will it do to me?'

I shook my head. 'I don't know. Not for certain. I'll have Ash sort out the scrolls that relate to cures from dragon-parts. I'll have him read through them, and set aside for me any that seem relevant.' I didn't tell him that Chade regarded most of what was written in such scrolls as chicanery. We were in unknown territory, groping our way through the dark. 'Do you feel well enough to talk to me?'

He smiled. 'At the moment, I feel I could walk to the Mountains with you. But a little while ago, my guts were burning inside me and I wept on Kettricken's shoulder as if I were a dying child.' He blinked his golden eyes. 'I see more light than I could before. I slept for a long time after he gave it to me. Or so he says. I do not really believe I was fully awake when he poured it in my mouth. And such dreams I woke from! Not the dreams of a White Prophet, but dreams full of power and glory. I flew, Fitz. Not as when I rode on the back of Girl-on-a-Dragon. I flew. Me.' For a time he sat, silently staring. Then he came back to me. 'My hands ache horribly, but I can move them. Every finger! My skin itches so badly I wish I could tear it off. And my foot, my bad foot?' He lifted the hem of his night robe and displayed it to me. 'I can walk on it. There is pain, great pain in it all the time. But it's not the pain that I had before.'

I realized then that his smile was gritted teeth as well as amusement. I rose to see what herbs I might have to ease the deep ache of healing bones. I spoke over my shoulder as I moved about the room. 'I need to talk to you about the people who attacked Withywoods. They took my little girl, my Bee. And they took Chade's daughter, a grown woman named Shun.'

'No.'

'What?'

The panicky expression was back on his face. 'Chade does not have a daughter. She, too, would count as a Farseer heir. I would have seen her. Fitz, none of the things you tell me can be so. I would have known. It would have revealed other paths to me.'

'Fool. Please. Be calm. Listen to me. You and I, we changed the world, as you said we would. And when you . . . came back, I think we changed all the paths. Chade came out from behind the walls of Buckkeep Castle because of what we did. And he fathered not one, but two, offspring. Shun and Lant. And I had a daughter you had not foreseen. We changed things, Fool. As you said we would. Please, for now, accept that. Because you are the only one who may know why the Servants would take my daughter. And where they would take her and what they intend.'

I turned back to him. I had selected a mixture of valerian and banwurt, willowbark and some shaved ginger to make it a bit more palatable. I found a mortar and pestle on a different shelf and brought them to the table by his chair. As I ground them together, their fragrances mingled. I wrinkled my nose and went back for more ginger and a bit of dried lemon peel.

He spoke in a low voice. 'You left me here. Alone.'

Arguing with him that he had not been alone would have been useless. 'I had to,' I admitted. 'Have you heard what I found when I reached my home?'

He was looking away from me. 'Some of it,' he admitted in a thick voice.

'Well.' I put my thoughts in order. Sometimes to receive information, you must first share all you know. I did not want to think about it or relive any of it. Coward. It was other people's agony I would speak of, and I wished to hide from my shame? I took a breath and began. Part of me spoke the toneless words, relating the facts. Another part of me carefully composed the herbal tea that might ease his pain. Fresh water in a small kettle, put it to boil, warm the teapot with boiling water so the heat would not be lost when I poured the water over the herbs. Let them steep. Set out the cup and pour in the amber liquid without too much sediment. I found honey and added a fine stream of it.

'And here is a tea that might ease the pain in your foot.' I finished my account.

He did not speak. I stirred the tea with a spoon, tapping it on the edge of the cup to give him its location. His trembling fingers walked to the cup, touched it, and were pulled back. 'It was them. The Servants.' His voice was shaking. His blind eyes flickered a gold glance at me. 'They've found you. So they've found me.' He folded his arms and hugged himself tight. He was visibly shaking. It hurt me to see it. *A cold cell, a distant fire that meant only pain, never warmth for you. Men that would smile and shout with joy as they hurt you.* I remembered. I could barely breathe. He leaned his crossed arms on the table and put his face down on them. He collapsed into himself. I stood where I was. He was my last hope and if I leaned on him too heavily, he would break.

Wings flapped. Motley had been perched on a chair, dozing near the fire's warmth. She skidded to a landing on the tabletop and walked over to the Fool. 'Fool. Fool!' she said in her crow's voice. She leaned forward and took a lock of his hair in her beak. She groomed it as if it were his plumage. He took in a small breath. She scissored the tip of her beak against his scalp, selected another lock and groomed it. She made small concerned sounds as she did it. 'I know,' he replied. He sighed. He sat up slowly. He held out his fingers and Motley went to him. With one ruined fingertip, he stroked the top of her head. She had calmed him. A bird had done what I could not.

'I'll protect you,' I lied to him. He knew it was a lie. I had not protected my people at Withywoods, not Lant nor Shun nor even my precious Bee. The thought of my failures soaked me and sank me.

Then fury. Red fury suddenly blazed up in me.

Fitz?

It's nothing, I lied to Dutiful. I bottled and corked my anger. Private. So private. They'd hurt my Fool, possibly killed my friend Prilkop and stolen my daughter. And I had done nothing to them, and could do nothing until I knew more. But when I knew more . . . 'I'll protect you and we will kill them all,' I promised him savagely. I spoke my oath tightly, only to him. I leaned in close to whisper the words. 'They will bleed and die and we will take back our own from them.' I heard him draw a trembling breath. Tears, tinged gold rather than yellow, were creeping down his scarred cheeks.

'We will kill them all?' he asked in a small and shaky voice.

I walked my hand across the table, tapping my nails so he heard it coming. I took his bony hand in mine. I claimed a silent moment to gather my courage and chill my anger to edged cold. Was this right? Was I exploiting his fears for my own ends? Making promises I could not fulfil? But what else could I do? It was for Bee. 'Fool. Beloved. You have to help me now. We will kill them all, but only if you can help me. Why did they come to Withywoods? Why did they take Bee and Shun? What do they intend? Why were Chalcedeans there? And most of all, where would they take them? Where? The other questions matter, but even if all you can tell me is where, it will be enough for me to find them and kill them and take back my child.'

I saw him compose himself. I watched him think. I waited for him. He found the cup, lifted it, and took a cautious sip. 'It's my fault,' he said. I wanted to contradict him, to interrupt him and assure him it was not his fault. But his words had begun to flow and I did not want to divert them.

'Once they knew what you meant to me, they were bound to seek you out. To see if you held the secret that they had not been able to drag out of me. The Servants had your name; I've told you how that came about. They knew of FitzChivalry and they knew of Buckkeep. But of Tom Badgerlock and Withywoods they could not know. The messengers I sent to you – I did not tell them your name. I gave them pieces of information they could use as they travelled to find the next place and ask the next question that might bring them to you. Fitz, I did my best to protect you, even as I sent you my request and my warning. I can only suppose that they captured one of my messengers and tortured it out of him.' He took a noisy sip of his tea, sucking in air with the scalding brew.

'Or perhaps they just followed me. Perhaps they could see what I could not, that it was inevitable that I would make my way back to my Catalyst. Perhaps they even were counting on you to kill me. How sweet they must have found that!

'But now I fear a thing even darker. If they knew I had asked you to find the Unexpected Son and keep him safe, they might have suspected you had already done so. And perhaps they descended on Withywoods hoping to find him. You heard that they were asking for him.

'But here is the darkest thing of all. What if they know more than we can possibly know? What if they have generated new prophecies since you brought me back from the dead and rendered so much of the old future impossible? What if they knew that if you found me in the marketplace, you would kill me? Or what if they knew that if you nearly killed me, you would try to save me? That you would take me and leave your own home unguarded, so they might go in to rape and plunder and search for the Unexpected Son with nothing to fear?'

His words filled me with uneasiness even before he said, 'What if we are still dancing to their tune? And we do not hear it, so we cannot change the step of how we prance and turn to their wills?'

I was silent, trying to conceive of such an enemy. An enemy who would know what I would do before I decided to do it.

'It is no use fearing that,' he said sadly into my silence. 'If it is so, we are helpless against them. And the only logical response to that would be to stop struggling. And thus they would win. At least, if we fight them, we can be a nuisance to them.'

My anger, briefly banked, flared again. 'I intend to be more than a nuisance, Fool.'

He had not withdrawn his hand from my grip. Now he turned it and grasped my hand firmly. 'I have no courage of my own left, Fitz. They beat and twisted and burned it out of me. So I shall have to borrow yours. Let me think, for just a moment longer, on all you have told me.'

He released my hand and took another slow sip of his tea. His eyes stared past me. I had forgotten the crow, so still and silent had she been. Abruptly, she opened her wings and leapt from her perch to land on the small table, nearly oversetting the teapot. 'Food,' she demanded raucously. 'Food, food, food!'

'There is food left on the tray beside my bed, I think,' the Fool told me, and I fetched it for her. There was a bread roll, and the carcass of a small fowl with meat still clinging to its bones. I carried it to the worktable, and she followed me there. I tore the bread for her, poured water into a bowl and left it for her. Once it was in the circle of our lamplight, she found it easily.

The Fool spoke before I had seated myself. 'There are things in your tale I do not understand. And only a few things on which I can enlighten you beyond what you already know. But let us take our bits of facts and see what we can build. First, the kindly woman with the round face. I know her. She is Dwalia, and she will have her luriks with her. She is a Lingstra, that is to say, one who has advanced solidly within the ranks of the Servants, but not so high that she remains in the school interpreting the prophecies. She is useful and clever enough that she has been given luriks to teach and to serve her, but not so precious that the Servants will not risk her out in the greater world. She seems kindly; it is a knack she has, and one she uses well. People assume that she likes them, and in turn, they want to curry favour with her.'

'Did you know her then? In Clerres?'

'I knew of her.' He paused for a moment and for just that instant I wondered if he lied to me. 'She can so easily make others desire to please her, and to make almost anyone feel important and cherished by her.' He cleared his throat. 'Several other things you say puzzle me greatly. Chalcedean mercenaries. Are they just her hired tools or do they have an additional interest? The currency of the Servants is seldom gold. Will they trade a prophecy for what the mercenaries do? Give them a tipping point where they can seize power or glory? The Servants' mission seems clear to us. They were seeking for the Unexpected Son. But when they discover Bee, it is she they carry off, after garbing her as if she were a shaysim, an untrained prophet. But they take Shun as well! Shun! Such a dreadful name.'

'I gather she took it to herself. It is not what Chade named her. But Fool, are you saying they took Bee because she is a prophet?' Uneasiness was a cold coiling of worms inside me.

'Is she?' he asked me quietly. 'Tell me about her, Fitz. And hide nothing.'

When I was silent, gathering my thoughts, he spoke again. The most peculiar smile trembled on his lips and tears glimmered in his eyes. 'But perhaps you have already told me as much as I needed to know, even if I did not put the sense in your words. She is small, and blonde and pale-eyed. And clever. Tell me. Was she long in the womb?'

My mouth went dry. Where was this leading? 'Yes. So long that I thought Molly's mind had turned. For more than a year, almost two, she insisted she was pregnant. And when finally the child came, she was so tiny. And so very slow to grow. For years, we thought she would never do more than lie in her crib and stare. Then, slowly, she began to be able to do things. To roll over, and then to sit without support. Even after she could walk, however, she did not speak. Not for years. I despaired of her, Fool. I thought her mindless or very slow, and wondered what would become of her after Molly and I were dead. Then, when she first began to speak, it was only to Molly. She seemed . . . wary of me. It was only after Molly died that she talked freely to me. But even before that, she proved her cleverness. Molly taught her to read, and she taught herself to write and to paint. And, Fool, I suspect she will be able to Skill, eventually. For she was aware of me. "Like a boiling pot, with your thoughts spilling over," she said. And that was why she avoided my touch and being close to me. But we were getting to know one another, she was starting to trust me as a child should trust her father . . .' I suddenly choked and could not go on. It was sweet release to speak aloud of my child, to trust someone with the full truth of her, and sharpest pain that I described a child stolen from me.

'Does she dream?' he demanded suddenly.

And then it poured from me, the full story of her desire to

have paper on which to write her dreams down, and how she had so frightened me by foretelling the death of the 'pale man' and then the messenger in her butterfly cloak. I hated to tell him how the messenger had died, but by then the sharing of that barbed secret seemed a necessity.

'She helped you burn the body?' the Fool asked, incredulously. 'Your little girl?'

I nodded silently, then forced myself to admit it aloud. 'Yes. She did.'

'Oh, Fitz,' he rebuked me. But I had more to confess to him, and I did, with the tale of our aborted holiday in Oaksbywater, and how I had killed the dog and longed to kill her master, and how I had carelessly allowed Bee to slip away from me. And then, I had to admit the worst. I told how I had come to stab him thinking he was a danger to her.

'What? That was your child who came to me? The boy who touched me and opened me to all the futures? I didn't dream it, did I! He was there. The Unexpected Son!'

'No, Fool. There was no lad anywhere near you. Only my daughter, my little Bee.'

'Then it was her? It was Bee I held in my arms for that one moment? Oh, Fitz! Why did not you tell me instantly!' He stood abruptly, swayed and sank down. He grasped the arms of the chair and gripped them as if a storm blew around him. He stared at the fire as if he could see through the walls of the keep and into some other world. 'Of course,' he whispered at last. 'It would have to be so. I understand it all now. Who else's could she be? In that moment, when she touched me, ah, it was no dream, no illusion or delusion. I saw with her. My mind was opened once again to all possible futures. Because yes, she is Shaysa, even as I once was. And I did not see her in the futures I glimpsed for you because, without me, you would never have had her. She is my daughter, too, Fitz. Yours and mine and Molly's. As is the way of my kind. Ours. Our Bee.'

I was torn between utter confusion and deepest insult. I had a faint memory of him telling me once that he'd had two fathers, brothers or cousins, in a place where folk accepted that arrangement. I'd assumed that it meant that in that place no one would care whose seed had actually ripened in the wife the husbands shared. I forced myself to calmness and looked at him carefully. His golden gaze seemed to meet mine. His eyes were more unnerving now than when they had been colourless. The metallic gleam in them seemed to shift and flow and swirl as if they were liquid while the black dots of his pupils seemed too small for the dim light. I drew a deep steadying breath. Don't be distracted. Stay on the trail. 'Fool. Bee is not your child. You were never with Molly.'

He smiled at me. 'No, Beloved. Of course I was never with Molly.' His fingertip tapped the table, once, twice, thrice. He smiled gently. Then he said, 'I was with you.'

I opened my mouth and stood in gaping silence. It took a long time for coherent words to find their way out. 'No.' I said it firmly. 'No, you were not! And even if . . .' And then I ran out of words and logic.

He laughed aloud. Of all the reactions he could have had, that was the last I expected. He laughed as I had rarely heard him laugh, for while the jester makes others laugh, he seldom betrays his own amusement. But now he laughed unabashedly and without restraint, until he was breathless and had to wipe tears from his sightless eyes. I stared at him. 'Oh, Fitz,' he gasped at last. 'Oh, my friend. What a thing for me to miss! Such a terrible time to be deprived of my sight. Still, all I could not see on your face, I heard in your voice. Oh, Fitz. Oh, my Fitz.' He had to stop speaking to take in air.

'Of all your jests upon me, that was the least funny.' I tried not to sound as hurt as I felt. In the midst of my fears for Bee, he would do this?

'No, Fitz. No. It was the best, for it was no jest. Oh, my friend. You've no idea what you've just told me, even though I have done my best to explain it to you before.' He drew breath again.

I found a bit of dignity. 'I should go see Chade.' I'd had my fill of the Fool's peculiar humour for now.

'Yes. You should. But not just yet.' He reached out and unerringly seized my hand. 'Stay here, Fitz. For I think I know at least part of the answer to your most important question. And I have answers to the other questions that you do not even know to ask.

That last one is the one I answer first. Fitz. You can deny it. But I have been with you, in every way that matters. As you have been with me. We've shared our thoughts and our food, bound one another's wounds, slept close when the warmth of our bodies was all we had left to share. Your tears have fallen on my face, and my blood has been on your hands. You've carried me when I was dead, and I carried you when I did not even recognize you. You've breathed my breath for me, sheltered me inside your own body. So, yes, Fitz, in every way that matters, I've been with you. We've shared the stuff of our beings. Just as a captain does with her liveship. Just as a dragon does with his Elderling. We've been together in so many ways that we have mingled. So close have we been that when you made love to your Molly, she begat our child. Yours. Mine. Molly's. A little Buck girl with a wild streak of White in her.

'Oh, gods. Such a jest and such a joy. A jest I played upon you? Hardly! A joy you have given me. Tell me. Does she look like me at all?'

'No.' Yes. The twin peaks of her upper lip. Her long pale lashes against her cheeks. Her blonde hair, curly as mine, wild as his had been. Her round chin, not the Fool's as he was now but twin to him as a child.

'Oh, how you lie!' the Fool rejoiced. 'She does! I know it in your affronted silence. Bee looks like me! Yours and mine and doubtless the most beautiful and clever child that ever existed!'

'She is that.' Don't think of his ridiculous claim. Of all the people I could lie to, I'd always been best at lying to myself. Bee was mine. Only mine. Her paleness came from my Mountain mother. I could believe that. It was easier to believe that than to agree that the Fool had shared in her making. Wasn't it?

'And now the most important of your questions I answer.' His voice went deadly solemn. He sat straighter at the table. His shoulders were squared and his peculiar gaze distant. 'At this instant, I do not know where they are. But I know where they must take her. Back to Clerres and the school. Back to the den of the Servants. She will be a precious prize to them. Not an Unexpected Son, no, but a trueborn shaysa, unseen and unpredicted. And not created by them. How astonished they will be by that.' He paused and thought for a short time. 'And how determined to use her. Fitz. I do not think you need to fear for her life, yet. But all the same, we must fear for her and recover her as quickly as possible.'

'Can we intercept them?' Hope flared in me at the first possibility of actually doing something rather than simply floundering and agonizing. I pushed all else he had said aside. All those thoughts could wait until I held Bee in my arms again.

'Only if we are very clever. Exceedingly clever. It will be like that guessing game they play in the market, the one with the pea under one of three walnut shells. We must decide which route they will be smartest to take, and then that they will certainly not take the route as we will have deduced it. And then we must think of the route they would choose as the one we would think most unlikely, and discard that as well. We must thwart the future as they know it. It's a puzzle, Fitz, and they have far more information than we do. But there is one piece of information they may have but do not understand. They may know she is our child, but they have no idea to what lengths we will go to recover her.'

He stopped speaking. Cradling his chin in one hand, he turned his face toward the firelight. He pulled at his lips as if his mouth pained him. I stared at him. The scars on his cheeks were fading but his silhouette looked wrong to me. He turned his face back to me. The shifting gold in his eyes was like molten metal seething in a pot. 'I will need to ponder this, Fitz. I must try to dredge from my memory every prophecy or dream about the Unexpected Son that I ever memorized. And I do not know if any of them will be useful. Do any of them truly apply to Bee? Or is she a chance find for them, a treasure discovered when they were seeking something very different? Will they split their group, and send some home with Bee while others continue to seek the Unexpected Son?

'And since my Catalyst and I changed the world, have they harvested new prophecies from their stables of Whites and part-Whites? I think it likely. How can we outwit something like that? How do we outfox a fox who knows every path and den, when they seem able to fog every witness who might be able to help us?'

A shadow of an idea flitted through my brain. Before I could grasp it, the Fool broke the flimsy thought. 'Go on!' With the back of his fingers he shooed me away. 'Take some rest or visit Chade. I need to think alone.'

I shook my head, marvelling at him. In the space of a conversation, he had gone from a quivering, fearful wreck to dismissing me as if he were my king. I wondered if the dragon blood was affecting his mood as well as his body.

The Fool nodded a farewell, already lost in thought. I rose, stiff from sitting, and descended to my room. Ash had been there. It had been meticulously tidied with a precision I could never have achieved. A merry little fire on the hearth waited to be fed. I gave it a log and sat down in the chair before it. I stared into the flames.

The Fool was Bee's father. The thought pushed itself into my mind. Ridiculous. A wild claim by a desperate man. She did look like him. Sometimes. Not that much. But more like him than she looked like me. No. It was impossible and I would not consider it. I knew I was Bee's father. I knew that with complete certainty. A child could not have two fathers. Could she? Bitches could have split litters, with pups born that came from different males. But Bee was a lone child! No. A child could not have two fathers. An unwelcome memory intruded. Dutiful had been conceived by Verity's use of my body. Did Dutiful have two fathers? Was he as much my son as Verity's? I refused to think any longer about it tonight.

I considered my bed. I ached all over. My head was throbbing. My brow was puckered, and not with thought. I found the looking-glass in Lord Feldspar's travelling trunk. The slash on my brow was a wrinkled seam in my skin. The healer had botched his stitches. Picking them out myself would be long and painful. Later. Think about something else. Something that didn't hurt.

I would, I thought, go and find some food. No. Prince FitzChivalry would not wander down to the kitchens looking for cold roast or a dollop of soup from the cauldron kept for the guardsmen. I sat down on the edge of the bed. Or would he? Who could predict what Prince FitzChivalry would do? I leaned back and stared up at the ceiling. Patience, I thought to myself, had not changed to suit Buckkeep Castle but had remained her adorable, eccentric self. A regretful smile bent my mouth. No wonder my father had loved her so. I'd never considered how she had managed to remain herself despite the constraints of court life. Could I be as free as she had been? Set my own rules within the court? I closed my eyes to think about it.

NINETEEN

The Strategy

. . . *but the island is surrounded by a magic, so that only those who have been there can return there. No stranger can find his way. Yet, rarely, pale children are born, and without ever having been there, they recall the path, and so they importune their parents until they are taken there, to grow slowly old and wise.*

On that island, in a castle built of giants' bones, lives a white seer, surrounded by her servants. She has predicted every possible end of the world, and her servants write down every word she utters, scribing it with bird's blood ink onto parchment made from sea serpent hide. It is said that her servants are fed on the flesh and blood of sea serpents, so that they may remember pasts far beyond their own births, and these, too, they record.

If a stranger wishes to go there, he must find for a guide one born there, and he must be sure to take with him four gifts: one of copper, one of silver, one of gold and one made from the bone of a man. And those of copper and gold cannot be simple coins, but must be rare jewellery, made by the cleverest of smiths. With these tokens, each in a pouch of black silk tied with a white ribbon, the traveller must approach the guide and speak the following charm: 'With copper I buy your speaking, with silver I buy your thoughts, with gold I buy your memories and with a bone I bind your body so that you must accompany me on a journey to the land of your birth.' Then that one will take from the seeker the four pouches and speak to him and remember true and guide him to his birth-home.

But even then, the traveller's way may not be easy, for while the

336

guide is bound to take him to Clerrestry, nothing can bind him to take
him by the straightest road, nor to speak to him in plain talk.

An OutIslander minstrel's tale, recorded by Chade

I twitched awake to a soft tapping. I was dressed, on the bed.
Light through the shutters on my window told me it was day. I
rubbed my face, trying to awaken myself, and then wished I hadn't.
The puckering seam on my brow was sore now. The tapping came
again.

'Ash?' I called softly, and then realized it was coming from the
hidden door rather than the one that gave onto the corridor.
'Fool?' I queried, and in response heard 'Motley, Motley, Motley.'
Ah. The crow. I triggered the door and, as it swung open, she
hopped out into my room.

'Food, food, food?' she asked.

'I'm sorry. I've nothing here for you.'

'Fly. Fly, fly, fly!'

'Let me look at you first.'

She hopped closer to me and I went down on one knee to
inspect her. The ink seemed to be lasting. I could not see any
white on her. 'I'll let you out, for I know you must ache to fly.
But if you are wise you will avoid your own kind.'

She said nothing to that but watched me as I went to the
window and opened it. It was a blue-sky day. I looked out over
castle walls topped with an extra rampart of snow. I had expected
it to be dawn. It wasn't. I had slept all the night and part of the
morning away. She hopped to the sill and launched without a
backwards glance. I closed the window and then secured the
secret door. The cold air on my face had tightened the faulty
stitches. They had to come out. The Fool was blind and taking
them out myself would require holding a mirror with one hand
and picking at them with the other. I certainly did not want to
call back the healer who had done this to me.

Without thinking, I reached for Chade. *Could you help me*
remove the stitches in my brow? My body is trying to heal and the stitches
are puckering the flesh.

I felt him there, at the end of my Skill-thread. He drifted like a gull riding the breeze. Then he said softly, *I can see the warmth of the flames through the spy-hole. It's cold here but I must stay here for the whole watch. I hate him so. I want to go home. I just want to go home.*

Chade? Are you dreaming? You're safe home, in Buckkeep Castle.

I want to go back to our little farm. I should have inherited it, not him. He had no right to send me away like this. I miss my mother. Why did she have to die?

Chade. Wake up! It's a bad dream!

Fitz. Stop, please. Nettle shushed me. Her Skilling to me was tight and private. None of her apprentices or journeymen would hear us. *We are trying to keep him calm. I'm looking for a dream that might soothe him and give him a road back to us. But I seem to find only his nightmares. Come to his room, and I'll see to your stitches.*

Remember to come as Prince FitzChivalry! Dutiful cut in, riding her stream of thought. *You caused enough talk when you stole that horse. I've bought it for you, at twice what any horse should be worth! I've tried to explain it was a mistake, that you'd ordered up a horse and thought the roan was for you. But be circumspect with any you meet and try to avoid conversation. We are still trying to construct a plausible history for you. If anyone comments on your youthful appearance, imply that it's an effect from your years among the Elderlings. And please be suitably mysterious about that!*

I affirmed that in a tight Skill-sending to Dutiful. Then I considered myself carefully in the looking-glass. I was seething with impatience to go after Bee, but riding out randomly was as likely to take me further away from her than put me on her trail. I tamped down my frustration. I had to wait. Stand and wait. The Fool's suggestion that we dash off to Clerres, a journey of months, seemed premature to me. Every day that I travelled south was another day of Bee in captivity by Chalcedeans. Better by far to recapture Bee and Shun sooner rather than later, before they could be carried out of the Six Duchies. Now that we knew who and what they were, it seemed unlikely to me that they could elude our search efforts. The reports would come back here, to Buckkeep. Surely somewhere, someone had seen some sign of them.

And in the meanwhile, I resolved to be as tractable as I could.

I'd already created enough difficulties for Dutiful and Nettle. And I had a feeling I was going to be asking for a great deal of help from them and the royal treasury. They would do it for love of me and Bee, regardless of the cost. But it was going to be difficult for the king to lend me the men-at-arms I would require without anyone making a firm connection between Tom Badgerlock's stolen child, the raid on Withywoods and the long-missing FitzChivalry. It would be even more difficult with Chade wandering in a wound fever and unable to apply his cleverness to the problem. The least I could do was not make their political puppetry any more difficult.

Political puppetry. While brutes held my child captive. Rage swelled in me. I felt my heart surge and my muscles swell with it. I wanted to fight, to kill those Chalcedeans as I'd stabbed and bitten and throttled Chade's attackers.

Fitz? Is there a threat?

Nothing, Dutiful. Nothing. Nothing I had a target for. Yet.

When I emerged from my room, I was shaved and my hair groomed back into as much of a warrior's tail as I could boast. My clothing was the least colourful of the garb that Ash had set aside as fitting for Prince FitzChivalry. I wore the simple sword at my hip, a privilege of my rank within Buckkeep. Ash had polished my boots to a gloss and the earring I wore had what appeared to be a real sapphire in it. The frilly half-cloak with the lace edges was an annoyance, but I had decided I must trust Ash and hope such foolish garb was not a boy's prank.

The halls of the castle, that had been thronged with folk for Winterfest, were quieter now. I strode along them confidently, giving a smile to any servant I encountered. I'd reached the stair that would take me to the level of the royal apartments and Chade's elaborate rooms when a tall woman suddenly pushed off the wall she had been leaning on. Her grey hair was pulled back in a warrior's tail and her easy stance told me she was perfectly balanced on her feet. She could attack or flee in an instant. I was suddenly very alert. She smiled at me and I wondered if I'd have to kill her to get past her. She spoke softly. 'Hey, Fitz. Are you hungry? Or are you too proud now to join me in the guards' mess?'

Her eyes met mine and she waited. It took a time for my

memory to travel back that many years. 'Captain Foxglove?' I managed to guess.

The smile on her face warmed and her eyes gleamed. 'I wondered if you'd know me, after all these years. We're a long way from Neat Bay in distance and time. But I've made a bet and a large one, that a Farseer doesn't forget who had his back.'

I immediately extended a hand and we clasped wrists. Her grip was almost as firm as it had once been, and I was immensely glad she wasn't there to kill me.

'And it's many a year since anyone called me captain. But you, what have you been up to? That slash looks no more than a week old.'

I touched it self-consciously. 'It's a humiliating tale, of a very foolish encounter with the corner of a stone wall.'

She shook her head at that. 'Odd that it looks like a sword slash. I can see that what I have to tell you would have been better told to you a month ago. Come with me, please.'

Delayed, I Skilled small and tight to Dutiful and Nettle. *Captain Foxglove wishes a word with me.*

Who? Dutiful demanded worriedly.

She guarded your mother at the Battle of Neat Bay. Kettricken will recall her, I think.

Oh.

I wondered how much he knew of that tale, and as my recollection of that bloody day trickled through my mind, I strode along beside the old woman. She still had the upright bearing of a guardsman and the long stride of one who can quick-march for miles. But as we walked, she said, 'I haven't been a captain in the guards for many years, my prince. When the Red-Ship War was finally over I married, and we managed to have three children before I was too old to bear. And in their time, they gave Red Ross and me a dozen grandchildren. You?'

'No grandchildren yet,' I said.

'So Lady Nettle's child will be your first, then?'

'My first grandchild,' I confirmed. The words were strange in my mouth.

We clattered down the stairs side by side and I was strangely glad of the envious looks other servants bestowed on her as we passed them. Time was when friendship with the Bastard had not been something to prize, but she had given it to me. Down we went, to the level of the castle where the real work was done, threading past the laundry folk with their baskets of linens both clean and dirty, past pages balancing trays of food and a carpenter and his journeyman and three apprentices off to repair something in the castle. Past the kitchens where once Cook had reigned and made me her favourite despite the political ramifications. And to the arched doorway that led to the guards' mess, where the clamour of hungry folk eating seldom ceased.

Foxglove flung up a hand to my chest and halted me there. She met my gaze, looking straight into my eyes. Her hair was grey and lines framed her mouth but her dark eyes snapped bright as ever. 'You're a Farseer, and I know a true Farseer remembers his debts. I'm here on behalf of my granddaughter and a grandson. I know you'll remember the days when a few words from you made me and Whistle and a handful of other good soldiers leave King Verity's Guard to put on the purple and white and the fox badge for our foreign queen. You remember that, don't you?'

'I do.'

'Then ready a smile, sir. Your time has come.'

She gestured for me to precede her. I entered the room, braced with dread and ready for anything. Except for someone to shout, 'Hep!' and have every guard at the table suddenly surge to his feet. Benches scraped loudly against the floor as they were pushed back. One mug teetered precariously as the table gave a bounce. Then it settled and silence filled the room of men and women standing tall and formally alert to greet me. I caught my breath.

Many years ago, King-in-Waiting Verity had fashioned a sigil for me. I'd been the only one to wear it. It had been the Farseer buck, but with his head lowered to charge rather than the lofty pose that a king's son would wear. And across it there had been the red bend that marked me as a bastard even as the buck acknowledged my bloodlines.

Now I faced a room of standing guards, and half a dozen of them wore the slashed buck on their chests. Their jerkins were Buck blue, with a stripe of red down the breast. I stared, speechless.

'Sit down, you idiots. It's still just the Fitz,' Foxglove announced. Oh, she was enjoying this, and when a few of the youngsters in the room gasped at her temerity, she compounded it by taking my arm and tugging me to a place at one of the long benches at the table. 'Push the ale pitcher down this way, and some of the black bread and the white cheese. He may sit at the high table now, but he was raised on guardroom rations.'

And so I sat, and someone poured a mug for me and I wondered how this could feel so good and so strange and so terrible all at once. My daughter was missing and in danger, and here I sat, grinning foolishly as an old woman explained that it was time I had my own guard, and although her other grandchildren were all members of Kettricken's guard, her two youngest hadn't given an oath yet. As the rest of the guards settled at the table, smirking at one another to see a Farseer 'prince' sharing their common fare, they could not know that food had seldom tasted better to me. This dark bread and sharp cheese and the ale that foamed over the top of the tankard were the foods that had sustained me through many a dark hour. It was the best feast I could imagine for this peculiarly triumphal moment.

Foxglove herded two youngsters toward me, a hand on each of their shoulders. Neither could have been over twenty, and the girl visibly straightened herself to try to be taller. 'They are cousins, but as alike as two kits from the same litter. This is Sharp and here is Ready. They're already wearing your badge. Will you take their oaths now?'

'*Does King Dutiful know of all this?*' I spoke the words aloud as I Skilled them tightly to Dutiful. Thought is fast. He witnessed my dilemma instantly and I felt his amusement at it.

'If he doesn't, he should,' Foxglove responded tartly, and mugs thumped the table in agreement. 'I don't recall your asking permission before the white fox badge marked a guard troop.'

'Oh, that was you and Whistle, not I!' I rejoined, and she laughed.

'Perhaps. But I recall it differently.' Then her face grew sober. 'Ah, Whistle. She went too fast, didn't she?' She cleared her throat. 'My infants, draw your knives and present them to Fitz . . . to Prince FitzChivalry. We'll do this the old way.'

Old it was, so old I did not know it, but she walked us through it, and five others followed. She nicked the back of my left hand, and as the tip of her knife moved my blood onto the outstretched palm of the boy, she told him, 'The blood of the Farseers rests in your hands, for you to protect. You hold his life in your hands, now and whenever you draw blade in his name. Do not dishonour it, nor put your life ahead of his.'

There was more and I became aware of first Dutiful and then Nettle joining me as the guards wearing my badge came to me one at a time. They swore their blades to me and took my blood into their hands and I tried to breathe and keep some measure of royal poise as I did so. As the last one rose, taking back from me his sworn blade, I felt a breath of Skill from Nettle. *That was beautiful.*

I'll wager Fitz is weeping like a maiden. This from Dutiful, wryly, but I could feel that he was as moved as Nettle had been.

Or weeping like a man who is finally welcomed home, Nettle responded tartly.

What do I do with them now? I was a bit dazed.

Quarter them. Clothe them. Pay them. Make sure they keep discipline and practise daily. Isn't being royal fun? You're going to need staff, Fitz. The people who do all the things that need doing.

I don't have time for this! I have to go after Bee!

With them at your heels, Fitz. You'll need them. But most of them look as green as grass. Do you want me to choose one of my captains and send him to you?

I think I've a better idea. I hope.

My silence during my conversation with Dutiful had been taken for gravitas. I turned my gaze on Foxglove. 'Captain Foxglove, I'd like your blade, now.'

She stared at me. 'I'm an old woman, Fitz. I left the guard many years ago, after our king drove the Red Ships from our shores. I liked peace. I wed, I had children and I saw them every day. Now I'm old. I've a bad elbow, and my knees are stiff and my eyesight is not what it was.'

'But your mind is. You can refuse me if you wish. I imagine you've a home and a husband and . . .'

'Red Ross is gone for many a year, now.' She stood very still.

343

I watched memories flicker through her eyes. Then she spoke in a whisper as she drew a humble hip-knife from her belt. 'If you still wish to have my blade, I'll swear it to you, Fitz.'

'I do. I'll need someone to keep these puppies in order.'

And so I opened the small wound on my hand afresh, and put my blood into the palm of one who had already held the lives of Farseers in her hands. I would not allow her to go down on her knees to me, but took her promise from her standing. 'Face to face, as we once stood back to back,' I told her. She smiled and every guardsman in the room cheered her.

'And my orders, sir?' she asked.

'To do what you think best. You know far better than I how to captain them. Quarter them, clothe them, see they don't break discipline, and take them to the practice yards. And pay them when their pay is due.' I tried not to betray that I had no idea where those funds would be coming from.

Guards are paid from the treasury. I'll let Lady Lightfoot know that we've a new troop. Right now Chade is awake and almost sensible. My mother is with him. Nettle and I will meet you there.

On my way.

But it took me some little time to pry myself loose from the guards' mess. I had to lift a toast to my new Captain of the Guard, and confirm several tales she had told of the battle of Neat Bay. Thankfully none of them touched on my legendary ability to change myself into a wolf and rip out throats. Finally I was able to leave Foxglove at the head of the table with her two grandchildren beaming with pride in her as I slipped away.

I lowered my head as if in deep thought and strode hastily through the corridors and up the stairs of Buckkeep Castle, everything about me saying I was a man who had no time to stop for words. My concern for Bee vied with my concern for Chade. I needed him to help me sort through all the Fool had told me about the Servants. Chade, if anyone, would know how to outfox them. I needed him for every aspect of my return to life at Buckkeep. It was unmanning to realize how much I depended on him. I tried to imagine the court at Buckkeep without him. Or my life without him manipulating all sorts of events from behind the curtains like a very clever puppeteer. I'd been counting on

him to manufacture and release plausible explanations for where
I had been and my connection to Tom Badgerlock, if there was
to be one. How quickly would the news flow from Withywoods
to Withy and then to Oaksbywater? I would deal with it. Once
I had Bee back, I would deal with everything else, I vowed to
myself, and took the last flight of steps two at a time.

A page with a tray of emptied dishes was just leaving Chade's
room, and behind her came a cavalcade of healers with basins
and soiled bandages and baskets of supplies for treating wounds.
They bobbed greetings to me as they passed and I returned them.
As the last one left, I slipped in the open door.

Chade rested in grand fashion in the midst of his emerald
green bedding and cushions. The heavy curtains around his bed
had been pulled back. A large, cheery fire burned on the hearth
and the room was warmly lit with candles. Kettricken was there,
gowned simply in white and purple. She sat in a chair near the
head of Chade's bed, some bit of needlework in her hands. King
Dutiful stood at the foot of his bed, formally attired in heavy
robes. His crown dangled from his fingertips. I suspected he had
just come from the Judgment Chambers. Nettle was gazing out
of the window, her back toward me. As she turned, I fancied I
could see a slight swell in her belly. A growing child. A baby for
her and Riddle to cherish.

I turned back to Chade. Pillows propped him all around. He
was looking at me. The rims of his eyes were pink as if recently
cleansed of a crust, and the flesh looked loose on his face. His
long-fingered hands rested on the edges of the coverlet, still as I
had seldom seen them still. But his gaze met mine and recognized
me. 'You look terrible,' I greeted him.

'I feel terrible. That bit of scum's sword did more damage than
I thought it had.'

'But you still made an end of him.'

'I did.'

There we stopped. I had not told anyone there how Chade
had ended the traitor. Or had I? Oh. I recalled what Dutiful had
told me of the Rousters and I wondered what they would make
of cut hamstrings, a notched nose and a slashed throat. Later.
Deal with it later.

I wanted to ask if Shun's stepfather had already paid the price for his treachery. But that, too, was not a question to ask in front of others. I spoke to all of them. 'I may have a bit of good news for us. It's thin soup but better than nothing to feed our hopes upon. The Fool confirms what I've suspected. The attack came from Servants of the White Prophet. The Chalcedeans there were most likely mercenaries hired to wield swords, with the Servants directing the attack. The Fool has listened to all the Withywoods folk told us about that terrible evening. He is convinced from the way they dressed Bee in white and bundled her into their sleigh that they believe she is a, uh, a shaysa – that is, a White Prophet candidate. Or something like that. They will value her and will attempt to take her back to their home in Clerres.'

'And Shine?' Chade demanded.

'You heard what the folk of Withywoods said. Bee did her best to protect her. If the Servants value Bee as the Fool believes they do, I hope that means that Bee can continue to extend some protection to Shine.'

There was a silence. 'So we can hope,' Kettricken offered us quietly.

'Thin soup indeed.' Chade was slowly shaking his head. 'You should never have left them alone there, Fitz.'

'I know,' I said simply. Little else I could say to that.

Nettle cleared her throat. 'Chade's messenger has proven his usefulness. I had believed his level of Skill-talent too low for him to belong to a formal coterie, but in this he has functioned well and we will now train Sildwell as a solo.'

'You've word from Withywoods?'

'Yes. Once the Skill-fog was cleared, Chade's messenger was able to reach us clearly, as did my journeyman Grand. But little of it is cheery. FitzVigilant is on his way back to Buckkeep, accompanied by the remaining Rousters. I am leaving Grand in place there. They are bringing the bodies of those who attacked you on Gallows Hill. We have led them to believe you and Chade were attacked by unknown assailants, who fled after the Rousters had loyally protected your entry into the stones.'

'That galls me,' Chade said bitterly from his bed.

'But it best protects FitzVigilant and Thick as they journey with the Rousters back to Buckkeep. At least one of the dead men deserves a hero's funeral, Chade. When they are here in Buckkeep we will sort the sheep from the goats, and we are already digging to see how such treachery could occur within their ranks. The Rousters has always been a "final chance" troop among the guards. Perhaps it is time we disband them altogether.' Dutiful's voice fell on those last words.

Chade had a slight smile on his face. He pointed a finger at the king and said to me, 'He learns. An excellent trait in a king.' He gave a small sigh and added, 'When I feel a bit stronger, I will help in that digging. But don't disband my Rousters. I have a man . . .' His words trickled away. His mouth was slightly ajar as he stared into the flames. I turned my gaze to Nettle. She shook her head at me and lifted a finger to her lips.

Dutiful turned back to me and spoke almost in a whisper. 'Thick rides with them, of course. He and Lant will look after one another. And we have Sildwell with them, to keep us informed. Still, it will be good to have both of them safely home again. Lant will stay at court, and this time he will be safe here. As he should have been all along. The sons of Lord Vigilant will not be presented at court for five years.' There seemed some small rebuke for Chade there. Had he never informed Dutiful that Lant's 'stepmother' harboured hatred for him? Well, it meant that the boys had survived. I wondered about the stepmother's health but did not ask.

Dutiful drew a breath and informed me, 'We have had no reports of the raiders after they left Withywoods. It is as if they vanished completely. We think it is that fogging they can do. I've asked several of the Skill-journeymen to look through the scrolls for any mention of such a use of it and how it can be detected. But we will continue to search for them and to watch key locations. Grand is in place at Withywoods, with directions that he continue queries and report back daily.'

'How are my people there?'

'Our folk are as well as could be expected,' Nettle replied quietly.

A silence fell in the room. I pondered the full import of those words. Nothing I could do about what had been done.

Chade spoke suddenly. 'Ah, Fitz! There you are.'

I turned to Chade and forced a smile to my face. 'How are you?' I asked him.

'I am . . . not good.' He looked around at the others as if he wished them gone. No one moved to leave. When he spoke again, I knew he was not telling the full truth. 'I feel as if I have been away for a long time. A very long time. Dutiful and Nettle tell me we were less than the full turn of a day in the stones. But I feel as if we were there much longer. Much longer.' His eyes held mine, asking.

'It was almost a full day, Chade. Things can seem very strange in a Skill-passage.' I glanced at Dutiful. He was nodding, his gaze distant. 'I think they are more dangerous to use than we know. There is more to them than we understand. When we travel through them, we traverse something that is much more than distance. We should not use them as if they were simple doors that go from here to there.'

'There, we agree,' Nettle said softly. She glanced at Dutiful, deferring to him.

He cleared his throat. 'And how do you feel, Fitz?'

'I think I am almost myself.'

'I fear I have to disagree with you. And Nettle shares that opinion with me. Even now, both of you ring oddly against my Skill-sense, and you have ever since you returned from the stones. We believe your journey changed something in you both. And that perhaps both of you ought to refrain from using the Skill for a time.'

'Perhaps,' Chade agreed. He sighed heavily and then flinched.

I knew I would discuss the Skill-prohibition privately with Chade. I changed the subject. 'How bad is your wound?'

'We think the blade sliced into his liver. The bleeding has stopped. The healer says we are wisest to leave well enough alone, that searching the injury may do more damage that simply letting him rest.' Dutiful spoke. Chade rolled his eyes.

'It seems a good plan to me.'

'It is,' Nettle asserted. 'And we need another plan as well.' She came away from the window to stand directly in front of Dutiful. She cleared her throat. 'My king. Invaders have dared to bring

Chalcedean mercenaries into the heart of your kingdom. They have attacked my home, killing and injuring my servants. And they have stolen my sister, a child of the Farseer lineage, even if as yet unacknowledged!' Dutiful listened to her gravely. 'Such an invasion is not to be tolerated, not by me or by you. The Fool has told us that they will attempt to take them to Clerres. That is a place I have never heard of, but surely it must be on some map, somewhere in Buckkeep. And whether it be north, south, east or west of us, we can block their path! I beg you, as your subject and your cousin, send out our troops now. If we cannot find them on their road, at least we can put a watch on every kingsway, on every ferry crossing and in every harbour. Block them, stop them, and bring my sister and Lord Chade's daughter home safe to us.'

I spoke the little I knew. 'Clerres is a city far, far to the south of us. Past Chalced, past the Pirate Isles, past Jamaillia, past the Spice Isles. It requires a journey by ship. The question is, will their mercenaries take them to Chalced first, and set sail from there? Or will they make for the coast and hope to find a southbound ship?'

'Chalced.' Dutiful and Chade spoke together.

'No band of Chalcedean mercenaries would try to take ship from a Six Duchies port. They'd be singled out and questioned immediately, and once it was discovered Bee and Shine were with them against their wills, they'd be arrested.' Dutiful was absolutely certain.

I was silent, applying the Fool's backward logic. So. The Servants would not make for Chalced. Where and how would they go, then?

Dutiful was still expounding. 'They've a lot of territory to cross, then. And long before they reach Chalced they'll have to replace the sleighs with carriages or wagons. Or carts, I suppose. Or all go on horseback . . . How did they come? How is it possible for them to have penetrated so deeply into the Six Duchies, without alerting us at all? Do you think they came from Chalced? Crossing all that territory?'

'Where else would they hire Chalcedean mercenaries?' Chade asked of no one.

Dutiful stood abruptly. 'I need to speak with my generals immediately. Nettle, gather your Skilled ones and send out word to every outpost where they are placed. Explain as best you can the "fogging" and ask them to be alert for any strange Skilling – if, indeed, they are using the Skill as we know it. We'll be sending messenger birds to the lesser border outposts. Mother, you know our libraries almost as well as our scribes. Can you direct them to search out any maps or charts we may possess of the far southern lands and look for this Clerres city? No matter the age of the map. The legend of the White Prophet is very old. I doubt the city of its origin has moved. I want to know their most likely routes, ports they may visit, any information you can find.'

'Elliania will help me. She knows our libraries as well as I do.'

The wisp of an idea that had drifted through my mind earlier suddenly manifested. 'Web!' I said abruptly.

They all turned to look at me.

'What fogs a man's mind may leave an animal's untouched. Let us ask Web to send word to the Old Blood settlements, to ask if any of the partnered beasts have noticed a troop of soldiers and folk riding white horses. Those bonded to birds of prey or carrion birds might be our best hope. Such birds see for a great distance, and carrion birds often mark soldiers. Too well have they learned that soldiers on the move can mean battles, and battles mean dead flesh.'

Kettricken lifted her brows at me. 'Clever,' she said softly. 'Yes. Web departed a day ago, travelling to Bearns. The crow had visited him and conveyed that she had found a companion. He wished to stay and say farewell to you, but could not. A dragon has been seen regularly over Bearns and perhaps has taken up residence there. Web goes to take counsel with the Duchess and Duke of Bearns about how best to deal with it. The folk of Bearns are not happy to think of donating tribute animals to slake a dragon's hunger, but it may be their wisest course. It is hoped Web can have words with the dragon and persuade it to take what is offered rather than preying on their best breeding stock.' She sighed. 'Such a time we live in. I am reluctant to call him back but I suppose we must. This is too delicate a matter to entrust it to anyone else.'

I nodded to Kettricken. Another delay, with Bee and Shine moving further and further away. Another idea burst into my mind. 'Civil Bresinga. He was here at court, for Winterfest. He sent me a note, offering to be of service to me in any way he could.'

'That he was!' Dutiful smiled and I could see he was pleased that I had remembered his friend. 'Civil has many friends among the Old Blood. He can put out the word more swiftly than a messenger can seek out Web.'

'Even for my daughter, I still must wonder: Do we want to spread the news far and wide that we have had unseen invaders in Buck?' Chade spoke from his bed, his voice full of reluctance.

Kettricken spoke into the quiet. 'I have come to know Civil well. I've never forgotten that as a boy he led Dutiful into danger, even danger of losing his life, but we all recall too the threat Civil was under. In the years since then he has proven himself a true friend to my son, and an honourable bearer of the Old Blood. I trust his intelligence. Let me speak to him. I shall tell him to be circumspect in to whom the messages go. And we need tell them only that we are looking for a troop of men on horseback, sleighs, and folk dressed in white furs. But my own tendency is to shout it from the rooftops. The more eyes looking, the better chance that someone will see something.'

'And sometimes people see what they are told they might see. Circumspect is my choice for now.' The king's word was final. My heart sank a little even as I saw the wisdom of his words.

Dutiful was already at the door. Nettle was on his heels and I sensed a stream of Skill-commands flowing as she moved to her task. Obedient to her request, I did not try to expand my Skill-sense to be aware of what she did. I did not wish to distract her by annoying her. Kettricken was last to the door. She paused and shook her head sadly at Chade. 'You should have trusted us more.' Then she closed the door softly behind her, leaving us two assassins alone.

Old habits. Left alone in the room, both of us reverted. Lord Chade and Prince FitzChivalry vanished, and two men who had long done the quiet work for the king's justice exchanged a glance. Neither of us spoke a word until no echo of footsteps reached us from the corridor. I stepped to the door and listened a moment longer. Then I nodded.

'What else?' Chade demanded of me after a long silence.

I saw no point in mincing my words. 'Ash revived the Fool by giving him dragon's blood.'

'What?' Chade demanded.

I said nothing. He had heard me.

After a time, he made a small noise in the back of his throat. 'Ash presumes a bit too much, sometimes. Well, what has it done to him?'

I wanted to ask him what he had expected it to do. Instead, I said, 'The lad said the Fool was near death. He trickled it into his mouth. It revived him. It more than revived him. He is better by far than when I first brought him here, more recovered than when I left him to race to Withywoods. It seems to be healing him, but it is also changing him. Bones that were broken and then badly healed in his hands and feet appear to be straightening themselves. It's painful for him, of course, but he can now move all of his fingers, and stand on that crumpled foot. And his eyes have turned gold.'

'As they were before? Can he see now?'

'No, *not* as they were before. Not a very pale brown. Gold. Like molten metal and as shifting.' It came to me suddenly. I'd seen Tintaglia's eyes. So had Chade. 'Like dragon eyes. And he still cannot see. But he claims to be having peculiar dreams.'

Chade tugged at his chin. 'Have Ash speak to him about how he feels, and record everything he says. Tell him he may use pages of the good parchment.'

'I can do that.'

'His dreams, too. Sometimes a man's dreams tell him things he doesn't admit to himself. Ash should write down everything the Fool dreams.'

'He may not wish to share what he dreams, but we can ask.'

He gave me a narrowed look. 'And what else is biting you?'

'The Fool fears that our enemies may already know our every move.'

'Spies among us? Here in Buckkeep Castle?' He sat up too suddenly, clutched his side and gasped for a few breaths.

'No. Not spies. He fears they have harvested prophecies gleaned from enslaved White and half-White children.' He listened intently as I explained what the Fool had shared with me.

When I finished, he mused, 'Extraordinary. Breeding humans for prophetic powers . . . Such a concept. Study the possible futures and select the chain of events that will most profit your order. It would demand extreme dedication, for you would be acting for the good of those Servants who came long after you, rather than for immediate gain. And they send out into the world the White Prophet they choose, the one who will do their will in shaping the future. Then along comes the Fool, a true-born prophet, outside their controlled breeding . . . Have you written all this down for me?'

'I haven't had much time for scribing.'

'Well, make time, if you can.' He folded his lips tightly, thinking. His eyes were very bright. I knew his thoughts were outstripping mine, racing up ladders of logic. 'Years ago, when the Fool isolated himself after getting Kettricken home to the Mountain Kingdom, when he thought you were dead and his plans all come to naught, folk came seeking him. Pilgrims. Seeking a White Prophet in the Mountains. How did they know where to find him?'

'I suppose from the prophecies . . .'

He spoke very rapidly. 'Or were the so-called "Servants" seeking for him even then? It's fairly obvious to me that they disliked him being out of their control. Put it together, Fitz. They made the Pale Woman. She was their game-piece. They set her loose on the gaming cloth to shape the world as they wished. They kept him there intending that no one could compete with her, but he got away from them. Rolling and tumbling across their gaming cloth like a bad throw of the dice. They needed him back. What better way to find someone than to seed a search for him by releasing prophecies and letting others be your pack of hounds seeking for him?'

I was silent. Chade's mind often made those sorts of leaps. He made a small sound, not quite a cough. Was the brightness of his eyes the light of fever? I could hear him breathing through his nose as his mind raced.

He held up another finger. 'When they started to arrive, he refused to see any of them. Denied he was a prophet and claimed to be just a toy-maker.'

I nodded to that.

'And when you left Jhaampe, you left very quietly.'

'We did.'

'So they might have lost track of him there. He vanishes. He follows his vision of the future, and helps you wake the dragons. He ensures that the queen returns to Buck, with a Farseer heir growing in her belly. He vanishes again, to Jamaillia, I suspect, and Bingtown.

'And years later, he reappears as Lord Golden at Buckkeep again, just in time to help you assure the survival of the Farseer heir yet again. He is determined to return dragons to this world. He manages to outmanoeuvre both of us and get himself to Aslevjal Island. And there, at last, the Servants capture him. And they torture him nearly to death. They think they've killed him.'

'They did kill him, Chade. He told me they would.' His gaze met mine. He didn't quite believe me, but I decided it didn't matter if he did or not. 'He went to Aslevjal believing that had to happen for IceFyre to be set free from the glacier and mate with Tintaglia. To bring dragons back to our world.'

'Yes, and how we've all enjoyed that!' Chade observed sourly.

For no reason I could explain, that stung. 'You've enjoyed it enough to obtain dragon's blood,' I retorted.

He narrowed his eyes slightly. 'It's an ill will that blows no good,' he observed.

I teetered on a decision. Conversations about morality were rare among assassins. We did as we were told to do. But Chade had undertaken obtaining the blood himself, not as a mission ordained by the king. I dared to question it.

'You don't feel a bit . . . uncomfortable buying the blood of a creature that obviously thinks and speaks? A creature that was possibly murdered for the harvest of that blood?'

He stared at me. His green eyes narrowed and glittered like glacial ice. 'That's an odd line for you to draw, Fitz. Witted as you are, you ran with a wolf. Did not you bring down deer and rabbits and eat them? Yet those of Old Blood who bond to such creatures would tell you that they think and feel even as we do.'

But they are prey and we are predator. It is how we are meant to be to one another. I shook my mind clear of wolfish thoughts. 'That's true. A man bonded to a buck would agree with you. But it's how the world is structured. Wolves eat meat. We took only what we needed. My wolf needed meat and we took it. Without it, he would have died.'

'Apparently, without the dragon's blood, your Fool would have died.' His tone had become acerbic. I wished I had not begun the conversation. Despite all our years together, despite how he had trained me, we had diverged in our thinking. Burrich and Verity, I thought to myself, were perhaps not the best influences for a young assassin. Like a curtain parting to reveal daylight, it came to me that perhaps neither of them had ever truly seen me as a royal assassin. King Shrewd had. But Burrich had done his best to raise me as Chivalry's son. And perhaps Verity had always seen me as his potential heir.

It did not lessen Chade in my sight. Assassins, I believed, were different but not inferior to gently-raised men. They had their place in the world. Like wolves. But I regretted beginning a conversation that could only show us both how far we had diverged. A silence had fallen between us and it seemed a gulf. I thought of saying, 'I do not judge you,' but it would have been a lie and only made things worse. Instead, I tried to resume an old role and asked him, 'I am in awe that you were able to obtain it at all. What did you procure it for? Did you have plans for it?'

He raised his brows. 'Several sources imply it's a powerful restorative. Word came to me that the Duke of Chalced was employing every means at his command to obtain that vial. He believed it would restore him to health and vitality. And for many years, I'd taken a keen interest in the duke's health.' A very slight but very triumphant smile twitched at his mouth. 'That vial of blood was on its way to Chalced when it was . . . diverted. Instead, it came to me.' He waited a moment to allow that thought to penetrate my mind and then added, 'The dragon was already dead. Refusing to buy it would not have brought it back to life. Diverting it from the Duke of Chalced perhaps saved lives.' The smile flickered over his face again. 'Or perhaps not having it ended the duke's life.'

'I had heard that he died when dragons tumbled his castle on to him. If it's so, there's some irony to it, isn't there? The creatures he was hunting to preserve his life sought him out and killed him.'

'Irony. Or fate. But you'd have to ask your White Prophet about fate.'

He wasn't serious. Perhaps. I answered as if he were. 'After I brought him back from the dead, he lost his ability to see all the futures. He lives day to day now, just as we do, fumbling forward down the path to the future.'

Chade shook his head. 'There is no path to the future, Fitz. The path is now. Now is all there is, or ever will be. You can change perhaps the next ten breaths in your life. But after that, random chance seizes you in its jaws again. A tree falls on you, a spider bites your ankle, and all your grand plans for winning a battle are for naught. Now is what we have Fitz, and now is where we act to stay alive.'

The wolfness of the thought jolted me to quiet.

He took a breath, sighed it out fiercely, and gave me a look that was almost a glare. I waited. 'There is something else you should know. I doubt it can help us regain our daughters, but you should know it, in case it can.' He sounded almost angry at having to share his secret, whatever it was. I waited.

'Shine has the Skill. And strongly.'

'What?' My incredulous reaction pleased him.

He smiled. 'Yes. Strange to say, the talent that is so thin in me that I still must fight to use it blossomed in her at a young age. The Farseer blood runs strong in her veins.'

'How did you discover that?'

'When she was very small, she reached out for me. I had a dream of a little girl tugging at my sleeve. Calling me Papa and begging me to pick her up.' The proud smile grew stronger. 'She is strong with it, Fitz. Strong enough to find me.'

'I thought she didn't know you were her father.'

'She doesn't. Her mother left her to be raised by her grandparents. Good enough people in their own way. I can recognize that, even if they bled me for money. Obviously they were not fond of me, but they were loyal to their own blood. She was undeniably their granddaughter, and they raised her as such. With the same haphazard raising they had bestowed upon her mother, I am sad to say. Benign but not intelligent. Keeping a child from harm is not the same as rearing one.' He shook his head, his mouth sour. 'Her mother disdained her from the beginning, and even as a small child, Shine knew that. But she also knew that she had a father, somewhere, and she yearned for him. And in her dreams, she followed that yearning. And our minds touched.'

The uncharacteristically tender smile on his face told me that was his real secret. His daughter had reached out and touched minds with him. And he was proud of her, so proud of her Skill. He regretted not being able to have her near him and shape the innate cleverness he sensed in her. Perhaps if he had had Shine from her beginnings, she could have inherited his role. Too late for that now, I thought. Those thoughts flashed like lightning through my mind, but my own concerns immediately overwhelmed them.

'Chade, I consider it very likely that you had actually touched her with Skill first. As I did with both Nettle and Dutiful, not even realizing what I was doing. And she then reached back to you. So you can reach her and she can tell us where she is and we can reclaim them! Chade, why didn't you do that immediately?'

The smile vanished as if it had never been. 'You'll judge me harshly for this,' he warned me. 'I sealed her. To everyone but me. While she was still small. Long before I brought her to you, I sealed her against the Skill. To protect her.'

I felt sick with disappointment, but the orderly part of my mind tidied my facts into a neatly dovetailed stack. 'Sealed to the Skill. Which was why she alone was still capable of fighting the Servants when everyone else were as passive as cattle awaiting slaughter.'

He bowed his head in a slow nod.

'Can't you reach out to her and unseal her? Skill the key-word to her and open her mind?'

'I've tried. I can't.'

'Why not?' Panic, anger at a lost opportunity. My voice cracked on the words.

'My Skill is not strong enough, perhaps.'

'Let me help you then. Or Thick. I'll wager Thick could batter down any wall.'

He shot a look at me. 'Battering. Not the best word to tempt me to try the experiment. But I suppose we shall when Thick gets here. Yet I doubt it will work. I think she has put up her own walls and that they may be stout ones.'

'Did you teach her to do that?'

'I didn't have to. She's like you. Some things she does by instinct. Do you not recall what Verity said of you? That he could often reach you easily, but the moment you went into any sort of a battle-frenzy, you were lost to him.'

That had been true and was apparently still true. 'But she's not in a battle. They were taken days ago . . .'

'She's a lovely young woman in the hands of Chalcedean brutes.' His voice grew thick. 'I'm a coward, Fitz. I refuse to imagine what her life has been since she was taken. She may very well be in an embattled state of mind at every moment of every day.'

Don't think about it, I warned myself. The dread was as engulfing as the fog had been at Withywoods. I scrabbled back and away from barbed speculation as to how our daughters might be treated. *But they had treated Bee as a prize. Surely that will protect her!* Such a grimy comfort to offer myself, that my little girl might be safe from all that threatened Chade's daughter. Burning sickness rose in the back of my throat.

Chade's voice was low. 'Stop feeling and think. Think and plan.' He lifted a hand, grimacing at the pain of the motion, and rubbed his forehead. 'Shine was able to resist the magic because she was sealed from the Skill. That may be an armour to use when we go against them.'

'But she was not the only one who resisted. Revel fought back. And Lant.'

Chade's voice was deep. 'Until they didn't. Recall what Lant said. That he was trying to hold the door and then suddenly the invaders were laughing at him and walking past him. However they netted that magic over Withywoods, it was not in place when they first began their attack. Why? Did they need to be closer to their victims for it to work? That Shine, sealed against all Skill-influence, was the sole person capable of continuing resistance hints to me that if they are not using the Skill itself, their magic is closely related to it.' He paused and pointed a bony finger at me. 'So. This tells us what, Fitz?'

I felt as if I were his student again. I tried to find the path his thoughts had already travelled. 'Perhaps their Skill-users are not as strong—'

He was already wagging the finger at me. 'No. The door-breakers and swordsmen came first. If they had multiple Skill-users, surely they would be the front ranks. Nullifying resistance is surely better than breaking doors and killing, especially if they were actually looking for this Unexpected Son. Why take a chance that your mercenaries will slaughter the very boy you are seeking? But none of that is what matters here. Think.'

I thought, and then shook my head at him.

He gave a small sigh. 'Similar tools often have similar weaknesses. How did we defeat their magic at Withywoods?'

'Elfbark tea. But I cannot see how we can deploy that resistance against them when we do not even know where they are.'

'Right now we do not know where they are. So, despite our desire to dash up and down every highway between here and Chalced with drawn swords, we muster our weapons and ready them as best we can.'

'We prepare packets of elfbark tea?' I tried not to sound sarcastic. Was his mind wandering?

'Yes,' he said sharply, as if he had heard my thought. 'Among other supplies. My explosive powders are much improved since the last time you experienced them. When Lady Rosemary returns from . . . her errand, I will have her package some of them for us. I would do it myself, if this wound were not troubling me so.' He touched it again, lightly with his fingertips, wincing as he did so.

I did not ask his permission for I was certain I would not get it. I leaned forward and set the back of my hand to his brow. 'Fever,' I confirmed. 'You should be resting, not plotting with me. Shall I fetch a healer?'

He had been sitting up. Now I understood that it was because he could not lean himself back because of the pain. He gritted his teeth in a smile. 'A prince does not run and fetch the healer. You ring the bell and send a servant. But here we are not princes or lords, but assassins. And fathers. We do not rest while beasts hold our daughters captive. So help me lean back. And bring no healers here, but go and find for me the remedies you think best. They will want me to sleep, when I well know that the fires of a fever can make my thoughts burn brighter.'

'I will. But then you will tell me Shine's key-word and together we will try to reach her.' On that I was determined. This was a secret he could not be allowed to keep.

He folded his lips. I stood firm. It was only when he nodded that I set my arm around his shoulders and supported him as he lay back on the bed. Even so he gasped and set his hand to his wound. 'Oh, the blood flows again,' he complained. Then he was quiet, his lips puffing in and out as he breathed against the pain.

'I think a healer should look at you. Poisons I know, and the sort of medicines that have kept me alive when no one else was near to help me. But I am no healer.'

I saw him almost give way. Then he bartered, 'Bring me something for the pain. Then we will try to reach Shine. And after that, you may summon a healer.'

'Agreed!' I said, and hastened out of the door before he could tie any strings to our bargain.

Back to my room I went, locking the door behind me and opening the secret stair. A tap, tap, tap startled me. I pushed back the curtain to find the crow clinging to the stone sill of my window. The moment I opened it, she was in. She hopped to the floor of my room, looked around, then spread her wings and flew up the stairs. Up I went, two steps at a time.

There a curious sight met my eyes. The Fool was at table with a young girl of about fourteen. Her hair was gathered back and pinned neatly under a ruffled cap. Humble as it was, it still boasted three buttons. Her neat servant's tunic of Buckkeep blue covered her modest bust. She was watching intently as the Fool moved a small, sharp knife against a piece of wood.

'. . . more difficult without my sight, but it was always my fingers that read the wood for me when I was carving. I'm afraid that I'd grown more dependent on my fingertips than I realized. I can still feel the wood, but it's not the same as when . . .'

'Who are you, and who let you into this chamber?' I demanded. I moved immediately to put myself between the Fool and the girl. She looked up at me with a woebegone expression. Then Ash spoke from her lips.

'I've been careless. Lord Chade will not be pleased with me.'

'What is it? What has alarmed you so?' The Fool was breathless with anxiety, his golden eyes wide. The carving tool in his hand he now gripped as a weapon.

'It's nothing. Just more of Chade's mummery! I've walked in on Ash dressed as a serving-girl. I didn't recognize him at first, and it gave me a turn. It's all right, Fool. You are safe.'

'What?' he asked in a flustered voice, and then managed a nervous laugh. 'Oh. If that's all, then . . .' But when he set the tool to the wood, his hand trembled. Wordlessly, he set it down. Then, swift as a snake striking, his hand shot across the table to grip Ash's arm. The boy cried out but the Fool held fast as he seized his other wrist as well. 'Why would you disguise yourself so? Who pays you?' Then, as his hand travelled further down the boy's arm to his wrist and then hand, he sat back suddenly in his chair. He did not release Ash's arm but said in a shaking voice, 'Not Ash in a serving-girl's dress, but a serving-girl who has masqueraded as Chade's young apprentice. What goes on here, Fitz? How could we have been so stupid as to have trusted so quickly!'

'Your trust was not misplaced, sir. Possibly I would have shared my secret sooner if Lord Chade had not forbidden it.' In a lower voice she added, 'You are hurting me. Please loosen your grip.'

The flesh of the girl's forearm stood up in white ridges between the Fool's fingers. I spoke. 'Fool. I have her. You can let her go.'

He did, but reluctantly, a slow opening of his hands. He sat back on his chair. His golden eyes whirled and gleamed angrily in the low light. 'And what have I done to deserve this deception from Lord Chade?'

She looked at me as she spoke, rubbing her arm. Her cheeks were very pink and now that the Fool had announced her as a girl, I wondered how I could have seen her as anything else, even in her lad's guise. When she spoke, her voice was a notch higher. 'Sirs, I beg you. There was no wish to deceive you, but only to remain as you had first seen me. As the boy, Ash. So I was when Lord Chade first met me, though he saw through my guise in less than an evening. He said it was in my throat and in the fineness of my hands. He has given me much scrubbing of floors to roughen them, which helps, but he says it is the bones that give me away. Is that how you knew, Lord Golden? By the bones of my hands?'

'Don't call me by that name. Don't speak to me at all!' the Fool declared childishly. I wondered if he would have regretted his words if he had seen how they devastated her. I cleared my throat and she turned her stricken gaze to me.

'Do speak to me, and give me the tale from the beginning. From the time your first met Lord Chade.'

She composed herself, folding her betraying hands on the table before her. I had forgotten the crow, and when Motley hopped closer, I startled. The crow bobbed and touched his beak to her hand, as if to reassure her. Ash-girl almost smiled. But when she spoke, I could hear how rattled she still was. 'My tale goes back quite a bit before I met Lord Chade, sir. You know that my mother was prostituted. That is where my tale of deception begins. I was born a girl, but my mother made me a boy within minutes of my birth. She birthed me alone, biting a folded handkerchief to keep her cries from betraying her. When I was discovered, I was already swaddled, and she declared to the mistress of the establishment that she had borne a son. So I grew up in that house of women, believing myself a boy. My mother was fastidious in her insistence that only she might care for me, and enforcing on me privacy for any moment when my body might be bared. I had no playmates, left the house only in my mother's company and was severely schooled that when I was not with my mother, I must remain in her small and private dressing chamber and keep myself quiet. This I learned so long ago that I do not even remember how it was taught to me.

'I was nearly seven when she revealed the truth to me. Having never seen anyone naked but a woman, I knew nothing of how a man's parts differed. I had believed myself a boy, all that time. I was shocked and distressed. And afraid. For in our house, there were girls not much older than me who toiled at my mother's trade sadly, though they must always pretend to be merry and giddy. That, my mother told me, was why she had made me a boy and why I must remain a boy. My true name, she told me, is Spark. Ash is what covers a coal and hides its light, and so she made my names.'

Despite himself, the Fool was rapt in her tale, his mouth slightly ajar in either wonder or horror. I felt a deep sadness for her.

'How is it that women work that trade as if they were slaves? Slavery is not permitted in the Six Duchies.'

She shook her head at my ignorance. 'No. But when one incurs a debt one cannot pay, often the judgment is that you must labour to pay it off. When my mother was young and new to Buckkeep Town, she learned to love the gaming tables. She was pretty, and clever, but not clever enough to see that the owner of the gaming establishment gave her credits too easily. And when she was deeply enmeshed, he closed his trap.' She cocked her head at me. 'She is not, by far, the first woman or man to be so coerced. It is well known that there is a judge, Lord Sensible, who presides over many debtors' judgments, and often sends comely men and women into the flesh trade. Discreet houses, such as the one where my mother worked, pay off the gambling debts and claim the new debt. If anyone complains, the owners threaten to sell the debt to the ones who put debtors on the docks and streets, to service their trade in the alleys. But once my mother was in the house, she was charged for the food she ate and her clothing and her bed and clean bedding. The whores can never emerge from their debts. When I was born and my mother kept me, I became an additional expense for her.'

'Lord Sensible,' I committed the name to my memory and vowed coldly that Dutiful would hear it from my lips. How had I lived so long in Buck and never known of such a thing?

Spark resumed her tale. 'The women of the house began to use me for their little errand-boy. I was allowed out and about, to run notes to their gentlemen or bring special items from the markets. Our lives went on. I met Lord Chade one evening when he asked for a lad to take a message from him to a ship at the river docks. I took it from him and did as he bade. When I returned, I gave him the written reply. I had turned to leave when he called me back, holding up a silver penny. But when I went to take it from him, he seized my hand, even as you did, and then in a whisper asked what my game was. I told him I had no game, that I was my mother's errand-boy and if he had questions, he should ask them of her. And that night he sought her out instead of his favourite, and spent the whole evening with her. He was very impressed with how well she had taught me. And after that, whenever he came for his visit, he always made excuse to see me, to send me on an errand and always to pay me a silver penny. He began to teach me more things. To push my chin out to have more of a jaw, and to roughen my hand with cold water, and to pad out my shoes to make my feet look bigger.

'My mother was very good at her trade, but it was not what she had wanted for herself, and still less for me. Lord Chade promised that when I turned fifteen he would take me as his servant and teach me a different trade.' She paused, sighing. 'Fate intervened. He took me when I was eleven.'

'Wait. How old are you?'

'As a girl? Thirteen. When I am Ash, I tell people I am eleven. I'm a rather spindly boy, even though I'm strong for a girl.'

'What happened when you were eleven?' the Fool demanded.

Spark's face lost all expression. Her eyes were unreadable. But she kept her voice steady. 'A gentleman thought it would amuse him to share a bed with a mother and her son. He had already paid the lady of our house a substantial sum for such a night when he came to our quarters. No one asked our permission. When my mother objected, the owner of the house said that the debt to her was mine as well as my mother's. And that if my mother and I did not comply, she would turn me out of the house that very minute.' Her face went paler, her nostrils pinched with distaste. 'The gentleman came to our rooms. He told me that first I would watch as he did his business with my mother. And then she would watch as he taught me "a new little amusement". I refused and he laughed. "You've raised him to have spirit. I've always wanted a spirited little mount."

'My mother said, "You will not have him, now or ever." I thought he would be angry but it only seemed to make him excited. My mother was wearing a pretty wrap, as the women of the house often did. He seized the neck of it and tore it open and pushed my mother down on the bed, but instead of fighting back, she wrapped her arms and legs about him and told me to run away, to leave the house and never come back.' She paused, her mind going back. Her upper lip twitched up twice: if she had been a cat, she would have spat out a hiss.

'Spark?' the Fool prompted her quietly.

Her voice was flat. 'I ran. I obeyed her as I always had and I ran. I hid. For two days, I lived on the streets of Dingyton. I did not do very well at it. One day a man caught me. I thought he was going to kill me or rape me, but he told me Lord Chade wished to see me. It was a different name, of course, from the name I knew him by when he patronized my mother's house. But he had a token I recognized, so even though I feared a trap, I went with him. Two days of hunger and cold had made me wonder if I had been a fool to refuse my mother's gentleman.' She sighed out a breath. 'The man took me to an inn, gave me a meal and locked me in a room. I waited for hours, fearing what would happen next. The Lord Chade came. He said that my mother had been murdered and he had feared for me . . .'

That was the point at which life and pain came back into her voice. She gasped her way through the rest of her tale. 'I thought I had left her to face a beating. Or to having the lady of the house dock her earnings. Not to be raped and strangled and left like a dirtied handkerchief on the floor of her chamber.'

Her words stopped and for a time she breathed like a bellows. Neither the Fool nor I spoke. Finally she said, 'Lord Chade asked me who had done it. The lady of the house had refused to say who had bought my mother's time that evening. I did not know his name but I knew everything else about him. I knew the name of the scent he wore and the pattern of the lace on his cuffs, and that he had a birthmark below his left ear. I do not think I will ever be able to forget exactly how he looked as my mother clutched him to herself so that I could escape.'

Her words dwindled away and a long silence followed. She hiccupped, a strangely normal sound at the end of such a dark tale. 'So I came here. To work for him, and to learn he was actually

Lord Chade. I came here as a boy and I live here mostly as a boy, but sometimes he bids me dress as a maidservant. To learn how to be a girl, I suppose. Because as I become a woman, I suspect that it will not be as easy for me to wear my boy's disguise. But also to hear the sort of thing that folk do not say in front of a serving-lad. To witness the sorts of things a lord or a lady does in front of a simple maidservant that they would not do before anyone else. And to bring such observations back to Chade.'

Chade. And with that speaking of his name, my errand flew back into my mind. 'Chade! He has a wound fever, and that was why I came here. To fetch something for his pain. And to send for a healer to come to him later to cleanse the wound again.'

Spark leapt to her feet. The concern on her face was not feigned. 'I'll fetch a healer for him now. I know the old man he prefers. He is not swift, but he is good. He talks to Lord Chade and offers him this or that treatment, and listens to what Lord Chade thinks would be best. I'll go for him now, though he will be slow to rouse, and then I'll come immediately to Lord Chade's room.'

'Go,' I agreed, and she hurried to the tapestry door and vanished from the den. For a short time we sat in silence.

Then, 'Poppy,' I said, and rose to go to the shelves. Chade had it stored in several forms. I chose a potent tincture that I could dilute with a tea.

'She was a very convincing boy,' the Fool observed. I could not identify the emotion in his voice.

I was looking for a smaller container to carry some of the tincture in. 'Well, you would know better about that than I would,' I said without thinking.

He laughed. 'Ah, Fitz, I would indeed.'

He drummed his fingertips on the tabletop. I turned in surprise to watch that. 'Your hands seem much better.'

'They are. But they are still painful. Any poppy for me?'

'We need to be careful with how much pain medicine we give you.'

'So. "No" is what you are saying. Ah, well.' I watched him try to steeple his fingers. They were still too stiff. 'I want to apologize. No. Not apologize exactly but . . . I get those surges of terror. Panic. And I become someone else. Someone I don't want to be.

I wanted to hurt Ash. That was my first impulse. To hurt him for frightening me.'

'I know that impulse.'

'And?'

I had given up my search. I'd have to take the little bottle to Chade's room and then bring it back. 'Ash is the one you should apologize to. Or Spark. And for that rush of fury? Time. Time passing with no one trying to hurt you or kill you will lessen that reaction. But in my experience, it never goes away completely. I still have dreams. I still feel flashes of rage.' The face of the man who had stabbed the dog in the market came to my mind. Anger surged in me again. *I should have hurt him more*, I thought. *Stop*, I told myself. *Stop remembering that.*

The Fool's fingers pattered lightly on the wood he had been carving. 'Ash, Spark. She's good company, Fitz. I like him. I suspect I'll like her as well. Chade is often wiser than I give him credit for. Allowing her to dress and live in both her roles is brilliant of him.'

I was silent. I had just recalled how casually I had stripped to the skin before Ash. A girl. A girl not that many years older than my own daughter, handing me fresh smallclothes. I do not think I had blushed so hotly in years. I would not mention that to the Fool. He'd had enough merriment at my expense lately.

'I should hurry this down to Chade. Fool, is there anything you need or want before I go?'

He smiled bitterly. He held up a hand and began to tick off items on his fingers. 'My sight. My strength. Some courage.' He stopped. 'No, Fitz, nothing you can give me now. I regret how I reacted to Ash being Spark. I feel oddly ashamed. Perhaps because, as you mentioned, I have played both those roles. Perhaps I understand a bit more of what you felt the first time you knew of Amber. I hope he will forgive me and come back.' He took up his wood and felt about for his carving tool. The crow hopped closer and cocked her head to see what he was doing. Somehow he sensed her. He extended his finger toward her and she hopped closer to have her head stroked. 'My time here would have been far lonelier without Ash. And Motley. Much harder to bear. And she was the one to give me the

dragon's blood that has done so much for me. I hope I haven't
driven her away.'

'Perhaps I can come back and share a meal with you this evening.'

'The duties of being Prince FitzChivalry Farseer will most
likely prevent that. But some good brandy, late tonight, would
be very welcome.'

'Late tonight then.' I left them there and threaded my way
back to Chade's bedchamber, arriving as two young men were
leaving. They halted where they were and regarded me with wide
eyes. Prosper and Integrity. Dutiful's sons. I had held them when
they were babies, and as small boys they had sometimes visited
Withywoods with their father. I had rolled them about in autumn
leaves, and watched them chase frogs in a stream. And then,
as they began to get older, their times on the OutIslands had
taken them out of my world.

Integrity elbowed his brother and said smugly, 'I told you that
was him.'

King-in-Waiting Prosper had a bit more dignity. 'Cousin,' he
said gravely and held out a hand.

We clasped wrists while Integrity rolled his eyes. 'I seem to
recall him rinsing you off in the horse trough after you fell in the
manure,' he observed to no one in particular.

Prosper strove to maintain his dignity as I lied carefully, 'I
don't remember that at all.'

'I do,' Integrity asserted. 'Grandma Patience scolded you for
fouling the horses' water.'

That brought a smile to my lips. I had forgotten that they had
considered Patience a grandmother. Abruptly I wanted those days
back. I wanted my little girl home, and I wanted that childhood
for her. Not burning bodies in the night, nor being kidnapped by
Chalcedean mercenaries. I pushed it all down and found my voice.
'How is Lord Chade?'

'Our grandmother asked us to visit him and keep his mind
busy. He just told us his mind was busy enough and asked us to
take ourselves elsewhere. I think his wound is bothering him
more than he wants anyone to know. But we are doing as he
bade and taking ourselves elsewhere. Would you like to come
with us? Lord Cheery is hosting cards today.'

'I— No, thank you. I think I'll take my watch at keeping Lord Chade's mind busy.' Cards. I knew a vague disapproval, then wondered what I thought they should be occupying themselves with. They stood a moment longer, looking at me, and I suddenly realized that we had next to nothing to say to one another. I had stepped back from their lives and now I scarcely knew them.

Prosper recovered before I did. 'Well. We shall certainly see you at dinner tonight. Perhaps we can talk more then.'

'Perhaps,' I agreed, but I doubted it. I did not want to tell them grandfatherly tales of how things had been. People I'd killed, how their great-uncle had tortured me. I felt suddenly old, and hastily entered Chade's chambers to remind myself that he was much older than I was.

'Fitz,' he greeted me. 'You were gone so long.'

I shut the door behind me. 'How bad is the pain?' I took the vial out of my pocket as I spoke. His mouth was pinched white and I could smell the distress in his sweat.

'It's bad.' He was breathing through his open mouth.

'Ash has gone for the healer. Or rather, I should say Spark has.'

His brief smile was a grimace. 'Ah. Well, better that you know. Did you bring the poppy?'

'Yes. But perhaps we should wait for the healer?'

He gave his head a quick shake. 'No. I need it, boy. I can't think. And I can't keep them out.'

'Keep who out?' I looked around his room hastily. Nothing here to mix with the poppy to make it go down more easily.

'You know,' he said in a conspiratorial whisper. 'The ones from the stones.'

That froze me where I stood. In two strides I was beside his bed. I touched his brow. Hot and dry. 'Chade, I don't know what you mean. You have a fever. I think you might be hallucinating.'

He stared at me. His eyes were glittery green. 'No one spoke to you during our passage? No one tries to speak to you now?' They weren't questions. They were accusations.

'No, Chade.' I feared for him.

He chewed on his lower lip. 'I recognized his voice. All these years gone, but I knew my brother's voice.'

I waited.

His fingers beckoned me closer. He flicked them toward the portrait on the wall. He whispered, 'Shrewd spoke to me, in the stones. He asked if I were coming to join him now.'

'Chade, your wound has gone foul and your fever has gone up. Your mind is wandering.' Why did I bother speaking the words? I knew he would not accept them. Just as I knew with plummeting despair that he could not Skill with me just now.

'You could come with us, Fitz. Whisper away with us. You'd find it a kinder awareness.' He spoke in a tone so like old King Shrewd's that a chill ran down my spine. It was too late. If I helped him reach out with the Skill right now, would he open Shine? Or wilfully tatter us both away to nothing?

'Chade. Please.' I did not even know what I was asking him for. I took a breath. 'Let me look at that wound.'

He shook his head slowly. 'It's not the wound, Fitz. It's not the infection. At least, not that one. It's the Skill. That's what festers in me now.' He paused. He stared at the wall, taking long, slow breaths. I could not resist the impulse. I turned to look at the portrait. Nothing there. Only paint on canvas. Then he asked me, 'Do you remember August Farseer?'

'Of course I do.' He'd been nephew to King Shrewd, and nephew to Chade, too, I supposed. Son of their younger sister, who had died giving birth to him. Not much older than me when we had both been sent off to the Mountain Kingdom. He was supposed to be the intermediary for Verity to speak his vows to the Mountain princess Kettricken. But even at that early stage, Regal's treachery had been at work. Verity had not meant to burn out August's mind when he had Skilled through him to assure Kettricken that he was an honourable man, and had had nothing to do with her brother's assassination. But he had. After that, August had come and gone like a flame dancing above a guttering wick. Some days he had seemed sensible. On others his mind had wandered like an old man succumbing to dotage. The Farseer throne had quietly moved him away from the court. I recalled now that he had died at Withywoods in the early days of the Red-Ship War. By then his passing had scarcely been noticed, for his mind had long since departed.

'So do I. Fitz. I should have listened to you. Maybe Shrewd was right when he said no. All those years ago. Envy cut me like a knife when he said you might have the Skill-training. They'd denied it to me, you know. And I'd wanted it so. So much.' He gave me a sickly smile. 'And then . . . I got what I wanted. Or perhaps it got me.'

There was a brisk tap at the door. The healer. I felt a burst of relief that ebbed as rapidly as it had risen when Nettle swept into the room. I felt her Skill come with her as if it were a strong perfume. It flavoured the air in the room and I could not step back from it. She looked at me in dismay. 'Not you, too,' she begged. She drew a sharp breath. 'I could feel him spilling out into the Skill. I've summoned the others. I didn't expect to find you here, spilling with him.'

I stared at her. 'No. I'm fine. But Chade has a high fever. I think his wound has become toxic. He's hallucinating.' I spoke quickly.

She looked at me pityingly. 'No,' she said quietly. 'It's worse than that. And I think you know that. It's the Skill. Once, you told me that it was like a great river, and that if a Skill-user wasn't careful, she could be swept away in it. You warned me of the danger of that pull.' She met my eyes and lifted her chin. 'Not that long ago, I caught you at it. Tempting yourself with it. Letting yourself unravel into that flow of threads.'

It was true. Allowing oneself to flow into the Skill-current was intoxicating. The sense of merging and belonging beckoned, as pain and worries flowed away. It felt powerful and right. I'd been tempted, and more than once. I would have felt ashamed if I had not been so frightened. And so desperate. 'We have to pull him back,' I told her. I teetered on the edge of telling her why it was so important. Then feared that even if she knew, she would not let us try.

'No. Not *we*. You have to stay well back from this, Da. Because I've sensed it in you since you came back from Withywoods. The current tugs at you both.' She took in a breath, her hand set on the barely-visible rise of her belly. 'Oh, that Thick were here now. But even if the weather holds fine, he is still two days away.' She put her attention back on me. 'It would probably be best if you left. And set your walls as tightly as you can.'

I couldn't go. Chade had clutched the blankets to his throat and was watching her as if he were a small boy and she had a switch behind her back. 'I brought him poppy. For the pain. If we dull the pain, he might have more control.'

She shook her head. 'He can't have it. We think that, right now, the pain is what is keeping him here, in his body. It's reminding him he *has* a body.'

'He seemed fine when we spoke earlier. Well, in pain from his wound, but he made sense. We took counsel together . . .'

She was shaking her head at me. There was another tap at the door and Steady entered. He nodded to me and actually smiled. 'Fitz! I'm glad that at last you can be yourself here at Buckkeep Castle.'

'Thank you,' I said inanely. My gaze was on Chade. He was staring up at the portrait of his brother, his mouth moving soundlessly as if he spoke to him. But Steady's full attention was on his sister as he asked Nettle, 'Should you be trying this? Shouldn't you be resting?'

She smiled at him wearily. 'Steady, I'm pregnant, not ill. Where are the others?'

He tipped his head toward me as if we were sharing a joke. 'When she snaps her fingers, she expects the king to come at a trot. He'll be here soon, Nettle.'

'It will be only the three of you? That's not much of a Skill-coterie. You'll need me here.' I tried not to sound as desperate as I felt. I reached my hand toward Chade, thinking that if we touched, I could reach him. Nettle sharply slapped it aside.

'No. We have two solos we can summon if we think that we need their help. Amethyst and Hardy are not very sociable but both are strong in the Skill. But for now, I think those most familiar with Lord Chade can best call him back and bind him up. But not you.' Nettle answered my question and then pointed at the door. I opened my mouth to object and she told me, 'You can't help us. You will only distract us, and that includes distracting Chade. And you may make yourself more vulnerable than you already are. Chade is haemorrhaging into the Skill-stream. And he's actively trying to draw you with him, whether you realize it or not.'

'I have to stay. You have to bring him back to his senses. Then, wise or not, he and I must attempt to Skill together.'

Nettle narrowed her eyes at me. 'No. The very fact that you are asking this shows me that you are strongly drawn to it.'

I met her gaze. *Oh, Molly, would that you could look at me with that same stubborn look your daughter wears.* I steeled my heart. Loyalty to the Farseer reign Chade had always taught me. Above all things, even loyalty to Chade. Right now, my judgment was clearer than his. 'That's not it at all. It's not the Skill-yearning. It's Bee. A short time ago, when we were talking, Chade revealed to me that his daughter Shine has the Skill. She is untrained. And worse, he sealed her to the Skill lest she be vulnerable.' The anger on Nettle's face was building to fury. More frightening was Chade's lack of reaction to my betrayal. He was watching the wall again, his mouth hanging ajar. 'He has been unable to reach her, to Skill the unlocking word to her so she can help us find her. He did not know if it was because he was weak or because the danger all around her has made her put up her Skill-walls. Together, we were going to try to break through to her.'

'After I'd told both of you to refrain from Skilling?'

'I'd forgotten that,' I said honestly.

'You expect me to believe that?' She bit off the words one by one.

'It's true! The chance to find Bee was all I was thinking of.'

Her look softened slightly. No, I had imagined that, for her next words were, 'And knowing that, you did not think to immediately come to me, the Skillmistress, to seek my advice and expertise in this matter?' She folded her lips tightly, then, as if against her will, asked me, 'Do you have any respect for me at all?'

'Of course I do!'

'You love me as your daughter. I don't doubt that. But respecting my knowledge and ability, I doubt that—' She stopped herself suddenly. She was still for a moment and then asked me calmly, 'What was the word to open Shine?'

'He didn't tell me.'

She nodded gravely. 'Perfect.' She pointed to the door. 'Now go. I have work to do here.'

'I can help. He trusts me. I know the shape of him, I can find him and bring him back.'

'No. You can't. Even now, you are spilling and you don't even know it. You are tangled with him somehow. And even now, he is holding on to you, trying to pull you with him.'

I opened myself, trying to feel if what she said were true. Was there a tugging? Pulling me in or . . .?

'Stop that!' Nettle hissed at me, and I snapped my walls back into place.

'Pull me back,' Chade said quietly. Every hair on my body stood erect.

'Verity?' I whispered. I took an inadvertent step toward him, looking into his green eyes, seeking the dark brown gaze of the king I had served. My mind darted back to a Skill-dream, of my weary king crouched by a river of pure and shining magic, plunging his hands and arms into the silvery burning flow. And then begging me to help him, to pull him back from the draw of that liquid magic.

'Stay back, boy!' he cautioned me as my daughter stepped between Chade and me. She put both her hands on my chest.

'Da. Look at me!' she commanded, and when my gaze met hers, she promised, 'If I must, I will call the guard and have you removed from this room. If I must, I will force elfbark tea down your throat until you cannot muster even a thread of Skill. I will not lose you. I need you and my sister needs you.'

'Bee,' I said quietly, and as a wave retreats from the beach, all desire for the Skill ebbed from me. I looked at Chade's glittering eyes and felt ill.

'Save him,' I begged her. 'Please. Save him.'

Then I turned on my heel and left them there.

TWENTY

Marking Time

Taking an unSkilled person through a portal can be accomplished, if it is absolutely necessary. But the dangers to both the Skilled escort and those being transported cannot be exaggerated. The focus of the Skilled one must be divided between the destination and those he escorts. Close physical contact can make the transition easier. Simply holding hands may be sufficient for two who know one another well, and is the recommended method.

On very rare occasions, it may be necessary for an escort to take more than one unSkilled person through one of the corridors. The hazard to both Skilled one and those who accompany him will increase with each additional person or creature. An apprentice should never attempt this. A journeyman, no more than two beings, and only in dire circumstance. The limit for a master is not set, but no more than five living beings are advised.

The dangers are several: that the journey will not be completed, and all will be lost within the passage. That the Skilled one will emerge exhausted, even to the point of dying shortly afterward (recall the account, by Skill-journeyman Bells, of the death of Skillmaster Elmund.) That those accompanying the Skilled one will emerge deranged in mind. Or not emerge at all.

There are several ways to make a successful transition more likely. It is best if the Skilled one has used that particular portal and passage before and is familiar with it. It often seems that if the Skilled ones and those with him are well known to one another, the passage is safer.

On no account should a pregnant woman make any passage. She will emerge with her womb empty. Transporting an unconscious person is to be avoided, and very small children are little better. Curiously, animals seem to fare better in passages than humans do.

Skill-pillars and passages, Skillmaster Arc

The best way I know to stop thinking is to pick up an axe and attempt to kill someone with it. I had no potential targets in the vicinity, but I've always had a vivid imagination. I took myself down to the practice yards and looked for Foxglove.

The day was clear and cold. She was well bundled, but had her charges already steaming as they went through drill after drill. She carried a wooden practice sword and employed it without restraint as she wandered down the rows of her combatants. 'This arm is unguarded, flopping about and begging to be cut off,' she told one as I arrived and gave him a sound thwack to remind him of it. I stood at the edge of her territory and waited for her to notice me.

I think she was aware of me for some time but let me watch what she was doing before she approached me. It seemed to me that she had already added five new recruits to my bastard's badge. She gave all of them permission to breathe and crossed the practice yard to me. 'Well. I can't exactly be proud of my work yet, but they're coming along. I immediately put out the word that we'd be willing to take on some experienced guardsmen. We've attracted some who were put out of their units as being a bit too old or too damaged by old wounds. I'll give them a chance and we'll see who we will keep.'

'Any axemen?' I asked her.

She lifted one brow. 'Lily, there, told me she used an axe. I've not seen her with one yet, so I can't say. Vital looks as if he might be one. Some day. Why? Do you feel as if we'll have need for that sort of guardsman in your company?'

'I thought I might find a practice partner.'

She stared at me for a moment. Then she took in a breath through her nose, stepped forward and with no hesitation felt my upper right arm and then my forearm. Her backhand to my belly took me by surprise but I didn't lose my wind. 'Are you sure you want to do this? It's not very princely.' I looked at her and after a moment, she nodded. 'Very well. Lily!'

The woman she summoned was my height and well-muscled. Foxglove sent her off for practice axes with weighted wooden bits. Then she asked me, 'In those garments?'

I didn't want to go back up to my chambers and change. Too much time, too many thoughts were nagging to explode in my brain. 'It will be fine,' I said.

'No. It won't. I think there are some leather jerkins in the equipment storage. Go now so you don't keep Lily waiting.' As I turned to go, she added, 'Here's something to think about. Your mind will remember how to do something and you will think you can still do it. Your body will try. And fail. Don't hurt yourself today. It will come back to you. Not quickly, and not all of it, but enough.'

I didn't believe her. But long before the end of her practice drills with her recruits, I did. Lily thrashed me. Even when I imagined her as one of the Chalcedean mercenaries who had taken my little girl, I could not defeat her. The wooden practice axe, weighted with lead to give it heft, weighed as much as a horse. I was not sure if it was mercy or pity that made Foxglove summon Lily to work with Vital. As soon as Lily left, she suggested I go to the steams and then rest. I tried not to slink as I left the scene of my defeat. The work had done its task of keeping me unaware of whatever Skill-cure they were working on Chade, but left me in a pit of bleakness that made my elfbark darkness look like a merry sleigh ride. I'd just proved to myself that even if I had the opportunity this moment to reclaim my daughter, she'd probably watch me die in the attempt. I think my morose expression kept anyone from speaking to me in the steams. I might appear to be in the midst of my fourth decade of life to others, but it had been more than thirty years since I'd been the muscled oarsman and warrior I'd been in my twenties. My body reflected the life I'd lived for the past twenty years as a gentleman farmer.

When I stumped up to the door of my chamber, I found Steady leaning against the door. I unlocked it and without a word he followed me inside. When I closed the door behind us, he spoke. 'That's going to be an amazing black eye by tomorrow.'

'Probably.' I looked at Burrich and Molly's son. The bottom of my despair opened and I fell through it. Burrich's eyes, Molly's mouth . . . 'I don't know how to save your little sister. Today, for one moment, we had that chance with Chade. And it's gone now. I don't know where Bee is and even if I did, I doubt I can win her back. My Skill is tattering, I can't wield a blade like I used to. Just when she needs me most, I can't help her.' The useless, stupid words tumbled from my mouth. His face went almost blank. Then he took two short steps toward me, seized me by my upper arms and put his face close to mine. 'Stop it,' he snarled. 'You're drowning us all in hopelessness when we need to be strong. Fitz, after my father died, you came to us. And you were the one who taught me to be a man. In El's name, live up to that! Get your walls up! And hold them.'

I felt like a man who suddenly realizes his purse has been cut. That sudden surprise and moment of checking to see if I could be mistaken. No. My walls were down and indeed I'd been letting my emotions overflow like a river in flood. I slammed them up and then realized that I'd drawn on Steady's strength to do so. True to his name, he stood before me like a rock, clutching my arms. 'Have you got them?' he asked me gruffly, and I nodded. 'Hold them, then,' he ordered, and released me, stepping back. I thought he staggered a little, but at my concerned look, he smiled. 'I caught my heel on your rug. That's all.'

I sat down on the edge of my bed and checked my walls again. 'Are they tight enough?' I asked him and he nodded slowly. 'I'm not myself,' I said, and hated the feeble excuse.

'No. You're not, Tom . . . Fitz. We all hate that we have to wait and hope for word, but it's all we can do. No one blames you for what happened. How could anyone have foreseen it? We are up against a magic as unstoppable as when the Red Ships were Forging our towns.' He smiled small. 'Or so I suspect. That was before my time.'

I nodded at him, unconsoled.

He sat down beside me. 'Do you remember anything unusual about your passage through the stones?'

'I think Chade fainted just as he pulled me into the stone, so he was not using his Skill to help us make the passage.' I didn't like to remember it. 'I was aware that we were in a passage. Aware of my identity in a way I hadn't been before when travelling through the stones. I was trying to hold onto Chade and keep him together. But to do that, I had to let down my own walls. If you know what I mean.'

He nodded, his brow furrowed. He spoke slowly. 'You know that I'm not talented in the Skill. I sense it. I have a lot of strength that I can lend, but I can't do much in the way of directing it. I can help someone else, but not really initiate it.'

I nodded.

'I'm not really sure that I'm Skilled at all. I think I'm just a person who can give strength. Like my father.'

I nodded again. 'Burrich excelled at that.'

He swallowed. 'I scarcely knew my little sister. Withywoods was far away, and she seemed to not really be a part of my life. I saw her a few times, but she seemed, well, too simple. As if she'd never really be a person. And so I didn't get to know her. I regret that now. I want you to know that if you need my strength in any way, you've but to ask me for it.'

I knew he was sincere. And I knew there was precious little he could do for me. 'Then look after your older sister and protect her in any way you can. I do not know what lies ahead for me. Be here for her and protect her.'

'Of course.' He looked at me as if I were slightly daft. 'She's my sister. And I'm part of the King's Own Coterie. What else would I do?'

What else indeed? I felt a bit foolish. 'When you left Chade, was he better?'

His face grew grave. He looked down and then lifted his eyes to meet my gaze squarely. 'No. He's not.' He ran his fingers back through his hair, then took a deep breath and asked me, 'How much do you know of his activities with the pillars and stones?'

My heart sank. 'Next to nothing, I imagine.'

'Well, he has always had a very keen interest in Aslevjal. He was convinced that the Elderlings had left a great amount of knowledge behind in those little blocks of memory-stone and in the carvings on the walls. And so he would go there. At first, he would let the coterie know where he was going and how long he expected to be gone. But as his visits became more frequent, Nettle endeavoured to restrict him, saying that as Skillmistress she had the right to do so. He countered that the knowledge he was gaining was well worth the risk to "one old man" as he put it. It took King Dutiful stepping in to stop his travels.

'Or so we thought. He was no longer leaving Buckkeep and going up to the Witness Stones. No. He had discovered from his studies of the markings on the stones that there was another passage-stone, one that had apparently been incorporated into the building of Buckkeep Castle itself. Or perhaps it was originally there. We have hints that sometimes portal-stones were actually inside strongholds. There is some information that leads us to believe that there was a circle of passage-stones built into the Great Hall of the Duke of Chalced's throne room. Long since toppled, our spies say . . . Oh. Sorry. Down in the dungeons of the keep, in one wall, there is a stone and on it is carved the rune for Aslevjal. He had been using it, and often. To conceal his use of it, he would leave Buckkeep late at night, and return by morning.'

My nails were sinking into my palms. It was the worst and most dangerous way to use the stones, according to Prilkop. Years ago, he had cautioned me against making such a passage twice in the space of less than two days. I had not listened, and I had been lost in the stones for weeks as a result. Chade had been taking very grave risks indeed.

'We only discovered it when he went missing one day. For a day and a half we could not find him, and then he came staggering up out of the dungeons, half out of his mind, with a sack of memory-stones slung over his shoulder.'

I knew a jolt of anger. 'And no one thought to tell me of this?'

He looked surprised. 'That would not have been my decision. I know nothing of why you were not told. Perhaps he begged them not to. Nettle, Dutiful and Kettricken were extremely angry and frightened by the incident. That, I think, was when he truly stopped his experiments.' He shook his head. 'Except for the amount of time he was spending delving into the cubes of memory-stone he had brought back. He had them in his apartments, and we think he was using them in lieu of sleep. When Nettle confronted him about his absent-mindedness, he explained what he was doing. When she ordered them removed to the library, and limited his access to them, he was furious. But not as a man is furious: more like a child deprived of a favourite toy. That was over a year ago. We thought he had mastered his thirst for the Skill. Perhaps he had, but maybe these last two trips, too close together, woke it again.'

I thought of the times Chade had come to see me. Of how he had brought Riddle through. Nettle, I decided, had known of those visits if Riddle had gone with him. Hadn't she?

'Does he know what is happening to him? Is he aware he's doing it?'

'We can't tell. He isn't making a lot of sense. He talks. He laughs and speaks of things from the past. Nettle feels he is experiencing his old memories, and then releasing them to the Skill-stream.

'I was sent to you for two reasons. The first was to help you set your walls more tightly; Nettle is afraid that Chade will cling to you and pull your awareness with him as he goes. The second reason is to ask you for delvenbark. The strong stuff from the OutIslands. The kind that completely quenched your Skill when it was fed to you.'

'I don't have very much left. We used most of it at Withywoods.'

He looked concerned but said, 'Well, whatever you have is what we'll have to use.'

It was still in my travelling bag. It had not been unpacked since they'd all but carried Chade and me to our rooms. I found it, and Bee's dream book, in the bottom of my pack. I rummaged carefully and took out all but two packets. I looked at the herb packets then reluctantly surrendered them. It was hard to come by. Would the dose save Chade? What if it destroyed the precious ability with the Skill that he had so painstakingly built up over the years? If he could not Skill, how could he help me find Shine in the Skill-stream and use her key-word to unlock her? I clenched my jaw. It was time to trust Nettle. Time to cede respect for her hard-won knowledge. Still, I could not keep from saying to him, 'Be careful. It's very strong.'

He hefted the little pouches. 'That's what we are hoping. Nettle thinks that if we can cut him off from the Skill, he may be able to find his centre again. That perhaps we can keep whatever is left of him. Thank you.'

He left me there, staring at the door he closed behind him. Whatever was left of him . . . I rose, Bee's book in my hands, and then sat down slowly. As Chade was, he certainly could not help me find Shine. The first step had to be to stabilize him and persuade him to share Shine's word with us. And I could not help with that. Until then I had to wait.

I was sick with waiting. Waiting had scraped me raw. I could not think about Bee. It was agonizing to imagine what she might be going through. I had told myself, over and over, that it was a useless torment to dwell on thoughts of her in pain, terrified, cold or hungry. In the hands of ruthless men. Useless. Put my mind to what I might do to get her back. And how I would kill those who had put hands on her.

I was gripping her book savagely. I looked at it. My gift to her, a bound set of good paper between sturdy leather covers with images of daisies pressed into it. I sat down with it on my lap and opened the first page. Did I break confidence with her to look at her private writings? Well I knew how often she had spied upon mine!

Each page contained a brief description of a dream. Some were almost poems. Often she had illustrated them. There was the image of a woman sleeping in a flower garden, with bees buzzing around her. On the next page was a drawing of a wolf. I had to smile. It was obviously based on the carving of Nighteyes that had occupied the centre of the mantel in my study for years. Under it was a poem-story about the Wolf of the West, who would race to the aid of any of his subjects who called upon him. The next page was plainer. There was a simple border of circles and wheels and a couplet about a man's fate: 'All he could dream, all he could fear, given to him in the space of a year.' A few more pages, poems about flowers and acorns. And then, on a page that was a riot of colour, her dream of the Butterfly Man. In her illustration, he was truly a Butterfly Man, pale of face, transcendently calm, with the wings of a butterfly protruding from his back.

I closed the book. That dream had come true. Just as the Fool had when he was a lad, she had written down a dream and it became a prophecy. I had buried the Fool's wild talk that Bee was his daughter, born to be a White Prophet. Yet here was the evidence I could scarcely deny.

Then I shook my head. How many times had I accused the Fool of warping one of his prophecies to make it fit the events that followed? Surely this was more of the same. It had not been a 'butterfly man' but a woman, and a cloak with a pattern that suggested butterflies. I tamped my uneasiness down firmly with a mallet of disbelief. Bee was mine, my little girl, and I would bring her home and she would grow up to be a little Farseer princess. But that thought sent my stomach lurching into a different gulch. I sat for a moment, finding my breath and hugging her book as if it were my child herself. 'I will find you, Bee. I will bring you home.' My promise was as empty as the air I breathed it to.

I lived in a space between times. There was the time when Bee was safe. There was the time when she would be safe again. I lived in a terrible abyss of doubt and ignorance. I plummeted from hope to despair, and found no bottom to that dive. Any clatter of boots in the corridor might be a messenger with news of my child. My heart would lift and then it would be only a courier delivering someone's new jacket, and again I'd drop to despair. Uncertainty chewed me and helplessness manacled me raw. And I could let none of it show.

The next three days were as long as any I had ever known. I paced through them like a sentry making endless rounds on the same parapet. As Prince FitzChivalry, I ate my meals with my family, but exposed to the eyes of everyone else in the Great Hall. I had never paused to think how little privacy the Farseer royals enjoyed. I received numerous invitations. Ash still tended my room and sorted the missives into piles. Bereft of Chade's guidance, I presented the ones Ash considered important to Kettricken for her guidance. Just as I had once advised her on how to navigate the tricky currents of Buckkeep politics, so she now advised me as to which invitations I must accept, which I should politely decline, and which ones I could postpone.

And so, after an early morning axe session with my guard, I went out riding with two lesser lords from minor keeps in Buck and accepted the invitation to play a game of cards that evening. All that day, I remembered names and interests and made conversation with words that conveyed almost nothing. I smiled politely and dodged questions with generalities and did my best to be more of an asset than a liability to the Farseer throne. And all the while the thought of my little daughter boiled in the back of my mind.

So far, we had been successful in tamping down rumours and keeping word of what had happened at Withywoods to less than a whisper. I was not sure how we would contain it when the Rousters returned to Buckkeep. It was, I felt, only a matter of time before the connection between Tom Badgerlock and FitzChivalry Farseer became common knowledge. And once that happened, what then?

No one knew that a Farseer daughter had been stolen, and precious few knew that Nettle's younger sister had been kidnapped. We had kept it within the family. To release news of Chalcedean mercenaries able to infiltrate Buck and travel our roads unseen would trigger panic and outrage that the king was not protecting his folk. Keeping my tragedy unspoken was like swallowing back acid vomit. I despised the man who put a pleasant expression on his face, who held a hand of cards or nodded to a noble lady's discussion of the price of a blooded horse. This was Prince FitzChivalry, as I'd never hoped to be him. I recalled Kettricken, head held high and her demeanour calm in the days when her rebellious son Dutiful had vanished. I thought of Elliania and her uncle Peottre, keeping the secret of their kin held hostage as they trod the careful dance of betrothing her to Dutiful. Bitter to think that the same folk who had directed the kidnapping of Elliania's mother and small sister were behind the raid on Withywoods. So I was not the first to have to conceal such pain and it could be done and every morning I looked into the mirror and set my face to stillness. I cut the whiskers from my face instead of my own throat and vowed I would do it well.

Daily, I visited Chade. It was rather like visiting a favourite tree. The delvenbark had quenched his Skill. He no longer dwindled but it remained to be seen how much of himself he could regain. Steady kept watch over him. I spoke banalities to him. He listened, it seemed, but spoke little in response. A servant brought food for all three of us. Chade fed himself, but would sometimes pause and seem to forget what he had been doing. When I spoke of Shine he seemed to take no more than a polite interest. When I asked directly if he could recall the words with which he had sealed her from the Skill, he looked more puzzled than troubled by the question. When I tried to press him, to insist that he at least remember his daughter, Steady intervened. 'You have to let him come back. He has to find the pieces of himself and put them back together.'

'How do you know such things?' I demanded.

'The tiny blocks of memory-stone that Chade brought back offered us all sorts of knowledge. Nettle thinks they were cut into small pieces to be safer to use. We do not let anyone experience many of them, and no one explores them alone. As each one is studied, an account is given of what is learned. I myself was entrusted with one that dealt with those who lost themselves in pursuing knowledge too deeply. I wrote my account of what I learned. And Nettle and I believe it is similar to what has befallen Lord Chade. We hope that if we give him time and rest and keep any more of him from leaking away, he will come back to himself.'

He paused. 'Fitz, I can only guess what he is to you. When I lost my father, you did not try to step into his place. But you sheltered my mother and brothers and Nettle to the best of your ability. I do not think it was solely because of your love for my mother. I think you understood all we had lost. I'll always feel indebted to you. And I promise you that I will do all in my power to bring Chade back to us. I know you think he holds the key to regaining Bee. We all hate that we must stand by and do nothing as we wait for word of her. Please trust that what I do now, I do because I believe it is the fastest way to see Chade regain his senses and be able to help us.'

And that comfort, thin as it was, was the best I could gain from those visits.

That night, when I could not sleep, I tried to occupy myself. I read several scrolls on the Skill, and the accounts of what had been learned from the memory-blocks. Kettricken and Elliania had put their scribes to scouring the libraries of Buckkeep for any mention of Clerres or White Prophets. Four scrolls awaited me. I skimmed them. Hearsay and legend, with a dollop of superstition. I set them aside for Ash to read to the Fool, and comforted myself by imagining that I could poison all the wells in Clerres. The required amount of toxin would depend on the flow of the water. I fell asleep to my calculations.

The next day slowly ticked by. I passed that day as I had the one before. And another day came, with a storm of wind and snow that would delay the Rousters' return. There had been no word from any of the Witted of soldiers on the road, and nothing from the patrols that Dutiful had dispatched. It was hard to cling to that hope, and harder to let go of it. I told myself that if the storms let up, Thick would get home and we might pry Shine's word from Chade and Skill it to her. I busied myself as best I could, but each moment seemed a day to me.

I went to see the Fool at least twice every day. The dragon's blood continued to affect him, with changes that overtook his body so rapidly they were frightening. The scarring on his face, the deliberate tracks of the torturer across the planes of his cheeks and brow, began to fade. His fingers became straighter, and although he still limped, he did not wince with pain at every step. His appetite was the equal of a guardsman's, and Ash saw to it that he could indulge it.

Spark was most often Ash when I saw her in what had become the Fool's chambers, though now I caught glimpses of her as Spark about the keep. I marvelled at what I saw. It was not merely a change of clothing and a frilled cap with buttons. She was an entirely different creature. She was industrious and thoughtful as Ash, but the occasional smile that came and went on her face was all Spark. A sidelong glance from her was not flirtatious but mysterious. Several times I encountered her in Chade's rooms doing minor tidying or bringing cool water to replenish his ewer. Her eyes slid by me at such encounters so I never betrayed that I knew her in any other guise. I wondered if anyone other than Chade, the Fool and me knew of her duality.

It was Ash I spoke with one morning when I had climbed the stairs after what had become a daily practice bout with my guardsmen. I had come to see how the Fool was doing. I found the Fool garbed in a dressing-gown of black and white, sitting at Chade's worktable as Ash tried valiantly to tame the Fool's growing hair. To see him garbed so woke my memories of his days as Shrewd's jester. The new growth on his scalp stood up like the fuzz on a newly-hatched chick's pate, while the hanks that remained of his longer hair hung lank and coarse. As I climbed the final step, I heard Ash say, 'It's hopeless. I'm cutting it all to the same length.'

'I suppose that's the best solution,' the Fool agreed.

Ash snipped each lock and set it on the table, where the crow immediately investigated it. I had come near silently, but the Fool greeted me with, 'What colour is my new hair?'

'Like wheat ready for the harvest,' Ash said before I could respond. 'But more like dandelion fluff.'

'So it was when we were boys, always floating in a cloud about his face. I think you will look like a dandelion gone to seed until it is long enough for you to bind.'

The Fool put his hand up to touch it, and Ash pushed it away with an annoyed grunt. 'So many changes, so fast. Still, each time I awake I am surprised to find myself clean and warm and fed. The pain is still a constant, but the pain of healing is a bearable thing. I almost welcome the deep aches and even the sharp twinges, for each one tells me that I am getting better.'

'And your vision?' I dared to ask.

He fixed his whirling dragon eyes on me. 'I see light and darkness. Little more than that. Yesterday, when Ash walked between me and the hearth-fire, I had perceived his passing shadow. It is not enough, but it is something. I am trying to be patient. How is Chade?'

I shook my head and then recalled he could not see me do that. 'Little change that I can see. The sword cut he took is healing but slowly. The delvenbark has cut him off from his magic. I know he was using the Skill to maintain his body. I suspect he was consuming other herbs as well. And now he is not. I do not know if I am imagining that the lines in his face are deeper and the flesh fallen from his cheeks, but—'

'You are not imagining it,' Ash said quietly. 'Every time I venture into his room, he seems to have aged. As if every change he did with his magic is falling away, and his true age catching up with him.' He set his scissors down, his task finished. Motley pecked at the shining shears, and then decided to groom her feathers instead. 'What good have they done if they save him from dying of the Skill only to let him die of his years?'

I had no answer to that. I had not considered it.

Ash followed it with another question. 'And what will become of me if he dies? I know it is a selfish thing to wonder, but wonder I do. He has been my teacher and protector here at Buckkeep Castle. What will become of me if he dies?'

I did not want to think of such an eventuality but I answered as best I could. 'Lady Rosemary would assume his mantle. And you would remain an apprentice to her.'

Ash shook his head. 'I am not sure she would keep me. I think she dislikes me in direct proportion to how much Lord Chade favours me. I know that she believes he is lenient with me. I think if he were gone, she would dismiss me and take on apprentices more dutiful to her.' In a softer voice, he added, 'And then I would be left with the only other profession I have ever studied.'

'No.' The Fool forbade it before I could.

'Would you take me on as your servant, then?' Ash asked in the most wistful tone I had ever heard.

'I cannot,' the Fool said regretfully. 'But I am sure Fitz would see you well placed before we go.'

'Go where?' Ash asked, echoing my own thoughts.

'Back to where I came from. On a dire mission of our own.' He looked blindly toward me. 'I do not think we should wait, Fitz, for your Skill or my eyesight. A few more days, and I believe I shall be fit to travel. And we must set out as soon as we possibly can.'

'Did Ash read you the scrolls I left? Or Spark perhaps?' The girl grinned. But my foray did not distract the Fool.

'They were worthless, as you well know, Fitz. You don't need old scrolls or a map. You have me. Heal me. Restore my sight, and we can go. I can get you there, to Clerres. You took me through a stone to bring me here; we can get to Clerres the same way that Prilkop took me.'

I made myself pause and draw a deep breath. Patience. His heart was fixed on destroying Clerres. As was I, but both logic and love anchored me where I was and doomed me to the suffocation of waiting. I was not sure if rationality could move him, but I would try. 'Fool. Do you not understand at all what has befallen Chade, and how it affects me? I dare not attempt to Skill, not to try to heal you nor to enter a stone alone. Taking you with me? No. Neither of us would ever emerge.'

He opened his mouth to speak and I raised my voice.

'Nor will I leave Buckkeep until my hope of finding Bee within the Six Duchies is exhausted. Those of the Wit search for her now. And there is a chance that Chade will recover enough to help us reach for Shine. Shall I race off to Clerres, a journey of months by ship, leaving Bee to her captors' whims for all those days when word of her here in Buck or in Rippon may reach us any moment? I know you are impatient to go. Standing still and waiting for word feels like being slowly burned alive. But I will endure it rather than rush off and abandon her here. And when we do go to Clerres, when we take our vengeance to them, it had best be on a ship with troops. Or do you truly believe I can journey to a distant city, beat down their walls, kill those you hate and emerge with my life and their captives intact?'

He smiled and it was frightening when he said softly, 'Yes. Yes, I do believe we can. Moreover, I believe we must. Because I know that where an army would fail, an assassin and one who knows their ways will succeed.'

'So let me be an assassin! Fool. I have said that you and I will take our vengeance on them. And we will. My hatred for all they are burns just as hot as yours. But mine is not a raging forest fire, but a bed of tended coals in a smithy's shop. If you wish me to do this as an assassin, then you must allow me to do it as I was trained to do it. Effectively. Efficiently. With ice in my blood.'

'But—'

'No. Listen. I've said their blood will run. It will. But not at Bee's expense. I will find her, I will take her home, and I will stay with her until she is recovered enough to be without me for a time. Bee comes first. So become accustomed to delay and use it wisely. Rebuild your body and your health, just as I spend my waiting days honing my old skills.'

The fire crackled. Ash stood silent as a sentry, breathing raggedly. His eyes darted from the Fool to me and back again.

'No,' the Fool said at last. He was adamant.

'Have you not heard a word I've said?' I demanded.

It was his turn to raise his voice. 'I have heard them all. And some of what you say makes sense. We will wait, for a time, and though I think that wait will be fruitless, how sweet it would be for both of us if it were not. For all of us. I held her in my arms for but the briefest moments, but in that time, the connection we made. I do not know that I can describe it to you. I could see again. Not the sight of eyes, but my sight of what might be. All the possible futures and the most crucial turning points. And for the first time, I held in my arms someone who shared that with me. Someone to whom I could pass on all I had learned. Someone to come after me, a true White Prophet uncorrupted by the Servants.'

I said not a word. Guilt was choking me. I had broken that embrace, had torn Bee from his arms and punched my knifeblade into his belly, over and over.

'But if tonight a message about her whereabouts reaches you and if you recover Bee tomorrow then we should leave the day after.'

'I will not abandon her again!'

'Of course not. Neither will I. She will be where she is safest. She goes with us.'

I gawked at him. 'Are you insane?'

'Of course I am! As well you know! Torture does that to a man!' He laughed without humour. 'Listen to me. If Bee is truly your daughter, if she has your fire at all, then she will WANT to go with us, to bring down that hive of cruelty.'

'If?' I sputtered in outrage.

A horrible smile lit his face. His voice sank. 'And IF she is my child, as I am certain she is, then when you find her you will discover that she already knows she MUST go there and aid us. She will have seen it on her path.'

'No. I don't care what she has "seen" or what you advise. I would never take my child into slaughter!'

His smile only grew wider. 'You will not have to. She will take you.'

'You are mad! And I am past weariness.'

I walked away from him, to the far end of the room. This was as close to a real quarrel as we had come since the Fool had returned. He, of all people, should be able to understand my anguish. I did not want to be at odds with him right now. And I had so little faith left in myself or my judgment that when he questioned it, it felt like an attack.

I heard Ash's whisper to him. 'You know he is right. First, you must rebuild your strength and endurance. I can help with that.'

I did not hear the Fool's muffled response. But I heard Ash say, 'And I can help with that as well. When the time comes, all will be ready.'

I spoke when I knew I had control of my voice. No anger, no hurt rode my words. 'Tell me of those who follow the woman. Not the mercenaries she hired, but the pale folk. They puzzle me. They are Whites or part-White. If the Servants treat the Whites so badly, why do they follow her and do her bidding? Why must we kill them? Surely they would welcome being free of her?'

He shook his head slowly. His voice was calm and inform-ative. Did he wish to smooth things over as badly as I did? 'Children believe what they are told. They are on "a path" Fitz. They know nothing except obeying her. If they are not useful to her, then they are useless. And the useless are discarded. Euthanized when they are small, gently if they are fortunate. They will have seen some of their fellows given a night draught of poison. The ones who were intractable or did not manifest any talent become as slaves. Those who have a little talent are kept if they are obedient. Some come to believe everything they are told. They will be ruthless in following her orders. They will obey her even to giving up their lives. Or taking any life that opposes them. They are fanatics, Fitz. Show them any mercy and they will find a way to kill you.'

I pondered silently for a time. Ash had gone very still, and was listening as if he were absorbing every word. I cleared my throat. 'So. There will be no hope of them rising against Dwalia. No hope of converting them to our cause.'

'If you find the ones who took her . . . not just the mercenaries they've hired. I mean the ones who made this plan. The luriks. Dwalia. They may seem kindly to you. Or young. Misguided. Or as if they were simply servants, obeying orders. Don't trust them. Don't believe them. Have no mercy, feel no pity. Every one of them dreams of rising to power. Every one of them has witnessed what the Servants have done to their fellows. And each has chosen to serve them rather than defy them. Every one of them is more treacherous than you can imagine.'

I fell silent. And they were the ones who held Bee captive? I could pit my new guard against them, or ask Dutiful for seasoned troops. But my fury went cold as I imagined Bee, small as she was, scuttling for shelter in the midst of such a melee. Trampling hooves, swinging blades. Would Dwalia and her luriks kill my child rather than allow us to win her back? I could not bring myself to phrase that question.

'They will never turn against Dwalia,' the Fool admitted reluctantly. 'Even if you could engage them while they are within the Six Duchies, which I consider very unlikely, they will fight to the last death. They have been told so many tales of the outside world that they will fear capture much more than death.'

He fell silent for a time, pondering. Ash had put away his scissors and was sweeping up fallen hair. 'So. Enough of badgering one another. We have agreed that we will go to Clerres. Let us set aside for now *when* we will go. And even how we will travel there. Let us lay what plans we may. Once we reach Clerres the school has its own fortifications we must win past. Even once we are inside, there is such a nest of evil spiders that it will take cleverness to root them all out. I think we must rely on stealth and cunning more than force of arms.'

'I am cunning,' Ash said quietly. 'I think I might be of great use to you on such a mission.'

The Fool turned a speculative glance toward him but, 'No,' I said firmly. 'Despite all you have known in your short life, I do not take someone as young as you into a situation like that. We are not speaking of a knife in the dark, or a dose of poison in the soup. Dozens, the Fool has said. Perhaps scores. It's no place for a youngster.'

I dropped into a chair beside him at the table. 'Fool, this is not a light undertaking you are asking of me. Even if I can accept that every one of the Servants must die, I still must wonder if I can do it. I am as rusty at assassination as I am at axework! I will do all I can. You know that. Those who have taken Bee and Shine, yes. They ended their lives when they came to my home. They must die, but not in a way that endangers my daughter or Shine. And those who hurt you. Yes. But beyond that? You are speaking of slaughter. I think you imagine my abilities to be far greater than they are.' My voice dropped as I had to add, 'Especially my ability to deal death and not feel the cost. And when we reach Clerres? Do all of them truly merit death?'

I could not read the cascade of emotions that flickered over his face. Fear. Despair. Incredulity that I would doubt his judgment. But it ended with him shaking his head sorrowfully. 'Fitz. Do you think I would ask for this were there any other way? Perhaps you think I seek this purely for my own survival. Or vengeance. But it's not. For every one we must kill, there are ten, a dozen, twenty held there in an ignorant slavery. Those, possibly, we can free, to go about whatever lives they can build for themselves. Children bred to one another like cattle, cousin to cousin, sister to brother. The malformed children they create, the ones born with no sign of their White bloodlines are destroyed as carelessly as you might pull a weed from a summer garden.' His voice shook and his hands trembled against the table. Ash reached toward him. I shook my head at him. I did not think the Fool wished to be touched just then.

His words halted. He clasped his hands together tightly and I watched him try to find calmness. Motley left off grooming herself and hopped closer to him. 'Fool? Fool?'

'I'm here, Motley,' he said as if she were his child. He extended his hand toward the sound of her voice. She hopped to his wrist and he did not flinch. She climbed up his sleeve, beak over claw, until she reached his shoulder. She began to preen his hair. I saw his clenched jaw relax. Still, his voice was flat and dead as he spoke. 'Fitz. Do you understand that is what they intend for Bee?

For our child? She is a valuable addition to their breeding stock, a strain of White blood they have not yet been able to add. If they have not already deduced she is mine, they soon will.'

Ash's eyes flew wide open. He started to speak. A sharp gesture from me stopped him. I moved my hand to my heart and tried to calm it. I drew a deep breath. Ask the questions. 'So. How long will this journey to Clerres take us?'

'In truth, I can't say with surety. When first I travelled from the School to Buckkeep, it was by a very roundabout way. I was young. More than once I lost my way, or had to take ship to a port other than the one I desired in the hope of finding a ship there that would take me closer to Buck. Sometimes I was months in one location before I had the wherewithal to travel on. Twice I was held against my wishes. Back then, my resources were very limited, and the Six Duchies little more than a legend to me. And when I returned to Clerres with Prilkop, we travelled part of the way by the stones. It still took us quite a time to reach there.' He paused. Was he hoping that I would offer to take him by that route again? If so, he would wait for a long time, even when my control of the Skill was restored. Chade's current state had only increased my reluctance ever to enter them again.

'But however we go, we had best start as soon as we are able. The dragon's blood Ash gave me has had a remarkable effect on my health. If I continue to improve, if you can help me regain my eyesight . . . Oh, even if neither happens. We will wait for the messenger you hope for. But how long? Ten days?'

There was no reasoning with him. I would not give him false promises. 'Let us wait until the Rousters return with Thick and FitzVigilant. It will not be many days. And perhaps by then your eyes will have improved as much as the rest of you. And if not, we will ask Thick and the rest of Nettle's coterie to see if they can restore your vision.'

'Not you?'

'Until Nettle judges my Skill to be controlled again, no. I will be in the room but I will not be able to help.' I repeated aloud the promise I'd made to myself. 'It's time for me to cede to her true authority as Skillmistress. And respect her knowledge. She has warned me not to Skill. So I will not. But the others can help you.'

'But I . . . No, then. No.' He suddenly lifted one scarred hand to cover his mouth. Both his fingers and his voice shook as he spoke. 'I cannot. I just can't let them . . . Not until you are recovered. Fitz. You know me. But those others . . . They could lend you their strength but you must be the one to touch me. Until then . . . No. I will have to wait.' He snapped his mouth shut suddenly and abruptly crossed his arms on his chest. I could almost see hope depart from his body as his shoulders rounded in. He closed his blind eyes and I looked away from him, trying to give him space to compose himself. So quickly he had lost his dragon-blood courage. I almost wished he were quarrelling with me still. To see him suddenly shaking in fear again was like a bellows blowing on the coals of my anger. I would kill them. All of them.

Motley muttered to him. I stood and walked away from the table. I did not speak again until he could hear that I was not sitting and staring at him.

'Ash. You have a deft hand with those scissors. Do you think you could take the stitches out of my brow? They are too tight.'

'They look like a puckered seam in a badly-made dress,' Ash told me. 'Come. Sit down here near the fire where the light is better.'

Ash and I talked while he worked, mostly his small warnings that he would now tug out a stitch or asking me to blot away the blood that welled where the threads had been. We both pretended not to notice when the Fool gently set his crow down on the table and carefully groped his way to his bed. By the time Ash was finished with me, he was either truly asleep or feigning it well.

The slow days ground by. Whenever I found myself pacing, I took myself down to the practice yards. I had one chance encounter with Blade's grandson. He barely concealed his satisfaction in the drubbing he gave me. The second time I accepted his invitation to try our skills with staves against each other, he very nearly laid me out. Afterwards, Foxglove drew me aside and asked me sarcastically if I enjoyed the beatings I was taking. I told her that of course I didn't, I was simply trying to regain some of my old physical skills. But as I limped away to the steams, I knew I had lied. My guilt demanded pain, and pain was one of the few things that could drive Bee's predicament from my thoughts. I knew it for an unhealthy tendency, but excused myself on the grounds that when finally I had a chance to use a blade against her kidnappers, I might have regained some of my ability.

So it was that I was in the practice yards when the shout went up that the Rousters had returned. I touched the tip of my wooden blade to the earth to signify my surrender to my partner and went to meet them. Their formation was ragged and they rode as defeated and angry men do. They had their comrades' horses, but were bearing no bodies home. Most likely they had burned them where they fell. I wondered what they had made of finding one man hamstrung, with his throat cut. Perhaps in all the blood, no one would have noticed his specific injuries.

They ignored me as they led their horses to the stables. FitzVigilant had already dismounted and stood holding the reins of his mount and waiting for someone to take the horse. Thick, looking old and weary and cold, sat slumped on his sturdy beast. I went to his stirrup. 'Come down, old friend. Put your hand on my shoulder.'

He lifted his face to regard me. I had not seen him look so miserable in a very long time. 'They're mean. They made fun of me all the way home. They bumped me from behind when I was trying to drink my tea and I spilled it all down my front. And at the inn, they sent two girls to tease me. They dared me to touch their breasts and then slapped me when I did.' Tears came into his little eyes.

He told me his troubles so earnestly. I pushed down my wrath to speak gently to him. 'You are home and no one will hurt you any more,' I promised him. 'You are back with your friends. Come down.'

'I did my best to protect him,' Lant said behind my shoulder. 'But he could not seem to stay clear of his tormentors, or ignore them.'

Having had the care of Thick more than once, I understood well enough. The little man did seem to have the knack for putting himself into the most trouble he could find: despite his years, he still had difficulty telling mockery from good-natured joking. Until it was too late. And like a cat, he was inevitably most attracted to those who had the least tolerance for him. Those most likely to torment him.

But once he had been able to evade actual physical damage.

I spoke very softly. 'Could not you Skill them, "Don't see me, don't see me"?'

He scowled at me. 'They tricked me. One would say, "Oh, I like you, be my friend." But they would be mean. Those girls, they said they would like me to touch them. That it would be fun. Then they slapped me.'

I winced for the hurt in his eyes and drooping mouth. He coughed, and it was a wet cough. Not good.

'Every one of them deserves a good thrashing is what I think. Sir.' I turned to find Perseverance approaching. He led three horses. The roan, Priss, and a dappled gelding from my stables. Speckle. That was his name.

'What are you doing here?' I demanded and then took in the boy's appearance. His right eye was blacked and that cheek well bruised. I recognized that someone had backhanded him. I knew that type of injury well. 'And what happened to you?' I demanded before he could answer my first question.

'They hit Per, too,' Thick volunteered.

Lant looked flustered. 'He tried to intervene that night at the inn. I told him it would only make things worse and it did.'

I was confronted by incompetence, inexperience and stupidity. Then I looked at Thick's woeful face and mentally changed stupidity to naïvety. Thick had never outgrown his innocence. I was silent as I helped him dismount. Thick coughed again and could not seem to stop. 'Lant will take you to the kitchens and see that you get a hot, sweet drink. Per and I will take the horses. Then, Lant, I suggest you present yourself to King Dutiful to give your report. Thick will give his at the same time.'

Lant looked alarmed. 'Not Lord Chade?'

'He's very ill right now.' Thick was still coughing. He finally caught a wheezing breath. I relented a little. 'Be sure Thick eats well and then take him through the steams. Then I will hear your report at the same time as the king does.'

'Badgerlock, I rather think . . .'

'Prince FitzChivalry,' I corrected him. I looked him up and down. 'And do not make that mistake again.'

'Prince FitzChivalry,' he accepted the correction. He opened his mouth and then shut it again.

I turned away from him, holding his horse's reins and Thick's. 'That wasn't the mistake,' I said without looking back. 'I meant your trying to think. But do not call me by that name again. Not here. We are not ready for it to be common knowledge that Badgerlock and FitzChivalry are one and the same.'

Per made a small choking sound. I did not look at him. 'Bring those horses, Perseverance. You'll have time to explain yourself to me while you settle them.'

The Rousters had gone into what I still thought of as the 'new' stables, the ones built since the Red-Ship Wars. I did not want to see them just now. I wanted to be calm when I dealt with them, not merely appear calm. Per followed and I led him and the horses behind the new stables to Burrich's stables where I had grown up. They were not used as much as they once were, but I was pleased to see they were kept clean and that there were empty stalls ready for the horses we brought. The stableboys were in awe of me and scampered so swiftly to the needs of the beasts that Per found very little to do. The other stableboys seemed to recognize him as one of their own, and perhaps thought the bruises on his face were my doing, for they were very deferential to me.

'Isn't this Lord Derrick's roan?' one of them dared to ask of me.

'Not any more,' I told him, and was taken aback by the warm confirmation I received from the mare. *My rider.*

'She likes you,' Per told me from the next stall. He was brushing Priss. He'd let one of the other boys take Speckle but Priss he was doing himself.

I didn't ask him how he knew. 'What are you doing here?'

'She's muddy, sir. We were crossing an iced-over stream and she broke through and got her legs muddy. So I'm grooming her.'

Technically, a truthful answer. This boy. I admired him grudgingly. 'Perseverance. Why did you come to Buckkeep?'

He straightened to look over the stall wall at me. If he was not genuinely surprised at my question, he was very good at dissembling. 'Sir, I am sworn to you. Where else should I be? I knew you would want your horse brought to you, and I did not trust those . . . guardsmen to bring her. And I knew that you would need Priss. When we go after those bastards and take Bee back, she will want to ride her own horse home. Your pardon, sir. Lady Bee, I meant to say. Lady Bee.' He caught his lower lip between his teeth and bit down on it hard.

I had intended to rebuke him and send him home. But when a youngster speaks as a man it's not right to reply to him as a child. A stable-girl had just arrived with a bucket of water. I turned to her. 'Your name?'

'Patience, sir.'

That jolted me for an instant. 'Well, Patience, when Per is finished, would you show him where to get some hot food and where the steams are. Find him a bed in the . . .'

'I'd rather stay near the horses, sir. If no one minds.'

I understood that, too. 'Help him find some bedding, then. You can sleep in one of the empty stalls, if that's what you wish.'

'Thank you, sir. It is.'

'Should I make him a poultice for that cheek? I know one that can draw the swelling down by morning.' Patience looked very pleased to be put in charge of Perseverance.

'Do you? Well, then, you should do that as well, and I'll be pleased to see how well it works by the morning.' I started to leave and then remembered the pride of a boy. I turned back. 'Perseverance. You are to stay well away from any of the Rousters. Am I understood?'

He looked down. 'Sir,' he acknowledged me unhappily.

'They will be dealt with. But not by you.'

'They're a bad lot,' Patience said quietly.

'Stay clear,' I warned them both, and left the stables.

TWENTY-ONE

Vindeliar

*So let us speak of forgetfulness. We all recall episodes of forgetfulness.
We have missed a meeting with a friend, burned the bread or set down
an object and forgotten where we put it. That is the forgetting we are
aware of.*

*There is another kind, one we seldom think about. Until I mention
the phase of the moon, chances are that it is not in your thoughts. It
is pushed aside by the food you are eating, or the path you are walking
upon. Your mind is not fixed upon the moon, and so for that moment,
you have forgotten it. Or, perhaps it is better to say, you are not
remembering that bit of information at this time.*

*If I enter the room as you are fastening your shoe, I can say, 'There
will be a lovely moon tonight,' and then you will call it to mind. But
before I call it forth for you, you have forgotten the moon.*

*One can swiftly understand that for most moments of our lives, we
have forgotten almost all of the world around us, except for what
currently claims our interest.*

*The talent of the part-Whites is most often to be able to glimpse
the future in dreams. There are a rare few who can find a future that
is but a breath away, a future in which a chosen person will not be
remembering that which we wish to hide from him. Those rare few
can persuade a person to remain in that non-remembering state. And
thus one with that rare talent can render an event or person almost
invisible, almost forgotten. We have records of part-Whites who could
do this and hold it for a single person. We have records of some few
who could cause up to six persons to continue forgetting something.*

But in the young student Vindeliar, I believe we have found a truly extraordinary talent. Even at seven years old, he can master the minds of twelve of my students and cause them to forget hunger. And so I ask that he be given over to me, to train specifically in that capacity.

Lingstra Dwalia – from the Servants' Archives

I was better. Everyone told me so, even Shun. I was not sure they were right, but it was too much trouble to argue with them. My skin had finished peeling and I no longer had a fever. I did not tremble and I could walk without staggering. But it was harder to listen to people, especially if more than one person was talking at once.

The travelling had become harder. And there was more tension between Dwalia and Ellik. We had to cross a river and they wasted most of an evening arguing about where. It was the first time I'd seen conflict between them. They had a map, and they stood not at our fire nor at the Chalcedeans' fire but between the two and pointed and argued. There was a ferry at one village. Dwalia argued it would be too hard for Vindeliar. 'Not only must he keep anyone else waiting to cross from recalling us, he must fog the ferrymen. Not once, but three times before we have all the sleighs and horses across.'

There was a bridge that Dwalia favoured but to reach it we would have to travel through a large town. 'It is the perfect place for an ambush,' Ellik objected. 'And if he cannot fog the ferry workers, how can he fog a city?'

'We travel in the dead of night. Swiftly through the city, across the bridge and then swiftly away from the trading town on the other side.'

I leaned against Shun. Her whole body was tense, she was so focused on eavesdropping on them. I was tired of them talking and longed for quiet. Quiet and real food. The hunting had been bad and all we had had for two days was porridge and the brown soup. The sleighs were loaded, the horses harnessed. The Chalcedeans were mounted and waited in formation. The luriks stood by their mounts. All were waiting for Ellik and Dwalia to find an agreement. The bridge tonight or the ferry tomorrow? I didn't care. 'How did they get to this side of the river in the first place?' I asked Shun quietly.

'Shut up,' she said in such a snip of voice that only I heard it. That had made me struggle to be alert and hear more.

Dwalia was speaking. I could tell she was nervous. Her hands were fists, clasped to her bosom. 'The ferry is too close to Buckkeep. We need to cross soon and then be away. Once we are across the river, we can go through the hills . . .'

'The hills, again. Unless you are willing to travel on the roads the sleighs will bog down in the unpacked snow,' Ellik spat. 'Abandon the sleighs. They have only slowed us down since you stole them.'

'We no longer have the cart. We'd have to abandon the tents.'

'Then leave them,' Ellik shrugged. 'We will travel more swiftly without them. Your female insistence on these comforts is what slows us down.'

'Don't look at them,' Shun hissed by my ear. I'd been staring. They did not usually quarrel for long. Usually Vindeliar came, and smiled and bobbed, and then we did as Dwalia wished. I slitted my eyes and pretended to be dozing. I could see Dwalia's frustration. She glanced over at us and Shun leaned forward and poked at the dying fire.

Then Vindeliar came wandering over. He was smiling as he always was. He paused by our fire and looked around, puzzled. 'Why aren't you on the sleigh? Shouldn't we leave soon?' The night was darkening around us. Usually by that time we were well away from the day's campsite.

Dwalia lifted her voice to respond to him. 'Yes. We should be leaving very soon. Be patient, Vindeliar. Come wait with me while Ellik decides what we must do.'

Then, for the first time, I watched and saw clearly what Vindeliar did. He smiled and almost wriggled like a chubby little boy as he sidled up to Dwalia. He looked at Ellik, tilting his head. The man scowled at him. Dwalia spoke softly. 'So, as the duke has said, he considers the ferry crossing too dangerous for us. It is much too close to Buckkeep. But if we make haste, he says we could reach the bridge tonight. And perhaps cross and even be in the foothills before the sun is very high. And thence to Salter's Deep and the ship.'

Ellik scowled. 'That is not what I said,' he growled.

Dwalia was suddenly and immediately apologetic. She clasped her hands under her chin and bowed her head. 'I am so sorry. What was it you had decided?'

He looked well pleased at her chastened demeanour. 'I decided we would take the bridge. Tonight. If you can muster your lazy folk and get them mounted and on the road, we may well be in the foothills before the sun is too high.'

'Of course,' Dwalia said. 'When you put it like that, it's the only sensible thing to do. Luriks! Mount! Commander Ellik has made his decision. Odessa! Get the Shaysim into the sleigh right away. Soula and Reppin, get to the final loading! He wishes us to depart immediately.'

And Ellik had stood, smiling with satisfaction to see us all scramble to his orders. Snow was kicked over the dying fires and I was hurried into the sleigh. I feigned weakness and the luriks quickly gave me over to Shun's care. Vindeliar and Dwalia were the last to climb on board. I had never seen anyone look more satisfied than the two of them.

Ellik barked his commands and our company began to move. When we had gone a little way, I breathed to Shun, 'Did you see that?'

She misheard me. 'I did. We are not far from Buckkeep. Be quiet.'

And I was.

We made the crossing that night. As we drew closer to the river town, Vindeliar left the sleigh. He mounted a horse and rode at the head of our procession beside Ellik. And later that morning, when we finally reached a forested area of the foothills and made a camp, Ellik bragged to all about how simple it had been. 'And now we are on the northern side of the Buck River, with little between us and our goal but a few small towns and the hills. As I told you. The bridge was our best choice.'

And Dwalia smiled and agreed.

But if she and Vindeliar had tricked him into choosing the bridge instead of the ferry, it still did not make our journey through the hills any easier. He had been right about the sleighs. Dwalia insisted we must do our best to avoid roads, and so the soldiers and their horses broke trail for the heavier beasts that pulled the sleigh. Our passage was not easy and I could tell that Ellik chafed at how little we moved forward each night.

Shun and I had little time to speak privately. 'They mentioned a ship,' she said to me once as we crouched in the bushes, relieving ourselves. 'That may give us a chance of escape, even if we must leap into the water. Whatever happens, we must not let them take us out to sea.'

And I agreed with that, but wondered if we would have any opportunity to flee our captors.

I was slowly recovering but the poor food and the constant travel and sleeping cold made me feel as if they created an illness of their own. One evening as we rose to commence our route, I felt almost dizzy with hunger for something more sustaining than porridge. As I followed Shun from the tent to the fireside, I spoke carelessly to her. 'I'm going to die soon if I don't get a real meal.'

Several of the others halted and turned to stare at me. Alaria lifted a hand to cover her mouth. I ignored the gawkers. As always, the luriks had built two campfires, one for us and one for the soldiers. The luriks did all the cooking, but there was no shared meal at the end of the day's rest. Always two of them carried a steaming pot of the porridge they cooked and left it with the soldiers. We always ate separately. Tonight the soldiers had killed something and were roasting it over the fire. Their fire was closer to ours than it usually was, for the clearing we were in was small. The meat smelled very good and I snuffed at the hearty scent on the cold night air.

Careful of that, too, Wolf-Father warned me. I looked around our fireside and then frowned to myself. 'Where is Vindeliar?' I asked.

'He goes ahead of us this night. We must travel on the roads tonight. We will pass through a little town and he goes to smooth the way for us,' Dwalia told me.

I decided that she only spoke to me in the hope of having me say something back to her. I took a chance. I sniffed, loudly. 'The meat smells good,' I said and gave a small sigh.

Dwalia folded her lips. 'A serving of that meat would cost more than any here are willing to pay,' she said sourly.

I had not realized that the soldiers had been listening in. One brayed a boorish laugh. 'For a piece of meat from the Buck woman we'll give you a piece of this rabbit!' Then they all laughed. Shun had taken a seat beside me on the log. She huddled into herself, going smaller. Panic grew in me. She was the adult whom my father had bade look after me. I could not tell if the look on her face was anger or fear. But if she was afraid, how much more terrified should I be? It made me more frightened than I'd ever been, and somehow angrier, too. I stood up.

'NO!' I shouted the word at the leering men. 'That never happens in any future I see. Not even the one in which her hidden father leaves every one of you in bloody shreds!' I swayed, sat down suddenly and would have fallen if Shun had not caught me as I collapsed toward her. I felt sick. I had given away a piece of my power. I had not meant to share that dream. It still made no sense to me. They had not been men in the dream but pennants, hung in tattered shreds from a laundry line, dripping blood. A dream that made no sense. I could not have said why I mentioned a hidden father.

'Shaysim!'

There was shock in Dwalia's tone. I turned my face toward her. I looked into her disapproving eyes and tried to appear like a younger child surprised in mischief.

'Shaysim, it is not our way to speak dreams to any who might be listening. Dreams are precious and private things, our guideposts to the many paths that exist. Choosing among the paths requires great knowledge. When we reach Clerres you will learn many things. One of the most important things will be to record your dreams privately or only with a scribe chosen for you.'

'Clerres?' The old soldier, Ellik, had come to stand behind Dwalia. He stood straight but his belly still pushed out from his vest. In the light of the fire, his eyes were pale like shadowed snow. 'After we board the ship, we are bound directly for Chalced, and Botter's Bay. That was our agreement.'

'Of course,' Dwalia agreed smoothly. Despite her bulk, she lifted herself gracefully from her crouch to stand beside him. Did she avoid having him stand over her?

'And I won't have bad luck wished on me and my men. Certainly not by a moon-eyed pup like him.'

'The boy meant nothing. You need not be concerned.'

He smiled at her, an evil old man's confident smile. 'I'm not concerned at all.' Then, without warning, he kicked me in the chest. I flew backwards off the log, landing on my back in the snow. It knocked the air out of me. I lay gasping. Shun leapt up – to flee, I think – but he backhanded her across the face, knocking her sideways into a flock of luriks who had risen like birds to flutter to our aid. I expected them to fling themselves on the leader of the soldiers, to swarm over him and pin him down as they had the handsome rapist. Instead they seized Shun and dragged her away.

I felt Dwalia's fear soar. In a flash of insight, I realized that fog-boy was away from the camp, telling people that they would not notice when we moved through their village tonight. Vindeliar was not there to exert his strength over Commander Ellik, so she stood alone against him. Odessa circled the log and seized me under the arms. She dragged me backwards through the snow as Dwalia spoke. She seemed calm. Could no one else sense the fear that stormed inside her?

'He's just a boy, with a boy's way of shouting when he is angry. Or frightened. Were not you once a boy yourself?'

He looked at her flatly, not taken in by her effort at all. 'I was a boy once. I was a boy who saw my father strangle my older brother for failing to show him respect. I was a smart boy. I needed only one lesson to learn my place.'

Odessa had dragged me to my feet. She stood behind me, her arms crossed over me to hold me up. I still didn't have my breath back. When Commander Ellik pointed his thick-nailed finger at me, I gave up any thought of taking a breath. 'Learn. Or die. I don't care what name they call you by, boy or what value they place on you. Still that tongue, or you and your whore-tender will be thrown to my men.' He turned and stalked away.

At last, I drew air into my lungs. I desperately needed to piss out my fear.

Then Dwalia spoke, boldly calling her words after the man. 'That is not our agreement, Commander Ellik. If this boy is harmed in any way, we will not be obliged to pay you when we reach Botter's Bay. The one who holds the gold for you will not release it to you unless I am alive to tell him to do so. And unless the boy is unharmed when we arrive there, I will not tell him to pay you.'

Her tone was firm but reasonable. On another man, perhaps it might have worked. But as Ellik turned back to her with a snarl on his face, I suddenly knew that she should not have mentioned money, as if money could rule him. Money was not what he lusted for.

'There is more than one way to turn you and your pale servants and your precious boy into gold when we reach Chalced. I need not even wait until we reach Botter's Bay. There are slavers still in every port in Chalced.' He glanced about him at the staring luriks and spoke with disdain. 'Your pretty white horses might fetch me a better price than your bloodless serving-girls and flimsy men.'

Dwalia had gone pale and still.

He lifted his voice to fill our night. 'I am a Chalcedean, and a commander and a lord, not by birth but by virtue of my own good sword-arm. I am not ruled by whining women or cowed by whispering priestesses. I do as I think best for myself and the men who have sworn to me.'

Dwalia pulled herself straighter. Her followers had bunched like sheep, each striving to be behind someone else. Odessa still held me in front of her. Was she bravely protecting me or using me as a shield? Shun had recovered herself. She stood alone and apart from the luriks and stared fiercely at the Chalcedeans. I had breath in my body now. I readied myself to run.

Stillness. Be still as the hunter and listen.

I settled myself into my motionless body. Dwalia mastered her fear and spoke back to Ellik. Was she insane? Or so used to being in command that she did not see the weakness of her position? 'Your men are sworn to you. Promised to you, then? Promised to you, just as you gave your word to me when we set our bargain? And you believe in their promises when you do not honour your own? A generous advance on the payment was given to you, that you need not loot. But loot you did, in defiance of my order. You promised there would be no violence beyond what must be. Yet there was. Foolish destruction, breaking doors and slashing tapestries. Leaving signs of our passage that need not have been left. Killing beyond what was needed. Rapes that served no useful purpose.'

Ellik stared at her. Then he threw back his head and laughed, and for a moment I saw him as he might have been in his youth, wild and reckless. 'No useful purpose?' he repeated. He roared with laughter again. His men were appearing, by twos and threes, to stand in witness. They shared his mirth. I knew that his display was actually for them. 'There speaks a woman who knows nothing of her true purpose in the world. But let me tell you, I am certain that my men found those women useful enough.'

'You broke your word to me!' Dwalia tried to put certainty and accusation in her voice. Instead she sounded like a whining child.

He cocked his head to look at her, and I saw on his face that she had become even less powerful in his eyes. So insignificant that he bothered to explain the world to her. 'A man has his word. And he can give his word to another man, for both of them know what that means. For a man has honour, and to break his word to another man defiles his honour. The breaking of a man's word merits death. But all know that a woman cannot give her word to anyone, for women cannot possess honour. Women promise, and later they say, "I did not understand, I did not mean it that way, I thought those words meant something else." So a woman's word is without worth. She can break it, and always she does, for she has no honour to defile.' He gave a snort of derision. 'It is not even worth killing a woman who breaks her word, for it is what women do.'

Dwalia stared at him, her mouth ajar. I pitied her and feared for the rest of us. Even I, a child, knew that was the Chalcedean way. Every scroll I'd read of them, every time my father mentioned them, they were the ones who always found a way to break their word. They fathered children on their slaves, and then sold their own offspring. How could she not have known the sort of folk she bargained with? Her luriks were gathering behind us, a pale mirror of the soldiers behind Ellik. But his men stood, legs wide and braced, hands on their hips or arms crossed on their chests. Our luriks huddled and leaned against each other, whispering like a wind shivering through aspens. Dwalia seemed drained of words.

'How could I exchange a promise with you? I would give you my man's word, my word of honour in exchange for, what? The thought you held in your silly little head for that moment?' He barked in disdain. 'Have you any idea how foolish you sound?' He shook his head. 'You bring us all this way, deeper and deeper into danger, and for what? Not treasure or coin or fine goods. A boy, and his serving-woman. My men follow me and in return they take a share of all I take. And what could we take from there? A bit of wenching for my soldiers. A few blades of good quality. Some smoked meat and cured fish. A few horses. My men make mock of your raid! That is not good, for they must doubt why they came so far through such dangerous territory, for so little plunder. They must doubt me. And now what must we do when we are so deep in an enemy's territory? We dawdle and avoid the roads and villages, until a journey that should have been a few days stretches toward a month.

'The boy we have stolen dared to mock me. Why? Why has he no respect? Perhaps he thinks me as foolish as you make me seem. But I am not a fool. I have been thinking and thinking. I am not a man to be ruled by a woman. Not a man to be bought with gold, and then commanded like a sell-sword. I am a man who commands, who will undertake a task and do it as seems best to him. Yet, as I look back, time after time, I have bowed to your will. I look back and each time, it makes no sense to me. Always, I give way to your will. Why? I think I have discerned it.'

He pointed an accusing finger at her. 'I know your spell, woman. It is that pale boy you keep at your side, the one who speaks as if he were a girl. He does something, doesn't he? You send him ahead through the town, and we pass through and no one turns to watch us go. It's a good trick, a very good trick. I admired it. Until I came to see that he has been playing a similar trick upon me. Hasn't he?'

I would have lied. I would have looked at him in consternation and then demanded that he explain. She gaped like a fish. Then, 'This does not happen,' she said faintly.

'Really?' he asked her coldly.

A sound. All heads, even mine turned toward it. Horses coming.

Vindeliar returning with his escorts. Dwalia made her second mistake. Hope lit in her eyes.

Ellik read it as clearly as I did. He smiled the cruellest smile that I had ever seen. 'No. That is what does not happen.' He turned to his men. They had packed behind him, their eagerness straining like hounds on a huntsman's lead. 'Go meet them. Stop them. Take Vindeliar. Tell him we know his tricks. Tell him we are amazed and think him wonderful. Pump his vanity like you'd stroke yourself!' Ellik barked a crude laugh the others echoed. 'Tell him this woman has bid you command him not to use them on us any more, for his path now lies with ours. Take him to our tents and keep him there. Give him every good thing we have there. Praise him. Slap him on the shoulder, make him feel he is a man now. But be wary of him. If you feel your resolve weakening at all, kill him. But try not to. He is very useful, that one. Worth more than any gold this old whore can offer us. He is the true prize we will take home.' He turned his attention back to Dwalia. 'He is even more useful than a woman ready to be raped.'

TWENTY-TWO

Confrontations

The princess may confront, or the king may make demands. The queen or prince may even threaten or issue ultimatums. The diplomat or emissary will mediate, cooperate or negotiate. But the royal assassin, the one who wreaks the king's justice, has none of those tools at his disposal. She is the ruler's weapon, deployed as the Farseer king or queen sees fit. When the assassin is called into play by the one who rules her, her own will shall be suspended. She is both as powerful and as powerless as a game-piece deployed upon the gaming cloth. She goes and she acts and then she has finished with it. She makes no judgment and takes no vengeance.

Only in that way can she maintain her virtue and her innocence of true crime. She never kills of her own volition. What is done by the royal assassin's hand is not murder but execution. The sword never bears any guilt.

Instructions to an assassin, unsigned

'I did not know how to stop them.' FitzVigilant stood very straight before an odd court of judgment. We had convened in Verity's Tower, where once my king had defended the Six Duchies coast from Red Ships, and where later Chade and Dutiful and I had done our best to master the Skill-magic with the limited information we had. How it had changed over the years! When first Verity had used it as a look-out over the water to help him focus his search for the Red Ships attacking us, it had been dusty and disused, a refuge for retired bits of furniture. The dark circular table in the centre of the room now was warmly polished, and the chairs that surrounded it had high backs with carvings of bucks on them. I pitied whichever servants had carried the heavy furniture up all those spiralling stairs. Lant stood, and seated at the table were the king and queen, Lady Kettricken, Nettle and myself.

Lady Rosemary and Ash were also there, dressed entirely in blue so dark it was almost black. They stood, motionless and silent, their backs to the wall. Waiting. Like sheathed blades.

Dutiful sighed. 'I had hoped for better from them. I had hoped that when the conspirators were cut out of their ranks, something worthy of duty might remain among the Rousters. But it appears not.' He had been looking at his hands. Now he looked at Lant. 'Did any of them threaten you in any way? Or give any sign that they had been aware of the plot to kill Lord Chade?'

Lant stood straighter. 'When I rode with them, I was only partially aware of what had happened to Lord Chade and Prince FitzChivalry. If I had been better informed, I might have taken a different tack with them. And been more watchful and wary of all they did and said.'

'That's valid,' King Dutiful concurred, and once again, I thought to myself that it almost seemed as if Lant were on trial here rather than giving testimony that would decide the fate of the Rousters. Thick had been entrusted to a healer. He had already given a long and wandering account of his ill treatment at the hands of the men who were supposed to protect him. Then he had wanted his own bed. The steams had warmed him through but he was still coughing when he left us. Perseverance, very pale and nervous at being called to speak before such an august board, had corroborated all that Thick had recounted.

Queen Elliania spoke. She did not raise her voice but her clear words carried. 'Sir, did you at any time outright forbid their ill behaviour? Did you remind them that Thick was entrusted to their care?'

Lant paused to think, and my heart sank for him. He hadn't. 'I remonstrated with them. I pointed out that they should behave as befitted a guard company, especially when in a public place such as a tavern. It did little good. Shorn of their officers, they seemed to have no self-discipline.'

Dutiful's brow furrowed. 'But you never ordered them directly to cease their ill treatment of Thick?'

'I . . . did not.' He cleared his throat. 'I was not sure I had that authority, sire.'

'If not you, then who else?' the king said heavily. Lant did not reply. Dutiful sighed again. 'You may go.'

Lant went, walking stiffly. Before he reached the door, I spoke. 'If I may offer some words, my king?'

'You may.'

'I would point out that FitzVigilant arrived at Withywoods in poor condition owing to a severe beating he had taken in Buckkeep Town. And that he had been battered again, in both mind and body, when Withywoods was attacked.'

'His behaviour is not being judged here, Prince FitzChivalry,' the king said, but as Lant reached the door, he shot me a look that was both ashamed and grateful. The guard on the door allowed him out. At a gesture from Dutiful, the guard followed Lant out of the door and shut it behind him.

'Well. What shall we do with them?'

'Disband them. Flog those who mistreated Thick. Send them away in shame from Buck forever.' Elliania spoke dispassionately, and I had no doubt that in the OutIslands such would have been their fate.

'Not every man of them mistreated Thick. Find the ones who should bear the blame, and judge them individually.' Kettricken spoke quietly.

'But those who did not directly injure him did not oppose those who did!' Elliania objected.

The king shook his head. 'There was no clear chain of command. Part of the fault must be borne by me. I should have directed FitzVigilant to take command of them and conveyed that to all.'

I spoke. 'I doubt they would have accepted his authority. He has never soldiered. These men are the barrel-scrapings of the guard. Discarded by other guard units, they are the ones with the least self-discipline, ruled by the most ruthless and least honourable officers. At the least, disband them. Some will perhaps find places with other guard units. But keeping them as a company will only invite the worst from them.' I spoke for mercy in a calm voice. But privately, I planned to work a bit of the prince's justice on the ones that Thick had named to me.

Dutiful looked at me as if he could hear my thoughts. I hastily checked my walls. No, I was alone in my mind. He had simply come to know me too well. 'Perhaps you would like to speak with each of them and see if any meet the standard to be included in *your* new guard company?'

'And then he smiled at me.' The irritation I felt with my king was not ameliorated by the smile that bloomed on the Fool's face.

'He does know you well, to set you to this task. I'll wager that in that barrel of rotten apples, you'll find a few sound ones. And that when you give them a final chance, you'll win their loyalty forever.'

'Not the sort of men I'd want at my back,' I objected. 'Nor the sort of troops I want to hand to Foxglove and expect her to manage. I'd like my honour guard to actually be honourable men.'

'What of the ones who taunted Thick, and backhanded your stable-lad?'

I took breath to speak and then gasped in surprise as an arrow of Skill from Nettle penetrated my walls effortlessly. *The Queen's Garden. Tidings of Bee and Shine. Come now. Do not try to Skill back to me.*

Hope flared in my heart. 'I am summoned by Nettle to the Queen's Garden,' I told him and stood. 'They may have word of Bee's whereabouts.' I was shocked to find that the sudden hope cut me as sharply as fear.

'Light! Air!' the crow demanded as I stood.

'I'll return as soon as I can,' I offered. I ignored the Fool's disappointed look, and did not even object as Motley hopped from the table and with a single flap of her wings gained my shoulder. In my chamber, I paused only to release the crow from my window before I hastened to find Nettle in the Queen's Garden.

The Queen's Garden was no traditional garden, but a tower top. I was panting when I reached it, having run through half of

Buckkeep Castle to get there. In summer the pots there over-
flowed with greenery and fragrant blossoms. Some even held
small fruit trees. Simple statuary and isolated benches completed
Kettricken's retreat from the petty annoyances of life at court.
But as I emerged onto the tower top, winter greeted me. Snow
mounded the planters and the small trees had been swaddled
against winter's cruellest bite. I had thought to find only Nettle
waiting for me. But Kettricken, warmly cloaked against winter's
chill, was present, as well as Dutiful, and Queen Elliania. It took
me a moment to recognize Civil Bresinga. The boy had grown
to a man. When he saw I recognized him, he bowed to me
gravely but kept silent. I had wondered why they had chosen
the Queen's Garden as a meeting place. As Dutiful's hound
rolled a young lynx around in the snow, I understood. The two
Wit-companions, obviously well acquainted with one another,
suddenly raced off between the planters. I knew a moment of
sharp envy.

'We've had word,' Dutiful greeted me.

He seemed so solemn that I wondered if bodies had been found.
I left formality behind as I demanded of him, 'What news?'

'It's not certain,' Dutiful cautioned me, but Civil did not wait
to speak.

'As my king requested, I sent out discreet queries, particularly
to those of Old Blood who are bonded to birds of prey. I am
sure you understand that even Witted partners pay small attention to things that don't concern them. But two reports came
back to me.

'Yesterday a messenger pigeon brought me a message from
Carter Wick, an Old Blood bonded to a raven. The raven had
found a company of folk camped in the forest. When she tried
to pick over the bones of some rabbits they'd eaten, they threw
sticks at her. She said that there were white horses there.'

'Where?'

He held up a cautioning finger. 'Today, Rampion, a youngster
whose Wit-bird is a merlin, sent word to us. The merlin complained
of people ruining her hunting by stopping for the day in a clearing
where she can usually take mice. The white horses had trampled
the snow, giving the mice much better hiding-places when they

emerged from their burrows to seek seedheads still sticking up out of the snow.'

'Where?' I demanded again, my temper rising to match my urgency. Finally, finally, I could take some action. Why were all of them just standing about?

'Fitz!' Dutiful spoke sharply, as my king rather than my cousin. 'Calm yourself. Wait until you have heard all. The Wit-beasts have given us two possible sightings, a day apart. Both were in Buck. One on this side of Chancy Bridge. And the other approaching the Yellow Hills. It puzzled me greatly, for they were moving slowly.'

I bit the inside of my cheek to keep from demanding why I had not heard those reports as soon as they had come in. Dutiful was still speaking. 'Now I have reason to suspect that we know where they are bound. They can only be headed for the coast, and there are only three close ports where a ship of any size could dock. If there are forty of them, with horse, they will need a substantial vessel to depart.

'We have Skilled journeymen stationed at all the old look-out towers along the coast. I ordered two to ride together, one of them well-dosed with elfbark looking for anything unusual in Forge, Notquite Cove and Salter's Deep. At Salter's Deep, we found what we were looking for. There is a ship tied up at the docks there, one that everyone overlooked except for my Skill-deadened emissary. Her partner could not see it at all. No one knew when it had arrived, what cargo it brought or what it waited for. Some professed to know nothing of a ship tied up in full view, others could not be stirred to interest. Unfortunately, the local forces cannot capture what they cannot see. But I've already sent orders for the king's guard stationed at Ringhill Tower to procure elfbark, dose the troop, travel to Salter's Deep and seize the ship.' He grinned triumphantly. 'We have them. We've cut them off from escaping!'

My guts tightened. I have always preferred stealth to confrontation. What would happen when the kidnappers arrived at Salter's Deep and found their escape route cut off? What would I do? 'The Chalcedean mercenaries will be desperate. They may kill their captives, or threaten to when they find they are discovered.'

'They may,' Dutiful conceded. 'But look here.' He unrolled the map he'd carried tucked under his arm. Without words, Civil held it while Dutiful pointed at it. 'The Ringhill Guard will be at Salter's Deep in less than two days. The Chalcedeans are travelling slowly and stealthily. We think it will take them three or perhaps four days to reach Salter's Deep. The outlying areas around Salter's Deep are thickly forested. Mounted men might ride through there, but the sleighs will not go there. They will have to take to the roads or abandon their sleighs. Once the Ringhill Guard has secured the ship, they will split their men. Some will block the road down to the harbour. The others will circle through the hills and come at them from behind.' His finger pinned a point where the road descended from the hills to the rocky shores of Salter's Deep. 'They'll capture them and rescue Bee and Shine.'

I was already shaking my head. 'No. I have to be there. It has to be me.' I could hear how foolish I sounded as I desperately added, 'I lost them. I have to get them back.'

Dutiful and Kettricken exchanged a look. 'I expected you would say that,' Dutiful said quietly, 'as irrational as we all know it to be. And yet I understand it. What would I not do if one of my lads were taken? If you ride out tomorrow morning with your guard, you should arrive shortly after the Ringhill Guard does. You will be there to escort her home.'

'Are there no Skill-stones near Ringhill or Salter's Deep?'

'That goes beyond irrational to plain stupidity. You cannot use the Skill safely for your own ends right now, let alone take troops through with you. The Ringhill Guard is a substantial force, and we have a Skilled journeyman among them. She will report to us everything that happens. Fitz, you know this is the best tactic. What could one man do against twenty Chalcedean mercenaries?' He paused, giving me an opportunity to agree with him. I could not. He sighed. 'And looking at your face, I am glad to tell you that no, we know of no Skill-pillars that would shorten that journey.'

I stared at the map a moment longer. Then I looked out of the window, over the vista where Verity had once scanned for his enemies. Salter's Deep. I had to get there. Dutiful spoke behind me. 'Fitz, you well know that a military campaign must be carried out with precision. Everyone follows orders. If each soldier did as he thought best, well. Then it's a brawl. Not a battle-plan.' He cleared his throat. 'In this, I am in command. I have set it in motion. It needs to go as I have planned.'

'You are right,' I admitted. I didn't look at him.

'Fitz. Must I remind you that I am your king?' Dutiful spoke the words gravely.

I met his eyes and spoke truthfully. 'I am ever aware of that, my king.'

I had been outnumbered. Outmanoeuvred. They'd withheld information from me. Worse, all logic and rationality was on their side. They'd told no one who did not need to know. Their plan was good. I knew that they were right, if one considered only logic and rationality. Yet in my father's heart, I knew they were wrong. It felt awful to stand before them and be lectured by my king and my daughter, to be told that the plan was already made and that my only real option was to fall in with it. I felt suddenly old, and stupid, and useless. The bruises I'd taken in my efforts to once more feel like a warrior, my muscles that screamed at me when I moved, all confirmed my incompetence. My softness. My age. I'd lost my daughter and Shine both by my failed ability to think three steps ahead. I could look back and see a dozen simple things I could have done that would have prevented the kidnapping. For days, I had been burning inside to make it right, to correct my mistakes and go forward and never, never again allow my little girl to fall into such danger.

And today, with the possibility of action dangled like fresh meat before me, I was instead told that others would rescue her and return her to me. Someone else would pick her up and hold her tight and tell her she was safe. Days later, she'd be returned to me, like a lost purse. I could sit home by the fire and wait for her. Or ride out with my guard to meet her rescuers.

I left them there on the tower top, dismissed to inform my small troop of new recruits and salvaged oldsters that we would be riding out on the morrow. I was allowed to tell them that we might actually encounter an enemy, but Dutiful and Elliania, Kettricken and Nettle had all decided that it would be best if alarm were kept at a low level in Buck Duchy until the matter had been settled. The Ringhill Guard was well-trained and very experienced at dealing with the robber bands that sometimes plagued the king's highway. They were the best men for the job. And if any escaped them, my guard would shortly arrive to tidy up any loose ends. The Chalcedeans would have to yield or fall as the jaws of the split force closed around them.

And my Bee would be caught there with them, in the teeth of those jaws.

I went to Chade. Had there ever been a time when I did not flee to him for advice? I tapped on his door, received no answer, and slipped quietly inside. To my disappointment, Steady was there, seated in a chair by the fireside, whittling at something and throwing the bits into the fire as he worked. He did not seem surprised to see me. Nettle had probably warned him I might be coming. 'He's asleep,' he said before I could ask.

'Has anyone told him that we think we know where Bee and Shine are? That we are going to try to recover them?'

He frowned. He was a member of the King's Own Coterie. My news was no surprise to him but perhaps he was surprised to discover that I now knew of it. He spoke softly. 'I was told that all of it was to be kept secret. Surprising them is of the essence. As for Lord Chade, I am not sure he could mind his tongue. I do not think we should raise either hope or anxiety in him. We are trying to keep him peaceful and calm. Letting him gather himself.'

I shook my head and did not lower my voice. 'Do you truly think he can feel any peace while his daughter is in the hands of Chalcedean mercenaries? When all is quiet around me, my fears for your small sister still run rampant in my mind. I have not known a moment of peace since I knew she was taken.'

Steady stared at me, stricken. From his bed, Chade gave the groan of an old man awakening. I went to him and took his hand. He stirred very slightly. After a moment, he rolled his head toward me. His eyes were half-open.

'We've had news, Chade. The kidnappers were spotted. We believe they are on their way to Salter's Deep. Dutiful has dispatched troops and we'll seize the ship that is waiting for them, and then close in on them from behind.'

Chade blinked his eyes slowly. I felt a brush of Skill against my mind, softer than a butterfly's wing. *Go now.* 'Lant,' he said, his voice a bit rusty. 'Take Lant. He feels so guilty. That they took her. Left him alive.' He paused and swallowed. 'Save his pride. It's taken a beating.'

'I'll share the news,' I promised. For a moment, our gazes held. His look mirrored what I felt. He lay there, an old, aching man in his bed, while his daughter was in danger. And no one had even told him that she might be rescued, lest such news alarm him. Or prompt him to rash action. 'I have to go,' I apologized but he knew it was a promise. 'I need to give orders for my guard to prepare for tomorrow.'

For a moment, his gaze brightened. 'Roust them out,' he told me. One of his eyelids sagged shut, then he opened both eyes wide. 'We're not done yet, boy. You and I, we're not done yet.'

Then his eyes closed, he heaved a great sigh, and his breathing became regular again. I lingered a bit longer, his hand in mine. I glanced at Steady. 'I doubt he's a threat to our secrecy.' Then I tucked his hand back under his covers and left the room quietly.

I had not seen much of Lant since he had returned from Buckkeep. He had not really crossed my mind at all. And when he did, he left an unpleasant scent in my thoughts. He was a stony reminder of all the ways I had failed. I hadn't protected him, or Shine, or protected my little girl. And in a dark corner of my heart, despite knowing he could not have done so, anger burned in me that he had not given up his own life before allowing Bee to be taken.

A page passed me, carrying someone's laundry. 'Lass, I've a task for you, when you've finished that one.'

She very nearly rolled her eyes, and then recognized me. 'Of course, Prince FitzChivalry.' It's difficult to bob a curtsey with both arms full of laundry, but she managed.

'Thank you. Find Lord FitzVigilant. Tell him I've urgent news to share with him. And remind him to visit Lord Chade today.'

'Of course, my prince.'

My prince. I wasn't anyone's prince today. I was a father.

I went directly to the practice grounds. I found Foxglove sitting on a bench outside the weapons sheds, rubbing liniment into her hand and wrist. She'd changed since I'd made her the captain of my guard. Her greying hair was severely braided into a warrior's tail and her garb was more leather than fabric now. She rubbed the ointment into her ropy, veiny wrist and hand. I cleared my throat and she looked up at me. Before she could rise, I sat down on the bench beside her. 'I have to ask you to have my guard ready to ride beside me at dawn,' I said.

Her eyes flew wide. I held up a hand. As quickly and simply as I could, I told her all. She was my captain, my right hand. It would not have been right to ask her to ride blindly beside me. I doubted we were going into a confrontation. We'd simply be there in time to take charge of Bee after she had been rescued. But if by any chance we did have to cross swords with anyone, I wanted her to know why. And to know what was at stake.

She was the perfect second-in-command. She listened to me and accepted what I told her. Then she glanced at her boots and said, 'Were it my operation, I would not go about it that way.'

'I'm listening.'

'Stealth. Get up on them while they are resting or asleep. Find out where the captives are and worry first about protecting them. Or employ simple bargaining. They're mercenaries. Mercenaries can be bought. Whatever they're being paid, we offer them more and safe passage. Later, after the girls are safe, we can decide if we are bound by our words. We can always poison the stores on board that ship and then let them go their merry way.'

I stared at her dumbly for a moment. Then I said in honest admiration, 'I like how you think.'

She gave a brief snort of laughter. 'Do you? I'm a bit surprised. I know when you asked me to take this duty that you meant it as an honour to me. And as a way to keep yourself from being bothered with it. But I've seen war and I've seen peace and I know well that there is never truly one or the other. And being ready for war is better than being ready for peace, if peace is what you truly hope for. So. I've only had them a few days, but I started with quality, and I've seen a lot of improvements since then. But if we are riding into real fighting, then the first thing I'll tell you is, we don't have enough soldiers and what we do have are not ready. They'll die.'

She spoke as if she were talking about seeds that would fail to sprout, not as if she were speaking of her grandchildren.

'I can get more,' I said unwillingly. 'King Dutiful put the fate of the Rousters into my hands. If there's anyone there worth having, you can take them.'

She made a face. 'As men, they're worth nothing. As swords, we'll take them all. They won't respect me, and in all honesty, I'm not sure I can win their respect without killing one of them. I've never killed anyone wearing the blue, and I don't want to start at this stage in my life.'

I stood up. I knew what she was asking me. I didn't wait for her to put it in words. 'I'll put them on notice to be ready to ride tomorrow. And I'll see that they respect us.'

She gave a tight nod.

The delay chafed. I'd already delegated my task from Chade. This was one I had to do myself. So do it swiftly, even if it had to be done dirty. Get clear of it and go. Failure to do it could result in losses for my guard. Do it. I owed this to Foxglove.

A pang of guilt. Dutiful was my king. Did not I owe him obedience? The prince did, I decided. Bee's father did not.

As I walked away from her, I wondered if I were truly up to this any more. Foxglove's puppies were still battering me when I took up an axe, and I was just holding my own with a sword. Sixty years sat on my shoulders. I was many years out of practice at real fighting. All the discouragement I had felt earlier in the day came to whisper in my ears. Maybe Dutiful and Nettle were right to tell me that the best I could do was to comfort my child. I knew how far it was to Salter's Deep. One man alone on a good horse, pushing himself and his animal and going cross-country instead of by the roads could make it there in a day and a half. The younger Fitz would have been in the saddle as soon as he heard the name of the place.

And I, I calculated men and odds and knew with an old man's experience that I'd likely be dead before I got near Bee. She would watch me die and then who would there be for her? Don't be stupid, I counselled myself. At the head of my guard, leaving at dawn tomorrow, there was still a chance that we would be in time to at least lend our strength to the Ringhill Guard. Dutiful was giving me that.

Wisdom tasted as bad as rancid meat. I'd need the Rousters. I didn't want them, but Foxglove would need them. I made a brief stop in my room and then went in search of them.

I did not find them on the practice yards or in the steams or even in the guards' mess. I hated the wasted time so much that I took a horse from the stables and rode down the hill. I did not have to go all the way to Buckkeep Town. On the edge of the sprawling growth from the town, I entered the tavern called the Lusty Buck, just past the blackened ruins of the Bawdy Trout. It was exactly the sort of place I had expected it to be. The door did not fit tight in the jamb; a door can only be knocked off its hinges so many times before it always hangs askew. Inside, the candles were few and dark corners many. The air was ripe with cheap coarse Smoke, and the vinegary smell of spilled wine never completely mopped up. A woman smiled wearily at me as I came in; one of her eyes was swollen near shut and I could feel only pity for her. I wondered if debt had put her here. I shook my head at her and stood just within the door, letting my eyes adjust to the dimness.

The Rousters were scattered around the room. They were a small troop, and the losses Chade and I had inflicted on them had reduced them even more. There were perhaps twenty-seven troops in the dark-blue livery. There were a few sodden regulars mixed in with them, a handful of soldiers from other guard companies, and a scattering of weary whores, but the Rousters dominated with their dark jerkins and darker expressions. One or two had turned to look at me as I ran my eyes over them, trying to appraise them.

'Rousters. To me!'

The command should at least have brought them to their feet. Heads turned toward me and many who stared were blearily the worse for drink. Only a few lurched unsteadily upright. I suspected they had been here since they'd stabled their horses on their return from Withywoods. I didn't repeat my order. Instead I asked of the air, 'Who's in charge, Rousters? I know some of your officers went down near Oaksbywater. Where is Sergeant Goodhand?'

I had expected one of the older guards to stand. Instead it was a youngster with a patchy beard who spoke without rising. The heels of his boots rested on the corner of his table. 'I'm here.'

I waited for someone to laugh or contradict him. No one did. Very well. 'Sergeant Goodhand, muster your troop and bring them up to the practice fields. I need to speak to them.' I turned to go.

'Not today,' he told my back. 'We're just home from a long ride. And we're in mourning. Maybe a couple days from now.'

That brought a mutter of suppressed laughter.

There were a hundred ways to deal with that level of insubordination. I sorted through all of them as I turned and made my unhurried way through the tables to him, stripping my left glove from my hand as I came. I smiled at him, sharing his amusement. He did not move.

'Ah. I think I've heard of you,' I said as I slowly walked toward him. 'My stableboy. Perseverance. I believe you backhanded him when he came to the defence of Thick. The king's companion.'

He gave a single guffaw. 'The king's half-wit!'

'That's the one.' I did not lose my smile but I suddenly moved faster. I reached him as he was just moving his feet from the table to the floor. He was sneering at me as I hit him so hard I felt his cheekbones crunch under my fist. He'd already been off-balance. As he teetered in his chair, I kicked the legs out from under it. He went all the way to the floor. I added a solid boot to his midsection where his ribs did not protect him. He curled up tightly.

'And now I'm in charge,' I told him.

The silence that fell was not a good one. It simmered with anger. I spoke into it.

'King Dutiful gave you to me to keep or discard. Right now, I have a use for your swords. If you want to continue to be members of any guard company, form up on the practice grounds. Report to Captain Foxglove. Respect her. She'll be selecting which of you we keep. Now. Anyone who chooses not to form up is dismissed from the Buckkeep Guard. Forever.'

I stood still one breath longer. Then I walked unhurriedly toward the door, every sense prickling in case someone attacked me from behind. As I stepped back into the snowy street, I heard one of the women say, 'That was the Witted Bastard, that was.

What he did was mild compared to what he could've done. You're lucky he didn't turn into a wolf and rip your throats out.'

I smiled as I drew my left glove on, mounted the horse and rode away. Inside the weighted gauntlet, my right fist still ached, but not as much as it would have if my fist had been bare. Chade had taught me always to protect my knuckles.

Go now, my heart urged me. *Prepare*, said my head.

For a change, I took the wiser advice.

I did not think about what I was doing as I carefully measured the elfbark and made my tea. It was not the OutIslander stuff, but the weaker herb we harvested in the Six Duchies. And this was freshly harvested, by me, from an elf tree near the old well outside the walls. Winter-harvested, so I was making it strong. But not too strong, or I'd disappear from the coterie's awareness entirely. Strong enough that I could stop thinking about my walls constantly. Strong enough to deaden my Skill and leave my Wit completely unaffected.

I drank it and went up to visit the Fool. I found him stretched out on the floor flat on his back. 'I'm fine,' he said before I could express alarm. As I watched, he lifted both his feet off the floor and, legs straight, raised them as high as he could. It was not high. I winced for him as he held them, breathing stiffly. I did not speak to him until he lowered his feet to the floor again.

'I'm feeling restless. I think I'm going to go for a long ride. Want to come with me?'

He turned his head toward me. 'Not yet. But thank you for thinking I might. I'm feeling stronger. And . . . braver. The dreams help.'

'Dreams?'

'I have dragon dreams, Fitz. I battle for a mate I desire. And I win.' A very strange smile suffused his face. 'I win,' he said again, softly. He lifted his feet off the floor. He held them off the floor, toes pointed. They began to tremble and he lowered them again. He bent his knees and tried to curl to meet them. Limbering himself. Even I was more flexible than that. But he would fight his way back. I heard him groan.

'Don't push yourself too hard.'

He lowered his feet. 'I must. When I think it is too hard, I think of our daughter. And I find determination.'

I had been moving about my task. Those words halted me in place.

'What are you doing?' he asked me.

'Chade's shelf of herbs and elixirs is a bit untidy. I need to remind Ash to be more careful.' A very unfair lie. I was able to find everything I needed immediately. Distract him. 'I'm glad of your dreams. I just wanted you to know that you might not see me tonight.'

The smile twisted. 'Even if you were here, I wouldn't see you,' he reminded me.

I groaned, he laughed at me, and I left.

My saddle-pack was not heavy. Carris seed and elfbark weigh little. Some carryme, willowbark, valerian. I prayed Bee would not need it. I chose a warmer cloak. I exchanged the weighted gloves for warmer ones. A good wool scarf around my throat. The change of clothing for Bee. Only the most basic supplies. Done.

I shut my door and turned as Lant reached the top of the stairs and bolted toward me. Damn my luck.

'Fitz!' he cried and halted a few steps from me, clutching at his half-healed wound.

'Catch your breath,' I suggested to him. In a lower voice, I added, 'And speak softly.'

He was panting. 'Yes,' he agreed. He put his hand out and leaned his weight on the wall. 'I went to Chade. There were two healers in his room. He told me to come to you.'

I had no time to be oblique. I spoke quietly. 'We've had word of where we might find the mercenaries who took Shine and Bee. The Ringhill Guard will ambush and surround them. Tomorrow at first light my guard rides out to Salter's Deep. They will probably miss the Ringhill Guard recapturing them, but at least they can be there to lend some comfort.'

'Shine,' he said and a conflict of emotions trampled his face. 'Of course. Of course I want to ride with you.'

'Lord Chade thought you might. But are you sure you're ready for a long ride like that? If you cannot keep up—'

'You'll leave me. I know. Of course you must! No, I'll be ready to ride with you at first light.'

'Fine. I'll see you then. I've things to prepare.' I walked away, hoping he would cling to the wall a bit longer. Instead he gave a groan and a grunt as he stood almost straight and then followed me. He walked beside me in silence for a time. Just as it began to grow awkward, he spoke.

'I didn't know she was my sister.'

Sweet Eda, please don't let him confide in me! 'Neither did I, Lant. I had not even realized you were my cousin.'

'Cousin,' he said softly as if that had never occurred to him. Then he said slowly, 'It will be awkward for us when first we meet again . . .'

The least of my worries. 'I will speak to her first, if there is privacy to do so. But if not, you will have to handle it discreetly. Especially if there are others within earshot.'

'I have no wish to hurt her.'

I sighed. 'Lant, I know this is foremost in your thoughts. But in mine is the fear that she may already be grievously hurt. Or that the Ringhill Guard will not prevail, or that the mercenaries will either harm, kill or use their captives as bargaining chips. Those are the things I must give my thoughts to.'

As I spoke his face grew paler. So gently reared was this young man. I knew with sudden certainty that I should not let him go with me into any kind of an armed encounter, let alone what might be the end of a pitched battle between the Ringhill Guard and the Chalcedean mercenaries. I needed all my attention on Bee, not worrying that I might have to protect Lant. I stopped walking and he was grateful. 'Are you sure you are well enough recovered from your injuries to ride with us? Or swing a sword?'

'I must go,' he said. He knew my thoughts. Pride stiffened his spine. 'I must go, and if I fail, then you must leave me. But I must try. I didn't protect Shun at Withywoods. I cannot fail her now.'

I gritted my teeth together and nodded. He hadn't even mentioned Bee. My anger was pointless: he was blind where my child was concerned. I reminded myself that he was Chade's son and Nettle thought well of him. I forced myself to recall how stupid Hap had been at his age. Then I admitted to myself that I'd been even more obstinate and foolish than either of them. I put my hand on his shoulder. 'Lant. Perhaps for her sake, and yours, you should not be there. Go to the healer and get a fresh dressing on that shoulder. Rest. Look after Chade for me.'

I patted his shoulder and walked away. As I went, I heard him say to the air, 'Because that is what you would do? I doubt it.'

The Rousters had assembled in the practice yard. It was on my way to the stables. When I went to meet them, Foxglove walked at my side. Sergeant Goodhand hadn't come. I doubted we'd see him again. Twenty-one of the Rousters had seen fit to form up. I recognized some of them from the Withywoods contingent; others were new to me. I introduced Foxglove as their new commander, and summoned the three most senior in their ranks to come forward. Their length of service had possibly contributed to their battered appearance, but the missing teeth and crumpled ears spoke to me more of brawling than combat. It did not matter. They were what I had. Foxglove took their names and assigned them rank. None of them looked pleased but they did not argue with her. They followed her as she walked down the line of Rousters and immediately dismissed four of them. I did not challenge her decision.

After that, I let Foxglove give them their orders. They were to be mounted and ready at dawn, with four days' dry rations. They were to be sober enough to ride and dressed for winter travel, with weapons for close-quarters combat. At that, I saw interest kindle in their eyes, but we gave them no more information than that. I delivered my own message to them. 'King Dutiful gave you into my hands. Those of you who acquit yourselves well in the next ten days will remain as part of my guard, but not in the Rouster colours. The Rousters are to be disbanded. Those of you who prove cowardly, lazy, or simply stupid will be dismissed. That's all I have to say to you.' Foxglove released them and we watched them slouch away.

'They hate you, right now,' she observed.

'I don't care.'

'You'll care if you get an arrow in the back.'

A sour smile twisted my mouth. 'You think I'd be leading the charge?' I considered my next words carefully. 'Leave at dawn. I'll catch up with you. And don't put anyone wearing my Bastard's badge in the way of an arrow in the back. Let the Rousters go in first.'

'The Charging Bucks Guard will be ready,' she promised, and I nodded at her correction. She squinted at me, the lines in her brow getting deeper. 'What are you planning, Fitz?'

'I'm planning to take my daughter back.'

I turned and left her scowling after me.

In the stables, I saddled the roan. I secured my saddle-pack. I found I was humming, exhilarated. So good to be doing something, to have stopped waiting. I filled a grain bag for the roan and added it to my supplies. I was just finishing when Perseverance came around the corner.

'I'm supposed to do that for you!' he exclaimed indignantly.

I smiled at him. 'Would you like it if another man saddled your horse for you?'

His indignation deepened. 'Of course not!'

'There you have it,' I said, and laughed. He looked startled. I suppose he'd never heard me laugh before.

'What are you doing?' he demanded.

'Going out for a long ride. I grew up here, but it has been a long time since I rode through these hills. I might be late coming back. There's an inn down near the river that I used to frequent when I was a young man. I've a mind to dine there tonight.'

'With a battleaxe?'

'Oh. That. I'm dropping it off for Foxglove with a smith she likes. She wants a longer haft put on it.'

There was a heartbeat of silence. I lifted one brow at him. He quailed.

'Very well, sir. Do you wish me to ride along?'

'No, no. There's no need for that.'

In a much softer voice he asked me, 'Has there been any news of Bee, sir? Lady Bee?'

I took a breath. Not a lie. 'We've had all manner of folk out looking.' He nodded, then opened the stall door for me and I led the roan out. Excitement shivered over her as if she shook a fly from her withers.

Me, too, I told her. *Me, too.*

TWENTY-THREE

Bonds and Ties

I believe this is the oldest scroll in the Skill-library and I have subjected it to twelve different translations by my students and scholars. Two of the scholars were Jamaillian priests of Sa. Two others were OutIslander sages. Of the twelve translators, two suggested the scroll was a clever forgery, created to be sold.

If we accept the original scroll as authentic, then it is mostly likely a translation from a much older source, possibly one that was perhaps written by the creators of the Skill-pillars.

I believe this scroll was intact before Regal the Pretender sold it away during the Red-Ship Wars. The loss of this information is both insurmountable and infuriating, even at this late date. What follows is my best interpretation of what remains of the scroll. I discovered it, scorched and rotting, on the floors of a hall in Aslevjal. The burning meant that only the beginning and end of the loosely rolled scroll remained readable. From the account of FitzChivalry Farseer, the burning may have been the last vengeful act of the Pale Woman. This was a tremendous loss for us. What little remains is enough to tell us that.

Title: On the construction and use of portal-stones
'The construction of a new portal should not be undertaken without extreme caution and a consensus of the Elders. Never lose sight of the fact that all magic is an exchange, a bargain, and a purchase. From the cutting of the stone to the selection

of the site to the final inscribing of the runes, the process of creating a portal is dangerous and expensive to the spirits and physical health of those who do the work. Let those who labour in this process be rewarded appropriately, for they are surrendering years of health to provide for those who come after them. In their youthful dotage, let them still be cared for and honoured. Let their families be spared any burden, for the care of those who give their bodies and minds to this work should be the welcome task of those who enjoy the yield of that labour.'

The main portion of this scroll is heavily damaged. Words that can be reliably translated on the charred fragments:

Being toll corporeal language emphasis 'deliberate alignment' accompany sibling blood rune dragon bond relationship hands touch 'paid in blood' repository willing perpetuity 'physical contact' first entry concealed.

Those of the translators who chose to guess at the information loss believe it related to how to construct and safely use a portal-stone. Some speculated that the sequence of the readable words can be interpreted that one can more safely escort people who are close to the one who goes first, by blood relationship or emotional ties. But this interpretation of the scattered words may be completely incorrect.

'One uses a portal and pays the price. The price for every portal will be different. The one who opens it pays the greatest price, and should be full of health and capable of sustaining that price, especially if one is escorting others less able to pay the price of passage. Before and after the use of the portal, those who benefit from it should pause to reflect on the sacrifice made by those who created these passages. Speak them well when within and without their corridors.'

Chade Fallstar

The roan was a pleasure to bestride.

I did not leave the stables at a gallop though I had that desire in my heart. No. I rode like a man on a pleasant and casual errand, a bemused look on my face. I nodded graciously to the guards who bade Prince FitzChivalry a good day as he rode out of the gates. I took the road that led away from Buckkeep Town toward the River Road. Even there, I set an easy pace. I could feel my horse's impatience. She sensed my desire for speed and was very willing to deliver it to me.

Soon, I promised her.

We will run and then we will fight! As one!

My heart smote me. Unfaithful.

Unfaithful to whom?

Horse. I am sorry. I did not mean to start this. This is not a good bond for me.

I am not 'horse'. I am Fleeter.

I held stillness. She did not.

I have waited for you for a long time. Five humans have claimed to own me, but none did. And all of them, I think, knew that. Why else would they sell me for money, as perfect a mount as I am? They could not buy my heart and so they sold me again and again. And then you saw me and in that moment, you knew I was for you. In two strides you claimed me and we both know that was right and is right. Do not say to me that you can undo what is done.

I guarded my thoughts. I did not want this attachment. There could not be this attachment. I groped within me for my wolf, for Nighteyes, but nothing stirred. I sat on her back as still as if I were a sack of grain. I thought of everything else. How far I would travel before I pushed her into a gallop. I reviewed my mental map of where I would leave the king's Highway and go cross-country to Salter's Deep. I'd memorized that bit of the map and hoped it was accurate. I was fairly certain the roan could handle a long cross-country gallop. If I were wrong—

I can. For a time, I was used as a hunter's mount.

I began a meticulous catalogue of the weapons I had selected. I had tried to provide for every exigency. Sword and knife. A dust poison that could be flung. One suitable for poisoning food if the opportunity presented itself. Six tiny darts tipped with a very potent poison. A sling. I wondered if I could hit anything with it; I hadn't practised in years.

I am your best weapon. The man who trained me was like you. He refused me. I was young then, and did not know there were three other horses he spent just as much time with. They were all stallions. His friends mocked him for training me, saying I would never learn the kicks and jumps. That only stallions know how to fight. He proved them wrong. And he collected the wagers and before the summer was over, he sold me.

How does a horse know of such things as wagers? The thought escaped me before I could quell it.

She tossed her head, taking a bit more of the reins. I gave it to her. *What do you think stableboys do when they are waiting to be told what to do? They roll bones and shout and pass coins. And that was what I was to the man who trained me to fight. Bones to roll.*

I felt a pang of sympathy for her. *Horse, we can be—*

Fleeter. I am not 'horse' nor 'roan'. I am Fleeter.

Fleeter. I accepted the name reluctantly, felt the binding go tighter as I did so. *We can be friendly with one another. But I am not seeking—*

What is your name?

I breathed out slowly.

I feel the shape of it in how you think. Must I guess it?

I heard the sound of galloping hoofbeats behind us. Horses. More than two. *Move to the side of the road and be unworthy of notice.* Even before I tugged the reins, Fleeter had moved to the side of the road and slowed. She was too swiftly becoming attuned to me. Setting her aside from me was like trying to be rid of a feather with honey-sticky fingers.

So you are Changer?

No. This can't be allowed. I blocked myself from her.

I thought the riders would be messengers or lads out for a gallop. When I glanced back furtively and saw Perseverance bearing down on me, leading a saddled and riderless horse, my heart sank. Priss. Bee's horse. I did not recognize the second rider until they drew closer. Then I was shocked and almost angry to see Lant. As he reined in his mount beside me, he was pale, his face drawn with pain. Could there possibly be any more problems for me today?

'You should be recovering, not taking a horse for a gallop,' I greeted him. I tried to keep my words bland before Perseverance.

Lant's expression went sour. 'And should not you be at Buckkeep, preparing to ride out tomorrow with your guard?'

There were a hundred possible lies to answer that question. The most believable would be to say that I was limbering my horse and myself for tomorrow's long ride.

'I'm going after my daughter,' I said. 'Now.'

He stared at me, then gave a tight nod. 'Lady Shun,' he added.

I looked at Perseverance. He met my glare calmly. 'Lady Bee will wish to ride her own horse home.'

Fleeter resumed her pace and the others fell in on either side of us. I itched to ask but waited.

Lant gave in first. 'I went to visit Lord Chade, to let him know I'd be leaving tomorrow morning. It is my habit to visit him at least once every day, even when he is incapable of reasoned conversation, and I did not wish him to think that I was abandoning that courtesy. Today, he was rational for a short time. He asked me to recount our conversation. When I did, he told me I'd best make my way to the stables right away if I were to catch up with you.'

'And I thought for a bit when he told me to saddle his horse,' Perseverance added calmly. 'And then I followed.'

I held my words behind my teeth. I did not want either of them with me. I had no idea what I would find, if indeed I found the raiders at all. I wanted to be free to travel swift and alone, and in the end to be as stealthy or as savage as I judged necessary. I had brought the carris seed for my own use. I did not want to offer it to Lant, injured as he was, and I would never give it to a mere boy like Perseverance. When I had control of my voice, I spoke calmly.

'I told you that if your injuries held you back, I'd go on without you, Lant. That still holds. And Perseverance. You are to return to Buckkeep Castle right now.'

'I understand that,' Lant said, but his words had the sharp edges of humiliation. It was hard for me to care about that.

'Perseverance?'

'Sir.' He had not changed his horse's pace and he did not look at me.

'Did you hear my order?'

'I did, sir.'

'Then obey.'

He did look at me then. His eyes were very bright and I knew he fought the tears forming in them. 'Sir, I cannot. I made a promise to Steward Revel. He found out I was teaching Lady Bee to ride. He was not sure he approved, but after I promised him I'd see she came to no harm on a horse, he said he did not think he had to report what we were doing. And when our lessons with Scribe Lant were to begin, he summoned me again, and said I must always be ready to defend her, in the schoolroom or indeed anywhere in Withywoods. And I promised him again. Defend her I did. Even though she and I had had a bit of a tiff a few days earlier. It's as if I swore my loyalty to her first, before I swore to you. So I think only she can tell me to abandon her.'

'That's the most convoluted logic I have ever heard.' It wasn't. The Fool could do much better than that to get his own way.

Perseverance said nothing. I thought of ordering him even more sternly to return. And if he still refused, what then? Kick him? Poke him with my sword? The boy was more than stubborn. He was intent on becoming a man. Soon enough, Fleeter and I would outdistance both of them. And then he could be helpful to Lant in returning to Buckkeep. A fine prince I was. I could not get even a stableboy to obey me. I tried to summon the will to insist.

My Wit made me aware of her a heartbeat before her weight hit my shoulder. I flinched at that landing, and Fleeter flicked an ear back in a query.

'Fitz—Chivalry,' the crow announced. She set her feet more firmly in the fabric of my coat and used her beak to push the flap of my collar out of her way.

'What are you doing here?' I demanded of her, not really expecting an answer.

'It spoke!' Perseverance exclaimed.

'It's a crow!' Lant exclaimed as if perhaps we had not noticed. Breathlessly he asked, 'Is she your Wit-beast?'

'No. She's not my Old Blood companion.' I had never demanded the current usage of anyone and I did not have time to wonder why I did so now, for Per immediately pleaded, 'Would she come to me, do you think? She is such a beauty.'

Motley leaned forward and pecked my cheek lightly. 'Nice boy!' she squawked.

Eyes wide, Per extended his forearm hopefully to her, as if she were a falcon. She hopped from my shoulder to the offered perch with the barest lift of her wings.

'Aren't you fine?' Per breathed as he drew his arm in to admire her.

'Fine,' she agreed in mutual admiration, and I suddenly dared to hope she'd found a more permanent home than the Fool or I could offer her.

'Would you like the care of her? She's a few white feathers and because of them the other crows mob her. You'll have to ink them black for her if they start to fade.'

'Truly?' Per looked as if I'd conferred an honour on him. 'The poor thing! What's her name? How did you come to have her?'

'We call her Motley. Her owner died and a mutual friend asked if I could look after her for a time.'

'Motley. Well. Aren't you fine? Would you ride on my shoulder, do you think?'

The bird's bright gaze met mine for an instant, almost as if she begged pardon or asked permission. Then as Perseverance slowly lowered his wrist, she climbed up his arm until she sat on his shoulder. Per shot me a grin and then as he recalled our mission, it faded. 'Sir? What are we riding into? Has Bee been found? Is she well?' He tipped his head toward the axe that rode across my back. 'It doesn't need a new handle, does it?'

'No. It doesn't. And I don't know what we're riding into, or what condition Bee is in. Which is why I don't think either of you should be accompanying me.' The words felt like stones as they fell from my lips.

Lant spoke up suddenly from my other side. 'Well, whatever you do know, I'd like to know as well. Did you receive more tidings since we last spoke? I've only Lord Chade's directive that I follow you.'

I spoke more to the boy than to him. 'We've had reports of

her captors riding toward the coast. The ship they hoped to escape on has been seized. We believe we know the path they intend, and the king's forces are on their way to cut them off. We may discover her captors before they do. Or after. In either case, I know I must be there.' I recounted the details tersely. Then we all rode silently for a time.

When Per spoke, his words came slowly. 'So. We're actually riding ahead of your guard, aren't we? Are you hoping then to get to the soldiers and Bee before the king's soldiers do? You hope we can fight them and rescue her by ourselves?'

'That's would be insane!' Lant declared. 'There were at least a score of mercenaries, not counting the pale folk.'

Per had a more pragmatic worry. 'All I've brought with me is my belt-knife.'

Lant snorted. 'Lad, we are not going to charge into a band of trained mercenary soldiers with nothing but your belt-knife and FitzChivalry's axe. I'm sure he has a better intention than that.'

But I didn't.

Lying was suddenly too much effort and rather pointless. 'I don't have a plan, really. When and if I locate them, I'll decide what to do. And that is why you should both go back. Now.' I turned to look at Lant. 'Ride with my guard tomorrow. You can let Foxglove know that I've ridden ahead to scout. That would actually be a very useful thing for you to do, if you'd carry that message to Foxglove for me.'

Lant appeared to consider it. I hoped it would offer him a dignified way out of following me into what was, truly, an ill-considered venture. For that brief time, there was only the sound of the horses' hooves on the packed snow of the road, the creaking of saddle leather and the wind shushing as it smoothed the coverlet of snow that covered the meadow. I looked at the distant trees and then at the sky. Overcast. No snow tonight, I hoped fervently.

We topped a small rise and looked down the broad barrier of the Buck River. The edges of the moving water were frozen but a stripe of dark water still showed at the centre of the current. Just past that crossing I'd leave the road and cut across country. I could see the trail I'd follow. I watched a farmer's wagon pulled by a heavy team of greys come down to the ferry on the other side. Good timing. There were three houses and a barn and several large pens on the far side of the river. The ferry was a rickety old one, used mostly by farmers and shepherds wanting to move flock. We rode down to the splintery timbers of the landing and sat our horses in silence as the ferry bumped and sloshed its way across to us. I glanced at my companions. Lant looked dismayed and Per uncertain. The nose of the ferry dock was coated with ice. Priss bridled as we approached it.

The ferry slowly drew closer and then thumped against the landing. A lad leapt off and made it fast, first one line and then the other. The wagon driver lifted a hand in greeting and nodded to us without curiosity as his team stoically thudded across the wooden timbers of the landing. The wagon followed with a lurch and a thud. The sounds of the creaking wagon and the rushing river masked the hoofbeats of another horse. Only my Wit made me turn to see who came.

Yes. I could have more problems today.

'Fitz!' Riddle exclaimed, half-angrily, as he pulled in a rangy white gelding. 'What are you thinking, to bring these two? Lant should be resting and healing! And that lad is no more than a boy!'

'I didn't "bring" them. They've followed me.' I took in the light leather armour he wore under his heavy wool cloak. The sword he bore was nothing like the elegant gentleman's accessory that graced Lant's hip. Riddle was dressed for serious fighting. 'Nettle sent you?' I guessed.

He dropped his head guiltily. 'No. She doesn't know I've gone. I told her I wanted to ride with you tomorrow and she agreed to that. Reluctantly. When I couldn't find you and the roan was gone from the stables, I knew. And here I am.' His expression changed abruptly. 'Thank El! I'm so tired of sitting and waiting and worrying.'

Any fears that he'd been sent to bring me back were dispersed. I returned his grin despite my effort to restrain it. 'You are going to confront a very angry woman when you get back to Buckkeep Castle.'

'Don't I know it. My only hope of mercy is to have her small sister with me.'

The smiles we exchanged were tense. We might jest about it but we both knew that Nettle's anger was going to be a very real storm we'd have to weather. In some dim corner of my mind, I suspected her anger would be justified. I knew that my charging off to save Bee could be seen as foolhardy; what could one man do against a band of mercenaries? I was not directly disobeying my king, I excused myself. I'd stopped arguing before Dutiful felt he had to absolutely command me to follow his plan. I could not trust a band of guardsmen to rescue my child. I could not stand idly and wait for her to be restored to me.

And so I'd defied my king. But now I had three followers, two of them noblemen and somehow that seemed very different to me. As it well might to King Dutiful. A lone kinsman disobeying his king is one thing; this appeared closer to a mutiny. I cast a sidelong glance at Riddle. In the set line of his jaw and pinched lips, I read much the same sentiments. He spoke without looking at me. 'Not far past that ferry, there's a cart track that goes up toward summer pasturage. If we leave the road there and follow the track, we can probably overnight in the shepherds' huts in the hills before we push on toward Salter's Deep.'

'Or not spend the night. Just push on,' I suggested.

'Leave the road?' Lant asked in dismay.

Riddle has always had a talent for sharing a glance without being obvious. He spoke kindly to Lant. 'I think you should turn back now. Take the boy with you. If you must, ride with Foxglove tomorrow. If we're riding into direct conflict, then four of us are not enough to do battle with a mercenary troop. It's more likely Fitz and I will be doing something more . . . covert. And in that situation, two of us are less visible than four of us with five horses.'

Lant said nothing. I wondered where his true inclination lay. He had to be in moderate pain still. Which hurt worse, his injured pride that he had done nothing when Bee and Shine were taken, or the wound to his body? And how much did he dread encountering Shine not as her suitor but as her brother? I think he was on the point of turning back when Perseverance spoke.

'You can go back if you need to, Scribe Lant. No one would blame you. But I can't go with you. When we find Bee, she will want her horse. And as she was in my care when I lost her, I have to be the one to bring her back.' He looked at me and perhaps realized he had been less than tactful. 'Or at least, I have to be one of the ones who is there,' he added lamely.

The ferryman spoke. 'You want to cross or not?'

'I do,' I said. I dismounted. He held out his hand and I dropped my fare into it. I led Fleeter. Her hooves thudded on the timbers of the landing. She eyed the gap between it and the ferry, but when I stepped across, she followed me. The ferry bobbed slightly at our weight and I led her to the centre of the flat vessel. I didn't look back at any of them. I hoped they would all turn back.

But then I heard Riddle speaking to his mount and felt the mild lurch as they boarded. Perseverance led both of his horses. Priss was unhappy and jigged a bit, but he spoke to her and his own mount boarded calmly. 'I'm with them,' he said to the ferryman, and he let him pass without paying. I allowed myself one glance back.

Lant was shaking his head. Then he sighed, 'I'm coming,' and gave the ferryman his coins. He boarded with his horse, and the ship's lad cast off the lines.

I watched the water and the far shore. The current pushed and surged against the ferry but the ferryman and his boys moved us steadily across the river. Fleeter stood steady, but Priss was white-eyed, tugging on her reins.

Riddle led his horse to stand beside me.

As the ferry approached the far bank, Riddle spoke to Lant. 'Our horses are swifter and we can't wait for you and the lad,' he said bluntly. 'You can follow, or you can go back to Buckkeep. But we can't wait. Ready, Fitz?'

I was already swinging back up into Fleeter's saddle. 'I'm ready,' I replied.

'Wait!' Perseverance cried out, and I felt disloyal as I shook my head. Lant said something that I didn't catch but I heard Riddle say to him, 'Follow as you can, then,' and we were off, our horses lunging up from ferry to landing, and off we went through the tiny settlement, hooves clattering on icy cobbles. Beyond the little cluster of houses, a cart track diverged from the main road. Fleeter did not wait for me to guide her. She diverted, stretching into first a lope and then a gallop. The roan had been waiting for this all afternoon, and having the nose of Riddle's horse at my stirrup only urged her on. The packed snow of the wagon tracks gave both horses good purchase and my cheeks began to burn from the wind.

Go! I said to Fleeter and felt her joyous assent. She surged forward, and the world swept past us.

In a short time, I heard the beat of hooves behind us. I glanced back to see Perseverance urging his horse on and actually gaining on us. Lant came behind, one hand on the reins and one clutching his shoulder, his face grim. Nothing I could do about that, I decided, and we rode on.

My body settled into the rhythm of Fleeter's motion and we moved as one creature. She was a magnificent mount and I could not prevent my admiration seeping through to her. *We go well together, we two,* she said and I could not deny it. I felt her take joy in our headlong run, stretching her stride and pulling ahead of Riddle and his mount. My mind leapt many years, to another cross-country gallop. I'd been little more than a youth and had followed Chade as we tore through forest and over hills to the town of Forge and my first encounter with Forged ones. I reined my thoughts away from that memory, and immersed myself in the day, the horse, and the wind on my face.

I let go. We were just running, we two. Nothing more. Think only of how well we moved together. I let her set her pace. We slowed, she breathed, and then she ran again. We startled a fox with a rabbit limp in his jaws. At the bottom of a small incline, she leapt a trickling brook rather than fording it. *I am Fleeter!* She rejoiced and I with her.

The early winter evening began to shadow the snow with pale blues. We encountered a wagon drawn by a team of heavy black horses and driven by a boy scarcely older than Perseverance. It was loaded with firewood and we gave way to the steaming team. Fleeter broke trail through the deeper snow beside the track and Riddle and his mount followed in her wake.

I did not have to push her. She knew I wanted speed and her heart was in giving it to me. Lant was soon left far behind us, and then Perseverance. Riddle kept up, somewhat. He was no longer at our side but whenever I glanced back, I saw his face, red and set with cold, his dark eyes determined. Each time I glanced back, he'd give me a stiff nod, and on we would go. Light bled slowly from the day, colour seeping away with it. The cold deepened around us and the wind woke. Why, I wondered, did it seem that always I rode into a cold wind, never pushed by it? The skin of my face grew stiff, my lips cracked and the ends of my fingers grew distant with cold.

But on we went. Fleeter's pace dropped as we rode up into the hills. The skies were overcast and I relied more on Fleeter's vision than my own. We followed the wagon trail as much by feel as by sight. We entered a stretch of forest, and the looming trees made the night much darker. The trail was more uneven here. I began to feel old, cold and foolish. Had I imagined myself afire with carris seed, galloping away the night to go to Bee's rescue? I could barely see my hand in front of my face and the full length of my spine ached with cold. We passed the woodcutter's clearing. Beyond it, the trail we had been following became a shallow indentation in the snow.

The wind rose as we left the forested slope behind. The cold slapped me but the wind pushed some of the clouds aside. Light from the stars seeped down to show the windswept snow that covered the summer sheep- and goat-pastures. Fleeter slowed as she moved forward through the unbroken snow. She lowered her head and pushed stubbornly on.

I smelled a barn. No, Fleeter smelled a barn or some sort of animal shelter, and shared that sensation with me. It was different from when Nighteyes had conveyed information to me. For the wolf, it had always been about hunting and killing and food. The horse smelled something familiar, something that was possibly shelter and rest. Yes, rest. She was tired. And cold. It was time to be out of this wind, and time to find water. Ahead of us on the white-coated hillside there was a huddle of structures: a stock pen and a slant-roofed, three-sided shelter. Beside it was a snow-covered mound, a haystack. And sharing a wall with the animal pen was the shape of a humble cabin.

I did not have to pull Fleeter in. She halted of her own will and stood, sides heaving softly, taking in the scents. Sheep, old dung. Straw. I dismounted stiffly and walked first to the pen, feeling my muscles moving differently, feeling warmth trying to seep back into my feet. My hips hurt, and my back shouted at me with every step. Had I imagined I could ride all night and be capable of stealth, let alone fighting?

I was an idiot.

I found the gate to the corral and moved the bar and dragged it open, fighting the snow that blocked it. When it was one horse wide, I led her in. She stabled herself as I burrowed past snow to get an armful of hay. I carried it into the shelter and made three more trips to heap the manger full. She was grateful to be standing out of the wind. I fumbled the sack of grain free of my saddlebag.

Water?

I'll see what I can do.

I left her standing in the shelter as I explored the area. I beat my hands against my thighs as I walked, trying to stir enough warmth into them that I could unsaddle Fleeter. The overcast thinned and pale moonlight opened the night around me. There was a well, with a bucket and windlass. When I lowered the bucket, I heard it break thin ice before it tipped and filled. I brought the bucket up as Riddle arrived. I lifted a hand in silent greeting. He dismounted, led his horse into the shelter and I followed. I held the bucket while Fleeter drank and then offered it to his mount.

'I'll get a fire going in the cabin,' he offered.

'I'll take care of the horses,' I replied.

My stiff fingers struggled with stiffer leather and buckles. The two horses moved close together, sharing the warmth of their bodies. By the time I had both horses made comfortable for the night, a dim light was showing through the cracks around the doorframe of the cabin. I drew another bucket of water and headed for the cabin with my saddle-pack slung over my shoulder. Inside, the cabin was a humble but mostly snug retreat from the night. It had a plank floor and a stone fireplace took up one wall. Riddle had laid a fire and it was beginning to burn well. The furnishings were simple. A table and two stools. A raised platform spanned one end of the cabin and was intended as sleeping space. A shelf held two pots with bales for cooking over the fire. A candle-lantern. Two earthenware cups and two bowls. The shepherds had left a supply of firewood in the lea of the cabin. I went back to the hayrick and raided it ruthlessly to cushion the sleeping platform while Riddle heated water in one of the pots.

Riddle and I were near wordless as we moved around the cabin. We had stepped back into our old relationship and did not want or need much conversation. He made tea with the hot water. I spread the hay on the sleeping platform and then pulled a chair closer to the fire and sat. It seemed a great deal of work to bend down and work my boots off my numbed feet. Slowly, so slowly, the heat of the fire began to warm the cabin and then to penetrate to my chilled flesh. Riddle wiped dust from a mug and filled it with tea. I took it. My face felt stiff and sore. A single day of hard riding and the cold had taken this toll on me. What was my little daughter enduring? Was she still alive? No. Don't consider that thought. Perseverance had seen her carried off in a sleigh, surrounded by furs and blankets. They valued her and were taking good care of her.

And I would kill them all for doing that. That thought warmed me as the fire and hot tea could not.

I heard the thuds of horses coming at a dogged trot. I rose stiffly but Riddle was at the door of the cabin and swung it open before I could even fully stand. He lifted the candle-lantern and by its faint light I perceived Lant riding into the clearing. Perseverance was already dismounting.

'You look terrible,' Riddle greeted Lant.

Lant said nothing, but as his foot hit the ground he gave a stiff grunt of pain.

'Go inside. Get warm by the fire,' Riddle told him, taking the reins of his horse.

'I can do that, sir,' Perseverance offered, and Riddle handed the reins to him with thanks, and then passed him the candle-lantern.

'Want help?' I asked from the doorstep. I was already dreading the idea of putting my boots back on.

'No. Thank you. Sir.' He was curtly furious with me. So, let him be. He led all three horses off to the shelter.

Lant came slowly into the cabin. I stepped back to make way for him. He moved stiffly, his face red and white with cold and pain. He wouldn't look at me as he came in and took my chair by the fire. Riddle offered him his cup of tea and Lant took it without a word. 'You would have been wiser to turn back,' I told him.

'Probably,' he said shortly. 'But Chade's regard means a great deal to me.'

There was nothing to say to that. When Per came in, stamping the snow from his boots as he entered, Riddle surrendered the other chair to him. The crow came with him. She lifted from his shoulder and landed on the table, fluffed her feathers and then smoothed them, and kept silent. I refilled my mug with tea and when I offered it, Per took it from me, muttering his thanks to the floor.

'Water!' Motley demanded. 'Food. Food, food, food!'

Riddle and I had brought food, of sorts. I'd believed I was provisioning only myself. Lant had brought nothing, probably assuming that we'd be stopping at villages or inns along the way. The boy had brought grain for the horses. 'My da always said see to your horse first, as he can carry you but you can't carry him. And not to be too proud to cook up some grain for yourself if you have to. Because if it's not clean enough for you to eat, you shouldn't be feeding it to your horse.' This Per announced as he set a small sack of oats on the table after I had put out dried meat and a few withered apples. *Burrich would have liked you and your father*, I thought to myself.

Riddle shook his head at my meagre offering. From his saddle-bags, he produced a loaf of dark, sweet bread, a generous chunk of cheese, a nice slab of ham and a sack of dried plums. It would have been ample for the two of us, and was adequate for all four of us to make a meal. Motley was happy with the scraps. I made a fresh pot of tea, and as Lant and Per sat slackly before the fire, I went out for more wood and built the fire up well for the night.

They were all yawning when I returned. 'Have we a plan for the morrow?' Riddle asked me wearily.

'Up early. Ride. Find Bee and Shun. Kill the men who took them. Bring the girls home.'

'That's a plan?' Lant asked incredulously.

'Based on what I know, that's the best I can do,' I told him.
Riddle nodded agreement and smothered a tremendous yawn. Per
was already nodding before the fire. I took the half-full mug of
tea from his lax hands. 'Go to bed,' I suggested to him. 'Remember
that tomorrow is another day.' He managed a yawn before he rose
and stumbled toward the sleeping platform. He was asleep with
his boots on almost as soon as he lay down.

'How's the wound, Lant?' I asked him.

'Aches,' he muttered. 'Everything aches still. I was tired when
I began today. Now I've got nothing left.'

'Not your fault,' I told him. 'You're still healing. If Chade were
himself, he'd have realized that he shouldn't send you. No reason
to be ashamed. You need this rest and you should take it.'

I wondered why I was attempting to comfort him and then
put my finger on it. Guilt. He felt guilty for not defending Shine
when she was taken, and guiltier now that he could barely
participate in a mission to rescue her. And tomorrow, I knew,
he would feel even worse. I watched him as he rose from his
chair. He staggered two steps sideways and then trudged to the
bed. He lay down, wrapped his cloak more closely around himself
and was still.

'Fitz?' Riddle asked thickly.

'I'm sorry,' I lied as he stood. I caught him as he sagged and
eased him down onto the floor. Taking him by the shoulders, I
dragged him closer to the fire. I snapped his cloak out and spread
it over him. He was fighting to keep his eyes open.

'Take care of Lant and the boy,' I told him. 'That's the best
way to help me. What I may have to do, I think I'll do best alone.
Don't feel bad about this. I've always been a treacherous bastard.
And you know that.'

'Fiiiizs,' he managed and then his eyes closed. I sighed heavily.

'Oh, Fitz,' the crow said in a voice oddly like the Fool's. It felt
like a rebuke.

'I do what I have to do,' I told her. 'I'm not taking you with
me, either.'

I put a piece of wood in the fire.

I lay down beside Riddle, my back against his, covered us both with my cloak and closed my eyes. I did not allow myself to fall asleep. I did not have that luxury. I let myself rest for as long as it took my propped log to burn through in the fireplace.

When I heard it fall, I arose. I sprinkled seed on another piece of bread and went out to the stable. I moved softly, waking Fleeter with my thoughts as much as with my touch.

I didn't deceive her. 'If you eat this, you will have the strength to carry me through the rest of the night and the day tomorrow.'

I thought she would question me. Nighteyes would have questioned me. Instead, without hesitation, she lipped the piece of bread from my hand. Her trust shamed me. I did not think it would do her any harm. Nonetheless, I did not feel comfortable with what I had done. I went back to the cabin to allow the seed to work.

I ate lightly, pressing carris seed into what was left of Riddle's cheese and toasting it on the now-stale bread. Carris seed was often used on festive cakes for a lift of energy and spirit. I was judicious with it. The effects often ended quite abruptly. I recalled well how Chade had once dropped in his tracks after depending on it too heavily. The bread, melted cheese and tangy seeds were delicious and I felt its invigorating effects almost immediately. I felt almost light-hearted as I moved around the small cabin. The other three were sleeping heavily and probably would not waken until well past noon. I gave the crow a small cut of the bread and put water in one of the mugs for her. I checked on Perseverance before I left, slightly worried that perhaps he had consumed a heavier dose of my tea than I'd intended for him. But his breathing was strong and he even muttered as I felt the strong pulse at his throat. He'd be fine. I washed out the cup very well and packed the pot with snow, which I heated and added to it all the delven-bark that I carried. Time to disappear from the Skill-current. I hadn't told Chade that I'd retained a measure for myself. At the time, it had simply seemed a good idea. Now as I drank the bitter brew, I reflected that no one could hide my daughter from me or cloud my mind. I felt it deaden the Skill in me immediately, and felt also both the dampening of spirit and unnatural energy it bestowed. I washed the kettle with snow and put it back on the table. I packed some of the food, built up the fire for them. As I went out of the door, I heard the sharp clap of wings and felt a slap of black feathers against my cheek as the crow escaped. She flew to the top of the horse's shed and kicked down some snow from the ridgepole as she landed. The moon was well risen now, but even so she was just a darker bit of blackness against the sky. I looked up at her.

'Are you sure you want to be out here? They won't wake up for some time.'

She ignored me, and I decided to do the same to her. She was a crow. She could look after herself. She'd either wait for the others to awaken or fly back to Buckkeep Castle. I watered all the horses and put more hay for the other four beasts before I saddled Fleeter.

'Are you ready?' I asked her and felt her cheery response. I wondered if she could sense the energy of the carris seed coursing through me and if it affected her willingness for our mission. I could certainly sense its effect on her.

It's good to move, she assured me.

'It's good to be doing something,' I agreed. I took my frustration and helplessness and used them as fuel for my growing anger at Bee's captors. We had a bit more of a climb and then we'd traverse the pass called the Maiden's Waist and down into the valley beyond. There was a village on the other side of the hills and probably a cleared road. I still wasn't sure that I'd find them before the king's troops, but it would be close. 'I have to be there,' I told Fleeter.

Then we shall, she agreed. I gave her loose reins and we swiftly left the cabin behind us.

TWENTY-FOUR

Parting Ways

The dream begins with a distant bell tolling. In this dream, I am myself. I am trying to run away from something, but I can only run in a circle. I rush as fast as I can, trying to run away but always I find I am running directly back to the most dangerous place. When I tumble too close, they reach out and catch me. I do not see who they are. Only that they capture me. There is a staircase of black stone. She puts on a glove, slipping her hand into his anguish. She opens the door to the staircase, and grips me by the wrist as she drags me down. The door slams shut behind us, soundlessly.

We are in a place where the emptiness is actually made of other people. They all begin speaking to me at once, but I plug my ears and close my eyes.

Bee Farseer's Dream Journal

Everything changed once Ellik had Vindeliar in his control. I was not sure of the reason for this, save that he seemed to take pleasure in the distress it caused the luriks and Dwalia. The night he seized the fog-boy and kept him over at his camp, we did not load the sleighs or travel at all. He told us nothing and left us waiting.

Ellik went to greet his soldiers and Vindeliar. He welcomed him to his fire and to the meat his men had taken that day. His standing soldiers ringed them so that we could not see what went on. Lingstra Dwalia stood at the edge of our firelight and stared toward them, but did nothing to interfere. Ellik kept his voice low. We heard him speak, and then Vindeliar striving to answer him. At first Ellik sounded affable, then serious and finally angry. Soon we could hear Vindeliar sobbing and his voice went high on his words, but I could not make out what he told them. I did not hear anything to make me think they physically struck him. But sometimes the men would erupt into a roar of laughter at something. Dwalia's fists kneaded her skirts, but she did not speak to any of us. Two of Ellik's men stood near our fire, watching her. Once, when she took two steps toward them, one drew his blade. He smiled as he did it, inviting her to come closer. She stopped and when she turned back to our campfire, they both laughed.

It was a very long night. When morning came, perhaps she thought they might give Vindeliar back to us. They did not. Half of the soldiers went to their bedrolls, but the others put more wood on their fire and kept watch on the fog-man. When it was clear that Ellik had gone to sleep, she turned to us. 'Go to bed,' she ordered us angrily. 'Tonight we will travel again, and you should be rested.'

But few of us slept. Before the winter sun reached noon, we were awake and moving nervously about our campsite. Ellik arose, and we saw the guard around Vindeliar change, as did the two men watching our campsite. The pale Servants tried not to stare at them. No one wished to invite their scrutiny. With straining ears and sidelong glances, we tried to hear Ellik's orders for his men. 'Hold them here,' I heard Ellik say as he mounted his horse. 'When I return, I expect to find all exactly as I left it.' Dwalia's anxiety soared when Ellik ordered an additional horse saddled for Vindeliar. We watched in dread as Ellik rode away, trailed by four of his men surrounding Vindeliar. They rode toward the town in broad daylight.

I think that was the most frightening day, for Ellik was away and his soldiers were left watching us. And oh, how well they watched us. With sidelong glances and smirks, with pointing fingers that dismissed some of the luriks and hands that sketched the measure of breasts or buttocks of another, they watched us. They did not speak to us, or touch any of us with their hands, which somehow made the stroke of their eyes and their muttered words all the more threatening.

But his men kept Ellik's discipline. He had ordered them to leave us alone, 'for now', and they did. But the dreadful suspense of knowing that at any time he might rescind or change that order hovered over all of us. All that afternoon, the luriks went about their tasks with grave faces, eyes darting constantly to see what the soldiers were doing in their adjacent camp. Twice I heard whispered conversations. 'This was never seen, never foretold! How can it be?' They scrabbled through remembered writings, citing quotes to one another, trying to interpret them in new ways that would allow them to believe that what was happening had somehow been foreseen or foretold. Dwalia, it seemed to me, broke those conversations as often as she could, ordering servants off to melt snow for water or bring still more firewood. They obeyed her, going off in twos and threes, for safety and, I think, so they might continue their whispering.

While Dwalia tried to keep our camp bustling, Ellik's men remained idle and staring, commenting on particular women as if they were horses being auctioned. The males in our party were scarcely less nervous, wondering if Dwalia would order them to defend us. None of them were hardened fighters. They were all of the kind of folk I thought of as scribes: full of knowledge and ideas, but slight as willow saplings and bloodless as fish. They could hunt well enough to keep food on the spit, and Dwalia ordered them off to do so. My blood ran cold when I saw several of the soldiers rise and slouch after them, grinning maliciously and laughing low together.

We waited around our fire, cold in a way that the flames could not warm. Eventually, our hunters came back with two thin winter rabbits and drawn faces. They had not been assaulted, but the soldiers had followed them, speaking in whispers just loud enough to reach their ears about what they might do to them. Thrice they had scared off game just as the hunters let their arrows fly.

I waited as long as I could, but eventually I had to relieve myself. I went to Shun, who was very annoyed but in just as desperate a circumstance. We went together, looking over our shoulders, until we found a slightly more private spot. I still pantomimed pissing standing up before joining her in crouching in the snow. I was getting better at it. I no longer peed on the backs of my boots. We had both finished and were refastening our clothing when a shadow moved. Shun sucked in her breath to scream.

'Don't,' he said softly, more a plea than a command. He came a step closer and I could make out in the gathering dusk that he was the young soldier who had been making cow eyes at Shun since we had left Withywoods. He spoke quickly, softly. 'I just wanted to tell you. I'll protect you. I'll die before I let anyone hurt you. Or her.'

'Thank you,' I said as softly, preferring to believe he spoke to me rather than Shun.

I could not read his eyes in the dimness but I saw a smile twitch his mouth. 'Nor will I betray your secret,' he said, and then he stepped back into the shadow of the evergreens. We stayed where we were for some time, before we both cautiously approached that grove of trees. No one was there.

'He's spoken to me before,' Shun admitted. I looked at her wide-eyed. 'Several of the soldiers have spoken to me. Just as they whisper vile things to the pale people when they take them food or gather their dishes.' She stared off into the darkness where he might have gone. 'He is the only one who has said anything kind.'

'Do you believe him? What he said?'

She looked at me. 'That he will protect us? One against so many? He can't. But knowing that he thinks he might have to protect us from his fellows tells me that he knows something bad is coming.'

'We all knew that,' I said quietly. We walked back to the camp. I wanted to take her hand, to hold onto someone, but I knew she wouldn't welcome it.

Dusk was falling when Ellik and his men returned. Dwalia gave a wild gasp of relief when she saw that Vindeliar was with them and appeared intact. The saddle-packs on all the horses were bulging, and Ellik's companions were laughing and shouting to their fellows before they reached the fire. 'We've plundered a town in daylight, and not a soul the wiser!' one called, and that brought the men around the fires scrambling to see what they had.

From their packs they took bottles of wine and rich foods,

hams and loaves of bread studded with currants and swirled with spices, smoked fish and winter apples. 'In broad daylight!' I heard one man say, and another, as he swirled a homespun dress in the air, 'Took it right off her and she stood like a cow waiting to be milked! Had a feel or two, but no time for anything more! And when we walked away, her husband took her arm and they walked off through the town without a backwards glance!'

Dwalia's jaw dropped open in horror. I thought it was at what the man had said but then I followed her gaze. Vindeliar still sat his horse beside a grinning Ellik. The fog-man wore an uncertain half-smile and a necklace of pearls and a fur hat. A brightly figured scarf swathed his neck, and his hands were gloved in red leather with tassels. As we watched, one of the men who had ridden with him slapped him on the thigh and told him, 'This is just the beginning!' Vindeliar's smile broadened and became more certain.

That broke Dwalia's resolve, I think. 'Vindeliar! Remember the path! Do not stray from what has been seen!' Dwalia shouted at him.

Ellik wheeled his horse and rode it right up to her, pushing her back until she stumbled and nearly fell into the fire.

'He's mine now! Don't speak to him!'

But the smile had faded from Vindeliar's plump face and he watched in dismay as Ellik leaned down to backhand Dwalia. She did not move but accepted the blow. Courage, or did she fear worse if she avoided it?

Ellik stared down at her for a moment until she lowered her eyes. Then he rode back to his own fire, announcing, 'Tonight, we feast! And tomorrow, another test of our fine friend's abilities!'

Some of the Servants were staring hungrily and longingly at the soldiers' camp. As Ellik dismounted, his men offered him the best of the loot. For a time, a stricken Vindeliar looked toward our camp like a dog that longs to return to its familiar kennel. Then Ellik's men surrounded him, handing him an opened bottle of wine and a sweet cake. A moment later he was down and one of his riding companions had thrown a familiar arm across his shoulders and drawn him into the thick of their comradeship. I recalled a dream I had had, of a beggar sucked down and drowned in a whirlpool of jewels and food.

Cold rose in me. None of them had foreseen this. But I had. Only me.

I didn't understand how that could be and suddenly I knew that I had to understand. There was great danger in me not understanding these dreams. I was the only one who could seize the tiller and steer the boat, but I did not know how.

Hush, Wolf Father bade me sternly. *Say nothing. Not to these people.*

I have to know.

You don't. You don't have to be that. Take a breath. Breathe now, smell the scents of now. Be alert to the danger that is now. Or you will never have to fear tomorrow's danger. There was sad finality in his warning, as if he knew too well the meaning of it. I tamped down my questions and opened myself to all that was happening around us.

'At least they did no worse than take her clothing,' Odessa said quietly.

Dwalia, sitting dispiritedly by our fire, guessed the reason for that. 'Until they know the limits of Vindeliar's power, they will not risk putting themselves in a position in which the whole town might suddenly turn on them. But while they are playing childish pranks on merchants, we sit here exposed for any who might decide to wander through this stretch of woods. We can be seen now. Anything might befall us.'

Odessa's brow wrinkled. 'Anything?' she asked, as if the concept puzzled her.

Dwalia looked ill. 'Anything. We are so far from the path, I do not know how to recover our way. I do not know if we should act or hope that the path reclaims us. Anything we do may take us further from our correct choices.'

Odessa nodded almost eagerly. 'So we were taught in the School. "Trust the way of the White Prophet. Avoid extreme actions. Only the Prophet through her Catalyst may steer the future best." But when we are so far from the path, is it still true?'

'So we must believe,' Dwalia replied, but she sounded uncertain to me. Her luriks had ventured closer as she spoke. They huddled around her like a flock of sheep clustering close to their shepherd. A remembrance of a dark dream came to me. I clenched my teeth, feeling I held back vomit rather than sounds as the words of the dream echoed in my head. *The sheep are scattered, given to the wind's teeth while the shepherd flees with the wolf's cub.*

I heard a raised voice from the other campfire. 'Why? Why not? For a celebration! For those of us who stayed here and waited while you tested the boy in town.'

'They are mine,' Ellik replied, but his stern words were laced with tolerant amusement. 'When they are changed to coins, then be sure you will be given your rightful share. Have I ever cheated you of your rightful due?'

'No, but . . .'

I craned my neck. It was the handsome rapist speaking. By the firelight, his nose and cheeks were red with more than cold. They had been drinking the stolen wine. I caught a glimpse of Vindeliar. He was sitting flat in the snow, a foolish smile on his face.

'It's all his fault,' Dwalia said in a poisonously bitter voice. I thought she was speaking of Ellik but she was staring sightlessly into the darkened forest. 'He did this to us. He could not be content with the role he was given. He was treated well. He had no reason to run off, to choose a Catalyst of his own, to destroy the path with his wilfulness. I feel his influence in this. How that can be, I do not know. But I am certain it is so, and I curse his name.'

'So spare us two or even one!' Hogen suggested boldly. 'One will not make that big a hole in your purse, commander!'

I thought that Ellik would be furious at the question, but perhaps Ellik had been made more mellow by drink and by his enjoyment of his prize that day. 'Commander? No. Duke. Duke I will be again, with this boy on my lead. Name me so from now on!'

At that proclamation, some of his men cheered.

Did Hogen judge him mellowed with wine and success? He flourished an elaborate bow to Ellik and said in a mockingly elegant voice, 'Duke Ellik, your excellency, we your most loyal subjects beg a boon of you. Will not you spare us one of yon womanflesh for us to enjoy on this cold night?'

The other men erupted in laughter and cheers. Duke Ellik joined in. He slapped the man firmly on the back and spoke loud and clear. 'Hogen, I know you well. One will never be enough for you. And by the time all of you have finished with one, there will be nothing left for the market!'

'Then give us two, and she will have half the work!' Hogen proposed boldly and at least three of the men shouted their approval.

Beside me, I felt Shun stiffen. She set her hand on my shoulder and her grip was like a claw. She bent to say by my ear, 'Come, Bee. You must be weary. Let us go to our rest.' She clutched the shoulder of my coat and almost lifted me to my feet as she pulled at me. Around us, the luriks crouched frozen around the fire, their gazes turned toward the other fireside. Their eyes grew wider in their pale faces.

'Can we not flee?' I heard one whisper. 'If we scattered into the forest, some of us might escape!'

'Do nothing,' Dwalia hissed. 'Do nothing.'

But Shun paid her words no heed. She had me on my feet and we were moving, stepping quietly back from the circle of firelight. In their terror, the luriks did not seem to notice our departure. Dwalia did. She glanced at us but did nothing, almost as if she wanted us to flee.

I had lost track of the conversation from the other campfire, but the rough burst of laughter I heard was more frightening than merry. Ellik lifted his voice and sounded almost jolly in his tolerance.

'Oh, very well, Hogen. All here know that your brain cannot work when your dick is lonely for a dip. I will give you one. Just one. Chosen especially for you. Come, subjects! Follow your duke.'

I dug in my heels and, with an angry hiss, Shun halted. I stared back. I was terrified but I had to see what was happening. Shun gripped my shoulder hard but she stopped trying to drag me. I think she felt the same paralyzing curiosity. The same dread and horror.

Ellik came toward our fire, a wide, drunken grin on his seamed old face. His hand was on Hogen's shoulder as if he steered the man, but I think he more leaned on him as he staggered through the snow. The rapist was as handsome as ever; his golden hair gleamed in the firelight, and he smiled with his even, white teeth. So handsome and so cruel. Some of the luriks had been perched on their bundles around the fire. They stood as Ellik came on and retreated, but not far. They clustered closer to Dwalia as if she would protect them. I knew she would not.

'Do nothing,' she warned them in a stern voice as Ellik came closer. His men clustered behind him and the handsome rapist, leering like panting dogs. Hogen's mouth was wide and wet, his left hand gripping his crotch loosely as if to contain himself. His pale eyes wandered over the luriks like a beggar child staring at a display of sweets. The Whites froze like rabbits. Shun made a low sound in her throat. She crouched down low and I allowed her to move me some paces sideways to the flimsy shelter of some willow saplings. We both stared.

'Here she is! Here's the lovely for you, Hogen!'

Ellik stretched forth his hand and it hovered near a slender girl with a face as pale as the moon. She gave a low cry and cowered closer to Dwalia. Dwalia did nothing at all. She stared at Hogen and Ellik with a stony face and made no sound. At the last moment, Ellik's hand darted sideways and he seized Odessa by the front of her coat, pulling her from the shelter of the others as if he had just selected a piglet for the spit. Her mouth sagged into a cave of woe, her homely, unfinished face contorting as Ellik dragged her forth to the mocking cries of his men and Hogen's cry of disappointment. 'She's ugly as a dog's arse. I don't want her!'

All the men behind him roared with laughter at his protest. Ellik laughed until his face was bright red and then wheezed out, 'Your cock has no eyes! She'll do for you. She wouldn't bring anything at the market anyway!'

Odessa had half-fainted, sagging to her knees, held up only by the wiry old man's grip on the neck of her shirt. Ellik was stronger than he looked. He gave a sudden heave, pulling her to her feet and swinging her into Hogen so that he had to catch her in his arms or fall himself. 'Take her, you hound!' All humour suddenly fell from the commander's face. His expression was savage as he said, 'And remember this night well when I deduct her value from your share of our take. Don't lean on me, boy, and think you can whine and bargain with me. I set the bargains. And this ugly rag of skirts is what you get from me tonight.'

Hogen stared at his commander over Odessa's bowed head. She had come to her senses enough to be struggling feebly, her hands paddling at Hogen's shirtfront. Hogen's face had gone dark with fury but as he met Ellik's gaze, his eyes dropped. 'Stupid bitch,' he said disdainfully, and I thought he would cast Odessa back into the other luriks. But instead he shifted his grip on her, catching her one-handed under the throat and dragging her off with him. The other soldiers, gone silent for a short time at their commander's rebuke, followed him with sudden shouts and offers of wagers and demands to be next upon her.

Dwalia did nothing. Her followers huddled behind her like sheep. I wondered if each was secretly glad the wolves had dragged off Odessa and not herself.

Not wolves. Wolves feed when they are hungry. They do not rape.

I'm sorry. I could tell I had offended Wolf Father.

'Come.' Shun dragged me behind a snow-laden bush. 'They won't stop with her. We have to escape now.'

'But we've nothing with us . . .'

From the other campfire, we heard short bursts of screams. The men mocked Odessa, whooping along with her. Shun's grip on my shoulder began to shake. 'We have our lives,' she whispered angrily. 'That's what we flee with.' I could tell she could scarcely get breath into her lungs. She was terrified. And trying to save me.

I could not take my eyes off the huddled luriks. Dwalia was a standing silhouette against the firelight. Abruptly she moved. 'Ellik!' She shouted his name angrily into the night. 'We had an agreement! You gave us your word! You cannot do this!' Then, as I saw the two men he had left watching the luriks move toward her, she shouted at them, 'Do not block my way!'

'That's . . . stupid.' Shun's voice shook out of her body. 'We have to run. We have to get away. They'll kill her. And then there is nothing between them and us.'

'Yes,' I said. I listened to Wolf Father. 'We must leave no fresh tracks. Move where the snow is trampled already. Get as far from the camp as we can while they are busy. Find a tree well, a, a place under an evergreen where the branches are heavy with snow and bent down, but the ground around the trunk is almost clear of snow. Hide there, close together.'

I'd reached up to take her by the wrist. She let go of my collar and abruptly I was the one who was leading her, away from Dwalia and her paralyzed luriks, away from the campfires and into the dark. Odessa's screams had stopped. I refused to wonder why. We moved furtively, until we were at the edge of our campsite. Shun was not speaking. She simply followed me. I took her to the trail the horses and sleighs had made through the snow when we first arrived. We were moving steadily, both of us breathing raggedly with fear, backtracking the trail of the sleighs and horses. The forest was black, the snow was white. I saw a game trail crossing our path. We turned and followed it, leaving the runner tracks behind us. Now we moved as deer did, ducking our heads to go under low-hanging, snow-laden boughs. 'Don't touch the branches. Don't make any snow fall,' I warned. On a rise to our left, I saw a cluster of evergreens. 'This way,' I whispered. I went first, breaking trail through the deep snow. I was leaving tracks. We couldn't help that.

The snow will be shallower in the deeper forest. Go, cub. Do not hide until you are too weary to run any further.

I nodded and tried to move faster. The snow seemed to clutch at my boots and Shun made too much noise. They would hear us running away. They would catch us.

Then we heard Dwalia scream. It was not shrill, it was hoarse. And terrified. She screamed again and then shouted, 'Vindeliar! Come back to us! Vinde—' And her voice was cut off, as swiftly as one quenches a torch.

I heard frightened voices, a chorus of them, some shrill. Questioning, like a flock of chickens wakened in the dark of night. The luriks.

'Run now. We must run now!'

'What are they doing to her?'

'Vindeliar! He must help us.'

Behind us in the night, I heard Dwalia's voice rise in a desperate choked cry. 'This must not happen! This must not happen! Make it stop, Vindeliar! It is your only chance to return to the rightful path. Forget what Ellik told you! It wasn't true! Forget Ellik!' Then, in a desperately hoarse voice, 'Vindeliar, save me! Make them stop!'

Then a different kind of scream cut the night. It wasn't a sound. It hurt me to feel it; it made me sick. Fear flowed through the air and drenched me. I was so terrified I could not move. Shun froze. I tried to speak, to tell her we had to get further away, but I could not make my voice work. My legs would not hold me up. I sagged down in the snow with Shun falling on top of me. In the wake of that wave, a deadly silence filled the forest. No night bird spoke, no living thing gave voice. It was so still I could hear the crackling of the fires.

Then, a single shrill, clear cry. 'Run! Flee!'

And then, the hoarse shouting of men. 'Catch them! Don't let them steal the horses!'

'Kill him! Kill them all! Traitors!'

'Stop them. Don't let them get to the village!'

'Bastards! Traitorous bastards!'

And then the night was full of sound. Screams, cries. Men roaring and shouting. Orders barked. Screeched pleas.

Shun was the one to rise and drag me to my feet. 'Run,' she whimpered, and I tried. My legs were jelly. They would not take my weight.

Shun dragged me through the snow. I staggered to my feet.

We fled from the rising screams into darkness.

TWENTY-FIVE

Red Snow

I but recount the rumours and gossip as it comes to me. The tales I am hearing seem too wild to be true, but as you have ordered me, I do. This is what news reached me. The Duke of Chalced is no more. A horde of dragons bearing armoured riders came out of the wilderness and attacked the city of Chalced. They spat fire or something just as destructive. They ringed the city with circles of destruction. Finally they targeted the palace of the duke himself, destroying it with their spew and the battering of their wings and the lashing of their tails. It is said that his towering stronghold crumbled to a quarter of its height and is no longer inhabitable.

The elderly and ailing duke, it is said, came out of his palace to stand before his troops. A tower fell, crushing him and much of his soldiery. Chancellor Ellik, long the duke's most trusted adviser and a sword companion from the time of their youth, survived. The Chalcedean forces were reduced to a retreat that became a rout.

By the next morning, the daughter of the Duke of Chalced had emerged as allied with the dragons and their tenders and now claims to be 'rightfully' the Duchess of Chalced. Ellik has proclaimed that he was the duke's chosen successor and accused the so-called duchess of witchcraft. One Redhands Roctor, formerly a minor nobleman in the west of Chalced near Heastgate, has challenged both of them. His military forces were untouched in the attack and in my opinion is most likely to prevail. Chalcedeans are unlikely to accept the rule of a woman, even one with the goodwill of dragons. Duke Ellik's forces were greatly diminished in the dragon rout of Chalced city.

It would take divine intervention for him to return to power and influence, especially since he failed to protect the city. The 'Duchess' of Chalced has offered a reward for his severed head, and the people of the city of Chalced call him a coward who abandoned them to the dragons.

Unsigned report to Lord Chade Fallstar

Fleeter and I made good time. The moon silvered the snow and I had the stars to keep my bearings. The cart trail soon joined a wider way as we neared the Maiden's Waist, though the wide passage through the rolling hills scarce merited the title 'pass'. Fleeter was glad to be on trodden snow again. The roan employed her long-legged stride as we climbed the last stretch, and then we loped through an evergreen forest, and down a narrow trail that wound through bare-limbed oaks and alders. The slow winter dawn gradually came to light our way. Fleeter dropped our pace to a walk and breathed. The trail widened and I passed several small homesteads. Smoke rose from their chimneys and candle-light told of farmers awakening early. I saw no one outside.

Dawn grew stronger and I pushed Fleeter to a canter. The trail became a road as the morning passed. I rode through a small village without pause and on, past smallholdings and grainfields that dreamed of furrows beneath gently-mounded snow. We trotted, we cantered, we trotted. Then more forest. Over a bridge we went, and now passed occasional travellers: a tinker with his painted wagon full of knives and scissors, a farmer and her sons riding mules and leading pack animals laden with earthy-smelling sacks of potatoes, and a young woman who scowled at me when I bid her 'Good afternoon.'

Dark thoughts of what Bee was enduring, how Dutiful would react to my disobedience, how angry Riddle would be, and Nettle on his behalf, besieged me. I tried to push them down. Elfbark brought sad memories to the front of my mind and rebuked me for stupidity and failures of all sorts. And in the next moment, the carris seed would make me believe I was invulnerable, and I would fantasize about killing all twenty Chalcedeans and sing aloud to Fleeter as we travelled on.

Calm down. Caution. I could feel my heart beating in my chest, almost hear it in my ears.

More forest. Trot, canter, trot. I stopped at a stream to let her water. *How tired are you?*

Not at all.

I have need of speed. You will let me know if you tire?

I am Fleeter. I do not tire before my rider does.

You will. And you must let me know.

She snorted, and as soon as I was back in the saddle, she pranced a few steps. I laughed and gave her a free head. For a short way she galloped and then dropped back into her easy, rocking canter.

I entered a town of more substance, with an inn and a hostelry and three taverns. Folk were up and about now. On the outskirts of it, I passed a rare shrine to Eda. The goddess slumbered under a mantle of white snow, her hands open on her lap. Someone had brushed her hands clean and filled them with millet. Small birds perched on her fingers and thumbs. And on we went, and the road became one of the king's highways. I did not pause as I reviewed my mental map. This road went directly to Salter's Deep. It was wide and open and direct, the shortest route.

If I were fleeing the Six Duchies with captives and a troop of Chalcedean mercenaries, it was the last route I would take. The Fool's words came back to me. He had insisted I would not be able to find them, that the only way to regain my daughter was to go directly to where they must be taking her. I took another pinch of the carris seed, crushed it between my teeth and rode on. It was sweet in my mouth, a tangy, heady taste, and in a moment I felt the surge of both energy and clarity it always gave.

The likeliest unlikeliest, the likeliest unlikeliest drummed in my head, the words keeping rhythm with Fleeter's hooves. I could follow this highway all the way to Salter's Deep. If I saw nothing along the way, then I could join the Ringhill Guard and wait near the captured ship. Or once there I could work my way back along a less-used route and hope to be lucky. Or investigate some of the back roads. I rode on. I passed one diverging road. The next one, I decided. I'd take the next one and follow it.

I heard a sudden caw overhead. I looked up and saw a crow,

wings spread, sliding down the sky toward me. Suddenly it was Motley and I braced myself for her to land. Instead she swept past me in a wide circle. 'Red snow!' she called suddenly and clearly to me. 'Red snow!'

I watched her as she circled again and then veered away. I pulled Fleeter in. What did she mean? Did she want me to follow her? There was no road, only an open field and beyond it a sparse forest of birch and a few evergreens that soon thickened into true forest. I watched her as she glided away, then tilted her wings and beat them hard to come back to me. I stood in my stirrups. 'Motley!' I called and offered her my forearm. Instead, she swept past me so low that Fleeter shied from her passage.

'Stupid!' the crow shouted at me. 'Stupid Fitz! Red snow. Red snow!'

I reined Fleeter away from the road. *We follow her*, I told the horse.

I don't like her.

We follow her, I insisted, and Fleeter conceded her will to mine. It was not pleasant for her. We left the packed and level road, pushed through a prickly hedgerow and entered the farmer's field. The snow here was untrodden, and the frozen ground uneven beneath the wind-blown snow. Our pace inevitably slowed just as I wished that we could gallop. But a lame horse would be even slower. I tried to contain my impatience.

The crow flew away from me, into the shelter of the trees. We moved steadily toward where she had vanished. A short time later, she looped back to us, then circled away again. This time she seemed content that we were following her and called no insults.

And there we intersected a trail: not a road, merely an open space that left the field and wound into the scant forest. Perhaps a woodcutter had made it. It could be a cattle-track that led to water. I looked back along it. Had it been used recently? It was hard to say. Were there deeper hollows under the blown and polished snow? We turned and followed it.

When we reached the outskirts of the birch forest, I saw what I could not have seen from the road. The white horse had seemed but another mound of snow in the distance. I did not see the fallen rider until I was almost beside the fur-clad body. And only the crow, looking down from above, could have seen the trail of melted red-and-pink snow that led back into the forest.

The horse was clearly dead, its eyes open and frost outlining the whiskers on its muzzle and coating its out-thrust tongue. Droplets of blood had frozen around its mouth. An arrow stood out of its chest, just behind its foreleg. A good lung shot but not one that had penetrated both lungs. I knew that if I cut the animal open, I would find its body cavity full of blood. There was no saddle on the horse, and only a halter. The rider had fled in haste, perhaps. I pulled in Fleeter despite her distaste for the scene and dismounted. The body that lay beyond the horse was too large to be Bee, I told myself as I floundered through the snow toward it. The hair that showed beneath the white fur cap was the right colour, but it could not be Bee, it could not, and when I reached her and turned her over, it was not. The pale youngster I revealed was as dead as her horse. The front of her furs was scarlet. Probably an arrow, one that had gone right through her. And she was a White or at least a part-White. She had lived for a short time after she'd fallen face down in the snow. Frost had formed heavily around her mouth from her last breaths, and her cloudy blue eyes looked at me through ice. I let her fall back into the snow.

I could not get my breath for the shuddering of my heart. 'Bee. Where are you?' My words were not even a whisper for I had no air to push them. I wanted to run back down the blood-trail shouting her name. I wanted to mount Fleeter and gallop there as swiftly as possible. I wanted to use my Skill to scream to the sky that I needed help, that I needed everyone in the Six Duchies to come and help me save my child but I forced myself to stand, sweating and trembling, and do nothing until that fit of reckless urgency had passed. Then I went to my horse.

But as I lifted my foot for the stirrup, Fleeter sank to her front knees. *Tired. So tired.* She shuddered down, her hind legs folding under her. *So tired.*

Fleeter! Dismay choked me. I should never have trusted her to know when she was wearied. Carris seed filled one with energy, until it left the user exhausted. *Don't lie down in the snow. Up. Up, my girl. Come on. Come on.*

She rolled her eyes at me and for a moment I feared she would drop her head. Then with a shudder and a heave, she stood. I led her slowly from the trail to a stand of evergreens. Under them, the snow was shallower. *Stay here and rest. I will be back.*

You are leaving me here?

I must. But only for a time. I'll be back for you.

I don't understand.

Just rest. I'll be back. Stay here. Please. Then I closed my mind to her. I'd never ridden a horse to exhaustion. The shame I felt was overwhelming. And useless. I was doing what I had to do. I took from my saddle-packs items that I thought I might need. I shut my heart to Bee. I did not recall Molly or wonder what she would have said, thought or done. I put the Fool and all his warnings and advice from my mind, and set aside the man that Burrich had hoped I would become. I cut Holder Badgerlock from my heart and banished Prince FitzChivalry to the shadows where he had lived for so many years. I squared my shoulders and closed my heart.

There was another person in the depths of me. Chade's boy. I took a breath and summoned those memories. I recalled in full that which Chade had shaped me to be. I was an assassin with a mission. I would kill them all, as effectively and efficiently as possible, without remorse or emotion. This was a task to do coldly and perfectly. As I had killed the Bridgemore twins when I was fourteen, as I had killed Hoofer Webling when I was fifteen. I could not remember the name of the innkeeper I had poisoned. Knowing his name had not been part of that task.

I thought of all the assignments that I had banished from my thoughts as soon as they were accomplished, the quiet work which I had never allowed to be a part of my memories or image of myself. I summoned them back now and allowed them in. I recalled now the times I had followed Chade through darkness, or acted alone at his behest. Once Chade had cautioned me that assassins such as we were did not ask one another about their kills, did not flaunt them or record them. I recalled, not scores, but dozens of assignments. King Shrewd had not been a callous or murderous king. Chade and I had been his weapons of last resort, the solution that was applied when all others had failed.

The twins had been rapists and unusually cruel ones. Twice they had stood before his judgment throne, received punishment and promised repentance. But their father was unable or unwilling to keep them in check, and so my king had sent me out, reluctantly, as he might send a huntsman to put down mad dogs. I never knew what Hoofer had done, or why the innkeeper had to die. I had been given a task and I did it, silently and well, without judgment, and then walked away, setting all thoughts about them aside.

Assassins did not share those grim little triumphs. But we kept them, and I did not doubt that Chade sometimes did as I did now. I thought I knew now why he had cautioned me to set those memories aside. When you are fourteen and you cut the throat of a man of twenty-three, it seems a contest between equals. But two score and some years later, when a man looks back, he sees a boy killing a youngster who was foolish enough to get drunk in the wrong tavern and take a dark pathway home. I told myself that such insights did not destroy the finesse of what I had done. As I told my horse to stand and stay, as I pulled my hood up and laced my sleeves tight to my forearms, I counted my kills and recalled that this was something I could truly do well. This was, as the Fool had reminded me, something I was good at.

I did not walk back over the blood-trail the girl and the horse had left. I moved through the trees, keeping the wallowed and red-spattered trail in sight, but never coming too close to it. I let my mind consider only exactly what I knew. This girl was part of the force that had taken Bee. She and the horse had been shot, most likely as they fled in haste. They had been dead long enough for frost to form. I felt a small lift of my heart. One less person to confront, one less person to kill. Perhaps the Ringhill Guard had already engaged with the Chalcedeans. The quiet of the forest told me that battle was over. Perhaps Bee and Shine were already safe. I regretted the elfbark now. Something had transpired, and Dutiful would know of it by Skill or messenger bird. If I were not deadened to the Skill, doubtless I'd know, too. I'd outfoxed myself. I had one choice. Follow the blood-trail back. I scowled as I reflected that a lung-shot animal does not often run far. Either the battle was over and all combatants had departed the scene or something was very odd.

Until I knew, I would be cautious. I moved quietly and irregularly along the trail. The eye is drawn to motion, especially repeated motion. I stepped softly, I paused, I waited. I breathed quietly, taking in air through my nose, trying to scent smoke or other signs of a camp. I heard the distant caw of a crow. Another. Then I saw her, flying low through the forest. Motley spotted me almost instantly and alighted on a tree branch over my head. I fervently hoped she would not betray me as I continued my measured stalk along the horse's trail.

I heard soft wind in the trees, the occasional fall of snow from branches and distant bird calls. And then the normal hush of a forest in winter was cracked by more bird noises. The hoarse croak of a disturbed raven, followed by the squawking of crows. My own crow now landed on my shoulder as lightly as a friend's hand. 'Red snow,' she said again, but quietly. 'Carrion.'

I thought I knew what I would find but I did not drop my caution. Instead I moved on. I crossed tracks of other horses. They had ploughed through the snow, running between trees and in some places crashing through brush. At least one of them had been bleeding. I did not turn aside for any of them. My first goal was to find where the escaping animals had come from, and perhaps what they had been fleeing. I continued my ghosting walk.

When I came to the edge of what had been their campsite, I stood still. I looked carefully at everything I could see before I moved again. I studied the fallen tents and the burned-out fires. There were bodies, some in soldier's harness and some in white furs. The crows and three ravens that had come to clean the bones made no difference between them. A busy fox looked up, studied my stillness for a time, and then went back to tugging at a man's hand, trying to pull a meaty forearm free. Two crows on the corpse's belly made small protests as the fox's efforts disturbed their probing beaks. The softer tissue of the man's face was already gone. The merciful cold kept the stench of death at bay. I judged at least a day had passed since this carnage had been wrought.

Unlikely to be the Ringhill Guard. The timing was off, and they would have burned the bodies. Who, then? *Oh, Bee.*

Pacing slowly, the crow still on my shoulder, I circled the camp. Three sleighs, incongruously gaudy and elaborate, had been deserted. Frost dimmed their scarlet sides. I kept a mental tally of the bodies. Four in white. Five. Six soldiers. Seven. Eight soldiers. Six Whites. I examined the disappointment welling in me. I'd wanted to kill them myself.

I saw no sign of a body of Bee's size, no corpse with Shine's lush hair. I circled the entire camp. Nine dead soldiers. Eleven dead Whites. The dead Whites were scattered. Six of the dead mercenaries were in pairs, as if they had fought and killed each other. I scowled. This was definitely not the work of the Ringhill Guard. I moved on. Three dead horses, a white one and two brown ones. Two white tents collapsed on themselves. Three smaller tents. Three brown horses on a picket line. One lifted his head and watched me. I lofted the crow from my shoulder. 'Go quietly,' I told her, and she did. The horse's eyes followed the bird's flight as I slipped behind one of the white tents.

I approached the first white tent from behind. My Wit told me that it held no living creature. Crouching, I used my knife to slice an opening. Inside, I saw tousled blankets and sleeping furs. And a body. She was lying on her back, her spread legs making plain her fate. Her hair looked grey in the dimness. Not Shine. Twelve dead Whites. Her throat had been cut; black blood matted her long pale hair. Something had gone badly wrong in this camp. And Bee had been in the midst of it. I withdrew and went to the next white tent.

This one had not fallen as badly. Again, I quested toward it and sensed no life within it. My knife made a purring sound as it sliced the canvas. I cut a cross in the fabric and peeled it wide to let in light. No one. Only empty blankets and furs. A waterskin. Someone's comb, a heavy sock, a discarded hat. A scent. Not Bee's. Bee had very little scent. No this was Shine's, a fading trace of one of the heavy fragrances she favoured. Sweat masked it but there was enough to know that she had been there. I enlarged the slash and crept into the tent. The scent was strongest in the corner, and on the furs next to hers, I caught the faintest whiff of Bee's elusive scent. I picked up a blanket, held it to my face and inhaled her. Bee. And the smell of sickness. My child was ill.

Captive. Ill. And gone. The cold-hearted assassin in me warred with the panicked father. And suddenly they merged, and any doubts I had felt about what I could or must do to get Bee back vanished forever. Anything. That was what I could do to regain my child. Anything.

I heard sounds outside the tent. I froze, breathing silently. Then I edged back out of the tent to where I could see the campsite. A Chalcedean soldier had just tumbled some pieces of firewood down next to the burned-out campfire nearest one of the smaller tents. He was leaning on a sword. As I watched, he went down on one knee with a groan. His other leg, bandaged stiff, hampered him as he sank down to stir the ashes. He leaned forward to blow on them. After a moment, a tiny trickle of smoke rewarded him.

He broke bits from the wood he had brought and fed his fire. When he bent forward to blow on it, his hair dangled down in a fat blond braid. He muttered a curse as he drew it away from the flame and tucked it into his hat.

There was a sudden stirring from the other tent. An old man, his greying hair wild around the edges of his woollen hat, emerged. He moved stiffly. 'You! Hogen! Make food for me.'

The man building up the fire did not respond. It was not that he ignored the man. It was as if he had not heard him. Deafened somehow? What had happened here?

The old man shouted, and his voice rose to an infuriated screech on the words. 'Pay attention to me! Hogen! Cook up some hot food for me. Where are the others? Answer me!'

The one he called Hogen did not so much as turn his head. Instead, he picked up his sword and using it awkwardly levered himself upright again. Without a glance at the shouting man, he limped over to the horses. He checked their picket line, and then looked off into the forest as if he were expecting someone. Then he limped off toward a fallen tree whose dead branches protruded above the snow. He waded slowly through the unbroken snow until he reached it. He began to attempt to break more firewood from it. He was working one-handed as he leaned on his sword

for support. No. Not his sword. My sword. With a start of recognition, I knew the blade as the one that had hung over the mantel
in my estate study for so long. Now it served as a crutch for a
Chalcedean mercenary.

'Answer me-e-e-e!' the old man was roaring at the soldier
who paid him not a whit of attention. After a moment, he
ceased his yelling. He stood still, chest heaving in frustration,
and then stalked over to the fire. He opened gnarled hands to
it, and then threw another piece of firewood onto it. There was
a leather bag on the ground by the fire. He rummaged through
it and drew out a stick of dried meat. He stared at the soldier
as he bit it savagely. 'When you come back to this fire, I'm going
to kill you. I'm going to run my sword through your guts, you
traitorous coward! Then let's see you ignore me.' He took a deep
breath and roared, 'I am your commander!'

I unslung my battleaxe from my back and hefted it. Then,
stepping softly but not hiding, I crossed the unbroken snow into
their camp. The old man was so intent on shouting Chalcedean
obscenities at the soldier that he did not see me until I was almost
within axe range. Obviously he was not accustomed to being
ignored or disobeyed. An officer then. When he glimpsed me,
startled, he shouted a warning to Hogen. I shifted a glance that
way. Hogen did not behave as if he'd heard him at all. The old
soldier swung his gaze back to me. I met his gaze. I did not make
a sound.

'You can see me!'

I gave him a nod and a smile.

'I am not a ghost!' he announced.

I shrugged at him. 'Not yet,' I said softly. I hefted the axe
meaningfully.

'Hogen!' he roared. 'To me! To me!'

Hogen went on wrestling with a branch, working it back and
forth in a vain attempt to break it free from the fallen tree. I
widened my smile.

The old man drew his sword. I found myself looking at the
point of Verity's sword. I had never seen it from that vantage.
My uncle's sword, his last gift to me, carried by me for many years.
And now it threatened me. I stepped back. I'd happily chop the

man to pieces, but wanted nothing to mar that fine blade. My apparent retreat lit sparks in the man's eyes. 'Coward!' he shouted at me.

I breathed the words to him. 'You raided my home. That's my blade you are holding. You took a woman and a little girl from my home. I want them back.'

It infuriated him that I whispered. He scowled, trying to make out my words, then shouted, 'Hogen!'

I spoke softer than the wind. 'I don't think he hears you. I don't think he sees you.' I threw down my wild guess. 'I think their magic-man has made you invisible to him.'

His mouth sagged open for an instant and then he clapped it shut. That barb had struck true. 'I'll kill you!' he vowed.

I shook my head at him. 'Where are they? The ones you stole from me.' I breathed my question at him, moving silently sideways and his eyes tracked me. He kept his sword at the ready. How good was he, I wondered? I gauged his age and how stiffly he moved.

'Dead! Dead or run away with the others.' He turned his head and shouted, 'Hogen!'

My smile became mostly teeth. I stooped and seized a handful of snow. I crushed it into a ball and threw it at him. He dodged, but not fast enough. It hit his shoulder. He was stiff. And slow.

He took a step toward me, sword at the ready. 'Stand and fight!' he demanded.

I'd manoeuvred to the far side of the tent, out of Hogen's view. The old man moved slowly, keeping his eyes on me and his weapon up. I rested my axe on the snow for a moment, to see if I could tempt him to charge me but he kept his place. Keeping one hand on my axe, I drew my knife and stuck the blade into the canvas of his tent. I dragged a long cut in it and watched it sag. 'Stop that!' he roared as he saw his shelter destroyed. 'Stand and fight like a man!' I glanced at Hogen. He was cursing and fighting with the tree branch, completely oblivious to us.

I widened my cut in the tent. The old man advanced further. I stooped and reached in through the cut and began to drag his supplies out into the snow. I found a sack of food. I seized it by the bottom and soundlessly flung the contents wide into the deeper snow. I kept one eye on him as I reached in, groped, and found a bedroll. I dragged it out and threw it.

My behaviour was frustrating him. 'Hogen!' He actually screamed the man's name. 'An intruder raids our camp! Will you do nothing?' With an angry glance at me, he suddenly veered and began to stump off toward Hogen. Not what I wanted.

Axe down, knife sheathed. I stripped off my gloves, then took out my sling and the carefully selected stones that went with it. Nice round stones. A sling makes a sound, but not a loud one. The old man was shouting as he went. I hoped it would cover the whirling of my sling. I hoped I could still hit with it. I threaded the loop over my finger, set the stone in the pouch and gripped the other knotted end of the cord. I swung it and then gave the snap that sent my missile flying. It missed. 'You missed!' the old man shouted and tried to hurry. I chose another stone. Launched it. It went winging through the trees.

Hogen was trudging back to the camp, awkwardly, using my wall-sword as a crutch and gripping the ends of several branches under his arm as he dragged them back to the fire. My third stone struck a tree trunk with a loud thwack! Hogen turned toward the sound and stared. The old man followed his gaze and then turned to look at me. And my fourth stone glanced off the side of his head.

He went down, half-stunned. Hogen had resumed his trek toward the camp, dragging his firewood. He passed an arm's length from his fallen leader and never once looked aside at him. Using the tent for cover, I slipped toward the forest and circled the camp. My prey had fallen onto his back in the deep snow. He was thrashing feebly, disoriented but not unconscious. Hogen had his back to us. He had dropped his branches near the fire and was examining the slashed tent and scattered supplies in consternation. I raced toward the downed man.

He was struggling to sit up when I dived on him. He gave a wordless cry and groped for the sword. Wrong tactic. I was inside the range of it and I let all my frustration power my fists. I hit him hard in the jaw, and his eyes went unfocused. Before he could recover I rolled him face down in the snow. I caught one of his flailing hands and took a tight wrap around his wrist with the sling cord. I had to set my knee between his shoulder blades and struggle before I could catch and control his other arm. He was old and half-stunned, but also tough and fighting for his life. When I finally controlled his other arm, I took two tight loops of the sling cord around it at the elbow and then bound it as tightly as I could to his other wrist. Elegant it was not but I hoped it was as uncomfortable as it looked. I checked my knots, and then rolled him onto his back on top of his bound arms. I picked up Verity's sword, seized him by the back of his collar and dragged him kicking through the snow. He came to himself enough to shout obscenities at me and call me, with absolute truth, several different varieties of bastard. I welcomed his shouting. While Hogen was unable to respond to hearing it, it might mask whatever small sounds I made as I panted and heaved to haul him well away from the camp.

I stopped when I could no longer see the tent or the campfire. I let go of him and stood, my hands on my knees, catching my breath. I tried to judge how much time I had alone with him. The other mercenaries might be returning. Or might not if they'd encountered the Ringhill Guard. Riddle, Lant and Perseverance might be coming. Or they might not. It was entirely possible that they'd chosen to follow the direct road to Salter's Deep. I evicted these thoughts from my mind and crouched down in the snow next to my captive. I pushed my Wit-awareness down. I did so reluctantly, knowing it would leave me more vulnerable to stealth attack. Yet it was essential that I quench shared sensations in order to be able to do what I needed to do.

'Now. We are going to have a conversation. It can be friendly, or it can be very painful. I want you to tell me everything you know about the pale folk. I want to know all about the day you invaded my home. Most of all, I want to know about the woman and the girl that you took from my home.'

He cursed me again, but not in a very inventive way. When I wearied of it, I scooped a great handful of snow and pushed it into his face. He sputtered and shouted, and I added more until he grew silent. I sat back on my heels. He shook his head and dislodged some of it. Some had melted and was running down his wet, red face. 'That doesn't look comfortable. Would you like to talk to me now?' He lifted his head and shoulders as if he would sit up. I pushed him back down and shook my head at him. 'No. Stay as you are. Tell me what you know.'

'When my men return, they will cut you to ribbons. Slowly.'

I shook my head. I spoke Chalcedean. 'They won't return. Half lie dead in that camp. The one you have left can't hear or see you. Any that fled have run into the Buck troops by now. Or if they made it to Salter's Deep, they found the ship has been moved. Would you like to live? Tell me about the captives you took from my home.'

I stood up. I set the point of Verity's sword in the soft spot just below his sternum. I leaned on it, not hard enough to make it penetrate the fur and wool he wore but hard enough to hurt. He kicked his feet wildly and yelled a bit. Then, abruptly, he went limp in the snow and glared at me. He folded his lips stubbornly.

I was unimpressed. 'If you won't talk to me, you're useless. I finish you now, and go after Hogen.'

The crow cawed loudly overhead and then suddenly swooped down to perch on my shoulder. She cocked her head and stared down at my captive with one bright black eye. 'Red snow!' she rejoiced.

I smiled and tipped my head toward her. 'I think she may be hungry. Shall we give her a finger to start with?'

Motley sidled closer to my head. 'Eye! Eye! Eye!' she suggested rapturously.

I tried not to show how unnerving that was for me. I had not taken my weight off the sword. The tip of it was slowly and inexorably nudging its way through the layers of clothing that protected him. I watched the corners of his eyes and the set of his mouth. I saw him swallow, and in the instant before he tried to roll out from under it, I kicked him as hard as I could just where his ribs ended in the softness of his belly. The sword sank through clothing and into flesh. I did not let it go too deep. 'Don't.' My word was a pleasant warning.

I leaned over him, Verity's sword still in his wound and made a suggestion. 'Now. Start at the very beginning. Tell me how you were hired and for what. As long as you are talking, I won't hurt you. When you stop talking, I will hurt you. A lot. Begin.'

I watched his eyes. His glance darted once to the camp. Once to the crow. He had nothing. He licked his chapped lips and spoke slowly. I knew he was trying to gain time for himself. I had no objections.

'It began with a message. Almost a year ago. A pale messenger came to me. We were surprised. We could not decide how he knew where to find our camp. But he had found us. He came with an offer of a great deal of gold if I would perform a service for people who called themselves the Servants. They were from a distant country. I asked how these far-away people had heard of me, and he told me that I had figured in many prophecies in their religion. He said they had seen my future, and over and over, they had seen that if I did as they willed, not only did great good come to them, but I achieved the power that I had rightfully earned. In their prophecies, I was a figure of change. If I did what they asked, I would be changing the future of the world.'

He paused. Obviously, he had been flattered by such claims and perhaps expected that I would be impressed. He waited. I stared at him. Perhaps I jiggled the sword a tiny bit.

He grunted breathlessly. I smiled at him and he resumed. 'He assured me that helping them with their task would put me on the path to glory and power. The path. They spoke so often of "the path". He came with funds, asking me to bring a picked force of men and come with him to a port in the Pirate Isles. There he had an army of soothsayers and visionaries, ones who could guide us to success because they could foretell what would be our best tactic. They could pick "the one path of many" that would best lead us to success. And he hinted then that they had with them a very special person, one who could make it impossible for us to be seen or tracked.'

I heard the sounds of a hatchet working on firewood. The lad had finally found a tool. The crow had moved to perch in a tree over my captive. She cawed at him derisively.

'And you believed that?'

He looked at me almost defiantly. 'It was true. They showed us. When we travelled to the Pirate Isles. He made one of my men forget where the door to the room was. He made another forget his own name. They put food on the table, hid it from us, and then revealed it again. We were amazed. They had a ship and a crew there. They gave us the gold they had promised us just for coming to speak with them. They promised that if we helped them find the Unexpected Son, they would give us more gold, much more.' He scowled darkly.

'Only one part I disliked. The one who bargained with us in the Pirate Isles was a woman. We had not expected that. The messenger they sent to us first was a man. Then when we were shown the man who could do the magic, he was a soft and pudgy creature, one who quivered and cowered to the woman's commands. This made no sense to us. Why would a man of such power not do as he wished in the world?'

I wondered that myself but did not speak.

'I am cold,' he said into my silence. 'As you said, I am old. And I have not eaten since yesterday.'

'It's a hard world. Imagine being a child torn open by a rapist. I have as much mercy for you as you had for her.'

'I did nothing to a child!'

'You allowed it to happen. You were the commander.'

'It was not my doing. Have you ever been in battle? A thousand things happen at once.'

'It was not a battle. It was a raid against an unguarded home. And you stole a little girl. My child. And a woman who was under my protection.'

'Heh. You blame me when you were the one who failed to protect them.'

'That's true.' I eased the sword a finger's breadth deeper into his chest and he shrieked out loud. 'I don't like to be reminded of that,' I told him. 'Why don't you go on with your story? About how proud Chalcedean soldiers sold themselves like whores for gold to be the servants of a woman and a soft man?'

He said nothing and I turned the sword slightly in his chest. He made a sound as if he would vomit.

'I am not just any commander, not just any man!' He drew breath and I eased the sword slightly from its burrow. Blood welled. He bent his head to see it and began to pant. 'I am Ellik. I was second only to the Duke of Chalced when he sat his throne. He promised me that I would follow him in ruling Chalced. I was to be Duke Ellik of Chalced. Then the damn dragons came. And his whore of a daughter, she who was given to me by her father, turned against her own people and proclaimed herself duchess! She squats on my rightful throne! And that is why I sell my sword. So I can regain what is rightfully mine! That is what they saw, those pale prophets and soothsayers! It WILL come to pass.'

'You are boring me.' I squatted next to him, put my sword aside and took out my knife. I held it up and studied it. Long and sharp. I caught the winter light on the blade and tilted it so it travelled. 'So. The woman and the child.'

He panted for a time. I made a gesture with my knife and he shook his head wildly. He gasped in air and spoke in short bursts. 'We came on a ship. We hid with our weapons as her crew brought it into port. We thought there would be questions . . . at the docks, tariffs and . . . demands. But there was nothing. It was as if we were not there at all. The soft man led us . . . and we trooped off the ship and . . . offloaded the horses and . . . rode off through the town. And not a head turned toward us. We were like ghosts. Even when we all began to laugh . . . and even to shout at the people on the street. No one saw us.'

For an instant, his eyes rolled up, showing too much white. Had I gone too far? The blood from the sword-hole seeped and darkened his shirt. He gave another gasp and looked at me.

'She told us where to go. The boy kept us hidden. We soon chafed with it. We stole the sleighs and the teams. The pale folk knew exactly where to find them. We passed through towns unseen: fat, rich towns. So much we could have done – taken. But that woman, always saying, No. And no. And no. And each time, to my men, I said No. And they obeyed. But they thought less of me. And less. And I felt . . . odd.'

He paused and for a time he was silent, breathing noisily through his nose. 'I'm cold,' he said again.

'Talk.'

'We could have taken anything. Could have gone to Buckkeep. Taken the crown off your king's head if that boy had been ours to rule. We could have gone back to Chalced and walked in and killed that whore who squats on my throne. If the boy favoured us over her. My men knew that. We spoke of it. But I could not do it. We just did as she told us. So we went to that place, that big house.' He moved his eyes without shifting his head to look up at me. 'It was your home, wasn't it? Your holding?' He licked his lips and for a moment, avarice shone in his eyes. 'It was rich. Fat for the taking. We left so much. Good horses. The brandy kegs. "Take only the son" she said. And we obeyed like slaves. We took the boy and his maidservant and turned back toward our ship. Moving through your land like sneaking cowards.'

He blinked. His face was getting paler. I found I didn't care.

'Then. I knew. She was using the boy on me. Clouding my mind. To make me weak. To enslave me! So I waited. And we planned. There were times when my mind was clear, when the boy was using his magic on others. So I waited until the magic-boy was away from her and me. I knew it would happen. I made it happen. I sent him off with my men. And while he was working on the town, not thinking of controlling me, I confronted that woman. I put her in her place, and I took her magic-boy from her. It was easy. I told my men what to say to him and he believed us. We kept him at our fireside and tried to wake the man in him. The next day, we tested him. We raided the town, in broad daylight, with no challenge from the inhabitants. We simply told Vindeliar it was what the woman wished him to do. To enjoy himself for that one day. To take whatever he wanted in the town, to eat whatever he wished. He asked us if it were his true path now. We told him it was. It was so easy. He was foolish, almost simple. He believed us.'

He coughed. 'It could have been so good. If not for that stupid woman. That stupid woman. She had the real prize. That boy that could cloud minds. But she didn't use him as she could have. She wanted . . . your son.'

I didn't correct him. 'What became of the captives? The woman you took, and the child?'

'Disrespectful little rat. I knocked him down. Ugly little bastard. Those staring eyes. All his fault that it fell apart.'

It took everything I had not to shove my knife in his eye. 'Did you hurt him?'

'Knocked him down. That was all. Should have done more. No one speaks . . . to me . . . like that.'

He took a sudden gasping breath. His lips were going dusky. 'What happened to him?'

He laughed. 'I don't know. That night it all went wrong. That damn Hogen. Whining and sniffling for a woman like some table-fed lapdog. So I gave him one. One he deserved. She screamed a lot. Someone brought the magic-boy over. He stared. We asked if he'd like a turn. Then that woman. Dwalia. She came running over, shouting that we had no honour. That we were not men at all.' He rolled his eyes toward me. 'I could stomach her no longer. Two of my men seized her, for she came at me with her claws out. And I had to laugh at her, held between them, struggling, those plump breasts and that round belly jiggling like a pudding. I told her that I thought we could prove to her that we were men. We began to strip her. And it all . . . went bad. The fear. I think it was the boy. He was more tightly bound to her than we thought. He swamped us with his own fear. Fear everyone felt. The pale folk were screaming. They scattered like rabbits. That woman, Dwalia. Shouting at them. Shouting at her magic-boy. Telling him to forget everything we'd promised him, to forget me and return to the path.'

He turned his whole head to look at me. His greying hair had come free of his wool cap to hang in wet locks around his face. 'My men forgot me. I stood and shouted my orders, but they ran past me as if I didn't exist. They released Dwalia. Perhaps they could not see her any more. She called to the magic-boy and he went to her like a whipped dog.'

He shook his head against the snow that pillowed it. 'No one heard me. A man crashed into me, picked himself up, and kept on running. The men chased the pale folk. They were like mad things. The horses broke loose. Then . . . then my men began fighting each other. I shouted my orders. But they did not obey me. They did not hear me. Or see me. I had to watch. My men, my chosen warriors, brothers-in-arms for more than four years . . . They killed each other. Some of them. Some ran. The boy drove them mad. He made me invisible to them. Maybe Dwalia and the boy didn't realize that I was the only thing keeping my men in check. Without me . . . Dwalia fled and left the others to their fate. That's what I think.'

'The woman and the child you took from my home. What did they do? Did the pale folk keep them?' He smiled at me. I set the edge of my blade to his throat. 'Tell me what you know.'

'What I know . . . what I know very well . . .' He fixed his eyes on mine. His voice had fallen to a whisper. I leaned closer to hear him. 'I know how to die like a warrior.' And he surged suddenly up against my blade, as if to cut his own throat. I pulled my knife clear of him and sheathed it.

'No,' I told him pleasantly. 'You don't die yet. And you don't die like a warrior.' I stood and turned my back on him, leaving him trussed like a hog awaiting slaughter.

I heard him take in a great breath. 'Hogen!' he roared. I stood up and backed away from him with Verity's sword in my possession. Let him shout as much as he wanted. I wagged a remonstrating finger at him as he yelled again and then turned back to my second target. Sword or axe? Suddenly it seemed as if Verity's sword was the only choice for this.

Hogen had lifted his head and was looking through the forest toward the distant road. So he expected the others to return. No sense in waiting until I was dealing with more than one person.

My years of doing quiet work had convinced me that surprising my target was most often my best technique. Sword drawn, I approached him stealthily. What made him turn? Perhaps that sense that many warriors seem to develop, an awareness that might be a touch of the Skill or the Wit or both. It mattered little; my surprise was lost.

Perhaps my second best technique was to challenge a man who could not stand without leaning on the sword he had looted from my wall. Hogen saw me, dropped his hatchet, seized the sword that he had planted in the snow and challenged me with it. I stood still, watching him balance on one good leg, holding the sword at the ready. I smiled at him. He could not fight me unless I brought the battle to him; he could neither advance nor retreat on his injured leg unless he used the sword as a cane. I stood and watched him until he lowered the sword to touch the snow. He tried not to lean on it too obviously.

'What?' he demanded of me.

'You took something of mine. I want it back.'

He stared at me. I studied him. A handsome man. White teeth. Bright blue eyes. His long wheat-coloured hair hung in two smooth plaits with a few charms braided in. Every hair stood up on my body as I recognized who he must be. The 'handsome man' who had raped the women of my household. The one who had attacked Shine, and in turn been attacked by the pale folk. And now he was mine.

'I have nothing of yours.'

I shook my head at him. 'You burned my stables. You hacked your way through my home. You took that sword from my cousin Lant. You raped women of my household. And when you left, you took a woman and a child. I want them back.'

For a moment he stared. I advanced a step. He lifted his blade but the pain it cost him showed in his face. That pleased me so much. 'How long can you stand on one leg, holding a sword? I think we will find out.' I began to walk slowly around him. Like a wolf circling a hamstrung elk. He had to hop and hitch to keep his eyes on me. The tip of the sword he held began to waver. I spoke as I walked. 'I had a nice discussion with Commander Ellik. You don't remember him, do you? You don't remember the man who led you here from Chalced. The man who convinced you to serve the Servants, to come to my home to kidnap a child and a woman. Ellik. That name means nothing to you, does it? The man who once thought he'd be Duke of Chalced.'

Every time I said the name Ellik, he flinched as if poked. I herded him now, as if I were Shepherd Lin's dog. Step by limping step, he retreated from the fire, from the trampled snow of the campsite toward the unbroken snow of the forest.

I kept talking. 'Do you remember the raid on my home? The woman you tried to rape, the pretty girl in the red dress with the green eyes? You remember her, don't you?'

A flicker of wariness in his eyes and a droop of dismay on his lips.

'I've come to take blood for blood, Hogen. Oh yes, I know your name. Commander Ellik told me. I've come to take blood for blood, and to give pain for pain. And to help you remember. You took that wound to your leg from your fellow mercenaries. They had sworn to you, sworn to one another, and of course sworn to Ellik. Commander Ellik. Who thought he would be Duke Ellik.'

The flinch and the lack of focus were what I watched for. The third time I said the name, I struck. The point of the sword was already drooping and, as he shuffled to face me, I stepped in abruptly, beat down his guard and struck off three of his fingers. The sword dropped into the snow. He cried out aloud and hugged his mangled hand to his chest. In the next instant, he stooped and tried to seize the sword with his remaining hand, but I stepped in close and kicked him in the chest. He fell back in the deeper snow. I stooped, seized the fallen sword and held it. Both my swords reclaimed. I wished I held my child instead.

'Talk to me,' I suggested pleasantly. 'Tell me about the hostages you took. What became of them, the woman and the little girl?'

He stared at me from where he sat in a snowbank. 'We took no little girl.' He was instinctively holding tight the wrist of his maimed hand. He cradled it to his chest and rocked back and forth as if it were his child. He spoke through clenched teeth. 'Coward! You've no honour and no courage to attack an injured man.'

I stood both swords in the snow behind me. I drew my belt-knife again and crouched beside him. He tried to sidle back from me but the deep snow resisted him and his stiffly-bandaged leg hampered him. I smiled as I waved my blade toward his crotch. He went paler. We both knew he was completely at my mercy. I shook his blood from my glove, letting it spatter him. I spoke softly but clearly in my best Chalcedean. 'You came to my home. You stole my sword. You raped women in my household. I am not going to kill you, but when I am finished you will never rape anyone again.'

His mouth fell open. I touched my finger to my lips. 'Quiet. I am going to ask you a question. You will answer right away. Do you understand me?'

He was breathing in gasps.

'You have one chance to remain a man.' That was a lie, but one he was eager to believe. I saw hope startle in his gaze. 'You took a child from my home. I am here to take her back. Where is she?'

He stared at me, eyes wide. Then he shook his head. He could barely get words out for terror. 'No. We took no girl.'

I glared at him. I whetted the blade of my knife on my leg. He watched it. 'You did. You were seen. I know this is true.' Oh. Silly me. 'You thought she was a boy. You took a woman, and you took my little girl. Where are they?'

He stared at me. He spoke slowly, perhaps from pain, perhaps to be sure I understood him. 'There was a big fight. Many of us went mad. We had hostages . . .' His eyes were suddenly confused. 'They ran away. The others pursued them. They'll be back once they catch them.'

I smiled. 'I doubt that. They don't remember Commander Ellik either, I'll wager. I think that each man of them will catch whatever he can and keep it for himself. Why come back to share with you? What good are you to them? Oh. Maybe the horses. They might come back to take the horses from you. And then they will leave you here.

'Tell me about the child you took. And the woman you tried to rape.' I spoke each word in careful Chalcedean.

He shook his head. 'I didn't. There was no little girl. We took only—'

I leaned forward. I smiled. 'I think a rapist should look like a rapist instead of a handsome man.' I set my knife to the bottom of his left eye socket. He caught his breath and held very still, thinking it was a threat. Foolish man. I sliced him from eye-socket to jaw. He shouted and thrashed away from me. Blood began to sheet down his jaw and the side of his neck. I saw his eyes roll back as he struggled not to faint from the pain. Fainting, I knew, has nothing to do with courage. The right amount of sharp pain and anyone will faint. I didn't want him to become unconscious but I did want him to fear me. I leaned closer to him and set the tip of my knife to his groin. He knew now that some things were not merely threat.

'No!' he shouted and tried to scoot away.

'Tell me only about the woman in the red dress and the child with her.'

He took three slow shallow breaths.

'Truth,' I suggested to him. I leaned on the knife a little. I keep my knives very sharp. It sliced the fabric of his trousers.

He tried to crawl backwards in the snow. I leaned on it harder and he grew still.

'Tell me everything,' I suggested.

He looked at his groin. His breath was coming in small pants. 'There were little girls there, at the house. Pandow has a taste for them. He raped one, perhaps more. I do not think he killed any of them. We did not take any of them.' He scowled suddenly. 'We took very little from that house. I took the sword. But we only took two captives. A boy and his servant. That was all.' I saw confusion grow in his eyes as he tried to assemble his memories of the raid while not remembering Ellik.

'Where is the boy, and his servant?' My knife widened the slash in his trousers.

'The boy?' he said as if he could not recall what he had just told me. 'The boy is gone. With the others who fled. They went in all directions, running and screaming.'

'Stop.' I held up a hand. 'Say exactly what happened when you lost your captives. From the beginning.'

I lifted my knife blade and he took a long shuddering breath. But quick as a cat I sprang closer to him. I set the tip of the blade to the hollow beneath his eye on the good side of his face. He lifted his bloody hands to defend himself. 'Don't,' I suggested, and forced him to lie back in the snow. Then I cut him. Not deeply, but enough to wring a tiny shriek from him.

'Softly,' I said. 'Now.'

'It was night. We were drunk. Celebrating.' He paused suddenly. Did he think he would keep a secret from me? 'Celebrating what?'

He took several breaths. 'We had a prisoner. One that could do magic. Could make people not see us . . .' His voice trailed away as he tried to make sense of shredded and dangling recollections.

'I hate you,' I told him affably. 'I enjoy hurting you. You might not want to give me an excuse to make you bleed more.' I cocked my head at him. 'A rapist does not need to be handsome. A rapist does not need a nose. Or ears.'

He spoke quickly. 'We had the soft man. The man who looks like a boy. Vindeliar. The one who can make you forget things. We'd separated him from the pale folk and convinced him to enjoy himself. To use his magic for things he might want to do. We wanted to make him like us and think we were his friends. And it worked. He was worth more to us than any of the others, more than anything they offered us. We were going to take them all back to Chalced, sell them in the market there but keep the magic man.'

A bigger story here, but not one I cared about. 'You were celebrating. Then what happened?'

'I wanted a woman. I should not have had to ask for one. They were plunder, I had a right to my share, and there were plenty of them. But we had not had them . . .' Again, his words dangled. With no Ellik to recall, he would not know why they were working for women, let alone why he had refrained from raping them. He scowled to himself. 'I had to take the ugliest one. The one that most of us thought was probably not a woman at all. But that was the only one . . .' Again, he paused in puzzlement. I let him try to gather his threads.

'She started screaming before I even touched her. She fought so hard when I tried to strip her. If she hadn't, I wouldn't have . . . I did nothing to her that a woman is not meant to have done to her. Nothing that would have killed her! But she screamed and screamed . . . And someone brought Vindeliar to have a turn . . . I think. I don't know. Something happened. Oh. A woman, older and fleshy, and we were going to have her. But then . . . And everyone went mad. We chased them and hunted them, and the blood . . . and then we turned on each other. Sword-brothers. We'd eaten together, fought side by side for the last four years. But that one that she brought with her, the one who could make the villagers not see us? He turned on us and made us forget our brotherhood. All I could remember were the slights, the times they had cheated me at dice or taken a woman I wanted or eaten more than their share of the best food. I wanted to kill every one of them. I did kill two. Two of my fellow warriors. Two I had taken my oaths with. One slashed my leg before I killed him. Chriddick. He did that. I'd known him for five years. But I fought him and killed him.'

The words were pouring out of him now, heedless of the pain it cost him. I did not interrupt. Where in that mad night had my little girl been? Where were Bee and Shine? Somewhere beyond the camp, fallen bloody in the snow? Captured and dragged off by the fleeing mercenaries?

'The ones who hired us, the pale ones, the white ones? They did not do this to us. They could never have fought us. They were weak, stupid with weapons, with little stamina for the march or the cold. Always, they begged us to go slower, to rest more, to find more food for them. And we did. Why? Why were warriors commanded by snivelling women and sapling men? Because of a dirty magic they put upon us. They made us less than warriors. They shamed us. And then they turned us upon each other.' He gave a noise between a sob and a cry. 'They took our honour!'

Did he hope to win sympathy from me? He was pathetic, but not in a way that roused any pity in me. 'I care nothing for your lost honour. You took a woman and a child. What became of them?'

He balked again. My knife moved, slicing his nose. Noses bleed a lot. He flung himself back from my knife and lifted his hands defensively. I slashed both of them and he shrieked.

'Bastard! You cowardly bastard! You've no sense of a warrior's honour! You know I cannot do battle with you or you would not dare treat me so.'

I did not laugh. I set my knife to the base of his throat. I pushed and he lay back on the snow. Words came out of my mouth. 'Did the women of my holding know your warrior's honour when you were raping them? Did my little kitchen-maid think you honourable as she staggered away from your friend Pandow? When you cut the throats of my unarmed stablemen, was that honour?'

He tried to pull back from the tip of my knife but I let it follow him. With his lamed leg he could no more flee than my little kitchen-girl had. He lifted his bloody hands. I dropped my knee on his injured leg. He gasped at the pain and found blurred words. 'They were not warriors! They had no honour as warriors. All know women can possess no honour. They are weak! Their lives have no meaning save what men give to them. And the others, those men, they were servants, slaves. Not warriors. She was not even right as a woman! So ugly and not even right as a woman!'

He screamed as my blade bit deeper, opening a gash in his neck. Careful. Not yet.

'Strange,' I said quietly when he ran out of wind. I moved my knife up to his face. He lifted his hands. I shook my head. 'My women gave this meaning to my life: I hurt those who hurt mine. Without regard for their imaginary honour. Warriors who rape and kill the helpless have no honour. They possess no honour when they hurt children. If it were not for my women, the women of my household and my serving-men, I would think it dishonourable for me to do this to you. Tell me. How long did it take you to rape one of the women of my household? As long as my knife has been playing with your face?'

He bucked away from me, cutting his own face as he did so. I stood over him and picked up Verity's sword. He was squeezed dry of all information. Time to end it. He looked at me and knew it.

'That night, that night they all ran away. Kerf might know. He fancied the woman in the red dress, mooned about her like a baby that wants his mother. We mocked him. He watched her all the time. Sneaking around in the bushes to watch her pee.'

'Kerf.' One tiny bit of information. 'The magic-boy and the woman who commanded him. What became of them?'

'I don't know. It was all madness and fighting and blood. Maybe they were killed. Maybe they ran away.' He gave a sudden sob. 'I'm going to die here in the Six Duchies! And I don't even remember why I came here!'

Two things happened simultaneously. I heard a horse whinny and the picketed animals answered it. And the crow screamed, "Ware your back!'

My quenched Wit had not warned me. The old training kicked in. Never leave an enemy behind you. I cut Hogen's throat, and went low and to the side as I spun around.

I'd underestimated the old man. Working his hands loose of my sling cord must have limbered his arms, for the stolen sword rang loudly against mine. He was a sight, his wet grey hair wild around his face, his teeth bared in fury. The glancing blow of my stone had purpled his brow and shot one eye with blood. Blood had darkened a swath of his shirt. I had a knife to his sword. I

489

could see Verity's sword behind him, still sheathed in the snow-bank where I'd stupidly left it. He grunted, our blades screamed a kiss, and then he disengaged, caught a breath and swung again. I parried him, but not without effort, and stepped forward and pushed him back hard with my blade. I leapt back. He smiled and took a step forward. I was going to die. He had the reach.

I gave ground and he grinned as he advanced. Ellik was old but he was powered by battered pride and a thirst for vengeance. And, I decided as he made yet another reckless attack, the desire to die as a warrior. I had no wish to assist him in that. I gave ground again. Bloodied as he was, I was fairly certain that I could simply let him attack until he exhausted himself. Fairly certain. Not absolutely certain. I tried to back toward Verity's sword and he cut me off. His smile grew broader. He wasted none of his labouring breath on words. He surprised me with a sudden leap forward. I had to both duck and retreat.

Hoofbeats, muffled by snow. I was not at all certain that I could hold out against the number of riders I could now hear coming. I dared not look to see if they were Chalcedean or the Ringhill Guard. Then someone shouted, 'Get the horses!' In Chalcedean.

Ellik looked aside for an instant. 'To me!' he shouted to his men. 'To me!'

I forced myself to believe that they could not and would not respond to his shout. I had to do something he didn't expect, something stupid in any other setting. I stepped in, beat my knife-blade hard on his sword and very nearly disarmed him, but he managed to step forward and shove me off with a display of strength I had not expected. It so startled me that I felt a moment of giddiness. I sprang back from him, disengaging and had to endure his mocking grin. He shouted then, 'Men! To me! To me!'

As the Chalcedeans swept in on horseback, I doubted that any of them gave him so much as a moment's thought. The riders appeared completely unaware of Ellik. One even passed so close behind him that he was nearly trampled. They must have seen me and yet none of them took time to challenge me, for they were fleeing for their lives. I heard a more distant shout of 'This way, they went this way!' and decided that the Ringhill Guard unit was after them.

The Chalcedean mercenaries were intent only on winning fresh mounts for themselves. They rode straight for the picketed horses, flinging themselves from their spent mounts and each racing to try to seize a horse and be gone. The picketed horses were spooked by the frenzy and danced and pulled at their leads, near-trampling the men in their distress. There were not enough fresh horses for all of them.

'FitzChivalry! Prince FitzChivalry!' The shout came from behind me, and I knew the voice. Perseverance was charging toward me.

'Perseverance! Wait!' And that was Riddle's voice, with panic in his warning.

'Stay back!' I shouted. While I'd been distracted, Ellik had seized his opportunity. He leapt in recklessly, determined to either slay me or force me to kill him. I tried to fall back from him but deep snow and a tangle of brush were behind me. A terrible wave of vertigo swept over me. I barely kept to my feet. I staggered sideways, the deeper snow clutching at me. The weariness that now claimed me could not be denied. I felt a general slackening of all my muscles. My knife fell from my limp hand as my knees folded under me. I stumbled backwards and the snow and the brambles received me.

Ellik never questioned his good fortune. He staggered forward, and the sword from my own home darted toward my chest.

'My lord! FitzChivalry!' And with that shout, I found myself looking up at Perseverance. He'd ridden in and somehow snatched Verity's sword from the snowbank where it had stood. He clutched it as if it were a poker; I saw that he'd never held a weapon before. 'Get back!' I shouted because Ellik was turning and lifting his sword to meet the boy's charge. Verity's sword was too heavy for the stableboy. It wasn't skill. The weight carried the blade down and the horse's charge provided momentum. He more speared than stabbed Ellik. The would-be duke dropped his blade and clutched at the one going into his chest. Perseverance screamed and I saw fury and horror in his face. He came off the horse, clinging to the sword, falling with the weapon onto the collapsing Ellik.

The carris seed was failing me. My heart was leaping like a

hooked fish in my chest. I gasped for air as I fought my way free of snow. I could hear men shouting but I could barely make sense of what was happening. I knew only one solution. I dropped my knife and groped at my waist for the pouch there. A twist of paper, a tiny cone of seeds left in the bottom. I tipped some into my mouth and ground them between my teeth. I shuddered and I thought I would vomit. The world went white and spun. It was all noise and cold and then everything was suddenly bright and light and clear.

I reached for Perseverance, seizing him by the collar and hauling him off the dying Ellik and back to his feet. I stooped, groped in the snow for my knife and sheathed it. I turned, trying to take in what was happening. I saw Lant swing his fancy sword and take off a Chalcedean's arm, sword and all. More shocking was that Riddle was on the ground. The Chalcedean had dragged him off his horse and tried to seize his mount. Lant had saved him.

I stooped and pulled Verity's sword out of Ellik's chest. The man made a sound. He wasn't quite dead. Another thrust finished him. Perseverance was staring at me. His mouth was hanging open, his chest heaving and I feared he would cry. 'Pick up that sword!' I bellowed at him. 'To me! To me, lad!' For a wonder, he obeyed. He picked up the wall-sword and stepped away from Ellik's body. 'Follow me,' I commanded him and he came behind me as I moved toward Riddle and Lant. They had dispatched the Chalcedean who had tried for Lant's horse. Per whistled and his mount came to him. Priss followed, nostrils and eyes wide. 'Secure those horses,' I ordered him. To Lant I said, 'Help him. I don't want any of those bastards riding off on fresh mounts.'

I heard a wild shouting and turned to see my Rousters sweeping in behind the Ringhill Guard. Two lengths behind them came Foxglove and the rest of my guard.

'Capture! Don't kill!' I shouted with all my strength. But one of the Chalcedeans had already gone down, caught between two Ringhill guards and slashed from both sides. Before I could draw breath to shout again, I saw two more fall. The final man got a horse loose and nearly managed to get onto the panicky animal. As I started toward the melee, he fell and was trampled.

'Stop!' I shouted. If anyone heard me, they paid no heed. One of my Rousters was off her horse. She'd put her sword through two of the downed men before I reached her. The third did not require a killing thrust. He was dead.

'WARE!' shouted Riddle. 'Prince FitzChivalry! Guards! Put up your swords!'

I'd never heard him shout like that. He had regained his horse and was thrusting his mount between me and the battle-maddened men I'd heedlessly charged.

'Prince Fitz!' someone else shouted, and suddenly my Rousters were turning to me, grinning and shaking bloody swords, as proud as puppies that had just killed the barn cat. I stared at them. A tremor of fatigue, of giddiness, of drugs and of despair passed through me. I reached up to seize hold of Riddle's thigh. I didn't fall.

'Is Bee here? Is she safe?' Perseverance's voice had gone high and boyish again in his anxiety.

'No,' I said. 'No Bee. No Shine. At least not here.' I summoned every bit of strength that was left to me. My knees were shaky. I drew breath and felt the carris seed surge. 'We organize a search. Now.'

TWENTY-SIX

A Glove

Of the naturally-bred one named Beloved, we have only a brief genealogy. This was due to carelessness on the part of the Servant who received the child at the gates. Although he claimed that he took a complete account of his parentage and siblings, the document either does not exist or was separated from the child and misplaced during his acceptance and orientation time. Some have suggested the candidate himself stole and destroyed the document, but I find this unlikely. His cleverness has been overestimated by far too many of his caretakers.

While at first the child was cheerful and obedient as his family had assured him that Clerres was where he belonged and he would be cared for, as days passed, he became morose and impassive. He shared little with those who attempted to ascertain his lineage. We can say with relative certainty that he had lived with his parents for over twenty years, that all three of his parents were elderly and becoming unable to continue to care for themselves or Beloved. He initially asserted that he had two sisters that he missed badly. Later, he denied having any siblings. An effort to locate them and harvest their offspring for interbreeding with our established pool of those who carry White lineage was not successful.

Thus Beloved remains the only member of his lineage that we have in our records. Our efforts to have Beloved contribute a child to our stock have been in vain. He is stubborn, occasionally violent, argumentative and incites like behaviours in the other Whites if allowed to be in contact with them. When it was decided that he should be marked for easy identification no matter where he might go, he resisted the tattooing process, even to attempting to burn the completed markings from his own back.

While it is an extreme solution, in my opinion he should be eliminated. Even the accounts of his dreams should be excised from the regular listings and placed separately in our records as I judge them to be unreliable reports. His rebellion knows no bounds and he exhibits no respect. It is my considered opinion that he will never be useful to us. On the contrary, he will be destructive, kindle rebellion and disrupt the order and peace of Clerres.

Yarielle, Servant

The first day and a half of fleeing from Dwalia were brutal for Shun and me. We found a tree well the first night, and huddled together there, shaking as much from terror as cold. Close to the trunk of the massive spruce tree, the earth was bare of snow but carpeted thickly with generations of fallen needles. The down-swooping branches were like the walls of a tent. We'd been unable to hide the tracks we'd made crawling into that space. We could only hope that no one would attempt to track us.

In the distance, we could hear screams and angry shouts and a peculiar sound that I could not at first identify. 'Is that sword against sword?' I whispered to Shun.

'The pale people didn't carry swords.'

'Maybe they snatched some up.'

'I doubt it. Here. Put your coat on the ground for us to sit on. I'll open my coat and you sit on my lap and get inside it with me. We might be warmer that way.'

The kindness of the offer startled me as much as how pragmatic it was. As we arranged ourselves, I asked, 'How did you learn this?'

'Once, when I was very small, my grandmother was taking me home from a visit when our carriage wheel hit a pothole and broke something. It was winter and night and our coachman had to ride off to get help for us. She took me inside her coat to keep me warm.' She spoke to the top of my head.

So. Her childhood had included rides in carriages and a kind grandmother. 'Not all of your life has been horrid, then,' I said.

'Not all of it. Only the last four or five years.'

'I wish it had been nicer for you,' I whispered and strange to say, I meant it. I felt closer to her, as if I were older this night or she were younger.

'Sshhh,' she warned me, and I kept silent. Excited and angry cries still tore the forest night. A long scream rose and fell and rose again. I thought it would never stop and I buried my face in Shun's shoulder and she gripped me close. Despite how we huddled, we were still cold. The dark and the forest seemed so huge that I felt we were a stubborn nut that it clutched and tried to crack with cold. I heard a horse galloping and it passed us, and though it was not at all near, I still trembled with fear. At any moment I expected to hear someone shout that they had found us. They would seize us and drag us out and this time there would be no Dwalia to protect us. Or that Vindeliar and Dwalia would come with his misting lies and her soft, cruel hands and claim us to be Servants. I closed my eyes tightly and wished I could close my ears.

No, cub. The ears keep watch while the eyes sleep. So sleep now, but be wary.

'We should sleep if we can,' I whispered. 'Tomorrow we will need to move far and fast.'

Shun settled her back against the tree. 'Sleep then,' she said. 'I'll keep watch.'

I wondered if there was any sense in keeping watch. If they came and found us, could we fight and escape? But maybe it would only be one or two of them. Maybe we could run. Or turn and fight. And kill them. I was cold and shaking, but somehow I fell asleep.

I awoke once in the night to Shun shaking me. 'Move off me. My legs are numb!' she breathed by my ear.

I didn't want to get off her lap. When I moved, it opened her coat and the little warmth my body had stored around itself slipped away into the night. She shifted around, grunting a little as she did, and settled her legs into a different position. 'Sit next to me,' she directed. She slipped one arm out of the white fur coat and I crawled inside it. I put my arm down the empty sleeve and she put her arm around me. My bottom did not like the hard, cold earth. I tugged at my coat and found enough slack to fold an edge up around us. We huddled. The night had become colder, darker, and much more quiet. Two owls began a conversation, and I slid into shivering sleep again.

I woke shaking all over. My toes were numb and my bottom ached and my spine was painful ice in my back. I had buried my face in the fur of the coat, but one of my ears was painfully cold. Morning light was fingering its way through the snow-laden branches that had sheltered us for the night. I listened but heard only the morning challenges of birds.

'Shun. Are you awake?' She did not stir and I felt a bolt of terror that she had frozen to death in the night. 'Shun!' I shook her, gently but insistently. She abruptly lifted her head and stared at me without recognition. Then she gave her head a sudden shake and knew me.

'Listen!' she hissed at me.

'I did.' I kept my voice low. 'Nothing but birdsong. I think we should get up and try to get as far from here as we can.'

We both began to move stiffly. We could not stand upright under the branches. It was hard for me to untangle myself from her coat, and harder for me to pull my coat from under her and wallow my way into it. It was cold and full of fallen needles. I was suddenly hungry and thirsty.

I led the way out of the tree well and Shun wallowed up after me. The winter day was bright and clear and for a moment I stood blinking. Then I scooped a handful of snow and put it in my mouth. It melted into a very small amount of water. I stooped for more.

'Don't take too much at once. You'll chill yourself even worse.'

Shun's advice made sense. I could not have explained why it irritated me. I took a smaller scoop and put it in my mouth. She spoke again. 'We have to make our way home. We can't follow the sleigh tracks back. If they're looking for us, that will be the first thing they'll expect us to do.'

'If they're looking for us?'

'The soldiers quarrelled with the Servants, I think. The Servants will still want you, if any of them survived. But we can hope the soldiers won't care about us.'

'Can't we go to that town and ask for help? Or one of those houses?'

She shook her head slowly. 'They were doing bad things in that town. Making people forget they were there. I don't think we should go there. Because I think that's what they'll expect us to do. And the same for knocking on someone's door and asking for help. I think that today we should walk as far as we can, away from here, but not on a road where we can be seen. And not where people can see us. They might ask people if they've seen us.'

Everything she said made sense but I didn't want her to be in charge of all our plans. I thought hard, trying to be as clever as she was being. 'We should go by ways where it would be hard for a sleigh to follow. Or a horse. Through brushy places. Up and down steep places.'

'Which way is home, do you think?'

'I'm not sure,' I said.

She looked around us and then, almost randomly, said, 'We'll go that way.'

'What if it takes us deeper and deeper into a forest and we die of cold and hunger?'

She gave me a look. 'I'd prefer that to what will happen if they find us. If you want to retrace our tracks and see if they'll take you back, go ahead. I'm going this way.'

And she started off. After a moment, I followed her. It was slightly easier to walk in her broken trail than to force my own way through the snow. The path she had chosen led us up one hill and down the next and away from the mercenaries' camp, and all seemed like good things at the time. As we continued, the hillside grew steeper and the brambles thicker. 'There will be a stream at the bottom of this,' I predicted, and 'Maybe,' she agreed. 'But the sleighs can't come this way, and I don't think the horses would do well here, either.'

Before we reached the bottom, the incline was steep enough that we slid several times. I feared sliding all the way and ending up in water, but when we did reach the bottom, we found a narrow stream that was mostly frozen. The narrow thread of moving water we easily jumped. It reminded me of my thirst, but

I took another mittenful of snow rather than put my bare hand in the water. My heavy fur coat was like walking in a tent. The bottom hem gathered snow and added to my burden.

Shun led us along the path of the stream, moving against the current, until she found an easier place for us to try to climb the opposite bank. While it was easier than it might have been, it certainly was not easy, and the brambles on this side of the stream were savagely thorned. By the time we reached the top of the steep bank, we were both sweating and I opened the neck of my coat.

'I'm so hungry,' I said.

'Don't talk about it,' she advised me, and we hiked on.

As we crested the second hill, my hunger began to tear at my insides as if I'd swallowed a cat. I felt weak and angry and then nauseated. I tried to be a wolf. I looked around the white-swept landscape and tried to find something I could eat. This hill was cleared and in summer was probably used as pasturage for sheep. Not even a seedhead of wild grass peeped up above the snow, and nothing sheltered us from the wind that swept across it. If I had seen a mouse, I think I would have pounced on it and eaten it whole. But there were no mice and a useless tear dared to track down my face. The salt stung on my cold, chapped cheeks. *It will pass*, Wolf Father breathed to me.

'Being hungry will pass?' I wondered aloud.

'Yes. It does.' I was startled when Shun answered. 'First you get very hungry. Then you think you will puke, but there's nothing to vomit up. Sometimes you feel weepy. Or angry. But if you just keep on going, the hunger goes away. For a time.'

I toiled along behind her. She led me across a craggy hilltop and then down into a forested vale. As we reached the trees, the wind grew less. I scooped a bit of snow to wet my mouth. My lips were cracked and I tried not to lick them. 'How do you know about hunger?'

Her voice held little emotion. 'When I was little, if I was naughty my grandfather would send me to my bedroom in the middle of the day, with no supper. When I was your age, I thought it the worst punishment of all, for at that time we had a magnificent cook. His ordinary dinners were better than the best holiday feast you have ever tasted.'

She trudged on. The hillside was steep and so we were cutting across the face of it. At the bottom of the hill, she turned to follow the flat land instead of crossing it and clambering up the next snowy hill. I was grateful but I had to ask, 'Are we trying to find our way home?'

'Eventually. Right now I am just trying to get us as far away from our kidnappers as I can.'

I wanted to be walking back to Withywoods. I wanted each step to be taking me closer to my home and my warm bed and a piece of toasted bread with butter on it. But I did not want to clamber up any more snowy hills and so I kept my peace. After a short time, she spoke.

'But I was never truly that hungry in my grandparents' home. It was after they died and I was sent to live with my mother and her husband that I went days without food. If I said or did anything that my mother's husband thought was disrespectful, he sent me to my room and locked me in. And left me there. Sometimes for days. Once I thought I would die, so after three days, I jumped out of my window. But it was winter and the snow was deep over the bushes below. I was scratched and bruised and limped for ten days, but it didn't kill me. My mother was worried. Not for me, but for what her friends would say if I died. Or simply vanished. She had marriage plans for me. One suitor was older than my grandfather had been, a man with a loose wet mouth who stared at me as if I were the last sweet on the plate. And another family had a son who had no wish for the company of women but was willing to marry me so his parents would leave him and his friends in peace.'

I had never heard Shun speak so much. She did not look at me as she talked, but stared ahead and spoke her words to the cadence of her trudge. I kept silent and she talked on, speaking of being slapped for insolence, of a younger brother who tormented her with surreptitious pinches and shoves. She'd spent more than a year being miserable there, and when she adamantly refused the attentions of both her suitors, her stepfather expressed his interest, cupping a buttock as he passed, standing over her if she sat reading a book, trailing his fingers over her bosom as he became bolder. She had retreated to her room, spending most of her hours there and latching the door.

And then one day she received a message and slipped out of the house in late evening. She met a woman with two horses at the bottom of the garden, and they had fled. She halted suddenly. She was breathing heavily. 'Can you go first for a time?' she asked me.

And I did, and suddenly appreciated the work she had been doing since dawn. I led us by a more winding way, seeking shallower snow in the lee of trees and clumps of bushes. Even so, it was heavier work than I'd been doing and sweat began to run down my spine. I had no breath to speak and she seemed to have run out of words and stories. I pondered what I'd learned of Shun and rather wished she had shared such tales when first she had come to live with us. I might have been able to like her if I had known more about her. When we paused to rest the sweat cooled my body and I shivered until we trudged on.

I did not last as long as Shun had. I told myself it was because I was smaller and had to lift my feet higher at each step to push my way through the snow and work against the drag of my coat. Shun took the lead again when I had slowed beyond her patience and led us on along a widening vale. I hoped desperately for a shepherd's cottage or a farmstead. But I saw no chimney smoke rising and heard only birdcalls. Perhaps sheep or cattle pastured here in summer but they had been herded home to their pens for the winter.

The shadows of the hills began to creep across us as the sun moved and I realized we'd been travelling east. I tried to decide if that meant we were closer to Withywoods but I was too tired and my hunger had begun to creep back, setting claws in my belly and up my throat. 'We should look for some kind of shelter soon,' Shun announced.

I lifted my eyes. I'd been looking only at the backs of her legs. There were no evergreens here, but to the south of us I saw bare-limbed willows along a watercourse. They were grey and twiggy and the snow had penetrated to lie shallowly on the ground beneath them. 'Perhaps under the willows?' I said, and 'If we find nothing better,' Shun agreed, and we walked on.

It began to get darker, and the clear day that had seemed almost kind now seemed crueller as the cold began to descend from the sky. Ahead we could see the brushy line that indicated another watercourse would soon cut our path.

We had good fortune. Evidently that stream ran wild and raging in the spring, for it had cut a deep path through the meadow. Now it ran quietly under the ice, but along the undercut banks, roots of trees trailed down and there were hollows in the earth behind them. They dangled like ropy curtains. We beat the clinging snow off the lower parts of our coats before we pushed the roots aside and forced our way into the earthy darkness.

This is good. Settle here and be safe. I felt Wolf Father relax inside me.

'I'm still hungry,' I said quietly.

Shun was settling herself. She'd pulled her hood well up over her head and had sat down and pulled her feet up inside her coat. I copied her.

'Go to sleep. At least when you're asleep you don't think about food,' she told me.

It seemed good advice and I followed it, resting my forehead on my knees and closing my eyes. I was so tired. I longed to take my boots off. I fantasized about a hot bath and my deep feather bed. Then I slept. I dreamed of my father calling me. Then I dreamed I was home, and meat was roasting on the kitchen spit. I could smell it and I could hear the noises flames make when fat drips into them.

Awaken, cub, but make no sound. Untangle yourself. Be ready to run or fight.

I opened my eyes. It was deep night. Through the droop of my hood and the screen of the roots, I saw flames. I blinked and it was a little campfire by the edge of the stream. A spitted bird carcass was propped over the flames. I had never smelled anything so delectable. Then the silhouette of a man passed between me and the flames. A Chalcedean soldier. They'd found us.

I could have slipped quietly from our den and very slowly crept away but instead I put my hand into Shun's hood and softly patted her lips, and then covered her mouth more fully as she came awake. She struggled for an instant and then abruptly stilled. I made no sound as she pushed her hood back from her face. The firelight reached to paint stripes of shadow on her face as she stared. She leaned over and put her mouth to my ear. 'It's Kerf. The one that said he would help us.'

Caution, Wolf Father warned.

'I don't trust him,' I breathed back.

'Nor I. But he has food.'

She tried to be quiet as she pushed her feet out of her coat, but Kerf turned toward us. 'I know you're there. Don't be scared. I've come to take you home. Back to your family. Come out and eat something.'

His voice was deep and gentle, despite his accent. Oh, how I wanted to believe him. But Shun gave me a small push to show that she would go first. She pushed past our root curtain and then stood straight. 'I've a knife,' she lied. 'If you even try to touch me, I'll kill you.'

'I'm not like that,' he assured her. 'I don't rape women.'

She gave a short, ugly laugh. 'You're saying you're not a Chalcedean? Or that you're not a man?' Her words were edged. Oh, I didn't want her to make him angry. Couldn't we pretend we trusted him until after we'd eaten that bird?

'I am both,' he admitted. His laugh was uglier, bitter and old. 'Though my father might agree with you. He says I stayed too long with my mother, that I should have been removed from her care when I was seven, like his other sons. But he was away at the wars, and so she kept me until I was fourteen. Neither she nor I were happy to see him come home.' He was quiet for a time. He went down on one knee by the spit and turned it a bit. 'For five years, I have shamed and disappointed him. He sent me off with my brother, on this raid, to make a man of me.' Kerf shook his head.

He was not looking at us, and Shun made a small motion, bidding me come out of the den. I did, moving softly, and stood well back in the shadows. 'I'm going to fetch more wood and build up the fire,' he told us, and walked away into the night. We heard a horse snort and stamp. He spoke to it and walked on. Shun made a brief run and leapt the stream. I followed her immediately.

She knelt by the fire. 'I don't think it's cooked yet.'

'I don't care,' I replied.

She took the spit off the fire and waved the bird about to cool it a bit. It flew off the spit and into the snow. I sprang on it, picked it up and tore it in half. Some parts were too hot, some were cold from the snow and some were raw. We ate it standing, making small huffing noises as we hit the hot places. I could hear Shun swallow, and the cartilage crackling in her teeth as she ate the ends off the bones. It was not a large bird and was too soon gone but I found myself panting with relief at the easing of my hunger. 'The horse,' Shun said. I didn't want to leave the fire but I knew she was right. I felt not a morsel of shame for eating his food and stealing his horse. I followed Shun to where we had heard the animals. After the firelight, it took a moment for my eyes to adjust. Two horses. A brown one and a white one, both hobbled. Their saddles were stacked nearby. I looked at Shun. I'd never saddled a horse before. Nor removed hobbles.

'Be careful,' I whispered as she crouched down by the white horse's front legs. I saw her groping for the straps.

'I can't feel how they come off.'

'Take off your mittens.' I was struggling with the saddles. I could barely lift it to drag it. How would I get it up on the horse's back?

'Do they tie?'

'No. They buckle.' Kerf spoke from just behind us. 'Let me put the wood by the fire and I'll unhobble them. If you truly want to go riding off into the dark.'

We froze as we were. I felt only a little ashamed. Shun straightened up. 'I won't be in your debt. You were in league with those who stole us. So we owe you nothing for your righting the wrong done to us.'

'I know that.' He walked to the fire and dropped the wood. He crouched and carefully added a stick. He appeared not to notice that we'd eaten the bird he'd been cooking. 'I'm here for one reason. To take you back to your people.'

'And you expect no favours from me for your "kindness"?' Shun asked sarcastically.

'None.' He looked at her guilelessly. 'I won't deny that I find you beautiful. I think you must already know that from how I look at you. But I understand you owe me nothing. I won't try to take advantage of you.'

It was as if he had stolen all our weapons from us. Slowly we walked back to his fire. I held my dirty hands out to the flames and felt the warmth on my face. He was well supplied. He unrolled a piece of canvas so that Shun and I might sleep on it near the fire. We had to crowd to fit on it, but it was warmer that way. He had another piece for himself, and bedded down on the other side of the fire.

'I still don't trust him,' I breathed to Shun as I hovered at the edge of sleep. She said nothing.

He knew how to get food. The next morning when we awoke, he had already built up the fire and had a lean winter hare cooking over it. I lay still, curled in the weight of my too-large coat and watched him as he did things to his bow and to the arrow that had slain the hare. I wondered if he was the one who had shot at Perseverance and me as we fled. The one who had shot my friend. It was still hard for me to recall parts of that day. The moments when the fog-man had focused on me were all gone. But I knew they had not gone back to look for the boy they had shot. I had only that one passing glimpse of him. I hoped he had returned to Withywoods and not been too badly hurt. I suddenly recalled Steward Revel, dead in the corridor, and a deep sob ambushed me. It woke Shun.

'What's the matter?' she asked, and sat up quickly, staring at Kerf.

'They killed Steward Revel,' I choked out.

Her eyes flicked to me and then back to Kerf. 'Did they?' she asked flatly, but it wasn't really a question. Shun and I had spoken very little of what we had experienced and witnessed that day. We had been too drugged with the brown soup and too focused on getting from one moment to the next. There had been no privacy for comparing what we'd seen. Neither of us had wanted to bare our wounds in front of our captors. 'Stop crying,' she said to me, and by that sharp rebuke, I knew she still considered Kerf our enemy. Show no weakness before him.

She's right.

I rolled my face, rubbing my tears off on my hood and sat up slowly. It wasn't pleasant to move. My muscles ached and moving opened gaps that let in cold air. I wanted to cry. I wanted to throw myself down and wail and weep and scream.

'I only have one cup,' Kerf apologized. 'We will have to take turns with it.'

'You have something to drink from it?' Shun asked.

'Warm broth. Snow-water and the bird bones you dropped yesterday. But we can only make one cup at a time.'

Shun said nothing to that, did not offer thanks or rebuke. Instead we stood, shook our coats back into place. Together we shook and then rolled up the piece of canvas. She handed it to me to carry, a reminder to him that it was ours now. If he was aware of that subtle declaration, he ignored it.

There was little more talk. Shun and I had little to do to prepare to travel, other than eat the hare and drink what he offered us. He melted snow in a tin cup and added the bird bones and warmed it over the fire. Shun drank first, then he made more for me. It tasted wonderful and warmed my belly. I savoured the last of it as he saddled the horses and packed his gear. I watched him load it onto the horses and a vague discomfort stirred in me, but I could not place why it seemed wrong.

'You take the white. I'll put the girl behind me on the brown. He's sturdier and better trained.'

I felt sick. I did not want to be on any horse with that man.

'That's why Bee and I will be taking the brown,' Shun said firmly. She did not wait for a response from him, but went to the horse and mounted it with an ease I envied. She leaned down and reached out her hand to me. I took it, determined that somehow I would get up onto the animal's back if I had to shinny up his leg. But before I could try, the man seized me from behind and lifted me up onto the horse. I had to sit behind the saddle, with nothing to hold onto but two handfuls of Shun's coat. I settled myself silently, seething that he had touched me.

'You're welcome,' he said tartly, and turned away to mount the white. He tugged at her reins and rode away following the stream.

After a moment, Shun stirred the brown and we followed him. 'Why are we going this way?' I asked Shun.

'It's easier for the horses to get up the bank down here.' Kerf was the one who answered me. And he was right. The cut banks eased down to a gentler slope and we rode behind him in the tracks he'd probably made the night before. Once we were on level ground again, he began following his own tracks back.

'You're taking us back the way we came!' Shun accused him.

'You were going in the wrong direction,' he responded calmly.

'How do I know that you're not just taking us back to your camp, back to the other soldiers?'

'Because I'm not. I'm taking you back to your own people.'

For a time, we rode behind him in silence. It was discouraging to see how easily the horses moved through the snow that had so hampered us yesterday. A light wind had begun to blow, pushing a bank of grey clouds across the blue sky toward us. Midmorning, he cast a glance at the sky and turned the horses away from the trodden path. 'Is this right?' I whispered to Shun. My heart sank when she replied, 'I'm not sure. I'm turned around.'

Kerf glanced back at us. 'I promise I'm taking you back to your people. I know it must be hard for you to trust me. But I am.'

The horses moved more slowly through the unbroken snow. We crossed the face of a hill to gain the top of it, and when we did, we looked down on a lightly-forested meadow. In the distance, I saw a road, and beyond it, a small farmstead. Pale smoke was rising from the chimney and dispersing in the wind. I longed to go there, to beg to come inside and be warm and still for a time. As if he had heard my thought, Kerf said, 'We have to avoid the roads and we cannot go through towns or stop at houses. Chalcedeans are not welcome in your land.' Again he turned his horse's head, and we now followed him along the spine of the gently rolling range of hills.

The sun passed overhead and the clouds began to darken as the afternoon passed. Shun spoke aloud. 'I don't think we want to be on these hills if it starts to snow. And we've been riding all day. We should look for a place to stop soon, rather than ride until dark.'

He gave a sigh. 'I've been soldiering for four years now. Trust me. I'll find a good place for us to overnight. Remember, I'm taking you back to your people. You'll be safe with them.' He pointed ahead of us and said, 'Just there, where the evergreens are? We'll go down into that valley for the night.' I looked at a forested hillside where rough stones jutted out of the snow amongst the trees. I finally grasped what had bothered me earlier.

I tugged at Shun's coat and hitched myself closer to speak by her ear. 'That night everyone was screaming and fighting and running away. Why does he have two horses and everything he needs?'

'Not everything,' Shun muttered back. 'No food supplies, no pans for cooking. I think he was just lucky to catch these two horses.'

'Maybe,' I agreed reluctantly. It began to snow, big flakes that clung to our coats and flew into my face. I put my face against Shun's back. My face grew warmer, and the steady rhythm of the plodding horse tried to lull me to sleep. I felt a change in that rhythm and lifted my head. We were riding downhill now, threading our way between the trunks of big spruce trees. Here and there, stones stood up. It came to me that they were worked stone, as if walls and even buildings had once stood here. Our path meandered between the tumbled stones and the down-sweeping limbs of the trees. The snow was shallower here, but sometimes we brushed against one of the drooping branches and triggered a slide of snow.

'Not much further now,' Kerf called back to us, and I felt grateful. I was so tired and sleepy. The trees were blocking most of what remained of the day's light.

Then Shun stiffened in the saddle. 'Not much further to what?' she demanded.

He glanced back at us. 'Your people,' he said.

I had one glimpse of firelight through the trees and then Shun pulled the horse around hard. I clung to her coat, nearly sliding off, as she kicked the horse and shouted, 'Go, go, go!'

But it was too late. Their white coats had been almost invisible against the snow in the dimming light, but there they were. Two abruptly blocked the trail behind us and when Shun tried to rein the horse aside, Reppin jumped and seized its bridle. Shun tried to ride her down but the brown snorted and half-reared and then I was torn free of my grip on Shun's coat as another White seized me and pulled me from the horse. 'I have him! I have the Shayshim!' Alaria shouted.

'Don't hurt him!' Dwalia commanded, coming toward us. Shun was screaming and kicking at the lurik who held the brown horse's head, and Kerf was shouting at her, 'Be calm! You're safe now! I've brought you back to your people!'

'You bastard!' she shouted at him. 'You treacherous wretch! I hate you! I hate all of you!' She tried once more to stir the horse, but Kerf had dismounted and was tugging at her, saying, 'What is the matter? You're back with your people, you're safe now!'

I had ceased my struggling but Shun fought on, shouting and kicking. Vindeliar was there, smiling a warm welcome at me, and I knew then how Kerf had been used against us to do Dwalia's will. Alaria held me captive, firmly gripping the back of my coat and my arm as she pulled me toward the small campfire. I had dreaded to see the soldiers still there, but there was just one horse, a blanket pegged from the ground to a tree as a sort of shelter, and a small fire burning. Dwalia's face was bruised. She rushed at me and seized my other arm.

'Hurry!' she whisper-shouted at the others. 'They are still hunting for us. Two of them passed at the bottom of the hill not long ago. We must get the Shaysim away from here as quickly as we can.' She shook me roughly by the sleeve. 'And don't think to pass yourself off as a boy any longer! A girl. Not what we were sent after. But you're the only coin we have to buy our way back into good graces at Clerres. Hurry! Get her under control! Don't let her scream! She'll bring them down on us if she hasn't already!'

They had dragged Shun from her horse and Kerf had a firm grip on her wrist. 'What's wrong with you? You're safe now!' he kept saying. She bared her teeth at him, still struggling.

'Hold her!' Dwalia ordered the two luriks and thrust me at them. Alaria seized my wrist and Reppin took my other arm. They gripped me between them, holding my arms so tightly that they almost lifted me off the ground. From a pouch at her hip, Dwalia had pulled out a scroll and a single strange glove. I could not tell what it was made from. The hand of it was pale and thin, almost translucent, but to three of the fingertips a shrivelled silvery button had been attached.

'I don't even know if this will work,' Dwalia said, and her voice shook. She unrolled the scroll and held it by the tiny fire. They had shielded it with packed snow on all sides to keep us from seeing it too soon. She had to bend close. She studied something written on it, then straightened and ordered, 'Bring her, bring both of them to the stone. I will go first, then Vindeliar. Alaria, take Vindeliar's hand and grip the Shaysim tight. Reppin, you take the Shaysim's other hand, and also Kerf's. Kerf, bring the woman. Soula, you are last. We'll have to leave the horses.'

My head was spinning. Still caught, still dragged along with them, into ever greater danger. I could imagine no good ending for us. I had no idea why she wished us all to hold hands. Reppin gripped my wrist as if she wished to break it. Perhaps she did. Kerf was not as mean but he had stripped his mittens off to grip my other wrist. There would be no tugging free. I tried. He smiled benignly as I struggled. How had I not seen how dazed he was?

I heard voices through the trees. Chalcedean. They were calling to one another in Chalcedean. 'Now!' Dwalia cried, and she sounded almost hysterical. I could not make out what she intended to do, and then I saw the standing stone that now leaned drunkenly, nearly toppled by the immense spruce that had grown up beside it.

'No!' I cried as Dwalia gripped Vindeliar and reached toward the faded glyph with her gloved hand. 'No, it's dangerous! My father said it's dangerous!' But her hand touched the stone and I saw her dragged in. She did not release Vindeliar and he followed her, and then Alaria. I screamed and I heard an answering scream from Shun. Then, in an instant as brief as a flash of lightning, I saw. I understood. Change it. One tiny chance to change it. Not for me. My escaping was too unlikely. Reppin would never release me, and if she did, they'd come back for me. But I could change it for Shun. I suddenly coiled down, mouth wide, to where Kerf's bared hand gripped my wrist. I bit his forefinger as hard as I could, sinking my teeth into the second joint, tasting his blood as he yelped. He let go of Shun to slap at me but I held tight to his hand, teeth and fingers as I dragged him with me into a tarry darkness dotted with distant stars.

TWENTY-SEVEN

Aftermath

The Black Prophet has likely been at the root of our near failures.
Without his alliance, it is doubtful that Beloved would have enjoyed
any success with his rebellion. Prilkop vanished from our records
generations ago and we are beyond any doubt that his disappearance
was deliberate. Since he was discovered as a natural-born rather than
bred at Clerres, his time at our school was too short to be certain of
his loyalty.

Perhaps the most astonishing part of this disaster has been that both
Prilkop and Beloved returned to Clerres of their own volition. And
initially both he and Beloved were inclined to share a complete and true
report of all their activities. But something in our questions caused both
of them to soon become recalcitrant. When gentler means failed and we
could not lull them into contentment with their situation, we were forced
to move into more energetic methods of questioning them. All know that
knowledge gained by such means is often untrustworthy. We have
recorded separately information garnered from questioning both Beloved
and Prilkop, and recorded as reliable only that which corresponds.

Our knowledge of the travelling stones, of those who made them
and how they were constructed, and even what locations the runes
signify is fragmented but fascinating.

North Countries Gleanings, Lingstra Dwalia

That long, cold day faded slowly.

The lone surviving Chalcedean died quickly. I tried to ask

him about Bee, but he only shook his head and groaned. Any information the others knew had been lost with their lives.

I stood, shaking my head. The commander of the Ringhill Guard, one Spurman, was already giving his men orders to gather the bodies. Foxglove rode over to me. Her face was full of hope as she dismounted. 'No,' I said softly to her unspoken question. 'She was here and so was Shine. But the Chalcedeans and the captives fought a day or more ago. Bee and Shine fled when the Chalcedeans turned on each other. They are at least a day gone, perhaps two. Where they are now, no one seems to know.'

'I'll organize a search,' she replied calmly. 'They can't have gone far. Fitz, we'll find them.'

'So we all hope.' I lifted my voice as I turned to my guard. 'Captain Foxglove will be conducting a search for escaped Chalcedeans. Watch for any of their captives or any stragglers.' I turned a firm gaze on my Rousters, where they had assembled in a rough formation separate from my guard. 'Alive,' I cautioned them. 'Any pale rider in white furs, any captive of theirs, or any Chalcedean mercenary you find, take them alive.'

Foxglove was shaking her head. 'Not likely. We've seen two bodies in white furs. Both looked as if they'd cut their own throats. Probably rather than be taken by the Chalcedeans. We ambushed some Chalcedeans on their way to the ship. And chased what remained of them back here.'

'Do what you can, then,' I said quietly.

I left Foxglove to organize the search while I returned to the tent where Bee and Shine had slept. A more leisurely search of it turned up nothing that I connected to either of them. A very pale Lant had followed me there. He stared at the corner where they'd slept.

'How do you know they were here?' he asked me as Riddle came into the tent.

I picked up a blanket and tossed it to him. 'Shine's perfume lingers on some of the bedding. It's not strong, but it's there.'

He nodded slowly, and held the blanket to his breast. Slowly he turned and left the tent, still clutching it. 'He shouldn't be here,' Riddle said to me in a low voice.

'On that, we agree.'

'I mean that he's injured. And heartsick. Not that he's incompetent.'

I kept silent.

'You're too hard on him, Fitz. He can't help who he is, or what he isn't. I, for one, am glad for what he isn't. And I was very glad of his sword a very short time ago. Nettle was nearly a widow before she was a mother.'

'I don't dislike him,' I said, and wondered if that were true. 'He's just not the sort of man I need backing me right now.'

'Nor am I, then, I suppose.'

I stared at him. He turned and left the tent. I followed. In the thin winter sunlight, he stretched and then turned to look back at me. 'You drugged us and left us. Like discarded baggage. I understand the other two. Per is just a boy yet, and Lant is injured. But why me?'

'I couldn't get them to drink it without your sharing it, too.'

He looked away from me. 'No, Fitz. I can think of a dozen ways around that, from joggling my arm when I started to drink to telling me what you were doing.'

It was hard to admit the truth. 'I didn't want any of you to witness what I might have to do. I didn't want you to see me as . . . what I truly am. What I had to be today.' I glanced toward where Hogen's body had been. Foxglove was there, ordering it dragged away by the Ringhill Guard to join the other bodies piled for burning. I wondered if anyone would notice how I'd mutilated him.

'I think I know who you are.'

I met his gaze and gave him honesty. 'Probably you do. I'm still not proud to have you see it. Let alone watch me do it.' I looked away from him. 'I'd rather that my daughter's husband, the father of my grandchild, not be a party to things like this.'

He looked at me.

I tried to explain. 'Once you are a father, you have to try to be a better man than you truly are.'

He stared. Then he laughed. 'Me especially?'

'No. No, not you. I meant myself. That I tried.'

He clapped me on the shoulder. 'The carris seed is catching up with you, Fitz. But I do know what you mean.'

'How did you know?'

'Your breath reeks of it.'

'I needed it,' I excused myself.

'So. Share with me, now. And let's get started on our own search. If you were Bee and Shine and able to flee, where would you go?'

'I'd probably backtrack to that town, assuming they passed through it.' I passed him the folded paper that had held the carris seed. He shook the few remaining seeds into his palm and then clapped them to his mouth. He chewed.

'Me, too,' he agreed. 'Let's send Lant and the boy and your roan horse on to Ringhill Keep. Have Lant give a report to the Skill-user there to relay to Nettle and Dutiful while you and I begin our search.'

It was past dark when Riddle and I rode through the gates of Ringhill Keep. Our searches had yielded nothing, nor had Foxglove's soldiers discovered anything. Four times, Riddle and I had followed tracks. We'd found one wandering horse that had probably just bolted, a Chalcedean body, and twice the tracks had merged with well-travelled roads. We'd asked in the village, and visited four different isolated farmsteads. No one had seen anything or anyone. By the time we returned to the campsite for a final visit, the area had been so over-ridden that there were no longer any tracks worth following. The smouldering remains of the bonefire gave off a greasy smell. Night was coming on, and I was finished.

As its name suggested, the Ringhill Keep fortification ringed one of the hills that overlooked the coast of Buck. From its vantage, one could watch ships approach Forge, Salter's Deep and the smaller fishing villages that fringed that part of the coast. It was not a grand keep, but like many settlements in Buck, it was growing. We allowed the stableboys to take our horses. I had used Perseverance's mount. The lad had ridden Priss and gentled Fleeter here. I thought of checking on her but as I knew it must, the carris seed had deserted me. I was weary past exhaustion and the dark mood of elfbark had claimed me.

I did my best to be civil as the commander of the keep greeted me. Commander Spurman invited Kesir Riddle and me to join him for a late repast. They put us in the best lodging the keep had to offer, and urged us to take advantage of the steams. I had no heart for cleanliness, but forced myself through the ritual. We shared the steams with a dozen or more guardsmen, still drunk on blood and battle. My efforts to remain unnoticed were useless, and I had to accept congratulations from them.

When we entered the dining hall, I found not only Spurman but a handful of his officers, Foxglove, Lant and several others convened. I had expected a small and simple meal, but Spurman had ordered up the best his keep could offer. For a moment, I was baffled. Then I recalled that I was a prince. Carris seed. My head felt full of wool. Time to tighten my thoughts and be very careful.

I do not know how I survived that meal. I decided it was better to be seen as taciturn rather than a man who made unrelated comments. When the meal was over, I hoped to be able to retreat to my bed, but killing Chalcedeans within Buck was an activity that seemed to require a thorough discussion. Over and over, Spurman and his officers marvelled at the Chalcedeans' audacity and wondered who their peculiar allies had been and what they had hoped to achieve. Riddle, Lant and Foxglove all expressed puzzlement, and I maintained my noble silence. When the talk ran down, the keep's Skill-user found a moment to draw Riddle and me aside. 'A private word before you retire, gentlemen, if you are not too weary?'

I was so tired my ears were humming, but as we bade everyone goodnight and left the gathering, she managed to catch up with us. Out of earshot of the others, she still looked embarrassed as she told us, 'I am to inform you, in the strongest possible terms, that you are to return to Buckkeep Castle as soon as you are able.'

Riddle and I exchanged a glance. 'Was the message from Skillmistress Nettle, or King Dutiful?'

'Yes. She relayed the king's will in this.'

I thanked the Skill-user and both Riddle and I moved slowly toward our rooms. At a bend in the corridor, I asked him, 'How angry is Nettle, do you think?'

'Very,' he said shortly. And in that terse response, I sensed that he wished to keep that aspect of our fiasco private. For a time I was silent. Nettle was pregnant and should have had a time of peace and happiness as she waited for her child. I had driven a wedge between her and Riddle. I tried to tell myself that it was outside my control, that her sister being stolen had destroyed peace and happiness for all of us. I could not convince myself of that.

I walked more slowly. 'Before we go back to Buck, I want to see the ship they came on.'

He shook his head. 'It's not tied up in Salter's Deep any more. It was confiscated days ago. Spurman told me that they removed the ship as part of the ambush. The crew claimed to know nothing except that they'd been hired and paid very well to simply stay aboard and wait for their passengers to come back. They came out of the Pirate Isles, and were hired new to the ship and each other. Most of them seemed glad to walk away from it.'

'No chart on board with Clerres marked on it?' I was half-jesting, but Riddle took me seriously.

'Nothing. Literally nothing. No extra clothing left aboard, not a trinket or a shoe string. Only the crew and their bits of possessions. Nothing to indicate there had even been passengers.'

Despair gaped like a dry well in front of me. I could not indulge in that. I could not curse nor weep. Such things prevent a man from thinking, and I needed to think clearly. I reached the door of my room and opened it. Riddle followed me in.

'So. We return to Buckkeep Castle tomorrow,' he told me.

'So I planned.'

'We are ordered back, Fitz. That's a bit different.'

'Oh.' It took a moment for me to consider all the ramifications of that. Prince FitzChivalry, so recently acknowledged and lauded, was being summoned back to Buckkeep like a recalcitrant page. This was not going to be pleasant for anyone. I grasped abruptly how much of my personal freedom had vanished when Chade had taken my arm and presented me to the court. What had seemed a family matter, my sidestepping my cousin's request that I not go off on my own, now loomed as a prince directly disobeying his king's directive. Dutiful had reminded me he was my king, and I'd admitted that to him. And then done as I thought best, as if I were merely Tom Badgerlock. No. Not even Tom Badgerlock should have defied his king that way. I chewed my lower lip.

Riddle sank down to sit on the edge of my bed. 'I see that you understand.'

I walked to the window and stared out at the lights of Salter's Deep. 'I wish you hadn't been dragged into it.'

'Oh, Fitz, I dragged myself into it. I could have just reported that I suspected you were going alone, and the Buckkeep guards would have brought you back.'

I turned to stare at him. 'Truly?'

He shrugged. 'I don't know. They might have just told me to drag you back quietly. A task that neither of us would have relished.' He gave a small sigh. 'No, I got myself into this.'

'Sorry to have put you in that position.' Loyalty to me or to Nettle, and he'd chosen me. That did not bode well for any of us.

And me? I'd chosen my duty as a father over my duty as a prince to a king. As I knew I would again. As I must.

Bee, where are you? My heart cried out for her, and shame wafted over me. Why couldn't I find and save my child? We'd come so close. I'd seen where she had slept, just days ago.

Riddle's voice jolted me. 'Fitz. This is a terrible question but it must be asked. At what point do we accept that Bee and Shine are lost to us?'

I turned wild eyes upon him. 'Don't even say that!'

'I have to say it. Someone has to ask it. You know as well as I do that they may both be already dead, out in the forest. We have no trail left to follow. The Servants and the Chalcedeans are all dead or fled.' He came to join me at the window. 'We've no clues left to follow. The best we can hope now is that they turn up on their own at a farmstead or inn.'

'And the worst that can happen is that things remain as they are now. With us having no idea whatever became of them.'

For a time, we both stood in silence. I tried to find a thread of hope. 'We did not find Vindeliar or Dwalia,' I reminded him.

'They may be bodies in the forest. Or hiding from us as they did before. They have not left us a trail we can follow.'

He was right. Reality and the bleakness of elfbark welled up in me like blood in Ellik's wound. 'I'm so powerless.' The words burst from me. 'Riddle, I had to come here and try to find her. Since Winterfest, she has been gone and I've been able to do nothing. Nothing! And now I've even less of a trail to follow.' Agony and anger were one force in me. I wanted to smash everything in the room but most of all, I wanted to destroy myself for how impotent I was. I had cut my hair to my scalp when Molly died, a symbolic destruction and punishment of myself because I had failed to save her. Now I wanted to slash my face, to batter my skull against the wall, to fling myself from the window. I hated myself for my total failure. I was a thing that was so useless as to be evil. I was an assassin and capable of torture, a man bereft of goodness. But even my wickedness was impotent. It had gained me nothing.

'I do not like the expression on your face,' Riddle said softly. 'Fitz. You cannot hold yourself responsible. This was a thing that happened to you, not a thing you did.' His voice was sympathetic.

'It was a thing I did not do. A neglected duty,' I said quietly. I turned back to the window and looked down. A drop but not a big enough one. The impulse would not work.

Riddle knew me too well. 'And then if we did find her, that would be the first piece of news she'd have about you.'

Slowly I turned away from the easy exit. 'Tomorrow we leave for Buckkeep.'

Riddle nodded slowly.

Mornings come, whether we want them or not. I dragged my body from my bed and trusted that my herb-addled mind would catch up with me. Breakfast was interminable and full of pleasant conversations I could scarcely follow. Someone had recognized Ellik as Chancellor Ellik of Chalced, and for some reason it was very exciting that a Buck stableboy had made an end of the old man. Spurman assured me twice that he'd sent word on to Buckkeep Castle concerning exactly who had attempted this peculiar invasion of Buck. My weary mind offered me no response for him, so I simply nodded.

And finally, finally, we departed Ringhill Keep. I rode at the front of my guard, with Riddle beside me. Perseverance trailed behind us, still leading Bee's horse Priss. He looked battered and wan. Lant rode beside him. Riddle leaned over and said quietly that the boy had had his first night drinking with men last night, and been feted as a hero for his 'first kill'. He tipped his head toward Lant. 'Lucky for the lad, Lant intervened right after he puked the first time. He forbade any more liquor and sent him off to bed. But I expect he has a bit of a head today.'

I rode Fleeter. The horse seemed to have recovered from my abuse of her, but exhibited a wariness in contrast to her former eagerness to please me. I let her feel that I regretted how roughly I had used her, but did not try to intrude into her thoughts.

Foxglove came behind us at the head of our troops. She was displeased with the Rousters and cool toward me. I could tell that her efforts to integrate them with my guard were not going smoothly. Yesterday her control of them had been tenuous at best. Today as they formed up with my guard, they still remained as a separate rank at the rear of the formation. I suspected that she was unhappy with me for saddling her with such troublemakers. We had not ridden far before Lant edged his mount closer to mine. He spoke while looking straight ahead. 'You humiliated me. You left me drugged and sleeping as if I were a child.'

You are. I shook my head. 'Lant, I left you sleeping as if you were a badly injured man who should not have been sent out on such a mission. That was true of Perseverance as well.' I fabricated some balm for him. 'I could scarcely have left the boy there alone. How is your wound?'

My diversion of the conversation baffled him for an instant. 'It's healing,' he said gruffly.

'Good. It needs time. Lant, I have a suggestion. It's a strong suggestion. When we return to Buckkeep Castle, report to Captain Foxglove. Let her direct you in your swordplay, going gently until your muscles are rebuilt. I do not propose that you become a soldier or a member of my guard.' How to phrase the next part. Become a man? No. I fumbled for words.

'So they can mock me for my lack of skills? So I could fail again for you?'

How had he ever become such a bubbling pudding of self-centredness? Here was another repair task I did not want. 'Lant. Muscles in your chest were cut. They need to heal and then grow strong. Let Foxglove help you with that. That's all I was suggesting.'

He was quiet for a time. Then he said, 'My father is going to be very disappointed.'

'In both of us,' I pointed out.

He sat back in his saddle. I think he took peculiar comfort from my words.

The day passed in a way that would have been pleasant at another time. The weather stayed mild for winter. Fleeter recovered enough of her spirits to want to be out in front of the other horses and I was happy to let her be. Motley flew ahead of us, and circled back to ride on Per for a time, and then flew ahead again. She seemed just a pet crow today, cawing wordlessly as she flew overhead. Once, when she was perched on Per's shoulder I asked her, 'How many words do you know?'

She cocked her head at me and asked, 'How many words do you know?'

Per almost smiled as he said, 'She sounded just like you.'

The well-kept roads avoided the hills and wound through several small towns. In each settlement, we paused to ask for tidings of Bee or Shine, and to tell each innkeeper that there was a large reward for two lost girls. No one had news for us.

That night, we found lodging at an inn. Riddle, Foxglove, Lant and I had rooms above the kitchens and they were warm. My guard and Perseverance had a loft over the stables and the Rousters would sleep in the common room. I enjoyed a well-prepared meal and a mug of ale, and an early bed in a clean room, followed by a late night fistfight when my Rousters did not go to bed but quarrelled amongst themselves. The ruckus awakened me and I pulled on trousers and dashed down the steps two at a time. By the time Riddle arrived, I had a black eye and two men on the floor and a third cornered. We exiled all three to the inn's stables for the night and promised the innkeeper that damages would be paid for. As we climbed back up the stairs, Riddle observed, 'Usually princes don't do that sort of thing.'

'I'm not prospering in this role, am I? All the times when I wondered what it would be like to be legitimate and recognized as a Farseer at Buckkeep Castle? I'm finding it more of a liability than a privilege.'

'You'll get used to it,' he promised me doubtfully.

In the morning, I had two fewer Rousters following me. Well, that was two fewer of them for Foxglove to deal with. They'd taken their horses and left their guard tunics. I counted it a small loss. Foxglove had slept through the row in the tavern and I said nothing of it to her. I was sure that word would reach her soon enough.

The day was overcast with snow clouds and a light breeze that woke sporadically to lift ice crystals against our faces. Riddle and I rode side by side, in a silence full of foreboding. I think we both dreaded our return to the castle. We had resumed our formation of the day before, with Lant and Perseverance riding side by side behind Riddle and me. I heard several snatches of conversation and deduced that their recent battle experience had given them something in common. The boy still led Priss. Her empty saddle was a fresh heartbreak every time I looked at it.

I felt I was going home with my tail between my legs. And somewhere, somewhere was my Bee and I was no closer to knowing where. The morning passed with little talk between Riddle and me. Sometimes the crow flew overhead and ahead of us, and then back as if to be sure we were following her. I had grown so accustomed to her that I hardly noticed her. More often she rode on Per's shoulder though once I was a bit surprised to see her on Lant's.

We crested a gentle rise in the road and saw a rider on a brown horse, trailed by a saddled white horse, on the road ahead of us. I studied them for a moment as they came toward us. The rider was stocky and wore his hood well pulled forward. They were moving at a dogged trot but even at the distance I could tell that the brown horse was being pushed hard and was at the end of his endurance. His head jounced too hard with every step. He tried to slow and his rider kicked him hard. Then Riddle said, 'White horse,' at the same time I said, 'White coat.'

I called back to Foxglove. 'Halt the guard. If I lift my hand, bring them at a gallop. If not, keep your distance.' She nodded, accepting the command but unhappy at not joining us, as both Riddle and I urged our horses to a trot. Lant followed and I knew Perseverance would copy him. I wished they hadn't. I kept my eyes on the rider. At first, he showed no sign he was aware of us. The white fur coat convinced me that this was one of the Servants who had escaped the slaughter. As we got closer, he seemed to rouse himself out of a daze. He looked up at us, screamed and kicked the brown horse he rode frantically even as he tried to wheel it about. It turned to the rider's command and broke into a trot, but we were already in motion and before the trot became a canter, we were on either side of him. Riddle leaned forward and grabbed the reins, turning the horse sharply as the rider continued to scream and kick it. I knew that scream.

'Shine! Shine, stop! You're safe! Shine, it's me, Fitz—Badgerlock! And Riddle. We're here to find you and take you home. You're safe! Shine. Where's Bee? Was she with you?'

The saddled white horse had jigged aside from us. It was evidently only following the brown because it had no idea what else to do. Riddle pulled his horse in, dismounted hastily and approached Shine. She kicked at him, shrieked again, and then fell off her horse and into his arms. I dismounted, took her reins and stood stupidly as he patted her back and told her she was all right, she was safe, she was safe now.

Her wailing slowly faded to deep sobs and then to breathless, shaking weeping. 'Bee? Shine, where's Bee? Shine, look at me. Do you know where Bee is?'

To Riddle's gentle questions, she only shook her head wildly and sobbed louder. A terrible certainty was building in me. The white horse came closer. I ignored it until it stood near enough that with a calm step I could take the end of the dangling reins. Two horses. Two saddles. One rider. No Bee. The saddle on the brown horse was definitely Chalcedean-made. The one on the white horse was like nothing I'd ever seen before. High in the front and low in the back. It looked uncomfortable to me.

Bee, where are you? Did you ride on this horse?

'Tom Badgerlock.'

I turned in surprise. Her voice was thick from weeping. She'd pushed back her hood. Her hair was matted and hung in wads about her face. She'd lost weight, and the boniness of her face made her look more like Chade. Her lips were rough and her cheeks chapped red. She was still breathing hard but she had stepped clear of Riddle. The white fur coat she wore was enormous on her, hanging in folds around her. Her hands clutched her forearms and she hugged her body tight as if she might fall into pieces. She faced me and looked directly into my eyes. This was a different woman than the one who had demanded that all life must stop until we had purchased green stockings for her.

'Bee,' she said. 'They took Bee.'

'I know,' I said. I tried to keep my voice calm and even. 'They took you and they took Bee. But you're safe now.' I drew a breath. 'Bee. Do you know where Bee is now?'

'They took her,' she said again. 'They took her into a stone with them.'

TWENTY-EIGHT

Repercussions

The depredations of this dragon are just as damaging as if we were facing an invasion by a small army. The creature is 'small', I am told, by dragon standards, and yet her hunger seems insatiable. The shepherds dare not put their flocks out into the higher summer pastures, for even with men and dogs watching over them the dragon swoops in and takes what she pleases. As many cattle and sheep die in their headlong flights as by her claws. The best breeding stock of cattle and horses were, for a time, safe if kept within barns or stables, but even that is no longer the case. There have now been three reports of the dragon using claws and powerful sweeps of her tail to demolish buildings to get at the cattle inside.

Will homes and humans be next? The situation is intolerable. As king, you must offer us some kind of solution, whether a negotiation or a military response. There are rumours that Skill-coteries are able to communicate with dragons. Those of my shepherds and farmers who have been brave enough to stand and either offer this dragon selected stock or threaten her have been ignored. At the least, cannot you send a coterie here to attempt to reason with this creature?

From the Duke of Farrow to King Dutiful

I stood as if turned to ice. I tried to make my mouth form words. 'What do you mean?' I managed at last, but I knew what she meant. As impossible as it seemed, there was only one explanation.

'Like you did,' she said. 'They went into a stone, like you did. And they took Bee with them.'

I felt the world halt around me. My ears rang. 'What stone? Where?' I could not find enough air in my lungs to make my questions more than a whisper.

Shine blinked. She spoke quietly, in a puzzled voice. 'He tricked us. The Chalcedean who had seemed kind. He found us and he took us back to Dwalia. And Vindeliar and a few of the others. They were hiding because Chalcedeans were near. Almost as soon as she saw us, she made us all hold hands.' She scowled suddenly. 'As if it was a game. A children's game. Soula held my hand too tight, digging her nails in. The bitch . . .'

Her voice ran down. I held my breath. Let her talk. Ask no questions. I could see how fragile she was, how tenuous her focus on us. She reached toward Riddle suddenly with a shaking hand and her voice went breathy. 'Dwalia took out a scroll. And a glove, a very thin glove with silver on the fingertips. But it wasn't pretty. She put it on. And she touched the stone and—'

'Shun! Sweet Eda be praised! It's you! Shun!'

Foxglove had halted my guard a respectful distance away and the Rousters had bunched behind them. Lant and Perseverance had ridden forward to see why they had halted, and now he flung himself from his horse and raced toward her.

'Lant!' she cried, and then she shrieked, 'Lant! Lant!' She flung herself into his arms and I did not want to see the terrible race of emotions that went across his features. I hoped no one else could know what they meant. He held her, but not as she clung to him. He held her as a thing lost to him, while she wrapped herself in his arms as if she had finally and safely reached home.

'I thought you were dead! I saw them kill you. And then they kidnapped me!' Her dull calm was gone. Safe in his embrace, her hysteria was rising.

'Shine. What stone? Where?' Riddle demanded. He seized her by the shoulders and turned her back to face him. She tried to hold onto Lant's shirt but at Riddle's warning glance, he surrendered her and stepped back. Did he look relieved to have her taken from his embrace? She looked confused and panicky, but Riddle put his fingers on her chin and turned her face to his.

'Shine. Look at me. We may be able to get Bee back right now. What stone did they enter? How long ago?'

She stared at him, blinking once as if she was trying to put her memory in order. I knew that feeling. Her crying had been too intense for tears. Her nose was running and her cheeks and nose were bright red. She finally spoke. 'Last night. Dwalia led them. They all held hands. I was at the end, with Kerf. And Soula. At the last moment, Bee leaned down and bit his wrist. He was so surprised he let go of me. But Bee didn't let go of him. She dragged him into the stone. He went in screaming.' Her voice lifted on her last sentence, as if that gave her satis-faction. She turned back toward Lant, obviously baffled at how he had released her.

Riddle tugged her back to face him.

I tried to keep my voice level and calm. 'Shine. You have to guide us back to that stone. Now. I must go after Bee.'

She moved her gaze slowly from Riddle's face to mine. Her eyes grew flinty and her voice childish. 'You left us through a stone. And then *they* came. You shouldn't have left us.'

'I know that and I'm so sorry. But you are safe now. And we need to find Bee so she will be safe too.' I spoke very simply, as if she were a child. I recalled that fragmented thoughtfulness that follows torture or extreme hardship. Shouting at her would do me no good.

She leaned toward me and whispered, 'No. We have to get far, far away. They may come back out of the stone. And there were still some soldiers roaming the forest there. I left the fire burning to lure them and I took the horse and left as quietly as I could. I wish the white horse hadn't followed me. So easy to see her in the night. I would have killed her to keep her from following if I'd had a knife. But I had nothing. Nothing at all. And it got too dark for me to find my way. So I found a thick grove of trees and hid there until daylight.' She drew a breath. 'I rode through the forest until I found a road. We galloped and galloped until the stupid horse wouldn't gallop any more. And then I found you.'

'You have to guide us back to the stone. See all the guards we have with us? They'll protect you this time.'

She lifted her eyes and looked at the waiting troops. Then she narrowed her expression. 'I don't think I could find that place again. Even if I wanted to. Please. We have to get far, far away from here.'

'We will,' Riddle assured her. 'But first we have to go back for Bee.'

She stared at him, taking deeper and deeper breaths until I feared she would break out into a shriek. 'You don't understand. I can't go back there!' Her eyes grew very round and black. 'After Bee dragged Kerf in. We, we were . . . There were more Chalcedeans nearby. Dwalia had said so. But they went into the stone and left us, Soula and me. And Soula, she started screaming and hitting me, and trying to follow them into the stone. I had to make her be quiet. And . . . she was part of them, the ones that had ruined our home and dragged us away. So I . . . I killed her. I think.'

'You had to kill her,' I said. I could not let her dwell on that. 'You had to kill her, and your father will be so proud that you did. It was the right choice. Shine. What stone?' My heart was racing. Nettle and Dutiful had told me there were no records of Skill-portals in this area. Had they lied to me? I felt a flash of anger, followed by the fear that the stones were unknown because they were defective.

But my effort to reassure her and focus her mind failed badly.

She turned her head slowly to me. 'My father?' she asked dully.

'Our father.' Lant's voice broke on the word and I wanted to strike him. Not now, not now. But he spoke on. 'Lord Chade is your father.'

She blinked at him. The look on her face reminded me of a foundering animal. She would go down soon and with her my chance to find Bee. She spoke slowly. 'Lord Chade is your father, you mean. You told me your secret . . . the night before . . .'

Her eyes widened. No, don't let her thoughts go back to the day she was raped and kidnapped. I tried to keep my voice calm. 'I must know where the stone is, Shine!'

Lant held up a shaking hand. 'Let me speak. Let it be said before your guard gets here. Let me tell her and have it over with! I can bear this no longer.' He looked at her, his face full of tragedy.

'Shun— Shine. You are my sister. Shine Fallstar. Lord Chade is father to us both.'

She stared, her gaze going from me to Riddle and then to Lant. 'It's a poor jest,' she said brokenly. Her bottom lip quivered. 'If you love me at all, you will take me away from here, as fast and as far as we may go.'

Lant gave me an agonized look.

Sometimes it is better to rip off the bandaging quickly. 'Of course he loves you,' I reassured her. 'He *is* your brother. He would never let you come to harm.'

She snapped her head around to stare at me. 'My brother?'

Riddle was staring at us, aghast. Some secrets could not be preserved safely, not without risking terrible consequences. I spoke softly. 'Lord Chade is father to you both.' I took a breath and tried to speak kindly. 'And now you must guide us back to the stone. Where Bee disappeared.'

She gaped at me. Then her head swivelled again and she looked at her brother. What did she see there? The same resemblances I had seen once I had known to look for them? 'Lant,' she said in a fading voice, as if she called to him from across a great distance. And then she went boneless, sliding to the road in a heap. The heavy fur coat collapsed around her and, lying there, she suddenly reminded me of a very thin winter-killed deer. Riddle dropped to his knee beside her and put fingers at the side of her throat. He looked up at me. 'It's been too much for her. She's done, for now. And we can't wait for her to come to her senses. We'll have to follow her tracks back. Summon Foxglove to take her?'

Lant made a sound of remorse and pain. I took his upper arm before he could fall to his knees beside her. I spoke close by his ear. 'Not your fault. And it would be best if you let someone else tend to her for a time when she comes round. She will need time, just as you did.' He tried to twist free of me, but I kept my grip and set my thumb in a certain spot and pushed it between his arm muscles in a way that would definitely be uncomfortable. As I hoped he would, he went from morose to angry in less than a heartbeat. Riddle was already gathering up Shine. I lifted my free hand and gestured to Foxglove and the troops.

'Let go of me!' Lant demanded in a low voice. At least he had the presence of mind to be somewhat subtle.

I smiled and spoke softly, gesturing as if speaking of concern for Shine. I gradually eased the pressure on his arm as I did so. 'When you can control yourself, I'll stop controlling you. There are too many people watching for you to indulge your emotions right now, or to have any heartfelt conversations with Shine about who your father is and what it means to her. So, you will mount up and ride beside Riddle and me, you will help us follow her tracks back to that stone, and we will leave her care to Foxglove and my guard. Understand?'

He did not like it. I did not care how he felt. I watched his face and I saw the moment when he recognized that logic was on my side. He ceased struggling and I left him standing with the horses while I went to speak to Foxglove and Riddle. Shine might have been awake but she was not stirring. Her eyes were open to slits and she made no comment as I asked Foxglove to create a travois for her to ride on. Foxglove nodded grimly and began to order some to find sturdy branches and others to gather firewood and create a fire so that Shine might have hot food and drink before moving her, and I conceded that to her. I took Lant, Riddle and my few remaining Rousters and began to ride slowly back down the road in the direction from which Shine had come. I chose not to notice that Perseverance trailed behind us, Motley on his shoulder. The boy had witnessed Lant's revelation. I'd deal with it later. This section of the king's highway traversed a forested area with some farms and smallholdings. The short winter day would soon fade. I wondered how far she had galloped the brown and how tired he had been to start with. I wanted to hurry. I could not afford to miss the trail.

I broke the Rousters into pairs and sent them ahead of us at a gallop with directions that at every crossroads, two should peel off from the main body and ride down each tributary. If anyone saw anything that indicated that two horses had emerged from the forest onto the road, he should halt near the disturbed snow and the other was to ride back to me immediately. They rode off at a breakneck gallop, perhaps hoping to redeem themselves to me.

For a time, Lant, Riddle and I rode in silence at a more measured pace, scrutinizing the road to either side. Perseverance, still leading Bee's horse, had fallen in behind us. I studied the snowy ground to the left side of the trampled road while Riddle watched the right. I thought about Bee. Last night, she had been riding on a horse with Shine. She'd bitten someone, and somehow that had helped free Shine. Why hadn't she been able to free herself? Again, she was snatched away from me, vanished, perhaps through a Skill-pillar. Sadness and despair deepened in me, enhanced by the lingering effects of the Elfbark. We watched not just for Shine's tracks but anything that might indicate sleighs or a mounted troop of men might have passed. Any sign of my little girl. After a time, Riddle observed aloud, 'I wouldn't be human if I didn't ask.'

I knew his question. 'It's true. Chade is their father.'

'I knew that about Lant, but not the girl. Why did he keep Shine secret?'

'Well, because he is Chade. He never told me that Lant was his son until a few days ago. Though I suppose I should have known it by looking at him.'

Riddle nodded to that. 'I think more people at Buckkeep know than Chade suspects. It was fairly obvious in how he treated Lant from the beginning. So why keep Shine a secret?'

I was silent for a pause. Lant asked acidly, 'Do you want me to ride ahead so you can gossip about my parentage and my half-sister in privacy?'

I stared at him. 'Lant. Riddle is married to my daughter. Skill-mistress Nettle. Your cousin. So I think that makes him family.'

Riddle fought the grin on his face. 'And actually I'm discussing your father, not you. Chade! I am scandalized!' The grin spread despite his best efforts.

'Chade,' I confirmed and a bark of laughter burst from me, defying my dark spirits. We both laughed aloud and shook our heads.

After a time, Lant asked, 'Why did he keep Shine a secret, even from me? He managed to bring me to Buckkeep and let me know he was my father. Why not Shine?'

I spoke heavily and reluctantly. Better he asked these questions now than before witnesses. 'He has kept her ignorant and hidden from all others because of dangers both to himself and to her. Her family was not pleased to be saddled with his bastard, and yet they did not mind extorting funds for her keep and education. Funds they apparently did not use for her benefit. He was allowed only sporadic access to her. Her grandparents took care of her at first and were, if not kind, at least not cruel. When they died and she was turned over to her mother and her mother's husband—'

'I know some of that,' Lant cut in hastily.

Riddle raised an eyebrow at me.

'About as bad as you can imagine,' I told him, and saw him wince.

'What will Chade do with her now, do you suppose?' he asked me.

'I don't know. I don't even know if he will be mindful enough to recognize her. But I think she would be safest at Buckkeep, given over into Kettricken's care, perhaps. She has always longed to be at court, and I rather imagine her maternal line will be a bit more cautious about crossing Lord Chade's will in that now.'

FitzVigilant took breath to ask a question I knew I wouldn't want to answer. I was glad to hear a galloping horse and see one of my Rousters headed back toward us. 'They must have found something!' I touched my heels to Fleeter and she broke into a grudging trot. Riddle's horse surged past us and *No!* I sensed from her. *I am Fleeter. I always lead.*

Show them! I suggested to her, and she lifted into an effortless gallop. She did not allow her mind to touch mine again, and I did not try to push my way in. I did not want to re-establish any sort of a bond but I was glad that my misuse of her had not broken her spirit.

Sawyer, one of my Rousters, began shouting before we had even reached him. 'We've found her trail. I told Reaper to stay off it, but I don't know how long he can resist it.'

'Well done,' I told him.

He wheeled his horse and led the way, despite Fleeter's disgruntlement at following him. It felt good to be in motion. We reached a section of the road that wound through a denser area of forest. There another Rouster awaited us, standing in the cold beside his restless horse. 'Can we follow it now?' he demanded. I did not answer immediately. I flung myself from Fleeter's back and in a heartbeat Riddle was beside me. I waded into the unbroken snow beside the wallowed trail. 'Two horses, one behind the other,' Riddle announced decisively.

'So I read it, too,' I replied. I swung back up into my saddle. 'Be wary!' I warned the others. 'Shine said some of the mercenaries were still prowling in the area. If you see them, we need to take them alive. I need to talk to them.'

Sawyer gave a tight nod and his partner grunted an assent. A small part of my attention noted that both of them were standing a bit straighter. They exchanged satisfied looks. These two, it seemed, might take a bit of pride in accomplishing a task. Possibly salvageable.

The trail was easy to follow. I focused on that and pushed Fleeter to move as quickly as she could go. The deep snow was trampled but it was not a well-broken path. I kept my head up and watched the encroaching forest for any sign of the mercenaries. Twice Riddle and Lant moved off to inspect other tracks we sighted. Each time they found only deer trail. I wondered if a terrified Shine had only imagined the Chalcedean trackers as she had the ghost in her room.

The forest became denser. Here evergreens towered and laced their branches overhead to steal the afternoon's greying light from us. The snow was shallower but the trail was still plain. We followed it up a slope, weaving among rocky outcroppings and ducking under leaning trees that had grown at angles among the stones. Under these giants, there was little underbrush.

'Fitz!' Lant called and I pulled Fleeter around, thinking he had seen danger. Instead he leaned down from his mount and brushed snow from stone. 'There was a town here once. Or something. Look how straight this stone still runs.'

'He's right,' Riddle confirmed before I could even speak. 'Most of it's buried in earth as well as snow. But look there. The trees lean in, and it's narrowed, but that might have been a road at one time.'

'It would make sense,' I said, and turned Fleeter back to the trail. Old structures. In the Mountain Kingdom we had often found standing stones near Elderling ruins.

'I smell old smoke,' Riddle declared, and just then Sawyer cried, 'There are more tracks over there, sir. Looks like they're headed in the same direction we are!'

I threw caution to the wind and urged Fleeter on. She surged up the steep trail in powerful bounds, and suddenly an abandoned camp was before us. Hasty shelters of branches and evergreen boughs surrounded a blackened place where a small campfire had burned. 'Stop!' I called to the others. We dismounted and Perseverance stayed with the horses as we moved forward more slowly. I quested with my Wit but felt no others near. If there had been Chalcedeans stalking Shine last night, they were here no longer. I squatted down to peer into a temporary shelter built of pine boughs. Someone had huddled in there. That was all I could tell.

'Fitz,' Riddle said, his voice soft but urgent. He pointed with a gloved hand.

White coat, pale skin, pale hair. Dead. Sprawled on her back in the snow, the only colour a bit of blood coming from her mouth. Riddle and I crouched over her, our heads close together. I slid a hand under her neck and lifted. It wasn't broken.

'That's a hard grip to get or maintain,' he said. 'I'm impressed.'

I nodded. Chade's daughter. Cup the back of the neck and drive the pinching fingers in hard to crush the windpipe. No air, choking on her own blood. Not the quickest death in the world nor the quietest, but it had done the job.

I let her fall back into the snow and stood. And there it was, right before me.

I'd seen the looming block of stone but not recognized what it was. The big tree that had grown up beside it had nearly toppled it. At the edge of the camp, the stone leaned drunkenly, one face of it touching the snow that had banked around it. Lichen had begun to encroach on the stone's edges. I approached it slowly, as if it were game to be stalked. Lant and Riddle followed, but my two Rousters stood by with Perseverance as if they could sense danger.

Someone had recently swept the snow from the uppermost

face of the stone. A hundred questions pelted me. How had the Servants known this stone was here? Were they Skilled, to be able to use it? Did they know more of that magic than we did? I'd been told there were no Skill-pillars in this area. How was it that the Servants knew of this and we did not? All useful questions; and the answers would have undoubtedly been even more useful. And pondering them now was a waste of time.

'Do you know where it goes? Do you recognize the rune?'

'I do.' It was one of the few that I knew very well. 'It goes to a crossroads market beyond the Mountain Kingdom. On our way to find King Verity we followed an Elderling road and came upon it. It's not far from where we found the stone dragons sleeping.' I recalled the place well indeed. Both the Fool and I had briefly fallen under the spell of that place. The memory-stone there was strong, and he had seemed to become someone else, a long-ago White who had passed that way, a poet or jester . . .

I drew off my glove.

'Fitz, no! Contact Nettle first, let her know what you—'

I pressed my hand to the cold black stone.

And nothing happened. I felt astonished. And sick.

'Maybe it's broken.' Riddle spoke doubtfully, and I heard his reluctance to encourage me at all.

'Shine said they went through the stone.' I centred my hand on the rune, dug my fingers into the cold, rough impression. I pushed. Nothing. I could sense nothing from the stone.

Elfbark.

No. I could not allow myself to be dead to the Skill right now. It could not be so, not when Bee might be only two steps through darkness away from me. 'No. NO!'

I rubbed my hand down the face of the cold stone, eroded by age. I felt the skin of my palm snag on it, felt callous sand away. 'NO!' I shouted.

'Fitz, it might be—'

I do not recall whatever else Riddle might have said. I shoved at the stone, hit it with a fist. I went into a rage. The edges of my vision went red and black. And when I came out of my rage, I had ruined a battleaxe against the Skill-pillar. I did not even recall pulling it from my back sling. My arms, back and shoulders hurt from the force of the blows but the stone itself showed little sign of my attack, other than a few grey scuffs on its black surface. I was out of breath, and sweat ran down my back to match the tears of frustration that had coursed down my cheeks. I found I was hoarse from roaring curses.

I dropped the useless weapon in the snow and stood, lungs screaming for the air that I gulped, my raw hands braced on my knees. When I could straighten up and look around me, I found all my companions standing in an awestruck circle, at a very safe distance away.

'Fitz?' Riddle's voice was soft.

'What?'

'Why don't you step back from that axe?'

Instead I stooped down and picked it up. I examined the peened-over edge, and then returned it to my back sling. I crouched, scooped up a handful of snow in my raw palm and ate it. The moisture eased my throat. 'I'm done,' I told them wearily.

'What happened?' Lant demanded.

'Stupidity happened,' I told him. 'I drank elfbark tea so their wizard could not use the Skill to hide Bee from me, and I deadened my Skill to the point where I can't use a portal. She might be only two steps away, and I cannot take them!'

'What now, sir?' It was one of my Rousters.

What now? I sank down and sat in the snow. It was cold. I didn't care. I tried to master my thoughts. It seemed to take a long time. I looked up at Riddle who was still keeping his distance.

'I'm staying right here. Perseverance, take Fleeter. She's fast. Ride ahead to Buckkeep Castle. Riddle and Lant, follow as swiftly as you can but I'll wager the boy will get there first. Go straight to Skillmistress Nettle. Tell her what has happened and ask her to send me Skilled ones who are experienced at using the stones to travel and who know how to use a blade. Riddle and Lant, if you will, give a full report to King Dutiful.'

Per spoke up fearfully. 'Sir. I don't know the fastest way.'

He still held the horses' reins. I looked at Fleeter. *Do you know the swiftest way to the stables at Buckkeep? Can you run that far?*

I do. Her Wit was contained. *You still claim we cannot bond, and you ask this of me?*

I do.

Then you will grant me a boon. When I ask it.

I promise it will be so, I replied humbly. She owed me nothing and I needed this so desperately. I held my breath.

I'll take the boy there.

Bear him well, Fleeter.

I know no other way. She tossed her head, dismissing me.

Thought is swift. The bargain was sealed in that moment. I met Per's gaze. 'Trust Fleeter. She knows the way. Go now.'

For an instant our gazes held. Then Per passed the reins of the other horses to Lant. He mounted Fleeter, turned her head, and she bore him away. I spoke to the others. 'Sawyer and Reaper. You ride back to Captain Foxglove. Tell her that she and my guard are to take Lady Shine to Buckkeep as swiftly as they can. Sawyer, pick the six best soldiers in the Rousters. Bring them back here, with whatever supplies you can muster for spending the night in the open.' I looked at Riddle, to see if I'd missed anything.

He was scowling. 'I don't like leaving you here.'

'There's nothing you can do for me by remaining.'

He tipped his head. 'The body?'

I just looked at him.

Riddle nodded slowly. 'I'll tell Sawyer and his men to burn it when they return.'

I didn't care. Riddle turned away from me and began to give his orders.

The forest seemed a different world after they had left. I'd sent my lightest follower on my swiftest horse. Per would reach Buckkeep before nightfall. I believed Nettle would listen to him. If not, Lant and Riddle would not be far behind. By tomorrow afternoon, someone should arrive who could use the stone. Someone else would go through the portal and face for me whatever lay on the other side. I might be sending them into an ambush, or into a scene of people deranged by a Skill-passage. They might find my child with her mind forever scrambled and leaking. They might find only tracks leading away. Had Dwalia known where she was taking them, or was it a random escape? Did she know how to use the pillars and was she strong enough with her wizard to take that many followers through safely?

If she was, we were up against an incredibly powerful opponent. If she wasn't, my quest might end with a child who would never recognize me again.

I knew I should build a fire and prepare for the oncoming night. The falling snow was not yet penetrating the interlaced evergreen boughs overhead, but it would. Colours were already fading from the day in the dimmer light of the forest. Pale grey, grey, dark grey, black. I watched it get darker and did nothing. More than once, I set my hand to the runes on the pillar, and hoped. In vain.

I heard my Rousters before I saw them. I could make out from the tone of their conversation that a night in the open while their fellows travelled on to the comforts of the barracks at Buckkeep Castle was not appreciated. They were carrying fire, probably from the cook-fire Foxglove had kindled earlier. The light of their makeshift torches wavered and danced as they approached.

Both Sawyer and Reaper had returned with six extra Rousters. 'Make camp,' I told them, and they did. They built a fire where Dwalia's had burned. Three shelters were thrown up rapidly, from tree limbs and pine boughs. They'd brought bedrolls, and they floored the shelter with those. They had food and they shared it amongst themselves. I had no appetite, but when they melted water for drinking, I heated some and made a tea for us. They exchanged some sidelong glances and did not drink until after I did. Evidently FitzVigilant or Perseverance had made complaint about my trickery.

Long after they had gone to bed, I sat and stared at the fire. I do not know how often I stood and walked to the stone and put my hand on it. It was foolish. I could feel that my Skill was quenched. It was the same ear-stoppered mental isolation that I had felt on Aslevjal the first time I'd accidentally eaten OutIslander elfbark. I tried to reach out with the Skill without success. I unfolded my Wit, and sensed the sleeping men, and an owl hunting nearby, and very little else. Towards dawn I crawled into the tumbledown shelter the Servants had left, and slept. I awoke after the others were long awake. My head hurt and my spirits were less than low. I was cold and hungry and angry with myself.

I walked to the stone and put my hand on the rune. Nothing.

The morning passed. More snow fell. I dismissed four of the Rousters to go and find meat. I wasn't hungry but it gave them something to do. We had seen no sign of anyone else in the forest and they were chafing with boredom. The sun wandered the sky behind a layer of clouds. The hunters came back with two grouse. They cooked them. They ate them. I drank tea. The afternoon meandered toward evening. Too much time had passed. Was no one coming?

The light was going away when they arrived and I saw the reason why they had taken so long. Riddle led the way, and Nettle rode behind him. She sat her horse, but a litter followed: she'd probably disdained it. A full coterie of six Skill-users, armed and armoured, followed them. And the baggage train, and attendants appropriate to Nettle's station, trailed after them. I went to meet them. Her public greeting to me was restrained, but I read anger, weariness, disappointment and sorrow on her face. Riddle was subdued to stillness.

She allowed Riddle to hand her down from her horse but I sensed the chill between them and knew I was the cause. She looked at me, not him as she said, 'The Skill-pillar?'

I led the way wordlessly. All around us her entourage was busy setting up a camp with a stout tent for her. I heard the ring of hatchets as firewood was gathered and horses were led away. Her coterie trailed her, their faces grim. When we reached the Skill-pillar, I touched the rune once again. 'I know where it goes.'

'The ancient marketplace on the trail to the stone dragons,' Nettle said. She met my gaze and said, 'Did you think I would not know that?'

'I would like to describe it for the coterie, so they can know what to expect as they emerge from the pillar.'

'Do that. But we all know that there is no assurance the pillar has not toppled, and we cannot know if there are people there or if it is deserted. The Killdeer Coterie has offered to risk their lives to rescue Lady Bee.'

I turned and bowed gravely to the six strangers. 'I thank you.' And I did, but I also hated them a little for being able to do what I could not. Then I told them of the pillar as last I had seen it, a stone standing in what might have been a market-circle at some ancient time. Any town that had once existed there was long gone. The last time I had seen it, it had been surrounded by forest with no sign of human occupation. It would be cold in the Mountains in the winter. They nodded. Their leader, Springfoot, knitted her brow and listened earnestly and then formed her coterie up as if it were a military patrol. Left hands on the shoulder of the Skill-user before them, and right hands holding bared blades, they advanced to the Skill-stone and then looked to Nettle.

She nodded gravely. I watched what I had never seen before: a line of Skill-users swallowed one after another by the black stone. The appearance of the pillar never altered. The coterie simply walked into stone and was gone. When the last of them had vanished I lowered my face into my hands and breathed into the darkness I cupped, imagining a thousand possibilities.

'Fitz.'

I looked up. Nettle's expression was strange. I saw her swallow and then she spoke again.

'Springfoot has Skilled to me. They found no one. Only the plaza as you described it. Unbroken snow. No tracks leading away from the pillar. No one is there.'

I stared at her. 'They must have gone on from there! Blowing snow must have covered their tracks.'

Nettle closed her eyes. I watched the lines of her brow deepen as she Skilled. She shook her head slowly, then met my gaze again. 'Springfoot does not think so. She reports it is a calm, clear evening there. The snow is not fresh. There are rabbit tracks across the surface. Leaf litter, pine needles. All the signs that there had not been fresh snow nor wind. Fitz. Springfoot does not think they ever emerged from the pillar.'

I spoke without breath.

'Did they not sense her at all? In the passage?'

She shook her head slowly as she Skilled to them.

'When Chade and I were delayed, Dutiful found us in the pillar. Cannot they . . .?'

She lifted her hands, gloved fingers spread. 'They are trying, Da. But they sense nothing there. Even to Skill back to me is a challenge, like shouting over the rush of a river. The Skill-fountains there, they say, and is hard to navigate.'

Riddle put his arm around her, shoring her up. I stood alone. Very alone. A trained coterie was barely able to function there. An untrained woman had led a following there; what chance could they possibly have had? 'Then . . . she is gone?'

'They will keep trying.' But I had uttered the unthinkable aloud. Gone. Lost in the Skill-current.

Nettle spoke on. The coterie had supplies for five days and would have to remain for at least three days before using the pillar to return. This particular coterie was as talented with weapons as with Skill. She dared to hope that perhaps Dwalia and the others would still emerge from the pillar, that they were only delayed and not lost. I'd had that experience. I knew it could happen. She reminded me that the old tales were full of instances of folk who had accidentally entered a stone and then emerged months or even years later, untouched by the time that had passed. Her words meant as much to me as the sound of water flowing over icy stones. I'd not had luck that good in a very long time.

After a while, I had become aware that she had stopped speaking. She was silent. Tears, silver in the last light of the day, were tracking down her face. Riddle stood beside her and wept unashamed. No one was talking. There was nothing to say.

We stood and we waited. Nettle Skilled. I attempted to Skill, without result. Eventually, exhaustion claimed her and Riddle guided her off to a sturdy tent and a warm meal. I sat down and put my back to the cold stone and waited. I spent the night staring into the dark.

TWENTY-NINE

Family

This is a true account of exactly what happened, penned by Scribe Simmer as told to me by the minstrel Drum, a man unlettered but sworn only to speak truth.

Kitney Moss, accused of the murder of his young wife, was dragged to the Witness Stones near Buckkeep Castle on the fifteenth day after Springfest. He did not go willingly. The brother of his wife, Hardy the tinker, had demanded that Kitney meet him there, to duel with staffs and fists for the truth of the matter. Hardy judged Kitney had strangled Weaver in a drunken rage. Kitney admitted to his drunkenness that evening but insisted that he had found Weaver dead when he returned to their cottage, and had fainted from grief, only to awaken to their son's terrified screams when the boy found his dead mother.

Hardy accused Kitney of murder and demanded that he be given his sister's son to raise.

The contest commenced, and Kitney was soon badly battered by Hardy. When Kitney's stave broke, Hardy laughed aloud and promised him a swift death. Kitney exclaimed, 'By Eda, I swear that I did not do this awful thing. To the goddess I turn for protection.'

He lifted his hands and ran. Some there said he only hoped to flee. But seven witnesses and Drum the minstrel said that he appeared to deliberately dash himself against the face of one standing stone. There he vanished, as if he had dived into deep water.

Summer has passed and still no one has seen Kitney Moss or heard word of him. But it has been discovered that Tag the miller had in his possession a silver chain and a ring that once belonged to Weaver.

When his cot was searched, other stolen items were discovered, and it now appears that perhaps Weaver discovered him robbing her house and she was killed by him. Kitney Moss was apparently innocent.

Scribe Simmer, *One account of the matter of Kitney Moss*

It was past noon when we reached Buckkeep Castle.

We had ridden slowly for Nettle's comfort. Riddle rode at her side, and any anger she had felt toward him had vanished, swept away by the even more terrible loss we shared. By way of the Skill, she had kept Dutiful and the others abreast of our tragedy. I was deaf to the Skill and numb to every sense except my loss.

We had camped for five days at the site. Nettle had summoned a fresh coterie from Buckkeep. They had joined us there and attempted to find Bee in the pillar from our location. Their efforts had exhausted them with no results. They had returned to us, frostbitten and hollow-eyed. Nettle had thanked them and the Killdeer Coterie for their heroic efforts. We'd struck camp and left the standing stone in the deeply-shaded winter forest. I carried that cold within me as we left.

I had Perseverance's horse as a mount, a beast so well trained he took absolutely no management. Bleak and silent, I dropped back to ride with my Rousters. Not thinking took my entire focus. Every time a blade of hope sprouted, I rooted it out. I refused to think of what I'd done wrong, of what else I might have done. I refused to think at all.

We rode by daylight, but all seemed dimness to me. Sometimes I felt thankful that Molly was dead and not here to witness how badly I had failed. Sometimes I wondered if I were being punished because I had not loved Bee enough when she was small and dumb and helpless. Then I would push my mind back into not thinking.

The Buckkeep Guard admitted us without pause and we rode to the courtyard. There was a flurry around Nettle's horse as servants emerged to welcome her home and all but carry her inside. I was dully surprised to find my Rousters standing in a row, holding their horses and waiting to be dismissed. I sent them off to their barracks and told them to report to Foxglove on the morrow. Time for Foxglove to integrate them, to change their livery and teach them discipline. I could not care about any of it.

I wondered why I had come back here. I wondered what would happen if I got back on the horse and rode away. I stood silent for a long time, aware that Riddle had come to stand beside me but I didn't turn to look at him.

He spoke quietly. 'King Dutiful has summoned all of us to his private audience chamber.'

There would be a royal rebuke for my disobedience. A report demanded. I did not care about any of it, but Riddle just stood there, a presence against my Wit-sense. I didn't turn to him when I spoke. 'I need to take care of the horse,' I said.

He was silent for a time and then said, 'I'll tell her that you'll be with us shortly.'

I led the horse into the old stables. I didn't even know his name. I found the empty stall between Fleeter and Priss, removed harness, hauled water and found grain where it had always been kept. The stablegirl named Patience came, looked at me, and then went away silently. No one else approached me until Perseverance appeared. He looked over the stall wall at me. 'I should be doing that.'

'Not this time.' He was quiet, watching me do meticulously every small task one does when a hard-used horse is returned to a stable. I knew how his hands must itch to watch someone else take care of his animal. But I needed to do this. I needed to do at least this small task correctly.

'She goes like the wind. That Fleeter. The horse you loaned me.'

'She does. *She's a good one.*' She was watching me over her stall door. I was finished. There was nothing more to do here. No more excuses for delay. I closed the stall door behind myself and wondered where I would go.

'Prince FitzChivalry? Sir?' He spoke in a whisper. 'What happened? Where is Bee?'

'Lost. Lost forever.' I said aloud the words that had been echoing endlessly in my mind. 'They took her into a Skill-pillar, boy. And they got lost in the magic. They never came out on the other side.'

He stared at me. Then he lifted his hands to his head and

seized two great handfuls of his own hair as if he would rip it out. He bowed his head to his chest. 'Bee,' he said in a voice so tight it squeaked. 'My little Bee. I was teaching her to ride.'

I set a hand to his shoulder and he suddenly butted into me, hiding his face against me. 'I tried to save her, sir!' It was a strangled cry, choked against my shirt. 'I did, sir. I tried.'

'I know, boy. I know you did.' My back was to the stall wall. When my knees gave out, I slid down, to sit in the straw. Perseverance collapsed beside me. He curled up and wept ferociously. I sat wearily and patted him and wished that I could let my sorrow out as tears or sobs or screams. But it was a black poison that filled me up.

His horse looked over the stall and down at Per. He stretched his neck and whiffled the boy's hair, then lipped at it. Perseverance reached up a hand. 'I'll be all right,' he told the horse in a dulled voice. The boy lied well. Fleeter reached for me.

Not now, horse. I can't. Nothing left to give or share. I felt her bafflement. Don't bond. If you don't bond, you can't fail. Not with Fleeter, not with Perseverance. Cut them off now before it got any deeper. It was the responsible thing to do.

I hauled myself to my feet. 'I have to go,' I told the stableboy.

He nodded and I walked away. I hadn't eaten, I hadn't slept, and I hurt all over. I didn't care. I entered by the kitchen door, as if I were still Nameless the dog-boy. I walked stolidly until I reached the door of Dutiful's private audience room. Once it had been King Shrewd's. Here judgment was passed and justice delivered to those of the nobler bloodlines. In older times, princes had been sent into exile from this room, and princesses found guilty of adultery and banished to distant keeps. What fate would Dutiful decree for me? I wondered again why I had come back to Buckkeep. Perhaps because thinking of something else to do was too difficult. The doors were tall, lovely panels of mountain oak. They were ajar. I pushed them open and walked in.

For all its gravitas, it was a simple room. An elevated chair, a stark judgment throne for the king or queen, presided over it. A lower chair beside it for any counsellor the ruler might wish. Other chairs, of oak with straight backs, lined the walls for possible witnesses to the misdeed or those bringing the grievance. And in the centre, a short wooden railing enclosed a low wooden block where the accused would kneel while awaiting his ruler's judgment. The floor was bare stone, as were the walls. The only decoration was a large tapestry of the Farseer Buck that graced the wall behind the judgment seat. At the other end of the room, a fire burned in a large hearth but it was not enough to banish the chill or dismiss the smell of disuse in the chamber.

They were waiting for me. Dutiful and Elliania, and the princes Integrity and Prosper. Nettle and Riddle. Kettricken, clad in simple black, her head cowled against the chill, looked older than when I had last seen her. Chade was seated, and next to him, in a heavy woollen shawl as if she would never be warm again, hunched Shine. She leaned on her father as if she were a child. Her cheeks, nose and brow were still scalded red from the cold she had endured. Lant sat straight at Chade's other side. Chade looked at me but his gaze betrayed nothing. Thick was there also, I noted, seated and looking about with round eyes. King Dutiful had not yet assumed the judgment seat, but he was formally attired and crowned. His queen Elliania had a fine scarf embroidered with narwhals and bucks over her head, and her crown upon that. She looked grave and ethereal. Nettle had changed her clothes but still looked cold and weary. Riddle, dressed in Buck blue with black trim, stood beside her. His arm sheltered her as I never had. Her brother Steady was beside her, as if to offer his strength.

I squared my shoulders, stood straight and waited. I was surprised to hear someone else enter. I turned to see Hap, my foster son, dragging a wool cap from his head, his cheeks still red with cold. Swift entered on his heels, and his twin Nimble behind him. Must they, too, witness my disgrace and failure? Chivalry, Burrich's eldest son, came in behind them. The page who had guided them up bowed deeply and then withdrew, shutting the doors behind him. No one had spoken. Chivalry looked at me with deeply-grieved eyes before joining his siblings. Swift and Nimble had gone to Nettle's side, to flank their sister. They huddled together. Hap looked at me but I would not meet his gaze. He hesitated, and then went to stand with Nettle and her brothers.

I stood alone.

I turned to look at Dutiful but he was watching the door. Someone tapped cautiously and then pushed the door open slowly. Spark entered, clad in sedate Buckkeep blue, the guise of a serving-girl. And walking slowly beside her, his pale hand on her shoulder, came the Fool. He was clad in a black tunic over a loose-sleeved white shirt, with black leggings and low shoes. A soft black hat covered his sparse hair. His sightless eyes roved the chamber but I knew that it was his hand on Spark's shoulder that guided him. She took him to one of the chairs along the wall and helped him seat himself. Steady looked around at the gathering and then at King Dutiful. The king gave a short nod. Steady walked to the door and shut it firmly.

I waited. I'd only witnessed this once, when I was twelve, and then it had been through a spy-hole in the wall. I remembered it well. I knew that Dutiful would walk to the raised chair and take his place. The others would find chairs along the walls. And I would be commanded to take my place standing at the rail and explain what I had done. And what I had failed to do.

Dutiful drew a deep and ragged breath. I wondered how hard this would be for him and suddenly I deeply regretted putting him through this. Not what I had done; no regrets there, save that I had not rescued my daughter. He did not speak loudly, but his voice carried. 'I think we are all here. I am sorry we must gather like this. Under the circumstances, we must keep this private. Within the family, in a sense.'

The lack of formality shocked me. He turned, not to me, but toward Hap and Chivalry and Nimble. 'We sent you word that Bee had been kidnapped. Today, we give you worse tidings. She is lost to us.'

'No!' Chivalry's voice shook as he uttered his low denial. 'What happened? How was she taken, and how is it possible you could not track down her kidnappers?'

Hap looked around at us. His trained voice broke as he said, 'She was so small. So delicate.'

Shine muffled a sob. Dutiful spoke. 'Fitz, do you want to tell them? Or shall I?'

So. A public confession before judgment. It was fitting. Dutiful had not taken his proper place but I knew how things should proceed. I walked to the railing. I placed both hands on it. 'It began two days before Winterfest. I wanted to give Bee a special day. She'd . . . things had been difficult in our household.' I hesitated. How much pain did I wish to cause? As little as possible. Chade, Lant and Shine had tragedy enough. However they had failed me, I had failed them even more.

And so I took it all upon myself. I did not speak of Lant's shortcomings as a teacher and I glossed over Shine's greed and childishness. Of all I had done, I spoke true, from my interference in the dog's death to how I had left my child to the care of others to try to save the Fool. I admitted that I had resisted the idea of having a Skilled one stationed in my home to relay information in my absence, and that I had never seen the need for a house guard.

Dispassionately, I recounted all that had happened in my absence. I did not stop for Shine's gasping sobs. I spoke of the lives shattered at Withywoods and all my futile efforts to find Bee. I said only that the two Chalcedeans I'd questioned had confirmed all our Withywoods folk had told us. I did not say why they had spoken so freely. I confessed that I had taken elfbark and been unable to follow my daughter into the stone. And to those who had never used a Skill-portal, I explained that Bee was now lost. Not dead: no, nothing so simple as dead. Lost. Gone. Unravelled into the Skill-stream. All efforts to recover her failed.

Then in all ways, I was finished. I swayed. I looked down at the wooden block before me and realized I was kneeling. At some time during my account, my knees had folded and I had crumpled.

'Fitz?' Dutiful said, and there was only concern in his voice. 'Fitz? Are you unwell?'

'Of course he's unwell! We're all unwell. None of this is right. Worst is that we have to gather here in secret to mourn the loss of a child. Fitz. Put your arm across my shoulders. Come. Stand up.'

It was Kettricken tugging at me, lifting my arm to put it across her shoulders. And then she stood, not effortlessly, for the years weighed more heavily on her than they did on me. I tottered as she escorted me to a chair near the hearth. I sat, feeling confused and older than I'd ever been. I did not understand what was happening until her cowl dropped and I saw that her head was shorn.

The others gathered around us. Dutiful spoke softly. 'Oh, Mother, I told you we must be restrained.'

'Restrained?' This from Elliania. She snatched crown and scarf from her head, revealing only a short brush of what had always been her glossy black hair. 'Restrained?' She lifted her crown as if she would dash it to the ground. Prosper caught her arm and she let him take it. She sank down to the floor, her royal robes puddling around her. She put her hands over her face and spoke through her fingers. 'We have lost a child. A little girl! A Farseer daughter! Gone, just as my little sister was gone for years. Must we have this agony again? The not-knowing? The secrecy of the pain? Gone! And we must be restrained?'

She threw her head back, baring the long column of her throat and keened as if she were a wolf mourning her cub. Prosper sank to his knees beside her and put his arm around his mother's shoulders.

Chivalry lifted his voice. 'Can we be sure she is gone forever? All know tales of folk who have emerged from the stones years later . . .'

Nettle replied. 'She has no training, and she entered the stone as part of a company of untrained folk. She would be like a drop of wine splashing into a rushing river. I will hold no false hopes. We have to let her go.'

I found I was shaking. Kettricken took the chair beside me and put her arm protectively around me. 'It's all my fault,' I confessed to her.

'Oh, Fitz, always you are . . .' She bit back whatever it was she had started to say. More gently she added, 'No one blames you.'

'I blame me.'

'Of course you do,' she said, as if I were a child insisting the moon was a cheese.

Elliania had overheard. 'No! Blame *them*! The ones who took her. They all must be hunted down and killed! Killed like pigs screaming before the butcher!'

'Elliania. Fitz killed those he could. The stone took the rest.' Dutiful tried to comfort her. I lifted my head. Blind or not, the

Fool's gaze met mine. He stood, groping for Spark's shoulder, and she slipped beneath his hand as if it were a well-practised trick. I saw his mouth move and knew that he whispered to her. He would go to Elliania and that alliance would be as unpredictable and explosive as one of Chade's fire-pots.

'Family,' Dutiful said. His voice had that indefinable ring of someone taking control of a situation. 'Please. We gathered here to mourn little Bee. We must keep our sorrow private until we have determined how magic was used against us, and if there is any further danger of attack from invisible enemies. We will strike back once we have a tactic and a target. Until then, we gather information and we plan. We should not alarm our duchies until we have a defence to offer them.' He shook his head, his teeth set in a grimace.

'We are threatened on more than one front. An immense green dragon has been raiding Farrow, not only taking livestock but destroying barns to get at the animals. Two other dragons have been menacing Bearns. The Dragon Traders simultaneously claim they have no control over them and threaten retaliation against any who attack them. The Pirate Isles have increased levies against our trading ships by thirty per cent, and have begun to insist those levies can only be paid in gold or Sandsedge brandy. Tilth is reporting a pestilence that is killing their sheep and their dogs. And in the Mountains—'

'It was ever so,' Kettricken interrupted his listing of woes. 'Tragedy does not mean that other problems cease. But you are right, Dutiful. We came here to mourn, and to give one another whatever small comfort we can.' She rose and extended a hand toward her son's wife. Elliania took it and Kettricken helped her to rise. 'Come.'

The two queens led and all followed them to the hearth. Chivalry, son of Burrich and Molly, came to me and offered me his arm. 'Can you walk?' he asked me without pity.

'I can,' but I accepted his arm to stand, and he stayed beside me.

Spark had scissors in her apron pocket. Both Kettricken and Elliania had brought their shorn hair in silken bags. Into the flames they went, and the stench filled the room. The smell reminded me of how Bee and I had burned the messenger's body. My little girl had been so brave that night. My gorge rose suddenly. Such a fond memory to cherish of my little child: how she had helped me conceal a murder. I could not speak as each person contributed a lock of hair to the flames and spoke a memory or a regret or bowed a head silently. Hap spoke of a dress he had given her, and how she had looked like a 'little holiday cake, trimmed with sugar and spice' when she wore it for him. Kettricken spoke, with regret, of how she had misjudged her viability when she saw my infant. Nettle shared something I'd never known, that she had passed a room and seen Bee dancing, alone, as she watched snow fall through the window. But when it came my turn all I could do was shake my head.

Dutiful took Spark's scissors. He cut a lock from the back of my neck, where it would scarcely show, and gave it to me to offer to the fire. He did the same for the others. There was no restoring Kettricken's or Elliania's hair, but we would give no others cause to wonder. When the Fool came forward to offer his lock of hair, he put his hand on my arm. 'Later,' he said quietly.

And that was all. There was no little body to set on a pyre. All felt it. Our small farewell ceremony was unfinished and always would be. In the midst of my family, I had never felt more alone. Nettle embraced me. Kettricken took both my hands in hers, looked in my eyes, and simply shook her head. Spark came to take me over to Chade. He smiled at me and thanked me, very softly, for bringing his girl back to him. I could not tell if he even knew that Bee was lost to me forever.

Each of them came to me, with a word or a touch, and then quietly left the audience chamber. Nettle's brothers bore her away and Riddle trailed after them. Chade's children had taken him back to his room. Spark guided the Fool away, and Hap slipped out on their heels, probably to have quiet words with him. I made a grave farewell to Queen Elliania. Tears still streaked her cheeks as her sons escorted her away.

I was left alone in the stark room with Dutiful and Kettricken. Dutiful looked at me woefully. 'I have to leave. Three of my dukes have travelled to discuss with me the depredations of the dragons and what can be done about them.'

He took a breath to say more but I shook my head. 'You must go and be the king. I know that.' And I did, but it was my desire to be alone that made it so easy for me to urge him back to his own life. He left, walking sadly, and I turned to Queen Kettricken.

'No.' She spoke firmly.

'I beg your pardon?' Her single word startled me.

'You are going to escort me back to my sitting room. There will be food waiting there. Fitz, you will not leave. Nor will I allow you to waste away. I see every bone in your face and your hands are skeletal. Come. Walk with me.'

I did not want to. I wanted to go to my room and sleep forever. Or get on a horse and ride off into the darkening winter night. Instead, Kettricken took my arm and we paced through Buckkeep and up the stairs and to the door of her sitting room, adjacent to her bedchamber. We entered, and she shooed away two ladies waiting for her.

A table and food and tea awaited us. The soup had been covered to stay warm, and the bread was soft and fresh. The tea had mint in it, and chamomile, and a rich spice I did not know. I ate without appetite, because it was easier than resisting her. I drank the warming tea and felt like a hard-ridden horse that had finally reached the stables. My sorrow had not eased, but it was giving way to weariness. Kettricken put another log on the fire. She came back to the table but did not sit down. Instead, she walked behind me, set her hands to my shoulders and kneaded them. I stiffened at her touch. She leaned down to speak by my ear. 'There comes a time to stop thinking. That time is now for you. Drop your head forward.'

And I did. She rubbed my shoulders and my neck and spoke of other times. She made me remember the Mountains and how she had tried to poison me the first time we met. She spoke of our long trek in search of Verity, and recalled to me my wolf and how we had once moved as one. She spoke of the pain of finding Verity, and finding him so changed. And giving him up to his dragon.

The fire burned low and outside the narrow window, the winter day faded. 'Get up. You need to sleep.' She led me to her bedchamber, and drew back the rich purple coverlet to expose the clean white linens. 'Rest here. No one will come to find you or ask you questions. Just sleep.'

'In the tea,' I said, and she nodded.

'For your own good,' she replied, 'and fitting, after what you did to Riddle.'

I could not find an argument. I lay down on her clean sheets in the clothing I'd worn for days. She pulled the boots from my feet and covered me over as if I were a child.

In the dead of night, I stirred. Wakefulness flowed back into me. I was a cup full of sorrow, but that sorrow was stilled, like a pain that abates as long as one does not move. Slowly it came to me that I was not in my own bed. Kettricken's scent was all around me. There was warmth and pressure down my back. She slept beside me, against my back with her arms around me. So wrong. So right. I took both her hands in mine and held them against my chest. I felt no desire other than to be held, for someone to sleep beside me and guard my back. She drew a deeper breath and sighed it out on a word. 'Verity.'

Sorrow and loss never die. We can put them away in a chest and lock it tight, but whenever it is opened, even a crack, the aroma of lost sweetness will rise to fill our lungs to heaviness. Verity, lost to the Skill just as Bee was. Sometimes, to share a loss is the closest to balm. I missed my king and wished I had his strength. 'Verity,' I agreed softly. 'And Bee,' I added. I closed my eyes and sleep pulled me under again.

Before dawn she awoke me. She wore her thick winter night-robe and her short hair stood out in a grey halo around her pink scalp. 'You should go by the secret door,' she said, and I nodded. There was enough troubling Dutiful without scandal between his mother and his cousin. My body ached and I did not put on my boots, but carried them. She followed me to the door of the garderobe. My concealed exit was in the wall of that small chamber. There she caught my arm, turned me, and embraced me again. I kissed her brow, and then her cheek. As I let her go, she leaned up to kiss my mouth. 'Do not punish yourself, Fitz. Grieve, but do not punish yourself. And do not run away from us, please. We need you here, now, more than ever.'

I nodded but did not answer. Did she know what a heavy harness she had just put upon me?

The passage I entered, like all things that touched Kettricken, was clean and bare. There were no mice droppings, no cobwebs there and I traversed the distance by touch to Chade's old den. I entered it as softly as I could, hoping not to wake the Fool.

But he was in a chair before the fire. His hands were held up in front of him, and he moved his fingers against the dancing light of the flames. 'There you are,' he greeted me. 'I was worried about you when you didn't come by.'

I stopped. 'You thought I'd run away.' It was a bit daunting to realize how many of my friends believed I'd do that.

He wagged his head in a dismissive way. 'There's a pattern.'

'I did that once!'

He folded his lips and said nothing. His fingers continued their dance.

'Can you see your fingers?'

'I see darkness against a lighter background. And it limbers them. Even though it hurts.' He waggled them again. 'Fitz. Words can't express—'

'No. They can't. So let us not try.'

'Very well.' Subdued.

Bee. Bee. Bee. Bee. Think of something else. 'I was glad to see you up and out of this room yesterday.'

'It was frightening for me. I wanted to come to you. To speak to Elliania. But . . . well. Not yet. I know that I must push myself. I cannot be a rat in the walls. I need to become lithe and strong again. So we can go back to Clerres, and end that place. Avenge our child.' Like a suddenly billowing flame, his fury, hatred and pain erupted in his voice.

I could not take him with me. I told him the truth in a way that seemed a lie. 'I have no stomach for plotting just now, Fool. All I can feel right now is sorrow.' And shame. I knew this stillness. I recalled it from Regal's torture chamber. One becomes motionless, assessing how badly one is hurt. One asks, can I move without dying?

'I understand, Fitz. Mourn you must. Your mourning is the

seed that will grow into fury. I will wait for you to be ready. Though it grieves me to think of those who suffer there, waiting for us.' His façade of calm was in place again.

The eyes he turned toward me were blind but I still felt the rebuke in his gaze. I spoke flatly. 'It's no good, Fool. You are putting the spurs to a dead horse.'

'You have no hope, then?'

'None.' I did not want to talk about it.

'I thought that surely you would go after her.' He sounded as hurt as he was puzzled by my lack of fire.

'I would have if I could. I took the elfbark tea to be proof against their fogging magic. It has blanketed my Skill. I can no more go through a Skill-stone now than you can.'

His fingers paused in their dancing. He rubbed the scarred tips of those fingers together and said, 'Ah, but once I could.'

'And now neither of us can.'

'But your limitation will pass. Your Skill will return.'

'I believe it will, though even that is not certain. Some of the older scrolls speak of quenching forever the Skill in those who used it for ill purposes. And they used elfbark to do it.'

'How much did you take?'

'Two doses. One of weak elfbark here. And one of delvenbark as I got closer. I believe it will pass. What I cannot predict is how long it will take.'

He was silent for a time. 'I had intended that the first part of our journey to Clerres would be made through the stones, as when Prilkop and I travelled there.' He was subdued.

'It seems you have it all planned out.'

The firelight glinted oddly on his skin as he shook his head. 'No. I have planned only the possible. The impossible I have yet to map out.'

'Truly?'

'Yes. We will leave from the dungeons of Buckkeep. I have learned from Ash that several times he was ordered to await the return of Lord Chade in a certain corridor. Once he crept forward and peered around a corner and saw his master emerge from a stone wall. A wall with a rune on it.'

'It goes to Aslevjal.'

The Fool made a sound of exasperation. 'You might at least pretend to be surprised.'

It came to me like a curtain parting. He was trying to distract me from my mourning. Trying to lift me from a pain we shared. I tried to find something new to tell him. 'It was part of Chade's downfall. His curiosity. He travelled by the stones too often, creeping off to Aslevjal to prowl the corridors there in search of more Skill-knowledge. Nor did he follow the precaution of waiting at least three days between journeys. He would go and return in a single night, and sometimes do so for several nights in succession.'

'No amount of curiosity could lure me back to that place,' he said, and there was a shadow of old dread in his voice. The fire crackled and we both recalled our torments there.

'Yet you would go back there as the first part of your journey back to Clerres?'

'I would. Such is my determination. Such is my need.'

I said nothing. The fire spoke in the silence, hissing and popping when it hit a pocket of sap.

'Very well, then,' he said at last. 'If you will not plan this with me, then what will you do, Fitz? What are your plans for the rest of your life?' He made a small dismissive sound and asked, 'What will you do tomorrow?'

His question was a dash of cold water in my face. What would I do? I had no woman to care for and protect, no child to raise. 'I just woke up. I don't even know what I'll do today.'

He frowned. 'It's morning? Not late at night?'

'Morning. Dawn.' Another day of Bee being gone. Tonight would be another night of the same. And tomorrow would be another empty dawn. What would I do with my life now? I knew. But it was not a choice I intended to share with anyone.

I became aware of her an instant before the tapestry moved. I was looking at it as the corner lifted and Spark appeared in her tidy dress of Buckkeep blue. She wore a little white cap on her head today, edged with lace and decorated all round with horn buttons steeped blue. A pretty girl who would grow to be a lovely woman.

As Bee never would.

'Excuse me, sir. I went by your room with a breakfast tray and left it there for you. But . . .'

She hesitated and I knew her difficulty. I hadn't been there and my bed hadn't been slept in.

'I'm here. I'll find my breakfast when I go down. Don't be concerned, Spark.'

'Oh, it wasn't the food, sir. I was given a message by the steward, to be given to you as soon as you were awake.'

'And?'

'The king will be meeting with the Duke of Farrow this morning, in his private chambers. He desires you wait in the antechamber so he can speak with you afterward.'

'Very well. Thank you, Spark.'

'You're very welcome sir, I'm sure.' She hesitated. She was going to offer me her condolences. I didn't want them. I didn't want to hear anyone say again how sorry they were that Bee was gone. She saw my face and just nodded. To the Fool she said, 'Sir, did you want your breakfast now, or in a while?'

The Fool made a sound between amusement and disgust. 'Actually, I'm just off to bed. Perhaps later, Spark?'

'Certainly, sir.' She dropped an effortless curtsey, and I thought I glimpsed a brief smile, as if this were a new skill and one that pleased her. Then she whisked herself away.

'Well, Dutiful has saved you for today. But I warn you Fitz: if you don't decide what you will do with the rest of your life, someone else will decide it for you.'

'Scarcely a new situation for me,' I reminded him. 'I'd best go and wait for Dutiful to see me.'

'You'd best head to the steams before you go to meet the king. I actually smelled you before I heard you.'

'Oh.' I scowled as I realized I was still wearing the clothes I'd worn when I left Ringhill Keep. And I'd slept in Kettricken's bed in them.

'One thing still bothers me,' the Fool said suddenly. He had leaned back in his chair and his fingers were once more dancing between him and the fire's light. His pale fingers gleamed almost golden.

'What's that?'

'Shine told you that Dwalia led them into the Skill-pillar. Not Vindeliar, who I suppose has some measure of Skill or a similar magic. But Dwalia. I knew her. She is a Servant, through and through. Not a drop of White in her, and certainly not Skilled. How did she do it?'

What did it matter? She'd done it. I cast my mind back for the details of Shine's account. 'Shine said that Dwalia made them all hold hands. Then she put on a glove before she touched the stone. A very thin glove with silver fingertips . . .'

We both understood in the same instant. I stared as he turned his scarred fingers toward himself as if he could see the sliced surfaces. 'I wondered why they took them,' he observed. 'Now we know.'

They had sliced the Skill from his fingertips, sewn it into a glove and used it to take my child into the stone. I had to gasp to remember how to breathe. I felt a surge of revulsion and then, for a blink, fury cracked through my sorrow.

I had to look aside from him for a time. When I looked back, he was rubbing the tips of his scarred fingers together, as if recalling when they were silvered with magic.

THIRTY

Prince FitzChivalry

In contrast to the days of King Shrewd, when Skillmaster Galen judged that the Skill and all knowledge of its use be confined to as few practitioners as possible, Lady Nettle, from the beginning of her service as Skillmistress, suggested that even those with lesser levels of ability be retained and given whatever tasks they could do. Under her leadership, the summons to Skill-students has been sounded every ten years and coteries formed as soon as practitioners reached journeyman status.

Thus over a dozen coteries now exist in service to the Farseer reign, and nearly a score of Solos. Each of the watchtowers along the coast and Chalcedean borders include a Skilled one among their troops, and every duchy has a coterie devoted to its needs. Skilled ones have been included in diplomatic parties sent to the OutIslands, Bingtown and Jamaillia. The ability to swiftly communicate information about threats to the kingdom has facilitated the dispatching of troops. Flood-destroyed bridges, highwaymen and pirates are but a few of the menaces that have been swiftly met because quick communication was available.

Scribe Tattersall, *An Account of Skillmistress Nettle's Use of the Skill*

In my room I found my cooling breakfast and clothing laid out for me. I stared at the food with no appetite, then moved it around a bit so it would appear I had eaten some. Even as I did it, I wondered why I bothered. Did I think Spark or Ash would report that I wasn't eating? To whom? Ridiculous.

I went down to the Buckkeep steams, my clean clothing under my arm. The steams were a grand tradition in Buckkeep, a place where roaring flames met icy water. There was a chamber for washing, a chamber for steaming and sweating, and then a place to wash off that sweat and clothe oneself. There was a section for guardsmen and servants. And another set of chambers that I had never visited, for nobility, including the royal family. Today I ventured there.

I was both disturbed and annoyed to find there was an attendant waiting to take my garments, both clean and dirty, to pour warm water over me in the bathing pool and offer me soap and a scrubbing cloth, to douse me again to rinse me, and then to offer to dash the water onto the red-hot sides of the iron firebox to create steam for me. I greeted his earnest ministrations with silence for the most part. I tried not to be surly and resentful. It was difficult. The steams had once been a place where I could be alone with my thoughts, or enjoy the rough camaraderie of the guardsmen. Gone.

Clean and dry, I assured the man I could clothe myself and waved him out of the small dressing chamber. There was a bench there, and even a looking-glass and brushes. I put myself into reasonable order.

The antechamber of Dutiful's audience chamber was a comfortable room with a fire in the hearth and benches and chairs with cushions. Large paintings of hunting scenes in gilt frames enlivened the stone walls. One could smoke or have a cup of tea. Two servants stood ready to bring whatever the waiting guest might request. I was not the only person waiting for time with Dutiful. One elderly woman in a button-cluttered gown and an elaborate hat was already deep in her cups. A simply clad fellow had spread several scrolls out on a table and was adding notes to them as he waited. Two young nobles were seated at opposite ends of a bench and glaring at one another. A dispute for Dutiful to resolve.

Eventually, the door opened and the Duke of Farrow emerged with his adviser. He was greeted by his two serving-men, afforded me a hasty bow and hurried on his way. I was surprised when the page immediately indicated that I should enter, as were the others who were waiting. One cleared his throat loudly, but the page ignored him cheerily and escorted me in.

This chamber was elaborately appointed and featured a more martial aspect than the antechamber had. The paintings were of battles and heroes, and the spaces between were occupied by weapons won in conquest. There was a throne for the king situated in the middle of the room, on a dais. At the other end of the room there was an area with a small table and comfortable chairs arranged around it. It was close to a cosy hearth and light refreshments were set out on the table.

That was not where Dutiful was.

He sat on his throne, robed and crowned, and I could not mistake that my audience was with King Dutiful of the Six Duchies, not my cousin. I advanced slowly into the room. When I glanced back, the page had vanished. But there was no welcoming smile on Dutiful's face to put me at ease, and no casual greeting.

When I reached what I judged was the proper distance, I bowed. 'My king.'

'Prince FitzChivalry.' The height of the throne was such that, even seated, Dutiful was looking down at me. I waited. He spoke quietly. 'You found Shine Fallstar and brought her home. My mother has taken charge of her. Her restoration to Lord Chade has brought him much comfort and eased his condition. Thank you for that service.'

I bowed my head. 'It was part of what I set out to do.'

He replied not to that, but said, 'Before you secretly left Buckkeep Castle, the last time we convened to discuss the kidnapping, in Verity's tower, I asked you if you remembered that I was your king.'

I gave a slow nod.

For a time longer, he sat looking at me. Then he slowly shook his head. 'Prince FitzChivalry, I speak to you as your monarch. I called you here today to remind you, again, that I am your king. To remind you also that you are Prince FitzChivalry, and fully in the public eye. I regret that in the midst of our grief, this is what we must discuss. But I dare not let you continue as you've begun!' He paused and I saw him strive to retain his composure.

'I repeat what I mentioned yesterday. There is more going on in Buckkeep than our private tragedy. More going on than Lord Chade coming unravelled and you being unpredictable with your Skill. More going on than announcing that Nettle is my cousin, and is married and with child. More than us trying to reconcile Tom Badgerlock and Prince FitzChivalry and dealing with someone trying to kill Lant, and Shine's stepfather attempting to murder Lord Chade. The Six Duchies and the Mountain Kingdom is a very large gaming board, and there are so many pieces in motion, always. And beyond our borders, we have Chalced, and the OutIslands, Bingtown and Jamaillia. And we have dragons, and each dragon is like dealing with a separate country, when they are interested in negotiating at all.'

His voice had begun to shake. He paused a moment and I sensed that he fought to get his feelings under control. Yet when he spoke again, it was the hurt that came through more than his displeasure with me.

'Always before, I've been able to count on you. To know that you had the best interest of the Six Duchies at heart, and would be honest with me even if it pained me to hear what you had to say. Always I felt I could trust you. At the very least, I knew that you would never do anything to cause me greater difficulties with my reign. I don't forget what you've done for me. How you brought me back from my ill-considered flight to the Old Bloods, and how you accompanied me to free IceFyre and win my queen. I know that you've intervened on my behalf with both my mother and with Lord Chade, to assert that I was to be king in truth as well as in name. I hold this throne in part because of your efforts to see me secure upon it.'

He paused. I was looking at the ground between us. He waited until I lifted my eyes to meet his. 'FitzChivalry Farseer, why did you take this action on your own? You could have challenged my plan, given me your reasons. I would have listened, as you have listened to me. Why did you not entrust me with your plans?'

I told him the truth. 'I knew you would forbid it. And then I would have to disobey you.'

He sat a little straighter on his throne. 'You did disobey me. You know that.'

I did. I felt childish as I tempered it with, 'Not directly.'

He rolled his eyes. 'Oh, please. This does no honour to either of us. Fitz, you have stepped out of the shadows and into the sunlight where everything you do will be scrutinized. Because you are so newly restored to us, even your smallest action is of great interest and fuel for gossip. I am not Chade, able to invent an instant veil of lies to drape whatever you do in respectability.' He drew a breath in my silence. 'Report. Leave nothing out. Tell me all you did not share with my mother and your daughter. Report to me as if I were Chade.'

I forgot myself. 'How is Chade?'

'Somewhat better. You may go from here to his chamber and see for yourself. Later. Prince FitzChivalry Farseer, I am not reporting to you. Give me an account of *all* you did since you decided to leave Buckkeep Castle. Spare me nothing.'

I made my decision quickly. Perhaps it was time my king truly knew me. Perhaps his assassins should not conceal the dirty work they did for the throne. And what I was capable of doing for myself. And so I told him, and left out no detail. I spoke of drugging my companions, and how I had taken both carris seed and elfbark. And then I told him in detail of what I had done to the handsome rapist and to 'Duke' Ellik.

He did not interrupt my account. His expression remained impassive. When I finished, he was silent for some time. I tried to be unobtrusive as I shifted my weight. He looked down on me. Did he evaluate me and find me wanting? Did he wish he had never drawn me out of the shadows?

'Prince FitzChivalry Farseer. You were a witness to my trying to run away from who and what I was. You reminded me of my duty and brought me back to it.

'I know you have not always been treated as if you were a prince. You have been given duties ill-suited to your bloodlines, trained to tasks that should never have been yours. Or Chade's. I know it was my grandfather's will that put both of you on that path.

'And now it is my will that removes you from it.' He waited

while I tried to make sense of his words. 'Do you understand me? I see you don't. Very well. Prince FitzChivalry Farseer. You are never again to consider yourself an assassin. Never to be the one to do the so-called "quiet work" or be the "king's justice". My justice will be rendered in daylight, before all. Not by poison nor a knife in the dark. Now do you understand me?'

I nodded slowly. My head was spinning. So many times, over decades of my life, I had protested that I did not want to kill any more. Over and over, I had said that I was no longer an assassin. But now my king snatched the title and those duties away from me, and it felt like a rebuke. I blinked. Not a husband. Scarcely a father. And not an assassin. What was left of me?

Had he sensed my question? 'You will behave as befits a prince of the Farseer line. With honour and dignity. With courtesy. You will share the wisdom of your years with my sons and assist in guiding them through their early manhood. If I choose to send you on a diplomatic mission, you will go to negotiate, not poison someone! As Prince FitzChivalry Farseer.'

Each time he said my full name with that title attached to it, I almost felt as if he were reciting a magic spell of binding. As if he would set a boundary around me. I found I was nodding slowly. Was this what the Fool had meant? Someone would find a life for me. And what he was describing was not so terrible. So why did it feel so hollow?

He was still staring at me.

I bowed gravely. 'I understand, my king.'

'Say it.' His words were stiff with command.

I drew a breath. The words I spoke seemed almost traitorous. 'I am no longer your assassin, King Dutiful. I am to comport myself always as Prince FitzChivalry Farseer.'

'No.' He spoke precisely. 'Not "comport". BE. You are Prince FitzChivalry Farseer.'

I hesitated. 'Lady Rosemary—'

'Is Lady Rosemary.' Finality in that.

Questions darted about in my mind like trapped fish in a barrel.

'Prince FitzChivalry, I will look forward to seeing you at dinner this evening.'

I winced at the thought of plunging back into court life. He said more quietly, 'Stand with your family, FitzChivalry. This is something we will bear together.'

That was a dismissal. I bowed again. 'My king,' I said, and withdrew.

I was completely distracted as I passed through the antechamber and back into the corridors of Buckkeep Castle. I had no destination in mind when I heard a soft patter of hasty footsteps behind me. I turned to find Spark hurrying to catch up with me. 'Sir, please, a moment!' Her cheeks were very pink and I knew a spike of terror. What had happened to the Fool?

But when she caught up to me, her news could not have startled me more. 'Sir, I wished to let you know that I've finished moving your things to your new chambers.'

'My new chambers?'

'Rooms more fitting to your, um, new standing, sir.' Spark was plainly as uneasy with this as I was. She dangled a shining brass key attached to a braided silk fob. 'You have the Heliotrope apartments now.'

I stared at her.

'I was told that they were once occupied by Lady Patience and her staff.'

Her staff. One serving-woman. But the suite was substantially larger than my single bedchamber. It was just down the hall from Lord Chade. With no access to the spy-warren. I was staring at Spark still.

'Of course, they've been redone since she lived there. Several times, I imagine. They're very nice, sir. There's a splendid view of the sea and you can look down on the gardens.'

'Yes. I know,' I said faintly.

'And your friend is to occupy the chambers once given to Lord Golden. Familiar rooms for him, though I am not to divulge that to anyone save you. I am to serve him, now. As well as you, of course. I'll have a room that is part of his chambers.'

A room I once occupied. I found my voice. 'It sounds as if you've had a change in occupation as well.'

She shook her head and a curl escaped from her cap to dance on her brow. 'Oh, no, sir, I've been a serving-girl since I came to

Buckkeep Castle.' She smiled but there was worry in her eyes. We shared that anxiety.

'Of course you have. Thank you.'

'Oh, your key, sir. Here. To your new chambers.'

'Thank you.' I accepted it gravely. 'I think I shall call on Lord Chade, now.'

'As you will, sir, I'm sure.' She curtseyed again, this time with a bit of a flourish, then turned and hurried off. I made my way to Chade's chambers, suspecting that he was behind these changes, for some arcane reason of his own. I expected he would explain everything to me.

I tapped on the door, and a servant admitted me. I turned toward his bedchamber, but the serving-man waved toward the sitting room instead. I breathed a sigh of relief. He was better, then.

His sitting room was decorated in moss green and acorn brown. A handsome portrait of King Shrewd in his prime hung over the fireplace. A warm and spicy aroma from a steaming pot flavoured the air. Chade, attired in a soft dressing gown, was seated by the fire. Shine sat in a cushioned chair across from him, a cup in her hands. She wore a simple and modest dress, and the green brought out her eyes. Her hair was braided and coiled at the back of her neck. Kettricken's influence, I was certain. They both looked toward me as I entered. Shine looked apprehensive to see me.

But it was Chade who stopped me in my tracks. He smiled at me benevolently. It was an old man's gentle, bemused smile. In the short time since I'd last seen him, he'd aged. I could see the shape of his skull beneath the thinning flesh on his face. His eyes looked almost glassy. I wondered for an instant if he recognized me. Then, 'Oh, there you are, my boy. Just in time. Shine has made us some tea. It's lovely. Would you care for some?'

'What kind is it? I don't recognize the fragrance.' I advanced slowly into the room. Chade gestured to a chair beside his own, and I cautiously sank into it.

'Oh, it's tea, you know. Made from spices and what not. Ginger, I think. Liquorice root, perhaps? It's sweet. And spicy. Very pleasant on a cold day.'

'Thank you,' I said, for Shine had already poured a cup and was offering it to me. I smiled as I took it. 'It's almost as if you were expecting me.'

'Oh, it's always nice to have company. I was hoping Lant would come by. Have you met my boy Lant?'

'Yes. Yes I have. You sent him to me at Withywoods, remember? To be a teacher for my little girl. For Bee.'

'I did? Yes, yes. A teacher. Lant would do well at that. He's a kind soul. A gentle soul.'

He was nodding as he spoke. No. Not nodding. It was a palsy, a shaking of his head. I glanced at Shine. She met my gaze, but said nothing.

'Chade. Please,' I said, not knowing what I asked for. 'Are you well?'

'He's well enough,' Shine said, warning me. 'When no one makes him fret. Or brings up unpleasant things.' I wondered if she were not in much the same state.

I lifted the cup of tea to my mouth and let it lap against my lip as I smelled it. No herbs that I knew as medicine. I watched Shine take a sip of hers. Her gaze met mine. 'There are some calming herbs in the tea as well. But they are very mild.'

'Very mild,' Chade agreed and again gave me an unnervingly genial smile.

I broke my gaze from his and addressed Shine directly. 'What's wrong with him?'

She gave me a puzzled look. 'My father seems fine to me. He's glad to have me here.'

Chade nodded. 'I am that,' he agreed.

Shine spoke quietly. 'He's stopped using the Skill to hide his ageing. He mustn't use it any more, nor the herbs he was using.'

I let my gaze wander the room, trying to suppress the panic that was rising in me. From his portrait, King Shrewd looked down on me. His keen glance and determined Farseer chin only reminded me the more sharply of how his mind had faded and faltered before his time, a victim of his wasting illness, his pain and the drugs he took to suppress it. Something in Shine's words snagged on my thoughts.

'How do you know that? That he can't use the Skill?'

She looked mildly startled, as if I'd asked a rude question. 'Lady Nettle, the Skillmistress, told me. She explained he had used it to excess, in ways that exceeded his ability to control the magic. She said she could not explain it to me perfectly, as I don't have that magic. But she said he was vulnerable now. That he must not try to Skill, and no one must try to Skill to him.'

I answered the question she didn't ask. 'I'm no danger to him. I drank a very strong elfbark tea, to be sure that Vindeliar could not cloak my thoughts and perceptions. It takes away the ability to Skill. And it has not come back.'

'Vindeliar,' she said and went pale. Her calm façade cracked and I saw a brutalized woman clinging fiercely to the reassuring trellis of clean clothing, a warm bed and regular meals. Once one knows what heartless people can do, it cannot be entirely forgotten. It always remains among the possible things that can befall you.

'You're safe,' I said uselessly.

She looked at me. 'For now,' she said quietly. 'But Bee is not. She bit him to set me free. And I fled.'

'It's a thing done,' I said woodenly. 'Don't dwell on it.'

Silence fell. Chade smiled on. I wondered what other herbs he'd been using.

Shine spoke suddenly. 'Badg— Prince FitzChivalry. I want to say I'm sorry.'

I looked aside from her. 'You already said that, Shine. When we first found you. It wasn't your fault they took Bee.'

'I'm sorry for more than that,' she said quietly.

I reined us away from that topic. 'Do you know why Bee bit the man holding onto you instead of the White gripping her?'

She shook her head. A silence fell in the room and I let it grow. Some things are not made any better by discussing them.

'The Skill,' I said quietly. That brought her eyes back to me. 'Has anyone spoken to you about it? That as a Farseer, you may have inherited a talent for it?'

She looked startled. 'No.'

'Well.' How did I approach this? Obviously, Chade had not removed the block he had put upon her. Nettle knew she had

Skill and knew she was sealed. Was it my place at all to intervene? I took a breath and set myself on the safer path. 'Well, you might. I am sure that when they feel the time is right, they will test you for the Skill. And if you possess it, they will give you the training to master it.' I was sure that any such training would be far different from the harsh lessons I'd been subjected to.

'She has it.'

We both turned to look at Chade. His head was still doing that tiny sideways wobble that was almost like a nod.

'I do?' Shine lit suddenly, glowed with excitement.

'You do. Of course you do. And you are strong in it.' Chade's smile grew stronger and for just an instant his green eyes were as piercing as ever as he focused his gaze on her. 'Do you not recall how you sought me out in my dreams? How you, untrained and unknowing, used your Farseer magic to find me? My . . . beloved . . . daughter.' He spoke each word clearly and separately. His eyes never left Shine's face. Something passed between them, something special and private and I knew with a lurch what he had done. Her Skill-seal had been words that he was certain only he would ever speak to her. Who else would call her beloved and daughter in the same breath?

Their eyes were locked and I realized they were breathing in unison. Shine's lips formed an unspoken word. *Papa.* The stillness in the room felt like a deep pool. I watched them, unable to tell what was happening, unable to decide if it was wonderful or terrible.

I heard the outer door of Chade's chamber open and Steady's voice preceded him. 'You know he isn't supposed to Skill, Fitz!'

'It's not me,' I said, and saw the shock on his face as he entered the room. He looked from Chade to Shine and then opened his eyes wide and in that instant, I knew that he called for Nettle. His gaze flashed back to me. 'She should stop! Lady Shine, please, please stop. It may be the death of him.'

'Stop?' she said and her voice was that of a dreamer who speaks in her sleep. 'It's my papa. I thought he had forgotten about me. Or abandoned me.'

'Never,' Chade vowed, and the strength in his voice made me wonder if she was not restoring him rather than destroying him.

'I don't know what to do!' Steady confessed.

'Nor I,' I admitted. It seemed a very long time before I again heard Chade's door open. This time it was Nettle, very pink in her cheeks, and a tall woman I had never met before. She seemed to take it all in at a glance. Nettle glanced at her companion. 'We separate them. Very gently. I will help Lord Chade restore his walls. See if you can help the girl. Steady, be prepared to help.' My daughter spared me one glance. 'It would be better if you were not here. I can feel him plucking at you again, trying to draw you into the current.'

'I'll go,' I said, stifling both my fear and reluctance. I was useless and perhaps worse than useless here. A hindrance to them. I did not doubt what Nettle told me and yet it stung my pride that she dismissed me so that she might do her work. What was Burrich's old saying? As useless as teats on a bull. That was me. I was becoming very weary of being useless and incompetent.

It was hard to leave the room, and harder still to know where to go. I made my way to my new chambers. The key turned smoothly in the lock and I entered. It was a strange and foreign place. All trace of Patience and Lacey's time here had long been tidied away. The chambers, like the rest of Buckkeep Castle, were far grander than they had been when I was a boy at Patience's mercy. Someone had smoothed the bony stone walls with plaster and painted them a soft yellow that reminded me of an old skull. There was a carpet on the floor of the main room, and framed paintings of flowers. The hearth was tidy, with a small fire burning and a hod of logs waiting my need. There were several chairs with embroidered cushions, and a small table with cats' feet on its legs and nothing at all to suggest that I lived in this room.

In the larger bedchamber, I found my garments neatly stored in a wardrobe. They were the less gaudy attire of Lord Feldspar and a few pieces that Ash had apparently chosen for me. It gave me a turn to see Verity's sword on the wall above my bed. Truly, the lad thought of everything. Or perhaps it had been Spark, I told myself, and wondered why it was so hard for me to reconcile them into one person. My pack from Withywoods was there, and I was relieved to find that my stores of poisons and small tools and weapons were still left to me, as was Bee's book. The battered pack held the only items in the room that were truly my own. I lifted it, opened the cedar chest, and concealed the pack beneath the soft woollen blankets.

I paced around the chambers like a wolf examining the limits of his cage. In the servant's room there was a narrow bedstead, a small chest for clothing and a basin and ewer. The clothing chest was empty. Doubtless Ash and Spark would be more comfortable staying with the Fool.

There was a pleasant little sitting room, much larger than I recalled it. Doubtless Patience's towers of clutter had diminished the size of the room in my mind's eye. A cursory examination of the walls showed me no signs of hidden doorways. I did note a small notch in the plaster that might have been the opening for a spy-hole. I sat down on the chair and looked out of the window. But there was nothing here to occupy my mind or my hands, nothing to distract me from the space where Bee was not. What was I to do with all the empty hours left in my life? I left my bland domicile, made my way to the Fool's chamber, and knocked.

I waited some time before I heard the door unlocked. It was eased open a crack and then with a look of relief, Ash opened it wide for me. 'I'm so glad you've come,' the greeting rushed from him. 'He's in such a state and I don't know what to do.'

'What's wrong?'

As soon as I stepped inside, Ash closed and locked the door behind me. 'He's terrified,' he said simply. 'He did not wish to leave the hidden apartments, but Lady Rosemary insisted. She's . . . I'm no longer apprenticed there. I'm glad to simply work here in Buckkeep Castle as a servant. I know that Lord Chade . . . but this is not time for me to be worrying you about my situation. All care was taken in moving him here, but he is still in shaking fear for his life. And I don't know how to reassure him.'

The lad looked up at me and then stepped back from the fury on my features. 'How dare she!' I burst out. 'Where is the Fool?'

'He's in the bedchamber. I brought him here by the secret passages, and I've done my best to bring everything familiar to him here. Physically, he's so much better than he was, but this move has upset him so—'

I knew my way through these apartments. When the Fool had masqueraded as Lord Golden, I'd lived here as his servant Tom Badgerlock. The chambers were much more simply furnished than they had been in the extravagant days of Lord Golden. I went to the door of the bedchamber, tapped loudly and said, 'It's me, Fitz. I'm coming in.'

There was no response. I opened the door slowly to find the room in semi-darkness. The shutters over the window were closed tightly and only the light from the hearth-fire lit the room. The Fool was sitting in a chair facing the door. He gripped a dagger in his hand. 'Are you alone?' he asked in a shaking voice.

'For now. Ash is right outside the door if we need anything.' I made my voice as even and calm as I could.

'I know you all think I'm silly. But Fitz, I assure you the danger is real.'

'What I think does not matter. What does matter to me is that you feel safe, so that your body can continue to heal. So. Here we are. Our situation has changed. No one acted out of malice, but I can tell you are badly unsettled.' I kept up a flow of words as I moved closer to him. I wanted him to know where I was as I approached. 'I was as surprised as you when I was moved out of my old rooms. And today King Dutiful has told me, quite formally, that I am a prince and not an assassin. Changes for me as well, you see. But what matters, as I started to say, is that I want you to feel safe. So tell me. What can I do to make you feel safe?'

His grip on the knife loosened. 'You aren't irritated with me? Annoyed at my weakness?'

I was startled. 'Of course not!'

'You went away so abruptly. When you didn't come to tell me yourself, I thought . . . I thought you had wearied of having me depend on you for everything.'

'No. That was not it at all. I thought I had a chance to rescue Bee. And I had to take it immediately. If only I had acted a day earlier . . .'

'Don't. You'll drive yourself mad.' He shook his head. 'She can't just be gone, Fitz. She can't!'

She could, and we both knew it. I veered my thoughts away from that path. 'What would make you feel safer?'

'You do. Being here.' With an almost convulsive gesture, he abruptly clacked the knife down on a table. 'There.'

'I cannot be here all the time, but I will see that I am here often. What else?'

'Is Ash armed? Has he been taught to fight?'

'I don't know. But those are things I can remedy. He is to be your serving-man now, I understand. I can teach him to be your door-soldier as well.'

'That would be . . . reassuring.'

'What else?'

'Fitz, I need to see. More than anything else, I need to be able to see! Can you use the Skill to restore my sight?'

'I can't. Not now, I fear. Fool, I took elfbark. You know that. You were there when I first reported to Dutiful.'

'But the effects will pass, won't they? As they did on Aslevjal?'

'I think so. I already told you that.' Not the time to tell him what such a healing might cost me. 'You've improved remarkably since Ash gave you the dragon's blood. Perhaps your vision will come back on its own. How is the pain?'

'Much less. I can still feel my body . . . changing. It's healing but the repairs are changes as much as restoration. Ash has told me that my eyes look different. And my skin.'

'You look more Elderling,' I said honestly. 'It's not unattractive.'

His expression brightened with surprise. He lifted his hands to his face and touched the smoothed skin then. 'Vanity,' he rebuked himself, and I think we were both surprised when we laughed.

'This is what I would like you to do,' I proposed. 'I would like you to eat, and rest, and continue to get better. And when you feel you are ready, and only then I assure you, I'd like to see you moving about Buckkeep Castle. Discovering pleasure in life again. Eating good food, listening to music. Going outside even.'

'No.' He spoke softly but forcefully.

I softened my tone. 'When you are ready, I said. And with me at your side—'

'No,' he said more harshly. He pulled himself up straight. When he spoke, his voice was judgmental, almost cold. 'No, Fitz. Do not coddle me. They took our child. And they destroyed her. And I cower and weep at the change of a room. I have no courage, but it does not matter. Being blind does not matter. I came here sightless, and if I must go sightless to kill them, then I must. Fitz. We must go to Clerres and we must kill them all.' He set his hands flat and calm on the table before him.

I clenched my teeth. 'Yes,' I promised him in a low voice. I found I was as calm as he was. 'Yes. I will kill them. For all of us.' I leaned closer and tapped the table as I walked my hand toward him. I took his thin hand in mine. He flinched but did not jerk away. 'But I would not go to that task with a dull blade. So it makes no sense to take to that task a man who is still recovering from grievous injuries. So hearken to me. We prepare. I have things to do, and so do you. Find your health and your courage will come back to you. Begin to move about Buckkeep Castle. Think who you will be. Lord Golden, again?'

A faint smile hovered. 'I wonder if his creditors are still as angry as they were when I fled.'

'I've no idea. Shall I find out?'

'No. No, I think I shall have to invent a new role for myself.' He paused. 'Oh, Fitz. What of Chade? What has befallen him, and what will you do without him? I know you had counted on his help. In truth, I had counted on his help in this.'

'I hope he will recover, and that we will not have to do without him.' I tried to speak heartily and with optimism. The dismay on the Fool's face only deepened.

'I wish I could go and visit him.'

I was surprised. 'You can. You should. Perhaps tomorrow, we can go together.'

He shook his head wildly. His pale hair had grown a bit longer but did not have enough substance to lie down and the slight motion made it wave about. 'No. I can't. Fitz, I can't.' He took a deep breath. He stared at me, misery written on his face. Reluctantly he added, 'And so I must. I know I must begin. Soon.'

I replied slowly, 'Indeed, you must.' I waited calmly.

'Tomorrow,' he said at last. 'Tomorrow we will go together to visit Chade.' He took a deep breath. 'And now I am off to bed.'

'No,' I said pleasantly. 'It isn't night and as I've nothing to do right now, I'm determined that you will stay awake and talk with me.' I walked over to the curtained and shuttered windows. I drew back the drapery and then opened wide the old-fashioned internal shutters. Winter daylight streamed in through the thick, whorled glass. 'It's a wild day out there. Storm over the water is blowing the spray and every wave is tipped with white.'

He rose and took slow, careful steps, his hand groping the air before him. He felt for me, then linked his arm through mine and stared out sightlessly. 'I can see light. And I feel the chill off the glass. I remember this view.' He suddenly smiled. 'The wall is sheer below this window, is it not?'

'It is. Unclimbable.' I stood there until he suddenly sighed and I felt some of the tension leave him. An idea came to me. 'Do you remember my foster son, Hap?'

'I never knew him well, but I recall him.'

'He has come to Buckkeep. To mourn Bee. I have not had much time with him, indeed I've scarcely spoken to him. I've a mind to ask him to sing for me tonight. Some of the old songs and some of Bee's favourites.'

'Music can be very easing to pain.'

'I'm going to ask him to come here.'

His arm tightened on mine. After a moment, he said faintly, 'Very well.'

'And perhaps Kettricken would join us.'

He inhaled unevenly. 'I suppose that might be pleasant.' His hand gripped a fold of my sleeve and held it tight.

'I am sure it will be.'

And the lift of heart I felt surprised me. Patience had once counselled me that the best way to stop pitying myself was to do something for someone else. Perhaps I had accidentally discovered what I would do with my life for at least a short time: bring the Fool out of his terror-stricken state and back to a life in which he had some small pleasures. If I could accomplish that, it might ease my conscience a bit when it came time for me to go. So I spent an hour with him planning for the evening's gathering. Ash was happy to be sent off to the kitchen to request refreshments, and then to seek out Hap and convey my request. An additional errand sent him down to the old stables to find Perseverance and bring the crow up to the Fool's rooms.

When I finally left the Fool's room, I encountered the two boys coming up the stairs, the crow riding on Per's arm as if she were a hawk, and the lads deep in conversation. I decided that introducing Per into his small circle of friends would do all of them good.

I moved slowly down the corridor toward my new room. Hap would meet me there. I felt a sharp stab of remorse. What was wrong with me? Arranging a party in the Fool's room just days after Bee was lost. My mourning came back like the rising wind that comes before a squall and swept through me, freezing my heart. I mourned but it was the uncertain mourning of one with no proof of death. She had been gone since Winterfest. Lost to me for much longer than a few days.

I searched my heart. Did I truly believe she was dead? She was gone, as Verity was gone from Kettricken. Unreachable and unseen. Somewhere out in the Skill-current that I could no longer navigate, threads of her might linger. I wondered if she would connect somehow with Verity, if her grandfather King Shrewd would know those threads as kin.

A pretty fancy, I chided myself. A childish comfort to offer myself. It had been so hard to believe in Molly's death. Time would erase my doubts. Bee was gone. The rest of the day passed in drops of time. Hap came to me, and wept into his hands, and showed me the gift he'd been carrying for Bee since the end of summer. It was a doll with a wrinkled apple head and twiggy little hands. I thought it both grotesque and oddly charming with its crooked smile and seashell eyes. He gave it to me and I set it on the stand by my bed. I wondered if I could sleep with it watching me.

That night, in the Fool's room, he sang the songs Bee had loved best, the old songs, the counting songs, the silly songs that had made her laugh with delight. The crow bobbed his head in time and once shouted, 'Again, again!' Kettricken sat beside the Fool and held his bony hand. We had ginger cakes and elderberry wine. A bit too much wine perhaps. Hap congratulated me on becoming a prince instead of a Witted bastard, and I congratulated him on being a famous minstrel instead of an odd-eyed Red Ship bastard. At the time, it seemed terribly funny to us two, but Ash stared at us in horror and Perseverance, who had somehow been invited, looked insulted on my behalf.

I slept that night. The next morning I breakfasted with the Fool, and then received an invitation to game with Integrity and Prosper. I did not wish to go but they would not let me refuse. I knew they meant well and hoped to distract me from my grief. I dressed in fussy clothing. I wore no hidden knives and carried no poison. I rolled dice made of jade and hematite and lost badly in games of chance that I'd never learned. My bets were made with small silver coins instead of the copper ones that crossed tables in the taverns of my youth. That evening I returned to visit the Fool, to find Hap already there entertaining Ash and Per with some very silly songs. I sat and listened with a pleasant expression on my face.

Decisions. No. A decision. The Fool had been right. If I did not choose what to do with what remained of my life, someone else would. I felt like ore, pounded to powder, heated until I'd melted and poured away. And now I was hardening into something I'd never been before. My awareness of what I would be came to me slowly, like numbness wearing off after a heavy blow. Inexorably. In my sleepless nights, my plans took shape. I knew what I would have to do, and in my cold evaluation, I knew I would have to do it alone.

Before I began, I would have to finish, I told myself. Late one night, I found myself smiling sourly as I recalled how the Fool had finished his role as Lord Golden. His plan to exit had not gone exactly as he'd imagined. He'd had to make a headlong flight from his creditors. Mine, I resolved, would be a gentler fading. A kinder vanishing than his had been.

Gradually I blundered into a peculiar normality. I looked at each person I would leave behind and considered well what each needed, as well as how I must prepare for my undertaking. I kept my word to the Fool and took Ash down to the practice grounds and gave him over to Foxglove. When she demanded a training partner of a suitable size for him, I gave her Perseverance, and she started both of them with wooden swords. Foxglove penetrated Ash's disguise far more swiftly than I had. The second day she had the lads she drew me aside and obliquely asked me if I had noticed anything 'odd' about Ash. I replied that I knew how to mind my own business, and that made her smile and nod. If she varied Ash's training at all, I did not notice.

I gave my guard over in Foxglove's keeping. The few remaining Rousters accepted her hammering discipline and began to be useful. She demanded they surrender their Rouster colours and that they integrate with my guard. Privately, I asked her to make them available for any special duty that Lord Chade might require of them. With his network of spies and errand runners tattering away, I wondered if he might not require a guard of his own, something the old assassin had never supplied to himself. She nodded her head gravely and I left it in her very capable hands.

The next time Prosper and Integrity invited me to game, I countered with an invitation to the practice yards, and there I took my cousins' measures. They were not the pampered castle cats that some might have thought them, and it was there, wooden blade against wooden blade, that I began to know them as men and kin. They were good men. Prosper had a sweetheart and looked forward to her being announced as his intended. Integrity did not bear the weight of the crown of the King-in-Waiting, and had a dozen ladies vying to ride and game and drink with him. What I gave to them was as much as I could give of what Verity had supplied to me. I became the man older than their father, telling them the stories of their grandfather that I thought they should hear.

I allowed myself my own farewells. Winter at Buckkeep Castle took me back to the days of my childhood. It was true that if I had wanted, I could have joined the lords and ladies elegantly attired and perfumed, rolling dice or playing other games of chance. There were singers from Jamaillia and poets from the Spice Islands. But still, in front of the Great Hearth, huntsmen fletched arrows and women brought their spinning or embroidery. There the working folk of the castle listened to the younger generation of minstrels or watched apprentices endlessly rehearse their puppetry while doing their tasks by firelight. When I was a lad, even a bastard had been welcomed there.

I took comfort there, coming and going quietly, enjoying the music, the awkward courtships among the younger staff, the pranks of the boys and girls and the soft firelight and slower pace. More than once I saw Ash there and Perseverance, and twice I saw Spark there, watching Ash's friend from a distance with a pensive look on her face.

Chade remained genially vague. He took his meals in his room. He was welcoming when I called on him but never addressed me in a way that indicated he clearly recalled who I was and what we had been to one another. He always had an attendant. Often it was Steady or Shine. Sometimes it was a pretty Skill-apprentice named Welcome. He delighted in her attention and she seemed fond of him. I walked in once to find her combing out his white hair and singing a song about seven foxes. The few times I contrived to be alone with him by asking her to run some small errand, she went quickly and returned before I had more than the briefest opportunity to try to jostle some true response from Chade.

Kettricken had taken Shine in hand. The girl dressed more sedately yet elegantly and was always occupied whenever I glimpsed her. Nettle began her Skill-lessons. Shine seemed content to be at court and to be part of Kettricken's circle. No young men were allowed to court her and Kettricken chose industrious and intelligent young women to be her companions. Shine blossomed in the light of the queen's interest. I could not be certain, but I wondered if some of her calm was due to herbal teas. Having found her father and his doting affection, she seemed to accept that Lant was lost to her as a suitor. In darker moments, I wondered if her experiences at the hands of the Chalcedeans had dampened her enthusiasm for the company of men. My even darker conclusion was that if it was so, there was nothing I could do about it.

I knew I'd have to wring from her a fuller account of her experiences with her kidnappers. I made my request to Nettle, as I feared answering upsetting questions might trigger some sort of Skill-storm with her. Nettle agreed immediately that we must know everything we could of her experience. Kettricken was less willing to subject her to a detailed interrogation, but when the matter was placed before Dutiful, he agreed it was necessary but suggested it be done as gently as possible. I prepared a list of questions, but it was Kettricken who asked them, with Nettle present in the room to monitor Shine's level of distress. I was there also, but behind the wall, back in my old spy-hole, where I could listen and take my notes without my presence increasing her anxiety.

It went well, but not at all as I had expected. Kettricken summoned Shine to help in sorting out a large basket of brightly dyed yarn that had become mingled. Nettle joined them, seemingly by chance and, as women seem always to do, joined in the task of sorting and rewinding the yarn. Their talk wandered until I thought I would go mad with waiting for my information. But somehow Kettricken shepherded Shine's thoughts to that terrible day when she had been snatched out of her old life. Then she did nothing but listen, with occasional exclamations of sympathy or a soft word or two that invited the girl to confide more in them.

I think Shine was almost relieved to tell what had befallen her. Her words were hesitant at first, and then came in a torrent. I learned the names of some of her captors, and listened in sick horror to how they had neglected my child in her grave illness. It was only when Shine mentioned Bee's shedding of her skin that I recognized what had happened. Just as it had with the Fool, it seemed that as she approached whatever it was she was fated to do, her colour darkened. Only to hear Shine tell it, Bee had become paler. I pushed all implications of that aside, stubbornly telling myself that I must stay fixed on Shine's every word. Later, I would think of what it meant to me. And would mean to the Fool.

I took careful note of every painful detail and became ever gladder that neither the handsome rapist nor Duke Ellik had reached a gentle end at my hands. But as Shine wound the tale to an end, to my horror she confided to both of them her pain at discovering that the man she had regarded as a suitor was actually her brother. She wept then, a girl's broken-hearted weeping that even when her long nightmare was over, she had awakened to the fact that the man she loved could never be hers in the way she had desired.

Nettle covered her shock and Kettricken said simply that there was no way either of them could have known. Neither woman offered any rebuke or advice. They allowed her to weep herself clean and when she fell asleep in the big cushioned chair, Nettle simply covered her and left her there while Kettricken went on with her yarn tasks.

FitzVigilant did not, however, take the revelation that he and Shine were siblings in stride. To my surprise, he did not discard his bastard's name to take Chade's surname. He subjected us all to several weeks of morose quiet. When seated near Shine at table, he kept his eyes on his food and contributed nothing to conversation. I was grateful that Chade took most of his meals in his room and that Shine frequently joined him there, for the old Chade would have quickly discerned Lant's discomfort. The looks he sent after her when they passed in the corridors were too transparent for my comfort. I dreaded stepping in but just when I was certain I must, Riddle intervened.

One evening he steered Lant firmly to a seat between us and demanded he discuss the virtues of his favourite taverns in Buckkeep Town. That led to a late-night expedition to visit three of them. At the end of the night, all three of us staggered back to Buckkeep Castle together. At one point as we all but groped our way up the dark and icy road, Lant burst out with a wail of 'but no one understands what happened or how I feel!' Riddle rounded on him and said bluntly, 'And that is the most fortunate thing that can befall you, or any of those you care about. Put it behind you, and think about it again in twenty years. Whatever it was, you can't change it. So stop clinging to it, and let time and distance do their work.'

I trudged along beside them in the dark. The night was cold enough that my face felt a stiff mask. I tried to think, but then Riddle began singing the old song about the woodcutter's son, and after the second verse, both Lant and I joined in. When Lant came to the table the next night, he announced he had spent the day fishing in an open boat and had caught a flat fish the size of a small child. I was unendingly pleased when I saw Nettle give Riddle a very special smile over Lant's bent head as he set upon his food with an appetite we had not seen since Winterfest.

So the slow moons of winter ticked past us all. I was more alone than I had ever been in my life and it suited me. It was a solitude that I cultivated. I let nothing touch me too deeply. Alone, I made my plans. With a hunter's heart, I waited for winter to fade and better travelling weather to come. I wrote several very long letters, one for Hap, one for Kettricken and another to Nettle and Riddle. I considered writing one to my unborn grandchild and decided I was wallowing in sentiment. The one to Chade was hardest, for I wondered if he would ever read it with a whole mind. As Verity had done, I signed and secured my missives and set them by.

I endured each day, waiting, as slowly broken things began to heal. My Skill came back to me, in tickles of chance thought, and then in whispers. I used it as little as possible at first, respecting my daughter's advice and wishes in that regard. Then I exercised it, but rigorously, in tight sendings to Thick, or a general comment to Nettle. I became aware of the various coteries within Buckkeep, and shamelessly listened in when their sendings were careless. I built my Skill-discipline as systematically as I rebuilt the muscles of my body and my fighting skills. By day, I took my bruises in the practice yard, and by night I practised throwing knives and materializing poison from my cuff. I watched for the weather to grow kinder for travel and I waited for myself to grow deadlier.

Every creature entrusted to my care, I settled into safekeeping. The crow was a jocund addition to the Fool's chamber, for Perseverance brought her daily to see him. She was company for the Fool in a way no human could be, and at times I almost wondered if they did not share a thread of the Wit. She picked up words from him as a pigeon pecks up corn. Despite his blindness, he endeavoured to teach her tricks, and I was never so astonished as I was on the day when he told her to 'take Fitz's spoon' and she promptly hopped across the table and stole it for him. Motley did not seem to respond to my Wit, but her language and responsiveness were that of a Wit-bonded animal. She puzzled me.

As for Fleeter, I had little use for a horse while I lived in the castle. I still visited her sporadically in the stables. Several times,

I found Patience leaning on the door of her stall, apparently admiring the horse. So I was not surprised on the day that Fleeter swung her head toward me.

My boon?

Ask it.

I've found my partner. See that I stay with her.

Done.

And that was it. After that, Fleeter disdained me completely. Perseverance bridled a bit when I asked the girl to take over Fleeter's exercise and grooming, but I refused to be moved. I saw the light in the girl's eyes when I gave her the duty and knew that she would enjoy the horse with an open heart that I could not offer her. I visited the stables less and less often, and as I saw Fleeter bond to her, I did not intervene. The beautiful partner I had spurned lavished herself on another. I deserved the regret that stung me. It was too late to change it, and I would not if I could have.

The Fool continued to heal but very slowly. The evening that he came to join me at the hearth in the Great Hall, I felt a lift of relief. Ash had obviously chosen his garments, for I saw him pleased with the stir they caused. The Fool wore a long robe of black in a style half a century old, spangled with moons and stars cut from other fabric and quilted onto the garment. He wore the slouch hat that had once belonged to Lord Feldspar, now adorned with green buttons and charms of brass and tin. His walking stick carved with serpents and dragons was his own handiwork, and I was glad to see he had taken up his old pastime. Motley rode on his shoulder and contributed to his peculiar appearance. Ash guided him to a seat beside me, and to those who greeted him, he introduced himself as Grey, a traveller from far Satine. He claimed no title of lord, but presented himself as a foreign mage come to Buckkeep to study the legendary magic of the Farseers. His garments and accoutrements were peculiar enough that his gold eyes and scarred face seemed appropriate to them. That first evening, he did not stay long but, as winter passed, he began to move about Buckkeep Castle. He courted no new friends as Mage Grey but did begin to call on those who had known him. I saw him taking a small pleasure in this new role, and both Ash and Spark seemed to take great enjoyment in assisting him in it. The two youngsters, I thought, would care well for my old friend. So even from the Fool, I caged my feelings and thoughts.

I watched Nettle grow heavier with the child she carried and Riddle became ever more solicitous of her. Both Kettricken and Elliania could not contain their joy for her. I took comfort that she was surrounded by their love even as I kept a careful distance. If I let no one depend on me, I could fail no one.

On most nights, sleep eluded me. I did not really care. In the dark of night, the libraries of Buckkeep were empty save for me and my lamp. I began a careful combing of them. At one time, Chade had developed a fascination with what he had called the religion of the White Prophet. I found the scrolls he had collected. Some I translated afresh and others I renewed with painstaking pen-work. Here I finally found the references I sought. Clerres was distant, further away than ever I had travelled. The accounts of travelling there were old and sometimes contradictory. I discussed my work with no one. The slow gathering of information consumed me.

I made time to go down to Buckkeep Town, and to frequent several of the taverns where the sailors gathered. I sought out those who had come furthest to Buckkeep's port and asked of them for any news of a place called Clerres. Three had heard of the place, but only one claimed to have ever visited that far port. He'd been a boy, on one of his earliest voyages. The garrulous old man did his best to tell me of nearby ports, but time, a harsh life and much rum had eroded his memory. 'Go to the Spice Isles,' he told me. 'There's folk there that trade with the White Island Servants. They'll put you on the right tack.' A tiny clue but one that gave shape to the journey to come.

I was relieved that my assassin's skills no longer belonged to my king. I even told Dutiful how relieved I was, at a private dinner one evening in Chade's rooms. My old mentor picked listlessly at his food as our king explained his decisions to move us into open view. 'I know it was uncomfortable for you, Fitz, but your status demanded appropriate chambers. And a son of the Farseer reign should not be lurking in hidden passageways and spying on his people.' He set down his fork with a sigh and gave me a weary smile. 'Fitz, I am finished with secrets. Look where it has brought us. Consider how it twisted childhood for Shine and Lant, let alone yourself. And the near-disaster of their meeting when they were unaware of their kinship.'

I chewed slowly, my eyes on my food, wondering how he had acquired that bit of insight and hoping that the meaning had slipped past Chade.

'Think of your crown and my father's last letter to you, hidden for years and known only to Chade. If he had perished in the Red-Ship Wars, none would have known of Verity's wishes for you. I look at Chade as he is now, smiling and nodding, and I wonder what else he knew and has now forgotten, what key bits of Farseer history will never be revealed by him.'

I raised my eyes to see how Chade was receiving such a rebuke, but he seemed intent on sorting his peas into two separate piles on his plate. He became aware of my gaze and looked up to meet me. His left eyelid slowly dropped and then opened again. I stopped chewing. Had he winked at me? Or was it part of the drooping of his features? Our glances met but his green eyes were as opaque as seawater.

Dutiful was still speaking. 'I know it was hard for the Fool, but I think it was the wise decision. Perhaps he will never be as gay as he was when he was Lord Golden, but he no longer cowers in the dark. Surely that is better for him than hiding away in Chade's dark old den.'

'What will become of those rooms?'

'Oh, eventually, we will move the wardrobe in Lady Thyme's chamber and restore the door to them. Lady Rosemary has begun to sort what is there. She told me that some of it must be handled carefully. There is no rush. An empty room or five in this rambling old castle is not as large a concern as a dragon in Bearns. Have you given any thought as to what might be done about the dragon Baliper?'

'I should be happy to help with the tidying of the old den. Rosemary is correct when she says there are items there that must

be disposed of with great caution. I will see to some of them.'
And many items that would be very useful to me. Already I was
planning that I would do that as soon as possible. I knew of
several entries to the spy-labyrinth. But now was not the time to
dwell on that lest Dutiful discern the direction of my thoughts.
I put a thoughtful expression on my face.

'And as to your dragon, well, there is always killing him. But
as he can speak to some humans, and as he has kin among the
dragons of Kelsingra, that might not be our best solution.'

'Indeed, it's to be our last resort. If we kill one, my dukes will
see it as the easiest solution. Right now I have forbidden any
warlike actions against any dragon.'

'Well, then the only solution is to treat him as you would
any ill-mannered guest. Choose what you will give him, offer it
freely, and hope he is satisfied with it. Do not make him comfortable. Hope he stays only a short time.' I tried to think of a fresh
solution. 'Contrast the farms they raid with the ones they leave
alone. Find out what conditions they prefer and don't create
them.'

'They eat so much,' Dutiful muttered in dismay.

'Too much!' Chade suddenly agreed. We both turned to him.
His eyes were bright with anger. He looked directly at me. 'There's
too much rosemary on this fowl! I can't stomach it. What is worse
than a journeyman cook who thinks she knows better than the
master! Heavy-handed! That's what she is!'

'Lord Chade, this is not fowl but good venison. And I taste
no rosemary in it at all!' Dutiful spoke gently but uselessly to his
complaint.

'Pah!' Chade pushed his plate aside. He pointed at me with a
finger gone knobbly. 'My boy would agree with me, I think! He
never liked her stirring the pot, Fitz did not.' He slowly surveyed
the room. 'Where is Fitz? Where is my boy?'

'I'm right here,' I said hopelessly.

He swung his gaze back to me. 'Oh, I doubt that,' he said. He
took a slow drink of his wine. As he set it down, he looked at
me again and said, 'I know my boy. He'd know his duty. He'd be
long gone by now, he would.'

I found a smile and patted his hand. 'The impulsive boy that ran through Buckkeep Castle with a bared sword? He's long gone indeed, Lord Chade.'

Chade twitched. For a single moment, his green eyes locked with mine. Then he smiled vacuously. 'Just as well,' he sighed slowly, 'though sometimes I miss him.'

THIRTY-ONE

Loose Ends

In this dream, everything stank. I was in a terrible place. Animals walked about without their skins. They looked like the hanging deer in the cooling sheds, after the carcasses had bled and when the hunters stripped the hides from the meat. I do not know how I knew that, for I had never seen hunters ride to the hunt, nor deer hung to bleed before skinning. The animals were dark red and purple and pink with glistening white muscles. The worst was around their staring eyes. They could not blink.

In the streets the men and women were wearing the animal's skins. It was so clearly wrong and yet all the folk there in Wortletree thought it the most normal thing in the world. I did not want to be there. On the water, a great seabird with broad white wings called for us to hurry. They made me go.

Bee Farseer's Dream Journal

That night, I slept not at all. I argued with myself and then I took out Bee's book. I paged through it slowly, marvelling at her illustrations and strange fancies. But not even that could distract me. Chade was right. The headstrong boy I had been would have been on his way a month ago. I reminded myself of the times when I had given in to such impulses. The first time, I'd ended up in Regal's dungeons. The second time, Regal's Skill-coterie had nearly killed me. I could afford no mistakes this time. I well knew it would be my last. So I inventoried my resources. My Skill was restored. My body was hardened, my weapons ready. Spring would soon break. I had seen to all at Buckkeep Castle as well as I could. I would settle my affairs at Withywoods and depart.

The next day I announced that I would return to Withywoods for a visit. No one objected. Nettle filled two panniers with gifts and tokens for the serving-folk. Perseverance would go with me, for I judged he should visit his mother and perhaps remain there.

Our travel day dawned blue and clear. I had invited the Fool to join me. He had refused. I'd expected that. What surprised me was the quiet anger in his voice as he said, 'While you dither and dally, I must make ready for my journey back to Clerres. When you said you could not go with me because of Bee, I understood. When you said she was stolen, and you could not leave until she was rescued, I understood. But they destroyed our child and still you do nothing.'

He waited for a response from me, and I think my silence only made his anger deeper. 'I do not understand you any more,' he said quietly. 'They destroyed our child. I lie awake and plan vengeance. I push my body to grow strong. Daily I strive for endurance. I am ready the moment that you say we are going to leave here and undertake our journey. And finally you propose a journey to me. To Withywoods.' His tone was one of disgust.

I told him the truth. 'I am not convinced that your health would allow you to journey back to Clerres, let alone take the vengeance you desire. You are not ready, Fool.' I did not add that he might never be.

'Yet with you or without you, it is something I must do. I have no choice. And so I make my own plans.'

'We always have choices, even when all of them seem bad.'

'I have only one path,' he insisted. He shook his head, then reached to smooth down the cloud of pale hair that stood up around his face. His voice changed. 'Fitz, I have begun to have dreams again. As I did when I was a child.'

'We all have dreams.'

'No. Not everyone has these sorts of dreams. These dreams are to ordinary dreams as drinking wine is to smelling it! They are unmistakably significant.'

'Are they from the dragon blood? I remember that you told me you had dragon-dreams. Of hunting and flying.'

He dismissed my question with a wave of his long fingered hand. 'No. Those were different. These are . . . Fitz, I know what lies ahead of us. In glimpses. We must be on our way. I dream of the Wolf from the West.'

He watched me carefully as he spoke. The words rang familiarly in my ears but I could not place where I had heard them before. It was my turn to shake my head. 'I must go, Fool. There are things there that must be settled.'

He folded his lips. 'With you or without you, old friend. With you or without you.'

And so I left him. It seemed a poor way to part and I was silent as we rode away from Buckkeep Castle. I rode a sturdy mare from the stables that did not mind the panniers. Perseverance rode at my stirrup, likewise silent. I think he more dreaded than welcomed the thought of a visit home.

Our journey was uneventful. The weather held fair, my guard was well behaved at the inns and Foxglove seemed pleased with them. As we drew closer to Withywoods my heart grew heavier and Perseverance morose. As we left the road and entered the long driveway, the drooping birches with their burden of snow arched over us and dimmed the day. At one point, Perseverance turned his head and stared, and I knew that was where he had fallen to a Chalcedean arrow. Neither of us spoke of it.

We saw the burned stables before we glimpsed the house. I'd given orders that the remainder of the barn and the bones of those who had perished there be burned on the site. Now the debris had been cleared away, leaving an ashy black area of tram- pled snow around the stone foundation. New timbers were rising and one end was already closed in. A bulldog came barking and snarling to meet us. A girl ran out to seize his collar and drag him back.

'It's the master!' shouted someone in the stables, and I saw someone hurry toward the house. Several hands came to take my horse and Foxglove's mount and direct the guard where they could stable their beasts and I released Perseverance to help them.

Steward Dixon greeted us in a coat festooned with bone buttons dyed yellow and green, obviously enjoying his elevated status. I could only think that he was not Revel. He told me that all had rejoiced at news of Lady Shun's rescue. He hoped she was doing well, for he recalled her fondly. He hoped she would soon return. I told him quietly she was settled now in Buckkeep. He asked after FitzVigilant and said he was missed. I replied that he, too, was settled in Buckkeep. Then, in an altered tone, he lowered his eyes and said all were saddened to hear of the loss of Lady Bee. 'Such a little thing she was, and still so sweet, even if she was odd. Some might say she was not meant for this harsh world.' I stared at him and he turned red. Abruptly he asked if I would rest or take refreshment, but instead I asked him to show me what had been done in my absence. I had already noted that the entry doors had been skilfully repaired.

So he walked me past mended hangings, empty places where tapestries had been removed for repair, reinforced doorjambs, and walls that no longer bore the scars of blades.

My bedchamber had been put to rights. The locked chest where I kept my personal items had withstood the raiders. Next was Bee's room. Dixon spoke as softly as if he were in the presence of a dying man. 'I allowed her maid to tidy it, sir, and put all back as it was kept before . . .' His voice trailed away. He opened the door and waited for me to enter. I looked at the smoothly spread bedding, at the little cloak on its hook and the paired slippers by the hearth. All tidy and neat. Everything there but the child. I reached past Dixon and closed the door. 'The key, if you please,' I said to him, and he produced his large ring of keys and indicated it to me. I held out my hand and he stared for a moment before he fumbled it free of the others. I locked the door and pocketed the key.

'Proceed,' I told him and we moved on to Shun's room. It was meticulously tidied as it never had been when she was in residence. 'Pack it all up,' I told the luckless steward. 'And send it on to her at Buckkeep.'

'As you wish, sir,' he sighed. He knew that he faced a monu-mental task.

I directed him to do the same for Lant's belongings. Dixon inquired whether I would send a new scribe to be teacher and help to keep the accounts. In my grief I'd neglected to think of such things. The children of the manor deserved better from me. I promised I would.

I dismissed him at the doors of my personal study. The shattered lock had been artfully repaired. Inside, the Fool's carving still rested on the mantel. The scroll-racks had been repaired and someone had attempted to tidy my desk. I had no heart for this yet. I closed and locked the doors and walked away.

Dixon had ordered a fine meal prepared to welcome us. Foxglove complimented him and the kitchen staff, and he glowed. I ate it and then retired to spend the night looking at the ceiling of the room I had shared with Molly. I have never been a man to pray, and if I were, El the heartless god of the sea would be more likely to listen to me than gentle Eda of the fields. But to someone or something or perhaps to Molly that night I poured out my apologies and deep desire to somehow redeem myself. I promised to exact payment: pain for pain, blood for blood. It seemed to me that nothing and no one listened to me, but in the very darkest hours of the night, I felt Nettle's touch on my thoughts.

Are you all right?

You know I am not.

Yes. I do. Set your walls, Da. You are singing your grief like one of Thick's melodies.

The children of Withywoods need a new tutor. Someone very gentle and kind.

You are right. I will find one for them.

Does all go well with you and the babe?

It does. I have not vomited for two days. I can eat with pleasure once more.

I am so glad to hear it. Good night, then.

So I set my walls and felt my heart batter and break against them like a storm on the seawalls of a shuttered town. I wondered in that dark night if I would ever again feel something other than pain and guilt.

I rose before dawn and followed my old habits to the kitchen. Tavia and Mild were hard at work, as was a youngster named Lea. There was a new kitchen girl, Chestnut. When I commented on this, Tavia recounted that after Elm drank 'the remembering tea' she had lost her mind. She was mortally afraid of men now, even her father and brothers. On her quiet days, they kept her in the inglenook, peeling potatoes or doing any undemanding chore. Today, knowing that I might walk into the kitchen, they'd sent her elsewhere, since the sight of grown men made her scream. Lea began to weep. I wished to hear no more.

But Nutmeg, our old cook, had come in to help with last night's meal and she gossiped ruthlessly about the various servants. Shepherd Lin had shocked everyone when he tried to take his own life, but he'd been cut down just in time by one of his own sons. They watched him more closely now even though he claimed it had been a moment of despair and nothing he would attempt again. He had nightmares of throwing bodies into the burning stables. Slight, one of the orchard women, had drowned. Some were saying she'd walked on the thin ice on purpose and others that she was slightly daft after what she'd endured. Servants had quit, and others had been hired. Nutmeg was full of every dreadful detail and I forced myself to sit still and listen even though I longed to flee. These were things I deserved to hear. These things were the fuel that would fire me if my own resolve faltered.

Tavia was white-faced and silent as Nutmeg spoke on. Lea continued to stir something bubbling in a kettle. I did not know if her face was red from the heat of the fire or suppressed emotion. One of the gardeners had been raped by the raiders. He had taken to drink and was almost completely useless now. 'Buggered him bloody,' Nutmeg reported darkly. 'Man stopped eating for fear he'd have to shit. But he drinks. Oh, does that man drink! The town men, they don't understand. His own brother said to him, he said, "I'd have died fighting before they did that to me." But they weren't here. We're the only ones who can understand.' She was kneading bread dough and she suddenly surprised me with the force with which she slammed it down on the board. She turned her gaze to me and her old eyes were full of tears.

'We know you'll make them pay, sir. We heard what you done to that Ellik, him on his high horse, looking down on us all. And that pretty boy, with his yellow hair braided like a bride, raping the girls like he couldn't get enough of it. You done them both good, so we heard, and they deserved every bit of it, and more!'

Her voice seemed to be coming from very far away. Who . . . of course. He had been with me. He'd seen the body. And the boy would talk, here at home, among his friends. And my guard would embellish, as all guardsmen did.

'We're proud of you, that we are, and we know you'll go after the rest of them. Track them back to their lair and smoke them out and kill them. Young Per might have finished that Ellik but he told us that you made him pay before he put a blade in him.'

Proud of me. I felt queasy.

Tavia took mercy on me, I think, reminding me that Foxglove would expect me to join her for breakfast. She shooed me out of the kitchen and I went gratefully. In the hall I encountered Perseverance. He looked pallid and his eyes were red-rimmed. I told him he would eat with us and took him to the table to wait for Foxglove. I didn't ask him what tales he had told the Withywoods folk. Instead I asked him how his mother was.

He took a slow breath. 'Well, she's not living here at Withywoods, sir. Not any more. She told Shepherd Lin there's nothing left here for her except nightmares and loss. She moved to town, to live with her sister and her husband. Her sister has six children, so they're crowded but she says it's all right. Her sister welcomes the help, for her youngest is colicky and my mother is patient. She takes in sewing and mending. I went to see her, but the moment she opened the door to me, she started weeping. She hugged me and she said she loved me, but then she went to bed very early. My aunt said that seeing me was hard for her, that I remind her of all she had lost. And that she can't forgive herself for how she turned me away from her door and didn't know me.' He suddenly squared his shoulders. 'If I may, sir, I'll return to Buckkeep with you when you go. I gave my aunt my pay to give to my mother, and she said it will help her a great deal. Her husband's a good man, but six children and then taking in my mother . . . I need to step up to my duty. I think the coin I earn is the best way I can help her.'

That did not sound right to me and yet something in his face convinced me it should be so. Lea brought us tea and looked very wide-eyed to see Perseverance seated at the table beside me, in his fine livery with my charging buck on his breast. She smiled at him shyly. He straightened his jerkin casually and I suddenly saw him with new eyes. He'd gone away a stableboy and returned a young man in service to a prince. A young man who had killed their nemesis and come home with coin in his pockets for his mother.

When Foxglove joined us, her face was grave. She kept silent while Lea brought her fresh tea, and set out breakfast bread and butter and jam for us. When the girl left the room, she spoke. 'I had no idea what had happened here, Fitz. Small wonder you seemed so dazed when you returned to Buckkeep. The girl who tended to my things used to be Lady Shine's maid. And helped with your little girl, she said. Oh, Fitz! I didn't understand the half of what had befallen you. Please forgive me.'

I stared uncomprehending at her. Lea came back with porridge and left again. 'Forgive what?'

'I was distant with you after . . . I saw your handiwork, Fitz, on those two men. Now I understand. That's all I wanted to say.'

I nodded as if I agreed. I just wanted everyone to stop talking. I ate food I had no appetite for.

The rest of the day dragged by. I did the things I had come to do. I inspected the rebuilding of the stables and requested a few changes. I found a man in the village who knew about training dogs and asked him to help the stablegirl turn the bulldog into a useful animal. I reviewed which horses and stock had been burned to death and which needed to be replaced. I asked the resident Skill-user to relay my decisions to Lady Nettle. I told Cinch that his position as stablemaster was now permanent. The other hands seemed relieved to have someone who was properly in charge of things. I arranged for our accounts in Withy and Oaksbywater to be settled and thanked the merchants for allowing us to trade on credit for so long.

All the ordinary business, all that I had neglected, I put in order now. I arranged that the accounts would be sent monthly to Riddle at Buckkeep. Nothing would I leave undone. Dixon was doing a credible job as steward; he showed me his tidy book of accounts and I decided to leave him in place. He could not help that he was not Revel. It was time to stop disliking him for taking the job of a man who had died.

I had come expecting to stay ten days. By the second day I was ready to return to Buckkeep. It was evening and I was in my personal den. I was gathering from there the more personal things I would take back to Buckkeep with me. I had a lively fire going on the hearth and was feeding it my old scrolls at a steady rate. I would leave nothing of myself here. I did not expect that I would ever return here to live. Most days, I did not expect to return to live anywhere. And so I gathered my treasures from the chest in my room, my keepsakes of Molly and the few I had of Bee and packed them carefully with the Fool's carvings and the more valuable scrolls that Chade had sent me for translation.

I looked at the objects I had assembled to take back to Buck with me. It was a pitifully small collection to define a man's life. The carvings the Fool had made for me in better times. The last shirt Molly had sewn for me, too precious ever to wear.

I thought of the things I would leave here. Everything of Molly's that I had given over to Bee would remain in her room. Her hairbrush and comb. The herb-books, with the carved and painted images that Molly had used to teach Bee to read. I imagined she had been wearing Molly's belt and small knife when she was taken. Doubtless discarded by her captors and lost forever now. I closed my eyes. I wanted her scent. I had let Bee take all the candles. She had squirrelled them away in her room. A few, I decided. I would take only a few, as a keepsake of both of them.

I made my way through the quiet manor. It was a cold and empty place, a nutshell emptied of its meat, a bottle drained of brandy. The house was full of a darkness that my candlelight could not disperse. I paused before Bee's door, and tried to pretend for that instant that she slept warm and safe in her bed. But I unlocked the door to a chill room that smelled of disuse.

I looked first in the fine new wardrobe that Revel had devised for her. There was a precision to its tidiness that had nothing to do with a child. My heart smote me and tears ran down my face as I saw that her maid Careful had put away the treasures I'd bought my little girl in town that day. Here was a little drawer full of seashells. The red belt decorated with flowers. The boots that had been too big for her. The bag of treasures I'd sent her from Buckkeep hung on a hook. Never opened, never amazing. Her new boots, delivered for a child who would never wear them. She would have fled in what she wore that day, low house shoes, no warm cloak, no gloves. I had not thought of that, of how she must have fled through deep snow in whatever she had worn to her lessons that day.

I shut the wardrobe door. No. The candles would not be there.

There was a stand by her bed, one brought from her old room. The guttered shell of a half-burned candle was in the holder. I lifted it and smelled the faint scent of lavender. I opened the compartment, and there they were, ranked like waxy sentries. Lavender and honeysuckle and lilac and rose. I would take only four, I promised, and like a child unable to choose, I closed my eyes and reached in to take them at random.

Instead, my fingers brushed paper. I crouched down to look inside. There, wedged to one side of the candles, was an older sheaf of bound paper, given to Bee long ago when she was first mastering her letters. I set a flame to the wick of the candle in the holder and sat down on the floor. I leafed through her book. I saw her own drawings, of flowers and birds and insects, all inked so meticulously and accurately. Leaf after leaf I turned, and suddenly there was a page of writing. Not a journal of her dreams, but accounts of her days. I read it very slowly. For the first time, I learned of how she had freed her bound tongue, a tale she had never entrusted to me. I read of a kitten, encountered again as a cat. For the first time I learned of Wolf Father and how she had been lost in the spy-labyrinth on the night I had gone to meet Chade. Wolf Father? Nighteyes, or a child's imaginings? No. The Wit did not work that way. Then I came to the page that told of how Lant had shamed her and mocked her before the other children and my heart burned with fury.

I turned the page. Here she had written in a firmer hand. She had recorded the promise I had given to her. 'He said he would always take my part. Right or wrong.'

It came then. Delayed for weeks, it burst in me. The throat-tearing sorrow that could not yield to tears. The killing fury. The need to rend. I could not make it right, but I could make someone pay for how wrong it had been. They had made me fail her. I had not taken her part. She had been stolen, and I had been helpless, and now she was gone, tattered to lost threads inside a Skill-stone. They had beaten and blinded the Fool, destroyed his courage and damped his merriment to nothing. And what had I done? Next to nothing. In a faraway place, they ate and drank and slept and thought not at all of the terrible wrongs they had done.

Bee had believed in me. Taken comfort and courage from my words that day. As had the Fool. He had come all that way, cold, broken and alone, to ask me for justice. Justice too long delayed. The sudden fury and the solid resolution to avenge them coursed through me, hotter than any fever. My tears were done.

Da?

Nettle broke into my thoughts. I sensed her confusion and worry. I must have spilled over. I could not contain what I was feeling. My hidden decision burst from me. *I can delay no longer. I will not see your child born, nor hold my first grandchild in my arms. Nettle, I am sorry. I have to go. I have to avenge her. I have to find the people who sent her killers and I have to avenge her. I've no idea how far I must go but go I must.*

For long moments, I felt nothing from her. She boxed herself in so tightly that all I could sense was that she was still there. She was a hollow of sound, a seashell held to the ear. I waited.

I knew that you would. I hoped . . . well. I know you must go. Riddle told me you would have to go. She was silent a time longer. *If you could have, you would have gone after her in that moment. Right into the Skill-stone.*

I would.

Another pause. *I will go to King Dutiful and tell him why I think he should not oppose it. And frankly, why opposing it would do no good. Will I see you before you go?*

I will be using the Skill-portals to travel. So, yes, I must first return to Buckkeep. I tried to put my thoughts in order. *I'll return to Buckkeep by horseback. I will need to consult the Fool as to my route. So, yes, you will see me before I go.*

Silently, we both wondered if I would ever return.

Actually, when I reached for you tonight, it was to give you news of the Fool. And then I stumbled into your storm.

News of the Fool?
He's missing.

A lurch of loss. With you or without you, that was what he
had said. He wouldn't leave without me. Would he? He'd been
so afraid. And so tired of waiting for me to act. *How long has he
been missing?*

*I don't know. Since this morning, at least. Kettricken went to call
on him, and he was not in his room. At first she was pleased, thinking
he had gone to visit Chade or had finally decided to take some air. But
this evening, when she went back, he still was not there. Chade does
not recall him visiting. No one has seen him.*

Have you asked his serving-boy Ash?

*The Fool sent him on an errand to town, to buy smoked fish. He
returned after we'd begun to search. He's as worried as we are.*

I started to lie to her. And stopped myself. Perhaps I was as
tired of secrets as Dutiful was. Perhaps I just needed an answer
swiftly. *Look in the lower parts of the castle. The dungeons.*

What? Why?

*He knew what Chade found there. A Skill-portal incorporated into
the foundation. A rune on it that would take him to Aslevjal.*

But he has no Skill! And no reason to go to Aslevjal.

Nonetheless, can you send someone to search that area?

*I will check, but Fitz, I don't think you need worry. Dutiful had a
door of iron bars installed across that end of the corridor to make it a
bit easier for Chade to keep his promise not to use it any more. It's
always locked. Dutiful and I are the only ones with keys.*

I doubted that. I knew Chade too well to think there was any
door in Buckkeep Castle he could not open. But that did not
mean that the Fool would have access to a key. Unless Chade's
former apprentice knew of one. But even if they got past the
locked gate, the Fool had not the Skill to enter a pillar.

Please, just ask the gaolers if they saw him down there. I hesitated,
not wishing to add what I knew I must. *And please discover if any
of your Skill-users are missing. An apprentice or a talented solo.
Anyone who might be restless and willing to be persuaded to try an
experiment.*

I felt her distress at the notion. *There may be a few,* she admitted
reluctantly. *Skilled folk tend to be odd in some ways. I will try to*

discover if any are missing. But it is late and most castle folk are abed by now. I may not know until tomorrow.

I hope to set out by first light tomorrow. Skill to me if there is any news.

I will. I could feel her thinking separately from me. It was almost a whisper in my mind as she said, *Do you remember when you were a wolf and came to me in my dreams?*

Her feelings for me as she had known me then blew like a breeze through our shared thoughts. I had been mysterious and powerful, almost a romantic image in her imagination of me. I felt a pang of loss that I had become so ordinary to her. *I remember.* Her Skill had first manifested in her ability to manipulate dreams, her own and those of others. I remembered her glass tower. Her gown of butterflies.

And I remember Shadow Wolf. I knew that he would have to hunt down those who attacked his pack. I knew you would become him again, when you had been alone long enough. A pause in our communication, as if she thought of things too personal to share with me. I could feel her resignation to what I would do. It hurt me. Then, shocking me, *I wish I had known her better. I wish I'd given her more time. I always thought there would be more time for us to be sisters.* Her blast of sudden fury hit me like a spray of fire. *I wish I could go with you and help you kill them!*

Skill-silence. I was stunned. Had I forgotten this was the woman who had stood up to Tintaglia when she was little more than a girl? When her mind engaged mine again, her polished control reminded me of her great-grandfather.

Riddle will know what must be prepared for your journey. I will put him to that task. And I will prepare Dutiful to accept your decision.

And with that thought she left me, drifting away from my thoughts like the scented vapours of an extinguished candle in a cold room. I gathered my feet under me and stood slowly. I held the book protectively, as I had not held my daughter. I thought a moment longer and then stooped and blindly chose my candles. I blew out my lights and in the dark, I sniffed one of the unlit candles. Honeysuckle. A long-ago summer day. Molly gathering the white-and-pink blossoms, as busy as her bees in collecting the blossoms that would scent the wax. A memory to hold.

I returned to my den. I put another log on my fire. I would not sleep in this dark before dawn. I kindled fresh candles and took up my old pack. It held my treasures, the things I would not be parted from. I added Molly's candles and Bee's journal. As I put her little journal in beside her book of dreams, I felt I joined two halves of her life. She had lived by day as my child, and by night as a dreamer of dreams. I did not want to name her a White Prophet. I did not want to mark her as more the Fool's than mine. I had not told the Fool she kept a dream journal. I knew he would want to hear me read it, would want to possess it as much as I did. These things were all I had left of my child, and I wanted to keep them to myself.

I returned to my bedchamber. I went to my clothing chest, and from the layer beneath the false bottom of the locked chest, I provisioned myself with poisons, unguents, powders, blades and all that an assassin-turned-avenger might need. For Dutiful had unwittingly freed me. A royal assassin was bound to his king's word, to slay only as directed. Now I would slay where I would.

I had a heavy belt, one of doubled leather. Methodically, I filled the concealed compartments. The sheaths that fitted inside of a boot and hugged my ankle, the ugly bracelet that concealed a garrotte, the belt-buckle that when snatched free became a short dagger. The gloves with the brass knuckles sewn into them. So many artful, deadly nasty little tools, to sort and select and compactly pack. I had to leave room for the supplies I'd already purloined from Chade's old lair. I would go prepared.

I carried my tidy pack down to my private den. Outside, darkness still reigned. Soon enough I would rouse Perseverance and bid him ready our horses. Soon enough I would bid Withywoods farewell. I knew I should rest. I could not. I took out Bee's books and sat down by the fire.

They were hard to read. It was not her clear handwriting or painstaking illustrations. It was my reactions to the pages. There was too much of Bee in them, too much of what I had lost. I read again the first part of her journal. The references to Molly and her account of the day her mother had died were agonizing for me. I closed that book and carefully set it down. Her dream journal was little better. Here again I found the Butterfly Man dream. And a reference to the Wolf of the West and how he would come from the Mountains to save all. I turned a page. Here was a dream of a well brimming with silver. Another of a city where the ruler sat on a giant skull throne. At the bottom of each page she had carefully judged how likely each dream was to be a true dream and likely to happen. The one of the Butterfly Man had been extremely likely. The dream of the beggar I had to recognize.

Alone by the fire, I could admit to myself that Bee had been precognizant to some extent. Some things she had right such as the butterfly cloak. Others were wrong. The one wearing it had been a woman. Did it mean she was truly more mine than the Fool's? The Fool, I had always felt, was adept at twisting his strange dreams into predictions that had come true. Often I had not heard about the dream until after the event that shadowed it. But Bee's seemed almost clear to me, even though each seemed to have parts that did not quite fit with what had happened. The Wolf of the West. I'd heard those words first from the Fool. The Fool and Bee had shared a vision? I recalled what Shine had said, that Bee had been feverish and then shed a layer of skin to become paler. I decided that no matter what she had taken from the Fool, it made her no less the daughter of Molly and me.

I came to her dream of a city and of standing stones with cleanly carved runes on them. That one, I felt, was obviously not a true dream, even though she had marked it as extremely possible. I had no idea of how many of my private scrolls she had read; likely my accounts were responsible for some of her dreams. I leaned closer, studying her illustration. Yes. The runes were mostly accurate. That was almost the rune for the Elderling city with the map-tower. It had a name now. Kelsingra. Yes. That she would have taken directly from one of my scrolls. She had marked it as likely to happen. So she had foreseen being snatched into a Skill-stone, although she had copied the wrong rune from my papers. The thought that she had foreseen her own end hurt my heart. I could bear to read no more. I closed her book and nestled both of them carefully into my pack.

As dawn broke, I did my final task. The hardest farewell of Withywoods.

The fire had nearly died in my private study. The scroll-racks were emptied, their contents either burned or packed for shipment back to the Buckkeep libraries. The secret compartment in my desk had gone undiscovered; if anyone found it now, they would find only emptiness.

I shut the tall doors, lit a candle and triggered the hidden door to the spy-passageways. For a long moment I debated. Then I picked up the triptych the Fool had carved of Nighteyes, him and me. I wondered if the peculiar hinge had been discovered in the course of the repairs, but inside Bee's tiny den, all was still as she had left it. Nothing had been moved since the last time I'd been here. I smelled a faint scent of cat, but if he was about, he took care not to let me see him. I suspected he laired here now, for Bee's supply of her mother's scented candles were not nibbled by mice. I refused to wonder how he came and went. Cats, I knew, had their ways. I took the key to her bedchamber from my pocket and placed it on her shelf with her other keepsakes. Beside it I placed the carving. Here, at least, we would all be together.

I gave a final look around the hiding-place my little child had created, and then left it behind me forever. The children of the keep would perhaps remember how they had hidden in a secret corridor, but they would search the walls of the pantry in vain for a way in. And I would take to my grave the trick of opening the study entry. Let her little things be safe there as long as the walls of Withywoods stood, as she had not been. I navigated the narrow corridor and shut the concealed door behind me.

Finished. All was tidied and finished. I blew out my candle, picked up my pack and left the room.

THIRTY-TWO

Travellers

For stone remembers. It knows where it was quarried. Always it will work best when installed near its home quarry. Stones that remain near their home quarries will always be the most reliable and they should be used in preference to others whenever possible, even if it means that one must travel by several facets to reach a destination.

For other crossroads, away from all quarries, let the core stones be brought and allowed to stand, in sun and rain, for at least a score of years. Let each become full of the passage of the sunlight across its face and which stars shine above it. Cut from it then the faces that will remember the place it has stood and the stone core it was cut from.

To a core stone that has become centred in that place, apply the shaved faces of the stones from the destinations. Mark the runes carefully as to which ones are for arriving and which ones are for departing, lest one enter a stone face backwards and face an opposing current. Renew the runes to keep them sharp and clear, to aid the stone in remembering from whence it came and where it must transport the traveller.

An expert mason must always make the choice. The stone must be strong, and yet rich in the Silver veins through which magic flows. Cut the core stones eight by eight by twenty. See they are well seated in the earth, to absorb the location and to assure that the stones do not lean nor fall.

Be patient in the ageing of a stone. This patience will be repaid for scores of years.

Summary of opening passages of memory-stone cube 246, a treatise on stoneworking. I have shelved it with the memory-stones related to Elderling construction.
Skill-apprentice Scribe Lofty

I announced my decision before breakfast to the kitchen staff. None of them seemed surprised that I was returning so soon to Buckkeep. In truth, they seemed relieved. Their recovery was slow and the presence of my guard, some of them rough fellows, had been more unnerving than reassuring to them. They would be glad when we were gone.

I did the final tasks that would finish my duties to Withywoods. I gave orders that as soon as the renovations were finished, the furniture should be draped in the Rainbow chambers and most of the East Wing. I told Dixon that he would be making his reports directly to Lady Nettle and Kesit Riddle now. I gave the same directive to each of my overseers. I was pleased to see Shepherd Lin's bent shoulders straighten a bit as I conveyed full authority for the flock to him. I made arrangements for the packed scrolls to be sent by wagon to Buckkeep with Lant's and Shine's things.

Before noon, all was settled. When I went out to depart, I found not only my horse and a pack animal waiting for me, but Perseverance. 'You are certain you don't wish to stay here?' I asked him, and his impassive face was my answer. Foxglove formed up my guard. I rode away from Withywoods.

We made good time, despite a wet wind that promised to bring snow by evening. We made our journey back to Buckkeep through unseasonably warmer weather that turned the snow into wet and clinging mush and promised an early spring.

As I had feared, the Fool had been found wandering the dark and damp corridors in the foundation of Buckkeep. Nettle Skilled to me that Ash had not been with him and had been extremely relieved when he was returned safely to his chambers. She was concerned for him. I thanked her for letting me know he was safe, and worried for him for the remainder of the journey home.

We had not even reached the gates of Buckkeep before I heard a shrill cawing and then, 'Per! Per! Per!' and Motley came swooping in. She spooked Perseverance's horse but still managed to land on his shoulder while he was mastering his mount. Our guard laughed among themselves, already familiar with the crow and Per grinned to be so welcomed. As if enjoying the attention, Motley tweaked the cap from his head and he had to catch it one-handed as she attempted to fling it aside. We rode through the gates unchallenged and as we drew in our mounts near the stable I was only mildly surprised to see Ash awaiting me.

Or so I had thought. Chade's erstwhile serving-lad went to greet Perseverance, and the crow transferred happily from one boy to the other. I gave my horse over to Patience, who delayed me to say Fleeter was prospering, and then I immediately sought out the Fool's chambers.

At first, there was no answer to my knock. I waited, knocked again, waited, and just as I was about to extract a lock-pick from my collar, a voice spoke from within. 'Who's there?'

'Fitz,' I said, and waited.

It still took some time for the door to be unlocked and then there was another pause before he opened it.

'Are you well?' I asked anxiously, for he looked haggard.

'As you see,' he replied dispiritedly. He attempted a smile. 'I am sure I will be better now that you are home.'

'I heard of your misadventure.'

'Ah. That is what you call it.'

The chambers were chilly, his breakfast tray not yet cleared away, and the fire burning low. 'Why is this room so ill kept? I saw Ash outside as I rode in. Has he become slack in his duties?'

'No, no. He has just become somewhat . . . aggravating to me. He was here this morning. I dismissed him and told him I would not need him until this evening.'

There was more to this story. I kept my silence as I built up the fire and tidied the hearth, trying to behave normally. The curtains were drawn and I pushed them back to bring light into the room. The Fool looked untidy, as if he had dressed in the dark and forgotten to comb his hair. I stacked his dishes and gave the table a swipe with his napkin. Better. Somewhat. 'Well. I've just returned from Withywoods and I'm ravenous. Will you come down with me?'

'I . . . no. I've no appetite. But you should go and eat.'

'I could bring food back here and share it with you.' Even as a prince, I could still raid the guards' mess if I chose to.

'No, but thank you. You should go and eat, Fitz.'

'Enough. What happened? Why did you vanish from your rooms, why were you in the dungeon corridors?'

He crossed the room slowly and groped his way into a chair by the fire. 'I got lost,' he said. Then, as if a dammed river had suddenly broken free, he confessed, 'I opened the door to the secret passages. The one inside the servant's chamber. I am sure you remember it from your days there. I thought I could recall the way to Chade's old chambers. I . . . there was something there I'd left behind, and Ash would not fetch it for me. So I resolved I would get it myself. But instead, I got lost.'

I tried to imagine being in those chill passages, blind. I shuddered.

'I kept thinking I would find a way back into a room or a proper passage. Twice I came to dead ends and tried to work my way back. Once I came to a narrowed way where not even I could pass. And when I tried to go back from that, I came to the dead end again, and suddenly it seemed to me that I was walled up and lost and no one even knew where to begin looking for me. I shouted for help then, until I was hoarse, but I doubt anyone heard me.'

'Oh, Fool.' I dashed the dregs of his morning tea onto the fire, and took the bottle of brandy from the mantelpiece. I poured some into the cup and handed it to him.

'Oh. Thank you,' he said and reflectively lifted it to his mouth. He startled when he smelled it. 'Brandy?' And before I could reply, he took a healthy swallow.

'How did you get out?'

'I came to some steps and went down them. And down and

down and down. The smell of damp grew stronger and the walls were moist and the steps became slippery. Almost slimy. And then they just stopped. My hands were so cold, but I stood there, tracing each brick and line of mortar. Oh, Fitz. I stood there and wept, for I did not think I had the strength to limp back up all those steps. I think I went a little mad. I pounded on the wall in front of me, and to my shock it gave way. Not much, but a little. I pushed and a brick fell out, and then I pushed and pulled at the next one and finally I had a hole I could wriggle through. I had no idea where I might be and I had to wedge my way out and I could not feel how far I would fall or what I would land on. But there was no help for it, and so I let go and then I fell onto ancient straw matted with damp and who knows what else. When I could get up and grope around, I found I was in a very small chamber. There was a wooden door, with a tiny window. I was terrified then, but the door of that cell was not fastened. I went out and down a corridor. I felt other doors, and I shouted, but no one answered.' He gave an odd laugh. 'Such a king he is. Dutiful's dungeons are full of empty cells!'

I did not speak aloud how happy I was to hear that.

'So out I went, blundering on and on. Then I smelled a torch and I turned a corner and I could sense a bit of light. Torches have to be tended. So there I stayed, and frightened the poor young guard who found me there. But she soon realized who I was and told me that Lady Nettle had had the whole castle and grounds searched for me. And she brought me back up here to my rooms, and Nettle came to see if I were all right.'

And now it was time to fill in the holes in his wondrously porous tale. I started with the obvious question. 'Why are you annoyed with Ash?'

The Fool stiffened up like a prim old duchess. 'He refused to obey me.'

'What did you ask him to do?'

'To fetch something for me.'

'Fool, this is already becoming tedious.'

He turned his face away from me. 'Dragon's blood,' he said quietly.

'El of the Sea, Fool! Are you mad? With all the changes it

already wrought in you, changes that may still be going on, you would take more of it?'

'I wasn't going to swallow it!'

'Then what?'

He held up his hand and rubbed his sliced fingertips together. 'These.'

'Why?'

He took a deep breath. 'I've told you that I've begun to dream again. And that sometimes when I dream, I am a dragon. And in those dreams, I know things. I dream of a place or perhaps a time when a river ran silver with Skill. And dragons drank it and grew strong and intelligent.'

I waited.

'And in other dreams, the silver was gone from the river and it was just water. And the dragons grieved and sought for it, and found a different source for it. Ash described dragon's blood to me, Fitz. Dark red, with threads of silvery stuff coiling and swirling in it. I think the silver is pure Skill. I think it's why that dose healed me, almost like a Skill-healing. And that more of it, on my fingertips, might restore them.'

'Do you not recall Verity, with his hands coated in Skill? He did that to himself, knowing he was going to give up his life. Have you forgotten having to glove that hand at all times when you did have touches of Skill on your fingers? Why would you wish for that again?'

He kept his face turned away from me but I thought I knew his motive. He needed to be able to see again. Had he thought to attempt to cure his own blindness? A wave of pity for him washed over me. He wanted his sight so badly. I wished I could give it to him. But I could not without risking losing my own. And I would need my eyes to fulfil my goal. And his.

He had left my question hanging and I let it be. I dragged a chair close to his and sat down. 'I need your help,' I said bluntly. As I had known it would, it brought his full attention to me. But he knew me even better than I thought he did.

'We're going, aren't we?' he asked almost in wonder. 'You've finally found your anger. And we will go to Clerres and we will kill them all.'

My anger had always been with me. It had been the fire I needed to forge myself into the proper weapon. My time in that fire had tempered me into what I needed to be. Now my steel had been quenched in grief. But I did not correct him. 'Yes. But I need to plan. I need to know all that you know, of how you travelled and how long it took to get there. Details, Fool. When you were so ill and injured, I did not press you. But now you must wring every detail from your memories.'

He shifted about in his chair. 'How I came back took far longer than how I went there with Prilkop. Almost as long as it took me to journey here the very first time I came. But I think you have the means to make at least the first leg of our journey as he did.'

'The Skill-pillars.'

'Yes. We came from the map-room in Aslevjal to Buckkeep, to your Witness Stones. Then we travelled to a place I did not know. Pillars on a windswept cliff. Then to the deserted market-place . . . you remember the one, the one that was on the road to the stone dragons? And from there, to Kelsingra. And then we went to an island and the city on it. I told you about that. How we landed face down in the dirt with barely room to scrabble out from under the stone. And how unfriendly the folk were.'

'Do you recall the name of this place?'

'Furnich, I believe Prilkop called it. But . . . Fitz, we dare not go that way! They quite likely would have finished their toppling of the stone by now.'

'Indeed,' I said to myself, thinking: *Furnich*. That was a name I had not searched for. Not yet. 'And after that?'

'I think I told you about the ship. We bought passage but it was more as if we paid them to kidnap us. From Furnich, we sailed to several places, a wandering voyage. They worked us like the slaves they intended us to be. Fishbones. That was the name of one place, but it was small, just a village. There was one other place, a city. It stank and the cargo we took on there was raw hides, and they stank. That place was called, what was it, something about a tree . . . Wortletree. That was it!'

'Wortletree.' The name rang oddly familiar in my mind. I'd heard it or read it somewhere. It was a place we could find. A destination. 'And from there?'

'To Clerres. And then to the White Island. Where the school is also called Clerres.'

'The White Island.' More ports to rattle my sailor friends' brains. More clues to give Kettricken and Elliania. I wanted to rush out of the room with my new information, but I looked at my friend and knew that I could not leave him so abruptly. 'Fool. What can I do to make you feel better?'

He turned his face toward me. His golden eyes, so unnerving and so unseeing, seemed to bore into me. 'Go with me to Clerres. And kill all of them.'

'I shall. But we need to plan now. How many people do you expect me to kill, and how shall we accomplish it? Poison? Knives? Explosives?'

My question triggered a terrible joy in his sightless gaze. 'As to how, I leave that to the expert. You. How many? Forty, perhaps. Certainly no more than fifty.'

'Fifty . . . Fool, that's a staggering number.' I had imagined six or even a dozen.

'I know. But they must be stopped. They must!'

'Who were the ones who were sent for the Unexpected Son? Who would have sent them?'

I could hear his breathing. I poured a bit more brandy into his teacup and he took a healthy swallow of it. 'Dwalia was sent, but she would have been eager to go. She is not of the top echelon of Servants but oh, how she longs to be! She is a Lingstra, rather like an emissary. They are sent on errands, to gather information or to tip events in the direction the Servants think they should go.'

'I don't understand.'

'Lingstras behave as Catalysts for the Servants. Instead of supporting a true White Prophet and allowing him to find his Catalyst and change the world as his vision bids, they study all the prophecies and employ the Lingstras to set the world in a path that will best benefit them. An example. Say there is a prediction that a disease that kills sheep will sweep through an area where all depend on sheep for a livelihood. The sheep will die and the livelihood of all will be destroyed. What might one do?'

'One might study to see what cures there are for a sheep plague? Or warn the shepherds to keep their flocks from mingling.'

'Or one might seek to gain from it, by buying up wool and good quality breeding stock, so that when disease makes wool scarce and sheep hard to find, one can sell them at a great profit.'

I was silent, shocked a bit.

'Fitz, do you remember the first time I came to you and asked you to do something?'

'Fat suffices,' I said quietly.

'A silly poem from a dream I had when I was barely seven. A dream that made you keep a lonely young woman's lapdog alive, and give her advice to make her step up into her role as a duchess. A little tipping point. But what if someone went there and deliberately poisoned her dog, and set her at odds with her husband. What then?'

'The Six Duchies might have fallen to the Red Ships.'

'And the dragons might have been extinct forever.'

A sudden question stung me. 'Why are the dragons so important? Why were the Servants so opposed to the dragons being revived?'

'I don't have the answers to those questions, Fitz. The Servants are a secretive folk. Dragons being absent benefited them somehow. On that, I would wager my life. Yet over and over, my dreams came to me and told me that dragons must be returned to the world, dragons, full of beauty and power and might. I did not even know what sort of dragons. Stone dragons? Real dragons? But together we brought them back. And oh, how the Servants hate us for it.'

'Is that why they took my child?'

I was surprised when he reached across and put his hand on my forearm. 'Fitz. It was an intersection of fates and futures, a very powerful one. If they could discover how much they have injured both of us, they would rejoice. They have struck us down, haven't they? Dwalia came looking for the Unexpected Son. She was so certain I knew where he could be found. I didn't, but she was willing to destroy me to find out what I did not know. And she has destroyed both of us, by taking and then losing our child. They have destroyed the hope of this world, the one that could guide us on a better course. We cannot restore that. But if we cannot give the world hope, we can remove some of its despair by killing those who serve only their own greed.'

'Tell me more about them.'

'They are tremendously wealthy. They have been corrupt for generations, and they use the prophecies to make themselves ever wealthier. They know what to buy to sell later at a much higher price. They manipulate the future, not to make the world a better place but only to add to their wealth. The White Island is their castle, their palace and their citadel. At low tide, there is a causeway. When the tide comes in, it becomes a sea-swamp. It is called the White Island not for the White Prophets who once were sheltered and taught there, but for the fortified city, all made of bones.'

'Bones?' I exclaimed.

'Ancient bones of immense sea creatures. The island itself, some say, is a heap of bones. When they existed, they came to that area to breed and to die. The bones, Fitz : . . . ah. I have never been able to imagine a creature so large as to have such bones. But the palisade that surrounds the city is made of thighbones, as tall and stout and hard as stone. Some say they are bones that turned to stone but kept their shape. And that the palisade and some of the structures are older even than the Servants and the legend of the Whites they once served.

'But if ever the Servants truly served, they have long ago forgotten that duty. There are ranks of Servants. The bottom level consists of the Servitors. We need not be overly concerned with most of them. They come, hoping to rise in the ranks of Servants, but most remain humble serving folk all their lives. When we destroy those who rule them, they will disperse.

'Some few are the children born to the Servants, the second and third offspring with ambitions. Those may present problems for us. Next come the Collators who read the dreams and sort them and make copies and keep indexes. The Collators are for the most part harmless. The clever ones are used as fortune-tellers by the Servants, to fleece folk of their coins by bending prophecies to suit their wishes. Again, they would be little threat if the upper hierarchy were gone. Like ticks on a dog. If the dog is dead, the ticks starve.

'Then there are the Lingstras, like Dwalia. The Lingstras largely do as they are told by the Manipulors. And no wickedness is beyond the Lingstras once their masters give their orders. The Manipulors are the ones who take counsel over the massed dreams of hundreds of years, to study them and to discover how best to build the wealth of the Servants. And above the Manipulors is the Council of Four. They are the root of the evil that the Servants have become. All descended from Servants, they have known no other life than wealth and privilege built on the stolen prophecies that should be employed to better the world. They would be the ones who would have decided that they must possess the Unexpected Son, at any cost.'

And I knew in that moment that they were the four I would kill. I pushed on with my questions. 'There were others. Shine said Dwalia called them her luriks.'

He pinched his lips tightly together. 'They can be seen as benighted children who believe too firmly in all they are told.' The set of his mouth told me he did not agree with that assessment. In a deadlier voice he added, 'Or you can see them as traitors to their own kind. They are the children of the Whites who did not breed true, or showed their talent for precognition in strange ways. Vindeliar is an example of that. Some see nothing of the future, but are adept at remembering every dream they have ever read. They are like walking libraries of the dream-scrolls, able to cite what they read and tell who dreamed it and when. Others are adept at interpreting an event and listing the dreams that foretold it in various forms. The ones who followed Dwalia and died here deserved to die. On that, you can absolutely believe me.'

'So you have said. Do you remain certain of that?'

'I speak of the ones who held and passed the tools of my misery. The ones who pushed the needles into my back to shoot the burning colours under my skin. The ones who so meticulously incised the slices in my face. The ones who cut the Skill from my fingertips.' He took a shuddering breath. 'Ones who chose to live free of inconvenience by tolerating the agony and degradation of others.'

I had begun to tremble but not as badly as he did. He shook.

I went to him, drew him to his feet and held him tightly, as much to still my own shaking as his. We had both known the torturer's touch, and that creates a common ground that is hard for others to understand. 'You killed them,' he reminded me. 'The ones who tormented you in Regal's dungeon. When you had the chance, you killed them.'

'I did.' My tongue stilled. I recalled a youngster, the last of his patrol, dying of poison. Did I regret him? Perhaps. But if I were in that situation again, I'd still do as I'd done. I squared my shoulders and renewed my promise. 'And when I gain the chance, Fool, I will do the same to those who tormented you. And to those who gave you over to torture.'

'Dwalia,' he said and his voice went deep with hatred. 'She was there. In the gallery, watching. Mimicking my screams.'

'Gallery?' I asked, confused.

He set his palms against my chest and pushed me suddenly away. I took no offence. I knew that sudden need not to be touched. When he spoke, his voice had gone high and he sounded as if he would laugh, but he did not. 'Oh, yes, they have a gallery. It's a much more sophisticated arena for torment than you Buckmen could ever imagine. There they might cut open the chest of a strapped-down child who shows no promise, to show the beating heart and swelling lungs to those who would later learn to be healers. Or torturers. Many come to witness torture, some to record every word that is spoken and others to while away a tiresome afternoon. Fitz, when you can control the course of events, when you can precipitate a famine or bring wealth to a seaport and all who live near it, the suffering of one individual comes to mean less and less. We Whites are chattel to them, to be bred or slaughtered as they please. Yes, there is a gallery. And Dwalia looked down on me as I bled.'

'I wish I had been able to kill her for you then, Fool. And for me as well.'

'So I wish also. But there are others. Those who raised and shaped her. Those who gave her power and permission.'

'Yes. So tell me of them.'

More the Fool told me that afternoon, and I listened well. The more he talked, the calmer he became. There were things he knew that might be useful. He knew of the deep spring that supplied the palace with water, and he knew of the four towers where the Council members each slept. He knew of the horns that sounded when folk could cross the causeway and enter the fortified city that was the White Island, and of the bell that tolled to warn folk that they must leave or risk being caught by the rising tides. He knew of the walled garden and the great house where the Whites and part-Whites were housed, knowing no other world than that. 'Raised like penned cattle thinking the pen is the world. When I first came to Clerres, the Servants kept me apart from their Whites, and I truly believed that I was the only White left in the world. The only White Prophet for this generation.' He sat silent, and then he sighed. 'Then the Pale Woman, at that time little more than a girl, demanded to meet me. She hated me from the time she saw me, for I was so certain I was all she was not. She decreed that I must be tattooed as I was. And when they were done, they put me in with the others. Fitz, they hoped I would breed for them. But I was young, too young to be interested in such things, and the tales I told the others of my home and my family, of market days and cows to milk, and pressing grapes for wine . . . Oh. How they envied me those memories, and how they insisted they must only be tales. By day they mocked me and set me apart, but in the evenings, they would gather around me and ask me questions and listen to my tales. They scoffed, even then, but I felt their hunger. At least for a time, I had had all that they had never known. The love of my parents. My sisters' fond teasing. A little white cat that trotted at my heels. Ah, Fitz, I had been such a happy child.

'And telling them my tales sharpened my own hunger, until I had to take action. And so I escaped. And made my slow way to Buckkeep.' He shrugged his thin shoulders. 'To wait to discover you. To begin our tasks.'

And so he spoke, and I was entranced, as he shared so much I had never known of him. I sat and I listened to him, afraid to break the spell of such honesty. When he ceased speaking, I realized the day was dimming to a close. There was still so much I needed to do.

I persuaded him then to let me ring for Ash and have food brought for him, and perhaps ask for a bath to be brought. For I guessed now that he had neither bathed nor changed his clothes since he had returned from his misadventure. When I rose to leave, he smiled at me.

'We're going there. We're going to stop them.' It sounded like a promise.

'I am but one man, Fool. Your quest demands an army.'

'Or the father of a stolen and murdered child.'

So he described me, and for a moment my pain and my fury were one emotion. I did not speak but I felt that thin shiver of awareness between us. And he replied to that.

'I know,' he said. 'I know.'

Later that day I tapped at Chade's door, and when no one answered, I slipped inside. He was dozing in a cushioned chair before the fire with his stockinged feet up on a stool. I stepped to the door of his bedchamber, expecting to find some attendant there, Shine or Steady or a Skill-apprentice.

'We're alone. For once.'

I startled at his words and turned to look at him. He had not opened his eyes. 'Chade?'

'Fitz.'

'You sound much better than the last time I saw you. Almost like your old self.'

He drew a deeper breath and opened his eyes. Awake, he looked more aged than he had asleep. 'I am not better. I cannot Skill. Nothing in my body feels right any more. My joints ache and my stomach seems angry no matter what I eat.' He stared at his feet, propped up in front of the fire. 'It's all catching up with me, my boy. All the years.'

I do not know what made me do it. I went to his chair and sat on the floor beside it, as if I were eleven again and he my master. He set his bony hand on my head and ruffled my hair. 'Oh, my boy. My Fitz. There you are. Now. When are you leaving?'

He knew. And for that moment, he was Chade as he had been always to me, knowing everything. It was a relief to speak to someone who understood me from the bones out. 'As soon as I can. I've waited for weather, I've gathered my information and regained my Skill. I've tightened my muscles and renewed some skill with a blade. So much time I had to waste.'

'Sharpening your knife is never a waste of time. You've finally learned that. Not an apprentice any longer, nor even a journeyman. This makes you a master.'

'Thank you,' I said quietly and was surprised at the heart I took from his words. 'I'll have to travel part of the way by the pillars, and from there, I'll have to travel overland, and then take ship. It will be a very long journey.'

He nodded. His hand still rested on my head. 'My son wants to go with you,' he said quietly.

'Lant?'

'Yes. He has spoken of it to me often, when he thought he was talking to my empty shell. He wants to go. And I want him to as well. Take him with you. Let him prove himself to himself and bring him back to me a man.'

'Chade, I can't. He's not . . .'

'He's not like us. He lacks our capacity for hate. Or vengeance. He was appalled at what befell his so-called stepmother, but it had to be done. I know that, but he can't see it. He would have gone to her and promised that he would make no claim on Vigilant's estates. He believed he could calm her.' Chade shook his head. 'He doesn't recognize evil, even when it's delivered a rib-cracking beating to him. He's a good man, Fitz. Probably better than either of us. But he doesn't feel as if he's a man. Take him with you.'

'I don't understand why he'd want to go.'

Chade gave a huff of laughter. 'You are as close as he has to an elder brother. And who was my boy before he was? The tales I told of that nameless boy fired him with rivalry and with a desire to be like him. And be liked by him. In his early training, I made you the rival for my regard that he could never best. The one he determined he would equal. He longed to step up, to be in our company. Then he met you, and he failed. And failed again, and again. Fitz. I cannot give him what he seeks. I know you mean to go alone. That would be a mistake. Trust me in this, and take

Lant. Until he wins your regard, he has none for himself. So take him. Let my son prove himself a man to you and to himself. Let both of you set aside all rivalry and jealousy.'

Jealously? I felt no jealousy of that pup! But it was easier not to dispute that with Chade. I did not want to take Lant and I knew I could not take him, but I didn't say no to Chade. For this moment, he was my old mentor as he had always been. I wanted no quarrel with him, not when I feared it might be my last conversation with him. I shifted our focus. 'Have you been feigning illness all this time?'

'No. Only sometimes. It suits me to seem weak. Fitz, I don't trust Rosemary. She has convinced Dutiful that he does not need assassins such as you and me. She's been letting all my nets unravel. All my informants have gone unpaid, and unable to report to me. Everything I built, all those years. It's falling apart.'

'Chade. I still have to go. I cannot stay here and take up your webs.'

'Heh!' He laughed and I looked up to see him smiling fondly at me. 'As if you could. As if anyone could. No, Fitz. I'm failing and I know it. And no one will come after me. The time for such as me is past. No, I do not ask that you stay and take up my work. Go and do what you must.'

'Chade. Why do you pretend to be feeble, with a wandering mind?'

He laughed again. 'Oh, Fitz. Because I am. Not every day and every hour. Sometimes I feel I am as sharp as ever. And then I cannot find my slippers, and I look and look, to find they were on my feet all that time.' He shook his head at himself. 'Better that people think I am wandering all the time than know the truth. I don't want Rosemary to see me as a threat to her assumption of power.'

I was incredulous. 'Do you fear her?'

'Stop. I can already hear you thinking of how you will kill her for me. A slow poison, a fall down the steps. No one the wiser and the old man kept safe.'

He was right. It made me smile, and then I tried to feel ashamed of that. I couldn't. He was right about me.

'So let her have it, my den and my bed, my tools and even

my writings. She won't find the key ones. No one will. Except perhaps you. When you come back.' He took a deep breath and sighed it out again. 'I have another task now. Shine. There is so much time to make up for. They thought to punish me by killing her or marrying her off to some cloddish brute, but what they did was worse. She is vapid, Fitz. And vain. Ignorant. But she need not be. There is a bright mind there, turned to all the wrong things. Kettricken teaches her now and I do not despise what she teaches my daughter. But for all her years, Kettricken is still naïve in some ways. She still believes that honesty and good will triumph in the end. So I must be here, for my Shine, to teach her that a little knife in her boot or a well-planned bolthole may be the key to a long life.

'And I want to be here to watch her bloom. They were all so astonished when I unlocked her Skill. They came on the run, they did, and helped her put up her walls and blocked her in until she can learn to master it. But she's going to be strong, Fitz. Strong. If ever they doubted the Farseer blood ran true in me, my daughter will disprove them.'

So strange, to hear him admit that old doubt. 'You are as much Farseer as I am,' I assured him.

He rumpled my hair again. 'I've a gift for you,' he said quietly. 'I sent for it some time ago. It's from Jamaillia, by way of Bingtown, where they enlarged and corrected it. You should take it with you. It's in the scroll-case on top of the shelf in my bedroom. The case is dyed blue. It's for you. Go get it now.'

I rose and went to his bedchamber. I found the scroll-case and brought it back to him. He took it from me and directed me, 'Find a chair and pull it up here.'

And by the time I had done that, he had opened the case and pulled out the rolled-up map. For such it was. The leather had been scraped thin and it uncoiled to twice the size I had expected it to be. It was done on calfskin, and inked all in gleaming colours. The lettering was wondrous tiny but still clear to read. There were the Six Duchies, and the Mountain Kingdom. Chalced, and the Rain Wilds. And beyond them, the Cursed Shores, with Bingtown, and then on, to far Jamaillia, with the Pirate Isles. And beyond them, the Spice Isles. 'It's beautiful,

Chade. But it's so different from every other map of Chalced or the Rain Wilds or—'

'Much more accurate,' he said brusquely. 'With increased traffic through that region, we now have far better charts and maps. Verity drew his maps based on what he knew himself, and the resources of the time. There were no freely available charts of the Rain Wild River, and those he bought were the work of charlatans intent only on gaining coin. The same is true for the interior of Chalced. And of course Bingtown and those regions. Charts of the Cursed Shores are notoriously bad because of the storms that change the shorelines and river mouths almost every season. But there it is. The best map that Six Duchies gold could buy. I intended to keep it, but I'm giving it to you. Along with this.'

His flick of his wrist was not as limber as it once had been. I was still impressed when a bone tube slid into his hand. He unscrewed a finely-tooled stopper and shook out a small roll of paper so fine it was almost translucent. 'This is my work,' he said, holding it coiled in his hand. 'The work I saw fit to do, knowing the danger but deeming it necessary. Aslevjal will not stand forever. As the ice caverns have warmed and the water has run, the old halls are leaking. Green slime and moss have begun to venture through the passages. Mould grows on the map they left there.'

He proffered the rolled paper to me. I opened it carefully. My silence was awe. 'Every detail,' I finally said aloud in slow amazement.

He chuckled his delight at my realization of what he had handed me. 'Every Skill-portal is marked. The engraving on the Elderling map there was fading, but I copied all I could see, Fitz. It will tell you what was graven on each face of every pillar. The destinations available to you. I intended to transfer it all to my new map, but my vision is fading. And I no longer feel inclined to share my hard-won secrets with those who do not appreciate the risks I ran to get them. If they wish to think me a foolish and reckless old man, then let them see me that way.'

'Oh, Chade. This is—' His flapping hand interrupted my gratitude. He had never been good at accepting thanks.

'You take it, my boy. Finish my work.'

He went suddenly into a coughing fit and gestured wildly for water, but when I brought it to him, he coughed so badly he could not drink it at first. When he could, he seemed to choke on it, and then finally to gasp in a free breath. 'I'm fine,' he wheezed. 'Don't delay here. Take it and go before Shine comes back. Curious as a cat is that one! Be away now. If she sees you carry anything out of here, she will natter me with questions until I cannot think. Go, Fitz. But bid me farewell before you leave. And come to me first when you return.'

'I will.' And moved by what impulse I do not know, I stooped and kissed his brow.

He hooked his bony hand around the back of my head and for a moment held me close. 'Oh, my boy. The best mistake Chivalry ever made was you. Go on, now.'

And I did. I carried the map-case under my arm, but the bone cylinder had gone up my sleeve as soon as Chade had said it was mine. Back in my fine new chamber, I found the fire burning brightly, my bed spread smoothly and my other boots polished to a sheen by the wardrobe. Someone had placed a decanter of amber brandy on my mantelpiece with two fine little glasses beside it. Servants gave one very little privacy. It took some thinking to come up with two different hiding-places that might withstand scrutiny and tidying. I stitched a loop to the back of a tapestry and secured Chade's pillar-map there. The other map-case was larger, but I found a spot atop the trim that held up the bed curtains. It was reassuringly dusty and I hoped it would remain so.

That done, I sat down by myself for the first time since I'd returned from Withywoods. I toed off my boots and peeled the damp stockings from my feet. I sat and felt the heat of the fire penetrate my body. The brandy proved to be of an excellent quality and I reflected wearily that drinking it on an empty stomach was not my best idea today.

Fitz. Da? I've heard you are back at Buckkeep Castle. Both Dutiful and I are very anxious to sit down with you. Will you join us in my sitting room, please?

Of course. When?

Now, please. Dutiful had rather expected you would come to see him as soon as you'd returned.

Of course. I should have. I was concerned for the Fool.

And Chade, too.

I found him better than I expected, I admitted, and wondered a bit woefully how she knew so clearly of all my movements since I had returned.

He has good days, and some that are not so good. Will you come now, please? The king has taken this time for us from a very busy schedule.

Immediately.

Dry socks. I started to pull on the cleaned boots and then looked at myself. Rumpled shirt. Weather-stained trousers. I opened the wardrobe and found an array of new shirts, variously afflicted with buttons. I'd never owned so many clothes in my life and I wondered who was arranging these for me. Ash? Nettle? Some poor servant in charge of dressing bastards elevated to noble status?

They fitted me well enough, though there was room for more paunch than was flattering. I'd chosen a blue shirt and I paired it with dark trousers. I added the waistcoat that had been hung with the shirt. There was a ribbony thing with it that I didn't know how to wear. I hoped it wasn't important. The waistcoat was long, hanging almost to my knees.

Neither the shirt nor the waistcoat had any hidden pockets. As I went to my meeting with them with little more than the knife in my boot, I wondered how I would defend either of them if danger threatened. I felt oddly naked. I hurried down the corridors to Nettle's chambers, stood outside her door, and hesitated. Then I knocked.

A serving-boy opened it and said, 'Oh! Prince FitzChivalry!' and then hit his head on the corner of the door as he dived into a low bow. I caught his elbow before he hit the floor and steadied him as he repeatedly apologized. I was still holding onto him when Nettle came to the door and demanded, 'What goes on here?'

'He hit his head on the doorframe,' I explained, and the boy babbled, 'Yes, my lady, that was exactly what happened!' in such a panicked voice that I scarcely believed him, let alone Nettle.

She gave me a horrified look and I tried to release the boy gently. He still sat down flat on the floor.

'This way, please,' she said and I followed her in silence.

'Really,' I whispered. 'He bowed too fast and hit his head on the door.'

For all that Nettle was my daughter, I had visited her chambers only seldom on long-ago visits to Buckkeep. Now I entered her sitting room to find it as stuffed with royalty as a pie is with cherries. The king and the queen were both seated facing the hearth while Kettricken stood by the window, holding the curtain back to peer out at the evening. Shine was beside her. Lant and Prince Prosper stood near the fireplace mantel. Prince Integrity was poking the coals, and Dutiful's Wit-dog gave me a piercing look as I entered. Chade was the only Farseer not present.

It was my turn to make a low bow to my king and queen. 'My lord, my lady, I regret my delay in coming here today—'

'There's no time left for formality,' Dutiful cut me off in a weary voice. 'Nettle already told us that you are determined to go after the people who sent raiders into Buck to steal Bee and Lady Shine.'

Bluntness called for honesty. 'Exactly,' I said.

'Your intent being?'

'Vengeance!' My queen spoke for me with a vehemence that surprised me. 'Bloody and righteous vengeance on those who stole a daughter of our blood. Just as he wrought when the Pale Woman stole my mother and sister! If we had known that they had a distant den to hide in, we could have carried the war to them then! And this would never, never have happened!' Elliania lifted a shaking hand and pointed it at Integrity. 'I give you my son. He will ride beside you, to avenge this grievous insult, this terrible loss to our mothershouse! I will send to my mother the narcheska and my sister Kossi, and she will muster the men of the Narwhal Clan to join you!'

Integrity's colour was very high. 'Mother, I vow . . .'

'Integrity! Vow not.' Dutiful shot me a desperate look. 'It puts my lady very much in mind of the time when little Kossi was stolen. And at night, she has evil dreams of when she was tormented and forced to offer herself as bait to lure us into the Pale Woman's trap.'

Oh. Never had I seen it that way, or considered what memories my own tragedy must wake in her. I dropped to my knees in front of Elliania and looked up into her face. Tears were streaming and by the look of her eyes, not for the first time this day. 'My queen. Please. Dry your tears and have faith in me. I promise you that I go, and soon, to discover where these snakes nest. Let Integrity remain here, at your side. If I have need of him, I will send word to Nettle to summon him, and then he can come, bringing whatever force you deem necessary, following a way I will clearly chart for them. But for now, Queen Elliania, let me go alone and secretly.'

It was not an easy posture to hold, on my aching knees, my head craned down and my face twisted up to look into hers. She bit her lip, and then gave a minuscule nod.

'Alone?' I had not realized Riddle was in the room until he spoke.

'Alone,' I affirmed.

'What of me?'

Nettle opened her mouth but I was faster. 'You already know the answer to that. If you do not stay, I cannot go. Nettle is heavy with child. Your place is here, guarding that which is precious to both of us.'

He bowed his head to that. 'Still. You should not go alone,' he said quietly.

'He won't be alone,' Lant interjected. 'I'm going with him.'

I turned to face him but spoke to the whole room. 'Lord Chade already suggested I take FitzVigilant. And I deeply appreciate his offer. But as I must make the first step of my journey via the Skill-stones, I fear I must go alone, even if it were not my preference.'

Lant set his jaw and gave me a baleful stare. I opened my hands helplessly and shrugged.

'And what of the Fool?' Dutiful demanded abruptly.

I hadn't wanted to discuss that. 'He must remain here, and for the same reasons. I have not had the heart to tell him so, but I will. I travel by the pillars and that will be risky enough for me to do alone. Last time I attempted to bring the Fool through a stone I drained Riddle's strength to take him with me.' I turned my head, speaking to all of them. 'It's very simple. I intend to go alone and swiftly. I will find the way to Clerres. I will study its weaknesses. And then I will send for who and what I need.' I forced a smile to my face. 'Not even I would be so foolish as to imagine I could carry out a solo attack against a city.'

For a moment, a silence fell, and I wondered how many of them did imagine I would be that foolish. Then the objections erupted.

'But, FitzChivalry—'

'Fitz, you will need—'

'What is your plan?' Kettricken spoke from her post near the window. Her low voice cut through the others and silence fell.

'It's not much of a plan.' I clambered to my feet. My knees made small noises. My body healed swiftly but it still objected to some things. 'I've gathered some tools and supplies. I've consulted with the Fool about my journey. He's given me some names of ports: Fishbones. Furnich. Wortletree. Clerres. And I am ready to leave. Tomorrow.'

Kettricken was shaking her head slowly. I turned to look at Dutiful. 'No,' he said succinctly. 'You can't do it that way, Fitz. There has to be a farewell dinner, and you must ride out of Buckkeep like a prince, not slink off like a—'

He fumbled for words. 'Lone wolf,' Nettle supplied in a low voice.

'Exactly,' Dutiful concurred. 'You have been reintroduced to the court. You can't simply vanish.'

Dismay rose in me like a tide. 'Must all know what I go to do?'

There was a moment of quiet. Dutiful spoke slowly. 'There have been rumours. Rumours from Withywoods, gossip among the guard companies. Bodies found. Evidently the pale folk would rather kill themselves than be captured or face hardship surviving alone. They leapt from the sea cliffs. They were seen doing so, and later the remains washed ashore. So there have been questions. And fears. We have to offer some answers.'

Chade would have been proud of me. The perfect deception came immediately to mind. 'Let us announce that I am going to ask counsel of the Elderlings, as to what I should do against such an enemy. And that is why I depart by the Skill-stone and alone.'

'The True Elderlings,' Kettricken supplied.

'True Elderlings?'

'Some of the correspondence we have received from Bingtown asserts that the Traders who settled in Kelsingra with their hatched dragons are insisting that they are now Elderlings. A claim I find both preposterous and offensive.' She had seen Verity absorbed into his stone dragon, but some part of her believed in the old legends of the wise Elderlings forever feasting in their halls of stone, their dragons sleeping but ready to awaken to the call of the Six Duchies. That same legend had lured Verity to the Mountains in search of the Elderlings, the legendary allies of the Six Duchies.

'I think that will be a very acceptable tale,' I suggested and looked around at my family. They were all nodding except Riddle. He had that weary expression that I had often worn when Chade would announce one of his masquerades.

'Give me five days to make all ready,' Dutiful suggested.

'I should like to leave in two,' I said quietly. One would have been better.

'Three, then,' he compromised.

I still had a difficulty. 'I must entrust the Fool to your safe-keeping. He will not be pleased about this, for he believes he must go with me. He thinks he can make the journey, despite blindness and his frail health. But I do not think I can care for him and still travel by the stones as swiftly as I need to.'

Kettricken had come to stand beside me. She set her hand on my arm. 'Leave our old friend in my hands, Fitz. I will see that he is neither neglected nor overwhelmed. It would be my pleasure to do so.'

'I will send word to my brothers and Hap, to let them know you are departing,' Nettle offered. She shook her head. 'I do not think they will have time to journey here and wish you farewell.'

'Thank you,' I told her, and wondered why such niceties never occurred to me. Then I knew. Farewells were always hard for me. And I'd left the most difficult one for last. The Fool was not going to be pleased with my plan.

It was difficult for me to extract myself from that gathering. Suggestions and ideas and warnings from those who loved me battered me until almost the dinner hour. As we left the chamber,

I informed them that I had to visit the Fool again. Kettricken nodded grimly. Riddle, ever pragmatic, said he would see that food and wine were sent up to Mage Grey's rooms.

I dragged my feet through the halls of Buckkeep, inventing and discarding a hundred ways of telling him that I was leaving him behind. I stood for a long time outside his door. At last I decided there was no good way to give him the news. Once more, I considered a coward's way out; I simply would not tell him. I would just go.

But I was certain that Ash would be a party to the announcement of my departure, and what he knew, the Fool would know. I lifted my hand and knocked and waited. Spark opened the door to me. She smiled to see me, and I decided that perhaps they had made up their quarrel. 'It's Prince FitzChivalry, sir. Shall I admit him?' she called merrily over her shoulder.

'Of course!' He sounded hearty. I peered past Spark to see Lord Grey sitting at his table. Motley was on the table, among an assortment of small items. I guessed at the game they'd been playing. I was glad at how quickly he'd recovered his spirits and miserable that I would soon destroy his cheerfulness. But I had no choice.

No sooner was the door closed behind me than he demanded, 'How soon do we leave?'

Just say it. 'I leave in three days.'

'I'll be ready.'

'I can't take you with me.'

He cocked his head at me. Shock was replaced with a desperate smile. 'And yet well you know you cannot find the way there without me.'

'I can.' I stepped around Spark and moved toward the table. I drew out the other chair and sat down opposite him. He opened his mouth. 'No,' I said firmly. 'Hear me out. I can't take you, Fool. I make the first part of my journey by the stones, using the same ones that Bee did. I dare not try to take you through with me—'

'I dare!' he declared over the top of my words, but I kept speaking.

'You are still healing. It's not just your body that needs time, as well we both know. It's best you take that time here at Buckkeep, where you are warm, safe and fed, among friends. It's my hope that as your health improves, the King's Own Coterie can attempt a fuller Skill-healing, perhaps even restore your vision. I know it must sound harsh to you, but if I try to take you with me, it will slow me down and may well kill you.'

The crow and the serving-girl regarded me with hard, bright eyes. The Fool was breathing hard through his nose, as if he'd just climbed a towerful of stairs. His hands gripped the edge of the table. 'You mean it,' he said in a shaking voice. 'You're leaving me here. I hear it in your voice.'

I drew a deep breath, 'If I could, Fool, I would—'

'But you can. You can! Take the risk! Take all the risks! So we die in a stone, or on a ship, or at Clerres. So we die, and it ends. We die together.'

'Fool, I—'

'She wasn't only your child! She was the hope of the world. And she was mine, and I only ever touched her for one brief moment! Why can you imagine I'd hesitate to risk my life for the chance to avenge her? To bring all Clerres crashing down around their ears! What, do you imagine I'll sit here and drink tea and chat with Kettricken while you go off without me? Fitz! Fitz! You can't do this to me! You can't!'

His voice had risen and he shouted the last words at me, as if shouting would somehow change the logic of my decision. When he paused to draw breath, we all heard the knocking at the door. The cadence indicated it had been going on for some time.

'Take care of that!' the Fool snapped at Spark.

With a pale face and folded lips, she did as she was ordered. The Fool sat across from me, his chest heaving. I sat still and silent, not listening to the words at the door. Spark closed it and came to the table bearing a tray. 'Someone sent food for this room.'

'I thought we might discuss this over dinner. I'd hoped to learn more that might help me.'

Spark set the tray down between us with a sharp clack. The savoury fragrance of seared meat seemed to come from some other world where such pleasures mattered.

Watching the Fool's anger build was almost terrifying. It seemed to come up from somewhere deep in his chest. I saw his chest swell and his shoulders bunched. His hands clenched and the tendons in his throat stood out. I knew what he was going to do an instant before he did it, but I made no move as he seized the sides of the tray of food and wine and upended it toward me. The gravy was hot and a wineglass bounced from my brow before dumping its contents in my lap. It fell to the floor with a soft chime of impact and then rolled in a half-circle.

Spark gasped. The crow uttered a harsh, 'ha, ha, ha!' before opening her wings and hopping from the table to the floor. Without hesitation, she began to sort through the food. I lifted my eyes from her to the Fool's frozen countenance. 'More that might help you? More that might help you to leave me behind here? You will hear nothing more from me. Get out. GET OUT!'

I rose. There had been linen napkins with the tray of food. I took one and wiped most of the food from my chest and lap. I folded the mess into it and set it quietly on the table. I spoke. I knew I should not, I knew it, and yet the words came out of my mouth. 'And this is yet another reason I cannot take you with me. You have lost all control of yourself, Fool. I came to tell you that I'm going alone. I did that. Goodnight.'

And I left him there, with the crow eating and Spark weeping noisily enough for all of us.

The next few days passed in a whirl. Two seamstresses came to my room early the next morning and measured me thoroughly for 'travelling clothes'. I told them to leave off any decorative buttons. A day later, they delivered to my room sturdy shirts and trousers in subtle browns and a tightly-woven cloak lined with fur. The lightweight leather armour came separately and was of a quality I had never experienced. The high-collared waistcoat would protect my chest, belly and throat. There were greaves and vambraces, also brown and unmarked by any insignia. I was pleased that Dutiful had known I would need to travel quietly and unremarked. But then came another delivery, of a lovely Buck-blue cloak and blue-dyed leather gloves lined with lamb's wool, and a doublet embroidered all over with bucks and narwhals. I began to guess that there was more than one kind heart supplying me for my journey.

My worn pack was replaced with one of weatherproofed canvas with sturdy straps. The first things I put into it were Bee's books and Molly's candles. Those would go with me to the ends of the earth.

The word had gone out that I would be leaving, and the farewell notes, invitations and gifts were overwhelming. And yet all must be acknowledged and politely refused. Every loose thread snipped or tied. Ash came to my room, grim-faced and silent, and every day presented me with all these missives sorted into tidy piles.

And daily, I returned to the Fool's room and daily failed at reasoning with him. I endured the Fool's constant imprecations and pleas that I reconsider. I continued to see him daily and he continued to batter me with anger, sorrow, sarcasm and silence. I held firm. 'You will never penetrate those walls without me. I am your only hope of gaining entry,' he told me more than once. The more I refused to discuss it, the more he talked only about it. It did not stop my daily visits but I counted down to the last one.

Two days before my departure, Kettricken summoned me to her audience chamber. That day no one else was waiting, having been warned she was busy for the whole day. I was admitted immediately and found her busy with pen and paper. A scroll-rack had been brought in, and it held perhaps a score of scrolls. She was kneeling on a cushion, pen in hand, head bent over a vellum.

'Just in time,' she said as I entered. 'I've finished.' She lifted a container and sanded her wet ink.

I opened my mouth to speak and she held up a hand. 'Many years ago, I suffered as I have watched you suffer. I waited in idleness, knowing nothing of the fate of my husband. Of my love.' Her voice broke slightly on the word. 'When I set out at last, I had nothing to guide me except hope and a map.' She tapped the sand from the vellum and offered it to me. 'A map. With Clerres on it. And Fishbones and Wortletree and all the other places you've been seeking. A map based on old drawings and hearsay and tales from that old sailor.'

I stared at her incredulously. 'The one from the tavern? He had little enough to tell me.'

She smiled. 'Him, and a few others. More than a little I have learned from our good Chade through the years. And informants love to be paid. A few were clever enough to move up the chain and come to me with empty palms waiting. A few coins and they are mine now, Fitz, and with them all they knew.' A steaming pot and two cups had been waiting on the table. She wore a little cat-smile as she poured a bit, considered the colour, and then filled our cups. As she set one before me, she blushed and said, 'Tell me you are proud of me.'

'Always. And astounded!'

Her hand was more delicate that Verity's but her work as precise. She had noted that sailing into Wortletree at low tide was inadvisable, and a few other snippets of information.

We had finished our tea when she asked suddenly, 'You don't expect to come back, do you?'

I gaped at her. Then I demanded, 'How did you know?'

'You've the look that Verity had when he was carving his dragon. He knew he'd begun something that he would not return from.'

We both fell silent for a time. Then she spoke in a husky whisper. 'Thank you for my son.'

I lifted my eyes from the map. I just looked at her.

'I've known for years. How it was done.'

I didn't ask how she knew. Starling had possibly told her. Perhaps Verity himself.

'Your body. Verity's will.'

'I wasn't there, Kettricken. I spent that night inhabiting Verity's body.'

'He's Verity's son. I know.'

And we left it there, and I was not certain if I felt better for her knowing and letting me know she knew or if I felt even odder about it. I only asked her, 'Are you telling me this because you don't think I'll come back?'

She met my gaze. 'I think you left when you lost Bee, and you haven't truly been here since. Go find out, Fitz. Come back to us if you can. But go do what you must.'

The farewell feast happened the next evening. It was interminable, with more food than anyone should possibly try to eat at a single meal, and far too much to drink. There were many toasts to me and a tableful of farewell gifts and tokens that would have required a baggage train. It was all well-meant and the food I managed to eat was delicious, but ever since I had announced my departure, it had felt as if every event were an obstacle to be overcome on my way to finally leaving. Chade was there but not truly present. The Fool did not come.

It was very late when we processed away from the table. There was another round of farewells in Dutiful's sitting room. Nettle wept and Chade dozed off and Elliania gave me a kerchief and asked me to dip it in the blood of any I slew, that she might bury it in the soil of her mothershouse so their souls would never know peace. I think she was a bit crazy, and wondered if my leaving would help her find calm again. Thick was morose. The little man had not been well since he'd returned from Withywoods and his Skill-song that evening was almost a dirge. Both the princes promised me that if I called for them to come to my aid, they would bring the might of Buckkeep and the Narwhal Clan with them. Shine and Lant were there, flanking their father. Shine promised to take excellent care of Chade in my absence. Lant looked at me like a woeful hound. He had presented himself to me two days earlier, asking again to go with me. I'd refused him again. 'What will my father say of this?' he demanded in an effort to sway me when his own demands failed. I was heartless. 'I suppose you will find out when you tell him,' I'd said. From Chade's calm demeanour, I doubted they'd had that discussion. It was not my problem. When tomorrow came and I was gone and Lant was not, then he and Chade could deal with it.

When finally I insisted I must sleep so that I could make an early departure, Riddle walked me to the door. 'I'll ride with you and your guard tomorrow,' he told me. 'But for now, I want you to have this. It's been lucky for me.' His token was a knife, not much longer than my hand, with the blade sharpened on both sides and a blood-groove down the centre.

'It goes in easy and pulls out easy and it's quiet,' he told me as he passed it to me in its well-worn sheath. And I left wondering if I knew Riddle as well as I'd believed I did.

I found Ash and Perseverance loitering in the corridor

outside my door. Motley was on Ash's shoulder. 'Good night,' I told them.

'It's not right to leave him,' Ash told me bluntly. 'He's despondent. He's been saying wild things, and I fear what he may do if you go without him. In all his stories, you two are together. How can you leave him?'

'I should go with you. And we should take Bee's horse. If we find her, she'll want to ride her own horse home.'

I looked from one to the other. Both so earnest. I had grown fond of both of them.

But not that fond.

I looked at Ash. 'After all of our years together, I believe I'm a better judge of what is good for us than you are. And he is in no condition to go on a long and demanding journey.'

I looked at Perseverance. 'And Bee is gone. There is no finding her, and she will never need a horse again.'

Ash's mouth was ajar. Perseverance had gone pale. I heard him trying to get his breath.

I opened the door of my room, entered, and shut them out.

THIRTY-THREE

Departure

I dreamed I was a nut. I had a very hard shell and I was curled up inside it. Inside my shell, I was me and there I kept all the parts of me. I had been swept into a river, and it tried to carry me with it but I stayed in one place and refused it.

Curious to say, I abruptly fell out of the river. I fell onto green grass and it was spring all around me. For a time, I stayed tight inside my shell. Then I unfolded myself and I was all there, in one piece.

The others who had been carried by the river were not so fortunate.

This is a dream that feels truer than most. It is a thing that almost certainly will happen. I do not understand how it can happen, that I shall become a nut and be swept away in the river. But I know it is so. And the mouth of the river looked like the shape I draw below. And the river sprang out of a black stone.

Bee Farseer's Dream Journal

Dawn came before I fell asleep. I had expected a sleepless night and put it to good use. I finished transferring Chade's information on the Skill-portals to the grand map he had given me. I did not wish to trust any portal-stone that I had not seen with my own eyes, lest it be fallen or sunken in a swamp. But if no other escape presented itself and I were hard-pressed, it was good to know which stone might lead where. I was astonished to notice that he had marked some as leading to the city of Chalced. I thought I'd best fight rather than ever consider those an escape.

I read over Kettricken's notes and studied her map. It held more information than I'd possessed before, but much of it was still vague. I would have to travel to the outer reaches of Chade's map and hope to find new maps of the lands beyond. From what the old sailor had told me, I should make the Spice Isles my destination and from there find a way. I found a faint smile as I considered his final advice to me. 'Oh, if I was going there, I'd never start from here.'

Verity's sword was going with me. Once more, it was back in a plain leather sheath, the hilt disguised with a wrap of worn leather. I had considered taking an axe; it was definitely my better weapon, but while a man might wear a sword for vanity, no one suffered the weight of an axe for any reason save to use it. I needed to look like an ordinary traveller, a bit of an adventurer, but not a father bent on vengeance. The sword would serve me well, as it always had.

As the day grew grey outside, I dressed carefully. I shaved with warmed water, wondering when next I might have that luxury. My hair had finally grown to the point that I could tie it back in a warrior's tail. I set out my fine cloak and my personal pack. Then, on a whim, I went down to the guards' hall and joined them there for a very early breakfast. There was hot porridge and honey, with dried apples chopped into it, an aromatic tea, bread and butter and slices of last night's roast. My guard was there and many of their Buckkeep fellows and they cheered me with rough jests and suggestions as to how best to deal with anyone who dared to come into Buck and raid a man's home. That was the most of what they knew, that my home had been raided and Lady Shine stolen and then recaptured. Only a few of my personal guard knew of Bee, and those few understood that I did not wish that knowledge to be shared.

So it was that at the formal breakfast I ate little and once more accepted farewell wishes. I wished to be away but I understood this was the fee that I owed Dutiful and Elliania, and I did my best to pay it gracefully. Chade was dozing, but I woke him to say goodbye. He seemed to be in a very genial mood and asked if I would play a game of Stones with him. I reminded him that I had to go to Clerres. He promised that he would remember that

I had kept my word and said farewell to him. I doubted he would remember it after I closed the door to his room.

I tapped in vain on the Fool's door. He would not answer, even when my knocking shook the door in its frame and I was not surprised to find it locked. I could have picked that lock. He knew that. But the locked door was a message. He was closed to me. I steadied my breathing and walked away from that stab. It was just as well, I told myself. Better a silence than another shouting quarrel. Who knew what he might fling at me this time?

I returned to what had been my room to gather my personal pack. I was only mildly surprised to find Perseverance waiting by the door. His expression was grim but he brusquely insisted on carrying my pack for me and I allowed him.

Down we went to the courtyard, where I found my guard drawn up in fine formation. The former Rousters now blended almost seamlessly with my troops. Foxglove was there, and Riddle was already mounted. Lant looked pale, and Perseverance had mounted up as well. He did not lead Bee's horse, and that struck a sharp pang with me. I had been harsh to him. Had I enjoyed the boy's foolish hope? Or was it just that I hurt to see him now as hopeless as I was?

Again, there was a crowd of folk to say farewell, and Dutiful and Elliania and the princes in full regalia as they saw me off. Nettle was pale and red-eyed. I held her for a long moment, and then Kettricken took her from my arms. 'Come back to us,' Kettricken pleaded softly. I nodded but made no promises.

We rode out of the gates of Buckkeep Castle to cheers. Motley flew overhead, occasionally cawing to remind us that she accompanied us. As we cantered showily away, I reflected that half my morning had been wasted with pomp.

'Necessary,' Riddle said, as if he had heard my thoughts and gave me a humourless grin.

The cantering soon gave way to an easy trot that would eat up the miles. We would overnight at an inn, and press on the next day. I hoped that the following evening would find me at the Skill-stone where Shine had seen my daughter vanish. There I would bid my companions farewell and journey on alone. I would go first to the ancient market-circle where once I had dreamed the Fool transformed.

It was a peculiarly routine journey. The inn had received word to expect us, and received us well. I actually slept that night, and in the morning, enjoyed a solid breakfast with Riddle and Lant and Foxglove. We spoke of very ordinary things, that the break-fast bread was fresh and good, and that we hoped the weather would hold fair. Riddle predicted an early spring, and Foxglove said she thought the snow was already softening.

I donned my fine Buck blue cloak and again we rode forth, with me at the head of a troop of guards. The innkeeper and his family saw us off with cheers, and sweet cakes of oats and dried fruit for our day's journey. We pushed our horses, for I thought to be kind to my guard. If we reached the Skill-stone by afternoon, there was a possibility they could return to an inn for the night instead of having to sleep out in the open. I had no such prospect before me. I knew that once I had passed through that stone I would encounter winter in the Mountains. I only hoped I would not step out into a blasting winter storm.

My plan from there was clear. Camp for three nights in the ridiculously bulky tent I'd been gifted with. I'd subsist on marching rations for that necessary interval between uses of a Skill-pillar. From there, Chade's chart showed me it was but a Skill-step through the pillar to Kelsingra. In that city, I would seek passage down the Rain Wild River and on to Bingtown and then Jamaillia. In Jamaillia, I was sure to find a ship bound for the Spice Isles. Once there, I'd trust to my luck and Kettricken's map to find my way to Clerres. And blood.

I almost rode past the turn. Riddle was the one who pointed it out. The tracks we had made in the snowy field were smoothed to dimples and pocks in the snow. It seemed years since I had last ridden this way. Years since Bee had passed beyond my reach forever. Years, and a moment ago. The closer we drew to the stone, the more impatient I was to be gone. We entered the forest and followed the fading tracks. When we came to the place where Dwalia and her luriks had camped, Foxglove halted our troops and gave the order for them to set up a camp.

'No need.' I spoke quietly to her. 'I'm not going to make this a dramatic moment, Foxglove. I'm going to walk to that rock, touch it, and be gone. And you will turn our guards around and head back toward an inn. And I hope that tonight you will sleep in warmth and comfort, and perhaps hoist a tankard to wish me good luck.' I cleared my throat and added quietly, 'Inside my chamber, there is a parcel addressed to you. Within there are messages for folk that are dear to me. If a year passes with no word from me, then you will know it is time to deliver them.'

She stared at me, then gave a stiff nod.

I dismounted, and she shouted to our guards to hold off on that order. She dismounted, handed her horse off to her grand-daughter, and followed me. Riddle came after us, and Lant. I glanced back, thinking I would see Perseverance shadowing us, but the boy had vanished. From somewhere, the crow squawked. They'd be together. Just as well.

In the gloom under the leaning evergreens, the winter after-noon already seemed like evening. The shadowed snow and dark trunks were shaded from black to palest grey. In that dimness, it took me a moment to pick out the Skill-stone gripped in the roots and leaning trunk of an evergreen. I approached it without reluctance. Nettle's Skill-users had travelled to the Mountains via this stone and returned days later without incident. It was as safe to use as any Skill-portal, I told myself. I pushed from my memory what had happened the last time I had travelled by stone. I sealed from my heart that this was the very stone that had devoured Bee and those who had taken her.

Only a light snow had fallen since last I had been here, and little of it had penetrated the interweaving needled branches overhead. With a gloved hand, I brushed snow and fallen needles from the face of the stone. I had my sword at my side, a pack on my back and a large carry-bag on my shoulder. Everything I thought I needed was in the pack and everything the others had insisted I take was in the carry-bag. I had privately resolved I would not carry it for long.

'Well,' I said to Riddle. He pulled off his glove as I did mine, and we clasped wrists. Our eyes met briefly and then we both looked aside.

'Travel well,' he said to me, and 'I shall try,' I replied. His grip tightened on my wrist and I returned that pressure. *Nettle, you've chosen well,* I Skilled to her. Through my eyes, I showed her the man she had chosen. *Care for his heart. It's a true one.* And then I swiftly set my walls to hold in all my fears and worries.

I bade farewell likewise to Foxglove and to Lant. The old captain met my gaze with her steely one and bade me, 'Uphold the honour of the Farseers.' Lant's hand was sweaty as he gripped my wrist and he seemed to tremble.

'You'll do fine,' I told him quietly. 'Take care of that old man for me. Blame it on me that I would not let you go with me.'

He hesitated. 'I'll do my best to live up to his expectations,' he replied.

I returned him a rueful grin for that. 'Best of luck with that!' I wished him, and he managed a shaky laugh.

They were watching me. I held up a hand. I closed my eyes, though I did not need to. *Through the stone,* I said to Nettle and Dutiful. I could feel Thick watching us drowsily. *I'll be sending Riddle right back to you. He should be home by tomorrow evening.*

And you will Skill to us as soon as you emerge from the stone?

I already promised I would. I will not leave you worrying. I expect to be told as soon as the child is born.

And I already promised that to you. Go carefully, Da.

I love you all. And then, because those words sounded too much like a final farewell I added, *Tell the Fool not to be too angry with me. Take care of him until I return.*

I turned back to those waiting around me. 'Nettle expects you home by tomorrow,' I warned Riddle.

'I'll be there,' he promised me, and I knew that he did not mean just for the next evening.

Foxglove looked weary and Lant looked as if he felt sick. I shared some of his nervousness. The world seemed to waver a bit around me as I stepped toward the stone. As I set my bare hand to the cold stone and pressed firmly against the rune, Lant leapt forward suddenly. He clasped my wrist and exclaimed, 'I go with you!'

Someone also clasped me suddenly around the waist. I thought perhaps Riddle would pull me back, but I felt the stone give way and draw me in. Lant came with me, with a drawn-out shout that cut off as the darkness snapped shut around us.

Travelling through a pillar had always felt disorienting. This time instead of twinkling darkness it was as if someone had snapped a hood over my head and then let a horse kick me. I had no sense of travelling a great distance; it was more like a sudden push off a ladder. I fell hard on snowy ground. Lant landed on top of me, and I was crumpled face down across the lumpy carry-sack and something else. There was snow in my eyes and the cold that engulfed me was far sharper than that of Buck. The wind had been knocked out of my lungs. I wheezed in snow, coughed it out, and then fought to breathe as I struggled to sit up.

Lant abruptly heaved himself away from me. He sat facing away from me in the snow. His shoulders shook but he made not a sound.

'Let me up!'

I pushed myself up off the noisy sack and wiped my sleeve across my eyes. I heaved myself into a sitting position. The struggling lump in the snow beneath me was wrapped in a butterfly's wing. Perseverance abruptly pushed one corner of the Elderling cloak aside and stared up at me. 'What happened? Where am I?' An instant later, there was an explosion of black feathers slapping me and an indignant Motley fled skyward.

'Stupidity happened!' I shouted. Except that I had no breath to shout, so it came out as a gasp. I floundered to my feet and looked around me. Yes. I was where I had expected to be. Loose, fresh snow had smoothed the rumpled tracks Nettle's coterie had left. Around me was the open circle of what had once been a market pavilion, and we had tumbled from one face of the lone standing pillar that centred it. Dark mountain forest glowered at us from all directions. Beneath me, I felt the distant humming of what I thought of as the Skill-road. Constructed long ago by Elderlings, it thrummed with the memories of those who had trodden it. Moss and grass always seemed reluctant to invade its surfaces. The forest leaned in over the decorative stonework that edged the plaza. I set my walls against the muttering of stone-memories.

I glanced at the sky. Night would soon be falling, it was very cold and I was unexpectedly saddled with two idiots. I felt vaguely ill in a way I could not define. Not dizzy or feverish. I felt as if I had just arisen from my bed after a long illness. Well, I had, without preparation, towed two unSkilled ones through a pillar, and the simmering memories of the Skill-road besieged my walls. I decided I was lucky that I felt only weak. And they were fortunate to be sane and alive. If they were.

'Lant? How do you feel?'

He dragged in a long breath. 'Like the morning after a night of drinking bad ale.'

I turned and glared at Perseverance. 'How did you do that?'

He looked surprised I would ask. 'I hid under the cloak near the stone. You know how it conceals things that are beneath it. Then, at the last moment, I jumped up and caught hold of you. And here I am.' He stood straight suddenly and met my gaze. He seemed totally unaffected by the passage. He draped the butterfly cloak around his shoulders. 'I followed to serve you as I vowed to do. To avenge my Lady Bee, whose colours I wear.'

I wanted to stamp and shout, to call them every demeaning and damning term I knew. They looked at me like puppies and suddenly I could not muster the energy. The cold that squeezed me was not a cold that had patience with human frailty. I looked down at both of them. 'Lant. Get up. There's a tent in that bag. Make camp over there, under those trees where the snow is shallower. I'm going to get a fire going.'

They stared at me, then exchanged astonished glances. Out of the corner of my eye, I saw Lant stand. He stumbled two steps sideways and then reached up to hold his head in his hands. The Skill-portal journey had not been easy for him. His own fault. My anger at how they had complicated my life drowned any sympathy I might have felt. Perseverance, wrapped in layers of butterfly wings, looked less affected. I walked away from them, pulling my cloaks closer. I'd worn the gaudy Farseer cloak over the plain one and was suddenly glad to have it. I found a dead and hanging branch, shook it cautiously to rid it and the branches right above it of loose snow and then began to break pieces off of it. I returned to find them struggling to erect the small tent

I'd been reluctant to bring. Now I was glad of it. I ignored their efforts as I scraped clear an area of the cobbles of the old market and set about my fire-making. I was rusty at this skill, light-headed from our passage, and the longer I struggled, the colder and stiffer my hands became. I panted and sniffled as I worked, for the cold does that to a man. I felt my lips dry and tried to remember not to lick them, as I knew they would immediately crack. Night was coming on and the cold was squeezing me harder. Patience was hard to find. I should have brought a fire-pot.

A spark caught and lingered, and then another, and finally a tiny trickle of smoke rose from my tinder. 'Go get wood,' I told the two watching me struggle. 'There's a hatchet in my pack. Don't dump it out on the snow, reach inside to find it.'

'I'm not an idiot,' Perseverance said huffily.

'You've not proved that today,' I told him, and he went.

Lant lingered a moment longer. 'I told my father you'd refused me. He told me it wasn't your decision to make. That I should find a way. So I did.'

That sounded like Chade. 'We'll need a lot of wood to last through the night, and the light is nearly gone,' I pointed out. Lant stamped away.

I fed the tiny fire twigs and then snapped off bits of the branch and then finally dared add some actual wood to it. I looked around at the gathering gloom. Motley had taken up a post in a bare-limbed tree and was watching me. I decided we would have a large fire tonight. Perseverance returned dragging a substantial branch. I broke some of the smaller limbs from it and then set him to chopping the rest. The fire was lending some warmth by the time Lant returned. He'd found a storm-broken evergreen and the resinous branches caught quickly and burned hot. I could tell he did not feel well. He kept pinching his lips together as if he feared he'd be sick and more than once he reached up to press the heels of his hands to his temples. I didn't care how he felt. 'We still need more wood,' I told them.

For a time, we all came and went, bringing whatever storm-dropped wood we could find. When we had a substantial reserve, we crouched around the fire, warming ourselves. 'You first,' I said to Lant. 'What supplies did you bring?'

I watched him try to order his thoughts. 'Warm clothes. Some dried meat and fruit. Bread, honey, some bacon, cheese. A blanket rolled small. A knife and a cooking-pot. A bowl and a cup and spoon. Coin for inns. My sword.' He looked around us at the forest. 'I thought there might be inns.'

'There aren't,' I told him. I looked at Perseverance. 'And you?'

The boy had the brilliant Elderling cloak hooded up over his head. It was too large for him. He peered at me from the recesses. 'I'm dressed warm. I brought food, mostly grain for porridge. Some smoked, dried meat. A cook-pot for it, and a spoon. A cup. My knife. A sling. Not a lot.'

'A bedroll?'

'I've got her cloak sir, the butterfly cloak. It's surprisingly warm.'

I looked at him. His cheeks were pink and the tip of his nose was red, but he looked comfortable crouched by the fire. I pondered for a time. I didn't like my decision. 'We'll camp here for three days. Then I'll take you back.' And I'd have to wait at least another three days before I dared another journey through the pillar. Setback after setback.

'No,' said Lant.

'Won't go,' Perseverance replied. He didn't look at me. Instead he went to his pack that he'd set inside the tent and came back with a cooking-pot. He moved away from the trodden area to pack it full of clean snow. He brought it back and set it by the fire. 'We'll have porridge for dinner,' he announced. He looked at Lant. 'I could add some of your dried fruit if you want.'

Lant was warming his hands. 'It's in my pack. Fetch it for me and I'll find the apples for you.'

'No,' I said. They both stared at me. I pointed at my cousin. 'Fetch it yourself, Lant. Perseverance is my man not yours. For the next three days, you'll do everything for yourself. Then we'll see if you don't want to go back to Buckkeep.'

He glared at me. Then, without a word, he rose and stalked off to the tent. He returned with his pack, opened it, and took out a packet of dried apples. I had to admire his self-control. He didn't take his temper out on the boy, but only selected a handful of dried slices and gave them to the lad. Perseverance thanked him.

I inspected their work on the tent. It had been intended only for me, and to be comfortably large for one man. Three was going to be more than snug. The tent was canvas, sewn like a big pocket that could be staked down and the top lifted with a line to a tree. I tightened several of the lines and tapped down one peg more securely. I hadn't wanted to bring it but I knew we'd all be glad of it tonight. I'd planned to abandon it as soon as I could.

The cold was not as daunting now that I knew I had a warm fire to return to. I walked slowly around the circular clearing that had once been a marketplace. I tried to imagine Elderlings converging here to trade goods and exchange news. I looked up at the pillar that had ejected us. It was a darker shape against a dark sky. I recalled the first time I had seen this place. Kettricken, the Fool, the old woman Kettle, Starling and I had come here on our long quest to find King Verity and persuade him to return to his throne and his embattled kingdom. The Fool had climbed the pillar, and when I looked up at him there, he had been someone else: another jester or songster, from another time. And Starling had slapped me, hard, to wake me from that vision. Later, the Fool and I had gone hunting with Nighteyes. And ended up in a waterfight in a creek. Boys. We'd been such boys, but I'd believed myself a man. So many years ago. How my world had changed since then. How we had changed.

I glanced back at Per and Lant. Per was crouched over his little pot, adding another handful of snow. The apples and the oats waited beside him. He was explaining to Lant that it would take a lot of melted snow to make a pot of water, and then it must boil before he added the oats or the apples. I felt a burst of disgust that Lant did not know such simple things as how to cook porridge over a fire in winter. Then it came to me that his life would never had taught him such skills, any more than mine had taught me the rules of the various gambling games that pleased the nobles of Buckkeep. I wasn't being fair to expect those things of him. But life wasn't fair. Life does not wait for any of us to grow up. Perhaps if it had been summer, they'd have been throwing water at each other.

I looked at Lant and tried to see him dispassionately. He had grit. He'd ridden after me with that half-healed stab wound. Even now, I saw his hand stray to his healed ribs and gently rub them. I knew the ache of old injuries in the cold. He'd known I would not welcome him, and still he'd followed me. I still didn't understand why. Lant said something in a low voice, Per chuckled and the crow copied him with her cawing laugh. Nothing could have made me smile tonight. I felt envy for their youth, and a spark of warmth for both of them. They'd made such a mistake today. And they'd have to pay the toll for it.

So I let them struggle. The water finally boiled, the oats and apples eventually cooked. We each had a small portion and then waited while Per cooked more. Lant looked a bit better after he had eaten. I gave the crow a stingy portion of bread. I filled my own little pot with snow-melt and made tea for us. We each had a cup and drank it slowly. I gave Per the first watch, with strict instructions that he was to keep the fire well fed. I no longer had a wolf to protect me through the night. This place and its memories were cutting my heart with loneliness and I longed for the Fool as he had been, for Nighteyes at my side. I could almost recall how the fur on the back of my wolf's neck would have felt, tipped with cold and then warm near his skin. I reached for him but found only silence.

I showed Perseverance a star, and told him to wake Lant for his watch when the star was over the top of a fir tree. I gave Lant the same instructions, and told him to wake me when the star had journeyed into the bare branches of an oak.

'Keep watch for what?' Lant looked around the silent forest.

'Wild creatures. Big cats. Bears. Anything that might see us as prey.'

'They're afraid of fire!' Lant insisted.

'And that's one reason why one of us stays awake and keeps the fire fed.' He did not ask me the other reasons and I did not offer them. That at least once the Servants had used this same portal. That sometimes forest creatures were hungry enough not to fear fire.

Lant and I tried to make ourselves comfortable in the cramped tent. When we had settled back to back, I was grateful for his body warmth. I had just begun to doze off when he spoke. 'I know you didn't want me to follow you.'

'Coming through the Skill-portal with me when I didn't expect you or Perseverance was incredibly dangerous. We were very lucky.' I thought about taking them back through the pillar. The obvious broke over me. Perhaps one of Nettle's Skill-users could come through and then take them back, so I didn't have to. Belatedly, I realized that I had not told Nettle that we were safe. I composed myself and reached out.

'Why do you dislike me so much?'

'Hush. I'm trying to Skill.' I pushed his blunt question aside. I reached out. *Nettle? Dutiful?*

I heard a distant music, like wind in the trees. I focused on it and tried to draw it closer to me. *Fitz? Fitz?* Hearing Dutiful was like listening to someone shout over driven surf. His thought was carried to me on Thick's Skill-music, like flotsam tossed on a wave. I pushed my thoughts at him. *We're all safe. Lant and Perseverance came with me.*

Perseverance?

The stableboy from Withywoods.

What happened? You were silent so long!

We needed to build a shelter and make a fire right away. It's very cold here.

Fitz, it's been a full day since you left, and a bit more than that.

Oh. I was silent for a time, absorbing that. *It didn't seem that way. It seemed as if we stepped in and out again.*

Fitz?

I'm here. We're fine. My distrust for that pillar flared anew. It had devoured Bee and we'd experienced a delay. I would not ask Nettle to risk one of her Skilled-ones in it, nor chance sending Lant and Per through it again. Thick's Skill-music rose and fell. I reached for it, and it slipped away. I arrowed my message to them. *Don't worry! We will be fine here. Tell Chade that Lant is with me.*

Nothing. No response. Distant music and then that faded. I came back to the tent and Lant's sullen silence. No. That was the deep steady breathing of sleep. I'd not have to answer his question tonight. I had others to occupy me. Was my Skill damaged somehow? How was it I'd not realized how long we'd been in the pillar? Why was it so difficult to reach Nettle and Dutiful? I should have lain awake worrying but I didn't. I realized that when Lant shook my shoulder.

'Your watch,' he said hoarsely. I sat up in the dark and beside me Perseverance muttered at my letting the cold air under the blankets we'd shared. I hadn't even awakened when Per and Lant had changed places. Not good. Dragging them through the Skill-portal had taken a heavier toll on me than I'd realized. I crawled out of the tent, every joint aching and reached back to take the cloaks I'd added to our blankets but, 'Here,' Lant said, and pushed a small bundle of bunched fabric at me. 'The boy let me use it. It was all I needed.'

'Thank you,' I said, but Lant was already crawling into the tent. The Elderling cloak was lighter than silk. I shook it out and wrapped it around me and pulled the hood up over my head. For a short time, I shivered and then my own warmth surrounded me. I went to the fire and sat down on a chunk of a log. It was too low and uncomfortable but it was better than sitting in the snow. When I wearied of that, I rose and paced slowly around the old market-circle. I came back to the fire, fed it, packed snow into the pot, melted it with a few tips of the evergreen needles, and drank it as tea. Twice I tried to Skill to Nettle with no success. I sensed a strong current of Skill and the muttering of the Skill-road, imbued with the thousands of memories of Elderlings who had passed over its surface. If Nettle heard me, I could not pick her voice out from theirs.

My mind ravelled through the years, and I had leisure to think of all the foolish decisions I'd made. In the dark I mourned the loss of Molly and how I had wasted Bee's little life. I indulged my hatred for Dwalia and her followers, and raged that they were beyond my vengeance. I lifted and studied my own ridiculous quest. I had to wonder if I would even find Clerres, and what one man could do to topple such an evil nest of cruelty. It was foolish even to try, but it was the last thing I had to give purpose to my life.

I wondered if I were a coward to refuse to risk my eyesight to bring back the Fool's. No. I was better suited to this mission than he was. I was sad to leave him, but glad he was somewhere warm and safe. If I succeeded in my quest and returned to him, he would forgive me. Perhaps. And perhaps by then, the dragon's blood he had taken would have restored his sight. I could hope.

For him, I could hope for a better life and good years to come. For myself, the only hope I had was that I could kill successfully before I was killed.

The steep thrust of the mountain peaks that surrounded us delayed dawn. When there was enough light to see, I built up the fire, packed both pots with snow and set them to melt and then shouted at the others to wake up. Per stumbled out first, and my reluctance to part with the butterfly cloak shamed me. The cold reached for me with greedy fingers. But my daughter had chosen to protect him under the cloak, and what she had given to him, I would not take away. Lant roused more slowly, and I hastened the process when I took back the two cloaks that had become part of his bedding.

'I'm going hunting,' I told them. 'You two are to stay near the camp. Gather lots of wood and keep the fire going. I may not be back until late evening. Or even tomorrow morning.' How far was it? I would travel swiftly and alone, unburdened by a pack animal or companions. I could do it.

'Where are you going?' Per was suspicious.

'I told you. Hunting. I'll bring back meat, I hope. A good meal for us.'

'You've no bow. How can you hunt?'

I was already tired of the conversation. 'As I used to. Like a wolf.' I turned and walked away from them. At the edge of the clearing, I stopped. 'Cut staves for yourselves. There are wild animals here, some big enough to think you'd be prey. Lant, practise with the boy. Teach him what you know.' I turned away from them. Whacking at each other with staves would both occupy them and keep them warm. As I walked away, Motley cawed derisively after me but did not follow.

I wondered why I was doing this. It was not part of my plan. But neither were Per or Lant. I reached for Nettle to let her know what I was doing and found only a roaring current of Skill full of strange voices. I pulled hastily away from it. I hiked on.

The trail was more overgrown than I remembered it. Trees and bushes had begun to encroach on the edges of the ancient Skill-road. Perhaps not even Elderling magic could hold out forever. Windblown dead needles and small branches littered the smooth snow. I relaxed into the cold, accepting it and felt my muscles loosen as my body generated its own heat. I moved swiftly but quietly, looking for movement. If I had the chance, I'd kill something for us to eat, but as Per had guessed, meat was not my primary goal.

The last time I'd walked this way, the foliage had been dense and green. Snow mounded on the moss that draped the tree branches now. I passed a tree where a bear had sharpened his claws. The tracks were old, softened with snow. Birds flitted through the trees. A deer trail crossed my path, but nothing moved on it right now. In a small clearing, I came across a tangle of wild roses still heavy with frozen red hips. The birds feeding on them cursed me as I stole from the edges of the prickly tangle. I filled my kerchief and tied it shut. If nothing else, they would flavour porridge or tea for us. I picked a final handful to chew as I walked.

The forest grew denser and darker. I hurried. Although the year had turned her steps toward spring, the days were still short. My feet got cold and I pulled my hood tighter around my ears. I ran then, ploughing through the snow across the path, pounding my feet until they warmed with the exercise. I ran carelessly, spooking a fat bird that might have made a good meal, if I'd had the means to kill it. After that, I walked, and ran, and walked again. I ate snow to keep my mouth wet, but avoided chilling my body with too much of it. Onward. I watched the winter sun pass over my head and shadows start to grow long. This was foolishness. Why had I yielded to the impulse? I was as stupid as Lant and Per put together. Then, as evening leeched all colours from the day, I came to the first buried hulk beside the snow pathway.

It had been years but some things a man does not forget. I moved from stone dragon to stone dragon. Here was the one shaped like a wild boar. Here was one with the shape of a dragon. The blue-winged buck's antlers were edged with snow. They still filled me with awe, each and every one of them.

Years ago, with blood and magic, Nighteyes and I had roused these sleeping shapes and sent them winging to Verity's aid. Verity. My king. He and the old Skill-user Kettle had poured all their memories and even their lives into a magnificent dragon, shaped from Skill-stone, from the same stuff that made up the pillars. And as a dragon, Verity had risen, and carried both Kettricken and Starling back to Buckkeep, so that his queen might bear his son and continue his lineage. The dragon he had made at such a cost led the battle against the Red-Ship Raiders and the OutIslanders.

And when all had been vanquished and peace returned to our shores, Verity-as-Dragon had returned here, to slumber with the others in the deep shade beneath the looming trees.

I found him. I brushed the snow from him, clearing it from the magnificent wings now folded close to his side. I swept his head clean of snow, wiping it away from his closed eyes. Then I pulled off my snowy gloves and set my bare hands to his cold and stony brow. I reached, not with the Skill but with the Wit, and I sought for the king I had served and then lost. I felt the dim flicker of some sort of lingering life in the stone. And when I did, I poured into my touch all the Skill and the Wit I could muster. I opened my heart and confided all to the cold stone dragon. It was not pouring memories into stone as Verity had done to waken his creation. This was a simple reaching to my uncle, to my king, an outpouring of all that had befallen me and all I hoped to do. All my anguish I shared with him, the loss of my wife and child, the Fool's torment, Chade's fading, all of it.

And when I was emptied far beyond tears or hopes of vengeance, I stood still and empty in the cold beside the frozen dragon. A foolish quest. I was here for the night now, with no tent, no fire. I pushed snow aside to bare years of fallen leaves. I sat down between his outstretched front legs and leaned back against his head, slumped on his paws in slumber. I drew my legs in close to me and pulled my hood well forward. I curled up against my king and hoped the cold would not deepen too much tonight. The Skill-stone he was carved from was cold against my back. Was Verity cold, somewhere? Or did he and Kettle play at Stones in some other world, beyond my reach? I closed my eyes and longed to join them.

Oh, Fitz. You feel so much.

Did I imagine it? I huddled perfectly still. Then I stripped my glove from my hand and set my bare palm to the scaled cheek of my king.

Nothing is really lost. Shapes change. But it's never completely gone. Verity?

Thank you. For my son. For my grandsons.

My king. Your thoughts warm me.

Perhaps I can do a bit more than that.

I felt a rising warmth. Snow melted and slid from the dragon's body, and he scintillated blue and silver. Warmth flowed up through my hand and into the rest of me. I leaned into stone that suddenly felt alive. But with that rising warmth, my Wit-sense of my king began to fade. I reached for him but could no longer touch him. *Verity?* I wondered, but he did not respond. Except with warmth. I found I could slide under his chin. I wedged myself under his long jaw, between his front legs. My back stopped aching from the cold. I felt cupped in wonder and safety. I closed my eyes.

Dawn came. I awoke to birds. My own body-warmth within my cloaks was all I felt now. I slithered out into the winter day, brushed dry leaves and needles from my clothes and set my hand on my king's scaled brow.

Chill stone and stillness. Tiny icicles had formed at the corners of his eyes like frozen tear tracks. The bleakness that rose in me was a steep price to pay for that time of connection and comfort. But I did not regret the price. 'Farewell,' I told the dragon. 'Wish me luck.'

I re-gloved my hands. The warmth that had infused me stayed with me as I turned my steps back toward the camp. I walked steadily and swiftly, hoping I'd see the yellow glow of our fire before all light went out of the day. Clouds covered the sky and slightly warmed the day. I walked, then ran, then walked, and pondered all the questions that I'd never have answered.

A flicker of one black-edged ear betrayed the hare that crouched under the rose thicket I'd passed the day before. Still as snow, he waited, his winter coat blending with the snow that was speckled with twigs and birds' droppings. I did not look at him, but continued my pace as I walked almost past him before I spun and fell on him.

I trapped him under my spread cloak. With gloved hands, I

gripped one wildly-kicking hind leg. When I was sure I had him, I stood, seized his head in my free hand, and gave his body a violent snap. In that instant, his neck was broken and his life was over. He hung motionless, warm and limp and dead as I gripped him by his head. 'Death feeds life,' I told him sadly, tucking his furry body under my arm and, pulling my cloak tighter, I continued back to camp.

The day faded around me. The trees seemed to lean in closer over the trail and the cold gripped me more tightly. I tramped on. It was the golden light of the campfire that guided me toward the end of my hike. I felt oddly successful. I had touched Verity again, if only for a short time, and I knew that somewhere my king continued in some other form. The rosehips in my kerchief and the dead weight of the hare made me simmer with pride. I might be old, my joints might ache in the cold, and I had failed in several dozen important ways in the last few months. But I could still hunt, and still bring back meat to share. And that was something, and a bigger something than it had been in a long time.

So I was weary but not tired as I came back into the circle of firelight. Lant and Perseverance were both crouched by the fire, looking into the flames. I shouted at them, held up my hare, and then tossed it at Per who caught it in a hug. They both stared at me. I grinned. 'What's wrong? Don't you know how to dress a hare for the pot?'

'Of course I do!' Per declared, but Lant spoke over him.

'The one you call the Fool? He was here. With a girl named Spark.'

'What?' The world rocked around me. 'Where is he? Why? How?'

'Gone,' Lant said, and Per added, 'They went back into that stone. The same one we came out of.'

'No.' I said it like a prayer, but I knew it was one no god would answer. Lant started to speak. I pointed a finger at him. 'You. Tell me everything, every tiny thing. Per, you do the hare.' I hunkered down on the opposite side of the fire and waited.

'There's little to tell. We were keeping watch here, bringing wood and feeding the fire. Per took out his sling and got a squirrel with it. We saved some for you, but when you didn't return by nightfall, we ate it. We cut staves, and I showed the boy a few moves he didn't know. We talked.' He shook his head.

'There wasn't much else to do. We gathered more firewood. Then, as full night came on, we heard a sound, like a thud. We both turned and there they were, sprawled in the snow. We didn't know them at first, for all the heavy clothing they were wearing. Then the smaller one sat up, and Per shouted, "Ash!" and ran toward them. He helped him to stand, and Ash said right away, "Help my master. Is he all right?" So then we helped the other one to stand, and it was a woman. Then I looked again, and it was the Fool. We brought them over by the fire. They were dressed warmly, but in very old-fashioned clothing, and both were dressed as women. Old furs, very lush but smelling a bit musty. Per called the girl Ash but the Fool said her name was Spark. She had an immense pack on her back, and the Fool had a tall walking stick.

'The Fool asked Spark who was here, and she told him Per and me, and then the Fool asked us why you weren't here. And we said you'd gone hunting. We heated water and gave them some hot tea and some of the squirrel broth to the girl, who looked poorly. The Fool said you were going to be very angry with him, but there was no help for that. Then he said, "Well, waiting isn't going to make it any easier or less dangerous. Spark, are you ready for another leap?" And the girl said she was, but we could all hear how sick she felt. And the Fool told her that she didn't have to go, that she could stay here and wait, but Spark told him not to be foolish, that he needed her eyes. Then they finished their tea and thanked us and went back to the pillar. When I guessed what they were going to try, I told them that it was dangerous, that you had said we had to wait at least three days before we used a Skill-portal again. But the Fool shook his head and said all life was danger and dead was the only way to be safe. He pulled off his glove, and the girl took out a tiny bottle and put just a few drops of something on his hand. Then the Fool held onto the girl's shoulder with one hand, and she took his stick and then the Fool put his other hand on the Skill-pillar. I called to them, asking where they were going. And the girl said, "The dragon city." And the Fool said, "Kelsingra." And they both just walked into it.'

I sat down flat in the snow. I tried to breathe. Dragon blood. That was why he had wanted dragon blood. I could understand why the Fool had come after us. He had always wanted to be a part of this quest. But why dragon's blood had worked to take him through the pillars, I was not sure. And it made no sense to me that he would go on without me, blind, with only Spark at his side.

'There was one more thing,' Per said. He'd made a tidy job of his skinning. The hare's head and paws were still inside the hide he'd stripped cleanly from the animal's body. The guts were in a pile. He sorted the heart and liver and tossed them into the pot. The rest of the hare, dark meaty red and sinewy white, was already cut into pot-sized pieces. Motley descended and began an inquest of the small gut-pile.

'What one thing?' I asked.

'He said, the Fool I mean, he said, "Don't let Fitz follow us. Tell him to stay here and wait. We'll be back."'

'He did say that,' Lant admitted.

'Anything else? Anything at all?'

They exchanged looks. 'Well, it wasn't a thing he said, but something they did,' Per said. 'Ash left the big pack and most of their supplies here. When they went back into the pillar, they took only a small part of what they'd brought.' He looked uncomfortable for a moment. 'Sir, why would Ash and Grey both dress as women?'

'Probably the only warm garments they could steal easily,' I said to him. 'Taken from a forgotten wardrobe that once belonged to an old woman named Lady Thyme.' Lant twitched at the name and I wondered how much he knew of his father's old disguise.

Per shook his head. 'Well, maybe. But their faces . . . Ash had red lips. Like a girl. So did your friend. So it looked like they did it on purpose.'

THIRTY-FOUR

Dragons

From Queen Malta and King Reyn of the Dragon Traders, greetings to King Dutiful and Queen Elliania of the Six Duchies!

We wish to express our great satisfaction with our recent trade negotiations. Our delegations have praised your hospitality, your courtesy and your willingness to negotiate. The samples of trade-goods we have received are definitely to our satisfaction, particularly the grain, brandy and leather.

Our long-standing agreements with our fellow Traders must prevail, however. Elderling-made goods will be released only through our contacts in Bingtown. We are sure you must be aware of our traditional and familial connections there. We are confident that you will understand our reluctance to abandon those generational alliances.

While we will not be trading Elderling goods for Six Duchies goods, we promise that our coinage is uniform and unadulterated. As a relatively new currency, we understand your reluctance to accept it but if you continue to refuse, we can only turn elsewhere to form our trade alliances, as we are certain you clearly understand.

As regards the dragons, we appreciate all your concerns. But we hold no authority over the dragons, nor do they owe us any obedience. While we enjoy a deep friendship with the dragons and savour their companionship, we cannot pretend to make any agreements on their behalf, nor do we claim any influence over them to moderate their behaviour when in your territory.

Some individual dragons are amenable to forming agreements about where they hunt or accepting designated largesse when they are visiting foreign countries. The best time to negotiate with dragons is when they awaken after they have eaten and slept. Attempting to greet or negotiate with an unfed dragon is not advisable. If you wish, we would be happy to share more of our knowledge of dragons with you, but claim no expertise that will bind them to any agreements.

Again we thank you for your gracious reception of our trade delegation. We look forward to a long and prosperous commerce between our domains.

'Did they say nothing of why they were going to Kelsingra? Did they tell you when they might return from Kelsingra? Why did they think they had to move on immediately? Why did the Fool not wait for my return?'

Neither Lant nor Per had answers to those questions or any of the others that I asked. I paced like a caged wolf, going from the fire to the stone-pillar and back again. I dared myself to follow them, but knew I'd be abandoning Lant and Perseverance to their deaths if I did not return. Then I asked myself if that duty was not just a cover for my own cowardice. A question to which I had no answer.

We ate the hare and drank the broth and made a fruity tea from the berries I'd found. While I'd been away, Lant and Per had made improvements to our camp. They'd dragged a longer piece of log to the fireside for us to sit on and had arranged our supplies more efficiently. I looked at the large pack that the Fool and Spark had left. Plainly they had packed for a substantial journey. But if these supplies were for Kelsingra, why had they left it here? And if the Fool had wished to journey with me, why had he and Spark gone on without me? I sat and stared at the fire and waited.

'Should I take the first watch?' Per asked me.

His voice startled me. I turned to look at his worried face. 'No, Per. I'm not tired yet. You get some sleep. I'll wake you when it's your watch.'

He sat down beside me. 'I slept while you were gone. There was little else to do. So I'm not tired either.'

I didn't argue with him. Later, when it was his turn to keep watch, he'd learn that he'd made a poor choice. Lant had already gone to bed. For a time, we stared at the fire in silence.

'Why were they dressed like girls?'

Secrets, secrets, secrets. Who owned the secrets? 'You'd need to ask them about that.'

He was quiet for a while. Then he asked, 'Is Ash a girl?'

'You'd need to ask Ash about that.'

'I did. And he asked me why I was dressed as a boy.'

'And what did you answer to that?' I prodded him.

He was quiet again and then said, 'That means he's a girl.'

'I didn't say that.'

'You didn't have to.' He hunched tighter toward the fire. 'Why would Ash pretend to be a boy?'

'You'd need to ask Spark about that.'

'Spark.' The name annoyed him. He scowled and wrapped his arms around himself. 'I'm not going to bother. I don't trust him any longer.' His face set into hardness. 'I don't need a friend who deceives me.'

I took a deep breath and then sighed it out. There were a hundred things I could say to him. A hundred questions I could ask him that might make him see things differently. But being told something is not the same as learning it. I thought of all the things Verity had told me. Burrich's stern advice. Patience's counsel. But when had I learned?

'Talk to Spark,' I said.

His silence was long. 'Maybe,' he said at last.

Since, as he said, he seemed wide awake, I left him sitting there, shoved Lant over to make room and crawled under the blankets. I gnawed on my questions. I must have slept, because I woke when Lant traded places with Per. The boy pushed his back up against mine, sighed heavily, and soon began to snore. I closed my eyes and tried to go back to sleep. After a time, I got up and went to join Lant by the fire. He was heating snow-water in a pot for tea. I sat down beside him and stared into the flames.

'Why do you dislike me so much?'

I didn't need to think about it. 'You made my daughter unhappy. And when I had to entrust her to you, you didn't care for her or comfort her. Revel was the one to come and take her in from the snowy wagon.'

He was silent. 'We were confused, Shine and I. We could make no sense of what you and Riddle were doing. You told us next to nothing. I tried to take Bee out of the wagon and she acted like . . . like a sulky child. I was tired, and cold, and angry with you. So I left her to find her own way in. If none of this had happened, would it have been so important? Fitz, I did not want to be a scribe, let alone a tutor to children. I wanted to be at Buckkeep Castle, with my friends, following my own life. I've never had the care of children, and even you must admit that Bee was no ordinary child.'

'That's enough,' I suggested pleasantly. He had stirred guilt in me, until his last words.

'I'm not like you!' he burst out. 'I'm not like my father. I tried to be, to please him. But I'm not! And I don't want to be. I'm here, I'm going with you, because yes, I failed your daughter. Just as much as I failed my sister. My sister. Do you know how it twists inside me to name her that? What they did to Shine, to my sister – it makes me ill to think of her hurt that way. I want to avenge her, I want to avenge Bee. I know I can't undo what happened. I can't change what I did, only what I will do. And I'm not doing this for you, or even for my father. I'm doing it for me. To give myself whatever peace I can find over what happened.

'I don't know how I'll help you or what you'll ask me to do or if I can do it. But I'm here. And I intend to try. And I can't go home until this is done. But I do want to go home, after all this is over, and I want to go home alive. So you'd better start talking to me and telling me what is going on, or teaching me what I have to do. Or something. Because I'm with you now until you go home. Or I'm dead. And I think that boy is, too.'

'I don't want you here. I didn't want you to come.'

'Yet here we are. And I don't think even you are spiteful enough to let me die of ignorance.'

That was true. I had almost thought of a response when I heard a muffled shriek. It burst suddenly louder and was followed by the sound of a wild struggle over by the Skill-pillar. Lant had the presence of mind to seize a flaming stick from the fire. I reached the pillar first but when Lant lifted the brand I shouted, 'Get back! Don't touch the Fool and don't let him touch you!' And in the next breath, I told him, 'Drag Spark over by the fire. Wake Per. Get water heating.'

Spark was twitching and yelping like a dog having a bad dream, but her eyes were open. I feared for her. Many years ago, I'd seen what a trip through a Skill-portal could do to unprepared minds. Regal had driven many of his young Skill-apprentices mad when he had attempted to send a small army through a pillar. Spark was unSkilled and had just experienced her third trip through a pillar in less than a day. I was angry at the Fool for risking the youngster, and heartsick that I would be helpless to aid her. I feared even more for the Fool. I prayed that the uneven light of the burning branch tricked my eyes, for it looked to me as if his left hand was unevenly silvered with Skill.

He lay on his back, staring up at me and panting. His blind eyes were wide and the torchlight danced in their golden depths. The skirts he wore were flung wide around him, like a collapsed tent.

I heard Per's sleepy voice raised in query, and Lant shouting at him to build up the fire, pack the pot with snow and get it melting and bring a blanket for him to put around Spark. I'd let them create and manage that chaos. They were doing as much for Spark as I knew to do. Keep her warm and try to get food into her. I moved carefully to the Fool's right side, away from the dangerously silvered hand. 'Fool,' I said in as even a voice as I could muster. 'Fool, can you hear me? Can you speak to me?'

'The dragon!' His words shuddered on a gasp. 'Is the dragon coming?'

I lifted my eyes to the night sky. I saw nothing except stars frozen and twinkling in the darkness. 'There is no dragon that I can see.'

'It chased us. And we ran, with Spark gripping my hand and dragging me through the streets. They were crowded with Elderlings laughing and talking, and we ran and ran, we ran right through all of them. Spark shouted they weren't real, that only the dragon was. But one of them was real, I think. One Elderling. I felt that arrow.' He paused, panting for breath.

'Were you hit? Was Spark?'

'I don't know.' With his right hand, he plucked at the loose

fabric of the shoulder of his blouse. 'I felt it, as if someone
had seized me hard for just a moment and then let go. Spark
kept running, dragging me along and I tried to keep up. Then
she shouted, "The pillar!" and I slapped it. And here we are.
Oh, here we are, Fitz. Don't be angry at me. Please don't be
angry.'

'I'm not angry,' I lied. 'I'm terrified for both of you.' That was
rock-hard truth. I spoke carefully. 'Fool. It looks as if you have
Skill on your left hand. As Verity did when he carved the dragons.
I'm going to help you stand and walk you to the fire. Don't touch
yourself with that hand and don't touch me.' The failing light of
the torch licked along his brightly shining fingers. I'd never
discovered precisely where Verity had obtained so much of the
raw magic. My king had coated both his hands in it, the better
to shape a dragon from stone. The raw Skill had penetrated his
flesh and stolen the focus of his mind. By the time we found him,
he had scarcely recognized his queen. Kettricken had wept to see
him so, but all he had cared for at that moment was to carve his
dragon.

'Yes,' he said, and his smile was beatific and frightening in the
torchlight. He held his silvered fingers up and I shrank back from
them. 'That much I managed. Against all odds. I brought a glove
with me, in the wild hope I might succeed. It's in the pocket of
my skirt.'

'Right or left side?'

'Right,' he said and feebly patted there.

I did not want to touch his garments. I didn't know how he
had got raw Skill on his left hand but I feared it might be spattered elsewhere. I thrust the base of my branch that now had but
a single dancing flame on it into the snow and found the edge
of a white glove peeping from a pocket concealed in the volu-
minous skirts. I tugged it free. 'Put your right hand on my wrist
so you can feel what I'm doing. I'm holding the glove open. Oh,
Fool, be so careful. I don't want that stuff on me.'

'If you could feel it as I do, you would,' he said. 'It burns so
sweetly.'

'Fool, I beg you, be careful of me.'

'I will. As I so seldom have before. Hold the glove wide, Fitz.'

And I did. 'Don't let your left hand touch the outside of it. Don't touch your left hand with your right.'

'I know what I'm doing.'

I muttered a small curse that expressed my doubt about that, and he appalled me by laughing. 'Give me the glove,' he added. 'I can do it myself.'

I watched him anxiously, worried that he would either silver his right hand or the outside of the glove. I was not confident of the failing torchlight but I thought he had managed. 'Can you stand and walk?'

'I put on a glove. Wasn't that enough for you?'

'I suppose it was.' I manoeuvred an arm around him and hauled him to his feet. It took more effort than I'd expected and I abruptly realized the weight of the skirts and the fur-lined cloak he wore. 'This way. We have a fire.'

'I can sense it.'

He was not steady on his feet but he walked. 'Sense it? Or see the light against the dark?'

'Both, and more. I think it's a dragon-sense, from the dragon blood. I smell the fire, I see the light it gives off, but more. There's something I can't quite describe. It's not my eyes, Fitz, but I sense warmth. The warmth of your body, and the greater heat of the fire. I can tell you that Lant stands to the left of it, and Perseverance crouches by Spark. Is she all right?'

'Let's find out,' I suggested, swallowing my fears. I had the Wit so I knew what it was to have a sense that others did not possess. If he said he could sense my warmth, why doubt him? I knew that on the far side of the market-circle, a bitch fox watched us from the darkness of the forest edge. My Wit told me that. I would not dispute what his 'dragon-sense' told him.

My heart sank as I steadied the Fool toward the fire. Spark sprawled in the snow, making pathetic little sounds. Like a kitten mewling for its mother. Her hands scrabbled and her booted feet kicked uselessly. Per was hunkered down beside her. The conflict on his face was as shifting as the firelight. Fear. Sympathy. Uneasiness. Confusion.

'There's a log here. Behind you. A little more. Sit down.'

The Fool sat, more abruptly than I intended. Uneasiness rippled through me as he carefully gathered his skirts around him. The white glove on his left hand was feminine, as was his movement as he adjusted the hood of his cloak. I saw Lant's lip twitch, as if he were a cat smelling something foul. I felt a surge of irritation with him. 'Spark. How is she?' I asked Perseverance, and he flinched at the name.

'I don't know.'

I crouched down beside the girl and spoke for the Fool's benefit. 'She's not unconscious. Her eyes are open and she's making sounds. But there is no awareness in her eyes.' I lifted my gaze to Per. 'May I please have the butterfly cloak? Let's keep her as warm as we can.'

Without hesitation, he stood up and shed the garment and handed it to me. I took off one of the cloaks I was wearing and gave it to him. He bundled into it gratefully as I tucked one edge of the butterfly cloak under Spark, rolled her onto it, and then snugged it around her, leaving only her face bare. She looked like a brightly-coloured cocoon. Her sounds grew softer and became a high soft humming. Her twitching eased. 'Tell me everything,' I commanded the Fool.

He pulled his cloak more closely around himself. Even in the cold winter air, I could smell the mustiness of it. It was thick wool, lined with fur, from Lady Thyme's closet. The heavy woollen skirts he wore came down to the top of his boots, which were leather, cut more for a city street than a snowy forest. He brushed his short, pale hair back from his brow and gave a small sigh. 'You left me. You told me you were going to do it, and I heard in your voice that you meant it. So I immediately made my other arrangements. I wasn't happy to do it, Fitz, but you left me no choice. I persuaded Spark that my place was beside you, as indeed it is in this venture. Lady Rosemary had dismissed her, to fend for herself in Buckkeep Castle, so it took little effort to make her completely mine. I persuaded her to attempt a foray back into Chade's old quarters. She procured the dragon's blood for me.'

'Why dragon's blood?'

'Hush. Let me speak.' He looked unerringly at Lant. 'There are tea herbs in that pack we left. Left front pocket.' He glanced over at the pot. 'The water will boil soon.' Lant did not move instantly, but then he rose and turned toward the tent. 'There are two cups in the pack also. The tea is a restorative one. It may help Spark,' he called after him, then shifted his attention back to me. 'The clothing was easier. No one bothered us about that. It's from Lady Thyme's wardrobe, of course. Spark said the lock on the door was a good one, but old. And she had been taught how to outwit locks. Once we were in, we took the greater part of an afternoon to select what we wished. And Spark proved to have a knack at adjusting clothing for size. That was what took the most time. She had to move it, a garment or two at a time, down to my rooms, and there she worked on the cutting and fitting and hemming. We were mostly finished with it the last time you came battering at the door. I dared not let you in for fear you would immediately guess our plan.'

It did not escape me that he had deflected my question about dragon's blood. I'd have to corner him later and pester it out of him. Lant came back with the tea herbs. He glanced at me and I nodded, and he went about that task. Per had drawn closer to listen to the tale. The Fool turned his blind eyes in the boy's direction and smiled at him. Per bowed his head. I did not blame him. The Fool's golden gaze had become a daunting thing to meet.

'How did you get to the Witness Stones?' I could not imagine the blind Fool and the burdened girl making that trek.

'We didn't.' The Fool spoke starkly. 'In the dark of night, we dressed warmly and Spark shouldered our pack. She had obtained a walking staff for me. And we went down to the dungeons of Buckkeep. It was a trick to get past the guards, but when they changed for the night, we managed it. And Spark had done it before, following Chade. She knew where to take us. Dutiful had put an iron grate across that corridor, and locked it securely, but again Spark knew the trick of making it open. And once we were through, we took our first big gamble. She spread dragon blood on the palm of my hand, then held tight to me. I pressed my palm to the old Skill-stone, the one that whoever rebuilt Buckkeep Castle from an Elderling ruin had used in the foundation. And it worked. We stepped out in Aslevjal.'

I recalled it well. I stared at him. 'How long did you stay there?'

'Long enough to locate the correct facet of the pillar to bring us here. Another smear of dragon blood and on we came. Only to find Lant and Perseverance here. I was startled to find them. Spark, however, seemed almost to expect Perseverance. Though I sensed a bit of a chill from him when he saw how we were dressed.' He turned his blind gaze on the lad again. Per said nothing and stared at the fire. 'I guessed where you had gone. I even considered following you. I would like to once more walk in the Stone Garden. To touch Verity-as-Dragon.' A strange smile curved his mouth. 'To touch, a last time, Girl-on-a-Dragon. Did you visit her?'

'No. I didn't.' In some ways, the thought of that stone dragon still put a chill up my spine.

He lowered his voice. 'Will she recover? Spark?'

I wanted to be angry with him, to demand why he had risked her so wildly. 'I don't know. Four portal journeys in less than two days? I'd never attempt it. We'll keep her as warm as we can, try to get a hot drink down her, and wait. It's all I know to do.' I bit back the recriminations and questions. 'I would love to understand why you seem so little affected.'

He suddenly sat up straight and stared around the ancient pavilion almost as if he could see. 'Fitz. We camped here. Do you recall? When I was dead?'

'How could I not recall it?' I ignored the peculiar looks that both Per and Lant were giving me. They had been staring at the fire but hanging on the edges of our conversation avidly. I had no intention of explaining to them what had happened here on that long-ago summer day. Just the Fool's mention of it had brought it vividly to mind. It was not that I had become him in death that still shook me to my core; it was the remembrance of how, as we had traded our bodies that he might resume his existence as the Fool, we had mingled and for that long instant, become one creature. One being.

And it had felt so correct. So perfectly balanced.

'It was here,' I confirmed again.

'It was. And when we left here, we left my things here. The Elderling tent. My little cooking-pot . . .'

'Decades ago,' I reminded him.

'But they were Elderling-made. And you made our camp on the pavilion stones. Do you recall where we camped? Could you look for what's left of them, under the snow?'

I could. I recalled where I had pitched the tent, recalled too where I had built the funeral pyre for him. 'Possibly.'

'Please, Fitz. Look for them now. It would be warm shelter for all of us. Even if only enough of it remains to be blankets, it will warm us better than wool and furs.'

'Very well.' I knew I'd get no more of the tale out of him until I had done as he asked. I found a likely branch and thrust it into the fire. As I waited for it to kindle into a torch, I asked Per, 'How is she?' He had gradually edged closer to his friend.

'She's stopped moaning and muttering. She's still now. Is that good?'

'I don't know. I think she's been through four Skill-pillar trips in quick succession. I'm not sure I could survive that, let alone an untrained mind like hers.'

'But Mage Gr— your friend seems unscathed.'

I said nothing to that. I didn't want to speak of dragon blood and how I'd seen the Fool changing since he'd drunk it, let alone smeared it on his palm. 'Keep her warm. Talk to her. Be her anchor to this world. Lant, come with me, please.'

He rose with alacrity, and as I held our pathetic 'torch' aloft, he followed me into darkness. I took a bearing from the Skill-pillar, and recalled where the ornamental stone wall had been in relation to our tent. And the funeral pyre had been there. I lifted the torch higher. Was there a slight mound there beneath the snow, the reminder of limbs and logs and branches that had rotted there for years? I walked toward it.

The tent had been beyond it. I walked more slowly, kicking my feet deeper into the snow, trying to get the soles of my boots all the way down to the stone of the pavilion. And suddenly my toe caught and dragged on something. Was it possible that anything of the Fool's grand tent remained after all these years? I hooked my toe under it and pulled it up to the surface. Fabric. Brightly dyed so that the colours shone even in our feeble torch-light. All those years ago, the Fool and I had donned winter clothing and just walked away from this camp. Through the

Skill-portal and back to Aslevjal I had taken him. All those years ago, and his grand tent was still here, collapsed under the snow.

'Help me drag this free,' I said to Lant, and he posted the flaming branch in the snow and bent to seize the edge of the fabric. We both pulled. It was heavy work, for more than snow weighted it. Fallen leaves and bits of moss, all the detritus that seemed to vanish from both the pavilion and the Skill-road were layered upon it. It came free slowly. As it emerged from the snow and I shook litter from it, the limber supports that held the tent up revived slightly, lifting the bright parade of dragons and serpents into view.

It took some time for us to drag it free. The torch burned out and still we struggled. There were objects inside the tent still, so abruptly had the Fool and I departed from it, and I dreaded we would tear it before it came free, but it held. I recalled well how it had held out the icy winds of Aslevjal, and how the warmth of our bodies had been enough to heat it. Even if it was no longer tight, it would be shelter for our enlarged party. We dragged it slowly to our fireside. Frost rimed the bright panels and it was hard to find the collapsed entry. 'We found it,' I said, and the Fool beamed like a child.

Spark was still, her eyes open and her lips moving slightly. From time to time, the direction of her gaze shifted and once she smiled at no one. Her lips moved, speaking silently. Revelation struck me.

'How can I have been so stupid? We have to get her off the stone flagging, away from the pavilion. Look at her. The stones are speaking to her.'

'That whispering?' Lant asked, alarmed. 'I thought it wind in the trees last night. Per did not hear it at all.'

'And you, too,' I announced.

It was hard work in the dark and the cold. I put Lant and Per to digging a small fire-pit under the evergreens where the snow was shallowest. I lifted Spark and placed her inside my tent. Then I took the task of shaking the last of the snow and moss from the Elderling tent and stretching it out to find the corners. I had never paused to look at the supports before. They were white but reminded me of baleen from a great whale. I set them aside, and went back to where we had salvaged the tent. Kicking and digging in the snow with my hands, I found the remaining supports and the rusty shell of the old fire-pot. It would do.

It took me longer to set up the tent than it should have. We installed the fire-pot in the pit, moved coals and soon had a fire to warm it. The Elderling pavilion was more spacious than my little tent had been. As soon as we had moved the bedding, I put Spark inside. We set a pot of snow to melt. 'Stay with her,' I told Per. To Lant, I said, 'Rummage in the packs. Put together some sort of meal for us.'

I went back to where the Fool sat by the fire still. 'Your tent is up. Shall I guide you inside?'

He was staring toward it, a faint smile on his face. 'I can almost sense the shape of it, for it traps the warmth so well.' He heaved a sudden sigh. 'So many memories that shelter holds for me. Did I tell you that the dragon Tintaglia was the one who commanded the Rain Wild Traders to help me? That tent was given to me, and a lovely robe. But the cloak, the one you call the butterfly cloak? That was something that Prilkop had found in Kelsingra. He managed to keep it, wadded small, even when we were slaves. He gave it to me in Clerres. And I gave it to Incalu. My messenger.' He fell silent.

I felt a wave of sympathy for him, but I firmed my will. 'You won't distract me from one tale by dangling another in front of me, Fool. You and Spark went through the portal to Kelsingra. It's claimed by Rain Wilders who call themselves the Dragon Traders now. Queen Malta and King Reyn rule there. Dragons live there, or near there. So. What happened when you emerged there?'

If I had hoped to push him closer to the truth with what I already knew of Kelsingra, I failed. 'Malta,' he said, and smiled. 'Possibly the most annoying young female I've ever encountered. Yet lovely. I named a horse after her. Do you remember?'

'I do. Nettle said that Burrich was stunned to receive her as a gift. So. You came out of the portal . . .'

He folded his lips for a moment, then spoke. 'It was night. And Spark needed to sit and recover for a time. It was hard for me to let her do that, for though I knew it was night, though I sensed no warmth from the surroundings, the city was lit with unfailing light, and I saw the brightly-clad folk you call Elderlings. I could see! We'd arrived in the midst of some sort of festival. At least, that was what the city remembered for us. And I could see! I do not think you can imagine what that is like, to be deprived for so long of my sight, to become accustomed and accepting that my vision is limited to the difference between light and dark, and then to suddenly see again. Colours and people's faces, to catch shifting expressions, to see the moving shadows on the walls, the glorious torchlight! Oh, Fitz!'

For a time he fell silent, just breathing, as if he were a starving man who had just described a feast. I waited. 'Well, I knew of course that it was a deception. Or a performance by the memory-stone of the city, if you will. That did not lessen its fascination for me. If anything, it sharpened it. I wanted to know more. Strange to say, it was when Spark began to attempt to speak to the passing people that I became alarmed for her rather than for myself. I got her to her feet, and we walked together through the streets. And it was wonderful, Fitz, to walk arm in arm with her, but not need her vision. Well, almost. There are still parts of the city that are in need of repair, for it is a large place, still far too large for the population it has now. I asked her to be wary, to watch for live folk like ourselves, people who walked through the shadow-population the city showed us. She said she would try, but her voice was vague and I was not sure she could discern what I meant.' He paused again, and again his sightless gaze wandered to the Elderling tent. 'I'm cold,' he said.

'If we go into the tent, all will hear your tale. Out here, we have some small privacy.'

'It matters little. Spark was with me, and I fancy that when she recovers, she will tell Perseverance all. They've become very good friends.'

I did not say that she might not recover. Nor did I mention that Per had doubts about that friendship. Instead, I helped him to his feet and guided him over the uneven ground to the Elderling tent's entrance. It was beautiful in the night, for the light from the little fire inside the tent lit the fabric so that the dragons and serpents gleamed in gold and scarlet and azure. Its beauty was both strong and delicate. My heart soared to see it. The little campfire crackled and danced behind us, scenting the cold forest air with pine resin. I could smell the porridge that Lant was cooking. The Fool was beside me and alive, despite his idiocy. My heart lifted in one wolfish instant of unadulterated satisfaction in the present moment.

In the next, shame scourged me. How did I deserve even an instant of peace when my Bee was forever lost? When I was on a mission to go to a land I'd never seen to kill as many Servants as I could find? When a young woman twitched and tattered away with the Skill-sickness in the beautiful tent before me?

'You are grinding your teeth,' the Fool pointed out quietly.

'I always fail the people I love the most.'

'Say rather that you judge yourself more harshly than anyone else ever has.'

We reached the tent door. 'Duck your head,' I suggested.

'Let me shed some of this first,' he responded. I took from him the heavy fur-and-wool cloak, an amply-padded embroidered waistcoat, and then he untied a sash and dropped several layers of skirts to reveal his wool-trousered legs.

I gathered it all up, a substantial armful. 'How much of a woman's shape actually comes from her garments?' I wondered as I mastered my load.

'More than you would suspect,' he responded.

We entered the Elderling tent. It was already capturing the warmth of the tiny fire in the pit. Per had put down a layer of small pine boughs and edged Spark onto them. He sat cross-legged beside the fire, looking both worried and sullen. 'A moment,' I told the Fool, and tucked his female garb into the cloak to transform it into a pallet. 'Here,' I told him, and he sat carefully. He held his hands, one bare and one gloved, out to the fire.

'That's so much better,' he sighed.

Lant entered the tent, carrying the bubbling pot of porridge with him. He served out a portion for each of us, even Spark, and it was not too badly scorched. He was learning. He passed out bread and cheese to go with it, and I judged that he was right, that we all needed a more substantial meal. 'Tomorrow, I'll try for some meat for us,' I offered.

'Tomorrow, we should try to move on,' the Fool countered.

'Only if killing Spark does not matter to you. I will not allow that girl to enter a portal for at least three more days, and even then, I doubt that she will be ready. If I can Skill to Buckkeep tonight, I will ask Nettle to send someone here, someone strong in the Skill, to take all of you back.'

'Well, that is not going to happen,' the Fool observed sweetly after a stretched moment of silence.

Spark turned her head toward us and then spoke. 'The dragon? The red dragon?'

'She's not here,' the Fool replied comfortingly. 'We escaped her. And when we return to Kelsingra, I will see that we go first to Malta and speak with her. She is a friend, Spark. If I could have gone to her first, we would not have been attacked.'

'And I think it is time we talked about that attack. Why did you go so swiftly to Kelsingra, why were you attacked and how did you get Skill all over your hand?'

The Fool made a small sound in his throat. I already knew he was dancing around the edges of the truth. He cleared his throat. 'As you know, my friendship with both Queen Malta and the dragon Tintaglia goes back many years, so I decided—'

'You are friends with a dragon AND a queen?' Perseverance broke in, astonished.

'It's news to me as well, lad. Though I had an inkling of it years ago. But, no, Fool, we will not be sidetracked with a story about how all that came about. We accept your peculiar alliances, while reserving the right to demand that tale at a later time. Go on.'

The Fool had moved to sit beside Spark. He felt for her hand to hold and when I saw her struggling, I stooped and unwound the butterfly cloak enough that she could get her arm and hand free. 'Do you think you would like some hot tea? Or something to eat?' She looked at me, her gaze still vague, but managed a nod. I ventured a tendril of Skill toward her, fearful of being pulled into the vortex of the portal, but I sensed nothing from her. I suspected she had been battered by the Skill but not shredded by it. I dared to hope she would recover.

The Fool drew a breath. 'Well, it was night there, and although the streets were dark and deserted, they did not seem so to me. They seemed wide and lit for a festival, the buildings themselves gleaming with a toadstool light that made the torches seem wild and bright. Yet sometimes I stumbled as we went, over fallen stones that the city did not show me, and once our way was blocked and we had to find a different route.'

'But you knew where you were going.' I allowed silence to take a breath. 'Fool, had you ever been to Kelsingra before?'

He hesitated. 'Not . . . not in person. Not as myself. But there is a dragon-sense in me now, Fitz. And from it, I've had dreams. Dreams that are more like memories.' His brows drew together and abruptly I allowed myself to see how much he had changed. His skin had the same fine texture you'd see on the belly of a tiny lizard. His eyes gleamed gold and yet anxious in the dim light from the fire-pot. 'I remember things. Flying over the ocean. The musky smell of an elk when it knows it cannot escape and turns to fight. The taste of hot blood over my tongue. Dragons are made of hungers and lusts that are beyond even human imagining. You others will not understand what I speak of, but Fitz will. I dreamed of silvery Skill, filling a well to brimming and flowing over. I dreamed of it rising to the surface of the river like an undulating silver ribbon after an earthquake. But most of all, I dreamed of drinking. Of plunging my muzzle into it nearly to my eyes and sucking it in, in long draughts.' He gave a short, breathless sigh as if even speaking of it inflamed his hunger. 'And I remembered where once I had drunk it. From a well in Kelsingra. So I went there.'

He still held Spark's hand but he turned toward me. 'That was how I knew the dragon blood had Skill in it. All dragons crave it, with every fibre of their beings. And why I believed the blood would carry me through the Skill-portals as it did.'

The pot of snow-water finally reached a grudging boil. Perseverance tended it, preparing cups of tea for each of us. For a time, the story was halted as we helped Spark to sit and hold a steaming cup and sip from it. I saw with relief that she was coming back to herself. She presented a thorny problem for me. I needed to be on my way, and the next step of my journey demanded that I go on to Kelsingra, unless the Fool had left it as stirred as a poked hive of bees. Spark sat up, the butterfly cloak draping her shoulders, and a second cup of tea warming both her hands.

'I meant to go first to Malta, to find her and greet her, and gain her assistance. I dared to hope that Tintaglia would be there and would recall my service to dragons and actually show her appreciation. A thin hope, that, I will admit. Dragons regard us as we might regard gnats. One is much like another, and our deeds matter little. Still. That was my resolution, and Fitz, I truly believed I was clinging to it as I led the way through the streets of Kelsingra. But then I came to a part of the city that was dark. Lifeless. No Elderling memories shimmered there to guide me, and yet I still knew where I was going. I could smell it, Fitz. I could taste it in the back of my throat with every breath I took. And suddenly I could not think of anything else except that brimming Skill-well. And how it would strengthen me and sate me.'

His eyes. Was it the firelight that danced and shifted in them, or was it the gold that swirled? I stared at him, wordless.

'I didn't drink of it, of course.'

'Only because he couldn't reach it,' Spark said. A very small smile was on her lips, a weary smile like a child's after an exciting day. 'He dragged me there like a dog on a lead. He knew the way, but I followed him through the dark as he gripped my wrist. We came to an open place. I could see little in the dark, but it seemed a shabby part of the city, not near as grand as the boulevards we had earlier walked. And it smelled rank there. We walked past an immense pile of dung.'

'Dragon droppings?' Per asked in awe, as if that were the most fantastic part of their tale.

'I suppose so,' she said, and the friends shared the first smile that I had seen pass between them since she had come back through the pillar.

'It stank,' the Fool confirmed. 'But the odd part was that it stank in a familiar way. Almost as if I should recall whose droppings those were and walk lightly in her territory.'

'Ugh,' said Lant, softly. I tended to agree with him.

'I tried to get the cover off the well.'

'Which involved a lot of tugging, then kicking and cursing it,' Spark confided to Per. He tried not to grin.

'True,' the Fool admitted reluctantly. 'Then I smelled Skill, very near me. There was an immense bucket nearby. It had been set down unevenly, and in the corner of it there was Skill. It was little more than a smear, as if someone had wiped it clean but missed a spot. And I could smell it.'

'I could barely see it,' Spark said, sitting up a bit straighter, now a partner in the telling. 'There was little moon, but it was so silver that it seemed to catch every bit of starlight. It was beautiful and yet terrifying. I wanted to move away from it, but he leaned on the edge of the bucket and reached as far down as he could and managed to get his hand into it.'

'Just barely, but I touched it.' He held up his gloved left hand and smiled as if the gods were pouring blessings upon him. 'The sweetest agony you can imagine.' He turned his face toward me. 'Fitz. It was like that moment. You know of what I speak. One and complete. I felt I was the music of the world, strong and sweeping. My throat closed and tears ran down my face and I could not move for joy.'

'And then the dragon came!' Spark continued. 'She was red and even in the darkness of the night she shone red, so that I saw her almost before I heard her. But then she made a sound, like all the horns of Buckkeep blasting, but it was full of fury. She ran toward us. Dragons are not graceful when they run. They are terrifying, but not graceful at all. It was like watching a very angry red cow charge at us! I screamed and seized Lady Amber and dragged him away from the bucket. I could scarcely see where I was running, but run we did. Not that he was happy about it.'

'Lady Amber?' Lant asked, confused.

Spark caught her lip between her teeth. 'So he— no, so she told me I must think of her, guised as we are.' She gave Per a look that asked for understanding and said softly, 'Just as sometimes I am Ash.'

Lant opened his mouth but before he could speak, the Fool took up the tale. 'I could sense the other dragon. The red dragon, I mean. Her roaring was full of threats and name-calling and absolute fury that we had penetrated the city and dared to come to the well of Silver. I could hear other dragons responding to her alarm, and then I heard a man's voice raised in anger. He was urging the dragon on!'

Spark shook her head. 'The dragons were so loud that I didn't even hear the man, and I didn't see him until he suddenly jumped out right in front of us. He had a sword, and he was wearing some kind of harness or armour. I dragged Lady Amber into a building. I just had time to slam a door closed behind us and then we ran in the dark, and we crashed into some stone stairs and we climbed those.'

I made a sound of despair. 'Upstairs? With an enemy in pursuit, you ran where you could be cornered?'

Spark looked at me with irritation. 'I've never been chased by a man with a sword, let alone a dragon. So, yes, we ran upstairs. It was awful there: furniture had gone to rot and it littered the floor. I kept stumbling and I could hear the man shouting as he searched downstairs, for like you he could not believe we would be so stupid as to run up the stairs. Then I found a window, and it looked out on an alley that I judged was too narrow for the dragon.'

The Fool took up the tale. 'So we held hands and jumped out of the window with little idea of what was below us. Oh, the terror of that jump for me! It was purest luck that we landed well. I still went to one knee, but Spark already had hold of me and was hauling me along. She flattened us against the wall and we went as silently as we could, staying to the narrow alley for quite a way. Once we came to where the buildings were wakeful, I could get my bearings and then I led the way. We could still hear the dragons trumpeting behind us, but it almost made me feel safer to know they were searching for us back by the well. I judged it was well and truly too late to seek an audience with Malta or to reach for Tintaglia, and that the pillar was our best way to escape, though I knew how much Spark dreaded it.

'I thought I could run no further. I had forgotten how heavy skirts can be, let alone a fur-lined cloak. And these boots!' He thrust one foot out before us. The toe was as pointed as a sword. 'Not for running,' he said decisively. 'But just as I slowed and told

Spark that we could probably walk for a time, I heard running feet behind us. It was strange. The ghost festivity was all around us, yet somehow I heard the sound of running footsteps. I felt I had no speed left in me and I shouted at Spark to flee but she would not leave me. Then I heard that sound just as I felt the arrow tug through the shoulder of my cloak. And I found that I could not only run but drag Spark along with me.'

'He was red,' Spark said suddenly. Her voice had gone shaky, a contrast to her earlier pleasure in telling the tale. 'I looked back. I didn't want to go into the pillar; I was terrified. I looked back to see if he might have mercy if I stayed. But he was like a creature from a nightmare. Tall and narrow and as scarlet as his dragon. And his eyes! When I saw him halt and set another arrow to his bow, I did not hold back. I may have pushed Amber into the pillar.'

'And here we are,' the Fool finished. He looked around at us, smiling blindly.

'Indeed. Here we are,' I said.

THIRTY-FIVE

Kelsingra

Wide gapes the gates of yellowed bone. A tongue of plank is our path between the teeth as we walk toward the gullet. Here I will be devoured. This is a true thing, near unavoidable on any path. I must enter those jaws.

From Bee Farseer's Dream Journal

We all slept in the Elderling tent that night, packed as neatly as saltfish in a box. I slept along one wall, the Fool against my back. Even against the fine fabric of the tent, I slept much more warmly than I had in our small tent. In the early hours of dawn Per came in from his watch. 'The porridge is nearly cooked,' he told me softly as I awoke. 'I put a bit of honey in it.'

I sat up, trying not to wake the others this early. Both the Fool and Spark, I thought, should take all the sleep they could. Then my Wit sent a sudden shuddering through me. A predator, one bigger than me, moved outside the tent, exploring our camp. In the next moment, Motley began a raucous cawing. I heard the clatter of an overturned pot.

I shifted as quietly as I could and reached across the Fool to seize Lant's shoulder. 'Sssh,' I warned him as he woke. 'Something's outside. Follow me, sword drawn.'

The others woke as we extricated ourselves but sensed our caution. Spark's eyes looked as big as saucers as I stepped over her, sword bared, and ducked to exit the tent. Lant came behind me, as barefoot as I was, naked steel in his hand. As soon as I saw our intruder, I reached back to grab his wrist. 'Don't look directly at him,' I warned. To the others inside the tent, I said in a carrying whisper. 'Bear. Come out. Don't dress, just get clear of the tent. You don't want to be caught inside it. Do not run, but be ready to scatter if I shout.'

The bear was a big fellow and the silvery hair on his shoulders and a greying muzzle showed that he was both old and wise. No bear gets that old without the wisdom that survival demands, but neither does a creature in the wild live to that age without infirmities. The breadth of his shoulders showed me what a powerful creature he once had been, but he was gaunt now. He was on all fours, sniffing through Lant's pack that had been left by last night's campfire. His interest was plain: food.

As the others emerged he became aware of us and made a leisurely decision to display his size for us. He lifted himself onto his hind legs and stood looking down at us with his glittering black eyes. He was a big one. Very big. His mouth was ajar, taking in our scent and incidentally displaying sizeable teeth. I could smell his hot breath on the cold winter air, and in it the carrion stink of infection.

'Spread out, but walk slowly,' I suggested to the others in a low voice as they came fumbling out of the tent. 'Move apart from one another. If he charges, we scatter. Don't bunch up where he can get all of us.'

I could hear Spark's panting breath. They emerged last, with the Fool caped in one of his skirts. Spark had the sense to keep hold of the Fool's sleeve as she began to tug him sideways away from the group. The bear's glittering gaze followed them.

Food, I reminded him. *Smell it. Apples. Maybe bacon or fish? Perhaps a pot of honey.* I could only suggest. The Wit-magic allows me to reach toward an animal but it does not assure that the animal will accept my thoughts. It certainly gives me no power to command a wild creature. And sometimes it is a mistake to try to touch minds.

It certainly was this time. I sensed his pain and he did not like that I knew his weakness. The bear gave a low huff, an angry sound. 'Stand still,' I warned the others. 'Do not run.' I lifted my sword. It had never felt smaller in my hand. The bear looked around at the human statues. I spared one sideways glance for Spark and the Fool. They were the most vulnerable, weaponless and the Fool unsighted. They were both in their stockinged feet. Spark still had the Elderling cloak bundled around her. The rest of us could run. Lant and I both had swords and Per had his staff in his hands.

But the bear decided we were no threat. He dropped back to all fours. He snuffed Lant's pack. His thick black claws were as big around as sausages, with deadly sharp tips. He demonstrated their power as he casually tore the pack open, scattering the contents over the snow. Lant made a dismayed noise. 'Stand steady,' I told him, and he obeyed. I tipped my eyes toward Spark. She looked haggard but her jaw was set with determination. Moving slowly, she had lifted one side of the butterfly cloak and was trying to drape it around the Fool. He was hugging himself against the cold, fear and misery on his face. What did he perceive? The warmth emanating from such a large creature, the sounds it made as it ransacked Lant's supplies? I studied the bear, estimated his size and strength. 'Per. Get up that tree behind you. He's too big to climb it. Go. Now.'

For a wonder, the boy obeyed. He moved silently and swiftly. The tree was not an easy one to climb but the boy was inspired. One safe.

'Lant. Now you go.'

'No.' His voice was deadly calm with terror. 'Two swords are better than one. I'm not going to attack him, but if he comes after you, I'll do my best.'

I shot him a sideways glance. Chade's son. Where had this man suddenly come from? 'Very well,' I conceded. The bear was struggling with something wrapped in several layers of waxed cloth. 'We're going to move back and away.'

Spark had moved the Fool slowly toward what she perceived as their only possible escape. The dense forest behind us offered them no clear place to run. She'd followed the edge of the pavilion and the old stonework, working her way around the curve until she was now nearing the stone pillar. With a sinking heart, I realized that the bear was now between them and me. I could see the panicky rise and fall of her chest as they edged closer and closer to the portal. I saw her lips move and watched the Fool tug the glove from his silvered hand. I could not hear what she said to him but I saw his tight nod. 'Don't!' I said in a low voice. 'Don't chance it. Once he's had all the food, he will likely leave. Stand still.'

The bear lifted his head at my words. He had attempted to eat the cheese, waxed cloth and all. It had tangled in his teeth and now he pawed irritably at his mouth, trying to dislodge it with his claws. He rumbled his displeasure and then gave an abrupt snarl of pain. Sometimes old bears have bad teeth and the cloth was wrapped around one. He gave a sudden roar of fury and Spark gasped shrilly. He turned his head sharply toward them. His eyes, small and snapping black with anger, focused on them. In terror, she dragged the Fool toward the pillar.

'No!' I shouted.

Bears walk and bears shamble. Bears also charge swiftly, swifter than a healthy man can run. He was an old bear but the Fool was blind. I could not outrun a bear. The Fool and Spark did not have a chance. The bear ignored my shout and went after them, closing the distance, roaring as he went. There was no time to think, no time to debate which was the lesser danger. 'Go!' I shouted at the Fool and Spark.

The bear would have them. His maw gaped wide and then he reared back, batting wildly at the crow as she flapped her wings in his face and stabbed at him with her beak. It was the instant that Spark needed.

She pushed the Fool through the pillar and turned to flee, but the Fool gripped her wrist and dragged her in after him. She went screaming, the fluttering crow fleeing with her. The charging bear slammed into cold black stone, and then fell back from it, mystified and angry. He swiped at it, the long black claws screaming against the face of the pillar. They were gone, to safety or oblivion, I could not tell. And Lant and I had one chance to live as the bear turned and chose his fresh targets.

'Trees!' I said to Lant. He needed no other word. I followed him as he ploughed through the snow toward a vast evergreen. It had no low branches. I gave him a leg up and then followed.

For a city boy, he climbed well. 'Higher!' I shouted to him. Up we went, stockinged feet digging into rough bark, fingernails bending and breaking as we climbed a stretch of trunk bereft of branches. He reached a thick branch. 'Move over!' I panted and he did.

If the bear had been younger or smaller, we'd have been in grave danger. As it was, he made several attempts to follow us, digging his claws into the bark and ripping chunks of it free, then hurling himself against the trunk so that the tree shook from his onslaught. When he could not reach us, he turned his fury on our tents. Mine presented no challenge to him. He shredded and tossed it, rooted through it for food, and then roared at the fabric still tangled in his sore tooth. He moved away from it with a festoon of canvas collaring him between his massive head and the hunch of his shoulders. I looked away as he attacked the Elderling tent, unable to bear its destruction.

'What stuff is that made of?' I heard Lant marvel and dared to look down. The bear had collapsed the tent and now battled the yielding fabric, rolling in a tangle of bear, dragons and serpents. His wrestling bared our still-burning fire-pot, our bedding and the rest of our supplies. He slashed at the fabric but I saw no rents in it. 'We'll have nothing left!' Perseverance cried from his tree, and I shouted back, 'We'll have our lives. Stay put, boy!'

I think the bear eventually felt he had vanquished the tent. He went back to our supplies, spilling and spoiling and eating and then roaring his fury at the pain. I hated what he was doing to us, and yet felt a pang of anguish for him. His death awaited him this season and it would not be an easy one for the old fellow.

It was when he tore open my pack and I saw Bee's precious book fall into the snow that I gave a cry of loss and started down the trunk. Lant seized the back of my collar. 'No,' he said.

'Let go!'

'Try to follow the advice you gave your stableboy. Don't give up your life for a thing, no matter how precious.'

He was not well seated on the tree, and for one berserk moment, I wanted to jerk him free and let him drop to the snow below. Instead, I leaned my forehead against the rough bark and to my shame great tremors of loss shook me. Lant kept his grip on me, fearing, I think, that I would simply let go and fall. I did not. I clung there while breakers of loss pounded me. I cursed the sorrow that would not let go of me, that ambushed me and unmanned me every time it woke. The book was a thing, not my child. The candles scattered like ivory bones across the snow were not Molly. But they were all I had left of my wife and my child.

From far away, I felt a plucking of Skill. *Fitz? Are you alive?*

Yes, I replied dully to Dutiful. *I live. Not that I wish to, but I live.*

Danger? His Skilling was thin as smoke.

I let down my walls, suddenly aware that I'd raised them against the whispering memories of the plaza and the Skill-road. The Skill is swift as thought. In a heartbeat, he knew all that had befallen us.

I can send help to you. I can . . . and whatever he was offering wafted away.

No. Send no one. We have to follow the Fool. I pushed the thought hard and wondered if he received it. The decision I had not known I was going to make was now obvious. As soon as the bear left, we'd salvage what we could and use the portal to go to Kelsingra. If the Fool and Spark had made it there, I was certain they would need help. If they hadn't, at least I would know. I could not leave Lant and Per here and go alone, for they'd be without shelter or supplies now, and it was likely the bear would come back. So, we would go on. I hoped there would not be a red dragon waiting for us on the other side.

The old bear had probably not had a decent meal in days. He dismissed us as a nuisance he had routed and got on with his pillaging. Our supplies were not equal to his appetite, but he was thorough in his snouting and tearing. His attempting to eat the cheese would probably hasten the inevitable end of his life. Often he stopped to roar in pain and anger and paw at his mouth and the twist of fabric snagged on his bad tooth. We sat in the trees, trapped and shivering, until nearly noon. The large pack that Spark had carried he exploded into a wild blossoming of skirts and scarves and petticoats. The Fool's pack was filled with a tinker's treasure trove of peculiar items. When he'd finally convinced himself there was nothing more to be found and eaten, he wandered off in a leisurely way that told me the pavilion was part of his regular territory. He would definitely be back.

Even after he was out of sight, we waited for a time. When we finally clambered down, we were all stiff and cold. 'Per, see if you can waken either fire. Lant, let's salvage what we can.'

My first thought was for Bee's books and Molly's candles. I found her old journal but not the dream book. The journal was in better condition than I had expected. It had snow on the cover but the little tie that held it closed had worked. I shook the snow from it, careful not to melt any with the warmth of my hands. There was little left of my pack. Of my four candles, I could find only three. I dug barehanded in snow for a time, until my fingers were numb and I had to admit defeat. I knew I was lucky the bear had not eaten all of them. Doubtless he had been attracted to the flower-scented beeswax. I tore a piece of canvas that was not wet with bear saliva and wrapped my treasures. My heart cried after Bee's other book. The bear had scattered things far and wide, and I held a tiny bit of hope that I'd still find it.

Which was worse? Bare feet or feet in wet socks in snow? Per had decided on bare feet and I marvelled at his toughness. He was working over the fire. Embers from the fire-pot and the last coals from our fire combined to become flames. 'Build it up large,' I told him, for if the old bear came back, flaming branches might be our best weapon.

Lant and I worked quickly. We shook out the bright fabric of the Elderling tent, and I was astonished to find it intact. Not all of the supports had survived, but we salvaged what we could. We left our swords thrust upright in the earth beside the fire yet we all knew how puny they would be against a bear's attack. We spread the tent out near the fire and began to gather anything useful that remained to us. Pots and cups, clothing, coin-pouches and knives. As soon as we found our boots and dry socks, we had them on, then our cloaks and gloves.

'What is our plan?' Lant asked at one point and I realized I hadn't spoken aloud since I'd given them their tasks.

'Gather anything useful. Follow the Fool and Spark as quickly as possible.'

'They said there was a red dragon there. And a bowman.'

'They did. So we will try to emerge from the pillar prepared to be attacked.'

Lant opened his mouth and shut it again.

'Somewhere in this wreckage, there's a bit of leather with a needle thrust through it and some stout thread wrapped around it. As soon as you find it, let me know. Make three piles of whatever we can still use.'

'Do we take Grey's things? And Ash's?'

'We salvage all and then choose. We carry as much as we can for I want to assume we will be reunited and that there was some sane reason for them packing so many garments.'

'Even the beads and string? All those gloves?'

I followed Per's gesture. The Fool's spilled baggage included a veritable rainbow of gloves, in all fabrics and weights. My heart listed a bit toward sadness. He'd always intended to silver his hand. He hadn't lied to me. The Fool and I seldom lied to each other. Except when we did. 'As much as we can carry of anything that might be useful. We don't know what we are going into.'

We worked as fast as we could but it was not an easy task. Some of Per's grain had been caught in a corner of the bag and he cooked it for us as we shook snow from clothing and pawed through snow to find our scattered gear. Under Burrich's tutelage, I had learned to mend harness as a lad, and the sewing skill had served me well all my life. Perseverance's pack was mendable. Mine was shredded and Lant's was worse. The torn canvas of my tent became two rough sacks, hastily stitched. Despite our need for haste, I spent time to make a smaller bag to hold Bee's book and Molly's candles and stowed them securely. I looked up from securing the flap to find Per watching me intently. Bee's dream journal was in his hands. He offered it to me uncertainly. 'I think I recognize her hand. Such pictures as she drew! Is this truly her work?'

'That's mine!' I said, my declaration harsher than I intended. The hurt in his eyes rebuked me as I took it from his hands. It was all I could do not to snatch it from him.

'Sir, if it's not too late . . . I'd still like to learn my letters. Perhaps some day I could read what she wrote.'

'It's private,' I said. 'But yes, I will teach you to read. And to write.'

He looked at me with dumb dog's eyes. My scowl sent him back to work immediately.

We hurried and yet time seemed to slip away from us. The early Mountain shadows of evening had begun to creep across the land when we were finished. The Fool's tent made a surprisingly small bundle. I could not say the same for the warm winter garments the Fool and Spark had packed. Woollen skirts and shawls were far heavier than I would have expected them to be.

'The packs are too heavy and awkward,' Lant observed. He'd kept his voice neutral; it wasn't a complaint. 'If we have to be ready for anything as we emerge from the pillar, carrying these is not a good plan.'

He was right. 'We won't carry them. We'll grip them as we go through, to be sure they travel with us. We've no idea what we'll find. Amber and Spark may be there and safe, or injured. Or captured.' In a quieter voice I added, 'Or not there at all.'

'Like Bee,' Per said in a small voice. He took a breath and squared his shoulders. 'Could that happen to us? That we go into the pillar and never come out?'

'It could,' I admitted.

'Where would we be then? What would happen to us?'

How to describe it? 'I think we would . . . become part of it. I've felt it, once or twice. It doesn't hurt, Per. In fact, that's the danger of the Skill to young users. That it feels as if it might be good to let go and tatter away and merge with it.'

'Merge with what?' His brow was furrowed. Lant's face was pale.

'The Skill-current. I don't know what else to call it.'

'Maybe merge with Bee?'

I took a breath. 'Highly unlikely, boy. And I don't want to speak of that, please. You can stay here if you wish. I can try to Skill to Dutiful and ask him to send a Skill-user through the pillar to take you back to Buckkeep. But you'd be here for at least two days, I think. In the cold, with little food, and a possible visit from a bear. But if you choose that, well, it's your choice. I'm afraid I can't stay here with you until they come for you. I have to go after the Fool and Spark as quickly as I can.' Too much time had already passed. I was now as eager to go as I was fearful.

Per hesitated. Lant spoke. 'You could just as easily be lost going back to Buck as you might going forward to Kelsingra. I don't really want to make either journey, but I'll follow you, Fitz.'

'I'll go with you, too,' Per said. 'How do we do it?'

We lined up at the pillar. I'd attached a hasty strap to each of my crude sacks. One was slung over my shoulder. Per wore his overstuffed pack and gripped my left hand. Lant rested a hand on my right shoulder and had the strap of the largest bag over his shoulder. In his right hand, he had his sword at the ready. I took a moment to myself. I'd never been trained to take others through a pillar with me, though I'd done it before, under duress. I loosed my Wit and made myself aware of both of them, their shapes and their smell, and then groped toward them with my Skill. Neither had any talent for that magic that I could detect, but almost all people have some small spark of it. I could not make either of them aware of my reaching, but I did my best to enfold them in it. I gave them no warning, no chance to hesitate. I gripped my sword in my right hand and pressed my bared knuckles against the cold stone of the pillar.

Blackness. Points of moving lights that were not stars. Per before me, swearing his loyalty. Lant staring at me, his lips folded tight. I held tight to my awareness of them. I wrapped them in myself.

Daylight blasted us. Cold seized me and suddenly I knew that I had to stay on my feet, drop Per's hand and protect us.

'Ware!' someone shouted as I sprang clear of Per and levelled my blade. My sun-dazzled eyes adjusted to the Fool sprawled at my feet and Spark fighting her way clear of the entanglement of the butterfly cloak. We had gone from a fading evening to the brilliant shine of a sunny winter day. Time lost, but even more unsettling, we seemed to have arrived only moments after the Fool and Spark had. I felt Per jostle into me as he got to his feet. He then staggered sideways, retching. Before I could look back to see how Lant had fared, I heard a roar.

I spun, or tried to, bringing my sword up to the ready. Even before my eyes found the great green dragon charging toward us, my Wit-sense reeled from the size and presence of the creature. It was coming toward us as fast as the wind blowing. I heard the clash of its silver claws on the stone street. His front legs reached, seized ground and flung it forward. His hide was rippled with silver like waterstains on fabric. This was no charging cow, but a powerful, angry creature. His roar struck me again, a sound with an edge of strange Skill and Wit. '*INTRUDERS!*'

I was no Burrich, to drop a stone dragon to its knees with the power of my Wit. I did not lift my voice but I set myself firmly before his charge and held my sword firm. That was the challenge I flung at him, my defiance, an animal-to-animal declaration, yet I was shocked to see him suddenly brace his front feet, claws screaming on the black stone as he slid to a halt. His tail lashed, a powerful limb that could probably have toppled trees. He threw his head back, jaws opened wide. There were bright flares of colour inside his open mouth, shocking orange edging to flaring red. Poison, such colours warn in a lizard or frog. He drew a great breath and I saw the sacs inside the sides of his mouth swell. I dreaded what I knew might follow, something I'd only heard tales about: a pale mist of venom that dissolved flesh and ate bones and pitted stones. But as he drew in the air, something changed in the dragon's stance. I could not read it. Anger? Puzzlement? He stood, a stiff ruff of silver spines erecting to stand out around his neck like a thorny mane. He breathed out, a hot exhalation of meaty stench, and then drew in more air, slowly wagging his head on his sinuous neck. He was taking our scent.

I had seen dragons before. I'd touched minds with Tintaglia, the first of the queen dragons to return to our world. I'd seen IceFyre's first flight when he emerged after years of being locked in a glacier. I'd watched mating dragons, seen them dive onto penned cattle offered to them as a bribe. I knew only too well how powerful they were, and how quickly they could reduce a bull to a bloody carcass. I had known that my sword was virtually useless against a bear; against a dragon, it was ridiculous. Lant abruptly stepped up beside me. He'd lifted his blade as well, but it wavered wildly. 'Sick,' he gasped, but he didn't retreat.

'Get under it!' I heard Per order someone hoarsely. 'Lie close. It can conceal both of you.' He staggered to my left side, his belt-knife out. 'Are we going to die now?' he asked in a quavering voice that broke to shrillness at the end.

'Where is the one who belongs to a dragon?'

Dragon-speech. Sound was only a part of it. Some, I knew, could not understand dragons when they spoke. They heard only the roars, grunts and snarls of a wild creature. I'd understood the words but could make no sense of them. I stood still and silent.

'I smell him. I smell one dragon-touched, chosen by a dragon we have long believed dead. Are you here by his command?'

I guessed what he smelled. The dragon's blood the Fool had used. Per made a retching sound. I heard no sound from the Fool or Spark. I took a breath. 'We mean no harm,' I called to the dragon. Then I swivelled my head. It was my Wit that had told me someone else approached, and the figure I saw striding toward me was one from my childhood nightmares. He was tall and scarlet-skinned, with blazing blue eyes, as if light shone through sapphires. His tall frame was cloaked in a flowing tunic of gold and loose black trousers. He was long-limbed in proportions that were appropriate to his height, but not human. He wore battle harness such as I'd never seen, but the sword that he pulled ringing from its sheath was all-too familiar a tool to me. Elderling, like the creatures that had stared down from the tapestry that had graced the wall of my boyhood bedchamber. He spoke as he strode toward us. 'Well done, Arbuc! I knew these invaders could not evade us for long! And now they will answer for . . .'

His words trickled away as he halted and stared at us. 'These are not the thieves I chased! Who are you and how do you come here and what do you wish? Answer with words or blood, it's all one to me.' He stood and held his weapon in a style I did not recognize. *Formality. Always choose formality first.*

I did not sheathe my blade but neither did I move it in a threatening way. I was glad now that I'd layered my pretty cloak over my serviceable one. I made as courtly a bow as I could with a bared weapon. 'Well met, good sir. We are emissaries to Queen Malta and King Reyn of the Dragon Traders. We come from the Six Duchies. We would be most grateful if you would escort us to their palace.'

My lack of aggression puzzled him. I saw that Lant had taken my cue and lowered the tip of his blade. Per stood at the ready. Of the Fool and Spark, I heard not a whisper. I hoped no betraying toe peeped out from under the butterfly cloak's camouflage.

The Elderling's gaze travelled from me to Lant to Per. I knew we were not particularly presentable but I retained my dignity and did not lower my eyes. 'How did you get here?' he demanded.

I avoided direct refusal in my answer. 'Sir, as you no doubt can tell, we have come a long and weary way. In the Mountains we dealt with cold and were even attacked by a bear. We ask only for audience with the most gracious rulers of Kelsingra. No more than that do we seek.'

I saw him turn his eyes toward the cliffs and mountains that backed the city we stood in. I tried to remember all I could of this city. I'd been here once before. Indeed, I had come here by my first inadvertent stumble through a Skill-portal, on my journey to find Verity. Without turning my head, my eyes marked the location of the tower where I had first glimpsed the intricate map the Elderlings had left. As I recalled what little I knew of it, I decided to take a risk. 'Or, if you are busy on errands of your own, we shall be happy to venture on to the Tower of the Map and wait there for your king and queen to receive us. We know our arrival is unannounced. We do not presume to hope they will see us immediately.'

I heard the clatter of boots and looked past the scarlet Elderling to see an armed troop advancing toward us. They were men, not Elderlings, and their weaponry and armour were of more familiar sorts than those the red man bore. Six in the front rank, and three more ranks behind them. Outnumbered. A conflict unwinnable with blades.

It took all my self-discipline to take my eyes off the scarlet Elderling. I looked down and carefully sheathed my blade as if it were an unfamiliar act. Then I smiled genially up at him, just a harmless emissary.

Another Elderling had come to join the dragon. He stood beside the powerful creature and despite his height, the dragon dwarfed him. This Elderling was lightly scaled in green and silver and he reached out a hand to touch the dragon's shoulder. The green dragon abruptly advanced two steps. He took in our scent again and said, '*One of them is dragon-claimed. I smell it on him.*' The immense head on the thickly muscled neck twisted. '*A dragon I have not smelled before,*' he said, as if dredging his memory for a name. '*A dragon unseen by us. Does he live yet?*' The head with its spinning silver eyes canted in the other direction but his gaze remained fixed on me.

The militant red Elderling's gleaming eyes narrowed as he regarded us. 'An unknown dragon? Which of you belongs to a dragon?'

How to answer that? I retreated toward truth. 'I do not understand the terms you use. Please. If you will escort us to where we can await audience with your rulers, I am sure all will be made clear.'

'I am sure it will,' he said after a long pause, but his voice was neither warm nor welcoming.

THIRTY-SIX

An Elderling Welcome

Select your Skill-couriers by these traits. First, let each courier be at least of journeyman status. Select for independence. Both arrogance and stubbornness may be seen as a virtue for this assignment. A highly developed sense of self is an asset for a courier. Vanity is sometimes a helpful marker, for the vain woman or conceited man is ever self-aware. Youth and a hearty constitution are also advantages.

A courier should serve no more than three years, with two years of rest between each year of service. A specific route of pillars should be assigned and the courier should travel the same routes over and over. Thus will his sense of place become well developed. The Skill-user who knows where he is going and recognizes where he is when he arrives is better able to maintain his self intact.

If the courier is strong enough to serve as an escort for the unSkilled, see that he is patient and responsible. Let those he guides always rest for at least three days between each leg of a journey.

Arrow, of Gantry's Coterie,
writing about the Qualities of a Courier

I kept my diplomat's poise and swept him a bow. 'We are so grateful to you. I am Prince FitzChivalry Farseer, of the Six Duchies. Lord Lantern Fallstar accompanies me, and our serving-lad, Perseverance of Withywoods.'

As I introduced them, Lant sheathed his blade and made a far more elegant bow than I could ever have mastered, one that involved much sweeping of his cloak. I smothered a smile as Perseverance made a brave attempt to copy him. I gestured casually at our tumbled baggage. 'Perhaps you could arrange for our things to be brought with us? The bear made short work of our picketed horses, and did great damage to our bags.' This was the gamble I was most reluctant to take. I knew that I would have taken an opportunity to search the baggage of any strangers who had mysteriously appeared inside the walls of Buckkeep Castle. The red fellow looked down at us in disapproval bordering on disdain.

'We keep no slaves here. As you have carried them this far, a bit further will not hurt you.'

'Very well.' I tried to conceal my relief. 'And sir, I do not recall that you favoured us with your name?'

A subtle reminder that I would know who he was and would perhaps speak of him to his queen. He had not sheathed his weapon and he did not look daunted by my request. 'I am General Rapskal, leader of the Kelsingra Militia. Gather your things. I will take you to my rulers.'

I glanced back at the dragon and his keeper. The Elderling said something to him and then hastened away. The dragon apparently decided we were not interesting. He turned and lumbered off in a different direction. In the distance, I heard a crow caw.

And so we loaded up with our heavy packs once more. I saw no sign of the butterfly cloak and what it concealed and I took care not to look for it. I had heard Spark speak when we arrived; perhaps that meant she was not in too poor a condition. Realizing one makeshift pack seemed to be missing, I gave a quick glance around, hoping it was under the cloak and not lost to the Skill-passage. Ah well: its absence allowed me to be mostly unencumbered and properly aristocratic as we were marched through Kelsingra.

It was a strange experience for me. I raised my Skill-walls and still the city spoke to me of a sunny winter day from its youth. A huddle of human merchants hastened past me, traders from some far city perhaps. They stayed close together and walked swiftly, glancing all about them as they passed us. A youth with a heavy line of scales on his brow and lizard-like wattles along his jaw swept the walkway outside a shop where meat hung on hooks over smoky fires. A girl with a basket on her arm passed us at a trot. Interspersed among these mundane forms, the ghosts of Elderlings strode and laughed and haggled with one another. I wondered if it was my Skill that made them seem so real. A sudden fistfight broke out between two of them and I instinctively moved away from it. 'So. You can see them,' Rapskal observed. He did not slow for the ancient altercation and I did not reply to him.

I wondered how Lant and Per perceived it, and wondered even more if the city whispered to the human guardsmen who walked ahead, beside and behind us. With a waft of smell and wind, a green-and-silver dragon passed over us, climbing steadily into the sky. I caught, not his thoughts exactly but his intent. He went to the hunt and for one peculiar moment I longed to hunt with him.

The day was cold and the wind off the unseen river had that wet bite to it that cuts through a man. General Rapskal did not slow his pace for weary travellers with heavy loads. Even so, I had time to notice that the city was sparsely populated. Some streets seemed to have inhabited structures, and the next would show signs of long desertion and disrepair. From my journey on the Skill-road, I knew that anything wrought from Skill-worked stone retained its shape and purpose far longer than any ordinary work of man. The wind might carry debris and scatter dust on the wide streets, but no errant seed had found a crack to take root in, no straggling vine struggled to tear down even the quake-cracked walls. This city had recalled for deserted generations that it was a city, and as if to mock its paltry number of inhabitants, it seemed to better recall its distant past as a centre of Elderling culture. I took note of all I saw and contrasted it with what Chade and King Dutiful believed of Kelsingra. Unless we were on the edges of a much more populous centre, Kelsingra and the Dragon Traders were presenting a far more prosperous face to the world than they truly could muster.

As I had surmised, we were walked to the base of the map-tower and then up those wide steps. The central steps had been scaled for a dragon's stride, as were the tall doors at the top. I dreaded such a climb but they took us to the human-scaled steps to one side. There, at least, folk were coming and going, some in robes as gaudy as the Fool's tent and the general's garb, and some in more prosaic leather and wool. A carpenter passed us, followed by his journeyman and three apprentices, all laden with their tools. I took in the grand art that graced the walls and then General Rapskal and his guards were escorting us into a vast and echoing space.

The immense entry hall was cleaner than I recalled it and much emptier. It was warmer as well, and seemed possessed of a sourceless light. The last time I had visited here, the floor had been littered with the fibres and dust of collapsed wooden furniture. The ancient debris had been cleared away, and a score of new desks and tables strove to occupy a space designed for hundreds. Scribes of various mien and garb occupied them, some perhaps diligently adding numbers, others facing a queue of people waiting with various degrees of impatience. I dreaded that we would be assigned to such a queue, but instead we were marched through that hall, drawing all manner of stares, and ushered through a wooden door and into a smaller chamber.

It was still too large a place for our company, but it offered warmth, and as soon as we halted Lant and Per gratefully set down their burdens. At a gesture from their leader, the troops ranged themselves around the wall. General Rapskal came to stand before me. 'I will be immediately calling on the king and queen to see if they are willing to give you an audience. I will not deceive you. I am unhappy with your account of yourself and I will advise them to regard you with the just suspicion that intruders to our city deserve. Wait here.'

He turned and I let him go three steps before I halted him with a genial, 'And will we be offered washwater and a place to tidy ourselves before we appear before them? We've no wish to insult them with a rough appearance.'

He turned back. A frown creased his brow. He made a swift gesture, and one of his men stepped forward to take hasty counsel with him. It did not take long. 'Captain Perling will see to your comfort and supervision while I am gone. Whatever you need, you may ask of him.' And with no more farewell than that, he turned and marched out of the room. The close-fitting footwear he wore made little more than a whisper against the stone. I turned a kindly look on the captain and smiled.

'When the Elderling Selden sojourned with us many years ago, he spoke glowingly of the wonders of your city. I see now that he did not exaggerate. Could we trouble you, good captain, for warm water and perhaps food and wine to restore ourselves? As you can imagine, our travels since the bear attack have been a journey of privation.'

I was following an axiom of Chade's. Always behave as if you are the person you wish to be perceived as. I was an emissary from the Six Duchies, a prince of the blood, and I had every right to be welcomed as such. Nonetheless, I had initially feared we would be thrown into a cell or dungeon until the king and queen could judge us. At the very least, I'd expected to be treated harshly, but the captain did not appear to share his general's trepidation about us. He dispatched a handful of his men for food and drink and washwater for us, and invited us to be seated and had his men bring a table and set it before us. The benches he offered us appeared hard and cold, but when we were seated, they warmed and became as soft as any cushioned chair.

That was enough to impress us, but it did not stop there. A vessel decorated with a pattern of leaves and dancers was set on the table before us. Cold water was poured into it, but within moments it steamed gently. We were grateful to warm our chilled faces and hands with it, and to dry them on the soft towels set out for us. The food served to us was less impressive. It was good meat, root vegetables, a cold fowl and bread, but plainly cooked and served. We were still glad to fill our bellies and if the wine they offered us was a rather sour vintage, it was still welcome.

Our guards gave us no privacy but we ignored them as we attempted to straighten our garments and smooth our hair. When we had eaten and made ourselves as presentable as we could, we sat on the comfortable benches and waited. And waited. Perseverance voiced the question that filled all our minds. 'Do you suppose they are safe?'

I deliberately misunderstood him. 'The King and Queen of the Elderlings? I am sure they will do their best to see us soon, and extend to us the same welcome we have offered their emissaries to Buckkeep.' I put a kindly smile on my face. 'You need not fear them, boy, no matter how strange their guise may seem to you. The Six Duchies has long had cordial relations with all the Traders.' Lant was nodding and the boy seemed to take my meaning. We sat and we waited. Endlessly. I comforted myself that I heard no alarm raised as the slow hours passed. I hoped that the Fool and Spark were using the time well.

I had begun to long to take a nap when finally the door opened again. General Rapskal appeared with a tall Rain Wilder at his side. His hair was tousled from wind and while he was clearly an Elderling, he was not as finely made as General Rapskal. He was older, I decided, though the scaling on his brow did not make it easy to guess his age. He entered the room, looked at me, and then turned to his general. 'Swifter would have been better, Rapskal. Later, I will wish to speak to you.'

I rose as he crossed to me and was startled when he extended his hand to me. I offered mine and he took my hand in a Trader's greeting rather than the warrior's wrist-clasp I had half-expected. 'You are Prince FitzChivalry Farseer, of the Six Duchies?' he confirmed with me. I nodded gravely. He still had not released my hand. 'I beg pardon for the rough welcome you have received. I am Reyn Khuprus.'

I tried not to start. I might call myself a prince, but I had not expected their king to clasp hands with me as an equal. I found my tongue. 'I am honoured, King Reyn. This is Lord Lantern Fallstar, and my serving-man, Perseverance of Withywoods.' Both were already on their feet, bowing.

The king finally released my hand and gestured to the door. 'I regret my delay in greeting you. My lady, Malta, was called away to deal with unexpected visitors and left me to finish a complicated accounting with one of our ship's captains. I had given orders I was not to be disturbed until the inventory was complete and somehow your arrival was not seen as an extraordinary event that demanded immediate attention. But, enough explanations for now. Please, accompany me to a more comfortable place. Rapskal,

summon someone to prepare chambers for them in the Greeting
Hall, and transport their belongings there. No, please, leave your
things as they are. I promise they will be delivered safely to your
rooms. Accompany me, please.'

The lack of formality was unnerving, and I suddenly and
desperately hoped that our arrival would not be an upset for
any treaties or pacts that Dutiful and Elliania had been carefully
negotiating. As I followed the king, I made a wild reach with
my Skill, only to founder in the vast chorus of the city that
surrounded me. No. Useless. I'd have to go very cautiously.

He took us back to the great entry hall and then to our
surprise, he ushered us out into the early evening. The city was
lit as I had never seen any city lit. When Per gasped at it, I
knew it was no Skill-trick but actual light emanating from the
buildings. They gleamed in dragon colours: gold and blue, scarlet
and verdant green, yellow as daisy hearts. Some were patterned
with vines of light or stylized waves and swirls while others
simply glowed. We needed no torches to make our way down
the steps to the street. There I fought my Skill clear of the
thronging ghost-Elderlings to see a far sparser population moving
in the streets. King Reyn walked briskly, responding with waves
or nods to those who greeted him. We attracted stares but he
did not permit anyone to detain us or ask questions. At the end
of the street, we reached a structure that was humbler than the
map-tower but taller and grander by far than Withywoods Manor.

'Our Greeting Hall,' he announced it with a gesture. 'We
find it a pleasant place to welcome our guests. It's scaled for
humans. Smaller doors, lower ceilings. Sometimes I feel rather
insignificant in some of the other structures here.' He tipped
me a small smile. 'A hazard of living alongside dragons, as you
may imagine. Please, come with me. There are many comfortable rooms here. And it is what we call a "quiet" place, meaning
that in the upper chambers the voices of Kelsingra do not
whisper so loudly.'

He maintained his brisk pace up the steps and weary as I was,
I strove to keep up with him. The entrance hall was furnished
in what I believed was a Bingtown style. There were clusters of
chairs around small elegant tables. The room still looked oddly

empty to me until I realized that it was a grand hearth with a fire that was missing. Despite the high ceilings and wide windows of thick yellow glass, it was still warm inside and I judged this further evidence of Elderling magic at work. We did not pause in this room, but entered a flagged hall and walked along it, our boots ringing while the softly-shod feet of the king whispered along. We passed half a dozen ornately carved doors before he opened one and gestured us in.

In the centre of the room was a table with an elegant cloth and fine dishes set out upon it. Chairs with carved wooden backs and green cushions awaited us. The art on the walls was foreign to my eyes, but pleasant. Images were suggested – the deep twining greens of a forest or the wide rippled face of a river – but nothing was precisely depicted. A woman had been straightening the silverware on the table, but she turned to greet us as we entered.

Queen Malta of the Dragon Traders. She was legendary for her exotic beauty and there was no mistaking her for anyone else. Her curling hair was not blonde but gold, gold as a gleaming coin. Delicate scaling followed the lines of her brow and emphasized her high cheekbones and decided chin. Like her king, she was dressed in an Elderling robe over loose trousers. The soft little slippers she wore sparkled gold. The fabric of her clothing shimmered from green to gold and back again as she moved to greet us. Caution made me drop to one knee before her, and Lant followed my example. She laughed, and I thought it was at me until I realized that young Perseverance, caught in her beauty, was standing behind us, staring at her with eyes wide and mouth ajar.

She shifted her gaze back to me, and her smile grew even broader. 'And that expression honours me more than any presentation of gifts,' she observed, and Perseverance abruptly dropped to his knees. Her eyes twinkled at me as if we shared some splendidly funny secret. She swept me a curtsey. 'Prince FitzChivalry, you honour us with this unexpected visit. Yet I feel as if we have met before. I do hope you will forgive General Rapskal. He is sometimes both officious and suspicious.' She transferred her gaze to her husband. 'Reyn, dear, as you can see,

I've added some extra place settings to our table. I was so glad to receive your message. And I think we shall have all our unexpected guests join us at table!' Again her sparkling gaze came back to me. 'Prince FitzChivalry, do you believe in coincidence?'

'I have known some that were passing strange,' I told her. Careful, Fitz. I knew I was treading onto unstable ground and would have to be ready to change my tale at a moment's notice. I turned my smile to Lant and Perseverance, hoping they could read my warning.

'And here is my coincidence,' Queen Malta exclaimed with a smile as a door on the opposite side of the room opened.

Spark, her hair freshly brushed and braided into tidy coils on her head, entered the room. Her cheeks were pink, and Lady Thyme's elegant black lace overskirt looked better on her than it ever had on that noisome old woman. Behind her came, not the Fool, not Grey, but Amber, and Amber as I had never even imagined her. The butterfly cloak hung gracefully from her narrow shoulders. The Fool's short hair had been damped and tousled into curls, and a touch of paint reddened his pale lips and cheeks. I knew the sparkling earrings were glass, but the sparkle was as convincing as the Fool's painted mouth and black-lined eyes. My boyhood friend had vanished and there was absolutely nothing of King Shrewd's jester. I stared and knew again that jab of betrayal. How could he be so completely this person that I knew not at all? The gulf of uncertainty I felt was painful. I felt both deceived and excluded.

But I had no time to indulge in my feelings. The play had begun and I must find my role. The fingertips of her gloved hand rested on Spark's shoulder as she was guided into the room. 'Oh, my lady, they are here!' Spark exclaimed when she saw us. 'Prince FitzChivalry and Lord Lant and even Perseverance. And they appear uninjured.'

At this news, Amber's fingertips fluttered up to the Fool's painted mouth in a completely feminine gesture of surprise and relief. He found my shape and exclaimed as Amber, 'Oh, Fitz! Lant and Perseverance! You are safe. I am so relieved to know that you have taken no harm! Oh, Queen Malta, thank you, thank you for finding them and rescuing them. I am forever in your debt.'

'Indeed, you are,' Malta said quietly. Had Amber forgotten she was dealing with a woman born a Bingtown Trader, one to whom every transaction in life was a bargain or an agreement or a deal? Then Malta added, 'As I and much of Bingtown remain in yours. For I believe that a debt can be as mutual as a promise.'

There was something of Chade in Lant after all. He had maintained his aplomb and did not gape. Perseverance struggled, coughed heavily and used it as an excuse to bow his head. I desperately longed to know what tale the Fool had already told Malta. I had said we were emissaries from the Six Duchies and had come down from the Mountains. Had we contradicted each other, and if so, could we find a way to mend it convincingly?

King Reyn looked puzzled and was not trying to cover his confusion. Malta gave him a significant look and I knew that she would be the one to handle us. 'Please, come to the table. Let us eat and drink together, and we will see what we can do to help you on your way.'

Reyn seated his queen and took his chair at the head of the table. We were ranged down one side of the table. A servant, very human in appearance, arrived to escort Spark and Perseverance away to refreshments of their own. Spark went as if fully comfortable with this while Per gave me several backward glances even as I nodded to him to go. King Reyn smiled around at us as the door closed behind them and exclaimed, 'I am ravenous! I hope you will not find it strange if we stand on little ceremony here.' He looked at Amber and smiled as he said, 'Even after years of it, "king" and "queen" sit a bit oddly with us.' With a glance at Lant and me, he added, 'After years of the Satrapy extorting money from the Bingtown Traders, we who were raised as Traders still wonder why anyone would think we preferred a monarchy. But it's a convenient way for the outside world to see us, as I'm sure you both understand.'

My thoughts scrabbled. Kettricken had said something of it to me once. Just as she had been trained to see herself as Sacrifice for her people, but outsiders had seen her as a Mountain princess, so Malta and Reyn, while known as the King and Queen of the Rain Wilds, were actually more the chief negotiators for a consortium of merchant traders. I nodded politely and Lant smiled. The 'king' was serving himself from a dish of food which he then passed on to his queen. As the dish moved down the table, we each took a portion and passed it on. Dish followed dish, and while it was of a better quality than what we had been offered earlier, it still did not surpass what I'd expect on the Buckkeep table. Lant rose in my estimation as I saw him lean toward Amber, identify the dish for her, and then allot her a serving if she desired it.

Reyn smiled around at all of us. 'Let us simply eat before we talk, shall we?'

'Of course!' Amber accepted for all of us. 'Bargaining and digestion are not the best companions, as well we must know.'

'Then you come to bargain?' Reyn smiled at her. 'And I thought Prince FitzChivalry and his party were emissaries from the Six Duchies.'

'Emissaries in search of a particular bargain. But let us say no more of that now, but only eat and drink together, as old friends and new.' Amber walked her fingertips on the table, found and lifted a glass filled with a golden wine. 'To friends well met!' she offered, and all drank to her toast. When she set down her glass, she added, 'I had so hoped to see Phron while I was here. He is well, I trust?'

Malta stopped chewing the bit of meat she had taken. Amber smiled innocently but I saw his dart had struck true and wondered why he had launched it. After a moment, Reyn said quietly, 'Phron's health remains delicate. Perhaps he will join us briefly after the meal, if he feels up to meeting guests.'

'I am grieved to hear that,' Amber replied softly. 'The last word I had of him was years ago. At that time, I believe he had begun to thrive.'

'Years ago,' Malta said softly. Sometimes, when a bell is struck, another vibrates in sympathy. The parent in me echoed the concealed pain in her voice and I wanted Amber to stop pressing her. Something was seriously wrong with her child. I would never make it a bargaining point and I was not sure what Amber was leading up to.

Reyn spoke and his tone was a bit acerbic. 'I'm surprised you had any tidings of Phron.'

Amber shrugged lightly. Her fingers danced delicately over her food, and then, almost as if she were sighted, she cut a bite from a slice of preserved fruit on her plate. I did not recognize the fruit and took a cautious bite of mine as she spoke. 'It was years ago. You know how such gossip travels, from friend to friend. You recall Jek, my shipmate on the *Paragon*?'

Oh, neatly done. I now guessed the true source of her news. Jek was one of the few names I knew from Chade's network of spies and information gatherers. I suspected that while news of this Phron was years old, the Fool had rummaged it out from Chade's scrolls. No: he was blind. It would have had to come from Spark. Or Ash. So the youngster was deeply, deeply the Fool's now, enough to purloin not only dragon blood but precious information for him. I was not sure if I were glad that he had such a loyal person at his command or resentful that such a useful resource had been lured away from Chade.

Malta's brow creased briefly, making the scaling wink. 'I do not recall her. Perhaps we did not meet.'

'She handled much of my business here after I had to leave Bingtown.'

'Oh, yes. I recall her now. The repayments of the loan were made through her.'

Amber nodded.

'We haven't forgotten,' Reyn said. 'Ready money was very scarce at the end of our war with Chalced. When you loaned out much of your share of Igrot's treasure, it helped many in Bingtown to rebuild. So many of our heritage merchants suffered the loss of their shops and stock. And it helped many of the Tattooed to make a fresh start here.'

'And it was financially wise of you,' Malta added, reminding all that Amber had undoubtedly shown a profit on her kindness. 'We were years paying it back to you.'

And now I knew the source of Lord Golden's stream of income in his wild gambling days at Buckkeep Court. What he had invested wisely in Bingtown, he spent with a shocking profligacy in Buckkeep Town. Because he had known then that he was going to die and saw no point in saving any of it. Oh, this was good. So many bits and pieces of the Fool's lives were being handed to me. I smiled at Amber across the table and somehow she knew, for she showed me her teeth. 'It helped me through a difficult time,' Amber responded congenially.

Malta spoke delicately. 'I cannot help but notice that life has put you through many changes since last I saw you. I mourn that you have lost your sight. And I had not realized that you had had enough contact with dragons to undergo a Change.'

There was a baggage-train of questions packed into that comment. I waited. 'I promised you my story when I came to you, and you have waited so patiently. Let us finish eating, then, and I shall tell it.' Ah, so I was not the only one he used his delaying tactic upon.

The rest of the meal passed uneventfully. Lant said little except to thank them for the meal and to compliment the food and I volunteered little more than that. Often I felt Reyn's eyes upon me, measuring me, and I strove to behave as a Farseer prince should, even as I wondered what sort of a tale Amber had spun around us.

Our meal over, a servant cleared the table, and then set out brandy and glasses for us, with a selection of spicy teas offered as well. The brandy was Sandsedge brandy from the Six Duchies and I wondered if that were intended as a compliment. I accepted a small glass with pleasure and sincere thanks. Reyn had just opened his mouth to reply when the door opened and a frail old Elderling came in. He moved slowly, a servant at his side and a cane in his hand. He breathed audibly through his nose, and took short cautious steps as he made his way toward the table. His hair was as golden as Malta's and his scaling as blue as Reyn's. Even so, I was startled when Malta said brightly, 'And here is Phron, come to wish us good night.'

Amber could not see but perhaps she could hear Phron's breathing and his hesitant step as he made his way to the table and then eased himself into a chair. The servant stooped, to ask if he would prefer brandy or tea. 'Tea. Please.' A gasp punctuated the man's request, for so his voice betrayed him to be. I looked at him afresh. His eyes were an intense blue, and the scaling of blue and silver that marked him was both intricate and fanciful. It was no chance growth, like a calico kitten's fur. The patterns on his face and bared arms were as deliberate and artful as a tattoo. But the purplish tint to his lips that puffed in and out as he breathed and the dark circles under his eyes were not part of that colouring. Phron. Malta's son. Not an old man, but a young one made old by illness.

Malta had gone to her son's side. She extended a hand to indicate us. 'Prince FitzChivalry, Lord Lant, Lady Amber, I am pleased to present our son, Ephron Khuprus.'

I stood, took two steps and bowed to him. The closer I got to him, the louder my Wit-sense of him rang. He extended his hand to me, and so I offered mine. He surprised me when he clasped my wrist in the Six Duchies style of warrior greeting warrior, but I returned it. The moment my hand closed against his skin, my awareness of him doubled in a way I had never experienced. It was not comfortable for me and yet it did not seem he was even aware of it. Dragon and boy, boy and dragon rang against my senses in a way I could scarcely stand. And with that doubled sense of him, an even deeper sense of wrong, wrong, wrong within his body. He was weak and breathless, starved and weary from the wrongness. It jangled against my senses unbearably, and thoughtlessly I reached out and touched the error.

The boy gasped. His head sagged forward on his chest and for a moment he was totally still. We remained as we were, our wrists locked in each other's grip. I reached to catch his shoulder with my free hand as he sagged toward me. I could not let go as the Skill poured through me and into him.

In a long-ago spring in the Mountains, Nighteyes and I had once witnessed an ice dam in a creek giving way. In a thundering roar, the pent-up water had burst through, and in a moment the white of the snowy creek bed had become a brown rush of water, sticks, and even logs tumbling as the flood gushed down the hillside. The Skill-tide that I had sensed all around me, that had surrounded me and prevented me from reaching Nettle, suddenly found an open channel. It coursed through me, powerful and pure and laden with pleasure in making things perfect. The Skill-joy that was as much sensory as it was intellectual flooded my mind and my body. The boy made a strangled sound and perhaps I echoed that muffled cry.

'Phron!' Malta cried out in alarm and in an instant Reyn was on his feet.

I shivered as if a chill wind swept through me as Phron's body aligned itself to my vision. Somewhere a vast distance away, the queen dragon Tintaglia was startled. Was not that human hers to shape? Then she dismissed me, as dragons dismiss humans and I sensed her no more. But Phron lifted his head and drew a deep breath and all but shouted his question. 'What was that? It felt amazing!' In sudden astonishment, he added, 'I can breathe! It doesn't hurt to breathe, I don't have to work at it! I can breathe and talk!' Suddenly, he released his grip on me and took the four strides that carried him to his father's worried embrace.

For myself, I staggered sideways. Lant shocked me when he leapt to my side and caught my elbow to steady me. 'What just happened?' he breathed the question and all I could do was shake my head.

Then Phron broke free of Reyn and turned back to me. He took a deep lungful of air in through his mouth and suddenly gave a shout of pure relief. 'Was that you?' he demanded of me. 'I think it was you, but it felt like what Tintaglia sometimes does, when she comes. She has not been here in, what, five years? When last she put me right, yes, five years.' He opened and flexed the long digits of his hands, and I guessed that whatever she had done then had restored his hands to him. Malta was weeping wordlessly, tears streaming down her cheeks. Phron turned to her, wrapped his arms around her and tried to lift her off her feet in a hug. He failed. Months of breathlessness had enfeebled him, but he was smiling now. 'I'm better, Mother. Better than I've been in years! Don't weep! Is there food left? Food I can chew and swallow now without gasping? Anything but soup! Anything I can bite and chew. Or crunch! Is there anything crunchy?'

Malta broke free of his hug, laughing wildly. 'I'll fetch it for you!' And that fine and queenly Elderling was suddenly just a boy's mother as she darted away from him toward the door. As she went, she was already calling for meat and fresh bread toasted hot and other words that were lost to us in the closing of the door.

I turned back to find Reyn standing behind me, grinning at his son. He looked to me. 'I don't know why you came here. I don't know what you did, even though I felt an echo of it. It felt like Tintaglia, she who touched me and made me an Elderling. How did you do it? I thought only a dragon could shape us like that.'

'He's a man of many talents,' Amber said. She stood, pushing back from her chair. Her fingertips trailed the table's edge as she came toward us, and when she reached us, Lant surrendered his place at my side to her. She took my arm in a way that was too familiar. Molly. Molly had always taken my arm like that, when we walked in the market and she wished my attention, or sometimes when she just wanted to touch me. It was different from how the Fool would sometimes link arms with me back in the days when we had walked side by side. He was Amber in that moment, and his hand rested possessively on my upper arm. I forced myself to stand still and accept it. Like a horse accepting a strange rider, I thought to myself, and reined in my impulse to break free of the touch. I did not know what game he played, and dared not spoil it for him. Very softly I said, 'A Skill-healing. And one that was beyond my control. I need to sit down now.'

'Of course,' she said, and Lant was already pulling out one of the unclaimed chairs for me. I sat down and wondered what had just happened.

'You look as if you could use this,' I heard Reyn say. He had my glass and was tipping a generous measure of brandy into it. He set it before me and I managed to thank him. I felt as if I'd fallen into a deep and swift current, been tumbled in it, and then pulled back to shore. It surged still, unbearably close to me, coursing through me with a pleasure beyond any appetite I'd ever known. *Pull me back*, Verity had once said to me. But there was no one near me to help me. I was not sure if I wanted help or to let go. The Skill-current beckoned, seething with power and pleasure. Why would I shut that out? I built my wall as if I were pushing a wall of mud against a flood. Did I really want to wall myself in? The Fool, or Amber, was standing behind me. I felt hands settle on my shoulders and steady me. I drew a breath and my walls held. I stepped back from temptation.

Malta came back into the room, carrying some flat yellow cakes on a platter. Two servants came behind her, bringing a roasted bird and a heaped mound of the dark orange roots we'd had at dinner. The boy's eyes lit to see them, and his father laughed out loud as he hastily seated himself. He did not wait, but took one of the yellow cakes and bit into it. It was crisp to the point of breaking when he bit it, and he devoured it with unabashed pleasure as a beaming servant forked a thick slab of meat on to a plate for him and mounded vegetables beside it. He spoke to me around and through a mouthful. 'I haven't been able to eat easily for more than a year. My throat had grown so tight and small inside. It burned when I swallowed. Soup. I could get down thin soup. That was all.'

'You had . . . they would have been right. In a dragon. They grew as if . . .' I felt very awkward saying it. I knew I'd seen them earlier, in the green dragon's open maw. 'Sacs,' I said. 'For spitting poison, I think. Growing in your throat.'

'What did you do? And how?' Malta was regarding me with wonder. Wonder touched with fear.

Amber spoke over my head. 'Prince FitzChivalry has the hereditary magic of the Farseer line. Of the royal blood. He can heal.'

'Sometimes!' I added hastily. 'Only sometimes.' I found the brandy. My hand was steady enough to pick it up and I had some.

'I think,' Reyn spoke slowly, 'that I would like for all of us to sit down. I'd like to hear Lady Amber's tale. To know why you came here. And how.'

She squeezed my shoulders, cautioning me to silence, just as Molly would have done if she thought I was about to offer too much coin for a market purchase. 'It would greatly please me to tell you all,' she said, and I was just as glad to let her. I felt relief when she let go of me and we were seated around the table again. Lant had taken his seat and remained remarkably quiet.

A tale the Fool told him, in the voice of a steady and practical woman. She and I were old friends, she began.

'That I guessed,' Malta said knowingly. 'When first I saw him, I felt as if I already knew him.' She smiled at me as if we shared a jest. I smiled back, without understanding.

Amber's tale skirted and leapt and wove through the truth. She'd come to Buckkeep, and there had a lovely time with all the beautiful money that Jek had sent to her from Bingtown. Too lovely a time, with too much fine brandy (and here she paused to take a sip of golden Sandsedge) and too many games of chance where neither cards nor dice nor scattering pins favoured her. She'd lost her fortune and decided to return to her homeland to reunite with her family and to visit friends. Instead she'd encountered old enemies. They'd taken over her ancestral home, and injured her kin. They'd captured her, and tormented her. Blinding her had neither been the least nor the worst of what they did to her. When she could, she escaped them. And fled back to me. To one who could avenge her, and help her free those still kept captive. To FitzChivalry Farseer, a man as adept at killing as he was at healing.

The tale had enraptured all of them, even Lant. It came to me that this contorted version of the truth of the Fool's tale was more than he'd heard of it before. Phron was now looking at me with a youngster's wonder. Reyn sat, elbow on the table, his chin in his hand and his fingers splayed across his mouth. I could not decide what he was thinking, but Malta was nodding to Amber's words, and accepted her claims for me with no argument. I controlled my face but ruefully wished she were less extravagant in her praise of me.

So I was dismayed by Malta's words when the Fool paused to sip brandy. 'There are other children,' she said. She looked directly at me. 'Not many. The children born here in Kelsingra are few and even fewer survive. If you could do for them what you did for Phron, you could ask of us almost any—'

'Malta, he is a guest!' Her husband began his rebuke, but she interrupted with, 'And they are children who suffer daily, and their parents with them. How can I not ask for it?'

'I understand.' I said it swiftly, before the Fool could speak. 'But I cannot make any promises. What Amber called a healing is more of . . . an adjustment. It may not be permanent. I may not be able to help any of the other children.'

'We need—' Amber began but I cut her off recklessly.

'We need nothing in return for helping children. The lives of children are not bargaining chips.'

'We need,' Amber resumed calmly, 'not speak of any bargain or desire of ours until after FitzChivalry has done what he can for the children.' She turned her blinded visage toward me. 'That goes without saying.'

And yet by saying it, she had reminded them that we could have held that back. I tried to watch Malta's face without seeming to stare. She was nodding slowly and then exchanged an unreadable glance with Reyn. Phron was still eating. Without thinking, I cautioned him, 'Slow down. You will have to give your body time to adapt to the change in your diet.'

He stopped, fork halfway to his mouth. 'I have been so hungry for so long,' he explained.

I nodded. 'But no matter how long you've been hungry, your stomach will only hold so much.'

'Trust me. That's very true,' Amber confirmed for him ruefully.

I glanced at his parents, suddenly aware that I had spoken to their son as if he were mine. Malta had a look of pleading desperation. Reyn was looking down, as if ashamed to hope.

I made the offer reluctantly. Had not I known what it was to have a child with a baffling difficulty? Had not I felt the pain of a parent who would pay any price to make my child's life better? 'I don't know that I can help all of them. Or any of them. But I am willing to try,' I said and attempted to keep my trepidation from my voice. It was not just that I was uncertain. It was the disquieting knowledge that my Skill-magic was moving strangely in me. Was it the Skill itself, was it stronger or more focused here in Kelsingra? Or was it me? Was the boundary between me and the Skill-current eroding? I had touched Phron, a boy I'd never met before, and healed him as effortlessly as if

I were Thick. No. Not healed, I reminded myself. Adjusted him. With no previous knowledge of how a young Elderling's body should be. I suddenly wished I had not agreed to try. What if my next effort did not correct but caused an error in a child's body? What would have become of us if Phron had died choking and gasping at my feet?

'I have not yet finished my tale,' Amber interjected softly. I was startled to the point of staring. The Fool never volunteered information about himself. Was Amber so different a person?

'There is more?' Malta was incredulous.

'It's quickly told, and perhaps a brief telling is best for you as well as FitzChivalry. The people who held me captive, tormented me and stole my eyesight knew that I would seek help from my old friend.' She paused and my belly turned over in me. He wouldn't. She did. 'They lured FitzChivalry away from his home. And then they attacked it with hired Chalcedean troops, led by a man whose name perhaps you may know. He called himself Duke Ellik.'

I actually heard Reyn's teeth grind. Malta had gone pale under her scarlet scaling. The crimson outline of every scale against her white face was beautiful and frightening. Was Amber unaware of the response she had wakened? She spoke on.

'They shattered his doors, burned his barns and stables, killed and raped and looted. And they stole his daughter. A small child of nine years. Her older cousin they took as well. Lady Shine was able to escape, not without harm, but alive. But little Bee, Lord FitzChivalry's daughter, a child beyond precious to both of us, they destroyed.'

So bald a telling of that tale. I should have been inured to that pain. I should have been past the point where it made me want to rage, to weep and to strike out at all around me. I found I was gripping the edge of the table, looking down at the edge of it and trying to cling to control as a storm raged within and around me.

'Destroyed.' Queen Malta spoke the word faintly.

'Gone forever,' Amber confirmed.

Reyn refilled my small blue glass with golden Sandsedge brandy and nudged it carefully toward me. It wouldn't help but

I tried to appreciate the gesture. I should not drink it. I'd already had too much, too quickly. I looked into it, swirled it and my thoughts went to Verity. How often had I seen him make that small gesture? What had he seen there?

Nothing, Fitz. Nothing at all. Drink up your false courage and move forward. It's the only direction a man can move in.

I lifted my eyes, listening. Imagination. I picked up my brandy and drank it down.

'Children are not bargaining chips,' Reyn confirmed. He looked to his queen. 'Yet I am unable to imagine a way to let you understand the depth of our gratitude.' He paused and added uncomfortably, 'Or the wild hope I feel for the other children. I know it must seem greedy of us, but if you will, please, let me summon the parents and speak with them tonight. To tell them that possibly you can help. Perhaps, tomorrow . . .' He let the request trail away.

I was shocked at the surge of anticipation I felt. 'I can make no promises,' I cautioned him.

Amber spoke suddenly. 'He will need to rest well before he attempts any more. These healings tax him in a way that is difficult to explain.' She paused and then dared to caution him, 'And when you speak to the parents, you must be honest, sir. Tell them there is risk as well, and not just that Prince FitzChivalry may not be able to help. Sometimes his healings take a heavy toll on the one he helps. I speak with a personal knowledge of that! Bid them consider well the gamble.'

'There is also General Rapskal. This will not please him.' Malta spoke anxiously.

'Few things do,' Reyn said with a laugh that had no humour in it. 'And some few of the dragons may be interested. There are not many here right now. Most are gone to warmer lands, for a season, or a year or a decade. They do not count time as we do.'

'They do not think of children who may need to be shaped or guided in their changes.' Malta spoke with an edge of bitterness. 'Those who have neglected their young Elderlings will express perfunctory regret, of course.'

I was not grasping the fullness of what I was hearing, but the offer of rest and time alone tempted me beyond words. I think my weariness must have shown in my face, for Malta added, 'I believe that comfortable chambers are ready for you and your young serving-folk. I will do all I may to assure you a night of rest and sweet dreams.' Her glance met her husband's and he nodded and added slowly, 'I promise I will caution the parents not to set their hopes too high. And give them a night to consider well their choice, to have you try. Or not.'

Amber nodded to that for me. 'Prince FitzChivalry does not have unlimited abilities. He has not been able to restore my sight, but much else that was wrong with me, he set right.'

Malta nodded. 'It grieved me when first I saw that you had lost your vision and been subjected to ill use. You have told us what befell you, but not why you have taken on some semblance to an Elderling. I know that you and Tintaglia had some doings, some years ago. I assume she is the one who began your changes?'

I wished Amber could have seen Malta's expression. She dreaded the wrong answer, but Amber danced all around a question as lightly as the Fool could. 'We did. It was many years ago, and she was more prone, then, to honour her debts to mere people. She persuaded the good folk of Trehaug to supply me for an expedition.'

'I recall something of that,' Malta replied. And then, as if both relieved by Amber's tale and recalling her duties as a hostess, she added, 'If you will excuse me, there is a small comfort I wish to send you.'

'And I am off, also,' Reyn added. 'Please, for now, be comfortable here.'

They left the room together, Malta's hand on Reyn's arm. Phron sauntered after them, the remainder of the cakes in his custody. At the door he paused, turned, and swept us a surprisingly gracious bow for a young man clutching a plate. I had to smile and then the door closed behind them.

For a time, the three of us sat in silence, each occupied with our own set of worries. Amber asked softly, 'Why ever did you do it, Fitz? Why attempt such a healing on your own and for a boy you scarcely know?' She leaned back in her chair and patted her own cheeks. 'When I grasped what was happening, I was terrified.'

'He took my hand and it just . . . happened. We connected in the Skill and I do not think I could have refrained from correcting his body.'

'That sounds dangerous,' Lant observed, and Amber choked on a laugh.

Then a servant entered bearing a tray with a large silver pot on it surrounded by tiny white cups, followed by Spark and Per. The servant poured each of us a tiny cup of dark and steaming liquid. 'A gift from the king and queen. Sweetsleep tea.' She wished us a good night and departed.

I lifted a cup and sniffed it. I passed it to Amber. 'Are you familiar with this? It's like a very dark tea, but thicker.'

She smelled it, and then took a delicate sip. 'I've had this before, in Bingtown. Sweetsleep. It's supposed to make one sleep well with very pleasant dreams. It allows you to forget your cares. It's very expensive. It's quite a compliment to be served this.'

'It is,' Perseverance confirmed heartily. 'The serving-woman who brought us here was astonished at being told to prepare it for you. It came all the way from Jamaillia, a gift to the king and queen from the Satrap himself! "Like drinking gold to have this tea", she said.'

'I would welcome a deep sleep,' Lant said quietly. 'With pleasant dreams, for a change.' He took up his cup and sipped from it. We watched him. He licked his lips. 'It's nice. An edge of bitter and then it tastes sweet.'

Amber was taking slow sips of hers. She paused as if she could see me watching her. 'It's safe,' she said quietly. 'Traders will drive a hard bargain with you, but poison is not part of their ethic. Nor do I think Reyn and Malta would do harm to the man who saved their son. Or to the man they hope will save the children of Kelsingra.'

Spark had been watching Amber. Without hesitation, she raised her cup to her lips and tasted it. 'I like it,' she proclaimed and took another sip.

'You're not drinking it, are you?' Amber smiled at me across the table. There was a bit of a challenge in that smile.

'I'm a cautious fellow,' I reminded her.

'Fitz. There's a time for caution. And a time to try something new. Something that might let you have a good night's sleep.' I do not know how she sensed my hesitation. 'Hospitality,' she said quietly. 'Do not turn away a very gracious gift. I promise you, it's no more than a restful tea. Less harmful than carryme. Courtesy demands we enjoy it.' She lifted her tiny cup and sipped from it.

Perseverance looked to me. I shrugged and tasted mine. It was pleasant, the bitter followed by the sweet. The boy watched me, and then took his down in a series of slow sips. 'Fitz, drink it,' Amber said in the Fool's voice. 'Trust my judgment in this. It will not harm you and may do you much good.'

And so I did. By the time two different serving-girls came to guide us to our rooms, I felt a pleasant lassitude. There was no heavy sensation of being drugged, simply the drowsy feeling that I would be easily able to fall asleep.

The serving-girls were not Elderlings, but were clad in bright garments similar to those Malta had been wearing. One was all in red, the other in blue. Amber took my arm and I guided her as we followed the girl in blue. Lant came with us. Spark and Perseverance came behind us and I heard Spark take up a conversation with the girl in red. Evidently they had all dined together earlier. 'I will move across the river tomorrow,' one girl said to Spark. It seemed the continuance of an earlier conversation. 'I decided tonight. The whispering has grown too loud for me to bear. I had hoped, though it seems silly to admit it now, to some day become favoured of a dragon and be Changed.' She shook her head. 'But I cannot endure it. All day, in the streets, the walls mutter to me. And at night, even in the quiet houses, my dreams are not my own. I will try my luck across the river, although I will miss the lights of the city and the warmth and comfort of these buildings. All winter, the workers there have been clearing land. In spring, we will dig and plant. And perhaps this time the crops will prosper.'

The girl in red paused at a door and looked at Lant. 'My mistress says she hopes you will find the chambers she ordered for you pleasing, but if you do not, you have but to ring a bell,

and someone will come to make it comfortable for you. Oh. And
to ring the bell, you need only touch the image of a tree beside
the door.' She opened the door and bowed to Lant. 'For Lord
Lant, this room has been prepared. Perseverance has told us
which pack to bring here. You will find the couch adapts to
your body. The jug with the figures of fish on it will keep your
washwater warm. A bath will be filling for you. I tell you these
things so that you may not be alarmed by them.' Lant listened
gravely, nodded to her with great equanimity, bade us goodnight
and entered. I judged he would soon be asleep.

The girl glanced back at us with a smile. 'Your quarters are
at the end of the corridor.' She led us on. I was definitely feeling
the effects of the soporific. The weariness I had been so long
denying was rising in me like an inevitable tide. Yet it was not
the aching tiredness that was too familiar to me but only the
gentle looming of easy sleep. She stopped at a door that seemed
a trifle grander than the one that had led to Lant's room. The
door was neither wood nor stone, but the unfamiliar substance
was carved in twists and twinings like the bark of a contorted
tree. It reminded me of ivory, in a darker tone. 'Your chambers,'
she said quietly. 'When you awake tomorrow, touch the flower
image by the door and food will be brought for you.'

'Thank you,' I said. She touched the door and it swung silently
open. I entered to find myself in a sitting room. My makeshift
pack looked sadly out of place on the delicately carved table in
the centre of the room. The floor was finished with hundreds
of tiny triangular tiles, and the walls were painted to resemble
a forest. The room smelled like a summer forest. Beyond the
sitting room, I saw a chamber with a large bed and beyond that
a sight I could scarcely believe. I crossed the bedchamber and
stared into the alcove beyond it. A pool twice the size of the
bed was filling with steaming water scented with forest herbs.
A table beside it was stacked with thick towels, squat pots of
soap and ewers of oils and several Elderling robes in bright
colours.

I heard the door shut behind me. I walked toward the water,
shedding clothes as I went. I sat down on the floor like a child
to pull off my boots, then stood to drop my trousers. I did not

hesitate at the water's edge. The lip of the pond slanted down and I waded into it and then sat down in the deepest end so that the water lapped my unshaven chin. Slowly the warmth penetrated my flesh and I felt my muscles relax. I leaned back as the water grew deeper until it lifted me and I hung in it. Slowly I cupped water and rubbed my face, and then ducked, rubbing salty sweat from my hair and head. When I came up the Fool was standing at the edge of the pool.

'How deep is it?'

'Not over your head.' I ducked again and came up. Water streamed from my hair and down my back. Had hot water ever felt so good? It was hard to think of anything besides the sensation. 'Why didn't you go to your room?'

'This is my room. Spark and I were here earlier. My things are already in the closet. When the servants asked Perseverance and Spark who you were, they said you were my protector. So, they did not separate us.'

'Oh.' I leaned back in the water and scrubbed at my face again. I wondered how unkempt I had appeared to the King and the Queen of the Elderlings. But I realized I cared little what they thought of me. I pushed wet hair from my face, stood up and shook water from my head. I was suddenly sleepy and the wide bed beckoned. 'I'm going to bed. If you go in the pool, don't drown.'

I walked to the shallow end and waded out. I took a towel from the stack but barely found the will to dry myself before walking toward the bed.

'Sleep well, Fitz,' the Fool said. And he was the Fool again.

'That tea. I can sleep, Fool. I can let go of everything. Stop worrying. Worrying doesn't solve anything. I know that. In one way I know it but in another it seems wrong. It seems as if I don't think about all the things that hurt, all the things I've done wrong, then I don't really care. Tormenting myself with Bee's death won't bring her back. Why do I have to remember it all the time?' The bed was large and flat. There were no pillows and no coverings. I sat down on it, my towel around my shoulders. The surface was firm and slightly warm. Very slowly, it gave to the weight of my body. I lay back on it. 'Molly is dead. Bee is gone. I can't feel Nighteyes any more. I should just accept those things and go on. Maybe. Or maybe you're right. I should go and kill all of the Servants. I've nothing better to do with what is left of my life. Why not do that?' I closed my eyes. When I spoke, I could hear the slurring of my words. I groped after what I was trying to say. 'I'm like you now. I've gone beyond the end of my life, to a place where I never expected to be.'

His voice was kind. 'Don't fight it Fitz. Don't question it. For one night, let it all go.'

I did. I tumbled into sleep.

THIRTY-SEVEN

Heroes and Thieves

Scrying is a little-respected magic and yet I have found it a small and useful talent to have. Some use a ball of polished crystal. That is well and good, for those who can afford such things. But for a boy born to a hard-scrabble patch of dirt scarcely worth the name of farm, a milk pail with some water in the bottom to reflect the blue sky above works well enough. It was my hobby when I was a smallish boy. In a life that consisted largely of chores and boredom, staring into a milk pail and marvelling at what I saw was a fascinating pastime. My stepfather thought me daft when he caught me at it. I was astonished to find that neither he nor my mother found anything fascinating in the water, while I watched a boy much like me but younger growing up in a castle.

My Early Days, Chade Fallstar

I awoke. I lay in the darkness. I could not remember that I had dreamed, yet words rang in my ears still. *Verity says you gave up hope too easily. That you always did.*

Bee's voice? If that message was the pleasant dream the Elderling tea had promised me, it was a sad misrepresentation of what the tea actually did. I stared up at a ceiling painted a dark grey. Stars had been painstakingly dotted over the entire surface. As I stared at them through slitted eyes, the deep of night became darkest blue. I blinked. I was staring up at the sky. I was warm, cradled in softness. I smelled forest. Someone slept beside me.

I lifted my head and stared. The Fool. Only the Fool. In sleep, with his strange, blinded eyes hidden, I could see the lines of Lord Golden's face with the colouring of my boyhood friend. But as the ceiling above me continued in its mimicry of dawn, I began to see the fine scaling along his brows. I wondered if it would progress until he looked fully like an Elderling or if the dragon's blood had finished with him. He wore an Elderling robe of white or pale silver; it was hard to tell in the dawn light. His bared hand clasped his gloved hand to his breast as if to keep watch over it while he slept. His head was bowed over his hands and he frowned in his sleep. His knees were drawn up to his chest, as if to protect himself from a kick. Men who have been tortured are slow to sleep carelessly. His curled body was too close to how I had found him, dead and frozen in the Pale Woman's icy halls. I stared at him until I was sure I could see him breathing. Foolish. He was fine.

I rolled cautiously away from him and sat up on the edge of the bed. I stood up slowly. I felt well rested, with no aching muscles. I was neither too warm nor too cold. I looked around the room. The magic of the Elderlings was all around me. How easily I had accepted it last night. How swiftly I had dropped my guard. 'Sweetsleep,' I muttered to myself.

I rose and left the Fool sleeping and went to the smaller room. The pool had drained itself, and my discarded clothing was where I had dropped it. One boot stood and the other sprawled on its side. I moved slowly, gathering my things and trying to clear my brain at the same time. I felt peculiar. One at a time, I gathered my worries with my clothing. Even drunk, I'd never behaved as selfishly as I had last night. It bothered me. I found fresher clothes in my pack, donned them, and tidied my discarded clothing. The water in the ewer was warm. There was a looking-glass, and beside it, brushes. I persuaded my hair into a warrior's tail and decided that it would be easier to have a beard than to shave. I turned my face from side to side, studying the grey in my whiskers. So be it.

'Fitz?'

'I'm right here. Up and dressed.'

'I . . . dreamed.'

'You said the tea would do that, give pleasant dreams.'

I turned to find him sitting up on the bed. The Elderling gown was silvery. It reminded me of very fine chainmail. Or fish scales.

'I dreamed of both of us here. Walking in this city, laughing and talking. But so long ago. In a time of dragons, when the city was fine and unshattered.' He paused, his mouth slightly ajar. He said softly, 'The air smelled like flowers. It was like that first time. In the Mountains at the market-circle.'

'We are deep in an Elderling city. The buildings are impregnated with Skill and memories. I'm not surprised you had such a dream.'

'It was a very sweet dream,' he said softly. He stood and slowly groped his way toward me.

'Wait. Let me come for you.' I reached his side and taking his hand, I set it on my arm. 'I'm sorry I left you to fend for yourself last night.'

'I was fine.'

'I didn't mean to be so thoughtless.' And yet, how good it had felt. To think only of my own needs and no one else's. How selfish, I rebuked myself. I guided him to the ewer of washwater.

'Don't apologize. The sweetsleep affected you exactly as I knew it would.'

His pack was overturned, Amber's wardrobe spilled out across the floor. 'Do you want me to put your clothing back in the pack?' I asked him.

He straightened from washing his face with one hand, groped for and found a drying cloth. 'Sweet Eda, no! I'll have Spark repack our things. Fitz, you've never had respect for fabric or lace. I won't trust you with it now.' He came toward me, his hands fluttering before him. His bared hand touched my shoulder, and then he crouched down over the spilled pack. He found garments by touch, considering texture. He paused once to hold up a skirt. 'Is this blue? Or turquoise?'

'Blue,' I said, and he set it aside. 'Are you hungry? Shall I ring for food?'

'Please,' he said as he shook out a white blouse.

I think he listened to my boots on the tiles, for just as I reached the entry to the sitting room, he said, 'If you would shut the door?'

720

I did so and then explored the room. I judged that the heavy furniture of dark wood had come from Bingtown. I found a flower painted on a twining vine on a trellis that framed the door. It was slightly raised, and I touched it. The petals blushed from pink to red and back again. I stepped back from it. I heard nothing, no bell in the distance. I walked to the window. I looked out in puzzlement, for the garden below was in riotous bloom. Out there, a fountain splashed and a caged bird hopped from perch to perch. Flowers were in bloom. Another step, and my perspective of the window changed. Despite the bird's motion and the flowers nodding in the breeze, there was no window. More Elderling magic.

I tapped on the door to the bedchamber. 'I've rung for food.'

'You may come in,' Amber's voice replied. And when I entered, she was seated before the mirror she could not see, pushing a brush through her short pale hair, and then patting at it. She seemed to feel me looking at her. 'Does it bother you?' she asked me.

I did not ask her what she meant. 'Strange to say, no. You are you. Fool, Lord Golden, Amber, and Beloved. You are you, and we know one another as well as any two people can.'

'Beloved,' she said, and smiled sadly. I did not know if she repeated my word, or if the Fool called me by his own name. She dropped her hands to the top of the table, gloved one atop the bared one. 'There was a time,' she began, 'when you would have hated this masquerade.'

'There was,' I agreed. 'And this is a different time.'

She smiled at that. And nodded. She turned her head as if glancing at me. 'Did you . . . would you like to be the Fitz you were last night? The man who had only himself to care for?'

I did not answer swiftly. I could have blamed it on the tea, or claimed not to recall it. But I did. Perhaps it had been the tea, but he was right. I had simply let go of everything and everyone and thought only of myself. Once, it was all I had longed for. I wanted to be free of obligations to family, to duty to the Farseer throne: I'd wanted to do only what I wanted to do, when I wanted to do it. Last night I'd had a taste of that. I had no idea how the

Fool had found his way around an unfamiliar room, how he had washed himself or found the garments he'd slept in. I'd abandoned him to his own diminished resources.

'I don't think you'd like him much,' I replied ashamedly.

'On the contrary. Why do you think I urged you to drink it?' Slowly he held out a hand to me. 'Fitz. Would you come here?'

I walked over to him. 'I'm here.'

His gloved hand groped over my belly and then found my hand. He took it in his. He sighed. 'I hate what I do to you. What I've done to your life. I am dependent on you, now more than ever, though I have always needed my Catalyst to accomplish anything. I am ashamed when I think of the danger, pain and the loss I've caused you. I hate knowing that you are ever mindful of me and my needs.'

'Loss?' I was confused.

'But for me, you might never have lost Molly for all those years.'

'No. I'd have been dead instead.'

His laugh was a hoarse bark. 'True. But against all odds, I became fond of you early in our acquaintance. The look on your face when Shrewd pushed that pin through the front of your jerkin. You gave him your heart, as I had given him mine, and for a moment I knew purest envy. Because I suddenly wanted you for my own. Not just as my Catalyst. As my friend.'

'We've been that.'

'And more. And that was what the Servants never grasped until I betrayed you. That you were more to me than my Catalyst. Yet even I did not realize the full import of that closeness. That a child who was as much mine as yours and Molly's would be the result. A child given to us. Because I used you so mercilessly. And a child stolen, because I betrayed you.'

'Fool. Stop. You gave me as much as you took from me.' The look of abject apology on his face was making me uncomfortable.

'Not really, Fitz. Not really.'

'You saved my life. More than once.'

'After endangering it, usually. Fitz. If you save a colt's life because you intend later to ride it into battle, it tinges the act with a high degree of selfishness.'

There was a knock at the door. He released my hand. For a moment longer, I stood still. He spoke quietly. 'Last night, you had one night without feeling obligations. For one night, you were able to let go of your grief. For one night, I released you to think only of yourself. One night of living as most men do every day. A very small respite.' He patted my chest. 'You should see who is at the door.'

When I answered it, it was Spark. 'I thought perhaps Lady Amber would need my assistance,' she said, and Amber immediately called to her to come and help. She hurried past me, pulling the door almost shut behind her, and for a time I listened to a lady give directions to her maid. When a second knock was a servant with a little wheeled table, they both emerged. Spark had painted Amber's lips and rouged the tops of her cheeks. It more accented the pale scaling than concealed it, but I said nothing.

'I can serve them,' Spark suggested and the servant-girl seemed only too happy to leave. Spark uncovered platters and poured tea for us both, and I sat down to a simple breakfast with Amber. Porridge with raisins cooked in it, and honey to sweeten it. Bacon. Stewed dried plums.

'Spark, have you eaten?' I asked the girl. She looked surprised.

'Of course. Hours ago, with the other serving-folk. They've made us very welcome. Everyone is very fond of Ephron. You are the hero of the day.'

'Hero,' I said softly. So strange.

'The bacon tastes a bit odd,' Amber observed.

'It's bear. Bear bacon,' I told her. There was a folded sheet of pale-blue paper on the tray as well. I unfolded it and perused it quickly. 'There's a note here, from Queen Malta. She asks that as soon as we have breakfasted, we join her downstairs. The children will be waiting there.' I tried to keep foreboding from my voice as I relayed the message.

'You will do your best, Fitz. You've warned them.'

'Warning does not prevent disappointment,' I said. Of Spark, I asked, 'Do you know if Perseverance is awake yet? And if Lord Lant has been summoned as well?'

'Yes to both, sir. Perseverance has leapt at the chance to be shown about a bit of the city by one of the other serving-boys. And Lant, I believe, went with them.'

I had not foreseen that. 'Very well,' I said faintly. How befuddled had I been last night, not to have warned them to stay close? Some of my trepidation must have shown on my face for Spark added, 'I'm sure they'll be safe, sir. What you did for the prince last night? It was all the servants could gossip about this morning. They were very impressed and eager to be kind to us.'

'I wish Lant and Per had been a bit more cautious,' I grumbled. Amber lifted one shoulder in a delicate shrug.

Spark seemed to already know her way about the Greeting Hall. Amber put her hand on my arm and I followed Spark down the passage I recalled from the night before. 'There are no windows at all,' I observed. 'Only painted images of windows with views that move as if real when one pauses to look at them.'

'I'd dearly love to see them,' Amber said wistfully in the Fool's voice.

'I wish you could,' I rejoined, and her grip on my arm tightened for a moment.

As soon as we reached the ground floor, a serving-man came to meet us. 'This way, if you please. King Reyn and Queen Malta await you in the Reception Hall.'

But when we approached the door of the chamber, General Rapskal stood before it, his arms crossed on his chest. Now that I was somewhat rested and alert, not to mention recovered from our Skill-portal journey, he looked less imposing. Part of that was that he had no dragon with him. Amber's grip on my arm tightened slightly. 'What is it?'

I lifted my voice. 'General Rapskal. So nice to meet you under more pleasant circumstances.'

'You escort a thief.'

My smile was bland. 'I do not take your meaning, sir.'

His gaze flickered to Amber, lingered for a moment on her eyes and then came back to me. 'Perhaps not. But you shall.'

He pushed away from the wall he had leaned on and stood blocking our way. The servant who had been leading us gave a small gasp of dismay and scampered away. No help from that quarter, then. I set my weight on the balls of my feet. Amber felt that slight shift and lifted her hand from my arm so I'd be free to move quickly if I had to.

'Let me be plain, then. The women who accompany you were prowlers in the streets of Kelsingra but four nights ago. They dared to invade a part of our city that is forbidden to travellers.'

Four nights. Four nights. We'd lost time in the portal again . . . I snapped my thoughts back to the present. 'And they supposedly stole something? What did they steal?' I tried to keep my voice bemused. The news of the time loss rattled me more than his accusation of theft.

He opened his mouth and then snapped it shut. His scaling flushed with sudden colour. I felt his anger as an undirected ripple of Skill. Somewhere, a dragon trumpeted shrilly. He glared at Lady Amber who stared blindly ahead, her expression puzzled. I heard footsteps approaching behind me and turned my head just enough to catch them at the edge of my vision. Two Elderlings approached, in battle harness similar to that their general wore. One was short and broad, almost squat for an Elderling. The other at his side had the tall, lanky build I had come to regard as normal. Both wore sheathed swords, as did their general. I was unarmed, assuming that, as at Buckkeep Castle, one did not wear a weapon when summoned to an audience with the king. This could go very badly for us in a very short time. Out of the corner of my eye, I saw Spark unobtrusively sidle up to be on Amber's unguarded flank. *Thank you, Foxglove.* I hoped she had a knife in her boot.

'Take them into custody,' Rapskal ordered his men. 'We need to confine them to a secure area for questioning.'

The Fool had always been an excellent actor, long trained to concealing his thoughts and feelings. But torture breaks many things in a man. He took a tiny, audible breath and then stood very still.

'If it please you, General Rapskal,' I intervened, 'we are summoned to a meeting with the king and queen this morning. Spark, have you the note we received?'

'Yes, my lord. It is here.'

I did not turn to look at her. I heard the rustle of her garments as she sought a note in her pocket. I hoped she also took the opportunity to be sure the smaller tools of our trade were ready to her hands. How well had Chade trained her? And where was Lant? Already taken into custody?

Before us, the double doors suddenly swung wide open and General Rapskal had to skip aside to avoid being struck. 'There is no need for her to produce a note when I am here to welcome my guests.' King Reyn stood suddenly in the open door before us. The manservant who had fled us was two steps behind him, wringing his hands. 'Welcome. Please come in. And you, too, General Rapskal. Did not you also receive my invitation? I see that Kase and Boxter are here. Excellent. I summoned all of the keepers, I believe.' He focused himself on me. 'Four children await you. As I told you, there are not many, but these four need your aid the most.'

'My lord, these people are dangerous. Especially the woman.' Rapskal's followers moved to form up behind him. Reyn sighed. 'General Rapskal, the "woman" is Lady Amber, long known to my queen since before our war with Chalced. She was an artisan in Bingtown in those days, with her own shop on Rain Wild Street. She made beads and charms carved from wood. Later, she served aboard *Paragon*, and was instrumental in the recovery of Igrot's treasure. Her generous loans from that wealth helped rebuild Bingtown and helped the Tattooed begin new lives in Trehaug. You will treat her with respect.'

Rapskal's glare met Reyn's flat stare. I sensed a power struggle in which, perhaps, we were no more than pawns. General Rapskal would not be the first military leader to believe he could rule better than his king. After a moment, Rapskal replied. 'Of course I will.' His words said one thing, his tone another. Quietly he added, 'I will be proved correct,' and preceded us into the room.

Reyn's facial expression did not change. He stepped aside to allow the general passage and then with a sweep of his arm gestured that we should enter. I heard a swift tapping of boots behind me and risked a quick glance. Lant and Per were hurrying down the corridor. Both were red-cheeked and smiling. They'd enjoyed their outing in the wintry streets of Kelsingra. I could not stop them from running into the same snare that held us.

I spoke calmly to Amber. 'Ah, here is Lord Lant and young

Perseverance come to join us. They look as if they've had a lively morning.'

'Oh, sir!' Per was gasping from his excitement as well as his pace. 'The magic of this place is everywhere. The things I've seen this morning!' His grin widened. 'And Motley is fine! I was worried for her, but she came and landed on my shoulder. She would not stay. The city makes her uncomfortable, but oh, sir, it's wonderful!'

'Later,' I warned him in a kindly voice. 'Compose yourself and show your best Six Duchies manners, boy. Just as Foxglove taught you.' They both gave me puzzled looks. Puppies. Little more than puppies. I could do nothing to make my warning plainer, and neither Lant nor Perseverance wore a blade I noted. At least not one I could see. I had two small knives concealed on my body. I hoped we would not be searched.

Rapskal's guard fell in behind us as we entered. King Reyn had gone ahead of us and was already speaking to Malta while General Rapskal stood nearby, scowling and shifting. I took in the details of the hall as quickly as I could. There were rows of the false windows down both sides of the chamber. No escape there. Not many folk were gathered. I estimated there were fewer than twenty Elderlings and about the same number of folk who bore the marks of dragon change without the beauty the Elderlings possessed. The serving-man who had escorted us was moving hastily about the hall, gathering other servants and escorting them out. I led my small party down the centre of the room. Malta was already seated in a tall chair on a modest dais. She regarded me with a tentative, hopeful smile. To the right of Reyn's chair but not on the dais, Ephron sat on a simpler chair. He grinned at us. Among the onlookers, a child coughed and then began to cry noisily. I heard a father trying to comfort it. All fell silent as the doors closed behind us with a thump. We were the only humans left; all around us, Elderlings lined the walls and looked at us. Reyn hastened to take his place. This was our formal welcome to Kelsingra, and as one who had seen many royal occasions, I did not find it especially impressive.

'I cannot see,' Amber reminded me in a soft whisper. Her hand on my arm was trembling slightly. I wondered what she imagined. A horde of armed guards ready to sweep us off to a torture chamber? I was not entirely certain that would not happen. At her words, Spark began a hasty and whispered description. I was grateful to her.

At what I considered a respectful distance from the dais I halted our party. 'Now we make our courtesies,' I told them in a low voice.

'Not too deep a bow. You are a prince,' Lant reminded me. A useful thought.

'Welcome to Kelsingra,' King Reyn greeted us. 'My friends and fellow traders, before us stand emissaries from the distant Six Duchies: Prince FitzChivalry Farseer and Lord Lantern Fallstar. Accompanying them is Lady Amber, known to some of you as a friend and to others by reputation. You will remember that her loaning of funds was instrumental to the rebuilding of Bingtown and the resettling of the former slaves in Trehaug. Prince FitzChivalry comes to us as not only an emissary but a healer. Last night, he kindly shared his ability to aid my son Ephron. All of you know that Phron has suffered badly from a breathing blockage. Now he can breathe, talk, and once more eat and drink, and move freely. For this, both Malta and I offer thanks.'

'And I!' Ephron injected with a smile. There was a scattering of laughter at his irreverence and I perceived that this was more like a merchant guild's meeting than a royal reception.

'King Reyn and Queen Malta, good morning,' I began. 'We are here, as you invited us to be. I was very glad to be of service to you yesterday. It is our hope that the Six Duchies and Kelsingra can remain trading partners and firm friends.' A general enough statement that I hoped I had not compromised any treaties that Dutiful had in mind. 'The wonders of your city have astounded all of us. Such a grand and wonderful hall! I see that there are other Elderlings in attendance here, their children with them.' I smiled and let my glance sweep the hall. I wondered if the Fool's dragon-sense could tell him how many there were.

I paused to draw breath, and in that moment, General Rapskal stepped out from the gathering. 'My friends and fellow dragon-keepers, I beg you to be wary. Malta and Reyn are too trustful of these travellers, blinded by parental gratitude. They are here not as emissaries, but spies and thieves!'

I did not miss that he did not accord Malta and Reyn royal titles. Amber's grip on my forearm tightened. I kept the dignity of a still face and wondered if Reyn or Malta would defend us or if I must cobble together a quick riposte.

A tall Elderling with lavender-and-black scaling stepped forward. He carried a small boy in his arms. The child looked to be about three but his head lolled weakly as if he were a newborn. The man's violet eyes were very large in his pale face and he blinked them at me slowly. His lips were dark. No wonder or alarm showed on his face, only weariness. 'Enough words. I came here for my boy's sake. Rapskal, I don't care if they've stolen IceFyre's back teeth. Help my child. That's all I care about just now.' The woman at his side was far more human than Elderling but still obviously marked by dragon contact. Her jaw was fringed with dangling growths like a sun-lizard's. She clasped her hands under her chin as if praying, and a line of silvery scales showed in the parting of her dark hair.

'Nortel, I understand that you feel—'

'No, Rapskal! You don't understand. You don't have a child, let alone a child that is slowly dying. So you can't understand and you don't understand. You don't need to be here, all dressed up like soldiers. Neither does Kase nor Boxter. You should all leave.'

'Hey!' One of Rapskal's guardsmen was clearly insulted. His copper eyes flashed and the colour in his bronze-and-orange scaling heightened. 'I've got a child. I understand.'

Nortel rounded on him. 'No, Kase, you don't understand. Skrim dotes on your little girl. A day doesn't go by that I don't see her climbing on his tail or sitting on his leg. He's scarcely been gone for over a week since she was born. But my Tinder left when Maude was still pregnant and hasn't returned. He's never even seen Rellik, let alone shaped him. And we can't wait any longer for my dragon to come back and do right by my son.'

'Not conducted like any monarchy I've ever encountered,' Amber observed under her breath. But Amber could not see what I could. Nortel marched toward me, his listless child jouncing in his arms. The child's eyes were dull and uninterested in his fate. Maude followed him, her hands over her mouth now. 'Please, sir, if you can help my boy, help him. Help him now. Please.' He tipped the boy away from his shoulder and held him out to me. The boy's head and legs dangled, and I did not even think as I reached out to support his lolling head.

I shot a questioning glance toward Reyn, but it was Malta who was nodding like a toy, her hands clasped as if in supplication.

'I cannot make any promises . . .'

'I don't ask any. Do what you can, for he grows weaker with every passing day. Please. Help my boy, and anything within my power is yours.'

'The lives and health of children are not to be bartered,' Amber said clearly. 'What he can do, he will. But it may take a toll on the child as well. His body will heal him; the prince will but guide the process. It can be taxing. I speak from experience.'

The parents did not hesitate. 'Please,' begged Nortel. I looked around at the clustered Elderlings. Some held children. If I failed, I had no idea what would befall us. I set my other hand on the boy that his father offered to me.

I lowered my walls.

The Skill immersed me, as if I had stepped into a surging wave. It filled and flooded me and then connected me to the child I touched. I knew this boy, this Elderling child, and knew how he should have grown, and saw what his body needed to do to correct itself. The Skill that flowed through me diverted to flow through him. The lure of the Skill, the terrible danger of that heady magic that every Skill-candidate is taught to block and suppress, shone before me in all its glittering, surging beauty. We dived into it and swam through it. His own body opened what was constricted, loosened what was too tight. It was a perfect alignment of purpose and solution. I guided the power as if I were tracing the lettering on a precious scroll. Perfect. He would be perfect. He smiled at me and I smiled back. I gazed at him and through him and saw what a marvellous creature was this child.

'I, I felt him heal!' Someone said this, at a great distance, and then he took from me the beauty of what I had mended. I opened my eyes, wavering on my feet. Nortel held his son. The boy was weak but smiling. He held his head steady and reached up a thin hand to touch his father's scaled cheek and then laughed aloud. Maude gave a shriek and embraced them both. They stood, the three of them a weeping, smiling pillar.

'Fitz?' Someone spoke close by. Someone shook my arm. It was Amber. I turned to her, smiling and puzzled.

'I wish you could have seen that,' I said quietly.

'I felt it,' she replied softly. 'I very much doubt if there is anyone here who did not feel it. The building seemed to hum around us. Fitz, this was a bad idea. You have to stop. This is dangerous.'

'Yes. But more than that, it's right. It's very right.'

'Fitz, you must listen to me—'

'Please. It's her feet. They started to go wrong about a year ago. She used to run and play. She can scarcely walk any more.'

I gave my head a shake and turned away from Amber. An Elderling woman with hummocked shoulders stood before me. But they were not her shoulders at all. What I had taken for fabric-draped hummocks I now saw were the tops of her wings. They were blue and the tops of them were as high as her ears and the trailing plumes nearly swept the floor behind her. A girl of about seven leaned on her, partially supported by her Elderling father on the other side. His markings were green, the mother's blue, and the child bore a twining of both colours. 'She is ours,' the father said. 'But from month to month neither of our dragons claim her. Or both do, and squabble over her growth as if she were a toy, one changing what the other wrought. Both our dragons have gone to a warmer place for the winter months. Since then, she has grown worse.'

'Tats, Thymara, do you think it wise to ask him to interfere? Will not both Fente and Sintara take this amiss when they return?' Queen Malta cautioned them.

'When they return, I will worry about it,' Thymara declared. 'Until then, why should Fillia pay for their neglect? Six Duchies prince, can you help her?'

I studied the child. I could almost see the conflicting plans for her. One ear was tasselled, the other pointed. The discord rang against my senses like the chiming of a cracked bell. I tried to be cautious. 'I don't know. And if I try, I may have to draw on her strength, on the reserves of her own body. It will be her own flesh that makes the changes. I can guide her, but I cannot supply what her body needs.'

'I don't understand,' Tats objected.

I pointed at her feet. 'You can see that her feet strive to become the feet of a dragon. Some bone must go away, flesh must be added. I cannot cut nor can I add. Her body must do that.' I could hear the muttering of the gathered Elderlings as they discussed my words.

The green father dropped to one knee to look into his daughter's face. 'You must decide, Fillia. Do you want to do this?'

She looked up at me, in fear and hope. 'I want to run again and not have it hurt. My face is tight when I try to smile so that I think my lips will crack.' She touched her scaled scalp. 'I would have hair, to keep me warmer!' She lifted her hands to me. Her nails were blue and tipped like claws. 'Please,' she said.

'Yes,' I responded. I held my hands out to her and she set her fate in them. Two slender hands in my sword-calloused ones. I felt her pain as she struggled to balance on her twisted feet. I sank down to sit on the floor and she folded gratefully. The Skill in me sent a tendril to touch her brow. This one, ah, this one was a puzzle. Here was her father and there her mother, and here the dragons that had touched her and quarrelled over her like two children ripping at a single doll. There were so many possible ways. 'What would you like?' I asked her, and her face lit. Her vision of herself surprised me. She did not mind her strong clawed feet, if only they would grow straight. She wished for a blue horse on one cheek, and for the darker green in her scaling to run up her back and down her arms like vines. She wanted black hair, thick and strong like her mother's and ears that she could move to catch sound. She showed me and with the Skill, I persuaded her body to follow her will. I heard as at a distance her parents speaking in worried tones but it was not their choice to make but hers. And when at last she stepped back from me, walking on the front pads of her high arched feet, shaking back a glossy mane, she cried out to them, 'See me! This is me!'

Another child they brought to me, born with nostrils so flat to his face that he could scarcely breathe. We found the nose he should have had, and lengthened his fingers and set his hips so that he might walk upright. This child moaned and I was sorry for how he ached with the turning of his bones, but, 'It must be done!' the Skill and I whispered to him. He was thin when I gifted him back to his fathers, and panting with pain. One stared at me, teeth bared, and the other wept, but the boy breathed and the hands that he reached to them had thumbs he could move.

'Fitz. You are finished. Stop.' Amber's voice trembled.

The Skill coursed through me and I recalled that this rush of pleasure was as dangerous as it was sweet. To some. To some it was dangerous. But I was learning, I'd learned so much this very day. I could control it in ways I'd never learned before, in ways I'd never thought were possible. To touch with a tendril, to read the make-up of a child, to allow someone to guide the Skill I wielded as if sharing a grip on a brush, all this I could do.

And I could cool the Skill, reduce it from a boil to a simmer. I could control it.

'Please!' a woman shouted suddenly. 'Kind prince, if you would, cannot you open my womb! Let me conceive and bear a child! Please. I beg you, I beg you!'

She flung herself down at my feet and embraced my knees. Her head was bowed, her hair hanging past her heavily-scaled face as she sobbed. She was no Elderling but one whose body had been distorted by contact with dragons. With every child I had touched, the influences of a dragon on a growing human body had become plainer to me. In some of the children, I had seen deliberation and even art in how dragons had marked them. But in this woman, the changes were as random as a tree planted in rocky soil and shaded by a boulder. As close as she was to me, I could not exclude her from my Skill, and as it closed around her, I felt her innate ability in the magic. It was untrained and yet in that instant I shared how deep her longing for a child was, and how it distressed her to watch the slow years pass and her cradle remain empty.

Such a familiar pang. How could I refuse such a request when

I knew so well what it was like to have it denied? Why had I never sought to use the Skill to find why Molly could not bear a child for us? Years wasted, never to be recovered. I set my hands to her shoulders to lift her to her feet and in doing so closed a circle. We were bound for that moment, the pain of loss tying us together, and what had been crooked in her the Skill straightened and what had been closed opened. She cried out suddenly and stepped back from me, her hands clasped over her belly. 'I felt the change!' she cried out. 'I felt it!'

'Enough!' Amber cried in a low voice. 'This must be enough.'

But there was suddenly before me a man saying, 'Please, please, the scales have grown down my brow and onto my eyelids. I can barely see. Push them back, I beg of you, prince from the Six Duchies.' He seized my hand and set it to his face. Did he have the Skill as the woman had, or was it that it was running so strongly in me that I could not deny it? I felt the scales retreat from his eyelids, from his brow-line, and he fell back from me laughing aloud.

Someone took my hand and held it tightly. I felt the fabric of a glove against my skin.

'King Reyn! Queen Malta, please, tell them they must step back! He heals them at great danger to himself. He must stop, he must take rest now. See how he shakes! Please, tell them they must not ask more of him.' I heard the words. They meant little to me.

'Good keepers and friends, you hear Lady Amber! Step back, give him room!' Malta's voice came from across the room. Closer to me were other voices.

'Please, kind prince!'

'My hands, if only you would mend my hands!'

'I wish to look like a woman again, not a lizard! My prince, please, please!'

In a lower voice, I heard the Fool give his orders. 'Spark, Per, stand before him and hold them back. Push them back! Lant, where are you? Lant?'

'People of Kelsingra! Keep order. Step back from the prince, give him room!' There was anxiety in Reyn's voice, bordering on fear.

It was hard to use my eyesight when the Skill flowed so strongly all around me, far more potent than any of my senses, far stronger even than my Wit. My eyes were poor things, relying on light to show me the outer shapes of things. Still, I looked for Lant and found him at my side, struggling to take something from his pocket. In front of me, Spark and Per had linked arms and stood between me and a wall of pushing people. They could not hold them back, not when such need consumed them. I closed my eyes and stopped my ears. Such senses only confused me when I could blanket the room with Skill and know so much more.

Amber's gloved hand still gripped mine and her free hand was on my chest now, trying to push me back and away from the reaching hands. It was a hopeless gesture. The room was large and the people had flowed to surround us. There was no 'back' now, only a noose of desperate people struggling toward us.

As mobs go, it was a small one, and no one meant me harm. Some pushed toward me out of hunger and need. Some strove to be first, others only to see what wonder I would next work, and some pushed to try and break through the wall of people in front of them so that they might have a chance to beg a boon of their own. One woman pushed because she did not want another woman to reach me and have her face changed, lest she win the man they both desired. Rapskal was in the thick of it, with Kase and Boxter, not to find order but to see if somehow Amber would betray she was sighted, for he was certain she had been to the Silver well, and he was consumed with hatred that anyone would attempt to steal Silver from the dragons.

'Fitz. Fitz! FITZ! You have to stop. Set your walls, come back to yourself. Fitz!'

I had forgotten my body. It was shaking all around me and Lant's arms were around my chest, trying to hold me up. 'Get away from us!' Lant roared, and for a moment the press of the crowd lessened. But those who could see me collapsing were pushed forward by those who wished to know what was happening. This I knew in a dispassionate way. I would fall, Lant would go down holding on to me, the grim youngsters trying to hold back the crowd would stumble backwards and we would be trampled.

The Skill told me that Amber had been pushed up under my

arm. 'Fitz,' the Fool said by my ear. 'Fitz, where are you? I can't feel you. Fitz, put up your walls! Please, Fitz. Beloved.'

'Give him this!' Lant cried out to her.

None of it mattered. Skill was a spreading pool and I was spreading with it. There were others here, diluted and mingled. They'd enjoyed what I had done. I sensed that there were some here who were larger and more intact, larger souls that were more defined. Older and wiser. I couldn't be one of them. There wasn't enough of me. I'd spread and disperse. Mingle. I could just let go. It would be like the sweetsleep. Stop the worries, give up the guilt. The worst were the sharp-edged hopes that I still clung to. The hope that somewhere, somehow, Bee still existed and would tumble intact from a Skill-pillar. But it was far more likely that she was here in this amorphous mingling. Perhaps letting go was the closest I'd ever get to reuniting with her.

Being Fitz had never been that enticing an existence.

Fingers prying at my lips, pressing on my teeth. Bitterness in my mouth. The Skill-tide that had surged so strongly against me became a lapping of calmer water. I tried to recede with it.

The touch of fingers on my wrist burned. Burned exquisitely, pain and ecstasy inseparable.

BELOVED!

The word echoed through me, rebounded from my fraying edges, found and bound me. I was there, trapped in an exhausted and shaking body, trembling as Lant hugged me from behind and held me upright. His hand was over my mouth and I tasted elfbark. Dry powder coated my lips. Per and Spark, arms locked, faced out into the press. They were crowded up against Amber, pushing her against me.

The Fool embraced me, his head bowed on my chest. One of his arms was around my neck, holding on to me. I clutched an empty glove in one hand. Slowly and dully, I lifted that hand to look at the glove. The Fool's hand, his fingers gleaming silver, clutched my wrist, burning my identity into me. The bond was shockingly and completely renewed.

'I told you!' Rapskal's shout was guttural with excitement and validation. 'I told you they were thieves! See there, see on her hand, my proof! Silver! She has stolen Silver from the dragons and she must be punished! Seize her! Seize all of them!'

A moment of horror and shock. I heard Spark give a shriek as someone grabbed her. In the next instant, the Fool was torn away from me. I struggled to remain standing.

I heard the Fool scream as the surging crowd engulfed us.

THIRTY-EIGHT

Emergence

In this dream, I am very small and I am hiding inside a tiny case, like a nut in a shell. I am floating in a wild and raging river. I am very frightened because I fear this journey has no end. Around me there are others who are flowing with the river. It seems I could come out of my shell and melt and be part of them.

Then a dragon picks me up. He holds me tight in his paw so that even if I wanted to come out of my shell and melt, I could not. I am scared, and then he lets me feel that I am very, very safe. 'As the wolf did for my young, so I will do for his cub. I will protect you here. When you emerge, come to me. I will protect you.'

I draw here the dragon. He is a terrifying creature, but to me he is a kindly uncle.

Bee Farseer's Dream Journal

After not being for so long, I was not sure how to exist.

Uncurl, Wolf Father commanded me. *You have to be ready before they are. Uncurl. Stand up.*

I couldn't. I tried. Somewhere, I knew I had legs and arms. A face. Sunlight. Wind. Slowly those words began to have meaning again. Sunlight was touching me and wind kissed my face. I was sprawled on my back. I blinked my eyes. I was looking up at blue sky. The sun was too bright. I tried to move but my body was weighted down with something.

I heard a terrible sound. I rolled my head toward it. The

Chalcedean who had liked Shun. He was making the sounds. I could not remember his name. He was on all fours and he was stretching his mouth wide open and making peculiar retching sounds. I thought he would be sick on the ground. Instead he collapsed back on to his belly. His face was turned toward mine, and he looked at me. Nothing human was in his eyes. They grew wider until I could see the whites all around them. He pursed his lips as if he would blow a horn and hooted at me. They were silly sounds that were somehow frightening.

Fear can help you do things. I rolled over onto my belly and suddenly knew what was holding me down. The heavy, floppy fur-coat I wore was like being rolled up in a rug. I tried to get my knees under me but instead I knelt inside the coat and could not move. The sounds the Chalcedean was making were getting stranger, as if he were trying to make squirrel noises.

I rolled onto my back. My floppy hands found the peg and loop fastenings that held the coat shut. I fumbled at them, trying to make the part of me that knew how to undo them connect with my fingers. His sounds were now like a dog trying to howl. I gave up on the pegs and sat up. I was suddenly trapped by the fur and getting out of the coat seemed more important than getting away from the mad man. I managed to stand up, staggered a few steps, and almost fell over someone. One of Dwalia's luriks. I could not think of her name. She was dead, I suddenly knew. I tottered away from her, still fighting with the pegs on my coat. I saw Dwalia. She was underneath someone and fighting to get out from under him.

Don't look. Run. Just run. You are safer in the forest than among these evil creatures. There is one here who will help us if I can wake him. Run. Run where I show you.

A wave of vertigo swept over me. I fell, going to my knees and my hands in the snow. I got up and staggered away. The coat I wore dragged on the snow. I hiked it up. Into the forest. Get as deep into the forest as fast as I could.

Behind me I heard Dwalia shout, 'Catch her! Don't let her get away! We can never go home unless we bring her with us.'

I ran.

And be sure not to miss the riveting conclusion:

ASSASSIN'S FATE

Book 3 of the Fitz and the Fool trilogy

Coming in spring 2017

Here's a special preview:

There is a peculiar strength that comes to a man when knows he is facing his final battle. That battle is not limited to war, nor the strength to warriors. I've seen this strength in old women with the coughing sickness and heard of it in families that are starving together. It drives one to go on, past hope or despair, past blood loss and gut wounds, past death itself in a final surge to save something that is cherished. It is courage without hope. During the Red-Ship Wars, I saw a man with blood gouting from where his left arm had once been, yet swinging a sword with his right as he stood protecting a fallen comrade. During one encounter with Forged Ones I saw a mother stumbling over her own entrails as she shrieked and clutched at a Forged man, trying to hold him away from her daughter.

The OutIslanders have a word for that courage. Finblead, they call it, the last blood, and they believe that a special fortitude resides in the final blood that remains in a man or a woman before they fall. According to their tales, only then can one find and use that sort of courage.

It is a terrible bravery – and at its strongest and worst, it goes on for months when one battles a final illness. Or, I believe, when one moves toward a duty that will definitely result in death but is completely unavoidable. That finblead lights everything in one's life with a terrible radiance. All relationships are illuminated for what they are, and for what they truly were in the past. All illusions melt away. The false is revealed as starkly as the true.

FitzChivalry Farseer

As the taste of the herb spread in my mouth, the sounds of the turmoil around me grew louder. I lifted my head and tried to focus my stinging eyes. I hung in Lant's arms, the familiar bitterness of elfbark suffusing my mouth. As the herb damped my magic, I became more aware of my surroundings. My left wrist ached with a bone-deep pain, searing as frozen iron. While the Skill had surged through me, healing and changing those I touched, my perception had shrunk, but now I was fully aware of the shouting of the crowd enclosing me as the sound bounced from the lofty walls of the elegant Elderling chamber. I smelled fear-sweat in the air. I was caught in the press of the mob, with some Elderlings fighting to get away from me as others were shoving to get closer. So many people! Hands reached toward me, with cries of 'Please! Please, just one more!' Others shouted, 'Let me through!' as they pushed to get away from me. The Skill-current that had flowed so strongly around me and through me had abated, but it wasn't gone. Lant's elfbark was the milder herb, Six Duchies grown and somewhat stale by the taste of it. Here in the Elderling city, the Skill flowed so strong and close I did not think even delvenbark could have closed me to it completely.

But it was enough. I was aware of the Skill but no longer shackled to its service. Yet the exhaustion of letting it use me now slackened my muscles just when I had most need of them. General Rapskal had torn the Fool from my grasp. The Elderling gripped Amber's wrist and held her silvered hand aloft, shouting, 'I told you so! I told you they were thieves! Look at her hand, coated in the dragon's silver! She has discovered the well! She has stolen from our dragons!'

Spark clung to Amber's other arm, trying to drag her free of the general's grip. The girl's teeth were bared, her black curls wild around her face. The look of sheer terror on Amber's scarred face both paralyzed and panicked me. The years of privation the Fool had endured were betrayed in that stark grimace. They made her face a death mask of bones and red lips and rouged cheeks. I had to go to the Fool's aid, and yet my knees kept folding of their own accord. Perseverance seized my arm. 'Prince FitzChivalry, what must I do? What must I do?' I could not find breath to reply to him.

'Fitz! Stand up!' Lant roared right next to my ear. It was as much plea as command. I found my feet, and pressed my weight against them. I strained, shuddering, trying to keep my legs straight under me.

We had arrived in Kelsingra just the day before, and for a few hours I had been the hero of the day, the magical Six Duchies prince who had healed Ephron, the son of the king and queen of Kelsingra. The Skill had flowed through me, as intoxicating as Sandsedge brandy. At the request of King Reyn and Queen Malta I had used my magic to set right half a dozen dragon-touched children. I had opened myself to the powerful Skill-current of the old Elderling city. Awash in that heady power, I'd opened throats and steadied heartbeats, straightened bones and cleared scales from eyes. Some I'd made more human and one girl had actually wished to embrace her dragon changes and I'd helped her do that.

But the Skill-flow had become too strong, too intoxicating. I'd lost control of the magic, become its tool instead of its master. Even after the children I'd agreed to heal had been claimed by their parents, others pushed forward. Adult Rain Wilders with changes uncomfortable or ugly or life-threatening had begged my aid, and I had dispensed it with a lavish hand, caught in the vast pleasure of that flow. I'd felt my last shred of control give way, but when I'd surrendered to that glorious surge and its invitation to merge with the magic, Amber had stripped the glove from her hand. To save me, she'd revealed the stolen dragon-silver on her fingers. To save me, she'd pressed three scalding fingertips to my bare wrist, and burned her way into my mind and called me back. To save me, she'd betrayed herself as thief. The hot kiss of her fingers' touch still pulsed like a fresh burn, sending a deep ache up the bones of my arm, to my shoulder, to my back and neck.

What damage it was doing to me now, I could not know. But at least I was again anchored to my body. I was anchored to it and it was dragging me down. I'd lost track of how many Elderlings I'd touched and changed, but my body had kept count. Each one had taken a toll from me, each shaping had torn strength from me, and now that debt had to be paid. Despite all my efforts, my head lolled and I could scarcely keep my eyes open amidst the danger and noise all around me. I saw the room as through a mist.

'Rapskal, stop being an ass!' That was King Reyn adding his roar to the din.

Lant abruptly tightened his hug around my chest, dragging me more upright. 'Let her go!' he bellowed. 'Release our friend, or the prince will undo every cure he has worked! Let her go, right now!'

I heard gasps, wailing, a man shouting 'No! He must not!' A woman screamed, 'Let go of her, Rapskal! Let her go!' Malta's voice rang with command as she cried out, 'This is not how we treat guests and ambassadors! Release her, Rapskal, this moment!' Her cheeks were flushed and the crest of flesh above her brow bloomed with colour.

'Let go of me!' Amber's voice rang with authority. From some deep well of courage she had drawn the will to fight back on her own behalf. Her voice cut through the crowd's noise. 'Release me, or I will touch you!' She made good her threat, surging toward Rapskal instead of trying to pull her hand free. The sudden reverse shocked him, and her silvered fingers came perilously close to his face. The general gave a shout of alarm and sprang back from her as he let go of her wrist. But she was not finished. 'Back, all of you!' she commanded. 'Give us room and let me see to the prince. Or by Sa, I *will* touch you!' Hers was the voice of an angered queen, pitched to carry her authority. Her silvered fore-finger pointed as she swung it in a slow arc around her, and people were suddenly stumbling over one another in their haste to be out of her reach.

The mother of the girl with dragon feet lifted her voice. 'I'd do as she says!' she warned. 'If that is truly dragon-silver on her fingers, one touch of it will mean slow death. It will seep down to your bones, right through your flesh. It will travel your bones, up your spine to your skull. Eventually, you will be grateful to die from it.' As others were falling back from us, she began pushing her way through the crowd toward us. She was not a large person but the other dragon keepers were giving way to her. She stopped a safe distance from us. Her dragon had patterned her in blue and black and silver. The wings that weighted her shoulders were folded snug to her back. The claws on her toes tapped the floor as she walked. Of all the Elderlings present, she was most heavily modified by her dragon's touch. Her warning and Amber's threat cleared a small space around us.

Amber retreated to my side and I heard her draw a shuddering breath. Spark stood on her left side and Perseverance took up a position in front of her. Amber's voice was low and calm as she said, 'Spark, retrieve my glove if you would.'

'Of course, my lady.' The requested item had fallen to the floor. Spark stooped and cautiously picked it up in two fingers. 'I will touch your wrist,' she warned Amber, and tapped the back of her hand to guide her to her glove. Amber was still breathing unsteadily as she gloved her hand but, weak as I was, I was horribly glad to see that she had regained some of the Fool's strength and presence of mind. She linked her unsilvered hand through my arm and I was reassured by her touch. It seemed to draw off some of the Skill-current still coursing through me. I felt both connected to her and less battered by the Skill.

'I think I can stand,' I muttered to Lant and he loosened his grip on me. I could not allow anyone to see how drained I was of strength. I rubbed my eyes and wiped elfbark powder from my face. My knees did not buckle and I managed to hold my head steady. I straightened up. I badly wanted the knife in my boot, but if I stooped for it, I knew I would not stop until I sprawled on the floor.

The woman who had warned the others stepped into the empty space that now surrounded us, but stayed beyond arm's reach. 'Lady Amber, is it truly dragon-silver on your hand?' she asked in quiet dread.

'It is!' General Rapskal had found his courage and took up a stance beside her. 'And she has stolen it from the dragon's well. She must be punished! Keepers and folk of Kelsingra, we cannot be seduced by the healing of a few children! We do not even know if this magic will last or if it is a cheat. But we have all seen the evidence of this intruder's theft, and we all know that our first duty is and must always be to the dragons who have befriended us.'

'Speak for yourself, Rapskal.' The woman gave him a cold stare. 'My first duty is to my daughter, and she no longer totters when she stands.'

'Are you so easily bought, Thymara?' Rapskal demanded with scathing disdain.

The father of the child stepped into the circle to stand beside the woman called Thymara. The girl with the dragon feet rode on his shoulder and looked down on us. He spoke as if he scolded a wilful child, rebuke tinged with familiarity. 'Of all people, Rapskal, you should know that Thymara cannot be bought. Answer me this. Who has it harmed that this lady has silvered her fingers? Only herself. She will die of it. So what worse can we do to her? Let her go. Let all of them go, and let them go with my thanks.'

'She stole!' Rapskal's shout turned to a shriek, his dignity flung to the wind.

Reyn had managed to elbow his way through the crowd. Queen Malta was right behind him, her cheeks pink beneath her scaling and her eyes fiery with her anger. The dragon changes in her were amplified by her fury. There was a glitter in her eyes that was not human, and the crest of flesh in the parting of her hair seemed taller: it reminded me of a rooster's comb. She was the first to speak. 'My apologies, Prince FitzChivalry, Lady Amber. Our people forgot themselves in their hopes of being healed. And General Rapskal is sometimes— '

'Don't speak for me!' the general interrupted her. 'Do not dismiss what I'm pointing out. She stole silver. We saw the evidence, and no, it's not enough that she has poisoned herself. We cannot let her leave Kelsingra. None of them can leave, for now they know the secret of the dragon's well!'

Amber spoke. She sounded calm but she pushed her words so that all could hear. 'May I prove that there was silver on my fingers for years? Before you were born, I believe, General Rapskal. Before your dragons hatched, before Kelsingra was found and reclaimed, I bore what we of the Six Duchies call Skill on my fingers. And your queen can attest to that.'

'She is not our queen and he is not our king!' General Rapskal's chest heaved with emotion and along his neck patches of his scales showed a bright scarlet. 'So they have said, over and over! They have said that we must rule ourselves, that they are but figureheads for the rest of the world. So, keepers, let us rule

ourselves! Let us put our dragons first, as we are meant to do!'
He pointed a finger at Lady Amber, from a safe distance, and it
shook as he demanded of his fellows, 'Recall how difficult it was
for us to find and renew the well of silver! Will you believe her
ridiculous tale that she has carried it on her fingertips for scores
of years and not died of it?'

Queen Malta's rueful voice cut through Rapskal's rant. 'I am
sorry to say that I cannot attest to such a thing, Lady Amber. I
knew you only briefly during your time in Bingtown, and met
you seldom during the negotiations of your loans to many of the
Traders.' She shook her head. 'A Trader's word is all she has to
give and I will not bend mine, even to help a friend. I cannot.
The best I can say is that when I knew you in those days you
always went gloved. I never saw your hands.'

'You heard her!' Rapskal's shout was triumphant. 'There is no
proof! There can be no...'

'If I may speak?' For years, as King Shrewd's jester, the Fool
had had to make even his whispered comments heard across a
large and sometimes crowded room. He had trained his voice to
carry, and it now cut through not only Rapskal's shout but also
the muttering of the crowd. A simmering silence filled the room.
He did not move as a blind man as he stepped forward into the
space his threat had cleared. He was a performer stepping onto
his stage. It was in the sudden grace of his movements and his
storyteller's voice, and the sweep of his gloved hand. He was the
Fool to me, and the layer of Amber but a part of his performance.

'Recall a summer day, dear Queen Malta. You were but a girl,
and all was in turmoil in your life. All your family's hopes for
financial survival depended on the successful launch of the
Paragon, a liveship so insane that thrice he had capsized and
killed all his crew. But the mad ship was your only hope, and
into his salvage and refitting the Vestrit family had poured the
last of their resources.'

He had them, and me. I was as caught up in this tale as any
of them.

'Your family hoped that the *Paragon* would be able to find and
restore to you your father and your brother, both missing for so
long. That somehow you could reclaim Vivacia, your family's own

liveship, for it was rumoured that she had been taken by pirates. And not any pirates, but the fabled Captain Kennit himself! You stood on the deck of the mad ship, putting on such a brave face in your made-over gown with last year's parasol. When all the others went below to tour the ship you stayed on the deck and I stayed near you, to watch over you as your Aunt Althea requested.'

'I remember that day,' Malta said slowly. 'It was the first time we had really spoken to one another. I remember . . . we talked of the future. Of what it might hold for me. You told me that a small life would never satisfy me. You told me that I must earn my future. How did you put it?'

Lady Amber smiled, well pleased that this queen remembered words spoken to her when she was a child putting a brave face on impending poverty. 'What I told you is as true today as it was then. Tomorrow owes you the sum of your yesterdays. No more than that. And no less.'

Malta's smile was like sunlight. 'And you warned me that sometimes people wished that tomorrow did not pay them off so completely.'

'I did.'

The queen stepped forward, unwittingly becoming part of the performance as she took her place on Amber's stage. Her brow furrowed and she spoke like a woman in a dream. 'And then... Paragon whispered to me. And I felt . . . oh, I did not know it then. I felt the dragon Tintaglia seize my thoughts. I felt she would smother me as she forced me to share her confinement in her tomb! And I fainted. It was terrible. I felt I was trapped with the dragon and could never find my way back to my own body.'

'I caught you,' Amber said. 'And I touched you, on the back of your neck, with my Skilled fingers. Silvered, you would say. And by that magic, I called you back to your own body. But it left a mark on you. And a tiny tendril of a link that we share to this very day.'

'What?' Malta was incredulous.

'It's true!' The words burst from King Reyn along with a laugh that was both relief and joy. 'On the back of your neck, my dear! I saw them there in days when your hair was black as a crow's wing, before Tintaglia turned it to gold. Three greyish ovals, like silver fingerprints gone dusty with age.'

Malta's mouth hung open in surprise. At his words, her hand had darted to the back of her neck beneath the fall of glorious golden hair that was not blonde. 'There was always a tender place there. Like a bruise that never healed.' Abruptly she sent her second hand to join the first. She lifted her cascading locks and held them on the top of her head. 'Come and look, any that wish. Come and see if what my husband and Lady Amber says is true.'

I was one of those who did. I staggered forward, still leaning on Lant, to see the same marks I had once borne on my wrist. Three greyish ovals, the mark of the Fool's silvered hand. They were there.

The woman called Thymara stared in consternation when it was her turn to see the nape of the queen's neck. 'It's a wonder it did not kill you,' she said in a hushed voice.

I thought that would be an end of the matter, but when General Rapskal had taken three times as long to stare at the marks as any had, he turned away from the queen and said, 'What does it matter if she had the silver then? What does it matter if she stole it a few nights ago, or several decades ago? Silver from the well belongs to the dragons. She must still be punished.'

I stiffened my back and tightened my belly. My voice must not shake. A deeper breath to make my words carry. I hoped I would not vomit. 'It didn't come from a well. It came from King Verity's own hands, that he covered in Skill to work his great and final magic. He got it from where a river of Skill ran within a river of water. Name it not dragon's silver. It is Skill from the Skill-river.'

'And where might that be?' Rapskal demanded in a voice so hungry it alarmed me.

'I don't know,' I replied honestly. 'I saw it but once, in a Skill-dream. My king never allowed me to go there with him, lest I give way to the temptation to plunge myself into it.'

'Temptation?' Thymara was shocked. 'I, who am privileged to use the silver to do works for the city, feel no temptation to plunge myself into it. Indeed, I fear it.'

'That is because you were not born with it coursing in your

blood,' the Fool said. 'As some Farseers are. As Prince FitzChivalry was, born with the Skill as a magic within him, one that he can use to shape children as some might shape stone.'

That struck them dumb.

'Is it possible?' This from the winged Elderling, a genuine question.

Amber lifted her voice again. 'The magic I bear on my hands is the same that was accidentally gifted to me by King Verity. It is rightfully mine, not stolen, any more than the magic that courses through the prince's veins, the magic you joyfully allowed him to share with your children. Not stolen any more than the magic within you that changes you and marks your children. What do you call it? Marked by the Rain Wilds? Changed by the dragons? If this silver on my fingers is stolen, why then any here who have been healed have shared in the prince's thievery.'

'Enough of this!' King Reyn commanded. I saw Rapskal's eyes flash anger, but he did not speak as Reyn added, 'We have abused and exhausted our guests. What the prince freely shared we have demanded in too great a quantity from him. See how pale he is, and how he shakes. Please, my guests, return to your chambers. Let us bring you both refreshments and our sincere apologies. But in the greatest quantity of all, let us offer you our thanks.'

He advanced and, with a gesture, moved Perseverance aside. Behind him came Queen Malta, offering her arm fearlessly to Amber. Reyn gripped my upper arm with surprising strength. I found myself a bit humiliated, but more thankful for the help. I managed to look back once to see Queen Malta and Spark escorting Amber while Per came last of all, slowly and with many a backward glance, as if wary that danger followed us, but the doors closed behind us without incident.

We walked through a corridor lined with curious folk who had been excluded from that audience. Then behind us, I heard the doors open and a gust of conversation belled out to become a roar. The hall seemed interminable. The stairs, when we came to them, wavered in my vision. I could not imagine that I could climb them. But I knew I must.

And I did, step by slow step, until we stood outside the doors of my guest chamber. 'Thank you,' I managed to say.

'You thank me.' Reyn gave a snort of laughter. 'I would better deserve a curse from you after what we have put you through.'

'Not you,' I managed to say.

'I will leave you in peace,' he excused himself, and remained outside with his queen as my small party entered my room. When I heard Perseverance close the door, relief swept through me and my knees tried to fold. Lant put his arm around me to help me to the table. I hated that my companions must know how close I was to the end of my strength. I took his hand to steady myself.

A mistake. He cried out suddenly and went to his knees in the same moment that I felt the Skill course through me as swiftly as a snake striking. He clutched at the scar from the sword wound that the Chalcedean raiders had given him. It had been closed, apparently healed. But in that brief touch, I had known there was more for his body to do, and known, too, of one rib healed crookedly, and a fracture in his jaw that was mildly infected and giving him pain still. All repaired and set right, if one can call such a harsh correction a repair. I collapsed merrily on top of him. Lant groaned under me. I tried to roll off him but could not summon the strength. I heard Perseverance's gasp: 'Oh, sir! Let me help you!'

'Don't touch—' I began, but he had already stooped and taken my hand. His outcry was sharper, a young man's voice taken back to a boy's shrill one. He fell onto his side and sobbed twice before he could master the pain. I managed to roll away from both of them. Lant didn't move.

'What has happened?' Amber's question was close to a scream. 'Are we attacked? Fitz! Fitz, where are you?'

'I'm here! There's no danger to you. The Skill . . . I touched Lant. And Per.' Those were all the words I could manage.

'What?'

'He did . . . the Skill did something to my wound. It's bleeding again. My shoulder,' Perseverance said in a tight voice.

I knew it would. It had to. But only briefly. It was hard to find the strength to speak. I lay on my back, staring up at the high ceiling. It mimicked a sky. Artfully crafted fluffy clouds moved across a pale blue sky. I lifted my head and summoned my voice. 'It's not blood, Per. It's just wet. There was still a piece of fabric caught deep in the wound. It was slowly festering there. It had to come out and the fluids of infection with it. So it did. And your wound closed behind it. It's healed now.'

Then I lay back on the floor and watched the elegant room swing around me. If I closed my eyes, it went faster. If I opened them, the forested walls wavered. I heard Lant roll over onto his belly and then stagger upright. He crouched over Per and said gently, 'Let's take a look at it.'

'Look at your injuries as well,' I said dully. I shifted my eyes, saw Spark standing over me and cried out, 'No! Don't touch me. I can't control it.'

'Let me help him,' Lady Amber said quietly. Two hesitant steps brought her to where I lay on the floor.

I pulled my arms in tight, hiding my bare hands under my vest. 'No. You of all people must not touch me.'

She had crouched gracefully beside me, but as he hunkered back on his heels, he was my Fool and not Amber at all. There was immense sorrow in his voice as he said, 'Did you think I would take from you the healing that you did not wish to give me, Fitz?'

The room was spinning and I was too exhausted to hold anything back from him. 'If you touch me, I fear the Skill will rip through me like a sword through flesh. If it can, it will give you back your eyesight. Regardless of the cost to me. And I believe the cost of restoring your sight will be that I will lose mine.'

The change in his face was startling. Pale as he was, he went whiter until he might have been carved from ice. Emotion tautened the skin of his face, revealing the bones that framed his visage. Scars that had faded stood out like cracks in fine pottery. I tried to focus my gaze on him, but he seemed to move with the room. I felt so nauseous and so weak, and I hated the secret I had to share with him. But there was no hiding it any longer. I wished we were alone but I dared not take the time to clear the others from the room. 'Fool, we are too close. For every hurt I removed from your flesh my body assumed the wound. Not as virulently as the wounds you carried, but when I healed the knife-stabs in your belly I felt them in mine the next day. When I closed the sores in your back they opened in mine.'

'I saw those wounds!' Perseverance gasped. 'I thought you'd been attacked. Stabbed in the back.'

I did not pause for his words. 'When I healed the bones around your eye sockets, mine swelled and blackened the next day. If you touch me, Fool—'

'I won't!' he exclaimed. He shot to his feet and staggered blindly away from me. 'Get out of here. All three of you! Leave now. Fitz and I must speak privately. No, Spark, I will be fine, I can tend to myself. Please go. Now.'

They retreated, but not swiftly. They went in a bunch, with many backward glances. Spark had taken Per's hand and when they looked back, they showed me the faces of woeful children. Lant went last and his expression was set in a Farseer stare so like his father's that no one could have mistaken his bloodlines. 'My chamber,' he said to them as he shut the door behind them and I knew he would try to keep them safe. I hoped there was no real danger. But I also feared that General Rapskal was not finished with us.

'Explain,' the Fool said flatly.

I gathered myself up from the floor. It was far harder than it should have been. I rolled onto my belly, drew my knees up under me until I was on all fours, and then staggered upright. I caught myself on the table's edge and moved around it until I could reach a chair. My inadvertent healing of first Lant and then Per had extracted the last of my strength. Seated, I dragged in a breath. It was so difficult to keep my head upright. 'I can't explain what I don't understand. It's never happened with any other Skill-healing I've witnessed. Only between you and me. Whatever injury I take from you appears on me.'

He stood, his arms crossed on his chest. He wore his own face, and Amber's painted lips and rouged cheeks looked peculiar now. His eyes seemed to bore into me. 'No. Explain why you hid this from me! Why you couldn't trust me with the simple truth. What did you imagine? That I would demand you blind yourself that I might see?'

'I . . . no!' I braced my elbows on the table and rested my head in my hands. I could not recall when I had felt more drained. A steady pulse of pounding pain in my temples kept pace with my heartbeat. I felt a desperate need to recover my strength but even sitting still was demanding more than I had to give. I wanted to topple over onto the floor and surrender to sleep. I tried to order my thoughts. 'You were so desperate to regain your sight. I didn't want to take that hope from you. My plan was that once you were strong enough the coterie could try to heal you, if you would let them. My fear was that if I told you I couldn't heal you without losing my sight, you'd lose all hope.' The last piece of the truth was angular and sharp-edged in my mouth. 'And I feared you would think me selfish that I did not heal you.' I let my head lower onto my folded arms.

The Fool said something.

'I didn't hear that.'

'You weren't meant to,' he replied in a low voice. Then he admitted, 'I called you a clodpole.'

'Oh.' I could barely keep my eyes open.

He asked a cautious question. 'After you'd taken on my hurts. Did they heal?'

'Yes. Mostly. But very slowly.' My back still bore the pinkish dimples of the ulcers that had been on his back. 'Or so it seemed to me. You know how my body has been since that runaway healing the coterie did on me years ago. I scarcely age, and injuries heal overnight, leaving me exhausted. They healed, Fool. Once I knew what was happening, I was more careful. When I worked on the bones around your eyes, I kept strict control.' I halted. It was a terrifying offer to make. But in our sort of friendship, it had to be made. 'I could try to heal your eyes. Give you sight, lose mine, and see if my body could restore mine. It would take time. And I am not sure this is the best place for us to make such an attempt. Perhaps in Bingtown, after we've sent the others home, we could take rooms somewhere and make the attempt.'

'No. Don't be stupid.' His terse words forbade any response.

In his long silence, sleep crept up on me, seeping into every part of my body. It was that engulfing demand the body makes, one that knows no refusal.

'Fitz. Fitz? Look at me. What do you see?'

I prised my eyelids open and looked at him. I thought I knew what he needed to hear. 'I see my friend. My oldest, dearest friend. No matter what guise you wear.'

'And you see me clearly?'

Something in his voice made me lift my head. I stared at him. After a time, he swam into focus. 'Yes.'

He let out his pent breath. 'Good. Because when I touched you I felt something happen, something more than I expected. I reached for you, to call you back, for I feared you were vanishing into the Skill-current. But when I touched you it wasn't as if I touched someone else. It was like folding my hands together. As if your blood suddenly ran through my veins. Fitz, I can see the shape of you, there in your chair. I fear I may have taken something from you.'

'Oh. Good. I'm glad.' I closed my eyes, too weary for surprise. Too exhausted for fear.

I slept.